Marian L. Jasper was born in Hertfordshire and worked in the publishing industry within that area for many years. On the sale of her company, she moved to Jersey in the Channel Islands and eventually owned a small telecommunications company which served all the islands. She and her husband now live near family in Mandurah, near Perth in Western Australia.

This book is dedicated to
Tim and Daniela
with love

Marian L. Jasper

PRIDE OF PLACE

Sixth in the Liza Marchant Series

Copyright © 2023 Marian L. Jasper

ISBN: 978-1-922788-72-6
Published by Vivid Publishing
A division of Fontaine Publishing Group
P.O. Box 948, Fremantle
Western Australia 6959
www.vividpublishing.com.au

 A catalogue record for this
book is available from the
National Library of Australia

Introduction

Ellie and Eddy Fuller arrived back in Belfast after their trip to see Jamie Edgeworth, and they had found Liza Marchant-Kelly-Edgeworth's grave and various documents and portraits which had been in the safekeeping of the subsequent vicars at the local church.

Liza had been removed from her resting place next to her husband of many years, Jamie Edgeworth, in a final vicious act of Jamie's previous wife Evelyn but the current Lord Edgeworth was making arrangements to have her placed back in her rightful place, and he would be contacting them when this was done so that they could witness whatever ceremony was necessary.

The portraits of Liza and Jamie had taken them by surprise as they had all seen Liza before in their various dreams and they had now seen them both put in pride of place in Edgeworth House as they always should have been.

Eddy was sitting and reading his e-mails and he let out a whoop of pleasure which startled Ellie. "I think we have managed to sell a large section of our offices and the buyers could be interested in renting some of the warehouses. We could have some money to make life a little easier for us, Ellie," he said.

"That's wonderful. How sure are you?" asked Ellie.

"It seems fairly certain, but I'll know more tomorrow. You know that means that we won't have to take anything from Jamie. I really want to find out all we can about Liza and what happened in America, but I was reluctant to take his money, although I know that it was something that he wanted us to help him research," said Eddy.

"Liza was really classed as one of our ancestors and she came to us to set her record straight, but it would be really wonderful if we can pay our own way. I wonder if Liza has helped us to get some funds; she has already led us in many directions which have proved useful. I think that she wants us to go to America because there is something important for us to find there and I have a feeling that it will be the reason why the jewellery is not ours to sell," said Ellie.

"If this deal goes through it will take quite a few weeks to finalise. We may not be able to travel when we would like, but we can go to Surrey to see Liza laid to rest properly. Jamie would understand that we have an important commitment to attend to," said Eddy.

"Having learned how the Marchant & Fuller business was successfully run all those years ago, it's such a shame that it has come to this. That business made them all multi-millionaires by the standards of today and Liza, with her Bradley & Company business, must have been a multi-multi-millionaire. It seems a terrible pity that all her achievements have been obliterated from every record. I would like to see what she had in Italy and the Daltons project was extremely interesting. It grew so large that several towns were renamed because of it, we must look into that also," said Ellie.

"No doubt there is a great deal that you can do from here," said Eddy. "That's the marvellous thing about the internet, there is so much research you can do from the comfort of your home, but it doesn't take the place of actually going and seeing what they are all about firsthand."

"You're right, but I can look into the year before Liza and Jamie travelled to the American south. I know that all the boys went to university that year and it must have been very hard on Liza to see them go," said Ellie.

The following day Eddy contacted the property agent who confirmed that a serious offer had been made for the offices and if they were interested the buyers would like to rent sections of the warehouses along the dockside.

"Which offices are they interested in?" asked Ellie.

"I believe the ones which were originally James Marchant's and Wendell's, plus the smaller rooms in that section. They are easily separated, and there is a possibility that they may wish to take up the option of the other ones which were once the Nedbury offices," said Eddy. "We had better go to the agent to get this ball rolling properly."

"I didn't think that you would want me with you," said Ellie.

Eddy looked at her strangely, "Why wouldn't I want you with me. They are also your offices Ellie. We don't go by nineteenth century rules now you know; everything is equal between men and women. It says an awful lot about the men in Liza's life, both Patrick and Jamie signed away their rights to her fortune. It just shows that they were not after her money, they just wanted her. That's very romantic, which must appeal to your nature."

"Well Patrick was a soldier and that's all he ever wanted to be, and Jamie Edgeworth had his farms and land and they became quite lucrative, but Liza's money eclipsed everything that they both had. Patrick and Liza lived quite simple lives in Benson, and I know that Patrick earned more than enough to keep the family in food and a roof over their heads and so did Jamie; Liza added all the luxuries, and they were many," said Ellie.

10

That afternoon Ellie and Eddy made their way to the Property Agent's office who confirmed that the interested party had placed a deposit with them to secure the offices and a rental price was agreed for the warehouses and all would be finalised in twenty-eight days.

Ellie contacted Jamie that evening, and he smiled happily on her computer screen when she said that she and Eddy could arrange a trip to America with him at the end of twenty-eight days. "We've sold one of our offices and rented out some warehouses. It's all come at the right time and much as we appreciate your offer to pay for our trip, we can now afford to buy our own tickets and hotel rooms."

"My offer was not to make you feel beholden to me Ellie; it was to help me put right what my family had done to Liza, and I can't do that without your help," said Jamie.

"If we hadn't had this stroke of luck, Eddy and I would have taken you up on your offer because Liza's story is very important to her and to us and I have a feeling that it is also very important to someone we have yet to meet," said Ellie.

"That seems logical when you have been told that those jewels are not yours to sell because if they aren't yours then whose are they? Did Matthew and John have any children?" asked Jamie.

"Not as far as has been recorded, but you never know if there are any offspring somewhere," said Ellie.

"I've spoken to our local vicar again and he doesn't seem to think that there would be any problems with moving Liza to be with her husband in the Edgeworth crypt, but he will be checking with his Bishop to make sure. He feels that as Liza adopted the then young James Edgeworth then I can be considered her descendent and therefore have the right to make the decision on behalf of the family and much as you consider her part of your family, I have a legal link to her. Anyway, I'll arrange for it to take place after your sale is completed and we have made our travel arrangements so we can move her before we go to America. I'm sure she'll be pleased," said Jamie.

"In the meantime I must look into the time leading up to their trip to the American south, which covers when the boys were preparing to go to university and beyond," said Ellie.

"I look forward to reading about that," smiled Jamie. "Goodnight, Ellie, it's always a pleasure to talk to you."

Chapter 1

Christmas 1859 was over and some of Liza and Jamie's guests did not seem anxious to leave. Bella, the Duchess of Berkshire, had already announced that she and her two sons would be staying until any harsh weather had cleared and her mother, Lady Redfern, had stated that as she was not needed at the Palace she would not mind also staying. The Duke of Berkshire had not committed himself to staying and Liza wondered whether he had a lady's bed that he would rather be sleeping in. Lord Douglas Carlton was quite happy to remain to enjoy the Edgeworth's hospitality.

Wendell and Amelia Fuller were staying with Liza and Jamie until around Easter time; they were family to Liza and the boys. However Peter Fuller and Edward, Nicole and little Edward would be staying until after the New Year, but then business commitments meant that they had to return to Belfast at that time. Joseph and Lily were with them until their apartment at the Langston Home was ready, which would be after any winter weather had cleared.

The Major and Jennifer were leaving for the Ffoulks Home after Boxing Day, but they would return for the New Year celebrations, which Liza had decided would be held for a few friends at Edgeworth House that year. She was determined that she was going to make this New Year as normal as possible; she still thought of Patrick who had been killed on that day seven years before, but life had to go on and mourning him as she had done each New Years' day had to stop. She had finally moved on and her love for her now husband, Jamie, had grown to such an extent that she now rarely thought about the past.

Jamie's mother, Miranda and her close companion, Lucinda, were enjoying the company, but everyone hoped that they would not have to close the Dower House and move in with Liza and Jamie as they had the previous year when the worst weather on record had snowed them in for some time. Uncle David and cousin Grace had also had to move from the gatehouse and take refuge in the main house as did the Reverend Bernard Collins, whose church and vicarage had been seriously damaged due to the fierce weather.

Young Derek, his mother and sister had to also come to the house as the roof on their home had collapsed because of the severe blizzard and their house had not been habitable. It had now been rebuilt and they were even cosier than they had previously been.

"With all the guests that seem to be staying with us we could certainly have to seriously think about doubling up in rooms if we have the same weather as last year and have to move the family into the main house again," said Liza.

"Yes," said Jamie. "It would be interesting to see Bella sharing her room with Grace or Nurse Dawkins," said Jamie.

"Surely she would have to share with the Duke if that was the case," said Liza.

"I doubt that the Duke will still be with us; he has another agenda," said Jamie and did not add to his comment but Liza knew that she had previously surmised correctly.

Each morning when the boys awoke, they looked out of the window hoping for snow but were disappointed. However all the boys found plenty to amuse themselves during the day and their highlight was always their supper.

"Are you sure that you are happy for us to host a New Years' Eve party Liza?" asked Jamie.

"I am Jamie and I'm looking forward to it. Everyone from the village and the farms are invited as well as Bernard and you know that Randolph and Penny Langston will be staying with us as will the Major and Jennifer. We are going to have quite a houseful, but all our staff and your mothers' will be pitching in to help and hopefully enjoy the evening themselves," said Liza.

It was going to be a lively evening as Liza had organised the village musicians to play for some of the time and Liza hoped that she would be able to dance as she had done on her wedding day when she had pretended not to know the steps of a particularly vigorous country dance to the amusement of all the local people.

"I wonder how Bella and Lady Redfern are going to react to our choice of musicians," smiled Jamie. "Do you think they will join in the dancing?"

"Give them enough champagne and they will join in with anything," said Liza.

The Duke left the day after Boxing Day, having thanked Liza and Jamie profusely for such an enjoyable Christmas and they did not expect to see him again for some time. His valet seemed disappointed that he would miss the New Years' Eve party.

Two days before the party Randolph and Penny Langston came to stay and Jamie approached them about the portraits that he wanted of himself and Liza.

"Do you really think that I am good enough for what you want?" he asked Jamie and Penny just raised a disbelieving eyebrow.

13

"We have seen much of your work Randolph and especially your portrait of Penny, which is superb and if you are agreeable, we would be happy to put this commission safely in your hands. We do not expect you to do this for no remuneration and would like to agree a price with you," said Jamie.

"I do not feel that I should take any money from you, you have been more than kind to us, and it could be my way of repaying you for your generosity," said Randolph.

"No, we cannot have that Randolph and I can only say what Liza would say if she were here and that is that you won't be working for us if that is the case," smiled Jamie. "If you do not know what to charge, I will look out the account that I had for portraits that I had painted some years ago and add a bit to it. Would that be acceptable?"

"That would be more than acceptable Lord Edgeworth," said Randolph. "To be able to do what I love and get paid for it is quite extraordinary."

"If I can call you Randolph then you can certainly call me Jamie," smiled Jamie.

They went into the drawing room where Liza was with Lily and Joseph, both of whom had become fast friends with Randolph and Penny. Bella and Lady Redfern were also there and as they were sitting and talking a carriage drew up and from it stepped the Duke of Berkshire. He was shown into the drawing room where everyone was surprised to see him.

"What are you doing here?" asked Bella not appearing too pleased to see him.

"I decided that I would really like to join you all for New Years' Eve; I trust you have no objections Liza and Jamie," said the Duke.

"You're most welcome," smiled Liza. "Come and sit down and warm yourself; it's turning quite cold. I'll just make sure your room is ready."

Liza left the drawing room and went into her study and rang for Mrs Frances and when she arrived she explained that the Duke had turned up and his room needed to be made ready for him and of course his valet would also need accommodation. Mrs Frances gave her knowing smile and told Liza that his room would be ready within half an hour.

"Thank you, Mrs Frances," said Liza. "I know it's not easy getting rooms ready unexpectedly."

"Don't worry your Ladyship, it will take no time at all," said Mrs Frances. "It does seem that everyone wants to be included in your New Years' Eve party. I'll tell Mrs Lambert to expect one extra for dinner and we will also have an extra person in the kitchen. We will cope, we've done it before and I'm sure this won't be the last time."

That night when Liza had made her way to Jamie's bedroom, she commented that she had been surprised to see the Duke return as she thought that the lure of the high life in London would have been too much for him to leave.

"I think that the Duke and his latest mistress have had a disagreement," said Jamie. "I heard him telling Douglas that his latest paramour became somewhat verbally vicious; apparently she did not appreciate him telling her how perfect his Christmas had been with his family in the wonderful home of Lady Edgeworth."

"It's our home Jamie, not just mine," said Liza with a frown.

"I believe the lady said that if he had enjoyed himself so much with his wife and family then he should go back there as she didn't want him around making use of her whilst he sang the praises of some other woman," said Jamie thoughtfully.

"Have I unknowingly made another enemy?" asked Liza.

"Quite possibly, but as you don't mix in those circles, I don't believe that there will be any repercussions," said Jamie but Liza could see that he was not pleased.

"You seem upset Jamie," said Liza.

"I'm sure that the Duke had a fairly respectable mistress, if any mistress can be deemed respectable, but I don't like the thought of your name being bandied around in such a situation by such a person. The Duke had got over his annoyance with his lady and now finds it quite amusing. I'm afraid I didn't laugh," said Jamie.

"Surely Bella is the one to be more upset by his return, because she must realise it was not of his choosing," said Liza.

"Bella had her own 'admirers' but she seems to have given up that way of life for the moment," said Jamie. "I think you have been a good influence on her."

Liza suddenly smiled and said, "Can I be a bad influence on you please Jamie?"

Jamie laughed and said, "Come on Liza, show me just how bad you can be."

***

It was the day of the New Years' Eve party and the Major and Jennifer had arrived whilst Amelia, Miranda and Lucinda were helping Liza organise the rooms to accommodate the number of guests that they were expecting. Mrs Frances and Harper were in their element; they enjoyed showing how well Edgeworth House could entertain so many people. Mrs Lambert had been barking orders in her kitchen for days and now the wonderful smell of a spit roast and freshly baked pies was wafting up the stairs and making everyone's mouths water.

The boys were quite excited as they were being treated like young men and would be allowed to stay up as long as they wished that night. They had planned

15

what they would be wearing with the help of Liza, Adam and April with Jamie adding in a word or two. They had eaten well at lunchtime and were going to save themselves for the food during the evening.

Bella and Lady Redfern came to see if there was anything that they could do to help and Liza set them the task of checking that the previous weeks' holly still looked respectable and they had the young driver, Ernie, with them and he was collecting up the old holly and would be cutting new branches later.

Grace, Lily, Jennifer and Penny came in carrying refreshments for everyone as those working in the kitchen were very busy as they wanted to finish in time to get ready to join in the festivities.

All was ready an hour before any guests were due to arrive and everyone within the house was relaxing and slowly dressing for the evening. Liza was dressed early so that April could get herself organised and she sat back and thought of all the New Years' Eves that she had experienced in the past but this year she was not remembering them with sadness.

There was a sound of voices outside her door, and someone knocked and before she could answer, the door burst open and six young men almost fell over themselves to come into her room. She stood up slowly and looked at them with pride; they all looked so young and handsome. Simon was the tallest and he was so like Gabriel, his father. Matthew was next and his hair was so fair that it was almost white, and Liza was startled at his likeness to his father, White Wolf as he was known to the Cherokees. James smiled at her, and she saw his father in him but also there was a look of Evelyn about him. Liza could see nothing of anyone in John, but he really had grown into a lovely looking young man with very gentle eyes. Nicholas was a young version of his father and Richard had both his mother and father in him.

Jamie came into her room and stood looking at the boys proudly. "Well Liza, you have some very handsome young men visiting you."

"Yes, I have, haven't I? You are right, they are no longer boys; when did they become men? It seems to have suddenly happened. I am so proud of you all. Shall we all go down together and greet our guests?" said Liza.

Miranda and Lucinda were arriving with all their staff as Jamie and Liza came down the stairs followed by their young men, and they looked up and they also had admiration in their eyes.

The village musicians had arrived and were setting up their instruments on a platform and Harper and Stewart, Miranda's butler, were arranging the drinks for the guests. All Liza and Jamie's house guests began arriving as well as many of the villagers and farmers. Derek proudly walked into the room with his mother

16

and sister, and he too had become a handsome young man. Liza walked over to the family and welcomed them warmly and Jamie followed smiling.

"It's wonderful to see you all and you, Derek, look so well tonight," said Liza.

"I may not be able to dance tonight, but I walked into this room unaided," he smiled at Liza.

"Does that mean that you won't be sliding down the banisters again?" laughed Liza.

"I can't promise that I won't. It does get me down the stairs quickly," said Derek. John came over to them and greeted Derek and his family and then guided him over to where the others were.

Liza turned to Mrs Price and told her that Derek had achieved so much and that she must be very proud of him.

"I am," said Mrs Price. "He was determined to come here tonight and walk without his stick, and he has done just that. It's his way of thanking you."

"That's kind of him," said Jamie, "but you are the ones to be thanked. You have all worked so hard to get him to this point. I just wish that it all could have happened earlier for him."

"It's happened now, which is something that we never believed could happen," said Mrs Price. "So we are delighted with the way it has turned out and it would not have been the case if you hadn't helped him."

Jamie and Liza brushed aside Mrs Price's comments and told her to go and enjoy herself. Susan was already with her friends from school and Mr and Mrs Rogers came over and joined in a conversation with Mrs Price. Liza and Jamie then carried on around the room making everyone welcome.

The musicians were beginning to warm up and then it all livened up with several people dancing. Jamie led Liza onto the dance floor which encouraged even more couples to join in.

"Are you going to pretend that you don't know how to dance, Liza?" asked Jamie.

"How do you know that I was pretending?" said Liza grinning up at him.

"Because Wendell told me, but I now know that you would do that just to make everyone realise that they could approach you quite happily. There is nobody who feels that they cannot talk to you, and I believe a little of that has rubbed off onto me now," said Jamie.

Bernard arrived and he and David talked together for a while. Peter was enjoying dancing with Grace and Liza had to admit that they did make a very good-looking couple. Amelia came over to her; she obviously had something on her mind.

"Do you think that Peter and Grace will eventually get together?" she asked bluntly.

"I really don't know Amelia. They seem to enjoy one another's company very much, but I have seen Peter working back in Belfast and his concentration is totally on business and I doubt that Grace could be persuaded to leave her father. Their relationship is different to most, but it is very interesting and seeing them together tonight it is obvious that there is something between them that is more than a cordial friendship," said Liza.

"I know that she is a good ten years older than him, but that doesn't matter if they are happy together and I really would like to see Peter settled with somebody nice like Grace," said Amelia.

"You have obviously realised that there is no point in trying to push either Peter or Grace into a relationship, it can only be their choice. They seem to be happy the way things are, and it must make you pleased that he is happy," said Liza.

"Peter would never have settled for someone who did not have the same or more intelligence than he has," said Amelia and she wandered off to find Wendell. Liza smiled as she watched her go; *a mother always watches over her children, no matter how old they are*, she thought.

There was no class distinction in the room. The Duke and Douglas were showing interest in what some of Jamie's farmers were saying and Lady Redfern was deep in conversation with Mrs Rogers. Bella was talking to April and Adam, presumably about her boys and Liza smiled to see Penny whizzing around the room in the arms of the Duke's valet; she made a mental note to find out his name. Randolph was staying safely in Lily and Joseph's company and Liza hoped that one day he would come out of his shy shell.

Matthew made his way over to her and smiled, "May I have the pleasure of this dance with you please Mother?" he asked. "I would be delighted," she replied.

Jamie looked across and saw Liza and Matthew whirling around the room, both laughing and enjoying their dance together. Her green eyes were sparkling and as Matthew turned around his green eyes also glowed happily. Jamie blinked, as did Wendell; she was seventeen years old again, which was when they had both first seen her. The music finished and Liza curtsied slightly to Matthew, and he bowed and led her over to Jamie before returning to his friends.

Mrs Lambert and Mrs Frances uncovered the food and Liza encouraged Lily and Joseph to lead the way and the Major and Jennifer followed. Miranda guided Mr and Mrs Rogers towards the table and then others started to join them. Liza led them towards the many tables that had been set up in diverse places.

Liza sat with Edward and Nicole and told them how happy she was that they had been able to spend this time with her. "It's a shame that Annalise and Arthur couldn't be with us this year, but maybe next year they will have the time," said Liza.

"Well Liza," said Edward. "I think I have managed not to say anything that could upset you. I know that I normally manage to put my foot in it."

"I hope you haven't felt that you had to watch every word you said. You know that we love you the way you are, and you could never hurt me, Edward. We have always been close, and you know that we both would forgive one another anything," said Liza.

"You know that Liza was my first love," Edward said to Nicole, much to Liza's horror, but then he added "We have always loved each other, but never been in love. That I saved for you Nicole."

Liza breathed a sigh of relief, especially as Nicole gave her a knowing smile.

Jamie was with Bella for a while and he noticed that she kept glancing at the Duke, and she was not looking too pleased. He asked her if something was upsetting her to which she replied that it was no more than usual. Jamie looked at the Duke and realised that he was watching every move that Liza was making, Jamie turned to Bella "I know that the Duke has always admired my wife, Bella. He admires the fact that she is only interested in me and our family, whereas many people in her position have outside agendas."

"You are very lucky to have such faith in Liza, and rightly so. You know my situation and the Duke's, but I class Liza as a close friend of mine and I would prefer that my husband did not make it so obvious that he would like Liza to be one of his conquests," said Bella.

"That will never be, and you know it," said Jamie. "I also know that the Duke quite enjoys the way that Liza avoids his advances, and I am sure that those advances are to see just how Liza rejects him, which you know amuses him and I think that Liza is also amused by them pitting their wits against one another. I know my Liza and I know where her heart is."

"You and she have such a good marriage Jamie, I envy you both very much," said Bella. "Still I must appreciate that I have everything that I could possibly want, apart from a loving husband. Of course he does not have a loving wife; we tolerate one another, and we are lucky to have our boys."

"I am sorry that you are not as happy as you would like, Bella," said Jamie.

"I am very happy when I am in your household Jamie. I feel very much at home here, which is why I impose myself so much on you. I do not dare to ask if I can stay, I just turn up. If I were to ask you may refuse and I don't want to take that chance. I even enjoy being here when the Duke is also with us," said Bella.

"You never need to ask Bella; you are always welcome as was I in your home when I was young. You were very kind to me then," said Jamie.

"Yes, you, Anthony and Binky were quite a threesome," said Bella. "Now you are just a twosome, but you both have wives that make you both happy, and that's nice to see. I must let you go now Jamie; you have many guests to speak to; I'll see you again soon."

Jamie watched her make her way to join her mother who seemed deep in conversation with the Major. He felt convinced that Bella was holding something back and he wondered whether it was to do with Binky, but he was not going to let it concern him that evening, especially as Liza was coming towards him with one of her brilliant smiles aimed only at him.

"Have you eaten yet Jamie?" she asked.

"No Liza, I was waiting for you," he smiled down at her. Bella was right; he was very lucky. He glanced up and saw his sons being perfect gentlemen, sitting at a table and at last they were allowing girls to be with them. They were definitely growing up.

The food and the drink carried on flowing and there was a great deal of laughter and dancing; then it was midnight, and they all raised their glasses and welcomed in 1860.

"Happy New Year Mother and Father," said Matthew followed by James and John, with Simon adding "Mother Liza and Uncle Jamie." Nicholas and Richard were wishing their parents a Happy New Year.

Liza and Jamie went around wishing everyone a Happy New Year and when they came to Wendell and Amelia, they both clasped Liza close to them and Wendell whispered how proud he was of her. He kissed her and said goodnight as he was feeling rather tired, and he and Amelia began making their way to their room but did not want to disturb any of the staff as they were still enjoying the festivities.

"Are you sure you don't need help," asked a concerned Liza.

"We haven't always had servants Liza; we'll manage quite well. Please don't worry about us," said Amelia.

Gradually the guests started making their way to their various homes. Derek walked over to Liza and Jamie and bade them farewell and then went to his mother and sister who were with Mr and Mrs Rogers and several others who would be travelling back to the village with them.

All the villagers and farmers had left by half past one and most of the house guests had gone to their rooms for the night. Miranda and Lucinda had left earlier, as had David, but Peter was going to see Grace to her home. Matthew,

John, James and Simon, together with Nicholas and Richard had tiredly but happily gone to their rooms.

Mrs Frances and Mrs Lambert were organising clearing the tables and Liza knew better than to suggest that they leave that until the morning.

The Duke and Douglas Carlton were having a final nightcap in the drawing room and Liza and Jamie joined them.

"I think that the New Year was welcomed in wonderfully this evening," said the Duke. "It's one of the first times that I have had long conversations with farmers and villagers, and some of their thoughts are extremely enlightening. They all think the world of you both. It's not many landowners who would open their house to them as you did tonight.

"Why not Duke, they are just the same as us; we are invited into their homes, so why shouldn't they be invited into ours. You know that we all spend a great deal of time together in the summer with the cricket matches. I consider them friends and I hope they feel the same about us," said Liza.

"Liza is right," said Jamie. "I have grown to know and appreciate all the people around the Edgeworth Estate and village, and I enjoy their company. It was so very different in my father's day; I don't think that he even knew the name of any villager or farmer. As long as they paid their rent, and it was enough for the gambling tables, then that was all he was interested in. However I should not speak ill of the dead."

"That is still very much the case with a great many estates," said Douglas. "Those landowners just do not realise that we all have to work together to be successful, which is something that has yet to be learned in Ireland. Even the repeal of the Corn Laws was too late, but that has become America's gain with the number of Irish now living there."

"Sadly many of the immigrants go there full of hope and finally end up on the streets of New York, which is where the lack of education has led them," said Liza.

"Do you really think that an education would make them any better off?" asked the Duke.

"I have seen how the lack of being able to read has fleeced them of the little that they still possessed. I have seen them believe what they have been told they are signing for and enslaving themselves and their children. I have seen them charged for goods that they would never receive because they had no idea what they were seeing. So my answer is yes, even basic reading and writing would make them much better off," said Liza.

"Liza is very passionate about education, and I can understand why," said Jamie.

"I have seen how you both have encouraged your children in that respect, and latterly encouraged mine in the same way. No doubt you have pushed others onto the right path at various times," said the Duke and with that they all finally went to their beds.

***

Liza spent New Years' Day surrounded by people, which gave her very little time to dwell on the past, but there were moments when she remembered that day seven years ago when Patrick had died. She could see in Matthew's, John's and Simon's eyes that they also remembered. James seemed not to be affected but of course he had not witnessed that terrible event, although he had liked his Uncle Patrick and, in the past, had remembered him fondly.

Jamie was very conscious of what this day meant, as were all the Fullers but nobody else would have realised the significance of the day as Liza carried out her duties as hostess with a smile that could not be seen through.

At one point through the day both Jamie and Liza felt that there was a certain amount of unease between Lady Redfern and the Duke. Sometimes Bella pursed her lips when approached by Lady Redfern.

"Do you think that there is something not quite right between Bella and her mother?" asked Liza.

"I believe the Duke has also suddenly become ill at ease. I had a feeling when I was talking to Bella yesterday that she was keeping something back from me," said Jamie. "I think that it must be about Binky."

"No doubt we will find out soon enough," said Liza.

After lunch the Duke whispered to Jamie that he would like to see him, and they quietly went into his study.

"Is this something to do with Binky? I have noticed that Bella has been a little on edge and normally nothing seems to worry her," said Jamie.

"Binky is on his way back to England," said the Duke and Jamie frowned.

The Duke continued, "I'm afraid that the despicable act that he tried to perpetrate on you and Liza has caught him out and he is returning to England to die."

"I'm sorry to hear that," said Jamie quietly. "I will just try to remember the good times that he, Anthony and I had when we were boys and forget about the other side of his life. I truly hope that he doesn't suffer too badly. How long have you known?"

"I picked up my correspondence just before I came here for New Year and only opened it after I had arrived," said the Duke. "You could say that it is poetic justice, but I know that you won't."

"How is Lady Redfern taking the news?" asked Jamie.

"What Lady Redfern feels is difficult to judge, but of course she must be very upset that she is losing her only son; although he has not been what she would have liked in a son," said the Duke.

"I don't believe that Bella was particularly close to him, if my memory of when I visited all those years ago is correct. I now think that she probably knew what his tendencies were," said Jamie.

"She may not have understood exactly what his leanings were, but she knew that he was not as he should have been," said the Duke.

"Anthony and I never saw it, but Hector did. He said that Binky only liked the younger boys so there was no reason for us to see it," said Jamie. "How very naïve we were. Do you know when he will arrive?"

"It took some time for his letter to reach me, so I can only assume that he is well on his way home. Unless of course he has already met his demise," said the Duke.

"I shall tell Liza, and Anthony when he returns from Belfast, but there is no need for anyone else to know. Thank you for telling me," said Jamie.

"I don't think that he will be with us for very long; apparently he has been ill for some time," said the Duke.

"I presume that Lady Redfern knows that you are talking to me," said Jamie.

"She specially requested that I talk to you Jamie. She knows that we owe you that. You were close friends when you were young, but unfortunately later his tendencies led to his attack on your son, and then conspiring with Evelyn to do you and Liza harm, as well as the attack on you in Belfast. His return does concern you, but I truly believe that he is beyond hurting you," said the Duke.

"We were always worried that he may have set in motion something to do us damage but as the time has gone by it appears that it was not the case. However we will be vigilant, but we always are as there are many who would prefer that we do not help the children in the care of the charity," said Jamie.

"It is always wise to be cautious Jamie," said the Duke.

***

Jamie thought it best not to tell Liza about Binky until they were alone that night. She was concerned that he was returning but also sorry that he was coming back to die.

"It seems to have happened very quickly; I thought that these diseases took years to come to their final conclusion. How long has he been gone?" asked Liza.

"Just over three years I believe," said Jamie. "It may be something that he contracted years ago, just because he's been in India for that time doesn't mean that he picked it up there. He was well versed in such things when he tried to do us harm in that respect, who knows, his knowledge could have been firsthand."

"I have never asked John exactly what happened to him in those few weeks that he was in that awful house, but you know that Binky recognised him, and he recognised Binky. If that disease takes years to manifest itself, I can only pray that John will not have been infected," said a very worried Liza.

"Oh God Liza, I hadn't thought of that," said Jamie. "That must be ten years ago, I'm sure that he would have had some symptoms in that time."

"You're right; he has been particularly healthy, apart from the usual coughs and colds. I am not going to panic," said Liza. "This is the very reason that we check the children when they arrive at our door before we place them in the Homes. If they have signs of anything untoward, we don't put them in the main Homes. Unfortunately, as you say, it could take years to come to the fore, although doctors say that a rash does show early on, but that can disappear, and it is no longer thought about. It's a risk that all these children have to live with, but we don't tell them, we just make sure that they have regular examinations."

"What happens to the ones who have been adopted Liza, surely they are just as much at risk," said Jamie.

"Mostly they have been well looked after in the places that they came from, after all they are their means of revenue. We get them examined by specialists and they normally have not been in those terrible places long. Most of them have not had to go through too much. Their adopted parents are well aware of where they have come from and they use their common sense regarding any problems which could arise," said Liza. "Of course, there are no guarantees."

"I knew that they were medically examined, but until now I had not realised how specialised it had to be; it is logical though," said Jamie.

"Binky slept with Evelyn, didn't he?" said Liza.

"Yes, he did, and under our roof also," said an annoyed Jamie. "I presume that they had a sexual relationship and didn't just sleep in the same room, in the same bed."

"Do you think that we should warn Evelyn?" asked Liza.

"It would be very ironic if she has such a disease after what she tried to do to us and no, I don't think we should tell her," said Jamie.

"You're right, why worry her unnecessarily. She is probably perfectly well, and it would only put fear in her mind which would be cruel," said Liza.

"She and Binky did not have a problem with wanting to watch you and I die miserably. You're being kind-hearted again Liza," smiled Jamie. "But I wouldn't have you any other way. I will have to tell Anthony when he returns."

"The three of you spent a great deal of time together when you were young, and you kept that friendship until Binky's terrible attack on John. Bella and Lady Redfern still think the world of you," said Liza.

"And the Duke thinks the world of you," smiled Jamie. "I think that all our guests have enjoyed their day. Our boys have been very good over the time, and how have you been today, Liza? I know it's not an easy day for you."

"It's been the best New Years' Day that I have had in years; thank you for that Jamie. You are very understanding, but I have to admit that I'm pleased that it is over," said Liza.

"New Years' Day may be over, but our guests seem to have no intention of leaving us soon and you know Bella is praying for snow; in fact I think that she will be staying regardless of whether it snows or not. She certainly is not contemplating going back to her 'mausoleum' soon; she may be with us until Easter."

"Well if she is she will have to appreciate that I have work that I must concentrate on. But there will be plenty of people around so that she will not be bored or lonely," said Liza.

"She told me yesterday that she is happier here more than anywhere else, and the reason that she imposes herself on us without asking is that she is frightened that we would refuse her if she were to ask and she doesn't want to take that chance," said Jamie. "I find that rather sad and can only think how unhappy she must be in her own home and indeed in her life."

"I think that she and the Duke have an understanding; she has given him what he wanted in Nicholas and Richard, and she has everything that she could possibly want," said Liza.

"To quote Bella; she has everything except a loving husband, but she did add that he did not have a loving wife," said Jamie.

"That's very sad for both of them," commented Liza.

"I don't think that the Duke finds it sad; they had an agreement and they have both fulfilled their side of the bargain and they now go their separate ways," said Jamie and he quietly added "which was the agreement that I had with Evelyn and we kept to our bargain until she met Felicity and started helping her to take what was yours and spreading lies about you which could have done you no end of harm."

"She probably felt more for you than you realised," said Liza.

"You know that she felt more for the title, and she still retains that title, so I have kept to my side of the bargain, and she gave me James, who happily is now yours," said Jamie. "I also have Matthew and John and of course Simon whilst he is with us."

"They are all growing into such young gentlemen now and they are all so good looking," said Liza.

"I think the time has come for them to have their own horses," said Jamie. "I know that they are capable of riding, but they have never owned their own horses and they also should have a carriage for their use. If you are in agreement, I'll look into that tomorrow and take Davis with me to help choose the right mounts for them."

"They'll be thrilled," said Liza. "How did they manage to be boys at Christmas and young gentlemen at the New Year? I'm very proud of them but sad at the same time."

"I'm afraid that they have grown up Liza, and they must be allowed to act on their own, even make their own mistakes, but at least you have given them the best start in life that they could possibly have, and I don't believe that they will ever let you down," said Jamie.

"You have been such an influence on them Jamie, and for a lot longer than the years that we have been married," said Liza. "When we came back from America you were a constant in our lives, and I do appreciate everything that you did for us, you gave us all love and stability. We could not have managed without you; we still can't."

"We had better get some sleep Liza, because we are going to have four young men all over us tomorrow, delighted that they are achieving more independence than they dreamed they would have at this time," said Jamie.

***

Jamie was right, the young men became boys again when they could not disguise their excitement at knowing that they would be getting their own horses and the bonus was that they would have their own carriage when they needed it.

They naturally wanted to rush off to get their mounts that day, but Jamie calmed them down by telling them that firstly they had to discuss their needs with both Davis and Hendry who were experts in horseflesh.

Simon was standing back and saying nothing, and Liza turned to him and said that when he chooses his mount, he had better not bring some of his American ways of riding to Surrey where it was considered a gentle and respectable pastime and that racing one another was not a good idea.

"Do you mean that I am also having my own horse?" asked Simon.

"Of course you are. You are part of our family for the next few years, and you need to go out and about with the others whilst you are here," said Jamie. "So far the weather is holding well, so I think we will be able to look around for the best animals shortly. Davis knows what is available and where; shall we go and see him?"

They were out of the door and on their way to the stables before Jamie had finished speaking.

The Duke came into the room and said that he understood that the boys were getting their own horses.

"That's right," said Jamie. "We thought that now was the right time. They have ridden around the grounds on a few occasions, but they are young men now and I remember riding here, there and everywhere when I was their age."

Jamie excused himself and left for the stables.

"Do all your boys ride?" he asked Liza.

"Matthew and John were taught in America by my previous husband, as was Simon," said Liza.

"I see," said the Duke. "I suppose the technique is a little different to here. They are probably more skilled than Jamie knows."

Liza did not respond to the Duke's comment; she just smiled at him which gave him the answer.

"I think that it is a very good idea; they are old enough to have a little independence and this is one way of giving it to them. If you have no objection, I'll join Jamie and the boys in the stable," said the Duke and Liza smiled and nodded her agreement. "Come on boys, let's go and see what is happening and we may be able to organise the same for you."

Nicholas and Richard moved quickly into the room, and it was obvious that they had been listening outside the door. Their faces were ecstatic, and they went with their father towards the stable.

I wonder if the Duke has any of his own ideas regarding his children, thought Liza as she made her way to her study where Grace was going through the correspondence which had not been tackled for a few days.

***

A week went by, and the boys' excitement had not abated. During that time a carriage had been purchased and the boys were taking it in turns at driving it around the estate until they felt confident enough to drive into the village to show Derek their vehicle as well as give him the opportunity to drive with them.

Finally the day arrived when Jamie, Davis and Hendry rode up each on a horse whilst leading another, with Ernie driving the carriage that they had used to reach their destination. The boys had been to the horse breeder earlier that week and with Davis' and Hendry's guidance they had chosen their animals. There had followed great discussions over naming their horses.

Once again, the boys became young men, each taking charge of their animal and gently leading them towards the stables and placing them in their individual stalls. The names had already been placed over the doors of each stall and immediately responsibility for the welfare of each horse was taken by its owner. Jamie and Liza looked on as all six horses were lovingly cared for and although it was tempting, all the boys had decided that they should just groom them that day and perhaps ride them the next day.

The Duke had already left but he was happy with what he had purchased for his sons, and it was decided that their mounts should be kept at Edgeworth House for the time being as he needed to get his stables in order before they could be taken to his estate.

Liza and Jamie watched the boys for a short while and then went back into the house leaving them to get to know their horses under the watchful eyes of both Davis and Hendry.

"I think that Matthew, John and Simon know more about horses than I realised," said Jamie.

"They were around horses for a few years and whereas we have stable hands here, we had to look after our own ponies and horses ourselves. Simon naturally has had more experience as Matthew and John left America some years ago, but I suppose they haven't forgotten what they were taught," said Liza carefully not mentioning Patrick or the army personnel who had helped them.

"I daresay that James, Nicholas and Richard will become just as skilled in time and no doubt the others will help them," said Jamie.

Liza nodded as they entered the drawing room where Bella was relaxing with Lady Redfern, Amelia, Miranda and Lucinda.

"All our young men must be very happy," commented Amelia.

"Yes, they are getting to know their horses and we probably won't see them until supper time," said Liza.

Peter, Edward, Nicole and little Edward had left for Belfast the previous day and Amelia was missing them and feeling a little sad.

Lily and Joseph were spending a great deal of time at Langston House, and they now had many members of staff to help them.

Douglas Carlton had no intention of leaving; he was quite happy spending time within the Edgeworth family, and he was in the library with Wendell and David. Jamie left the drawing room and joined the men in the library.

Penny and Randolph had spent some time discussing when the best time would be to start Liza's and Jamie's portraits and he would come to Edgeworth House and stay for some days in preparation. The forecast was for snow so he would not be with them until after that time.

Miranda and Lucinda, as well as David and Grace, were well stocked just in case they were cut off for a few days and should it really become as dire as the previous year they would pack everything and move into the main house.

Liza got up saying that she had some letters to sign, and she joined Grace in her study. They worked their way through a great deal of correspondence and when they had nearly finished there was a knock on the door and Lady Redfern asked to come in. Grace excused herself leaving them alone.

"I know that Jamie must have told you that Binky is returning and the reason why," said Lady Redfern.

Liza nodded, "I am sorry to hear that he is unwell."

"Yes, I believe that you are," said Lady Redfern. "I also believe that you know that his illness is of his own making, and it also saddens me that he may well have contracted this disease because of his strange tendencies. It does however concern me that he may have caused others to be ill, one of whom is very close to you and the other I could say would be what she deserves considering what she had in mind for you and Jamie."

"Since I heard about Binky, I naturally have been worried, but my son does have regular check-ups and he has never shown any signs of such an illness. I do not know whether he had any personal contact with Binky although I do know that they recognised one another years later. It must be about ten years since they could have known each other, and I would have thought that there would have been some symptoms by now. However, sadly nothing can be certain," said Liza.

"I suppose that you are cautious with all the children in your care," said Lady Redfern.

"Yes, they are all thoroughly checked and as I said to Jamie the other night, many of our children were good money earners for their so-called owners, so they were quite well looked after in that respect. Even to the extent that they were not starved. Sadly my John was not in such a house, but he had only been there for very few weeks," said Liza.

"What are your thoughts on Evelyn?" asked Lady Redfern.

"I do wonder at the wisdom of telling her. She seems fit enough at present and why worry somebody when there is no need. There is of course the other side to the problem which is to protect anyone that she might take a fancy to. Jamie and I decided not to contact her over this; she would have to live with the fear of possibly being infected for the rest of her life. However if somebody else were to let her know why Binky is returning, then she will come to her own conclusions," said Liza.

"Well Liza, somebody could do that if they knew where she was," said Lady Redfern. "I know that you spirited her away and the reasons being to protect the Edgeworth name and also I know that her child needed to be well away from the gossip that her mother had created with her behaviour."

"I do not have any contact with her, nor do I wish to," said Liza. "Does she not have any friends left?"

"No, she lost many of them with her antics with that Italian Count and the rest of them disowned her when she made an exhibition of herself by coming to Douglas' charity dinner with that obnoxious friend of Binky's," said Lady Redfern.

"I would like to discuss with Jamie the best way to get a message to Evelyn without us doing so," said Liza.

"I will write to her and tell her that Binky is returning to England and exactly what is wrong with him, all I ask is that you somehow get my letter to her. I will explain that I do not know where she is, but I took an educated guess that Jamie does. My conscience tells me that it is the right thing to do," said Lady Redfern.

"Thank you, Lady Redfern. I know you are right, but I am truly sorry that Binky is in this situation. I know Jamie is also; he remembers the friendship that he had with Binky and Anthony and how you took him in when his father was disinterested in him. It is such a shame that the friendship had to change," said Liza. "Do you know when Binky will be back with you?"

"He will probably arrive in two to three weeks from now. It will not be easy losing my child, no matter what faults he had, and there were many," said Lady Redfern.

"No, it isn't easy," smiled Liza.

"I'm so sorry Liza, that comment was thoughtless of me. I know you have had your fair share of losses in that respect. Forgive me," said Lady Redfern.

"There is nothing to forgive. It was all a very long time ago, and I now have three wonderful sons and Simon has always been like a son to me, so I am surrounded by four very caring young men," smiled Liza.

Lady Redfern got up to leave and suddenly said, "I think Bella is going to get her wish; it's snowing quite heavily now. Perhaps we will be snowed in together, which will be quite exciting."

Liza smiled at Lady Redfern, "It won't be the same as last year, no matter how Bella would like it to be, but it will start settling and the Dower House and gatehouse will be cut off from us, as will the village, but there is no sign of a blizzard, just regular snow in which our young gentlemen will become boys again, as will all the men in this household and unfortunately I shall be the target of their snowball enthusiasm."

"Will everyone be moving into this house?" asked Lady Redfern.

"Miranda, Lucinda and their staff are well supplied and will survive for a fortnight, as will David and Grace. However I am hoping that Lily and Joseph are on their way back but if you will excuse me Lady Redfern, I must check that Bernard Collins is well stocked as he has a habit of thinking that God will provide, when I'm afraid that it is only we lowly sinners who make sure that he is warm and well fed," said Liza.

"The vicarage seems to be weatherproof; he was telling me that the church has been rebuilt as well as his home. I suppose that was down to you," said Lady Redfern.

"He does tend to forget that kitchen cupboards need to have food placed in them and that there should be logs and coal to keep him warm, failing that he will move in with us again," said Liza avoiding answering Lady Redfern's question.

Lady Redfern just nodded and left to join her daughter. Jamie had seen her leave and came into Liza.

"I see that the snow has started, I hope that Joseph and Lily don't get caught in it. What did Lady Redfern want?" asked Jamie.

"She wants to write to Evelyn and asks that we get her letter to her as she seems well aware that you know where she is. She says that she will just tell her that it was an educated guess that you would know where she was," said Liza.

"I suppose she feels that she has a duty towards her," said Jamie.

"Not really, she feels that she has a duty towards anyone that Evelyn might be thinking of being with," said Liza.

"Of course, but I do not want that to be our responsibility. I'm glad that she is dealing with it. For once I feel sorry for Evelyn as she will have Binky's illness hanging over her for the rest of her life, and it could also prevent her from ever having a relationship with anyone else; that is always assuming that she slept with Binky," said Jamie and then he gave a slight smile. "I suppose she will think that it is your fault, after all you've been blamed for everything else."

"No doubt," smiled Liza. "I must go and see Bernard to make sure that he has everything that he needs; I presume that Mrs Price and her family are alright."

"They will be Liza," said Jamie. "You know that she has better work now and that Mr and Mrs Rogers will always make sure that she is well catered for."

"Hmmm," said Liza.

"I know that you want to see that for yourself," said Jamie. "I'll take you to Bernard and then onto Mrs Price. We had better leave now, before the snow gets any thicker."

Liza went down to the kitchen, whilst Jamie organised the carriage. Mrs Lambert quickly organised a couple of baskets of food for Bernard, and another two just in case Mrs Price needed anything. They took the baskets to the stables through the back door where Jamie was hitching two ponies to the carriage. Mr Lambert had placed some logs in the back of the carriage just in case Bernard needed them.

The boys were in the stable caring for their horses and making sure that they would be warm and well fed now that the snow had started. Hendry was watching over them and smiling. He commented to Jamie that their horses were going to be the most cared for of any animals on the Estate.

Liza pulled her cloak closely around her and climbed into the carriage beside Jamie. Hendry had offered to drive them; Jamie thanked him but quietly said that he was more use keeping an eye on the boys and their mounts.

Jamie smiled at her and said that they did not get many moments alone together during the day and he was going to enjoy the drive. When they reached the vicarage Liza found that she had been right, and Bernard was sadly lacking in food and fuel.

"You have two choices Bernard, you can either take this food and fuel, or you can come back with us until the snow clears," said Liza. "What would you like to do?"

"I think that I should stay here this year, especially as my home has been made so weatherproof now but thank you for the food and logs. I don't believe that this year is going to be as bad as last year. We will probably have just a few days being cut off: maybe up to a week. You know that I do appreciate your kindness Liza and Jamie," said Bernard.

"We hope that the farmers are right in their forecast but if by some chance we appear to start with a turn for the worse, we will come for you," said Liza.

Jamie did not know how they would go for him if there was a blizzard like last year's, but he nodded his agreement. He and Bernard unloaded the logs whilst Liza put the food away in his various cupboards and then they were ready to make the journey to the village to see Mrs Price.

Mrs Price was busy sewing when they called to see her. She was making curtains and cushion covers for one of the women in the village. Apparently she had several such commissions which she worked at from the warmth of her home and Susan was helping her. Derek was, as always, delighted to see Liza and

Jamie and said that Matthew and the others had taken him riding in their new carriage several times and that their horses were 'magnificent'.

"One day I may be able to ride; that's my next aim," said Derek.

"It's always good to have an aim and knowing you, Derek, you will achieve it," said Liza. She turned back to Mrs Price and asked her if she had everything that she needed as they would be snowed in for several days to come.

"Mr and Mrs Rogers have made sure that I have enough to keep us warm and well fed and this house is now weatherproof. We are well catered for thank you. The word is that it will not be as it was last year, so we are quite looking forward to being cosy in our home," said Mrs Price.

"Well if you are sure that you need no extra food, then we will leave you to your work in your cosy house," said Liza, "and we'll see you all as soon as the weather clears."

They made their way to their carriage and Jamie asked what she was going to do with the two baskets of food that she had planned for Mrs Price.

"I think we should see Mr and Mrs Rogers as they will know who may be in need," said Liza and Jamie drove them to the Inn.

"There is one family who are a little needy," said Mr Rogers. "You won't have met them yet; they moved into the old man Jacob's house just before Christmas. He is a widower and has four children and they are all a little undernourished."

"Is their house habitable?" asked Jamie.

"The roof has been mended since last winter, but it really is not in the best of conditions, and they have very little furniture. However they will be well out of the elements because they walked here and were sleeping rough on the way. I don't know if they should be in the house, but we are not going to enquire whilst this family are so needy and especially with the winter weather arriving," said Mr Rogers.

"Well we have a couple of baskets of food and some logs for a fire, so if you could get that to them then perhaps it will give them a little bit of warmth and something for their stomachs," said Liza.

"Certainly we will; I'm sure they will be very grateful," said Mrs Rogers.

"Will you tell them that we will be pleased to meet them when the weather clears and see if there is anything that we can do to help? Do you know if he has a trade?" asked Liza.

"No, I don't think so. I believe he would be happy to work at anything. He doesn't seem to be somebody who would be shy of work," said Mr Rogers.

The snow was now getting heavier, and Jamie and Liza quickly made their way home, and they were pleased to see that Joseph and Lily were also arriving at the same time.

"That makes you happy Liza," said Jamie. "All your charges are safely home, and all your villagers and Bernard are not going to starve."

In the drawing room Bella was smiling happily. "I got my wish; I will have to stay with you for some time. My boys will be pleased."

Lady Redfern and Douglas were also smiling; they now had an excuse to stay longer. Miranda and Lucinda were now going to make their way to the Dower House and David and Grace were going to see them safely home and then carry on to their own house.

"It's a shame that you will be leaving us," said Douglas.

"You have seen our home; Douglas and you know that it is very warm and cosy. Last year was exceptional and we were all worried that our supplies would run out, especially fuel, so it was sensible to all move in together, but this year is different, and our home is very inviting in this weather," said Miranda.

"As is ours," said David. "We have a lovely, comfortable home with everything that we could possibly need."

They made their way to their homes where they all seemed to be looking forward to being cut off from the outside world for a few days.

As everyone was assembling ready for dinner, they heard a carriage draw up and they all instinctively knew that the Duke had returned.

Before Harper could announce him, he walked into the drawing room and immediately said, "Bella you are right; our house is no place to be in the winter. I will have to see what I can do for the future. I trust you will forgive my intrusion yet again Liza and Jamie but the thought of the warmth of your hospitality as well as your house was too much for me to remain where I was. When the snow started I knew that I had to throw myself on your mercy."

They were all watching him, and Liza wondered whether she should let him carry on waffling inanely before putting him out of his misery and telling him that he was welcome.

Liza decided to give him one of her brilliant smiles and said, "We have kept your room for you Duke as we had a feeling that you would return. I presume your valet is with you."

The Duke looked a little awkward, "Yes he is with me, but I also have my butler and housekeeper."

Liza's eyes widened with shock and all she heard was Bella saying, "You have what?"

Lady Redfern and Douglas were staring at him also in shock. Amelia and Wendell both had their mouths open and Jamie was blinking quickly.

"Well, I couldn't leave them in that cold house, and I knew that there would be room here for them. All the other servants had homes to go to," said the Duke.

Lily and Joseph were sitting and looking everywhere but at the Duke.

Bella seemed now lost for words, as was Jamie but Liza was the first to recover and she smiled again and said that she would hold dinner up whilst the Duke got settled and ready.

"You know your way to your room Duke," said Liza. "I'm sure your valet is already there. I'll just sort all else out with Mrs Frances, Harper and Mrs Lambert. You do have your wish, Bella; we do have a full house now."

The Duke smiled at Liza and thanking her he made his way happily up to his room, seeming totally oblivious of the disruption that he had caused. Liza left the drawing room with all eyes following her and the last she heard was Bella apologising to Jamie and telling him how embarrassed she was.

Mrs Frances was coming to find her, and she had a questioning look on her face; Harper appeared behind her, and she ushered them into her study and at first she just did not know what to say. She looked from one to the other and decided that all she could do was accept the situation and tell them what had to happen.

"We seem to have surprise guests once again, but this time we must prepare for two others. However I have every confidence that we will handle it well. The Duke didn't bring a driver with him, did he?" said Liza with slight panic in her voice.

"No, he drove here himself," said Harper.

"I'll see Mrs Lambert shortly," said Liza. "What rooms do we have for the Duke's butler and housekeeper?"

"We do have room in the servants' quarters, but the rooms aren't aired. I'll get fires going as soon as possible, before I do anything else," said Mrs Frances.

"Do you know the butler and housekeeper, Harper?" asked Liza.

"No, I've never met them before. I hope we don't have any awkward situations because this house runs very smoothly without any outside interference," said Harper.

"This is your domain Harper and yours Mrs Frances and I know that you will both keep order in a way that upsets nobody. If you find that you have any problems, please come to me or his Lordship before anything becomes serious. I must see Mrs Lambert now," said Liza and they all made their way down to the kitchen where the Duke's butler and housekeeper were sitting and wondering what they were doing there.

Liza smiled at them and said that she remembered them from the times that she had dined at the Duke's house, and she hoped that they would be comfortable here. "Mrs Frances is arranging to have your rooms made ready for you as you will appreciate that she was not aware that you would be joining us for the next few days. I hope that you will settle happily here."

They both thanked her and looked slightly relieved. Liza then turned to Mrs Lambert and asked if she could hold dinner for about half an hour and if she knew whether there would be enough to make sure that everyone dining in the kitchen had plenty to eat.

"Yes, my lady, it may be a little 'make do and mend' but nobody will starve in this house," said Mrs Lambert.

Mr Lambert returned from taking fuel up to the rooms for the Duke's butler and housekeeper and he said that they had stocked up well this year having learned from the year before.

Adam and April were watching what was going on with resigned looks on their faces, and they could see that there was embarrassment on the faces of the butler and housekeeper as it would seem that they had no choice but to descend on the Edgeworth household without warning.

"We'll go to our rooms and get them ready, there is no need to bother anyone, we are able to at least do that for you," said the housekeeper.

"It would be better if you waited here for a while and had your supper with us as your rooms will have warmed up by then and aired a little, so you can get them ready later and we'll help you," smiled Mrs Frances.

Liza left them to it and thought that the offer to help was a good start to the relationship. The Duke's valet appeared and bowed to Liza. He asked Mrs Frances if he would be in his usual room and she nodded saying that they were making a fire for him, although his room was still aired from his previous visit.

All eyes went to Liza again as she entered the drawing room. "I am so sorry Liza," said Bella. "The Duke returning without warning is bad enough but bringing all the staff with him is inexcusable."

"Please do not worry Bella, everything is in hand. Nobody will starve and all will have warm and comfortable rooms by bedtime. We will be eating shortly; I hope you are all hungry," said Liza trying to lighten the mood in the room.

Jamie still did not look very happy, and Liza could understand that, as his hospitality was being stretched to the limit, but he was a gentleman and would act as such. Suddenly Wendell laughed, "It could only happen to you Liza, and you are handling it beautifully. Come on everyone, it is not a disaster, it's a compliment to the way you and Jamie run your household, people just want to be here. I know that Amelia and I always enjoy being with you both, so you have to appreciate that we are not the only ones."

Douglas also laughed and agreed with Wendell and on that note the Duke entered the drawing room, smiling broadly and obviously very happy to be in their company. Harper announced that dinner was ready, and they made their way into a quickly revised dining room. Liza took Jamie's arm and smiled up at him and at last he relaxed and became the excellent host that she knew he was.

Dinner went relatively well even though there were a few dark looks thrown at the Duke from Bella. Douglas and Lady Redfern acted as if there was nothing untoward and Amelia and Wendell appeared quite amused by the whole situation. Lily and Joseph regaled everyone with how the Langston House was progressing which they felt should be interesting to all around the table as they were involved with the charity. Liza and Jamie listened to what was being said but kept smiling at one another and Liza decided that she would sit next to Jamie at the next gathering around the table rather than so far away opposite him. She liked being near him.

In the drawing room after dinner the Duke seemed still oblivious of Bella's annoyance of him and once again Douglas and Lady Redfern carried on as if nothing was wrong. Liza excused herself by saying that she had to make sure that all the servants were settling into their places.

"I must go and check on the boys," said Bella suddenly much to everyone's shock as she had never been known to show such concern. She and Liza left the room together.

"I know that I impose myself on you Liza but initially it was truly for the sake of my boys. It was felt that they needed the friendship and guidance of others who were well adjusted, and that has worked wonderfully well. I found that I also enjoyed the friendship within this household, and you allowed me to feel welcome. I know why my husband keeps returning and it is not for Jamie's company, he is fascinated by you," said Bella.

"Surely not Bella and I can assure you that even if that were true, I have no interest in him in any way other than a family friendship and he is well aware of that. I love my Jamie and my family and there is nothing that I would not do for them, and I certainly would not jeopardise my happiness and theirs by encouraging a relationship with anyone else," said a concerned Liza. "You are my friend Bella, and even if in the unlikely event that I was attracted to your husband, I would not do that to you."

"I am well aware of that Liza. It is obvious that you and Jamie have an exceptionally good relationship and I will admit that I am envious of that," said

Bella. "My husband is now spoiling my enjoyment of your household Liza; it was my bolt hole away from my restrictive world, and that saddens me."

"Nothing has changed Bella," said Liza. "Jamie and I are the same, as are our boys. Miranda and Lucinda will be carrying on as usual, and David and Grace will continue enjoying all things to do with the Edgeworths. The cricket matches will start after Easter; sometimes the Duke will be with us, at other times he will not. Bernard will still need looking after and the villagers and farmers will treat us all like normal human beings. Anthony and Diana will come to stay with us occasionally whilst you are here."

"You are right Liza, but I am still annoyed," said Bella.

"Go up and check on your boys as you said you would and then when you come back down enjoy the fact that you are always welcome here and settle back to how you normally act in this household and ignore whatever agenda you think the Duke has. Treat him as if he needed to keep warm within our walls; you never know, maybe he did," smiled Liza. "Your mother and Douglas are doing just that. I must now make sure that all your servants are happy, warm and well fed."

Down in the kitchen Liza waved them down as they started to stand as she entered. They were enjoying their meal and she apologised for interrupting them and told them to continue eating.

"I just wanted to make sure that you are all settled and have everything that you want," said Liza and she added that they had a very full table and they all looked very cosy sitting there.

"We may well have to organise our evening meal in two sittings," smiled Mrs Lambert.

"That's a pity as you all look so comfortable together," said Liza.

"The rooms for the Duke's people will soon be nicely warm, and we can get them ready when we have finished our meal," said Mrs Frances.

"I know we'll be very comfortable here your ladyship," said the Duke's butler with his housekeeper nodding her agreement. Wendell's valet, Findley and Amelia's maid, Freda looked confused whereas Dawkins and Bella's maid seemed to accept the situation as normal. Adam and April quite often had their dinner with the boys, and they were thinking that they wished they had done so that evening as it was very late for everyone to be dining.

"Well, you're all very welcome and it's just as well you are here now as it is snowing quite heavily, and it would not have been nice for you to be in a cold place. I'm sure you will be warm and cosy here," said Liza. "I presume you have already organised what will be happening for breakfast tomorrow, Mrs Frances."

"Yes, we know what we will be doing thank you," smiled Mrs Frances.

"I'll leave you to enjoy your meal and thank you all for your support," smiled Liza to everyone.

Bella was back in the drawing room when Liza returned. She was smiling and talking to Lily and Joseph and Liza breathed a sigh of relief and hoped that Bella was going to relax and enjoy the rest of her stay with them.

Douglas and Lady Redfern smiled at Liza knowing that whatever she had said to Bella had settled her temper.

Jamie was with the Duke, Wendell and Amelia and there was a much happier look on Jamie's face as he beckoned her over to them.

"Is everything alright in the kitchen Liza?" asked Amelia.

"Yes, Harper, Mrs Frances and Mrs Lambert have everything in hand. Your butler and housekeeper will be very comfortable tonight," Liza said to the Duke. "We have a slight blizzard starting so you made the right choice coming here."

Jamie looked at her and his eyes told her that she was not a very good liar; Wendell's and Amelia's smile said the same, but the Duke had no idea and gave Liza a thankful smile.

***

"This has been a very difficult day for us," said Jamie when he came to her room that night. "I am rather concerned as I no longer feel that this is our home. It seems to have been invaded and has become a Berkshire residence where we have no say in what is happening within our household."

"Do you think that this is going to happen on a regular basis?" Liza asked Jamie.

"We are only a little way into the New Year and so far the Duke has descended on us three times, Lady Redfern and Douglas told us that they would be staying, and Bella and the boys come to us most of the time. I am not complaining about Wendell and Amelia, or Lily and Joseph; they were invited and are family to us. I enjoy their company, but I do not feel in control of my own residence," said Jamie.

"Hector was the same, but we could control him as we do Bella, however the Duke is a different matter, he does tend to appear as if he is running this household. He doesn't though, Jamie, you do. Nobody goes to him to arrange anything, they come to you," said Liza.

"Bella was right; to bring that many servants with him and expect us to feed them and make them comfortable was not just thoughtless, it was rude, and it wasn't just that he brought them, it was that he assumed that we could accommodate them at a moment's notice without an apology and without a good reason for doing so," said Jamie.

"Is his house really that cold in the winter? The first time we went to a function there I found it quite warm, and I believe that it was wintertime, although I suppose we were only in the dining room and the fires were going and there were a great many people there," said Liza thoughtfully.

"The Duke can afford to move his staff to somewhere warmer; he also has a gatehouse on his estate which could be made quite cosy, or he could take them to an Inn," said Jamie.

"But that would be very impersonal for them. I felt quite sorry for them because they knew that they had descended on us without warning and they appeared embarrassed but Mrs Frances, Harper and Mrs Lambert as well as April and Adam made them feel wanted and they in turn were helping where they could," said Liza.

"It seems that the Duke's servants have more etiquette than he does," said Jamie frowning and then his face changed, and he smiled. "I have just realised that I was exactly the same as he is. I used to find any excuse to come and visit you and then I stopped making excuses, I just used to turn up and impose on you but unlike him, my persistence was rewarded. I know his never will be."

"You're right, it never will be," smiled Liza. "I'm afraid that we have his company for quite a few days, the snow is getting quite thick now; our boys will be happy about that and no doubt I will be targeted if I venture outside."

"Why would you venture outside?" asked Jamie.

"Because I would like to make sure that your mother and Lucinda are alright as well as David and Grace; that is if it is possible to get to them and if it isn't, then nobody will be outside tomorrow, so I won't have to worry about being bombarded with snowballs," said Liza.

She moved towards the window and looked at how the snow was piling up and pulled the curtains tightly closed, walked to her bed and climbed in. Jamie smiled at her, took his dressing gown off and got in beside her.

"We have no need to worry about the Duke and his attitude, as we do exactly as we wish no matter what others demand. We do have a happy life unlike so many others," said Jamie.

***

The snow had piled up overnight, but the boys were determined to make sure that they horses were safe and well, even though those in the stable block could reach them quite easily. They spent half an hour clearing the snow from the back

40

of the kitchen to the stables and then spent several hours grooming their mounts. They all took their responsibility towards their horses seriously.

As Liza was about to attempt to reach the Dower House, the blizzard started again so instead she decided to catch up on some of her paperwork, but Amelia wanted to spend some time with her and came and sat with her.

"What's the matter Amelia, you obviously have something on your mind," said Liza.

"I think that you have a serious problem with the Duke. It is noticeable that he likes being here and it is not for the sake of his wife and children," said Amelia. "I think that he is infatuated with you and that could become quite dangerous for you. I can see that Jamie is uneasy with him being around and Bella is very annoyed with him, but he seems oblivious of the discontent that he has created."

"Thank you for your concern, Amelia. I am aware of the situation and so is Jamie although I don't believe that it is infatuation. I think that the Duke is just playing a rather foolish game and upsetting many people along the way. However, I have not acted on warnings before and paid a heavy price for not doing so. I will stay very close to Jamie, and of course to yourself and Wendell, for as long as the Duke is here. I understand that he has had a disagreement with his current mistress, so that is why he is at a loose end," said Liza.

"How does Jamie feel about the situation?" asked Amelia.

"He is fine now, but he has been feeling that he is not in charge of his own household and that it seemed to have become a Berkshire household rather than an Edgeworth one. He is over that feeling now, but I do understand how he felt as I felt the same," said Liza.

"As you know initially Wendell thought of it as a compliment to you that so many people wanted to be with you, but he is now a little uneasy. You know that he is very good at assessing people and I think that he saw something unsettling in the Duke's demeanour over dinner last night," said Amelia. "It was something that he has seen before."

"I know when that was," said Liza quietly. "It was a look that Jamie had some years ago before he and Patrick had that disastrous duel. Jamie has said that he was the same as the Duke in the past so he understands he must keep as calm as possible."

"It's unfortunate that the Duke is the biggest benefactor of the charity, and it would be a shame if we lose his sponsorship, but having his money is not worth you being hounded by him," said Amelia. "Perhaps he'll soon realise just how foolish he has been."

"Where is Wendell?" asked Liza.

"He's with Jamie and I believe that he is having the same conversation with him as I have had with you," said Amelia.

"Good, Jamie will look after me and I'm going to pretend that I don't realise what the Duke wants," smiled Liza. "Shall we go and find everyone. I know where the boys will be; they really are taking their duties towards their horses very seriously."

Jamie and Wendell came from the library at the same time that Liza and Amelia left the study, and they all went into the drawing room where everyone else had congregated. Douglas was at the window watching the weather and commenting yet again that Bella had got her wish.

The Duke and Lady Redfern appeared to be deep in conversation and the Duke was not looking too happy about whatever had been said. Bella was with Lily and Joseph, and she was regaling them with the terrible time she had experienced the previous year and how nice it was to walk into a room without having to wear a scarf, gloves, hat and an overcoat, not to mention several layers of underclothes.

"Are our boys still in the stables, Bella?" asked Liza.

"I believe so; those mounts are going to be brushed and fed to death," she commented.

"The snow is getting heavy again; they will be cut off from the house if they stay there much longer," said Douglas.

"I'll get them," said Jamie and Douglas said that he would accompany him. "Davis, Hendry and young Ernie are quite capable of making sure that all their horses are well cared for, but it's commendable that they are acting so conscientiously," added Jamie.

"Can I have a word with you please Liza?" asked the Duke.

Jamie stopped in the doorway and turned to look at the Duke as Liza said, "Of course Duke, shall we go to my study. Is it something very important; you are looking quite serious?" She smiled reassuringly at Jamie, and he stood aside and watched them go to the study.

Lady Redfern noted the concerned look on Jamie's face and moved to put an arm on him and whispered for him not to worry. "I believe an apology is being forwarded." Amelia and Wendell were watching what was happening and both were frowning slightly but looked relieved when Jamie nodded to them.

As Jamie and Douglas made their way to the stables, Douglas commented that the Duke seemed to have been playing a little game with Liza and had been trying to give everyone the wrong impression in his enthusiasm to create amusement.

"I didn't think that anyone had noticed, apart from Wendell and Amelia," said Jamie.

"I'm not sure that Lily and Joseph were aware, but they concentrate mainly on their new project at Langston House. Bella is furious and Trish took the bull by the horns and called the Duke to order before he made a complete fool of himself," smiled Douglas.

"So his approaches to Liza have been totally in fun and are harmless," said Jamie.

"Liza is a very attractive lady, and her skill at getting out of awkward approaches amuses all of us greatly; however it is felt that it was a little rude of him to descend on you with all his staff at a moments' notice, but you and Liza handled it admirably. He does think the world of you both and would certainly do nothing to jeopardise the close association that you have with his family. His sense of humour does leave a lot to be desired," said Douglas.

"Wendell and Amelia, and I of course, have been concerned. Liza was not, until we pointed it out to her. She took it just as a pitting of their wits, but by not taking notice of warnings in the past, she has suffered more than you would ever know and it is part of her life that she has desperately tried to obliterate," said Jamie.

"I have heard one or two things that have sounded quite horrendous and if they are true then she is indeed a remarkable person. You are a very lucky man Jamie, and one who needs not to worry that Liza is in any danger from the Duke, who behind his façade is a very caring man," said Douglas.

"So Lady Redfern's name is Trish, which I presume is short for Patricia. She has kept that quiet," smiled a relieved Jamie.

"That is correct, I call her Trish or sometimes Tricia," said Douglas. "Not many people know her Christian name, but I'm surprised that you did not, knowing your long association with the family."

Jamie just nodded.

***

The Duke followed Liza into her study and commented on how busy she must be judging by the correspondence on her desk.

"There are times when I seem to be inundated but Grace is very helpful and efficient," said Liza as she indicated towards a chair, and he sat down.

Liza watched him cautiously as he thought about what he wanted to say. "I want to apologise to you Liza; I have acted thoughtlessly and imposed myself and my staff on you and expected you to deal with it without question, which you have done wonderfully well, and I thank you for that. However, it has been pointed out to me that my enjoyment of your company has led to a certain amount of disquiet, not least with Jamie. To pit my wits against you and wait for your retorts gives me great pleasure. I have always admired you Liza and I would be a liar if I said that it would not be a dream come true to have a relationship with you; but it is just that, a dream, and I would never jeopardise the friendship that my family has with you and Jamie and your family."

"I have never thought that it was anything other than enjoyable banter between us," said Liza. "I was in a similar situation a long time ago and I'm afraid that it turned out very badly for me, but our association is different; there is no vindictiveness in you, although I have learned to be cautious through past experience," said Liza. "As far as accommodating you and your staff are concerned, it has been our pleasure to do so; I enjoy keeping everyone safe, especially through wintertime."

"It was very true that my house made me feel very cold and it is an unfriendly property at the best of times, and the thought of you all being together cosy and warm was too much of a draw for me. I could not in all good conscience leave my servants there to shiver uncomfortably whilst I and my family enjoyed the warmth and friendship of your hospitality," said the Duke. "They tell me that they are very happy under your roof, and you have made them very welcome."

"They have blended in well with our staff; I know that some of my servants were worried that they might try to take over their domain, but that has not been the case. They are all working very well together and seem to be delighted with the experience," said Liza.

"I do envy you and Jamie; especially your way of being able to communicate on every level; it is something that Bella also admires and now tries to copy with some success. I really can understand why my boys settle here so happily, and why Bella spends so much time with you all," said the Duke. "Once again Liza; I apologise for acting in such a foolish manner."

"There is no need," said Liza. "It would take a great deal more than you have done to create a barrier between our two families."

"I will talk to Jamie; I feel that he also needs an apology," said the Duke.

"I'm sure it's not necessary, but I know he would appreciate it," said Liza.

Chapter 2

The household settled back into a happy and relaxed atmosphere. The snow continued for the next two days and by the third day the conditions were ideal for the young and adult men to become boys. Liza and Lily put on their cloaks and made their way to the Dower House thinking that nobody had seen them leave.

They spent some time checking that Miranda and Lucinda were well and needed nothing and then made their way on to David and Grace's gatehouse. Grace decided to come back with them to the main house as there were one or two items that she would like from the kitchen.

Of course all the men and boys were in hiding and waiting for them and suddenly they were bombarded from all directions. *Not again,* thought Liza as she attempted to pick herself up and fight back. Help then came from an unexpected source as Bella ran down the front steps hurling snowballs as she went. It was such a shock to see her that momentarily the men stopped and stared, and she managed to hit the Duke full in the face, taking great pleasure in doing so.

The snowball fight went on for nearly an hour and it was a very unfair match with ten men and boys against four women. Finally Liza, Lily, Grace and Bella managed to get back into the house through the kitchen, much to the amusement of all the staff.

"I really thought that I had managed to avoid them this year," sighed Liza.

"I suppose that happens to you every year," said Bella. "I must make a note to be better prepared next year."

"How am I going to get back to the gatehouse without getting caught again?" asked Grace.

"You'll just have to wait until they finish," said Liza, "and I'm not going to help you because they'll all start throwing snowballs at me again."

They dried off quickly in front of the fire in the drawing room. "That was fun," announced Bella. "We got in some good shots, but there were too many of them for us. They're not very fair, are they?"

"No, I have always found that fairness is not part of any snowball fight," said Liza.

Eventually the fight finished and the smell of clothes drying came wafting up from the kitchen and all the protagonists came into the drawing room. The Duke pointed at Bella, "You hit me in the face," he said accusingly.

"I did indeed; you deserved it," said Bella triumphantly and the Duke laughed quite obviously pleased with the situation.

Grace went quickly to the kitchen and collected what she needed and then made her way back to the gatehouse and everyone else sat down to lunch, including the boys. Wendell, Amelia and Lady Redfern had enjoyed watching from the windows. "So this is why everyone wants to stay with you during a snowstorm," said Lady Redfern, "it's so that they can act like children and get away with it."

"That's right," said Jamie. "It has become a tradition. We count the number of snowballs that we can hit Liza with and now we are going to have to add some for all the other ladies."

The snow thawed slowly over the next few days and at the weekend preparations were being made for many of the houseguests to leave and before Lady Redfern was ready to go, she found Jamie in his study.

"Douglas and I will be leaving shortly, and I wanted to firstly thank you for your hospitality; I will see Liza before we leave but I wanted to say that although you have always been welcomed at Redfern House, it would not be wise to visit when Binky returns. I know you have no intention of meeting up with him, but I just want to say that when all is over with him, I do hope that we can resume our relationship. You and Liza have made my visit so enjoyable, even though it became rather difficult for me when I received the news of Binky's illness. I know that you both understood what I was going through but you allowed me the freedom and privacy to act on my feelings and I am sure that none of your other guests were aware of the situation," said Lady Redfern.

"I remember what you did for me when I was a boy and needed your comfort and guidance which was sadly lacking in my own home. I will not forget Binky either in those days; he was a good and loyal friend then. I am sorry that we lost that friendship and it turned to hatred. I would like to see Binky when he returns, but it may not be a wise idea and I will leave that decision to you. I am sorry that he now finds himself in such a deadly situation and I know that it is pointless asking if there is anything that I can do to help because I know sadly there is not. As far as our families are concerned, we will remain close friends. Bella would not have it any other way," and he laughed at that thought.

"Thank you, Jamie, I will keep in touch with you," said Lady Redfern.

"I don't like to ask, but do you know how long Binky is likely to be with us?" asked Jamie.

"I have no idea how long he has been ill; and as you know, Jamie, some people can last years, but Binky's letter to us does not sound that hopeful. We will know more when he is here. You will see Anthony when he returns from Belfast and let him know the situation, won't you?" said Lady Redfern.

"Of course I will. I know that he will also be saddened by this news," said Jamie and with that Lady Redfern left the study and found Liza who was wishing Douglas a safe journey. Lady Redfern kissed Liza and said that she would be in touch shortly and once again she thanked her for her hospitality.

The Duke was next to leave, as were his butler, housekeeper and valet. As the Duke had driven them to Edgeworth House, he had no option but to drive them back to their home, and he did not appear to be looking forward to the experience. Liza knew that none of his staff were happy about leaving as they knew that the Duke's house would be cold and would take some days to warm up.

Bella had decided that she was remaining with them for a few days more, which delighted Nicholas and Richard as their horses were to be stabled at Edgeworth House for a little while longer as their stable block had to be altered to accommodate them. Everyone was used to Bella announcing what she was doing without consulting anyone else.

During that time Liza decided that she should visit Mr and Mrs Rogers, and Miranda wanted to go with her. They were both concerned about the new family who had arrived in the village.

"We gave them the food and fuel that you had brought," said Mrs Rogers. "However they are in a very poor state. We have given him the odd job to carry out, but that is not enough to keep that family fed, clothed and warm."

"Do you think that there could be a problem with them living in Mr Jacob's old house? I have no idea who owns it, but it does not appear to be one of his Lordship's properties," said Liza.

"The roof is still in need of some repair; it was only temporarily mended by us nearly a year ago. We did nothing more as nobody was living there," said Mr Rogers.

"Do you know where they are from and what their name is?" asked Liza.

"He just said his name was Ken and forwarded nothing else. His children are all girls and the youngest seems to be around two years old; the oldest can't be more than eight years. None of them seem to be very happy, but who would be living like that," said Mr Rogers.

"I'll get some food from the bakers and grocers and call to see them. I hope it won't embarrass them, but they will need to eat. Can you arrange to deliver some wood for their fire please Mr Rogers?" said Liza.

"Are the children mixing with the others in the village?" asked Miranda.

"I've hardly seen the children; they don't leave the house very much, but I think that is more to do with them not having adequate winter clothing," said Mrs Rogers.

Liza, Miranda and Mrs Rogers chose some groceries and then went to the baker and picked up a couple of loaves and some sweet buns.

"I hope we're doing the right thing," said Liza. "He may be too proud to accept charity."

"If he's the father of four children then he can't refuse for their sakes," said Miranda.

"He won't refuse; he thinks the world of those children. They'll probably move on to somewhere else looking for work. I'll take you over to them and introduce you. He knows that you provided food for them before and I know he was grateful," said Mrs Rogers.

At the old Jacob's house Mrs Rogers called out a greeting and a male voice told her to enter. He was surprised to see three ladies on his doorstep. Mrs Rogers introduced Liza and then Miranda and he bowed to them.

"This is Ken," said Mrs Rogers. "I'm afraid I don't know your last name."

"It's Wallace," said Ken.

"I'm pleased to meet you Mr Wallace, and these are your children. They are all very pretty," said Liza.

"Yes, their mother was very pretty," said Ken Wallace.

"We just thought that we would like to welcome you to the village Mr Wallace. Are you going to make this your permanent home?" asked Liza.

"If I can find enough work then it does seem like a nice place to be. I think my girls could be happy here, but it does depend on what I can do," said Ken Wallace.

"Perhaps you could introduce us to your girls," said Miranda.

"Yes of course, this is Jeanette; she's the eldest. Then we have Millicent, we call her Millie, and Cora and the youngest is Libby," said Ken.

"We're very pleased to meet you all," smiled Miranda. "I hope you don't mind but we have some food that we thought you might like. We won't be offended if you don't need it."

"I'm not too proud to accept food. I know that you can see that we have very little; thank you, my girls will enjoy a meal tonight," said Ken.

"Do you have a trade Mr Wallace?" asked Liza.

"There is very little that I cannot do. I have done many jobs in my time, but work is scarce for someone who is unskilled. I am willing to do anything to put food on our table," said Ken.

"I'll bear that in mind and see if there is anything that we can do to help," said Liza. "May I ask if the owners of this house know that you are living here Mr Wallace. I don't want to create a problem for you, but if they aren't aware of you then when they find out they may put you out onto the street. I would not like to see that happen to you and your family."

"We travelled a long way and found this place. I had no choice but to move in. I don't know who it belongs to," said Ken.

"I wonder if old Mr Jacob owned it; if he did, I wonder if he had any family," said Liza.

"I've never seen anyone visit him and I never heard him talk about any family," said Mrs Rogers.

"It might be an idea for the Edgeworth Estate to lay claim to it legally and make it habitable, but firstly we must find out who did, or does, own it," said Liza. "Don't worry Mr Wallace, even if somebody does own it, we would never see you without some form of roof over the heads of you and your children. I am assuming that you wish to stay here."

"As I said, if I can find enough work, then I think that it's an ideal place, especially for the girls," said Ken.

"We'll see what we can do," said Liza and they left and spent a little while with Mrs Price before returning home.

***

"I've heard Mr Lambert say that he could do with some help around the place," Liza said to Jamie when she found him in his study.

"There's plenty of work for him and I suppose a regular assistant would be useful to him; why?" asked Jamie.

Liza told him about Ken Wallace and his four daughters. Jamie said that he would have a word with Mr Lambert as he did not want to tread on his toes, but if he needed an assistant then perhaps they should consider Ken Wallace.

"There's another thing, Jamie," said Liza and Jamie looked at her through half closed eyes.

"What might that be Liza?" said Jamie.

Liza then told him about the old Jacob's house and whether Mr Jacob had family or not.

"What do you want me to do about it Liza?" asked Jamie with a smile on his face.

"It would be nice if you could find out if anyone now owns it and if not, perhaps the Edgeworth Estate could lay claim to it and make it habitable," said Liza. "Or if there is an owner, perhaps you could buy it."

Jamie sighed and had a resigned look in his eyes. "Why do you think that they deserve our concern and help Liza? There are now many people in work because our Estate has been pulled out of the doldrums, admittedly by what you have put into it; do we really need another family to provide for?"

"No, we don't need another family to provide for, but we don't provide for any family, they work and provide for us and themselves. You are very good and cautious in business, but I know that you also care for people and especially people who are doing their best for their family under very difficult circumstances. I don't expect you to give this man money for nothing; I would want this man to earn a proper wage for a proper job and if he can't do that then he mustn't be employed," said Liza.

"All right Liza; I've said that I'll speak to Mr Lambert and let him decide and I will see our lawyer and find out if there is another owner of the Jacob house or if we can take it to become part of the Edgeworth Estate," said Jamie.

The next morning Mr Lambert went to see Ken Wallace and Jamie rode to see their lawyer. He was frowning as he rode out. *One of these days* he thought, *I'll be able to refuse Liza something; no, I probably never will be able to. She's normally right about people and this Wallace man is bound to turn out to be an asset.*

Liza watched Mr Lambert return to the house, and he had Ken Wallace with him and the first place they headed for was the kitchen. Liza knew that Mrs Lambert would give Ken a meal and something for his children. Liza was not going to interfere as she knew that they would sort everything out amongst themselves.

She wondered about the education of the children; however that was something she would look into when she returned from Belfast after Easter.

* * *

Two days passed and Anthony, Diana and Thomas drove up. Rose was also with them as was their nurse. Hasty arrangements were made to get their rooms ready and as always Rose would be staying with Miranda and Lucinda.

Thomas was now very sturdy on his feet, and it did not take him long to find Matthew who was just returning from the stables with the other boys. Matthew

50

greeted him with affection and told him that after lunch he would take him to the stables to see all their horses, which delighted Thomas.

Lily and Joseph were preparing to move into their accommodation at Langston House and they were planning to organise their stored furniture within the next couple of days.

Wendell and Amelia sat back and watched all the activity, enjoying the bustle of it all.

"I thought it was busy enough at Christmas and the New Year, but I believe it to be even busier now," said Wendell.

"Anthony and Diana are close friends and need no entertainment. They become part of the family as are you and Amelia," said Liza.

When they had all settled, Jamie called Anthony into his study and Liza assumed it was to tell him about Binky, and when they emerged they both looked rather sad, and she presumed that they were remembering their past times together as boys and young men.

Bella was happy to see Diana again and they were making plans to go to Langston House in the next few days because once Lily and Joseph had settled in, a few children would be arriving into their care.

Within the next week Randolph Langston would be arriving to make his preliminary sketches for Liza's and Jamie's portraits and Liza was not sure that she was looking forward to it, but she knew that Jamie was.

Lily and Joseph moved into Langston House and within two days the Major and Jennifer brought six children for them to look after. They did not appear quite so traumatised as those who had originally arrived at the Ffoulks house which Liza assumed was because they had been in the Major's care for just over a week. Amelia, Bella, Diana and Rose accompanied Liza to greet the children as did Penny and Randolph.

Liza admitted to Jamie that evening that although she was happy that the children were now in safe hands, she was not as emotionally involved as she had been with the first influx of children to the Ffoulks house.

Bella stayed with them until after the following weekend, as did Anthony, Diana, Rose and Thomas. Nicholas and Richard were reluctant to leave their animals, but they knew that they would be well looked after, and they were going to return the following weekend.

For just a few days they only had to share their house with Wendell and Amelia, which was a pleasure to them and then Randolph and Penny came to stay, and he began his work on their portraits. Jamie insisted that Liza wear the Edgeworth diamonds and Randolph agreed and commented that they would go well with Liza's exquisite green evening dress, which he knew would bring out the colour of her eyes. Jamie would also be in evening attire and Randolph was going to arrange that it would appear that they were looking towards one another.

Whilst Liza was sitting for her portrait Jamie would sit so that she could see him, and Randolph found that her eyes sparkled as she looked at him and she also had a happy smile on her face. He would arrange that when he painted Jamie's portrait Liza sat so that Jamie could see her as he was sure that it would add greatly to how he was portrayed.

The sittings were just for two hours a day and after a couple of days Penny left for her home as she wanted to help with the children as more would be arriving shortly. Randolph had settled into his room and was now no longer shy in their company.

Bella, Nicholas and Richard arrived for the weekend, and naturally the first place that they visited was the stable block. Ernie had been diligent in grooming and exercising their horses whilst they were away and after lunch Jamie and Davis were going to ride with all the boys to the local parkland. Wendell commented that he believed that it would be a wonderful sight to see. Randolph said that he would like to join them as one of his great pleasures was riding.

Randolph was well aware that Bella was Binky's sister, but he had come to terms with the family relationship and knew that both Bella and Lady Redfern were not approving of Binky's perverted way of life. He realised that Lady Redfern had manipulated his introduction to Liza and Jamie knowing that he and Penny needed to release the revenue in Langston House and that it would be ideal as a children's home. Life had become so much better since that introduction. He was under no illusions that many were aware that he had been assaulted by Binky and his friends when at university years before, but he was no longer embarrassed by them knowing.

Chapter 3

Time was passing quickly, and they were now planning their Easter Break. Wendell and Amelia had enjoyed their extended time with them, but they were now looking forward to seeing their grandson again.

Jamie had been made aware that Binky had returned although Lady Redfern did not contact him, and Bella never mentioned his name. He would have liked to have known how Binky was faring but felt that it would be an intrusion on the Redfern family at a very difficult time. Jamie had forwarded Lady Redfern's letter onto Evelyn, but he did not know the content. All he did know was that Lady Redfern had made it clear that it was just a guess that Jamie would know where she was, he had no other knowledge of the letter, but he assumed that it would be concerning to Evelyn.

Miranda and Lucinda had decided not to travel to Belfast that Easter and David had said that he would prefer to also stay during that time. Grace said that she would stay also, but David insisted that she went with the family and enjoy her time away from him. Miranda and Lucinda would be providing his meals each day and the household staff would make sure his house was kept in order.

Liza was finding it difficult to believe that nearly a year had passed since their trip to New York and that meant that Simon had also been with them for nearly a year. He had settled in so well that Liza kept forgetting that he had not always been with them. He wrote to Gabriel and Kate regularly and received letters from them also.

Hector and Estelle were very busy judging from their letters both to Liza and to Adam. Brendan kept in touch but was not as prolific as Hector. Garth and Tess were mentioned on occasion, and they appeared to be carrying out their duties over and above what was required. Estelle was happily teaching anyone who wanted to learn; Liza was envious of that.

Davis was very tolerant of the boys who were giving strict instructions on how each of their mounts was to be treated in their absence. They had forgotten that Davis and Hendry had spent their lives handling horses.

The Berkshire stable block was completed a week before the Edgeworths were due to travel to Belfast and the Duke's groom and stable boy arrived to collect Nicholas' and Richard's horses as they would be riding them back at the same time that Bella and her boys travelled back to their estate in their carriage. Nicholas and Richard wanted to ride them themselves, but it was thought too great a distance for inexperienced riders, much to their disappointment.

Finally they were packed and ready to leave. They were going to take the long route from London docks as it would be easier on Wendell and Amelia as it only took just over two hours to reach the docks and they could tolerate a slightly cramped carriage ride. Sadly this would possibly be the last trip that Adam and April would make with them to Belfast.

Edward and Peter were waiting to greet them when they docked in Belfast; Edward whisked Amelia and Wendell away to be with their grandson and Liza said that she would call around the next day. Peter went with the rest to Jamie's house, and he was obviously pleased to see Grace again.

"Will you be free for a meeting tomorrow afternoon?" Peter asked Liza.

"I would like to see Nicole and little Edward tomorrow morning, and I want to call in to see Mrs Edwards, but after lunch I believe I am free," smiled Liza as Jamie was nodding to her.

Liza spent some time at Nicole's the following day and enjoyed holding little Edward. He reminded her of Matthew when he was that age. She remembered that Patrick had come into their lives at that time and Matthew had loved him as much as Patrick had loved Matthew. She wondered why she was now thinking of Patrick, his memory was very strong at that moment. She was unaware that Amelia had said something to her and both Amelia and Nicole looked at her with concern.

"You didn't hear me Liza, are you alright, you look rather strange," said Amelia.

"Oh, I'm sorry. I was miles away; I seem to have developed a slight headache. It will pass," smiled Liza. "I must go and visit Mrs Edwards, and make sure all is well with her."

When Liza left Amelia sat frowning and Nicole asked her what was worrying her.

"I have seen that look on Liza's face before; she's sensing something that's unsettling her," said Amelia.

"Do you mean that she is having a premonition? I hope not because she has seen terrible things happen before," said a worried Nicole.

"She has also seen good things happen before, so I wouldn't worry too much Nicole. You must not forget that she's very tired. She has had to deal with so many unexpected visitors during and after Christmas and you know that she worries about the Edgeworth villagers as well," said Amelia. "We'll call around to see her tomorrow and you'll find that she'll be back to her normal self by then."

Mr Grouch was working in the garden at Liza's house when she arrived. "I heard you were coming for Easter; your boys have already been here this morning."

"I suppose they had cakes with Mrs Edwards. They know where to go to get help looking after their stomachs," smiled Liza as she went in to see Mrs Edwards and spend some time with her before making her way back to Jamie's house for lunch.

Peter called for her after lunch and at the offices the meeting was mainly concerning how much Joseph was missed. Edward enjoyed taking all the responsibility for what Joseph had undertaken in the past, but he was finding it a little too much and felt the need of an assistant. Also it had to be remembered that Brendan was no longer working with them and Edward was carrying out some of his tasks.

"You're so lucky to have Grace as an assistant," said Peter to Liza.

Liza smiled and told him that he would not be able to prize Grace away from her father no matter how much he could use her talents.

"Good heavens, I didn't mean for her to take the position Liza, it was just a general comment," said Peter which even made Edward smile and understand Peter's keenness.

"I presume that Mr Nedbury is fully occupied, so we will have to look elsewhere. I suppose there is nobody within the organisation who could be promoted," said Liza.

"Nobody springs to mind Liza," said Peter. "Anyway in principle you are in agreement with taking on an assistant for Edward."

"Yes, I'm sure there must be someone willing to work for our Company and I'm sure you will handle it beautifully and have no need of my input in the matter," said Liza.

"We always like you to see our main employees, Liza; you have an ability to see who is genuine and who is not, but we don't need to bother you yet on this occasion," said Peter.

Liza frowned and looked closely at Peter knowing that he was perfectly capable of undertaking such an interview without her assistance, but she wondered who Peter had in mind for the position and was keeping it as a surprise for her and as she turned towards Edward she noticed that he had an overly innocent look on his face.

"You are both looking very guilty; what have you been up to?" asked Liza.

"Nothing in particular; there is one person who may be eligible to fit the bill, but we are not really sure," said Edward.

"Is it somebody that I know and would not necessarily approve of?" asked Liza.

"No I don't believe you know him," said Peter. "I'm not sure he's the right person for the job, so we may not have to bother you with an interview yet."

"Why do I have an uneasy feeling about all this?" asked Liza. "Does your father know who you are thinking of?"

"No, but I'll be seeing him this afternoon," was all Peter would say.

She looked from one to the other and commented that she hoped that what they were thinking of would not jeopardise the smooth running of the Company. Realising that they were not going to say anything further she left the offices, but she was not happy with the situation. They were keeping something from her, and she made up her mind to visit Wendell later that day.

At home Jamie noticed that she was looking worried.

"I have never known Peter or Edward be less than honest with me before but today they are keeping something from me, and they are no good at deception. I think I'll visit Wendell to see if he knows what is going on," said Liza.

"Have you no idea what the problem is?" asked Jamie.

"It's something to do with someone they want to interview for the position of assistant to Edward. I thought that it may be somebody that I knew and didn't approve of, but they have assured me that I don't know the person that they have in mind. I don't even know the name of this mysterious person," said Liza.

"It's your Company Liza and you have every right to know who is employed in an important position. I think you are right to visit Wendell; I know you will be cautious of his health. I would like to come with you if you don't mind," said Jamie.

"I hoped you would offer and if you hadn't, I would have asked you to," said Liza.

She could hear the boys in the garden and this time they were kicking a ball around with Adam and Roberts and they were all enjoying the game.

"I can hear that the boys are well occupied, so they won't miss us," said Liza with a smile. "I must just check that all is in order for this evening and then we can leave. It's a lovely afternoon and the walk will do us good."

Within half an hour they were on their way and as always the door opened as they approached the house, but they were horrified to hear raised voices coming from Wendell's study. Amelia was standing in her drawing room and was close to tears. Liza could hear Peter arguing with his father and Edward joining in.

"I have never heard Wendell arguing like this before; what on earth is going on Amelia? Is it something to do with who should or should not be hired in the Company?" asked Liza.

Amelia nodded and burst into tears. Jamie looked towards Liza wondering what he should do, and Liza just shrugged. It was not difficult to hear what was being said in Wendell's study.

"You cannot do that to Liza," Wendell was shouting. "It will hurt her beyond belief. Choose somebody else; there are plenty of people who would want such a job. I'm surprised at your thoughtlessness Peter; Edward has always been thoughtless, but you are normally so caring of her."

"He's good and has been educated beyond the job that he has now and as Uncle James ensured that he would have a future then perhaps it is right that his future is with us," shouted Peter.

"I hope that you are not thinking of placing him in Liza's Company; that would be indecent of you; even in Marchant & Fuller it would never be acceptable to her, or to me. James purposely kept his existence from Liza and that's the way it should remain. He and his mother were adequately provided for; there is no need to go above and beyond that," shouted Wendell.

"Please calm down Father," said Edward. "Getting this excited is not good for you. It is probably best that we get someone else to help me, we are not duty bound to give him employment. It really is a very bad idea, and you know we do not want to hurt Liza."

"Liza would always agree that we should have the best man for the job and Harry Turner is the best man for the job. I'm surprised that she never knew of him, she normally has a way of finding out people's secrets," said Peter a little more calmly.

"I'm still chairman of Marchant & Fuller and own the greatest number of shares and I am telling you that you will not employ Harry Turner no matter how wonderful you think he is. How did you get to know of him?" asked Wendell.

"We've always known of him," said Peter. "You forget that we were three inquisitive boys and often heard what we shouldn't. However he did apply for a job, and I recognised his name. His qualifications are excellent."

"If that's the case then he is too qualified for the job on offer, so you'll be able to tell him that," said Wendell sharply.

Liza was standing open mouthed staring at the door into Wendell's study and Jamie had a hand reassuringly on her shoulder. Amelia was quietly sobbing into a handkerchief. The door flew open and Peter stormed out only to be stopped short at the sight of Liza's shocked face.

Edward followed him and could be heard saying, "Oh no!"

Amelia rushed into Wendell's study and was fussing over him and telling him that Liza had heard what was being said and Wendell also said, "Oh no!"

Peter and Edward slowly came into the drawing room looking very concerned. Liza finally sat down as Wendell and Amelia walked in.

Liza looked at each of them in turn and then said, "So the Fuller family are excellent at keeping secrets. You have all done very well, I had absolutely no idea. How old is he? Was he born after James and I married? I always believed that I was the only one in his life. How very naïve of me!"

"You were the only one in his life Liza," said Wendell. "After he met you there was nobody else for him. I am so sorry that you had to find out this way. In his defence I can tell you that he started his affair when he was married to Martha and a son was born to that association whilst she was still alive. Martha was a good woman but was very sickly after Frederick was born. She devoted all her time to him rather than James, and I'm afraid these things happen. Once you and he were to marry he cut all ties with his mistress, but he provided well for her and his son. He was very conscious that he had responsibilities in that respect, especially with regard to the boy's education."

"I see," was all Liza would say and Jamie recognised this as her way of not wanting to carry the conversation further.

"He never saw her or his son again; he only ever wanted to be with you. He neither needed nor wanted anyone else in his life," said Amelia.

"I see," said Liza again as she stood up and smiled and walked towards the door.

"Please don't leave like this Liza. We should settle down and talk about it all," said Amelia.

"There's really nothing much to say. I feel the need to go home now," smiled a very strained Liza. "Peter's right though Wendell; it should be the best man for the job, no matter who they are."

Jamie bade farewell to everyone and followed Liza out of the front door and as they made their way back home Liza was very quiet.

The boys were making their way up from the kitchen after their supper and they followed Liza and Jamie into the drawing room anxious to tell them what they had been doing that day. Liza was smiling at them happily and listened to everything that they were telling her. She asked the odd question, and they then went out for a short while into the garden to practice their batting and bowling. As they were leaving Matthew stopped and looked at her and she smiled and nodded to him, and Jamie was aware that the bond between them was so close that he once again knew her unease and quite possibly exactly why she was uneasy. Jamie always found it uncanny, but he felt that he had also developed the same closeness of mind with Liza.

"So," said Liza. "There is still a true Marchant on the earth. It's surprising that I didn't know. I should have been told, I would have understood or perhaps I wouldn't. I was so young then that James probably thought I would have been shocked and maybe I would have been then. I wonder why he has suddenly appeared; I suppose he thinks that he has the right to be part of Marchant & Fuller, and perhaps he has. I wonder what provision James made for him. He was left nothing in his Will, and I have seen no evidence of funds going to him from the Company."

"Wendell was right; it is very surprising that Peter and Edward are so keen to have him within the Company. I would have thought that they would have realised that it could create an unnecessary complication and alienate you to such an extent that it could drive a wedge between you and the Fullers," said Jamie.

"Did you know that James had a mistress?" Liza asked Jamie.

"It doesn't surprise me; many men do but you know that Liza. I know that he didn't have one when he was with you," said Jamie.

"How do you know that?" asked Liza.

"Because anybody who looked at you the way he did would never want to look at anyone else and you used to look at him the same way. There was no disguising how you both felt," said Jamie. "He had no room for anyone else in his life and I envied him that."

"I wonder how much money he wants," commented Liza.

"It seems likely that it is about money," said Jamie.

"I'm disappointed that James felt that he had to keep secrets from me; I always thought we had a more honest relationship than that," said Liza. "It just shows that you never really know anybody."

"I have no secrets from you Liza," said Jamie. "You also must appreciate that James would want to protect you from the seamier side of life, although I am sure that James would have had a relatively respectable mistress. You must admit that whoever she is has kept out of your life all these years; I wonder if she knows that her son is now in contact with the Fullers."

"Unless the Fullers have been in contact with her all these years and been paying her to keep away," said Liza. "I also wonder what hold her son feels that he has over Peter and Edward to make them so adamant that he works for us. I suppose it would have been to keep his identity hidden from me. Well there is no hold over them now that I know."

"You sound very bitter Liza. That is very unlike you. I know it has been a shock for you, but normally you try to understand and see a positive side to some difficulty," said Jamie.

"At the moment I can't see a positive side to this situation, but I can't let it ruin our holiday for Grace and the boys, so I am just going to let Wendell, Peter and Edward sort it out between themselves," said Liza.

"You and Wendell have the casting votes in Marchant & Fuller and you totally own Bradley & Company, so you can stop this man's employment without leaving the decision to Peter and Edward," said Jamie.

"Peter and Edward have got themselves into this situation, so they will have to get themselves out of it," said Liza and at last she smiled.

They heard a knock at the front door and a note was handed to Harper for Grace.

The boys came in from their game and sat with Jamie and Liza, and Matthew showed more concern for his mother than usual. Grace came in and said that she had a note from Peter who was unable to accompany her to dinner that evening as previously arranged and she hoped that it would not be too inconvenient for her to dine with them that evening.

"That's perfectly alright Grace, could you let Mrs Adams know please," smiled Liza.

Dinner that evening was rather subdued. "We're used to such large gatherings at dinner that it's strange to have just the three of us," said Liza.

"Something very important must have happened for Peter to cancel out on a dinner engagement," commented Grace and both Liza and Jamie nodded and agreed with her.

"What are your plans for tomorrow, Grace?" asked Jamie.

"I know that Peter has an interview tomorrow, but he said that he would come around at some time and possibly we would go for a walk," said Grace. "Are you going to be at the interview Liza?"

"No, I think that it's something that Peter can handle alone," said Liza.

***

"I don't think that Grace noticed anything at dinner tonight," said Jamie when they were alone that night. "Although I believe she was quite surprised at Peter cancelling dinner with her."

"Oh, I think that Grace noticed; she is the soul of discretion and has spent her life easing situations," said Liza. "She's no fool and has probably put two and two together."

"What are your plans for tomorrow?" asked Jamie.

"I want to take some flowers to the cemetery sometime in the morning and after that I'm all yours," smiled Liza.

"We were meant to be dining at Wendell's tomorrow night. I suppose that's not going to happen now," said Jamie.

"We'll just have to see what happens tomorrow," said Liza. "It's all down to the Fullers now; I'm not going to interfere with anything. I'm just going to let them sort it and we will just have to see what transpires."

Neither of them slept well that night and both were up early the next morning and breakfasting in the dining room when Harper announced Wendell and Amelia.

"Good morning Wendell, good morning Amelia," both Jamie and Liza chorused.

"Have you breakfasted?" asked Liza.

"We weren't very hungry," said Amelia.

"Sit down," smiled Liza. "Harper can you lay places for Mr and Mrs Fuller please."

"Liza, we don't know how to put things right between us," said Wendell when Harper had left and carefully closed the door.

"I was a little disappointed that your loyalties were to someone who has been dead for nearly nineteen years, rather than to the living, but I do understand that you wanted to preserve his good name to me. What I do not understand is why Peter and Edward are so adamant that James' son works for us, unless they feel that a true Marchant has a right to part of our Company. The two other reasons are that they were being blackmailed into giving him a job or he would tell everyone who he is, or he wants money to keep quiet. I find it difficult to believe that there is no motive behind his sudden appearance," said Liza.

"I have heard of no motive other than he would like to be Edward's assistant," said Wendell.

"I suppose yet another reason could be the fact that he was totally ignored by his father throughout his childhood. He probably felt the lack of any fatherly love and guidance keenly and now wants to make my life difficult as I was obviously the reason that his father left him and perhaps he feels that now is the time to gain some recognition," said Liza.

"Our loyalties and love are for you Liza," said Wendell. "You know that we have always felt that you are part of our family, and you also know that we love being with you, Jamie and all your boys who we feel are grandsons to us. We know that James loved you above all else and wanted you to think well of him. Having at one time had a mistress with a resulting son he felt would destroy some of the love that you felt for him. We just carried on not telling you about the situation as he had wanted that and after he died, we could see no merit in adding to your distress at the time."

"Liza, as time went by, I have to say that we forgot about her and her son," said Amelia.

"How very sad it must have been for them to have been forgotten not only by James but also by everyone else. No wonder his son has decided that he has a right to make himself known and perhaps feels entitled to part of the Marchant fortune," said Liza whose eyes belied her smile.

"Liza I can't bear the thought that we are no longer friends, or that you feel that you are no longer part of our family," said Amelia with a sob in her voice.

"I promised James that I would look after you Liza," said Wendell, "and I made a very poor job of it after James died, but I did make up for that when you returned to us and part of looking after you was to keep his secret and make sure you were not bothered by the mistakes of his past."

By then Amelia was crying bitterly into her handkerchief and kept apologising to Liza.

Jamie was frowning and feeling that he was caught up in a situation that he had no control over, and he was looking at Liza for guidance as this was a problem which was hers alone.

"I have been saddened by the losses that you have had to experience in your life Liza, but the last time that I felt this sad was when I found James' body and saw clasped in his hand the watch you had bought him," said Wendell quietly. "He died holding on to that, which was his prized possession, and I knew that his last thoughts were of you. I had to preserve how he wanted you to remember him, and it wasn't to add to your sadness by telling you of his past life which he had gone to such great lengths to hide."

"I'm so sorry Liza; please forgive us. I know it will take time for you to be able to trust us again. Your friendship and love have meant the world to us. We will miss you very much," said Amelia still sobbing.

Liza sat quietly for a while and then smiled brilliantly at both Wendell and Amelia. "It would take more than this terrible misunderstanding to ruin the years of trust and friendship that we have always had between our families. There is no need for you to think that you have to miss me; I will never let anything drive a wedge between us. There are questions that I need to ask, but they are mainly of Peter and Edward as I do not understand their insistence on employing this man," said Liza.

Everyone breathed a sigh of relief and Amelia carried on crying, but she looked much happier.

"I will answer any questions you have Liza, but I cannot also understand Peter and Edward's attitude and it surprises me because I would never have thought that either of them would have done anything to hurt you and I cannot get to the bottom of their reasoning. They have said many things but none of them ring true," said Wendell.

"Well, let's leave them to it and see what happens and eventually I will get them to tell me how they have got into this situation, and more importantly, how they are going to get out of it. In the meantime Wendell, I suppose we had better get back to running the Company as I have a feeling that they will be otherwise occupied for a while," said Liza with a smile.

Wendell gave her a watery smile, "Thank you Liza, but you can't hide the hurt you are feeling from me."

"I'll get over it Wendell, as will you and Amelia and we are already back to how we should be. Are we still invited to dinner tonight, or would you prefer to leave it a day or so, but don't leave it too long as we must have our usual Easter Sunday lunch together, which is the reason why we are here with the boys," said Liza.

"Oh please come; I presume Grace will be with you, that will please Peter," said Amelia who was beginning to ramble until Wendell quietened her telling her that they had better leave as he knew that she had much to do to prepare for the evening.

"So you would like us to leave Peter and Edward to do whatever is necessary about Harry Turner," said Wendell.

"I'm sure Peter will make the right choice and that may well be to hire him. We have pointed out our views on the matter and he will think about it and make the correct decision in the best interests of the Company," said Liza.

"We will see you later then Liza and I'm sorry that we disrupted your breakfast Jamie and have ignored you completely, it was very rude of us," said Wendell.

"You know I feel the same as Liza; you are family to us and there is never any need to apologise. I look forward to seeing you later," said Jamie.

When they had left Jamie turned to Liza and said, "You may have managed to hide your hurt from Amelia, but Wendell could see through your façade and so could I."

"I have no right to be hurt; I would think that James' son and his mother are the ones who have been hurt. I never thought that James was a cruel man, but to cut all ties with his son is something that I would not have believed he would do. It seems out of character for the man that I felt I knew so well. What a sad little boy he must have been," said Liza.

"He may not have been sad at all. His mother probably loved him, and she may have married, and her son may have thought of the husband as his father," said Jamie. "You don't know exactly what James arranged for them, but I would think that the boy did not suffer financially, although money does not make up for a loving father, but it helps if there is no alternative," said Jamie.

Later Liza collected up her flowers and made her way to the cemetery. She sat on the seat opposite James' grave and closed her eyes, until a gentle male voice said, *"So you know my secret at last Liza."*

Liza opened her eyes but there was no one there. She knew there would not be because she recognised James' voice; she had heard it on a few occasions when she needed his help.

"Yes James, I now know your secret," said Liza quietly. "It was a shock, but I do understand. I may not have done when I was younger, but I do now. What I do not understand is how you could have cut your son and his mother out of your life so completely. You were never a cruel man, but it does seem so very cruel to me. Why Peter is so insistent that he joins the Company I cannot comprehend. No doubt it will become clear to me in the fullness of time."

Liza felt a breath on her cheek and in her head she heard James tell her that Harry had a brain equal to hers and sometimes Peter needed more guidance than she could give him because of her frequent absences.

"But you have more on your mind than young Harry Turner, my Liza," said the voice in her head. *"It's Patrick, isn't it?"*

"I have very conflicting feelings on occasion. I do love Jamie, but there are times when I want Patrick so badly that I hurt in every part of my body. I miss him so much that my heartache is almost unbearable, but then I go weeks and months and am back to my normal self and my only thoughts are for Jamie. A sound, an action or a comment reminds me of him and my yearning for him engulfs me again. A while ago I believed that I had finally forgotten him, but I was wrong, and that terrible sadness washed over me."

Liza sat very still and had no idea what she was asking of James.

"Seven years have passed since he died, surely I should have just happy memories of him by now. I have very happy memories of you James, why can't I have the same for Patrick?"

"It's my fault Liza," said the gentle voice in her head. *"I taught you how to love and we were happy with that. Patrick put the passion into your love and that is difficult to forget. You will always remember us both, but Patrick even more than I. You know that Jamie loves you and has always done so and in your way you will always love him; you will be content with him, and you both would give your lives for one another. That love is probably the strongest love of all and will last you*

both for the rest of your lives. Enjoy your memories of me and of Patrick but enjoy your life with Jamie; it will be long, and it will be passionate and exciting. Don't feel guilty about your previous loves; they are part of what makes you what you are."

She felt the breath again on her face and in her mind she thanked him for listening to her and advising her and her mind was at peace. She placed her flowers on his grave and that of little Jonathan. She then moved on to Frederick's grave and put flowers there also and some on Martha's. She moved back and sat looking at them all but sensed that she was not alone. She patted the seat as she had done once before, and Jamie came and sat next to her.

"Did you give him a piece of your mind Liza?" he asked.

"There was no point, I just wondered why he had been cruel in disowning his son but I got no answer to that," said Liza.

"I'm under no illusions Liza, I know you probably got answers to other worries, but I know you would never tell me," said Jamie.

"I didn't think that you believed in ghosts," smiled Liza.

"I know that strange things happen and especially around you Liza, so the answer is yes, I believe that there are some spirits that guide us in the many things that we do," said Jamie.

Liza kissed him on the cheek and stood up saying that they had better make their way back and find out what trouble the boys had created in the household. At the cemetery gates they found Matthew waiting for them; Jamie was surprised but Liza was not.

"You could have joined me Matthew," said Liza.

"No, it was a private time for you, but I needed to make sure that you were alright as you have had a very upsetting time," said Matthew.

"We both needed to do that, didn't we Matthew?" said Jamie and Matthew just nodded.

"I think I'll go into the offices this afternoon and see what all the fuss is about," said Liza.

"Are you sure that's wise?" asked Jamie.

"Who knows, but there has to be a reason behind Peter's and Edward's thoughts and there is only one way to find out and that is to confront the problem," said Liza. "It will surprise them, but that's not a bad thing."

"I thought you had been given the answer to the problem just now," said Matthew.

Liza looked at Matthew and they smiled knowingly at one another. Jamie also knew what they were thinking, and it was a very comforting moment between the three of them.

Peter and Edward were shocked to see Liza arrive at their offices early that afternoon. She smiled sweetly at them and then made her way into the office that had been James' and now was only used by her.

"What time is your interview?" Liza called out to them.

"In half an hour," said Peter. "I didn't think that you wanted to be here for it. In fact it will be rather awkward that you are."

"Well Peter, I have more right than most to be here and I have every right to know who you are considering employing in such an important position. I would have to meet whoever it is sooner or later, so it might as well be sooner rather than later. I presume you would like to conduct the interview in this office," said Liza.

"Yes, but we didn't expect you to be here. We can use my office, I'll just have to organise it," said Peter.

"No, it's rather apt that you use this office, after all it was James'," said Liza. "You had better pull up a couple of chairs for yourselves."

"Are you going to stay then Liza?" asked Edward. "You know that would be rather embarrassing for everyone."

"I'm not embarrassed, so I don't see why anyone else should be. Does Harry Turner know that we are aware of his origins?" asked Liza.

"He knows that I do," said Edward. "Peter and I met him when he came here to see if there was any employment for him and I met him later at our hotel and I'm afraid I blurted out that I recognised the name and that he looked familiar, and then it all came back to me, and I remembered the talk in our house when we were boys about Uncle James' illegitimate son. I always make a hash of things, don't I?"

"Yes, quite often you do Edward, but we still love you," smiled Liza. "And you, Peter, why are you so keen for him to become part of our Company. By your own admission you have hardly met him; what hold does he have over you?"

"None Liza, there is no hold, but I have spoken to him, and I have seen his qualifications and they are excellent, and I did feel that it would be no bad thing to have a little of Uncle James' intelligence within the Company. We are lucky that you have the brains that you have Liza, but there are times when I would like to discuss financial matters with you face to face rather than by letter and I believe that in time Harry Turner is someone who could understand some of the complexities of the companies and the charity that we run," said Peter.

"I hope you are not suggesting that he becomes anything other than an employee of Marchant & Fuller and I hope that he does not believe that there is a family future here for him. He may be good at manipulating the finances but much of what we undertake is confidential, which is why we keep that within our two families," said Liza. "Your father is very upset with you both, I do hope that by the time we meet up for dinner this evening you have both made your peace with him. I have and I had more reason than you to create a rift."

Both Peter and Edward chorused, "Yes, Liza" and they both then smiled at the way they had answered like naughty schoolboys.

"Are you ready for this interview?" Liza asked and they both nodded. "I am not expecting him to like me, after all I was the reason that he and his mother were ignored by James and I'm sure he would find it hard to believe that I was totally unaware of his existence until yesterday."

"He has a great deal of his father's charm in him," said Edward.

"Does he think that it will sway us into giving him employment? I still believe that there is an ulterior motive behind his sudden appearance at our door, but we will see what transpires today," said Liza.

"He's not expecting to meet you today, Liza," said Edward.

"And I was not expecting to meet him today, so we will both be on an even footing. Are you ready as I'm sure he will be arriving any second; that is if he decides to turn up at all," said Liza.

There was a knock and their doorman announced that a Mr Turner was there to see Mr Peter and Mr Edward Fuller. "You can show him in here thank you," smiled Liza. A few seconds later he was announced, and Liza found it difficult not to show her shock. Before them stood a man whose similarity to James was astounding; she had expected to see some likeness, but he seemed to be a reincarnation of her dead husband. His hair was slightly lighter, and his eyes were hazel instead of deep brown, but otherwise she felt that she was looking at James. However, she hid her surprise well as Edward stood, shook his hand, and introduced her as Lady Liza Edgeworth and of course he already knew Mr Peter Fuller.

He in turn looked surprised and was staring intently at Liza. *So this was the woman who had taken his father from him and his mother all those years ago; she must have been very young, she's not old now,* he thought.

She smiled at him, and the sun seemed to come out, "Please sit-down Mr Turner and do tell me about yourself. I'm afraid it was only yesterday that I learned of you, and I have not had the opportunity to study your credentials as my colleagues have but I understand that keeping a close eye on finances is one of your many talents."

"I would not say that I have many talents, but finance is my speciality and of course a capacity to organise does go with that ability," said Harry Turner.

Peter handed Liza the documents relating to his education and qualifications as Harry Turner outlined his schooling.

Liza looked up and stared straight into his eyes and said, "There was no stinting on your education Mr Turner, and you were obviously very receptive to what you were taught. I congratulate you; your qualifications are very impressive. Do you not think that you may be overqualified for the position that we have to offer?"

"Lady Edgeworth," sighed Harry Turner, "the employment that I had just required someone who could add two and two to make four, which is good for those who have no ambition. I have studied your Companies and your charity, and I know that you do not leave employees in dead end jobs if they have talent and ambition and I have both of those requirements. You are right, I was well educated, I have my father to thank for that; I have little else to thank him for, but of course you know that already, don't you?"

"Mr Turner," said Liza. "Until around this time yesterday I had no knowledge of your existence or that of your mother. You might have got away with being employed by this Company as your name meant nothing to me, although I now understand that it did to the whole Fuller family. However you would not have got away with it for very long as you are definitely your father's son, there is no mistaking you."

"Am I so very like him; I do hope not in character," said a slightly embittered Harry Turner. Peter and Edward were nodding their agreement to what Liza had said.

"You are around the same height and build; your hair is slightly lighter and your eyes are hazel rather than brown. Since coming into this office you have rarely smiled but on the odd occasion that you have there is no mistaking the similarity in your countenance," said Liza. "As far as his character is concerned; you would be very lucky to have a quarter of what he was like, but I do understand that you have been somewhat embittered by your experience of him and I have to say that the decision that he took all those years ago I believe to have been very wrong, and I am sure that he would say the same now, but unfortunately there is no going back."

"Lady Edgeworth, Mr Peter and Mr Edward Fuller, I'd like to thank you for your time. I can show myself out," said Harry Turner.

"Mr Turner, I was under the obviously mistaken impression that you had come here to be interviewed for the position of assistant to Mr Edward Fuller and wherever else your talents were needed. So far we have discussed your education and your dissatisfaction with your parentage. Would you not like Mr Edward Fuller and Mr Peter Fuller to enlighten you about the position they have in mind for you?" said Liza.

"I did not think that you would now be interested in the talents that you believe I have," said Harry Turner.

"Well Mr Turner, I am interested but I have not been sure of your motives in coming here and if they are to embarrass me and disrupt the smooth running of our Companies, then you can leave now. If your motives are to improve yourself and our Companies then please remain," said Liza. "However, I will not give you false hope. Marchant & Fuller is wholly owned by Mr Wendell Fuller and me; with some shares in all the Fuller sons' names and it will remain that way. Bradley & Company is wholly owned by me and that will also remain that way. The charity has patrons but is run by Marchant & Fuller and much of my time is devoted to that enterprise. There are no openings for further shareholders no matter how hard you may work."

"I understand; that is quite clear and thank you for being so direct," said Harry Turner.

"If you are still interested in becoming part of the Company that your father and Mr Wendell Fuller embarked on all those years ago, then I will leave you in the very capable hands of both Mr Peter and Mr Edward Fuller, who can outline to you the duties that they would expect you to undertake," Liza smiled at him and stood to leave the office. Edward and Peter were a little taken aback but rose to the occasion.

Liza turned as she neared the door, "I hope to see you again before you leave Mr Turner."

"Thank you, Lady Edgeworth; I hope so too," said Harry Turner.

Liza moved towards Peter's office and caught sight of Samuel Nedbury on the way. He greeted her and opened Peter's door for her.

"Have you been giving a prospective new employee as hard a time as you gave me?" he asked smiling.

"I didn't give you a hard time Samuel; I just let you talk yourself into a job and it's worked out very well for us; I hope that it has done for you also," said Liza.

"You know that I would have liked to run my own business, but that wasn't to be. I am very happy here and enjoy the various sides to this business. I am now out of debt and can look to a worry-free future," said Samuel.

"I'm pleased for you Samuel and I know how disappointed you were to lose your ship; life can be tough, but hopefully you feel that you have landed on your feet," smiled Liza.

She went into Peter's room and sat waiting for them to finish their interview and in a little while Edward came to find her.

"Mr Turner is now leaving Liza and you did say that you would like to see him before he left," said Edward. Liza nodded and followed him into James' office. Peter stood up and moved from the large desk, freeing it for Liza to sit at. She looked from Peter to Edward and then to Harry Turner and all looked slightly ill at ease. *So they've left it to me to make the decision,* thought Liza.

"I presume that salary, duties and times have all been discussed," said Liza. "Although times can often mean as and when needed."

"Yes, they have, and they are acceptable to Mr. Turner should you decide to employ him," said Peter.

"I see," said Liza and Peter realised that she was making a decision that really he and Edward should have had the courage to carry out.

"So when do you start Mr Turner? Do you have to give much notice time to your present employer?" asked Liza.

"No, I gave up my employment when I moved to Belfast recently," said Harry Turner.

"We'll expect you tomorrow morning then Mr Turner, welcome to the Company and welcome to Belfast. I trust you have comfortable accommodation," said Liza.

"It is quite adequate thank you Lady Edgeworth. I'm sure that as time goes on I will become more settled," said Harry Turner.

When he had left, Peter and Edward sat quietly with Liza, all were deep in thought. Suddenly Edward said, "Who's going to tell my father?"

"You are," said Liza.

"Why me?" asked Edward.

"Why not you?" retorted Liza.

"That's right, you were the one who wanted an assistant, so it should be you," said Peter.

Liza was now laughing. "You both sound just like you did years ago when you were boys. All we need now is for Joseph to walk through that door and you would all be blaming one another for some wrong. Don't worry you cowards, I'll tell him. I'll go now."

Liza collected her cloak and bag and smiled at the 'two naughty schoolboys' and told them that she would see them later at dinner.

She arrived at Wendell and Amelia's house just as Jamie was guiding their boys down the steps to see them home.

"Hello Mum," they choroused with John going into great detail about the cakes that they had been eating and they offered to turn around and go back inside with her but Liza said that she needed to talk business with Wendell so it would be boring for them. Jamie said that he would go with them and then return for her.

Inside she found Amelia in the drawing room. "I see you have been feeding my boys well Amelia. Where's Wendell?" asked Liza.

"He's reading his newspaper in his study, but you can go in," said Amelia.

Liza knocked and entered Wendell's study and he dropped his newspaper down and looked at her cautiously. "You've employed him haven't you Liza?"

"Yes Wendell. It is better the devil you know," said Liza.

"I put Peter in charge with you by his side and I'm not sure that I made the right choice," said Wendell with some annoyance.

"I can understand you thinking that way, but I think you will be pleasantly surprised when you meet him. I had some help with the decision, although it was not an easy one to make," said Liza.

"I can still countermand that decision Liza," said Wendell.

"Yes, you can Wendell, but you are not going to do that, are you?" said Liza.

Amelia quietly came into the study and stood looking worried. "You two aren't going to argue please," she said.

"I hope not Amelia," said Liza. "I'm afraid Wendell doesn't agree with one of my decisions."

"It's that young man isn't it. What have you done?" asked Amelia.

"I went to the cemetery this morning as I needed to try to understand what was happening to us all," said Liza.

"Ah," said Amelia. "Did you get the advice that you were looking for?"

"Yes, I did Amelia," said Liza.

"So that is why you are giving him a chance," said Wendell.

"He has his fathers' intelligence and that could benefit the Company considerably, but that is not all that he has which is like his father. I felt that I was looking at James when I interviewed him, it was unnerving to start with but when you got through the enormous chip that he has on his shoulder, he has everything that James had. He has every right to have that chip; I just hope that he had some love from his mother because it was very wrong of James to abandon him, and James is well aware of that," said Liza.

Amelia smiled and nodded whilst Wendell frowned not wishing to accept that James had spoken to Liza.

"We cannot treat him like James; he can have no part in the running of the company," said Wendell.

"He knows that Wendell, I made it quite clear to him that the only shares in Marchant & Fuller were yours, mine and a few in the boys' names. I didn't bother to tell him about the few that Kate has, and I told him that it was how it was going to remain, no matter how hard he might work. I told him if his motive in applying to the Company was to create embarrassment for me and disruption to the smooth running of the Company, he would not achieve either but if he wanted to improve himself and the Company, then he would be encouraged in all that he did. He's starting work tomorrow and I just hope that Edward gives him enough to make his employment worthwhile. I can see from his qualifications that we could use him more on our financial side, but I didn't want to disappoint Edward. However I'm sure that Peter will monitor the situation and make his job stimulating. I can see him advising on both Companies as well as making the best use of the funds for the charity," said Liza.

"You studied him quite well then Liza," said Amelia. "Where is he living? Is his mother with him?"

"On a personal level all I know is that he has no love for his father, although he's thankful for his education, and that he recently moved to Belfast and his accommodation is adequate," said Liza. "At this point in the association I did not want to know more. I would not want to know more about any new employees; a time may come when we are told more. I do not know whether he is married, has children, or even if his mother is alive or dead. I am trying not to make his personal life my business," said Liza.

"You are right to keep some distance in your association and it's just as well that you mostly work from Surrey and only occasionally come here," said Wendell.

"I also felt that if he received yet another snub by his father's friends and family it could do untold harm not only to him, but also to the good name of our Companies. If he were to go away feeling disgruntled yet again, he would have that chip on his shoulder throughout his life, which could blight his future. At least we could try to knock it off for him and really, it's the least we can do," said Liza.

Wendell was thoughtful for a moment, "So your reasoning is to try to undo some of the perceived wrong that has been done to him and try to take some of the anger from him. I also know you Liza and you would not put the wrong man into our Company because you felt sorry for him; you will always put business first in that respect, so you must feel that he can genuinely benefit all that we do."

"You are right Wendell; I do think that he can be of benefit to us, and I believe that he will eventually enjoy working for us and that James would be proud. However initially we must watch him closely, although I don't believe he is likely to sabotage anything within our Companies, or the charity," said Liza.

"You truly believe that James regrets his decision all those years ago," said Amelia.

"Yes, he does," said Liza. "I can understand him wanting to leave a mistress; that's what often happens, but to ignore your own son was a very harsh thing to do."

"He provided for them more than adequately Liza and set up a fund with strict instructions relating to where the boy should be educated," said Wendell.

Liza gave him a sad smile, "It doesn't make up for not knowing your father and not having the love of that father."

"No it doesn't," said Amelia. "I do wonder why he has appeared now as he must be over thirty years old and could have come here any time in the last ten or more years. No doubt we will learn his reasoning at some time in the future."

At that point Jamie returned and she smiled at him remembering what she felt she had heard James say, which was that the love between Jamie and herself was possibly the strongest love of all. She would make sure that Jamie knew that also.

"I'm going to have to pull you away from here for a while Liza," smiled Jamie. "The boys, or should I say young gentlemen, want you to agree to one of their ideas and no, I am not going to tell you. It's up to them to twist you around their little fingers."

Liza laughed and told Amelia and Wendell that she would see them later.

On the way home Jamie asked her about James' son and she briefly told him about how the interview had gone. She added that she had been amazed at how like James he was.

"That must have been a little unnerving for you," commented Jamie and Liza nodded.

The decision that Liza was required to make was that the boys wanted to take a carriage and drive in the nearby parkland.

"As we don't have our horses with us here, we really should practice our carriage driving skills," said James who was their spokesman on this subject.

"Our carriage over here is somewhat different to those we have in Surrey, so initially you must have our driver with you. When he thinks you are proficient then you can go by yourselves, but it is a serious business and should not be treated as fun. I think you are all sensible enough to know that you can jeopardise other lives as a carriage is a dangerous weapon if not handled correctly," said Liza.

Jamie and the boys were smiling. "You have said exactly what I told them, so we are in agreement that you can carefully drive the carriage under the guidance of our driver. Hopefully you will soon be excellent carriage drivers."

"I presume that our driver will be quite willing to take his life in his hands," smiled Liza.

"We've already spoken to him," said Matthew.

"Of course you have," sighed Liza.

"I will nonetheless go and see him to make sure that he is happy with the situation," said Jamie and he made his way down to the stables with the boys trailing after him. Liza went to her room to get ready for the evening.

There was a knock on her door and Grace asked to see her.

"I know that we are dining at Wendell and Amelia's, but would you prefer that I did not join you. I know there seems to have been a problem and it seems that it is a personal one, so perhaps it would be better if I stayed here this evening," said Grace.

"No Grace, we have no secrets from you, and I'll just tell you what has been happening," and she briefly told her about the surprise of finding that James had a son and that she had decided to employ him within their Companies.

"That must have been difficult for you Liza; how did you get on with him?" asked Grace.

"He's a little disgruntled, but the biggest surprise of all is the fact that he looks just like his father. We may well talk about him this evening, but there are also a great many other topics of conversation," said Liza.

"That's good, because I am looking forward to this evening," said Grace and she left to get ready.

Jamie returned from the stables and said that the boys had already persuaded their driver to take them out the next day. All Jamie had to do was make sure that he was really happy to take on four young adults and he was going to have a serious word with them all before they embarked on their adventure.

"You are a good father, Jamie; our boys are very lucky to have you and they are also very lucky to have one another. Others have not been so fortunate," said Liza.

"I know what you are thinking, and I have to say that it was a very surprising decision for James to have made; I would never have thought that he would have abandoned his own child. He was such a kind man in so many ways and very thoughtful of others. I must admit that I am quite shocked," said Jamie.

"I don't like anyone to think ill of him. Unfortunately I know that he did it for me and that is something that I must live with and do the best I can to rectify the situation," said Liza.

"It wasn't your fault Liza," said Jamie.

"No, but it was because of me, and James didn't trust my love for him enough to tell me," said Liza.

"Perhaps he was just ashamed of his liaison with his son's mother; maybe she wasn't someone that he wanted anyone to know about. You must remember that he had been widowed for at least two years before he married you, so he could have married her at any time but obviously chose not to," said Jamie.

"I suppose she could already have been married; although she could not be living with her husband if that were the case," said Liza. "There is only one way to find out and that is to ask her son, but I have no intention of doing that. It is his business and not mine."

"You are not entirely right over that; it is partially your business as you have obviously been unwittingly blamed for the situation," said Jamie.

There was no embarrassment or awkwardness that evening; in fact it was dinner as usual in the Fuller household. Amelia had a look of great relief on her face and Wendell sat at the head of his table enjoying the banter that normally went on between his family and Liza and Jamie and now Grace was also joining in. Of course Peter was very contented sitting with Grace and Edward and Nicole were happy to be with them all and they were staying the night, so Liza had had the opportunity to play with little Edward.

Liza did not go to the office the next day. She decided that she must leave Harry Turner to Peter and Edward to welcome and settle into his position.

Both she and Jamie did have their hearts in their mouths as they watched James, Matthew, John and Simon go out in the carriage with their driver sitting next to James who was taking the first turn at driving.

"I know they have been driving around in Surrey, but this is so much bigger," said a worried Liza.

"They'll be fine," said a not very convincing Jamie.

He was right, the boys and their driver survived their excursion to the local park.

Liza and Jamie would be entertaining everyone on Easter Sunday. It was not going to be such a large gathering as Christmas had been, although it would not have surprised them if Bella and the Duke had turned up unexpectedly. Liza was looking forward to seeing Arthur and Annalise who would also be joining them.

The boys were with them for lunch, and they all looked so tall and so handsome. As always they acted impeccably and joined in the conversation. Although Liza was proud of them, she also felt a little sad that they were no longer her little boys and in six months they would not be at home, they would all be living at their university.

They would be staying for another ten days before returning to Edgeworth House and each day the boys went out driving in the park and Liza was dreading the time that their driver would say that they were ready to go out alone, but

Jamie told her not to worry as all the boys were very responsible. Liza wondered whether Jamie knew his boys at all, but she did not argue with him.

During the week after Easter Liza and Jamie were walking towards Liza's house to see Mrs Edwards and Mr Grouch and coming towards them was Harry Turner. Liza introduced him to Jamie who later admitted that there had been no need as it was obvious who he was.

"How are you settling in Mr Turner," asked Jamie.

"I am enjoying my employment Sir, there is a great deal to learn and undertake; I know I shall be kept busy in the future. I am however on my way to my lodgings as I have managed to secure much better accommodation and Mr Edward suggested that I take some time this afternoon to move my belongings and get settled," said Harry Turner.

"I hope Edward and Peter are stretching your mind Mr Turner as I know that you enjoy a challenge and sitting idle does not suit your character," said Liza.

"I have not seen you in the offices since I joined, do you not go in every day? Or was that because it was Easter?" he asked Liza.

"I work from wherever I am Mr Turner and I do have my assistant with me, who is also a cousin, but I am planning to be in the offices tomorrow. I have a meeting and some documents to look over, so I may well see you then," smiled Liza and once again he felt that the sun had just come out from behind a cloud.

"I know you don't wish to dwell on the past," Harry Turner said to Liza, "but I would be interested to know where my father had lived."

Liza said nothing for a moment as it was obvious that she was making up her mind over the question and then she said, "we are just on our way to the house, Mr Turner; you may join us if you wish and if you are really interested, I will show you around. It is, of course, my house now. Your father and I did spend a few very happy years there. However, I will understand if you would prefer not to visit."

Jamie was surprised at Liza's offer, but he did think that it was probably Liza's way of trying to understand this young man and to lay any ghosts to rest.

"Thank you and if it is no trouble to you, I would be delighted to see where my father spent his leisure time," said Harry Turner.

"It is no trouble, but I must warn you that you may give my housekeeper, Mrs Edwards, a heart attack as well as Mr Grouch, my gardener," smiled Liza.

"You certainly will Mr Turner," said Jamie and he laughed.

"So you still have the same staff? That's remarkable. I know you said that I look similar to my father, but surely there are many differences," said Harry Turner.

"If there are any differences, I have yet to find them," said Jamie.

"There are differences, but they are not immediately obvious. Take it as a compliment Mr Turner; your father was a very handsome man," said Liza once again smiling.

They continued their way to Liza's house and as always, she just walked in through the front door, she had no need of a butler to show her in. She called out to Mrs Edwards that they were there and that they had a visitor.

They went into the sitting room and Harry Turner was looking around curiously as Mrs Edwards entered, he turned, and Liza was right, Mrs Edwards clutched her chest and gasped.

"It's alright Mrs Edwards, you are not seeing a ghost; this is Mr Harry Turner who is a very close relative of Mr Marchant's. I admit that I was taken aback when I first met him," said Liza.

"I wasn't aware that Mr Marchant had any relatives apart from his son. I had better warn Mr Grouch, he will be just as surprised as I was," said Mrs Edwards.

"Perhaps this was not such a good idea," said Harry Turner when Mrs Edwards had left to arrange tea for them.

"Perhaps it was not, but sooner or later you would be seen by those who knew James Marchant and that could create unwelcome gossip, whereas now you will be known as a close relative and that is no lie. What you wish others to know is entirely up to you but for the moment I would think that being a close relative would have its advantages," said Liza.

Jamie was smiling at her manipulation of Harry Turner, and he realised that much as this young man wanted to be angry with Liza, he was finding it difficult to be so.

Mr Grouch knocked and entered asking if she was happy with the garden. Liza smiled, amused at Mr Grouch's excuse to look at James Marchant's close relative.

"Yes, Mr Grouch, the garden looks delightful and just as I like it. Mr Turner this is Mr Grouch who has been with this household since before my time here, and you must have noticed how well he keeps the grounds," said Liza.

"They are indeed well kept," smiled Harry Turner, who realised that Mr Grouch had no real reason to ask Liza about the grounds and just wanted to look at him.

Mr Grouch left the room and Liza said that Mrs Edwards could show him around the house if he was still interested in seeing it.

"Thank you, no. It was kind of you to offer but I really should sort out my accommodation. It was nice to meet you Lord Edgeworth and perhaps I will see you tomorrow, Lady Edgeworth," said Harry Turner.

"I'll get Mrs Edwards to show you out Mr Turner," said Liza.

"No need, I will find my own way, but thank you. Good afternoon to you both," he said as he left.

"I wonder if it was wise bringing him here," said Jamie.

"I don't think that it has done any harm, although Wendell may think differently," said Liza. "I will see how things are at the office tomorrow and I'm planning to take Grace with me. There is a meeting regarding the charity in the afternoon, I presume you were notified and will be there; I know that Wendell is planning to join us."

"That should be interesting, Wendell doesn't go to the office very much, I suppose his curiosity has got the better of him," said Jamie.

"Everyone's curiosity will pass. They will get used to him and his looks shortly," said Liza. "Let's go down to the kitchen and see Mrs Edwards and Mr Grouch and have tea with them."

Wendell found meeting Harry Turner a little unnerving the following day and before the charity meeting he came in to see Liza and said that she had been right and that he could believe that Harry Turner was the reincarnation of James Marchant.

"It must be creating confusion amongst those who knew James; he does appear to be quite intelligent and it would seem that he has taken advantage of his education. I hope that he is not here to create disruption," said Wendell.

"Well, don't let that be your worry Wendell," said Liza. "It was Peter and Edward who were keen to employ him, so let them take the responsibility."

"I will Liza, because I know that Peter would never let anything, or anyone disrupt business. I thought you would have been very hurt by his sudden appearance on our doorstep," said Wendell.

"I have been hurt; I thought that my relationship with James was open and honest, but I was wrong, and he did have secrets. I wonder if anything else is going to come out of the woodwork," said Liza. "I demand honesty in my relationships and so far, James hid his son, Patrick hid a wife and I now wonder what Jamie could be hiding."

"Jamie would never be able to hide anything from you Liza; you know that he would give himself away. He would not be able to face you if he had a secret," said Wendell.

Liza thought about what he had said, and he was right. She remembered back to when he had drunkenly thought that he had bedded his previous mistress and found it difficult to return home and when he did his face told her exactly what he had done.

"You're right Wendell, Jamie is unable to keep secrets from me; his face gives him away immediately," said Liza.

"I think that he kept many secrets from Evelyn, but certainly none from you," said Wendell.

Chapter 4

The time passed quickly and soon they were heading back to Edgeworth House. Harry Turner seemed to be relatively happy in his work and the chip on his shoulder appeared to be getting smaller. Liza still had no idea if his mother was alive or not; it was not her business, but she was intrigued.

The first place that the boys visited on their return was the stable block. Miranda, Lucinda and David found it amusing but Liza and Jamie would have to reprimand them as they had not acknowledged that their family were alive. Horses were obviously more important than relatives that they had not seen for weeks.

Bella arrived with Nicholas and Richard the first weekend that they were home. Her boys really would have liked to have brought their mounts with them, but James, Matthew and John allowed them to ride theirs on occasion and they helped to groom them also.

The cricket season was about to start, and that first weekend saw many people practising their batting and bowling skills on the green. Liza watched realising that when the season was over her boys would be away from her. She was sure that they would enjoy what they considered freedom, but she was not looking forward to them being somewhere other than under her wing.

Liza and Jamie never asked Bella about Binky but on one occasion she did forward the information that he was very sick, and she did not think that he was going to last much longer. Lady Redfern was with him most of the time, but she had not asked Jamie or Anthony to visit him, and they could only assume that it was Binky's choice. Jamie still had an uneasy feeling that Binky may still plan revenge on his family no matter how close his sister and mother were to them. He would have been happier if he could have seen him and make his own judgement on whether they were in danger or not. Anthony was also a little unnerved with him being back in England as he had been the one to confront Lady Redfern and the Duke of Berkshire with Binky's misdemeanours against Jamie's family.

During the week Liza noticed that Ken Wallace and Mr Lambert appeared inseparable, and Ken was a very keen employee. Liza wondered what his children were doing and whether they were at school. Rather than ask him, as she was going into the village later that day, she would find out for herself.

Mrs Price was with Mr and Mrs Rogers when Liza visited.

"I was going to visit you Lady Edgeworth as I have an idea for my Susan. Have you anyone in mind to take over from April when she and Adam move into the village," asked Mrs Price.

"No I haven't thought about when that time comes. I shall miss April very much and Adam also, but at least they won't be very far away," said Liza.

"I wonder if you would consider my Susan to take over those duties. She is a very good worker and has dreamed of the position since she knew that April was leaving," said Mrs Price.

"Susan is quite bright, do you not feel that with a little more tutoring she could make a very adequate teacher, which is a much better career?" said Liza.

"With all due respect Lady Edgeworth, we have all seen how you never stop teaching those you employ. April has furthered herself by being with you; she has travelled to places that she would never have dreamed possible and had the opportunity to learn more than most in her position. I am convinced that my Susan would never really end her education if she were with you," said Mrs Price.

"When Susan has completed her term at school and she is still of the same mind, please send her up to the main house and we can discuss her duties. You do realise that she would be living at Edgeworth House, but it is not so far away that you would not be able to see her," said Liza. "I presume that she is capable of sewing, mending and generally caring for clothes."

"She is very good at all those tasks," smiled Mrs Price.

"Of course she would be as I know that her mother is an expert," said Liza with a smile.

"Thank you, Lady Edgeworth; she'll be really pleased," said Mrs Price.

"I still have to establish that it is definitely what she wants," said Liza.

"I can assure you that it is definitely what she wants," smiled Mrs Rogers. "She has talked about it and nothing else for some time now."

"Hopefully both your children will end up with exactly what they want," said Liza. "I understand that Derek will be assisting Adam when he starts at the school in the new term. He will be very good with the children."

"Now that he is able to walk almost perfectly then he will enjoy it and he won't be laughed at," said Mrs Price.

"I'm sure that Adam would not allow that, but you are right, children can be cruel. However, Derek walks extremely well now, you would never know that he had a problem at one time," said Liza.

"I know he'll never run or dance, but he can do everything else now and I never thought that I would see the day when he would appear normal," said Mrs Price.

"You've all worked really hard to reach this stage, you must all be complimented on your dedication," said Liza. "I know that he'll be happy with Adam at the school and I'm sure Susan and I will get on well together."

Mrs Price smiled and left, and Liza turned to Mrs Rogers and asked how Mr Wallace and his children were getting on.

"The house is looking better, and the children are beginning to appear fairly well fed now," said Mrs Rogers. "I know what you want to ask. Are the two older ones going to school? The answer is no, they are too busy looking after the young ones and keeping house."

"Thank you, Mrs Rogers; you know me so well," smiled Liza.

As Liza drove back to Edgeworth House she was overtaken by Jamie and all the boys who had been out riding. The boys went on ahead and Jamie rode beside her.

"They are all getting on well with their riding," said Jamie. "James is a true English rider, but I have to curb the American enthusiasm of the other three."

"They did become used to the wide-open spaces, although Simon is the only one who has ridden for any length of time by himself. Matthew and John mostly went with Patrick or Sean, but of course they were very young then," said Liza.

"I remember how different it was when I went to America to find you. I must admit that once I got used to the saddle and then the speed that was sometimes necessary, there was quite a sense of freedom to the ride," said Jamie.

Liza was smiling at a memory. "You should have seen me riding an Indian pony without a saddle. I don't think I could do that now."

"Are you feeling that you are getting old my Liza?" smiled Jamie.

"Well I will be forty soon," remarked Liza.

Jamie looked at her out of the corner of his eyes, "You don't look it and you certainly don't act it; especially at night."

Liza grinned at him. "I left Liverpool twenty-three years ago and I met you soon after that. You are still as handsome now as you were then; you don't look quite so aloof though."

"Did I look aloof? I always thought that I was quite approachable," said Jamie.

"You were approachable, you just liked people to think that you weren't," said Liza and suddenly she added, "I haven't seen my parents for twenty-three years. I wonder if they are still alive."

"Do you want to find out?" asked Jamie.

"No, they have not contacted me; I don't need them. I have you and our boys and I also have your mother and uncle as well as Lucinda and Grace. They are proper family," said Liza.

"Are you planning a party for yourself Liza?" asked Jamie.

"Just family, friends and our staff; nothing very big," said Liza.

***

The day dawned and Liza stretched and yawned. It was her fortieth birthday, and she was still tingling from the way that Jamie had loved her that night. The door opened and April brought in her breakfast with Jamie following her.

"Happy birthday Liza, I hope you have a wonderful day, also I decided that I would once again like to watch you eat your breakfast in bed and mop up what you dribble down your chin. It's a while since I've done that," smiled Jamie.

There was a knock on her door and four boys entered before she could answer. "Happy birthday Mum," they all said in unison.

"I suppose Dad is here to clean your chin while you're eating," said James.

"Do you still do that?" asked Simon.

"I'm afraid that I have never learned the art of eating successfully in bed," smiled Liza.

Liza had visitors arriving. Bella and her boys were there before lunch, followed by Anthony, Diana, little Thomas and Rose. Douglas Carlton came alone as Lady Redfern was still looking after Binky. Peter had arrived the day before bringing gifts and good wishes from his parents and Edward and Nicole who would not be able to join them. The Major and Jennifer would be along later in the day, as would Joseph and Lily as well as Penny and Randolph.

All their staff would be joining them for the evening buffet as would Mrs Price, Derek and Susan and Mr and Mrs Rogers. Ken Wallace had firstly refused, mainly because he had nothing suitable to wear for the evening, but Mr Rogers gave him one of his older suits and Mrs Price altered it for him.

During the afternoon Jamie and Anthony sought out Bella to ask how Binky was getting on.

"I saw him this week, but I won't go again. I prefer to remember him the way he was. I know that he has done some terrible things in his life and gone with some very strange people; and although we are very different, he is still my brother," said Bella who just could not bring herself to say that she still loved him.

"We wondered whether it would be wise to find out if he would accept a visit from us," asked Anthony. "I know that it was necessary for us to go our separate ways, but we both remember our times when we visited and played together when we were boys."

For once Bella was finding it difficult to say what she thought, but finally she said, "My mother would have liked him to make his peace with you and she has suggested it on occasion, however Binky is still holding a grudge. He doesn't blame you for his disease; he knows that you could not possibly have anything to do with that, but he does blame you for his banishment and not being able to be treated in time for his disease, which could perhaps have cured him. He will never think differently no matter how illogical his arguments may be."

"I'm sorry to hear that Bella," said Jamie. "Although I do hope that he is not planning some form of revenge on us."

"I wouldn't like to guarantee that he has not thought about it, but my mother is keeping a close eye on him and there has been no contact with any of his old friends," said Bella.

"We will still be vigilant," said Jamie. "We would not take any chances with our families."

"He won't be with us very long now Jamie, so your worries will be over soon," said Bella.

When she had left to go to her room, Jamie commented that he hoped that Binky had no previous arrangements to do them harm as he was devious enough to take revenge when he was dead, the thought of which would please him until the day he died.

Amelia and Wendell along with Edward and Nicole were going to be missed as they had always attended Liza's parties, but at least Peter was representing them.

The Duke turned up unexpectedly; he had been invited but had a previous commitment, however he had rearranged his schedule specially to join them. His room was already made up for him as both Liza and Mrs Frances thought that he might make an appearance. Bella seemed pleased to see him as did his sons and Liza wondered whether they were coming to a better understanding. His valet was looking forward to the evening as he still remembered the good time he had experienced at the New Year's Eve party.

Once again the musicians from the village were employed for the evening and Mr and Mrs Rogers brought Mrs Price, her family and Ken Wallace, who looked remarkably good looking, as well as comfortable in his smart suit. *He's moved in higher circles before*, thought Liza.

Susan made her way over to April and Adam whilst Derek came to Liza and Jamie. "I am hoping that at your next party I will be able to ask you to dance," smiled Derek. "I have been practicing with my mother and Susan but I'm not yet ready to whirl around the dance floor."

"If you like Derek, should the musicians play a very slow waltz, we could try," said Liza.

"Would you really?" said Derek. "You know that I would only be walking around the dance floor, don't you?"

"I'm sure we could both walk to the music," smiled Liza and she noticed that Jamie was quietly talking to the leader of the musicians and in a short while they started to play a slow waltz. Derek bowed to Liza, and he took her hand and slowly led her onto the dance floor where they slightly stumblingly moved keeping in time to the music. People were holding their breaths, but Derek was oblivious of those watching; he was just enjoying his first experience of dancing and especially with the person who he believed had brought him to this point in his life and given him a future.

Liza and Derek were both grinning at one another triumphantly; they did not notice that Mrs Price was openly crying and surprisingly Bella was comforting her along with Mrs Rogers. Susan also was shedding a tear and both April and Adam were gently calming her. Nobody was talking, they were all watching and smiling, one or two ladies were a little watery eyed. As the music finished Liza curtsied and Derek bowed and began leading Liza back to where Jamie was standing and smiling; Matthew started clapping and suddenly the whole room joined in, much to Derek's embarrassment.

Liza made her way to the stairs so that she could stand above everyone and waited for the applause to subside and when it had she said, "I have received many wonderful presents tonight, but the best one of all has been this one. Thank you, Derek, for making my evening, and this birthday, so memorable."

Everyone clapped again as Derek joined the boys, but he was smiling happily, and he acknowledged to himself that he loved Lady Liza Edgeworth, however he was sensible enough to know that it was because she in turn loved him but not in a passionate way and he also knew that this crush that he had on her would change as he grew older.

Jamie came over to her and said, "That was a wonderful thing to do Liza; you have made a young lad very happy and made him feel that he is capable of achieving many things in life. I think that you now have one of your greatest fans."

"It's his achievement and that of his mother and sister. Our boys can also take some credit for it by treating him the same as they are," said Liza.

"And Matthew for teaching him to slide down banisters," laughed Jamie.

Food was consumed and drink flowed freely. Mrs Lambert proudly wheeled in an enormous birthday cake, and it was insisted that Liza cut it as she had done her wedding cake and when that ceremony was over the music and dancing started again. Liza was surprised to see that Ken Wallace was dancing with Penny Langston and he was not unfamiliar with the music or the steps. *He's definitely had a much better life than he has now*, thought Liza and she admired the fact that he was capable of turning his hand to any job to keep food on the table for his family. She was intrigued but felt it wrong to delve into his past circumstances; all she would do was try to ensure that his children had the best start possible.

Liza was in demand all evening, which was to be expected. Jamie found it difficult to get her to himself but at last he had her in his arms and he refused to let her go. Everyone had wished her a happy birthday and as it was one o'clock in the morning her birthday was over.

She was surrounded by well-wishers all getting ready to leave or make their way to their rooms. The boys had lasted until the end and they each kissed her before leaving. Derek came and also kissed her on the cheek as he was about to leave with his family, Mr and Mrs Rogers and Ken Wallace.

The musicians were packing their instruments as Mrs Lambert, Mrs Frances and the rest of the staff were helping to clear the tables. Liza came over to thank them for ensuring that her birthday had been such a happy time.

"I never thought that I would see the day that young Derek danced. I know that you said that it made your evening, but it made the evening for everyone here. I don't think he was planning to do that tonight; he didn't think that he was ready, but he was, and it was a delight to see," said Mrs Lambert.

"You've known him all his life haven't you Mrs Lambert?" said Liza.

"It was such a tragedy but good often comes out of evil and it's not only his mother who is proud of him, we all are, and I could see that you were also," said Mrs Lambert.

"He and his family have worked so hard to get this far; it has not been easy for them, but it has been wonderful to see how he has progressed, and we have watched him every step of the way," smiled Liza. "Good night, Mrs Lambert, don't stay up too late and once again thank you for everything."

April was hovering in her room, and she helped Liza out of her dress before making her way to her own room. Liza sat for a minute at her dressing table and before she could make her way to Jamie's room, he came to her.

"Thank you for my lovely birthday, Jamie; I've had a wonderful time," smiled Liza.

"Last night I went to bed with a young woman; tonight I'm going to bed with a middle-aged woman," laughed Jamie as Liza attempted to hit him. Jamie grabbed her and told her that she looked just the same as the first time that he had seen her.

"And so do you Jamie," said Liza. "We have had many traumas in between those years but we really haven't changed at all, maybe we have in looks; not in character though."

"I think my character has been through many changes, but I hope that it's as you would like it to be now," said Jamie.

"I wouldn't change you for the world Jamie and really you haven't altered; you've just mellowed a little," said Liza.

***

The cricket season was well under way and each weekend everyone gathered for the match, but it brought them nearer to the time that the boys would leave for university and each week Liza felt sadder and sadder at the prospect of their going.

Liza was not the only one to worry about the boys leaving; Miranda and Lucinda kept mentioning how quickly the weeks were passing by.

Adam was preparing for his role as headmaster of the village school and April was training Susan in her duties. They would be moving into their new home in the village in a couple of months. Everything was about to change and Liza did not like the prospect.

Ken Wallace began bringing his children along to the cricket matches and they began mixing with the other village children. The Edgeworth lawyers had investigated the ownership of the house that the Wallace family were using, but they could find no relatives of old Mr Jacob and nobody from the village knew where he had originated from. There was no record of rental payments to any other party, and it could only be presumed that the old man had just moved into the property and lived there for a great many years with no official ownership. All that could be done was to take the property and claim it as one owned by the Edgeworth Estate; if another owner turned up at a later date, then the problem would be dealt with at that time.

At one of the cricket matches Liza noticed that Ken Wallace was smiling whilst watching his children playing with others. The two-year-old and four-year-old were being played with by several of the older village children whilst his other two were enjoying the freedom of not having that responsibility.

Liza took advantage of the opportunity to talk to Ken.

"Your children seem to be enjoying the afternoon Mr Wallace; they appear to be mixing with the other children well, it's good to see them playing," said Liza.

"I understand that our house is now an Edgeworth one," said Ken. "Although I do also understand that if an owner turns up at some time, then we may have to look for somewhere else to live."

"It seems unlikely that anyone will turn up, but you never know who may appear in the future," said Liza. "We would not see you and your girls without a roof over your heads Mr Wallace."

"I believe that Lady Edgeworth; from what I am told by various people around here you make sure that not only your staff but also the villagers and farmers are treated well. It's a comfort to know that when you have children to consider. We were lucky when we came across this place; we had no idea where we were heading, we just needed to get out of the weather at that time," said Ken Wallace.

"It's nice to see more children in the village; have you enrolled them at the school yet?" asked Liza.

"Unfortunately I need the two older girls to look after the little ones and keep house for me. I would like them to go to school and mix with the others, but it isn't practical. It's lucky that I am able to teach them to read and write when I have the time," said Ken.

"I know it's not easy in your situation. If I could arrange for someone to come to your home for an hour or so to give your girls some lessons, would you be interested. Eventually they may be able to attend school as they get a little older," said Liza.

"I would be interested in anything that will give my girls an education, even if it means that I must wait for my evening meal. I want them to do well in life and they haven't had a very good start. I'm hoping that when I am a little more established, I would be able to afford to pay someone to look after the little ones so that at least Jeanette and Millie can attend school," said Ken.

"We'll see what we can work out; I am so pleased that you are a father who believes that girls should be educated just as much as boys," said Liza.

Liza would have liked to have asked him about his background as it was obvious that he had been well educated and although he was an excellent manual worker, he had not been born into that life. One day she may find the answer to his origins, but at the moment he did not forward any information and it was not her business.

***

The boys were taking advantage of the good summer weather and were out riding every day; sometimes Jamie would be with them and sometimes Randolph joined them.

Liza's portrait was well on the way and Randolph had also started Jamie's. Liza was fascinated that he was working on both their portraits at the same time. He was very happy undertaking the assignment and he also spent time back at Langston House guiding any child who showed an interest in art; he had become a very busy man. Penny was also busy helping Lily to guide the children in some lessons. Liza noticed that Penny often asked after Ken Wallace and she wondered whether there was an attraction there, unlikely as it seemed.

Jamie was very attentive to Liza and the boys as the time was approaching for them to leave to further their education. Bella and Nicholas and Richard were with them every weekend and all six boys were getting really excited at the prospect of leaving home.

A message came from Lady Redfern informing them that Binky was asking Jamie and Anthony to visit him. Bella was visiting at the time and Jamie asked her if she thought it wise for them to do so.

"He's harmless now Jamie," said Bella. "Although we don't know whether he set anything in motion in the past. I don't want to see him again as I was shocked by his appearance last time I was with him, and I must warn you that you will also be shocked."

"I'll go after the weekend and hope that Anthony can join me; I'll send a message to him," said Jamie.

Anthony arrived the next day and he and Jamie discussed their visit to Binky.

"This is not something that I really feel happy about," said Anthony. "However, I do remember the good times that we had when we were boys. It's such a pity that Binky had to turn out the way he has, and I am so sorry that we didn't see it sooner. Perhaps we could have stopped some of his excesses and saved some of those he assaulted."

"We just didn't see it, Anthony; we were very naïve in those days and Binky never approached us in that way," said Jamie.

They set off before lunch with Davis driving them. Liza was concerned as Binky had threatened her family in the past and there was no guarantee that he was not capable of paying someone to carry out his evil intentions.

"Please be careful," she had said to Jamie as he was leaving.

"Lady Redfern will not let anything untoward happen to us Liza. She would not have asked us to visit if she had not been sure of our safety," Jamie had replied.

Surprisingly they returned much earlier than expected and they both looked ill at ease. Liza came to find them and they looked up as she entered the room.

"It has obviously been very difficult for you both; is he in a very bad way?" asked Liza.

"Yes, he is Liza," said Jamie. "He really did not look like the Binky that we knew. He won't be with us for very much longer."

"Will you be visiting him again?" asked Liza.

"No, it isn't wise for us to see him again," said Jamie.

Liza looked from Jamie to Anthony and back again, "What is it? Something has happened and it's not because Binky is dying. Has he set something in motion that is going to hurt us?"

"I'm afraid so and we do not know what it might be. He will die happy thinking about it," said Anthony.

"Lady Redfern was shocked; she truly did not think that the reason he wanted to see us was so that he could take pleasure in letting us know that we are in danger. She does not believe that it is true as he has seen nobody since he returned. She thinks that it is just talk on his part. I hope that is the case, but we will of course be vigilant as we always have been," said Jamie.

"I should have thought that he would have wanted to make his peace rather than die in hatred and turmoil," said Liza. "So we will have to constantly look over our shoulders and watch our boys closely."

"Lady Redfern will try to establish exactly what he is talking about and let us know what she finds," said Jamie.

Bella knocked and entered. "Is he still threatening you Jamie?" she asked bluntly.

"I'm afraid so Bella, but we have no idea what he has planned for us," said Jamie.

"He'll tell me. He'll find it funny that he is worrying you and he will want to boast about it. I'll see him tomorrow and find out if he has really employed someone to do you harm. I hope that it is his illness that has affected his brain," said Bella. "I'll leave Nicholas and Richard here if I may."

Bella left the following morning and was back by teatime. She looked very sad and although they wanted to know what had happened, they gave her time to compose herself and when she had she told them that they had no need to fear what Binky had planned for them. She was asked how she had managed to dissuade him from taking his revenge.

"I pointed out that I and my family were constantly in your company and anything that was planned against you would affect me and my boys. If he damaged you, he would also be hurting his own family," said Bella. "The Duke is

90

in the process of undoing Binky's plans. He's paying off those who were employed by Binky and he's threatening them with incarceration or worse if they attempt to carry out anything which would harm either you or your family. The same goes for Anthony and his family," said Bella.

"How did he manage to arrange it without your mother knowing?" asked Liza.

"He did it on his travels before he arrived home. My mother is very upset; it was bad enough that she was losing her only son, but to have him try to take revenge on you all has distressed her considerably. I think I'll go and see my boys," said Bella much to their surprise.

When she had left the room Jamie said that no matter how she believed that the crisis was over, he was still going to be vigilant as he could not trust that those employed would not carry out Binky's instructions.

Dinner was a little subdued that evening and Liza was pleased when she made her way to her room where both April and Susan were waiting for her. She smiled knowing that she needed neither of them to help her that night, but they would be upset if she didn't use them, especially Susan who was taking her duties very seriously.

Finally they left and she made her way to Jamie's room.

"Are you alright Liza," asked a concerned Jamie. "You look a little worried. I suppose it's to do with Binky's last wishes."

"Yes, I felt a little insecure this evening and need you to hold me tonight because I always feel safe with you," said Liza.

"I will always do my best to keep you and our family safe Liza. We have a good life, it's just a pity that every now and again something worrying rears its ugly head," said Jamie.

***

The summer was passing too quickly for Liza, knowing that at the end of it she would be living without all her boys. Matthew had been with her all his life and the others so long that she could hardly remember a time without them. Jamie was very conscious of how she felt, and he experienced some of that sadness when he thought about how quiet the house was going to be. Over the past few years he had become used to the noise of children enjoying their lives. He would miss the jokes that they played on him and the questions that they asked. He liked riding with them and showing them the intricacies of grooming and carriage driving. He loved them all, even Simon who had only come to them just over a year ago; he knew that Liza loved him, and it was easy to see why.

Derek was also going to miss them; they had been fast friends for over five years. He was, however, looking forward to helping Adam at the village school. He was going to begin his teaching career by helping those who needed to learn how to read and write; Adam also had him in line for further tutoring tasks as time went by. It had also been agreed that he would spend an hour or so each day with Ken Wallace's girls until such time that they were able to attend school.

April and Adam were in the process of getting their home ready; it would be the first time that April had lived in a home of her own. Adam was also rearranging the school and bringing it up to date with the help of some of the village people.

Mrs Lambert said that she would not know what to do with herself when the boys left. She admitted that her highlight of the day was when they all descended on her for their supper. Their breakfast time and lunchtime were enjoyable, but supper time was special to them all.

Jamie wished that so many people would stop reminding them that they were going to miss the boys; they needed no reminders as it was constantly uppermost in both his and Liza's minds.

Bella turned up one day in the middle of the week with the news that Binky had died. She had Nicholas and Richard with her and an invitation to Binky's funeral for Jamie and Anthony. Jamie immediately forwarded Anthony's on to him.

Nicholas and Richard were a little subdued, but as Bella explained, they had hardly known Binky as she had kept them well away from him before he went to India.

"Will you stay with us Bella?" asked Liza. "You can travel with Jamie for Binky's funeral and no doubt Anthony will also be with you."

"If I may Liza; also may I leave my boys here? I have already ensured that my mother has all in hand and the Duke and Douglas Carlton are with her. She is of course sad, but knows that he's now free of his turmoils, and he did have many of those," said Bella.

"Will any of his so-called friends be at his funeral?" asked Liza.

"I doubt it; but you never know who may come out of the woodwork," said Bella.

"Your room's ready Bella, do you want to rest for a while. The boys will be fine, and I'll make sure that they don't disturb you."

Anthony turned up later that day and it was planned that they would leave relatively early the next day for the lunchtime funeral.

Dinner that evening was a quiet affair. It was lightened a little by Jamie and Anthony talking about some of the good times when they were all boys together and how they had played tricks on Bella.

"Yes Jamie, you did manage to get the smell from under your nose when you were with us, although you often tried to be aloof, but you frequently failed miserably," smiled Bella.

"Binky was the one with the affected voice but that used to change when we got enthusiastic over some game," said Anthony.

They then became very quiet, each with their thoughts and memories. Unfortunately all Liza could remember was Binky bringing Evelyn to their charity fund raiser and then attempting to sexually attack John. Paying ruffians to stab Jamie was also on the list of his misdemeanours and then organising setting fire to and killing all those in a London brothel. He was stopped in his final act against them, and Liza had no idea what that would have been.

The boys kept each other occupied the following day and Liza enjoyed watching what they were getting up to; it took her mind off Binky's funeral but not from the fact that in just two weeks they would be living away from her.

Anthony went straight home when they returned from the funeral and Bella went quietly to her room to rest. Liza asked Jamie how Lady Redfern had coped with the situation.

"It's the first time that I have ever seen her shed a tear and no matter how disappointed she must have been in Binky, he was still her son and no doubt she loved him. I know that behind all Bella's hardness she found it difficult today. Anthony and I were the only friends attending; I had wondered whether some of Binky's strange associates would be there, luckily they were not," said Jamie.

"I wonder who Lord Redfern will now be. Probably some obscure cousin; unless young Richard is now in line for the title," said Liza thoughtfully. "Nicholas will inherit his title from his father, but I don't know the rules of such inheritance."

"It would not be tactful to ask Bella today," said Jamie. "I shall be pleased when this day is over; it's been very trying."

"Of course it has; I'm pleased that you're home safely," said Liza who still had a nagging doubt that Binky's threats had been dealt with.

Chapter 5

It had arrived, the day that Liza had been dreading. They were taking the boys to Cambridge. Over the past few days Liza had become emotional on many occasions and had been in danger of becoming so doting that she knew that the boys were feeling claustrophobic. Jamie tried to tell her to give them the space that they needed but she found it difficult. She had had many conversations with each one on how they must look after one another but her main communications were with Matthew, and they needed no words to say how they felt.

"We will be alright you know," he said on the morning that they were leaving.

"I know that you will Matthew, and so will James and Simon, but John will need to be looked after more than the others. He has always been more vulnerable than the rest of you, he needs watching over," said Liza with a sob in her voice.

"I won't let anything happen to him, and neither will the others. We know that he's more sensitive than we are. I promise that we'll take care of him and each other; we always have, and we always will," said Matthew as he held his mother closely.

They were taking two carriages: the boys travelling in one and Liza, Jamie and Adam in the other. Adam's final duty for the boys was to see them settled into the next stage of their education. They arrived just after Bella and the Duke and their sons. They were all ushered into the headmaster's study. His name was Professor Reginald Cavendish and he greeted them cordially. He had only recently become headmaster of their college and he was very forward thinking educationally.

They were introduced to the tutors most of whom seemed approachable, however there was one who seemed to be nearing retirement and his ways appeared a little old fashioned. Finally they were shown to the boys' dormitory and each boy chose his bed and they started unpacking their cases.

Christopher Pound was the older boy in charge of their dormitory. He seemed a pleasant young man and Liza felt that he was not going to be too demanding of them. She noticed that he appeared to have a deformity to his left hand which he was trying to hide, but it had obviously not stopped him from becoming a prefect.

Reluctantly they had to leave and even Bella seemed a little emotional. "They'll be home for a week at half term, which is not far away," said the Duke but it seemed such a long while to Liza.

They dropped Adam off at his new home and Jamie and Liza continued on to the main house and when they arrived it seemed so quiet. Neither of them had realised how much sound the boys had made; it had just become part of the natural noises of the house.

Liza went up to her room and Susan had the sense to leave her alone. She sat on her bed and cried, Jamie came in and put his arms around her and she sobbed on him for a long while.

Nobody else was dining with them that evening; Liza could only imagine that Miranda and Lucinda were feeling as sad as she was, and David and Grace were probably feeling the same.

The next day was the last cricket match of the season and Liza really did not want to attend but knew that she really had no choice. Although it was difficult, she smiled at everyone who came to say how strange it was not to have the boys joining in. Derek was there and he looked dejected; he did not feel like playing as he did not have John there to take his runs for him. Several people had offered but he said that it would not be the same.

Ken Wallace and his daughters were there, and he spent some time talking to Derek and his two eldest girls seemed to be questioning and smiling at Derek. Adam was also joining in the conversation.

Finally the afternoon was over, and Liza could go back to the house and spend some time alone and resting. They just had a light supper that evening, and Jamie came into her room that night and comforted her yet again.

"The only time I have been away from Matthew and John was when I was taken by the Indians. I was desperate not to see them because if I did then they would have been taken also. They both knew that I would find a way to end their lives as I could not allow them to become part of the Cherokee nation. I really don't know how I would have been able to do that, but for their sake I would have done it before taking my own life," said Liza.

"That must have been the hardest decision that you have ever had to make," said Jamie. "They told me that you would have done that; I don't know how they knew but they did and neither of them had been frightened by it. Gabriel told me that they had said that you would send them to their father and that it was alright because he still loved them. I suppose it was Matthew who helped John through that time, and I also suppose that he knew that you would get back to

95

them. He has always seen things that the others don't. He's like you in that respect."

"He'll look after John, so will James and Simon. John will always need looking after. He's not as strong as the others. He's talented and artistic but doesn't have as much confidence as he should. I suppose his start in life has much to do with that. It's so sad that no matter how good his life has been since he came to me, what happened to him in his early years will always have its affect," said Liza.

"Derek missed him today; he wouldn't let anyone else take runs for him. Ken Wallace also offered, but John was his running partner, no one else would do," said Jamie.

"Did you settle easily when you went to Cambridge?" Liza asked Jamie.

"I was sent to boarding school at an early age so moving up to university was not a worry for me. I already knew Anthony and Binky; I was quite happy as home was not a comfortable place to be," said Jamie.

"Our boys are lucky that they've had loving homes and especially with you, Jamie. It's not many men who would take on two extra boys and another one this last year. Four boys all virtually the same age was quite a challenge for you, and then Nicholas and Richard arrived frequently, and of course Derek made seven. I suppose there were times when you wondered what you had done to deserve such chaos," smiled Liza.

"It has certainly livened up my life, but I wouldn't change it for the world. Neither would my mother or Lucinda and even David enjoys their company. We're all going to miss them," said Jamie.

***

Time was passing very slowly in the Edgeworth household. Bella still visited them every weekend and Liza took comfort from seeing her. Lady Redfern had returned to her duties at the Palace but there were occasions when she attended the same charity functions as Liza and Jamie.

Anthony and Diana visited on occasion and little Thomas constantly asked where Matthew was hiding, and he found it difficult to understand that he was not hiding and that he was staying away from home.

"They'll be home in less than two weeks; it'll be half term then," smiled Liza. "I'm looking forward to them being back here, even if it will be only for a week. Then it will be Christmas and they will be here for a few weeks."

They had received letters from each of the boys; the first ones were full of excitement, but the second letters seemed a little subdued and when Liza mentioned it to Jamie, he said that she had to appreciate that writing letters to parents could be considered boring.

Liza had not realised just how much the boys had taken up her time as she and Grace were getting through a great deal more correspondence while they were away and whilst they were working through various invitations to charity events, a rider came to the house with a letter for Jamie. Letters arrived at diverse times of day which were normally related to the charity and Liza just assumed that it would be one of those and she continued working with Grace.

Jamie burst in on them making them both jump and he looked like thunder.

"What on earth's the matter Jamie?" asked a surprised Liza.

"Our boys have been expelled," he said starkly.

"What?" was all that Liza could think of saying. Grace was still sitting there bemused.

"I have a letter from the Master telling me to collect them all as soon as possible," shouted Jamie.

"Why?" murmured a shocked Liza.

"They have attacked one of the teachers," said Jamie.

"Not our boys Jamie," said Liza. "There has to be a mistake. Our boys don't hurt people."

Jamie was calming down a little. "No they don't, something very strange must have happened."

"If they have attacked somebody, they will only have done it in defence of one of them. You know that," said a shaken Liza.

"I'll leave first thing tomorrow morning and find out what it's all about," said Jamie.

"I'll be with you," said Liza.

"There's no need Liza; this is something that I can deal with. I'll hope to persuade the Master to keep them there, but no doubt there will be some severe punishments if I can achieve it," said Jamie.

"There is a need for me to go Jamie. They are my responsibility just as much as yours. I will be with you no matter what you think," said a determined Liza. "I will find out from Matthew what has happened; he'll tell me."

"He'll tell me when I've finished with him," said Jamie.

"There will be no need to threaten him; he will tell me," said Liza and she looked at Jamie and he knew that she was right, Matthew would tell her everything.

Grace said she would leave them as they obviously had a great deal to discuss, and Jamie asked her to tell his mother what had happened, and it was not long before both Miranda and Lucinda appeared.

"Our boys wouldn't hurt anyone Jamie," said a slightly tearful Lucinda. "Something terrible must have happened for them to be accused of attacking a teacher."

"Lucinda's right, none of them have tempers which would make them do such a thing. How could all of them attack a teacher?" said Miranda. "Are you going to bring them home?"

"They've been expelled Mother, so unless I can persuade the Master otherwise, they will all be coming home tomorrow," said Jamie.

They both spent a very sleepless night and were up early and on their way before nine o'clock, arriving at their destination just before lunchtime. They made their way directly to the Master's office and although Jamie knocked, he did not wait for a reply and Professor Cavendish looked up surprised as Jamie escorted Liza straight into his room.

"What's all this about?" demanded Jamie. "You had better explain exactly what you think has happened."

Professor Cavendish seemed a little intimidated but soon regained his composure.

"Lord Edgeworth, you have obviously received my letter, so you know why your sons are being expelled; they attacked one of our teachers. He had occasion to discipline one of your sons and the other boys, including the Duke of Berkshire's sons, attacked that teacher who suffered quite severe cuts and bruises," said Professor Cavendish. "We cannot have such behaviour in our university; it would be a bad example to the rest of the pupils if we did not deal with it in this manner."

"Our boys would not do that without good reason," said Liza.

"So you condone violence in your children then Lady Edgeworth," said Professor Cavendish sarcastically.

"Don't be ridiculous Professor Cavendish; all you had to do was find what led to this situation," snapped Liza.

Jamie frowned at Liza, and she knew that she should leave Jamie to deal with Professor Cavendish.

"May I see my boys please Professor," said Liza. "And I'll leave you to discuss matters with my husband."

"Certainly, Lady Edgeworth," said Professor Cavendish and he called for a boy to take her to the boys' dormitory.

Christopher Pound was sitting in his small room opposite the boys' dormitory, and he came out when he saw her.

"Good afternoon, Lady Edgeworth. I'm afraid the boys are confined to their dormitory until they are able to leave with you. I'll take you in," said Christopher.

Liza smiled and thanked him. There was a chorus of "Hello Mum," "hello Mum Liza," and "hello Aunt Liza."

"Right," said Liza sternly, "tell me what has happened." Her eyes alighted on Matthew, and he held her gaze while nodding to her.

"Professor Grant was going to break John's fingers," said Matthew bluntly and Liza blinked with surprise. She turned and looked at John who was holding his left hand tightly closed and she could see that he was in pain. She moved over to him and gently opened it and saw bright red welts on his palm.

"Why have you been caned John?" asked Liza quietly and she could see that he was in danger of crying, and she knew that he would not like to do that.

"It's because he's left-handed," said Christopher also quietly and Liza looked at him and then towards his left hand and realisation was beginning to dawn on her.

"Matthew, did you say that Professor Grant was going to break his fingers?" asked Liza.

"Yes, he had a thick metal bar and he told John to put his hand on his desk and he was going to hit his fingers with it; we couldn't let him do that, so we stopped him," said Matthew. "We all did. You know that we all look after one another and that is what we did."

Liza looked from Matthew to James, who was nodding and then on to Simon who was agreeing with them. Nicholas and Richard also nodded their agreement. Christopher just stood there with pursed lips. Liza looked down at John's swollen hand and although she knew it was very sore and needed bathing, it could have been a great deal worse.

Liza looked up at Christopher and said, "And all this is because he's left-handed?" Christopher just nodded.

"Come with me," commanded Liza and she pushed John along in front of her and they made their way to the Master's study where she opened the door and pushed John inside. Jamie was talking heatedly to Professor Grant who was also in the room, and he stopped when he saw Liza's determined face. It had been a long while since he had seen her green eyes flash furiously as they were now doing. Professor Grant took a step backwards and Professor Cavendish was open mouthed.

"You condone teachers breaking pupils' fingers because they are left-handed, do you Professor Cavendish?" said Liza between gritted teeth.

Professor Cavendish looked shocked and even more so when Professor Grant said, "They have to be taught to write properly, and in some pupils it's the only way that they learn."

"I'm sorry but I don't know what you mean," said Professor Cavendish to nobody in particular.

"Liza, what are you saying?" said Jamie.

"I am saying that this man was going to break John's fingers with a metal bar because he is left-handed," said Liza. "He's already damaged his hand with a cane. Look at it." She grabbed John's hand and turned it showing Jamie the welts across his palm.

"He's left-handed, not right-handed," said Jamie. "Why try to change him?" He demanded of Professor Grant.

"It's not normal, that's why," said Professor Grant.

"It's normal for him, and for a great many other people," shouted Jamie.

Liza turned to Professor Cavendish, "John is a talented artist, and you were going to allow that man to take away that talent. How dare you treat pupils in that way?"

"Lady Edgeworth, I assure you I had no idea that such things were happening. I know young John is talented; in fact we have his work being prepared for display on our Christmas Open Day. I most certainly do not condone pupils being damaged in that way," said Professor Cavendish.

"Don't you Professor?" said Liza and she turned and grabbed Christopher Pound's left hand and pushed it towards Professor Cavendish. "I suppose you are going to deny knowledge of that also."

Christopher was shocked by the suddenness of Liza thrusting him forward. "When did that man break your hand, Christopher?" asked Liza.

"Nearly two years ago," he said quietly. "It hasn't mended well unfortunately."

Professor Cavendish was looking shocked again and the ferocity in Liza's eyes made him take a step backwards. The room seemed very crowded, Liza had not realised that all the boys had followed her, nor did she know that the Duke of Berkshire had marched into the room ready to deal with Professor Cavendish and was taken aback by what was happening and he was standing quietly at the back of the room with a look of horror on his face.

"You do not have to expel our boys Professor, as we have no wish for them to be educated in this establishment and we will ensure that others know the reason why," said Jamie firmly. "Come on boys, get your things together, we're taking you home."

"Nicholas, Richard, get your things also," said the Duke. "I'm taking you away from this place."

"Please, can we discuss this," said the Master. "I can only apologise for what has happened, and although I do not condone pupils attacking teachers, I can totally understand that they were defending one of their own from a punishment which was totally unwarranted. Will you please remain here whilst I deal with how I must rectify the situation for the future?"

"I would have thought that the time for discussion has passed," said Jamie. "But we will remain whilst we wait for our boys to ready themselves."

Professor Cavendish then asked Christopher to organise refreshments for everyone and he then pushed Professor Grant from the room and presumably had serious discussions with him.

"I am shocked by what I have heard Jamie," said the Duke. "I wonder how many pupils have been maimed by that man. I'm glad this has come to the fore early on; untold damage could have been done to your boy. I suppose we will now have to think about where we will send them all."

"The Master should have been aware of what was happening within his establishment, but in his defence, I know that this is his first year and I think we should give him the benefit of the doubt and hopefully he would have eventually realised what was happening. However, by that time our John would have probably lost the use of his left hand. You've seen what has happened to the other young man," said Jamie.

"Bella is with her mother at the moment, so may I impose my sons on you for a while. I'm afraid that my commitments mean that I have to get back this afternoon and I know that they enjoy being with you," said the Duke. "I believe that Bella can be with you tomorrow and she can then take charge of Nicholas and Richard."

Liza and Jamie smiled knowing that Bella may well arrive the following day but taking charge of her boys would not be her priority.

Christopher knocked and entered telling them that their boys were ready and waiting outside and at the same time Professor Cavendish returned and said that he had dealt with the matter.

"I can only apologise to you all and say yet again that I had no knowledge of such events. I can assure you that there will never be any further such actions against pupils. Professor Grant is taking early retirement. I completely understand that you wish to take your boys away, but will you please think about their reinstatement after our half-term break. I know that you must be very annoyed at the situation, as am I, but perhaps when we have all had a chance to calm down, we can think about your boys' future and I know that they will receive the best of education at this establishment, as indeed you did yourself Lord Edgeworth," said Professor Cavendish.

"We will indeed think about it, but our priority is to take John home and get him medically treated to ensure that he has no lasting damage," said Jamie.

Professor Cavendish nodded and Liza asked what he was going to do about the damage to Christopher Pound's hand.

"I doubt that there is anything that can be done at this late stage," said the Professor.

Liza turned to Christopher and asked him what his parents felt about his injury.

"They are unaware of the situation," said Christopher. "My stepfather is a diplomat in India and he and my mother have been there for some years. I am a ward of this university in their absence."

Liza rounded on Professor Cavendish again, "Are you going to at least attempt to help?"

"I really don't think that there is anything that can be done now," said the Professor.

"Rubbish," said Liza. "We had a child in our village that had been seriously injured when he was a toddler, and the result was that he could not walk. Everyone had given up on him, but I had the pleasure of dancing with him at our last function, so do not tell me that nothing can be done; there is always something that can be done. It may not be exactly as one would wish, but it can be improved."

"Liza," said Jamie. "This is none of our business. All I would say is that a specialist is returning to check on Derek during the half-term and I'm sure he would not object to looking at young Master Pound's hand. I'm sure you had that in mind, didn't you Liza?"

Liza had forgotten about the visit, but she just smiled and nodded at Jamie.

Christopher was looking at them hopefully and then he looked at Professor Cavendish.

"I would not want young Pound to have false hopes, but if he understands that it may be that nothing can be done; then you are right that there would be nothing to lose by getting a specialist's opinion. I could bring him to you next week; when is the specialist arriving?" said the Professor.

"We can take him with us now," said the Duke. "I'm sure that Lady Edgeworth can make room for him in her vast establishment, and as he is a ward of yours and therefore spends all his time here, a change of scenery would do him the world of good."

Both Liza and Jamie stared at the Duke, who once again had made an arrangement on their behalf without consulting them, but then Liza smiled and said that it would be a pleasure to have Master Pound as a house guest for a while.

"I will come and collect him towards the end of half-term and perhaps by then you will have had time to consider the future of your boys," said Professor Cavendish. "Go and get what you need Pound."

"We have not asked Christopher if he would like to spend time with us and see the specialist," said Liza. She turned towards Christopher and waited for his response.

"I would be most grateful Lady Edgeworth," smiled Christopher and he dashed off to get the few possessions that he felt he needed.

The boys were waiting outside the Master's study with their bags and Jamie and the Duke ushered them out and towards their carriages. Liza turned and smiled at Professor Cavendish and said that she was sure that they would be able to sort everything out satisfactorily and that she looked forward to seeing him when he came to collect Christopher.

"I can only apologise again Lady Edgeworth. It is something that should never have happened, and I will certainly make sure that nothing like it will ever happen again. I hope that something can be done for young Pound, and I must inspect all our students to make sure that no others have been damaged in that way. Thank you for being so understanding," said the Master.

"Goodbye Professor Cavendish," said Liza.

"It will do young Pound good to get away from this place for a short while. From what I gather, his parents have not returned for many years," commented the Professor Cavendish.

"He seems a nice young man; we will look after him," smiled Liza and she left him to think about all that had happened.

It did not take Christopher Pound long to gather up his belongings and join them at their carriages. Jamie was ushering the boys into their carriage, which would be somewhat crowded on the way home. The Duke was taking Nicholas, Richard and young Christopher in his carriage and it was not long before they set off on their way. Professor Cavendish watched them leave and hoped that they would return at the end of the holiday; it would be a very bad blot against him if he lost all those pupils. It was one thing to expel them because of bad conduct, but quite another to have them leave because of the university's dire management. It did not matter that Professor Grant had been carrying out such disciplines since well before he took over, to have it discovered during his time would damage his record considerably.

They arrived at Edgeworth House as it was getting dark, and they all tiredly made their way up the steps and were greeted by Miranda, Lucinda, David and Grace all talking at once and making a fuss of the boys. Liza arranged refreshments for the Duke as he had to make his way quickly to a delayed meeting.

Christopher seemed bemused by the fuss and pampering that all the boys were receiving from the family, especially John who was having his hand examined closely by everyone there. Liza introduced him to them all and he was welcomed as if he was also a family member. Mrs Frances was hastily making a room ready for him, but she was now used to unexpected guests.

The Duke left saying that Bella would be visiting the next day and he may well be with her if he had completed his commitments in time, and perhaps they could then discuss the options for the boys' education.

"I'll show you to your room Christopher as I'm sure you would like to freshen up before supper," said Liza.

"I'll show him," said Matthew.

"So will I," came the chorus from all the boys and they all left guiding a rather mystified Christopher, and Matthew could be heard asking which room Mrs Frances had put him in.

David said, "Is it true that a teacher was going to break young John's fingers because he's left-handed?"

"I'm afraid that's correct," said Jamie. "I know that you will all be tactful, but young Christopher received the same treatment some two years ago and we are hoping that the specialist who treated Derek may be able to suggest some treatment for him."

"I noticed that his hand looked deformed," said Miranda. "He seems a nice lad; I hope something can be done for him."

"I must go and see to John's hand as it looks very sore, but first I must see Mrs Lambert and find out what she can prepare for the boys' supper," said Liza.

In the kitchen Mrs Lambert had enough lamb chops for the boys and she was preparing vegetables to go with them. "It's not what they normally have, but it's the best I can do at short notice."

"I know Mrs Lambert," said Liza. "We always seem to be thrusting extra meals upon you and you always do so well. I'm sure the boys will enjoy whatever you have and of course we have an extra one to feed as well."

"Don't worry; they won't go hungry," smiled Mrs Lambert.

Miranda joined her as she made her way up the stairs. "I'd like to help you with young John; he's the last one who should be hurt, he's more sensitive than most," and off they went to pull John away from all the others.

John smiled as he came into his room; he was getting a great deal of attention and he loved it all. Miranda bathed his hand and Liza gently dried it. Miranda then held it gently as Liza put some soothing cream on it. He was then delighted to realise that it was going to be bandaged and he was going to wear his wound with pride. Liza drew the line at his request for a sling saying that it was taking his problem a step too far. Miranda laughed and putting her arm around him she kissed him on the head. He then looked at Liza and she said, "Come on then," and he enjoyed sitting on her knee whilst she cuddled him. He was a little big for that, but nobody was going to tell the others that he was being pampered in that way.

The word went out that supper must be ready and there was an exodus down towards the kitchen. John smiled and joined them. Liza and Miranda found Christopher wondering whether he should follow the others and Liza said that she would take him down and on the way they found Matthew returning.

"I'm sorry Christopher; we should have waited for you. Don't worry Mum, I'll take him down," said Matthew.

Down in the kitchen the boys were regaling Mrs Lambert, Mrs Frances and Harper with how they had saved John from a fate worse than death. John insisted that he needed his food cut up otherwise he would not be able to eat it.

"Don't be silly," said James. "Christopher manages to cut his food and he's much worse than you. You can use your fingers for your chop and your vegetables are small anyway. Is it still sore? The bandage must help."

"It is sore, but Mum put some cream on it and the bandage helps. I'll have to watch how Christopher eats his food," said John.

All eyes turned to Christopher, and they watched as he cut his meat. He was managing to stab the chop with his fork, hold it steady and cut it with his knife. It was quite skilled although looked quite clumsy.

"See," said Nicholas. "He does it alright."

Mrs Frances intervened telling them to get on with their meal before it got cold and to stop making young Master Christopher self-conscious.

"You're not self-conscious are you, Christopher?" asked Matthew.

"Well I don't normally have everyone watching how I cut my food, but no, I'm not self-conscious; I've got used to having to do things differently," said Christopher.

"Our mother and father will help to get you back to how you should be," said James. "They helped Derek walk and that has to be harder than getting a hand to work properly. We'll go and see Derek tomorrow, so you'll know what we mean."

Mrs Frances stood back and marvelled at the faith these boys had in their parents, she hoped that they would not be disappointed although she could see that Christopher was under no illusions.

***

"It's the happiest I've seen you for a while Liza," said David when they were at dinner that evening.

"She's got her boys back," smiled Lucinda. "Liza's always happy when they are around, and so am I."

"It has been rather quiet lately," said Jamie. "Today we certainly know that they are back, and we have to make a big decision regarding their future. Liza and I will discuss it over the next few days and in the meantime the boys will be enjoying being home."

"We do have a lot to sort out although I wonder whether it is better the devil you know but we'll worry about it later," said Liza. "I'll just keep enjoying having them home with us."

"Christopher seems a nice young man," said Miranda. "It's disgraceful what has happened to him, do you think that the specialist will be able to help him?"

"We never thought that we would see Derek walking, so miracles do happen. There is no harm in finding out if it's possible," said Liza.

Later when they were alone Jamie commented that it had been a long while since he had seen Liza so annoyed. "Your eyes flashed and Professor Grant thought that you were bringing the wrath of God down on him, Professor Cavendish was not much better."

"I don't think anything like what happened to John will ever happen again," said Liza. "It will be very difficult to find somewhere else for the boys."

"You're not taking into account the Duke of Berkshire. He's quite capable of getting his boys into any place that he wants," said Jamie.

"Well, we don't have to go along with his arrangements if we're not happy. I think that they will be fine back where they were," said Liza.

"You could be right, but we'll talk to the boys about how they have been getting on there; naturally John may not feel as happy as the others, but his protagonist is no longer there. The Master seemed to appreciate his talents," said Jamie.

The next morning Liza woke up to the noise of the boys making their way down to breakfast and she wondered why voices were so loud when telling each other to be quiet. She hoped that Christopher was amongst them, but she knew that Matthew would make sure that he was. She turned over in bed and realised that Jamie had already gone, so probably he was also making sure that they were all accounted for.

She smiled and stretched; it was going to be a good day. Susan came in with her breakfast which was unusual as she rarely ate in bed.

"His Lordship thought it best that you stay here this morning as your sons and their friends are making plans for the day," said Susan.

"Why should he want me out of the way?" asked Liza.

"Because he says that they can twist you around their little fingers," said Susan.

Liza just smiled knowing that they did exactly the same to Jamie and she had a suspicion that Susan knew it too.

She was finishing her breakfast when Jamie came in. He picked up her serviette and wiped her chin. "I didn't dribble down my chin," frowned Liza.

"Didn't you? Well done. I just naturally do it," said Jamie absentmindedly.

"What are they asking Jamie?" asked Liza.

"They're going to take their carriage and horses into the village to see Derek," said Jamie.

"Hmmm, what's wrong with that?" asked Liza.

"Nicholas will be driving the carriage and taking Richard, John and Christopher. James, Matthew and Simon will be riding," said Jamie thoughtfully. "It always worries me when they sound so logical."

"What time are they leaving?" asked Liza.

"Soon," said Jamie.

"Ask them to wait as I'd like to see them before they leave," said Liza and she slid out of bed and called for Susan to help her get ready quickly.

"What do you have in mind?" asked Jamie.

"Nothing much: just to let them know that we're keeping an eye on them. I might ask them to take me as I would like to see Mrs Price," smiled Liza.

"They won't like that," said Jamie.

"Don't worry, I'll change my mind at the last minute and ask you to take me. It will just give them pause for thought as they will think that we will be in the village at some time," said Liza.

Jamie made his way to the boys' room and told them that Liza wanted to see them before they left.

"I suppose she wants to tell us to be careful," said John.

"I think she wants to go to the village to see Mrs Price and you could take her," said Jamie to a chorus of groans.

Christopher was standing back and smiling as he realised that it was a ploy to calm their enthusiasm.

Liza walked down the corridor to their room with Susan following her to go down to the kitchen carrying the breakfast tray. Christopher stood to one side to let Liza pass and he caught sight of Susan and smiled at her, she looked shyly up at him and dropped some of what she was carrying. Christopher bent down and helped her retrieve what she had dropped, and she thanked him and carried on her way, whilst his eyes followed her until she was out of sight. Liza noticed all this and realised that there was a mutual attraction between them, and she guessed that he was probably seventeen years old, and Susan was just fifteen; they were both very young and had plenty of time to sort out their feelings.

"You're off to see Derek then," said Liza. "You do realise that he works with Mr Reece, so he may not be available now. No doubt he'll be free at lunchtime. Are you thinking of calling on April; I'm sure she'd be pleased to see you all."

"Oh, we hadn't thought that Derek could be working," said James which led to a great deal of discussion, and it was finally agreed that they would leave in a couple of hours and reach the village at lunchtime.

"It's going to take you a while to saddle up and get your carriage ready," said Liza. "Won't you be hungry?"

"No," said Matthew. "Everybody in the village likes to feed us."

Liza looked at them in horror, "You can't take food from the villagers. How long has that been going on?"

"It's always happened. The bakers like us to try their cooking and Mr and Mrs Rogers always have nice cakes and biscuits. We don't take much from Mrs Price because we know that she has to work hard for her money. I suppose April could now have something that we like," said John.

"You mean to say that you eat their food and then you come back here and eat again. Where do you put it all?" said Liza.

"We're still growing, you know," confided James.

Liza stared at them all and then turned to Christopher, "Is it your job to keep them in order?"

Christopher smiled and nodded.

"Do you manage to do that? If you do, can you please let me know your secret," said Liza.

"They do take notice of me. They know that they are my responsibility and wouldn't want me to get into trouble with our house master. Their attack on Professor Grant was totally out of character and it was an understandable action. I could support them in that," said Christopher. "However, I do seem to be in their hands whilst I'm here, so I have to do as I'm told." He laughed at the thought.

"I'll see you all later," said Liza and when she left she heard Nicholas ask if they would have to wait for her.

"No, she only said that so that we slowed our plans down," said Matthew. "I hadn't thought about Derek working though. Let's go and see if there's anything for us in the kitchen and then by the time our horses are ready Derek should be at lunch."

They know me so well, thought Liza with a smile.

"Have you slowed them down?" asked Jamie when she joined him in the library.

"Yes, I pointed out that Derek worked with Adam now. They hadn't thought that he might not be available. Did you know that the villagers feed them?"

"No, they don't need feeding; they get more than enough here," said a surprised Jamie.

"Apparently the villagers like them to try buns, cakes and biscuits. They are going to see what April now has to offer," said Liza. "At least Christopher says that they are well behaved at their university."

"They mustn't take food from the villagers. They can't afford to give food away," said Jamie.

"They don't take from Mrs Price; John said that they knew that she worked hard for her money. I suppose it's become a tradition now and people would be disappointed if the boys refused their offerings," said Liza.

"Perhaps it's their way of saying thank you for the food that you give to those who need it and it would seem that the boys don't take from those who can ill afford it," said Jamie.

Down in the kitchen they were being fed cake and milk, just as they had been when they were small. They let Mrs Lambert treat them like little boys; they knew she enjoyed it and they in turn enjoyed her cakes. Christopher was still bemused by the happy feeling and the fun in the household, and he was envious. He wondered what it would have been like to have lived with his parents, but they were just a distant memory now.

Mr Lambert came in and Christopher was introduced to him and a few minutes later Ken Wallace walked in, and Christopher stared at him; he was sure that he knew him, and his name seemed familiar. He was obviously a manual worker, but he did not sound like one; he was well educated. It was going to annoy him until he could remember where he had seen him before and then he forgot all about him as Susan came in and the boys shouted for her to join them, but she said that she was too busy. She was very pretty, and Christopher had his first feelings of attraction towards a female.

Liza and Jamie watched as they rode out towards the village. Nicholas appeared to manage the carriage very well and they could see that James, Matthew and Simon looked very confident on their mounts. This was one time that Liza and Jamie had to admit that they were indeed good-looking young men.

"Girls will soon be queuing up to meet our young men," said Jamie.

"I know it will happen sooner or later," said Liza. "I noticed that young Christopher seemed quite taken with Susan and she acted quite shyly with him."

"Stop matchmaking Liza," laughed Jamie. "Everyone finds their own partners eventually."

"Oh I'm not matchmaking. I hope it doesn't progress because I'm sure his parents already have somebody lined up for him," said Liza.

"I suppose it's something that we should do for our boys," said Jamie.

"You mean find suitable wives for them? I'm sure they will be able to do that for themselves," said Liza. "Did your father find Evelyn for you?"

"He would have liked me to have found somebody much richer than her family were. They were fairly well off, so he was quite pleased about that, but I have to admit that when he learned that James Marchant had died, he did suggest that I pursue you but by that time I already had done that and made a complete mess of it," said Jamie. "Wouldn't he be pleased now, but he would also be displeased because I know you would not have tolerated his gambling habits or paid off his debts."

"Are there many young girls in the families that we mix with; there seems to be a surfeit of boys. We meet many people but normally just at evening functions," said Liza.

"Don't worry Liza, when the time is right there will be no end of young ladies being paraded in front of our boys," said Jamie. "However, they will find who they want, no matter what background they come from."

Bella and the Duke arrived later that day and the Duke had several suggestions regarding other educational establishments for the boys, but really they were all in agreement that with Professor Grant gone, Professor Cavendish had the opportunity to bring the university back to the high reputation that it had held previously.

"The last Master obviously condoned such barbaric unwarranted punishments, unless he was unaware of them, which would not say much for his knowledge of his staff; but academically the university was sound. There are many places that our boys could be admitted to, but we had already chosen the best," said the Duke.

"You're right; academically it cannot be faulted, although they will need a new English teacher, but that should not be difficult. There are teachers queuing up to get a position there, so the vacancy has probably already been filled," said Jamie.

"I would think that John is the only one who would find it difficult to return, but we can assure him that he will not be victimised again, and I know that his brothers and Nicholas and Richard will also reassure him and look out for him, after all, they did it before," smiled Liza.

"Prior to the upset last week, they did seem to have settled in very well. Their house prefect seems to be a diligent boy; he's with you at the moment, isn't he?" said the Duke.

"Yes, he is, and they do seem to take notice of him," said Jamie.

The Duke had to leave but Bella was going to stay for the weekend and possibly longer, and as he was leaving the boys were returning. They stopped and it seemed that the Duke was impressed with what he was seeing.

Bella went to her room and Jamie went to his study to finally read his newspaper. Liza went to her study where Grace had been working and they discussed business for a while until Grace left to go to the gatehouse and eventually get ready to return with her father for dinner.

Whilst Liza was going through her correspondence, Matthew knocked and entered.

"Christopher would like a word with you Mother," he said as he ushered Christopher into the room.

"Thank you, Matthew, come in Christopher and sit down," smiled Liza and Matthew left closing the door after him.

"What is it Christopher, is something worrying you?" asked Liza.

"I met Derek today," said Christopher. "I find it difficult to believe that he was confined to a wheelchair before he met the specialist who's visiting next week. Did he have absolutely no use of his legs five or so years ago?"

"That's right. His sister is young Susan and she had to wheel him around and look after him whilst his mother worked. She could not go to school as he needed somebody to be with him all the time. I'm sure you realise that to get him to where he is today took a great deal of care and attention from his mother and sister. They have massaged him every day and with every day that passed he got a little bit better until I had the pleasure of dancing with him on my birthday and I said on that day that out of all the wonderful gifts I had received, dancing with him was the best one of all," said Liza.

"The specialist told them what to do and his family carried it out. If the specialist says that I can get the use of my hand back, I have no one to dedicate their time to me," said Christopher.

"If it is necessary, I will make sure that somebody massages your hand as often as needed. I know that Professor Cavendish will also ensure that your hand gets all the manipulation that it needs," said Liza.

"I watched Derek walk away today and apart from a slight stiffness there was no indication that he had been lame at one time," said Christopher. "Derek was telling me that he had to have his back and legs massaged every day after the specialist had pushed.and pulled him back into shape," said Christopher. "I hope he can do something for me."

"I hope so too," said Liza. "Professor Cavendish was right to worry that you might think that it can be put right only for you to be disappointed if there is nothing that can be done."

"At least we will have tried and yes, I will be disappointed if nothing can be done but I will know what I will have to deal with from now onwards," said Christopher. "I have never really accepted that this was how my life was going to be but maybe I will have to."

"We could be taking away all your hopes Christopher; is that something that you wish to take a chance on?" said Liza.

"Absolutely, I have a feeling that I will get more movement in my hand, but I know that I will never be able to draw again as I did prior to being hurt," said Christopher.

"You were just like my John then," said Liza. "It's surprising how many left-handed people are gifted artists. It's such a shame that talent such as that has been taken away from you, but it may come back to you in the fullness of time."

Christopher laughed, "Maybe that's true Lady Edgeworth."

"Nicholas and Richard call me Aunt Liza although I am not their aunt. I find that Lady Edgeworth sounds very unfriendly whilst under this roof," said Liza. "I will understand if you find it difficult."

"I won't find it difficult, Aunt Liza," said Christopher as he smiled cheekily at her.

"Tell me about your parents," said Liza. "Would they have objections to us undertaking any treatment that you might need?"

Christopher frowned and Liza knew that he was finding it difficult to reply as he did not want to be disloyal to his parents.

"Whatever you tell me Christopher will go no further than this room," said Liza.

"My mother remarried after my father's death, and you know that my stepfather is in the diplomatic service in India and I'm afraid that it has been some time since I heard from them. Professor Cavendish is now my guardian, and he has approved any treatment that may be necessary," said Christopher. "There is nothing secret to my situation."

"Well, I hope you enjoy your time with us, but don't let our boys run circles around you, difficult as that may be," said Liza.

"I'll try not to. Thank you, Aunt Liza," smiled Christopher. He left and Liza could hear Matthew taking charge of him and she had a feeling that he quite enjoyed being run rings around.

Liza went in to see Jamie who was still reading his newspaper, which he dropped slightly as she entered.

"Have you calmed young Christopher's fears?" he asked.

"I couldn't do that completely as nobody can judge the outcome of what the specialist may find. Apparently he was like John and had at one time been quite an adequate artist," said Liza.

Jamie's newspaper dropped a little further. "That's a shame," he said.

"He's going to call me Aunt Liza whilst he's here; I suppose that will make you Uncle Jamie," said Liza as Jamie's newspaper dropped right down.

"Liza, have we just taken on another person to add to our family?" he asked.

"Professor Cavendish is his guardian, so we can't do that," said Liza.

"Can't we? I'm sure you'll find a way," sighed Jamie as he watched her leave his room. He lifted his newspaper again but found it difficult to concentrate. He thought back to the time when he and James just lived in the house and how quiet it had been then and as he thought about it, he heard the boys racing down the stairs and on to the kitchen for their supper. Jamie sighed again but smiled as he would have his home no other way.

***

The boys accepted that they would be returning to their university at the end of the half-term. John was a little concerned, but he had been assured that Professor Grant was no longer there and using his left hand was not going to be a problem. Christopher also assured him that he would not allow anything to happen to him because he was left-handed, and all the other boys said that they would also protect him from any unwarranted punishments.

Dr Claude Phillips arrived at the beginning of the week and although he had come just to see Derek, he agreed that he would attempt to help Christopher regain the use of his hand.

"I have seen similar injuries, but normally in those returning from a war situation, or accidents in a factory. I am shocked that such an injury has been deliberate," said Dr Phillips. "I have helped most to recover but unfortunately few have completely regained the use as it was prior to the injury."

Christopher did not look too disappointed as he had said on several occasions that he did not expect to be as he was before.

"What is the treatment?" asked Jamie.

"The bones have healed incorrectly; each finger should have been splinted rather than left to mend without such support. The fingers will have to be broken and bandaged correctly; I can help a little with the pain of breaking the bones, but it will be painful whilst the hand is mending. When the bones have mended, massage, manipulation and exercise will bring it up to an acceptable standard. He will then have a great deal more use than he has now," said the doctor.

"If it is acceptable to his guardian for the treatment to be carried out, when can you undertake it?" asked Liza.

"From what you are saying, I gather that he is not your responsibility. If it is agreeable, I could treat him at your doctor's surgery as he has some very up-to-date facilities, which I suspect is your doing and I would arrange that I could clear my diary and return here say three weeks before Christmas and that will give him a chance to heal over the Christmas holiday. However it is essential that he is assisted with all the after treatment and that can be a long process," said Dr Phillips.

Liza turned to Christopher, "I know that we are talking as if you are not here Christopher, our apologies for that. We will talk to Professor Cavendish and hopefully he will agree to your returning to us so that Dr Phillips can work on your hand. I hope that you are in agreement to the treatment which is being advocated for you."

"I would like to have the treatment, I know that it will initially be painful but even if I cannot completely regain the use, I would be happy to have whatever improvement I can get. I hope that the Master agrees," said Christopher.

"I'm sure he will; I am so confident that we will make arrangements with Dr Phillips to return on a particular date prior to Christmas and I will suggest that you stay with us until it is time for you to return after the Christmas holiday. So if it is acceptable to you and Professor Cavendish, you will be spending Christmas with us," said Liza.

"It will be the first time that I have spent Christmas away from the university's environment for many years. All I can say is that it most certainly is very acceptable to me Aunt Liza, and I pray that it is also acceptable to Professor Cavendish," said Christopher.

Dr Phillips smiled at Christopher. "You know that you will be in pain for a little while, but you have experienced that pain before when the hand was broken, but this time it will not be to damage you but to put right a very great wrong, so I'm sure you will be looking forward to it."

"We will be able to undertake the after treatment and by the time he returns to university he will know what to do and I will also make sure that Professor Cavendish knows what must be done," said Jamie. "I'm sure that there must be somebody within the medical section who can continue with the treatment."

Dr Phillips left having said how pleased he was with Derek's progress and that he would look forward to seeing them and helping Christopher before Christmas.

Miranda commented one day that Christopher had settled in very well within the household and praised his excellent manners. Jamie and Liza looked at one another and realised that they had indeed taken in another person who was likely to become a permanent member of their home.

A carriage arrived on Friday morning, and it was Professor Cavendish who had come to collect Christopher. Liza and Jamie thought that it was unnecessary as they would be taking the boys back the following day. Liza wondered whether he had come to inspect where his ward had been staying to see whether it had been suitable which was a little late for him to be worried.

Jamie explained to him exactly what Dr Phillips had advised and said that they needed his approval to allow the treatment to be undertaken.

"Young Pound's parents left enough finance for his education; they did not make any allowance for such major medical treatments. Naturally I would like to see his hand restored but the funds just are not there," said the Professor.

Liza's eyes sparked but Jamie put a restraining hand on her.

"Professor Cavendish," said Jamie with annoyance, "as it was one of your tutors who inflicted such damage on the boy, I would have thought that you would have no alternative but to undertake the cost of his treatment."

"Of course, you are right Lord Edgeworth, it is my responsibility. Have you any idea what the cost may be?" asked Professor Cavendish.

"No Professor Cavendish, I have no such idea. If treatment is needed by us, then we ensure that it is undertaken. I suppose we are lucky that we do not have to worry about such things. I can however assure you that if it is found to be too expensive for your establishment to undertake, we will ensure that the medical account is settled," said Jamie.

"There will be no need for that Lord Edgeworth but thank you for offering. It will be enough that you are kindly having young Pound staying with you. I understand that he normally has to spend Christmas at the university. Occasionally there are others who must also remain during the holidays, but I have been informed that often he has been alone. I know that I am new to this situation, but I would not have allowed him to spend the time on his own, he would have been included in whatever my wife and I were organising," said the Professor.

"I did not know that you were married Professor and I'm pleased that you were kind enough to think about including young Christopher at Christmas. When he has had treatment on his hand and the splints are removed, he will have to concentrate on manipulating and massaging his fingers to help them regain some use, would your wife be able to undertake this, or even make sure that it is carried out by someone else as it is very important," said Liza.

"I will ensure that he gets all that is needed, even if I have to do it myself," said Professor Cavendish.

"I suppose we should put Christopher out of his misery as he was not sure that you would agree to the treatment," said Jamie.

"I have studied all the documentation regarding the university's guardianship of young Pound, and I am able to make any decisions regarding his welfare and it would be cruel not to allow him the chance of some improvement," said the Master. "I should not say this, but I do not feel that he has had any support from his parents in a number of years and at the end of his time with us I believe that he will be expected to make his own way in the world with nowhere to go and no money to give him a start in that life."

"That's very sad Professor," said Liza. "Has nobody contacted his parents on his behalf?"

"Yes, the previous Master wrote to them some two years ago; he did receive a response which was to tell him to do whatever was necessary for the boy and that the stepfather's diplomatic appointment meant that they were unable to return for some years," said the Professor.

"I find it difficult to understand how a mother is able to ignore her own child, but it is not up to me to judge. All I can say is that he will always be welcome in our household," smiled Liza.

Christopher was waiting in the hall and Professor Cavendish told him that he would be bringing him back to Edgeworth House the day before he was due to have Dr Phillips treat his hand and would collect him after Christmas ready for the new term, weather permitting.

Christopher was delighted that he would be returning, and he thanked 'Aunt Liza' and 'Uncle Jamie' for all they had done for him and said that he would make sure that their boys were treated well and fairly.

"I will especially watch over young John as I can see that he is not as confident as the others, particularly Matthew," he said. "I look forward to seeing you again on my return."

On their way back to the university Professor Cavendish wanted to make sure that Christopher knew exactly what was happening.

"I know that you have been treated exceptionally well whilst you have been with Lord and Lady Edgeworth, I am concerned that you may think that they have taken you under their wing for more than just your treatment. I noticed that you called them aunt and uncle, which is very familiar and I presume that they had no objection to that, but I do not want you to be under any illusions that you will become part of their family and I do not want you to be hurt or disappointed by the fact that probably, when you have had your treatment, your contact with them could well cease," said the Professor.

"I was made very welcome and treated as one of their family, but I understand what you are saying, and I have learned over the years to expect nothing more than I already have. I am looking forward to getting some use back into my hand which is something which will help me in the future, and it is very kind of Lord and Lady Edgeworth to organise it for me," said Christopher.

"I hope that by being with both the Edgeworth and Berkshire boys will not deter you from extending your authority over them when they return tomorrow," said Professor Cavendish.

"They are all full of life, even young John, but they are aware that if they disobey the rules not only do they get punished but I do also, which they would not in all honour want. They were more upset by my punishment because of their attack on Professor Grant, than by any punishment that they were to receive," said Christopher.

"Were you punished because of their attack?" asked Professor Cavendish.

"Yes, sir, six of the best as I was unable to control those under my care," smiled Christopher.

"I suppose that is part of the tradition of our school," sighed Professor Cavendish. "There are many such traditions which have become outdated, and I must study all the rules and make some decisions regarding them."

Christopher sat back and relaxed for the rest of the journey. He did not mind going back to the university as it was what he was used to. He thought about the enjoyable time he had had with the Edgeworths and Berkshires and smiled when he remembered how pretty Susan was. Suddenly he frowned as he tried yet again to recall where he had seen the man called Ken before, but it just would not come to him, and he knew that it had to be at least ten years since they had met. He thought that no doubt he would eventually remember who he was.

Chapter 6

Soon after Christopher and Professor Cavendish had left, the Duke arrived. He would be staying the night and the next day he would be going with Jamie to take the boys back to their university and see them settled. Liza was not looking forward to them leaving again but she was confident that they would have no problems when they returned and that both Christopher and the Master would be watching over them.

There were many long faces around the house as the boys left the following morning. John had been a little anxious, but he had been reassured and was looking forward to seeing some of the friends they had made before.

Plans were being put in place for Christmas and once again it was difficult to believe that a year had passed since the last one. Also Liza and Jamie had decided that they would visit Charles Enderby at Easter as 'The Amelia' was sailing directly to South Carolina at that time.

Wendell and Amelia would be with them well before Christmas with Peter, Edward, Nicole and little Edward arriving four days beforehand. Anthony, Diana, Thomas and Rose had decided not to travel to Belfast, and they would be coming to stay on Christmas Eve. Bella would also be with them and possibly the Duke. Lady Redfern would be at the Palace, and they had no news of Douglas Carlton. The Major and Jennifer, and Lily and Joseph would be joining them after Christmas lunch just for the night, as would Randolph and Penny Langston.

"We are going to have a houseful again this year," said Jamie. "Why is it that everyone comes to us?"

"Because we have the largest family and travelling with all our staff has become virtually impossible. It's much easier for everyone to come to us," said Liza.

"It's not easier for you Liza; you take on the responsibility for everyone; one day we may be able to just be alone," said Jamie.

"You know that you enjoy seeing everyone happy together and we do have time alone, we always make sure that we do," said Liza.

Dr Phillips arrived at the same time as Wendell and Amelia, and he went straight to Dr Bruce's surgery to make sure that all was in order for Christopher's operation.

Professor and Mrs Cavendish brought Christopher with them the next day and Mrs Cavendish and Liza spent time with Dr Phillips as he explained in great detail the treatment needed once the splints were removed.

"I'm so pleased to have met you Mrs Cavendish, I have been concerned that Christopher would not manage the treatment that is needed, but I can see that you will look after him well," said Liza.

"I can assure you that we will do the best we can for him," said Mrs Cavendish. "It is something that should never have happened to him, and I know that my husband was horrified when he found out how he had received his injury."

Amelia, Miranda and Lucinda were making a great fuss of Christopher, while Jamie was in conversation with Dr Phillips and Professor Cavendish. Liza came into the drawing room with Mrs Cavendish and saw that Christopher was rather overwhelmed by the attention that he was receiving from the ladies.

"Would you like to go to your room and get settled before lunch?" said Liza.

Christopher looked at her gratefully, "Where is my room?" he asked.

"You're in the same room that you had before," said Liza.

"I'd like to help him get settled," said Mrs Cavendish not realising that Mrs Frances had already unpacked his belongings.

"I'm sure Christopher would like to show you where he will be staying for the next few weeks," said Liza. "You can also show her where our boys' rooms are so that she can see that you will not be lonely for long."

"What a nice young man he is," said Amelia when they had left the room. "It's such a shame that he has to go through such an operation tomorrow, but we will make sure that he is well looked after."

Professor and Mrs Cavendish were going to stay for lunch and then return to the university directly afterwards, and over lunch they were asked many questions about the university and both Liza and Jamie were impressed by the improvements they were already making to the school. Christopher's table manners were impeccable although he did have difficulty using the cutlery.

Christopher appeared a little lost when the Professor and Mrs Cavendish had left, and he was in danger of being overly cosseted by Amelia, Miranda and Lucinda.

"I'm going to the village this afternoon," said Liza. "Would you like to join me, Christopher? I'm hoping to see Derek and call in on April, who used to be in Susan's position. Mr and Mrs Rogers and Derek's mother may be around, but I also want to call in on Dr Bruce and on the way back I will see if Reverend Collins has all that he needs."

Christopher smiled at her in relief, "I think I would enjoy that, Aunt Liza," he said.

"Get your coat and meet me at the stables," she smiled at him and off he went to his room to collect what he needed.

Derek was just leaving Ken Wallace's house and Liza explained that he had been tutoring the girls as they were unable to attend school yet as the two youngest needed to be looked after whilst their father was at work. Once again Christopher wondered where he had seen Ken Wallace before and at another time he would ask Liza where he had originated from.

They went with Derek towards his home and Mrs Price was pleased to see them; she had met Christopher before when he had visited with the boys at half term. Both Mrs Price and Derek wished Christopher well for the following day with Derek adding that Dr Phillips was a miracle worker.

Mr and Mrs Rogers also wished Christopher well and then on their way to April's, Christopher asked how so many people knew what was happening the next day.

"It's a small village and everyone is concerned for you. You must appreciate that when Dr Phillips visits they are interested in how Derek is faring; he's a great favourite amongst them and of course you will now be on their list of people to worry about. They are all very caring of everyone in the area," said Liza.

"But I'm not from this area," said Christopher.

Liza smiled, "You are now." And Christopher smiled back at her.

Dr Phillips was with Dr Bruce, and he explained a little of what was to be undertaken the next day. Christopher did not appear concerned at the prospect of the operation.

They then had afternoon tea with April and finally called in on Bernard. As always Liza opened his food cupboards and made a note of what he needed which she would send somebody down with later.

On the short drive back Christopher asked Liza about Ken Wallace, telling her that he knew him from somewhere, but where that was, he could not remember.

"Ken is a very private person; he arrived here nearly a year ago with his four girls. He is somebody who will work at anything to put food on his table. I believe that he has had a very different life to the one which he and his family are experiencing now, but his past is his business," said Liza.

"It just annoys me that I cannot remember where I have seen him before, but from what you say it would be wise not to ask him. I will still puzzle over it though," said Christopher.

Christopher joined them for dinner that evening, and Dr Phillips apologised for constantly watching him use his cutlery, but it was helping him to determine exactly how he would be treating the hand the next day.

Soon after dinner Christopher went to his room and once again it was commented how well-mannered he was.

"He must feel very nervous tonight," said Miranda. "He has no family to turn to at a time like this. It's such a shame."

Jamie smiled at his mother, "you must realise by now that Christopher has become a member of this household and he will not be alone when he undergoes his operation tomorrow. I presume you will be going with him Liza."

"Of course I will be; nobody should be alone at a time like this," said Liza.

"I would also like to be with him tomorrow," said Miranda. "Do you think that he would have any objections?"

"I doubt it, but we will ask him tomorrow," said Liza.

"I won't go with you," said Lucinda. "I know I would cry over him, which would do him no good."

"I would be just the same," said Amelia. "He seems very calm; I know if it were me, I'd be panicking."

"He's obviously looking forward to getting some use back in his hand which must be taking the edge off his nerves, and he knows that the only way that he can do that is to go through what he has to tomorrow," said Jamie.

"Will you go and see him shortly Jamie?" asked Liza. "I think that it would do him good to know that we are concerned for him. I would go but he may not appreciate a female fussing over him."

"I could see earlier today that he was bemused by being surrounded by ladies," said Miranda. "It is obviously something that he has not been used to. What a shame. It's surprising that he has not grown up very bitter."

"I believe that in his quieter moments he does feel very bitter, which is understandable. He hides his feelings well," said Liza. "It is so sad that some parents do not realise what they do to their children, although that does not surprise me when we see some of the children who come to our Homes."

"I don't think that he would mind you fussing over him tonight, Liza," said Jamie. "Shall we go together? I'll knock and go in first just to make sure he's decent."

"I think that Jamie's right; he's only a lad and could probably do with a bit of mothering, which has been sadly lacking for him over the years," said Amelia.

"I have always managed to love all children, but they have been much younger than Christopher. This is the first time that I have cared for someone his age," said Liza.

121

"Putting your arm around his shoulder would not go amiss," said Jamie. "Shall we go now?"

Liza nodded and she and Jamie made their way to Christopher's room. Jamie knocked and was asked to enter.

"Liza and I thought that we would just see that you are comfortable and not too nervous about tomorrow. May we both come in?" asked Jamie.

"Of course you may," said Christopher who was sitting up in bed and appeared to be attempting to read.

Liza came in and sat on the edge of his bed. "Jamie's mother will be accompanying us tomorrow; I hope you don't mind. She is a very caring person and will help us all to get home safely when the doctor has finished."

"She's very kind," said Christopher. "Will you be with me?"

"Yes, I'll stay with you the whole time. The doctors never object to my being in the room with them, but Jamie and his mother will be in the waiting room ready to help you home," said Liza.

"I'm glad you'll be there. It is a little frightening," said Christopher as a tear trickled down his cheek. Jamie discreetly left the room as Liza moved near to him and put an arm around him as his shoulders shook. "I'm acting like a baby," he sobbed.

"No, you're acting like a normal human being who knows that he will have to go through an ordeal. All you have to think about is that this time tomorrow it will all be over, and you will be on the mend knowing that you will be able to use your hand again," said Liza as she held him closely to her and they stayed like that until he felt better and the tears stopped.

"Thank you, Aunt Liza; it's a long time since I cried and it's even longer since someone held me as you just did. I am looking forward to being able to look at my hand without hating it and to being able to use it again. I will think about this time tomorrow and the following days. Perhaps I will be able to get some sleep tonight," said Christopher.

"I can help you with that Christopher," said Liza and she stroked his head and he held her gaze and gradually his eyes closed until finally he was in a deep sleep. She pulled the covers over him and put his book on the bedside table and quietly left the room.

Jamie was waiting for her outside. "Has he settled?" he asked, and Liza nodded. "I thought you would do that."

"Do what?" asked Liza.

"I've seen you soothe people to sleep before. I believe it's some sort of hypnosis. At least you didn't have to give him the foul-tasting concoction that you gave me," smiled Jamie.

"No, I'll save that for when he gets home and is in pain," smiled Liza.

***

Everyone was up early the next morning and Liza had organised just a very light breakfast for Christopher. Roberts took on the task of getting him ready for the day and told Jamie that he would be helping him dress each day until he regained the use of his hand and several people, including Susan, were going to cut up his food until he was ready to do it himself.

"How do you feel this morning, Christopher?" asked Jamie.

"Surprisingly well. I slept soundly last night which I didn't think I would be able to, and I feel very calm," said Christopher.

I wonder how she does that, thought Jamie. "That's good; we'll be leaving shortly."

Jamie drove the small carriage into the village. As they passed near the church Bernard came out and wished Christopher well and said he would see him later. They went on into the village and Derek was loitering, obviously waiting for them.

"You'll be fine Christopher, Dr Phillips is a brilliant doctor, and so is our Dr Bruce; you are in very safe hands," said Derek.

Mr and Mrs Rogers and Mrs Price were standing nearby, and they called out their good wishes, as did the baker and grocer. April walked down and said that Adam sent his regards and they both would be thinking of him, and several other people waved to him.

Christopher seemed a little overwhelmed by all the surprising attention. "These are really lovely people," was all Christopher could think of saying.

"Yes, there's very little that goes unnoticed in this village," smiled Miranda remembering how they had all cared for her when she was in need of help.

Jamie and Miranda went into the waiting room while Liza went with Christopher into the surgery. Liza helped him off with his jacket and rolled up the sleeve of his shirt. She helped him lay on the table and whispered something to him and he closed his eyes and was asleep.

Both doctors looked puzzled. "Have you hypnotised him?" asked Dr Phillips.

"He's just become very calm, but he still needs something to take the pain away. I presume you will be giving him a few drops of chloroform," said Liza.

"I doubt that we will be able to completely dull the pain, but stranger things have happened," said Dr Bruce as he looked closely at Liza who was looking very innocent.

123

They started the procedure and Liza found it difficult to tolerate the sound that each finger made as the doctors broke it and put it correctly in place. The thumb was already in place, but there was one last bone in the hand that had to be dealt with which was from the little finger near to the wrist. They had to cut open the skin and break the small bone. It was difficult but eventually they managed it. By this time Christopher was moaning and Liza moved close to him and whispered in his ear, and he settled again.

Three fingers had splints on them, and the little finger had one that held it in place from the wrist to the tip of the finger once the skin had been stitched together. The whole hand was then carefully bandaged.

"You can wake him up now Lady Edgeworth," said Dr Phillips.

"Surely it will take time for the chloroform to wear off," said Liza.

"That wore off a while ago; as I said, you can wake him up now as only you know how to," smiled Dr Phillips.

Liza looked at him and frowned, she did not like anyone knowing that she had that ability, which was something that she had picked up from the Cherokees. She leaned over Christopher and whispered to him that it was all over and he could wake up now.

He opened his eyes and slowly sat up, and then a look of pain crossed his face. Dr Phillips smiled at him and said, "Yes I know it will hurt, but look at your hand. It is open and your fingers are straight, and when they have knitted together in a few weeks you can start moving them. It has all gone very well. The doctor will remove the stitches in about a week."

Christopher nodded and gradually stood up. Liza pulled down his shirt sleeve and Dr Phillips put his arm in a sling, and they helped him out to where Jamie and Miranda were waiting anxiously. Jamie put his coat around his shoulders and Christopher staggered out to the carriage, where Jamie and Miranda helped him up the steps and settled him inside. Jamie gently drove them back to the main house and Miranda and Liza guided him from the carriage and up the steps.

Mrs Frances and Roberts came forward and guided him up to his room where Roberts helped him change and into his bed.

"Is it hurting very much, Sir," asked Roberts.

"It is beginning to throb and is getting quite painful," said Christopher.

"Her Ladyship will sort that out for you," said Roberts. "I'll tell her that you're ready."

"Ready for what?" asked Christopher.

"She has medicines that take pain away," said Roberts. "She'll be in shortly."

Christopher was sitting up in bed looking puzzled and in pain when Liza came in with a cupful of foul-smelling liquid; she also brought one of Matthew's favourite toffees with her which she knew would take the taste away. Miranda followed her in bringing her sewing with her. She was going to watch over him whilst he slept.

"Now you are not going to like this, but it will take the pain away and let you get some sleep," said Liza.

"Roberts said that you had something that would do that; does it taste so very bad?" asked Christopher.

"Yes, but I've got one of Matthew's favourite toffees which should take the taste away, but make sure you chew it and finish it before you go to sleep; I don't want you to choke," smiled Liza as she handed him the cup and watched him drink it and pull a disgusted looking face. "There that wasn't so bad, was it?"

Christopher looked up at her and said, "Yes it was. I can only think that anything that bad must be good for me." He took the toffee and sucked it noisily and both Liza and Miranda had to smile.

"I'll be staying with you for a while to make sure that you are alright," said Miranda. "Then when you wake you may feel like something to eat. You are going to be well pampered over the next few days, so enjoy it."

"Yes, do enjoy it because when the boys are back, they will want to examine your hand in great detail, so you won't have a minute to yourself once they are here," smiled Liza.

"I look forward to seeing them," said a very drowsy Christopher.

"Have you finished your toffee?" asked Liza and Christopher nodded and it was not long before he fell asleep.

Dr Phillips returned saying that all had gone well and that he would look at Christopher's hand again before he left the next morning.

After a couple of hours Amelia took Miranda's place and after that it was Lucinda's turn. Finally, just before dinner Liza took over, which was when Christopher woke up. He looked refreshed and said that he was hungry.

"I'll organise something for you to eat," she said and called Mrs Frances. It was not long before Susan appeared carrying a tray and she insisted that she would help him with his food. Liza smiled and left them to their own devices.

Liza looked in on him before she went to bed, and he was awake.

"How do you feel Christopher? Is it very sore?" asked Liza.

"If I say yes you'll give me that horrible stuff to drink," smiled Christopher.

"I can actually see from your face that you are in some difficulty, and you would be asleep if you were not, so the answer is yes, I am going to give you that horrible stuff to drink, but you can have another toffee to go with it," said Liza and she disappeared and returned a short while later with the cup of foul-smelling liquid.

Liza looked at Christopher, "It's no good Christopher; I know you are awake. There's no use pretending, so be brave and drink this down like a man."

He sighed and sat up, took the cup from her and swallowed it down, pulling a most disgusted face. Liza laughed and handed him another of Matthew's favourite toffees. She sat with him whilst he ate it and when he had finished, he was nearly asleep.

"Goodnight, Christopher, just call out if you need anything," she bent down and kissed him on the head which seemed to surprise him and then he smiled and closed his eyes.

Susan was waiting for her in her room and started to help her out of her dress. "Christopher seems very nice," said Susan.

"Yes, he does seem to be," Liza commented. "He's going to need quite some help over the next few weeks."

"I'll be able to help him," said Susan. "I helped Derek a great deal when he had seen Dr Phillips."

"That's very kind of you Susan; we'll all be helping him," said Liza.

When Liza went into Jamie that night, he commented how well Christopher had dealt with all that had happened to him that day. "I think that we have acquired a new member of our family."

"He may not wish to be with us. I have said before that he is the ward of Professor Cavendish, but I think that we can arrange to always have a room for him in the future should he like to join us. The Master may not wish him to be here, so I'm afraid that it is down to him whether or not he comes to us," said Liza.

"He'll only be in that situation until the end of the school year; that's when he will leave and have to make his own way in life," said Jamie.

"Oh well, that's when we may well have to help him, after all we have a number of companies that could employ him," said Liza.

"Firstly you'll have to find out what he's good at; but you probably have already, haven't you," said Jamie.

"Yes, he has some accountancy skills," said Liza as she climbed into bed and started making Jamie feel very loved.

**

The next ten days passed quickly. Christopher's stitches were successfully removed, and he was healing fast. His fingers still had to remain in splints, but he had feeling and some gentle movement. He now joined them regularly at dinner;

there was no getting away from the fact that he was now a young gentleman who would soon be embarking on a career.

The boys arrived home without Nicholas and Richard; they would be spending a few days at their home and would not be back with them until Christmas Eve.

After greeting Liza and Jamie and the rest of the family, they went off to find Christopher as they wanted to examine his hand closely. They found him reading in the library, he knew they had arrived home because of the noise that they made; the house was certainly becoming lively. Four faces were peering closely at his hand, although it was still bandaged and they could really see nothing, but they all discussed it in great detail as if they were fully knowledgeable with the procedure that Christopher had undergone.

"Do you realise that John would have had to go through that if we hadn't saved him," said James and they all nodded knowingly.

They asked a great many questions as they wanted to know all the gory details and then suddenly they were off to the stables to see their horses to make sure that they had been looked after correctly. Christopher felt that he had been caught up in a whirlwind. Miranda put her head around the door and said, "The boys are back" and went away laughing.

Wendell came into the library and sat down; he looked at Christopher and shook his head, "We're in for a lively time now, but we wouldn't have it any other way. That's why we love coming here," said Wendell as he laughed.

Christopher had recognised that it was a very happy household but now it was happy as well as chaotic and he knew that it would be even more so when the Berkshires arrived, and goodness knows who else. It seemed that this was where everyone liked to gather, and he could see Aunt Liza rushing around with Mrs Frances organising what looked like every room in the house. He had asked if there was enough room for him to stay and Aunt Liza had laughed and told him that it was his room as long as he wanted it.

Jamie came in to join them saying that he wanted some peace and quiet, so he was staying out of the way for a while. He picked up his newspaper and Wendell followed suit, Christopher smiled and enjoyed being with them. Everyone in this house had a wonderful character which went with their sense of humour. He was really looking forward to Christmas for the first time in many years, although he had no money to buy presents for anyone, but he knew that they all understood that.

Liza smiled as she came into the library and both Jamie and Wendell lowered their newspapers slightly.

"I've just had a letter from Douglas Carlton," she said.

"Have you Liza?" said Jamie.

"Yes. Don't you want to know what he said?" said Liza.

Both newspapers dropped a little lower. "What has he said Liza? Has he decided to join us again this Christmas?" asked Jamie.

"Yes, he will be arriving the day after tomorrow," said Liza.

"Isn't that when Peter and Edward and the family are arriving," said Jamie and now his newspaper had dropped to his lap.

"That's right, and Arthur and Annalise will be with them," said Liza.

"I've lost track of the number we will be entertaining this year," said Jamie.

"The trouble is, I think I have too," said Liza and she went off to see Mrs Frances and Mrs Lambert.

Wendell and Jamie looked at one another and then at Christopher who was looking rather bemused. "It will all work out, it always does," said Jamie. He and Wendell went back to their newspapers and Christopher went back to his book.

Liza was in her study with Grace and Mrs Frances, and they were all just sitting and thinking. Liza was muttering "Rose will be with Miranda and Lucinda, Anthony and Diana will have their usual room with little Thomas and his nurse in the small room next to them; Christopher is already in Nurse Dawkins' old room, Bella will be in her usual room, the Duke will have the room he had last year. Have you allocated a room for his valet Mrs Frances?"

"Yes, that's all taken care of," said Mrs Frances.

"Good, Amelia and Wendell are settled in their room and Peter will be in his room. Nicole and Edward are in their usual place, but little Edward will have to be in a room nearby with his Nurse. They didn't bring a nurse last year, but they needed one with them this year. Lord Carlton will have to be in a different room, as we have to put Arthur and Annalise in the room he had last year. The Major and Jennifer, and Joseph and Lily are only staying on Christmas night, as are Penny and Randolph Langston, they will all have to be accommodated in the east wing. Is that everyone? Have I forgotten anyone?"

"I think that's everyone," said Grace.

"The trouble is that we don't know how many servants they may be bringing. We can accommodate up to four drivers and I wonder if the Duke will be bringing his housekeeper and butler this year," said Liza.

"I'll organise that every room is made ready just in case we have any unexpected visitors," said Mrs Frances.

"I hope you are going to be able to have your own Christmas dinner as usual. I thought we were going to have less people here this year, but we seem to have increased. I'll have to go through the menus with Mrs Lambert, although I know that she will have everything in hand, but I do have to put my mind at rest," said Liza.

Bella turned up with Nicholas and Richard the next day instead of Christmas Eve as previously arranged.

"I remembered that you normally decorate the tree today and I didn't want Nicholas and Richard to miss out on the fun of that. Also they wanted to see Christopher to make sure that he was well," said Bella.

"Your rooms are always ready for you Bella," said Liza and Bella went and settled in her room with a look of relief on her face.

Later that day Mr Lambert and Ken Wallace staggered in with the tree and spent a great deal of time putting it safely in place with all the boys thinking that they were helping by directing them in the task. As with the previous year everyone helped with decorating it and by the end of the afternoon it was finished and looking splendid.

Christopher went down to the kitchen with the boys for supper; he could have remained dining later with everyone else, but the boys wanted him with them.

Peter, Edward, Nicole and little Edward arrived the next day along with Arthur and Annalise. Peter immediately sought out John to ensure that he was not affected by the problems he had had because he was left-handed, and his next thought was to find Grace and spend some time with her.

Anthony, Diana, Rose, little Thomas and his nurse drove up just before teatime and little Thomas immediately called for Matthew. His speech had improved and 'Maffew' had finally become 'Matthew'.

The Duke and Douglas Carlton came with just one valet later that day, so apart from those who were just arriving on Christmas Day, all the visitors were in place with two days to spare.

"This is the young gentleman I was telling you about, Douglas," said the Duke when he found Christopher reading in the library.

Christopher looked up startled.

Douglas smiled and asked Christopher how his hand was now feeling.

"The pain has eased considerably, thank you Sir," said Christopher. "I can also feel movement in the fingers, so it is all going to plan. Thank you for asking."

"I understand that the boys stopped the same thing happening to young John; I would not like to have been on the receiving end of either Lord or Lady Edgeworth's wrath. But good has come out of it all as nobody else will have to go through what you are currently experiencing. I'm pleased to meet you young man and wish you well in your recovery," said Douglas.

"Are you looking forward to Christmas?" the Duke asked Christopher.

"I am Sir. I cannot remember the last time I was with a family at Christmas," said Christopher.

"Are your parents no longer with us Christopher?" asked Douglas.

"My father died some years ago and my mother remarried not long after. My stepfather is in the diplomatic service and they live in India now. I have not seen them since they went there," said Christopher without looking for sympathy.

"Well, you will have a good Christmas here; that is guaranteed, which is why we return year after year. It is always a little chaotic, but good fun," said the Duke.

They sat with Christopher and discussed the book he was reading as well as the operation on his hand and made a few suggestions about his future and when they left Christopher realised that he had been talking quite naturally to the Duke of Berkshire and Lord Carlton as if he had known them for years. How strange his life had become but he remembered what Professor Cavendish had said about the fact that it could all end as soon as this holiday time was over.

Simon put his head around the door, "We're going into the village tomorrow morning Christopher: would you like to come with us. We want to see Derek and Mr Reece and April now that school has broken up. We'll see one or two of the others also."

"That would be good," said Christopher. "Do Aunt Liza and Uncle Jamie know what you are planning?"

"Yes, they do. I think Richard will be driving the carriage this time with you and Nicholas. We'll ride our horses," said Simon.

"I'll look forward to that. Is it supper time yet?" asked Christopher.

"Not quite, but we might as well go down to the kitchen and wait there," said Simon and they both went off following the smell of food cooking.

The boys set off the next morning for the village with the voice of Jamie telling them to be careful and a chorus of "Yes Dad," and "Yes Uncle" coming back at him. Liza had decided that a male voice would be the better voice of authority rather than hers.

Derek was visiting April and Adam when they got to the village and they all crowded into the April's kitchen, sniffing the air and eyeing up the cakes that had just come out of the oven and April knew that she was going to have to make another batch as the boys would be eating what she had already made.

Whilst April was giving out cakes to the boys, Adam and Derek had been discussing their plans for the term following Christmas as well as how Derek's tuition of Ken Wallace's children was progressing.

"Do you know where Mr Wallace is from?" asked Christopher.

Adam looked up and said, "No, I'm afraid I don't. Why do you ask?"

"I know him from somewhere, but I cannot remember where. It has to be at least ten years since I could have known him and I was born in Hertfordshire, so I can only think that he is from there," said Christopher. "Aunt Liza doesn't know, but of course she could be keeping a confidence as I know that people tell her things and she keeps them to herself, but it does annoy me that I cannot remember."

"You would have been very young then. Perhaps only six or seven-years-old," said Adam. "All I know is that he fell on hard times and when his wife died, he came here soon after. He is a very private man, but it is no secret that he has been well educated. I'm afraid that I can't put you out of your misery over him. It may come to you in time, although he may not wish to be remembered."

"It does annoy me that my memory has let me down, but I would not embarrass him by telling everyone about his past, I would just like to satisfy my own curiosity," smiled Christopher.

"Tell me a little more about yourself Christopher," said Adam and he listened as Christopher told him of his family and education.

"So at the end of the school year in July you will be looking for employment," said Adam. "I'm sure that Lady Edgeworth would assist you with that, however if you would like to think about a career in teaching, I have an opening for someone who could mainly concentrate on the mathematical side of education but also assist with other lessons. Derek and I manage at the moment, but we have quite an influx of parents wanting their children to be enrolled for the new school year."

"That does sound interesting. I had not thought of such a career. I hoped that I could possibly gain employment as a junior in some accountancy firm, which is something that really did not appeal to me, but I would have to take whatever was offered to me," said Christopher.

"I presume that I am correct that your leaning is towards mathematics," said Adam and Christopher nodded his agreement. "Why not discuss it with Lady Edgeworth; she is known for her sound advice. Of course it would solve a problem for you and one for me as I would have to find somebody to undertake such tasks. I think that you and Derek would make a very good team and children would definitely benefit from your input."

"It's kind of you to say so and I have to admit that I do feel very at home here. The people of the village seem to be very caring of one another. I have yet to meet any of the farmers but would think that they are just the same. I know that all the staff at Edgeworth House are very happy working there," said Christopher. "It would be nice to become one of them and feel that I belong somewhere."

"I know that you are young, but that means that you will be able to communicate well with children and I would not start you with the older ones; you could gradually move up to teach those in time," said Adam and then he laughed and said that he was talking to him as if he had accepted the position.

"If it all works out well, I presume that I would be able to rent a room in the village. I wouldn't want to impose on Lord and Lady Edgeworth, although I know that they would not think of it as an imposition, but I must be able to stand on my own two feet," said Christopher.

Derek had been listening to part of the conversation and said, "There is a spare room at our house now that Susan lives at Edgeworth House, and I know that my mother has mentioned once or twice that she could rent out the room. It's not large but it is comfortable."

"I will think about everything that has been said here and I'll discuss it with Lady Edgeworth, and I will make a final decision after Christmas and before I return to university, although I think that I have made my decision," said Christopher.

"It's always wise to seriously think about what you would like as a career. I'm pleased that we have had this talk as it has made me make up my mind that we could work well together, but as I have said, go away and think about your future," said Adam.

By this time the boys had eaten their way through April's cakes and now wanted to visit Mrs Price and the baker and Mr and Mrs Rogers. "Are you going to eat at all those places as well?" asked April.

"It would be rude to refuse their offerings," smiled Matthew and April just raised her eyes to heaven.

Derek and Christopher strolled to Mrs Price's house, whilst the boys went to the bakers first. Mrs Price said that she could accommodate Christopher if he decided to work with Mr Reece and Derek at the village school. She showed him the room and he said that he would not need it until around July, but she said that she was no longer desperate for money as she had been a few years ago. Christopher said that he would make his final decision before he returned to university, and he would let her know.

When they finally returned to Edgeworth House, Christopher sought out Liza and Jamie and told them of his conversation with Adam who had suggested that he discussed it with them.

"Is it a career that you feel you would like and is it something that you have thought about before?" asked Jamie.

"The only work that I thought I would be able to gain was a junior position in some accountancy firm, although that was not a situation that I truly wanted to undertake. My dream was to do something more artistic, but that dream was taken from me a couple of years ago, although it would not have been a very lucrative career and could possibly only be something that I would have indulged in during any spare time that I had," said Christopher. "Until today I had not

132

thought about a career in teaching, but it does appeal to me, and I know that I would be capable of guiding children in that respect."

"I believe that you already hold degrees in mathematics and English; you could quite probably have a career teaching the children in some prestigious homes and perhaps continue on to becoming a professor at some university," said Liza. "In other words, you could do a great deal better than teaching at a local village school. I had the same conversation with Adam Reece when I knew that he had decided to become the headmaster of a small local village school."

"I think I know why Adam Reece wanted to be that headmaster; it's because he was accepted as one of the villagers and he is happy and very contented with that life," said Christopher. "I feel that for the first time in many years this is somewhere that I have been made to feel welcome; in fact I feel that I belong here."

"I can understand that Christopher," said Liza. "You really have only had the university as your home for many years now and the people around here have welcomed you; they did the same to me when I arrived a few years ago, but it is a very big decision for you and one that only you can make."

"The word has spread about Adam's superb teaching abilities, and we now have children enrolling in the school from outside the area," said Jamie. "I have heard that some parents have arranged that their children stay with our villagers during the week and only return home at weekends, so Adam is going to need reliable help. I do not believe for one minute that you and Derek will be the only teachers that he will employ; the school is growing, and we will have to look at how the premises can be improved to accommodate the number of children that we expect will be enrolled in the future. To be in at the beginning of that expansion will be good for you."

"Mrs Price has offered me a room if I decide to take the position and that would be very convenient for me and would of course help Mrs Price also," said Christopher.

"You know you are always welcome here Christopher," said Liza.

"I knew that you would say that, but you have already done enough for me, and I am more than grateful for that. As I say, it would be very convenient to stay with Mrs Price, and Derek and I get on well and have a great deal in common. I do need to stand on my own two feet; however I don't want you to think that I don't appreciate your kindness," said Christopher.

"You must always do what makes you happy and I for one would be very pleased for you to be with us, but I want you to continue thinking about it before you make a final decision because I know you could do well in any career of your choosing," said Liza. "In the meantime you must relax and allow your hand to heal and enjoy Christmas and the New Year with us."

"I have heard that sometimes you get snowed in here, which could stop our return to Cambridge," smiled Christopher.

"Last year we did but only for a short while, whereas the year before it was very serious, and we were in danger of running out of food and fuel. We had to close some rooms and double up in bedrooms for quite some time. It was very concerning; however the boys thought that it was quite exciting. The forecast this year is virtually the same as last year, so you may get your wish," smiled Liza.

"I do not wish to dictate your life for you Christopher, but we would be pleased if you were to come to us again at half-term and at Easter, although we will not be here then as we are visiting friends in South Carolina, but you are most welcome to spend the time here and again during the following half-term, in fact for as long as you need to," said Jamie.

"We will get in touch with Professor Cavendish as he is your guardian, but I don't think that there will be any problem with what we are suggesting, but of course firstly you must determine that you would like to spend the time here," smiled Liza.

"You don't really need to ask me that Aunt Liza, being here is the happiest I have been in a very long time, despite the pain in my hand and I am really looking forward to Christmas," said Christopher.

"Is your hand still painful?" asked Liza with a smile.

Christopher was about to say that it was when he realised that Liza would give him some nasty tasting medicine if he admitted it, so he said, "No, it doesn't hurt at all."

"There are some people who are just no good at telling lies, and unfortunately you are one of them Christopher," smiled Liza, "So come with me."

Christopher groaned and Jamie said that it was for his own good.

Matthew was looking for Christopher when he saw Liza going towards his room with a cup of liquid and he grinned and put his hand in his pocket and pulled out one of his toffees and went with his mother into Christopher's room.

"So, she's going to give you her special medicine. You know you'll feel better in a little while, anyway here's one of my toffees, they do help to take the nasty taste away," smiled Matthew.

Christopher thanked Matthew and looked at the fluff covered toffee and said that he would eat it a little later.

"I thought of bringing him one myself," said Liza, "so you can enjoy your toffee yourself but thank you Matthew, it was very thoughtful of you."

"Oh, that's alright then," said Matthew as he put his toffee in his mouth as both Liza and Christopher looked on in horror. He went off to join the others.

"I suppose it won't do him any harm," muttered Liza.

"I suppose not," said a thoughtful Christopher and then he gulped down his medicine and followed it with the toffee which he once again sucked noisily.

"Supper won't be for at least two hours, so you can rest until then. I'll ask the boys to wake you in time," said Liza.

Liza went to her study and before long Jamie joined her.

"Do you think that it is really the best career for Christopher?" asked Jamie.

"If we were to think about how well he could do by working his way up in an accountancy company, then this is not the height of careers, but I have thought the same for both Adam and Derek. However when I truly analyse what they are doing, what higher ambitions can anyone have than to give children the very best start in life and their successful future is the greatest of achievements," said Liza. "Also instead of doing a job just for the money, they are all doing it because they enjoy it. Doing a job that you love is also very rewarding."

"I wonder what Professor Cavendish will think of his decision," said Jamie. "Also what his parents may think, although I don't believe they are particularly bothered about him; any responsibility they think they may have stops at the end of the school year. He must feel isolated without his parents."

"I didn't Jamie, and I still don't," said Liza.

"You had people who loved you around you Liza," said Jamie. "I cannot see that Christopher has had that for a very long time."

"I know I had, but it doesn't make up for having parents who think nothing of you. Their only thought was a means of money and I have ensured that they no longer benefit from my good fortune," said Liza.

"You are so kind and thoughtful of people that it is difficult to understand your lack of forgiveness for them. You have always forgiven everyone everything; even Evelyn with the things she has tried to do to us both," said Jamie.

"My parents sold me Jamie; you know that. It did not matter to them who they sold me to; it would have been to the highest bidder; they did not know that James was a kind man, he could have been the cruellest and most evil person on this earth and that would not have worried them. Parents are meant to love and protect their children, not use them as a means of gaining money," said Liza with a pout. "You must also remember that when I was missing, my mother wanted me declared dead so that she could inherit. Wendell paid her five hundred pounds and told her that she was not named in my Will, although he had no idea whether she was or not."

"You sound very bitter Liza, which is very unlike you," said Jamie.

"I will always feel bitter when I think about my parents, but I was lucky to have been surrounded by people who cared for me as soon as I left Liverpool and you know that they became my family. I hope that Christopher can achieve friendships as I did, and hopefully those friendships will take away some of the hurt that he must feel about his parents," said Liza.

"Do you still hurt?" asked Jamie.

"No, I don't hurt. It now just annoys me. The life that I have is wonderful. I have you and our boys and our family and friends and they are all with us for Christmas. I suppose I should really thank my parents as I would not have all this if they had not sold me," smiled Liza.

***

Once again the young men became boys on Christmas morning and Edward and Arthur could be included in that description.

Breakfast was necessarily light as Christmas lunch would be relatively early so that the staff could have their Christmas dinner at a reasonable hour and Ken Wallace had been invited to bring his children to the dinner. April and Adam would also be joining them as would Mrs Price and Derek. Liza would have preferred that they joined the main party, but they were happy to be with the staff.

Most of Liza and Jamie's guests attended church in the morning and when the service was over Bernard was going to join them for lunch.

Twenty-eight sat down to lunch, which included little Thomas, who was delighted to be considered old enough to join them. He would have liked to sit next to Matthew, but Anthony and Diana kept him safely between them. As always the boys had been interspersed with the guests and Liza had made sure that Christopher was next to those he felt comfortable with, so he had Miranda on one side and Grace on the other and she had Peter next to her. It was all working out very well and once again Mrs Lambert had excelled with her cooking expertise.

It was a very lively lunchtime and finally the Christmas pudding was eaten, and everyone then moved into the drawing room and whilst presents were handed around, Harper and Mrs Frances cleared the dining room and made it ready for the supper later when they would all help themselves when they felt the need for food.

At around three o'clock the Major and Jennifer arrived and a short while later Lily, Joseph, Penny and Randolph joined them. Mrs Frances quickly took their bags to their rooms, and they followed and freshened up before joining everyone in the drawing room.

Everything was skilfully arranged and then all the staff disappeared to enjoy their own Christmas dinner.

Jamie called everyone to order which surprised Liza and she wondered what he was going to say.

"Over the past many months our friend Randolph has been working on portraits of both Liza and I, which he finished some weeks ago. However I thought that this would be a good time to show the excellence of his work and so I asked him to arrange for them to be shown for the first time today," said Jamie and he and Randolph brought in easels and then Randolph carefully put the covered portraits in place.

"Now we need these portraits to be unveiled and I could think of no better people than Wendell and Amelia to do this honour. They have seen both Liza and I through so many good times as well as given gentle advice and guidance through the traumas which we unfortunately have experienced over the years that we have known them. They are family to us as we are to them, and I know that without their support Liza and I would not be together and have such a wonderful life. We have a great deal to thank you for and I would like you both to be the first to see how Randolph has portrayed the love that Liza and I have for one another, and for our extended family and friends," said Jamie as he beckoned them to the easels.

Wendell and Amelia smiled happily and moved towards the portraits and virtually in unison they gently removed the soft silky coverings and there were gasps from around the room as the beautiful smiling, contented face of Liza was revealed with Jamie's showing the love and happiness that he so obviously felt.

"They are absolutely superb," said the Duke. "Young Randolph has captured you both wonderfully well and so accurately."

"Where will you be hanging them?" asked Wendell.

"I'm making room for them in our drawing room. I shall be moving my father and grandfather to one side so that Liza and I can dominate the room," said Jamie.

"Neither your father nor grandfather look particularly happy; it will be nice to see people smiling down on us when we are here," said Diana.

"I would really like Randolph to undertake a portrait of my mother, but she has expressed reluctance to take her place on our walls," smiled Jamie. "I may yet be able to persuade her."

"Does Randolph take outside commissions?" asked Douglas Carlton. "I could think of many who would like to use his talents."

"Me and my family for one," said the Duke and he moved away and could be seen talking to Randolph and Penny.

"I think Randolph is going to be very busy in the future," commented Jamie.

The portraits were a great talking point, and they were studied closely until Douglas Carlton suddenly said, "Aren't we going to play the Christmas game this year?"

"Yes," the shout went up and James and John went to the library and took it from one of the shelves and returned to the cheers of all who knew about it.

It was not long before there were shouts, cheers, laughter and cries of "Stop cheating" echoing around the room and "That's not fair". Edward and Joseph were the greatest protagonists with Peter trying to call them to order, but to no avail. He gave up when the Duke got on his knees and joined in, and it was not long before Douglas followed suit. Arthur was standing and frowning but eventually he could not resist the draw of the competition.

The boys were in the middle of it all and so was Liza, for although she had been determined to stay away from it that year, the pull was too much for her. Christopher was watching and laughing, and Matthew called him over to join in. "Come on Chris, you can do it. I'll keep everyone away from your hand. Next year you won't have to worry as it will be mended by then."

Nobody ever really won at it; there were just those who did better than others.

Five o'clock came and it was Matthew who suggested that everyone must be hungry by then and gradually they all went into the dining room and helped themselves to their supper. Liza stopped the boys going to the kitchen to see what was happening as the staff should still have been enjoying their Christmas dinner.

"You can go down in a short while. You mustn't disturb them at their dinner but I'm sure they will be pleased to see you when they have finished," said Liza.

Another hour passed and Mrs Frances and Harper came into the dining room to see that all was in order, which gave the boys the excuse to visit the kitchen and spend some time with the staff and their friends; they specially wanted to see Derek. Christopher accompanied them and Liza warned them all not to interrupt anyone who may still be eating.

The boys were always welcome in the kitchen and Derek was especially pleased to see them. Adam and April were getting ready to leave and they would be taking Mrs Price and Derek with them, but they stopped to enjoy the company of the boys for a short while.

Christopher was pulled into the crowd, and it took him a while to notice that Ken Wallace was there, as well as his four children: the two youngest being very tired. He nodded to Ken and then caught sight of his eldest girl who was pretty and fair haired, and then saw the second eldest who looked very similar and then he remembered who Ken Wallace was. The two girls looked very like their mother, who was the daughter of one of the Earl of Graystead's grooms and Ken Wallace was the Earl's second son.

Christopher could remember the groom's daughter because she was so very pretty and used to laugh a great deal. She had been kind to him when he had lost his father and then she and her father had disappeared and a little while later it was rumoured that the Earl's son had left after a terrible disagreement.

He knew that Ken could not have recognised him as he had been very young when it had all happened, and he had seen very little of him; the groom and his daughter had spent more time in the area where Christopher had lived. He wondered what had happened to Ken's wife and assumed that she was no longer alive.

Christopher could see that Ken loved his daughters, but his eyes told a very sad story. From what he had heard, Ken had arrived in the village just a year ago with nowhere to go and nothing to eat and he had since worked very hard to keep a roof over their heads. He had also heard that Aunt Liza and Uncle Jamie had helped him get back on his feet and he realised that they did not know who he was, and he was not going to tell them as he was sensible enough to know that if Ken had wanted them to know, then he would have told them.

The two youngest girls were very tired, and Ken gathered up his family and smiled at everyone whilst thanking them for a lovely Christmas. The four girls left, and they were clasping their Christmas gifts closely and waved goodbye to them all.

Christopher made up his mind that he would say nothing of who Ken Wallace was to anyone. He felt a little guilty that he was going to have to keep a secret from Aunt Liza and Uncle Jamie, but they would do the same if they were in his situation. He admired Ken for being both mother and father to his children and he felt a pang of annoyance at his own mother who obviously felt nothing for him, otherwise she would have done what Ken was doing and that was loving and caring for his children in very difficult circumstances.

"What wonderful manners those girls have," commented Mrs Lambert and everyone nodded their agreement.

The day finally came to an end with everyone well fed and happy. Gradually the boys made their way to their rooms. Little Thomas and baby Edward had been put to bed much earlier and now it was late and eventually just Liza, Jamie, the Duke and Douglas Carlton were the only ones left in the drawing room. They enjoyed a nightcap and discussed the day, and the main topic of conversation was Liza and Jamie's portraits.

"I have asked young Langston to undertake portraits of Bella and myself. I don't believe that my boys would yet be prepared to sit long enough for their portraits to be painted, but perhaps in the future they may be more willing," said the Duke.

"What about you Douglas?" said Jamie. "Wouldn't you like to have your portrait painted? Unless you have already, although I can't remember seeing it hanging on any of your walls."

"My parents had one done of me when I was quite young, but it wasn't very good and I have changed quite considerably," laughed Douglas patting his stomach. "I wouldn't mind if I had somebody to sit with as you did Jamie."

"It would be a record to go with your family tree," said the Duke.

"I'll think about it," said Douglas.

Chapter 7

Christmas was over and Edgeworth House was gradually emptying of guests. Liza and Jamie held a small New Year's Eve Party for those who were remaining with them and that also included the staff. As always Liza smiled her way through New Year's Day; her guests would never have known that the happenings of that day eight years before still held a sadness for her. This year she heard the boys telling Christopher about Patrick and how he had died, and she felt it best to find Jamie and stay with him for a while.

She found him in the library with Wendell, the Duke and Douglas. They were catching up on the newspapers that they had been unable to read just prior to the New Year and it looked as if they were sharing pages. Liza made a mental note to order extra papers when they had so many guests.

All their newspapers dropped slightly as she came into the room and each of them waited for Liza to say something which would interest them.

"Well gentlemen, have you recovered from last night's entertainment?" said Liza with a smile that did not reach her eyes.

"Yes, thank you Liza," said the Duke.

"I still have a slight headache," said Douglas. "That is my own fault for over imbibing on your excellent wine."

Anthony entered the library and looked around before finding a chair. He frowned when he realised that all the newspapers were already in use.

Jamie was watching Liza closely and knew her well enough to realise that she needed him but did not want to make a fuss in front of everyone there. He dropped his newspaper and carefully folded it before handing it to Anthony.

"Take my paper Anthony, I can read it at any time," said Jamie. "Liza, can you help me sort out what I'm going to need for Thursday's gathering at the Langston Home?"

Liza smiled gratefully at him and Wendell muttered, "Yes, that's seems a good idea to get organised, the children won't want you to look overdressed." He looked at Liza and smiled gently as he had realised that she needed Jamie to be with her.

"Is she alright?" asked Douglas.

"This is always a difficult day for her," said Wendell from behind his newspaper.

"Ah, of course," said the Duke.

"I'm afraid that Matthew, John and Simon were telling young Christopher all about how Patrick died eight years ago," said Anthony, "and Liza heard them. She was fine until then."

"Eight years is a long time," commented the Duke.

"Not when you see your husband gunned down in front of you and your boys," said Wendell still from behind his newspaper.

"I suppose it is something that you never really get over," said Douglas and he then retreated behind his newspaper.

In Jamie's room he sat her on his bed, and she was trying not to look sad. He stroked her head and told her that she could be as sad as she liked, and he was pleased that she wanted to be with him on that day.

"It's been eight years now and you would think that this day would pass with just the happy memories that I have, but I suppose if it was any other day then it would not have the same impact that New Year's Day has. Everyone seems so happy on this day and somehow that doesn't seem right," said Liza.

"You seemed quite bright earlier, has something happened to make you feel like this?" asked Jamie.

"I heard Matthew, John and Simon telling Christopher what had happened on this day eight years ago," said Liza. "I had thought that their memories would be less keen, but I was wrong, they remember it all in great detail. I suppose it helps them to tell others what they went through, because all three went through hell on that day."

"They weren't the only ones to go through hell, were they Liza?" said Jamie.

"No, that was a bad time, but there are no bad times now Jamie; all I have is the odd hurtful memory and it doesn't alter how I feel about you and our family and all our friends. I would not change my life with you for the world. I love you Jamie Edgeworth and I hope my little hiccup just now hasn't worried you at all," said Liza.

"If you can't show how you are feeling to me then there would be something wrong with our relationship," said Jamie. "I'm pleased that we can be this honest with one another and I love you too Liza Edgeworth."

"Thank you, Jamie," she said as she pushed herself even closer to him and his arms engulfed her, making her feel very safe, secure and loved.

***

New Year's Day was over, and Liza was back to feeling her usual self. She was organising with Mrs Lambert what she would be taking on her visit to Langston House as well as planning for the first anniversary of its opening in a month's time.

Mr Lambert and Ken Wallace came in for their morning break.

"Good morning gentlemen," smiled Liza and they both nodded and smiled back at her.

"Mr Wallace," said Liza. "Langston House will be having a small party in a month's time, and I wondered whether you would allow your two eldest daughters to attend. I would take them and make sure that they are cared for."

"Thank you, Lady Edgeworth, but sadly they are needed to look after the two younger ones," said Ken Wallace.

"I can see that it would be a problem, but if we could find someone to care for them, would you be willing to let them come with me?" asked Liza.

"They are all abused children there, aren't they?" said Ken. "Would it be safe for my girls to mix with them?"

Liza smiled and said, "Yes, they have all been abused and are now trying to learn to be children again."

"Of course, my apologies," said Ken. "I suppose that one way to learn is to be with children who have not had to go through such terrible experiences."

"Yes, you are right, but I can understand your reticence," said Liza.

"If I can find someone to look after the little ones, then I am sure that Jeanette and Millie would enjoy time with some other children. I am hoping that soon they will be able to attend school; they do see some of the children from the village but not regularly enough," said Ken.

"I think that one or two will also be at the party. Young Susan will be with us, and I know that she will make sure that they have no problems," said Liza.

The Duke and Douglas were getting ready to leave as Liza returned from the kitchen.

"Are you going to be warm enough at your home?" Liza asked the Duke.

"I had our Dower House renovated ready for the winter and I shall be returning there, so I will not be descending on you unannounced as I did last year," smiled the Duke.

"You know that you are always welcome," said Liza.

"I'm also having new windows made for the main house, but that is taking a considerable amount of time. I don't think Bella enjoys living in the Dower House, but she does appreciate that it is much warmer than the place she terms the mausoleum," said the Duke.

"Well, Bella can stay as long as she wants," said Jamie. "And if you feel the need to return, you are most welcome and the same goes for you Douglas."

Anthony, Diana, Rose and little Thomas left the following day and all those from Belfast, apart from Wendell, Amelia and Peter, were leaving the day after. The house was going to seem very quiet; then Liza remembered that there were still six boys and Christopher at home, so the house would never be quiet while they were around.

The day after all the guests had left, they made their way to Langston House; they started out early as they wanted to return before nightfall. Liza, Wendell, Amelia, Bella and Christopher took the carriage driven by Davis and Hendry, but the boys were riding, as were Jamie and Peter. They made quite a sight riding out of Edgeworth House and Liza could see that Christopher was looking rather envious.

"Do you ride Christopher?" asked Liza.

"I have ridden, although I have had little opportunity recently," said Christopher.

"When you are with us at half-term we will make sure that you get back into the saddle. Your hand will have healed by then and it will give you an incentive to keep manipulating and exercising it so that it has the strength to hold the reins correctly and safely," said Liza.

"I would do that even if I didn't have such an exciting incentive," said Christopher.

"How many children are at the Home?" asked Bella.

"There are thirty-five at the moment, but another ten are arriving early next week if the weather stays as it is now and we aren't inundated with snow, but they are only coming from London rather than travelling across country," said Liza.

"They'll have very few places left. Have they some space for emergencies?" asked Wendell.

"They would make room for an emergency," said Liza.

"All the children have been attacked in some way or other; haven't they?" said Christopher.

"Yes, they have Christopher, but we do try to help them get back to a normal life," said Amelia.

"I suppose that could be quite difficult," said Christopher. "I am going to find today very interesting."

"I hoped that you would," smiled Liza.

It took just over an hour to reach Langston House and the boys had enjoyed their ride. Lily and Joseph rushed out to greet them while the boys took their horses to the stables followed by several of the children, all of whom were willing to help groom and feed them, under the watchful eyes of both Davis and Hendry.

Penny and Randolph joined them, and everyone took their place at the lunch table between the children, and it was noticed that Christopher was quite at ease with them and answered all questions that were thrown at him.

Randolph proudly showed them his art studio and some of the works that the children had produced. Both John and Christopher were more interested than the others in that room and they both studied the paintings displayed, making favourable comments to Randolph and a couple of the children whose work was on display.

The other boys did also take notice of the children and as the weather was quite pleasant and not too cold, a game, which only vaguely resembled cricket, started much to the delight of all the children. Jamie and Peter helped to organise the game and Joseph joined them later.

Wendell spent his time mainly with Lily who was telling him about the difficulties with some of the children but that they were all gradually relaxing as the time went by.

Liza, Amelia and Bella went with Penny to the sewing room and there were several girls embroidering and others were attempting to make clothes.

On their way back they noticed that the snow clouds were gathering, and they arrived home before there was a problem. The boys took their horses to the stables and spent a while feeding and grooming them. Christopher helped as much as he could and when they had finished there was just a slight covering of snow.

The boys made their way into the house through the kitchen door and were delighted to see that their supper was ready.

"We may be snowed in tomorrow," said James.

"I hope not," replied Christopher. "I'm seeing the doctor tomorrow and he is hoping to remove my splints."

Matthew looked at Christopher's hand thoughtfully. "We could remove those for you. We'd be very gentle."

"That's kind of you to offer Matthew, but the doctor needs to see that it is mending correctly, so I will just have to wait until I can see him," smiled Christopher.

"Well the offer is there if you need it," said Matthew who then carried on eating.

"Thank you, Matthew," said Christopher who was both fascinated and amused by Matthew. He knew that he was the youngest of all the boys but was the undoubted leader who the others looked to for guidance. He was definitely his mother's son and he wondered what his father had been like as he knew that Lord Edgeworth was not his father. He supposed that the American soldier was, although there appeared to be some doubt about that, but it was none of his business and he had been welcomed into the home and the life of this family and he was not going to jeopardise that by being too inquisitive.

It snowed very little over night and Liza knocked on Christopher's door early that morning, calling out that today was the day when he would get his hand back and she laughed as she moved away, and he smiled sleepily and lifted his arm and studied his splinted hand. He knew that from today for a while he would find the exercises painful, but he was going to ignore that and work hard to get full use of his hand again.

Roberts knocked and entered as he was going to carefully help him get ready for this very important day. He liked young Christopher; he was always polite and very thankful for anything that was done for him. All the staff hoped that today would go well for Christopher.

Shouts of "Good luck" came from the boys as Christopher climbed into the carriage beside Liza with Miranda opposite. Hendry was driving that day and he took them to Dr Bruce's surgery. It did not take the doctor long to remove the bandages and splints and apart from a slight scar, Christopher's hand looked completely normal. He gently moved his fingers; they were stiff, but they moved.

Dr Bruce bent each finger carefully which caused some pain, but he commented that the treatment appeared to be successful, and it was now down to Christopher to make sure that the hand was manipulated and exercised religiously.

"The scar will disappear with time, and you will have the full use of your hand again," said Dr Bruce. "I understand that you were a competent artist at one time, but I'm afraid that there is no guarantee that you will ever regain that talent."

"That is not something that I had ever thought of as a career; it was always more of a hobby. I do miss being able to draw as a relaxation, but I have learned to relax in other ways, including reading," said Christopher.

"You have a lot in common with young Derek as he had to spend many years immobile and reading was his only outlet," said Dr Bruce. "I have seen that you and he get on well together and I've heard that you may well be joining the teaching staff at our village school. I hope that you do as you would be a great asset to our community."

"That's very kind of you to say so Doctor," said Christopher. "I believe that this village is a very happy place to be, and I know that I would enjoy helping the children with their education. Derek and I have much more in common than just reading, although his earlier affliction was far more serious than mine."

"It sounds as if you have made up your mind about your future Christopher," said Miranda. "I hope that is so as I know that we enjoy having you with us."

"Yes, we do Christopher, but the next few months will be useful for you to make sure that you are making the right choice. It is a very big decision for you, and you must think very carefully if it is what you want in life. But we have had this conversation before, and I know you will do what is right. Regardless of your decision, we would still like you to visit us as often as possible," said Liza.

All this time the doctor had been gently massaging and manipulating Christopher's hand and he smiled and said that as his mind had been taken away from what he was doing, he doubted that it had been too painful.

When they arrived home, the boys insisted on inspecting Christopher's hand closely and their verdict was that it almost looked normal and they also wanted to see him move it, which he did slightly.

"You'll soon get the use back in that," declared Matthew and the others agreed as they always did with whatever Matthew said.

"We'll help you with that," said James confidently.

"Would you like to rest?" asked Liza.

"If you don't mind, I think I'd like to spend a little while in the library reading. I'll try flexing my hand whilst I do that," said Christopher.

"Of course you may," said Liza. "I'll get Susan to bring you some tea and biscuits. Just relax and enjoy being free of those uncomfortable splints."

A carriage drew up and it was Mr Rogers bringing Derek to visit. The boys were delighted to see him and once they had caught up with all the news, he went into the library to see Christopher. A close friendship had developed between them, and Liza guessed that it was because they had both suffered physical injuries which had to take determination on their part to put right.

***

Peter was leaving the next day and hoping to get back to Belfast before any large snowstorms hit. He, Liza and Wendell spent most of that day going through mail and various documents and also made some decisions regarding business and the charity.

"Is Harry Turner still working out well?" Liza asked of Peter.

"There are times when I see a look of annoyance on his face, but it passes and he does throw himself into his work. I hate to say it, but really he is too qualified to be Edward's assistant. Edward does realise that, and we are gradually increasing his responsibilities in other areas of the business and especially in relation to the charity. He has invested some of the monies that we receive for the charity very wisely and increased our working capital quite considerably. I know that we have always done that with the profits from our business as well as the charity, but he seems to have an instinct for the right investments. He plays the market very well; it is quite a talent," said Peter.

"We do have a finance department; would we have any problems with those who already work there if he were to join that section?" asked Liza.

"It could create some difficulty as the head of that department has worked his way up to where he is today," said Peter.

"But those in that department do not make the decisions over where any monies are invested; we do that. Would there be enough work for him if we were to create a section devoted solely to investment?" asked Liza.

"It wouldn't be a full-time job," said Peter, "but it would be if you were to give him Bradley & Company's English, Irish and Welsh investments to handle. If you do that then we would have to get another assistant for Edward."

"I don't suppose that would be very difficult to do," said Wendell.

"Surely it's full-time employment for him to assist Edward and work on the investments as he does now," said Liza.

"Would you not consider him for any of your investments Liza?" asked Wendell.

"I think that we have to be very clear about the fact that he will always blame me for his unhappy childhood and that would not be a very sensible move on my part," said Liza.

"I don't believe he blames you for depriving him of his father," said Peter.

"Well, I know that I am to blame, albeit unwittingly, and if I know that then I'm sure that he does," said Liza. "Do you know if his mother is still around?"

"He doesn't mention her or his past," said Peter. "In fact that 'chip on his shoulder' that you saw and mentioned when you first met him seems to be easing quite considerably."

"I'm pleased about that, but I'm not ready to let him loose on Bradley & Company just yet," said Liza. "I wonder if there is a position more in keeping with his talents."

"Are you trying to get rid of him Liza?" asked Wendell with concern.

"I think that we should give James' son the opportunity to travel and help to create new projects. It is just a suggestion; it may not be something that he would like, and it may not be something that you would like either," said Liza.

"Would you feel more comfortable with him many miles away across the water, perhaps helping Hector in Daltons?" said Peter.

"He already is many miles away from me and across the water; so what I am suggesting would be a business decision, not a personal one," said Liza sharply.

"What do you have in mind for him?" asked Peter.

"If he is so clever at seeing opportunities for investment within Marchant & Fuller and the charity, then I'm sure that he could extend that in many directions. In fact we could let him form a financial advisory company, perhaps starting in London and then onto New York, although I suppose we could test the market in our hometown of Belfast," said Liza. "Once all starting difficulties are sorted out, we could then become listed as Brokers."

Wendell was smiling broadly. "I like that idea, Liza. It would be making best use of his abilities and creating yet another section to our company. What do you think Peter?"

"I hadn't thought of expanding into investments for those outside our enterprises, but there are many people who like to invest and to have someone who is as astute in reading the markets as Harry would be beneficial to them," said Peter.

"Do you really think that Belfast would be the best place to set up the operation?" said Wendell.

"London would be more prestigious, but getting it organised and to sort out any initial problems it would be better to be in a place where procedures could be easily discussed," said Liza. "I would think that by the time we are ready to expand into London then that would be the time to become fully fledged Brokers.

"It could work closely with our M & F banking section and could end up in many parts of the world, but I am getting over enthusiastic," said Peter. "We must study the markets closely and lay plans on how it is financed."

"The investment by us would initially be minimal as we already have premises. I would think that Harry would need a couple of staff members," said Liza. "We would have to discuss the amount of the consultancy fee as well as the percentage profit that we would require. We would encourage the profits to be lodged in dedicated accounts within our bank for safekeeping."

"What if there are losses?" asked Wendell.

"Hopefully there won't be any of those, but if there are then we only have the consultancy fee. Any documentation would give us total protection against losses as we would only be giving advice initially. Investment would be at the investor's risk. We'll get our lawyer to make that watertight for us; Arthur will help with that," said Liza.

"This could become quite a large enterprise, do you think that Harry Turner would be capable of undertaking something that could be potentially enormous," said Peter.

Liza laughed, "He wouldn't miss the opportunity to show us how clever he is. However when you put the proposition to him, he may decide that he is quite capable of undertaking such a project without us. Can you think of a reason why he should stay with us and use his talents to our benefit?"

"He earns a respectable salary with us currently, but I don't believe that he has unlimited funds to start anything alone," said Peter.

"I suppose we could tempt him with a percentage of the profits along with an increase in salary," said Liza. "Do you think that might help him get rid of that chip on his shoulder?"

"I think that the best person to persuade him is you Liza," said Peter.

"I'm not his favourite person," said Liza. "You've been working with him for a while now so I'm afraid that task is yours and besides you are offering him something that is a very large step up the ladder."

"I realise that Liza, but we need to sort out all the details of such a venture before we put the proposition to Harry Turner; I don't want it to seem that what we have is a badly thought-out business plan," said Peter. "I do have to return to Belfast tomorrow as I have important commitments there. Is there a possibility that you could return with me?"

"The boys are returning to Cambridge next week, if the weather permits. I could come to Belfast after that time for say a week, but then I must prepare for our trip to South Carolina," said Liza.

"Amelia and I could return with you Liza; nothing needs to be said to Harry Turner until you get there and during that time you and I could thrash out all the details of this new venture. All we must pray for is good weather over the next week. Would that suit you, Peter?" said Wendell.

"If you could manage that Liza then I would be grateful. I will of course discuss it with Edward, but I know that he is always keen on any future business and especially one that you have dreamed up. I remember how enthusiastic he was when you both came up with our banking project. I know that he also believes that Harry Turner's talents are not put to the best use," said Peter.

"We all have a great deal to think about over the next few days, but I do want to spend some time with the boys before they leave. We can talk again later; I'm sure we are all going to have many questions and be able to come up with the answers," said Liza.

The meeting broke up and Liza went to find Jamie, who was about to leave with his overseer to visit one or two of his farms.

"I have to go to Belfast when the boys have returned to Cambridge," said Liza.

Jamie frowned; he did not want her to make such a journey without him.

"Is it really necessary Liza; you know I would miss you and worry about you," said Jamie.

"I will be with Wendell and Amelia, but I wondered whether you had the time to come with me," said Liza.

"I will make the time," smiled a relieved Jamie. "How long do you need to be there?"

"Just about a week, unless we get snowed in while we are there," said Liza. "I'll ask Peter to let Mrs Trent know that we are coming."

Peter left the next day and two days later the snow arrived with a vengeance, but it only lasted until after the weekend much to the boys' disappointment.

The Duke arrived and he was staying until the time came to take his boys back to university and Liza and Jamie were pleased as it meant that he was taking responsibility for his sons and not leaving that task to them.

Susan was getting very excited as she was going with them to Belfast, and this was the first time that she had travelled further than Langston. She was also overjoyed because she would be travelling with them to South Carolina as well. Roberts would also be with them on both trips.

Freda and Findlay were rushing around getting all ready for Wendell and Amelia's departure and they told Susan how envious they were because she would be travelling all the way to South Carolina, which made her even more excited.

Sadly the day arrived when the boys had to leave. They were looking forward to meeting with their friends and once again Christopher promised to keep an eye on them. He would be travelling with the Duke, Nicholas, and Richard whilst the others would be with Jamie. Mrs Lambert had packed pies, cakes and biscuits as she wanted to keep them well fed as she was sure that they would not be eating well whilst they were away from her kitchen.

The Duke would be returning, and he and Bella would go to their home the following day when Liza and Jamie would start their journey to Belfast.

**

It was cold when they left Edgeworth House the next day, but they were all wrapped up well and the drive to London docks was not too difficult. Their cabins were quite warm, but as always it was a relatively long voyage from there to Belfast. It was a better route for Wendell and Amelia, and Liza and Jamie did not mind as they enjoyed their company.

Wendell and Liza had discussed in detail the idea of Harry Turner establishing an investment advisory company and had smoothed out many of the difficulties which could arise. The main difficulty that they could see was whether Harry Turner would like to take up the challenge.

"I believe that he will," said Liza. "He said at his interview that he knew that our Company encouraged workers to achieve greater heights, which was why he applied to us. Whether that was strictly true, I'm not sure, although I think that if he didn't feel that he had a family connection, it would have been completely true."

"You still don't really trust him do you Liza?" said Wendell.

"I believe that he does his job well, but I also believe that he likes to create embarrassment. Perhaps giving him his own business to run may well change his attitude towards us," said Liza.

Liza had briefed Jamie on the reason why she was travelling to Belfast, and he added to the conversation by saying, "He is probably looking for answers about his origins and why he never saw his father and many other things that have puzzled him over the years. You and Wendell are the only ones who can ease his curiosity."

"You may well be right," said Liza, "although it could be opening up old wounds."

"For you or for him?" asked Jamie.

"For both of us no doubt," said Liza, "but if that is what is needed, then that is what I must do."

"I knew you would say that," said Wendell. "Please don't upset yourself for the sake of someone else; I doubt that he would do the same for you."

"He must have some of his father's good nature in him; he's probably hidden it for years. Don't worry about me Wendell, just by seeing him surprises me. I get over it though," said Liza.

Peter and Edward were there to meet them in Belfast and Liza noticed that Roberts was helping Susan organise Liza's luggage as well as Jamie's and their own. Freda and Findlay had their hands full with Wendell's and Amelia's, which was quite considerable.

Harry Turner was watching thoughtfully from the window and he was joined by Sam Nedbury.

"You seem deep in thought Harry," said Sam.

"I didn't know that she would be here," said Harry.

"There's no reason why you should," said Sam sharply.

"Isn't there?" said Harry as he walked away.

He has a very large chip on his shoulder, which has hardly shown until now, thought Sam. *I wonder why he dislikes her so much. He had better watch himself as the Fullers won't tolerate antagonism towards her and neither will I.*

Peter had organised a meeting with Harry Turner for before lunch the next day and he had arranged dinner that evening so that they could discuss the plan of action. Jamie offered not to join them, but he saw the pout on Liza's lips as well as Peter telling him that it often happens that someone else could see what they could not. "My mother and Nicole will of course also be with us, they may wish to leave us after dinner, although it will not be necessary for them to do so, but we would definitely like you to stay."

"Thank you, although I'm not sure that I have much to add to your thoughts," said Jamie.

Dinner was lively and informative, and Jamie, Amelia and Nicole had thoughts on the new venture, although their main ideas were on how to approach Harry Turner. Liza and Wendell smiled indulgently as they knew that the best way was to be open and straight with him although Wendell was keeping to himself that the one person who could instil enthusiasm into the man was Liza.

The meeting with Harry Turner was not until eleven-thirty the next day and Liza was seeing Edward and Peter at eleven o'clock, but she had some correspondence to go through, so she got to the office much earlier. She waved at those she passed and made her way to what she always thought of as James' office. Sam Nedbury caught sight of her and quickly came to open the door for her.

"How are you, Liza?" he asked. "It's been a while since you were here."

"Yes, I am sometimes brought out to make up the numbers," smiled Liza.

"I doubt that. I trust that the Fullers are watching over you today," smiled Sam.

"Is there a reason why they should be?" asked Liza.

"I have heard that you often end up where there is trouble," said Sam.

Liza frowned slightly and said, "Do you think that there will be trouble today?"

"You never know what is going to happen; it's always best to be prepared," said Sam and he smiled and left the office.

Just before Peter and Edward were due to arrive for their meeting Harry Turner knocked and entered the office.

"I thought I would hand in my resignation before you have a chance to terminate my employment, Lady Edgeworth," said Harry Turner.

Liza looked at him for a minute and then said, "Have you given me a reason to want to terminate your employment Mr Turner?"

"Yes, the reason is that I am an embarrassment to you, and you are here," said Harry Turner.

"This is my business and I have homes here. I may be here for any number of reasons, all of which could have nothing to do with you," said Liza.

"The Fullers don't like awkward situations. Mr Wendell and Mr Peter would handle them, but they would not like it and Mr Edward would shy away from them completely. You are the one who would have the strength to deal with difficulties, which is why you have been brought here from your comfortable family home," said Harry Turner.

"Is that so, Mr Turner? But you are wrong, any one of the Fuller family has the strength to do what is right for themselves and for the Company. They just have different ways of handling affairs. However you are right that if it was necessary I would terminate someone's employment without hesitation," said Liza.

"It won't take me long to tidy my desk and leave," said Harry Turner.

"If that is what you want Mr Turner, then I won't stop you, but I would prefer that you stayed at least until you hear what it is that we want to offer you," said Liza.

"Oh!" exclaimed Harry Turner. "Have I just made a fool of myself?"

"Quite possibly you have Mr Turner, but I'm not going to tell anyone," smiled Liza and her eyes sparkled with fun. "I was going to have a meeting with Edward and Peter before our meeting, but I see that they have arrived already."

Much to Liza's surprise and pleasure, Wendell was also with them, and Liza rose to give him her seat. He waved her back down and told her that it was her office and had been since James' death. Harry Turner blinked a little at the comment.

"Do we need to talk before we have our meeting with Mr Turner?" asked Liza.

"No, I think that we have sorted out all the details now," said Wendell. "Please sit down Mr Turner. Liza, as this is one of your business ideas perhaps you should start the proceedings."

"We have discussed in great detail the pros and cons of forming a new Company for the sole purpose of advising others on financial investments. There are many individuals and companies who are placing their money in all types of wild investments with very little analysis from someone who understands the markets. To have such a Company we need someone who has the ability to look into the diverse opportunities to increase investments and who is quite capable of talking to customers from all walks of life. We believe that the person to run such a Company and take that responsibility is you Mr Turner," said Liza.

Harry Turner was surprised and said, "That was not what I expected."

"I dare say that it wasn't," said Wendell. "We can see that you are somewhat taken aback, and you must want some time to decide whether or not it could be what you would like as a career."

Harry Turner smiled, and Liza felt that she was looking at James Marchant sitting opposite her. "I need no time to decide; this is just the type of challenge that I would revel in," he said. "Naturally, there is a great deal to plan and sort out and that will be exciting. Where would I be based? Who would I be answerable to? I would require some help and I can think of one or two within the Company who could be useful. We would have to protect ourselves legally because giving advice has its pitfalls."

"Liza, will you answer some of Harry's questions?" asked Wendell.

"Of course I will," smiled Liza. "Initially you will be based here because there will be a great deal to organise getting the Company started and you will have everything at hand to deal with that. We can envisage that eventually we would become fully fledged Brokers so London and New York will have outlets which you would be responsible for, and who knows where else would be advantageous."

"France, Germany, Spain, Italy; in fact every country will have investors and markets that need looking into. Language could be a problem," said Harry.

"Liza speaks all those languages," said Edward, which seemed to surprise Harry and Liza had the feeling that he was about to make a sarcastic comment but thought better of it.

"That could be useful," he said quietly, and Liza smiled.

"Peter governs all of our various companies, so you would be answerable to him, although you would be free to make decisions on the day to day running of the Company and of course you would not need to go to him for every investment that you advise on. It would however be necessary for you to have regular meetings to discuss what is happening and to keep him up-to-date on the markets."

Liza carried on, "We have discussed that legally we must protect ourselves totally. There may be times that some investments do not do as well as expected and we must not be held responsible for that, but our lawyer will handle all aspects of that, and we will arrange a meeting with him as soon as you are ready. As far as dependable people to work with you, I suggest you approach those you would like within the Company and put out feelers for those outside. There is a great deal to organise before you take on any clients Mr Turner."

"We are not very original with the names of our companies Mr Turner," said Wendell. "We would like to call it MF Investment Consultancy and eventually MF Investment Consultancy and Brokerage."

"I can see nothing wrong with that, it is exactly what it will be," said Harry.

"I'm pleased that you are working with us Mr Turner and that you will be heading our new project. I'm sure that you are going to be successful, I have every confidence in you," said Wendell. "I'll leave you to continue discussing it with Liza and Peter. Edward, will you see me down to my carriage please."

"We have a great deal to talk about Mr Turner," said Liza. "Firstly we must discuss your remuneration and the percentage profits that you will be entitled to and along with that we must home in on the consultancy fees that we must charge and what percentage profits we should expect from our clients."

Their meeting went on for many hours and Liza had arranged that they have a working lunch and Susan arrived with offerings from Mrs Adam's kitchen. They carried on talking with ideas being brought forward and discussed in detail. Liza realised that they had indeed been right in employing this man; he was definitely his father's son.

It was getting late when they decided to call the meeting to a close. One last item was where would the new consultancy operate from?

"I have been thinking about that," said Peter. "We have hardly used Sam Nedbury's old premises. We store some documents there and one or two items that have some value and need to be protected from the elements; it wouldn't take much to clean it and decorate it, and of course put a fancy name on the door. It isn't large but it is a place to start from."

"Yes, that would give some separation from the comings and goings of this premises, and it can be made to look quite prestigious to impress the clients that we are hoping to give advice to," said Liza. "I would like to see us set up in London as soon as we have this running smoothly. I know that there will be a great need of your services there."

Harry Turner was smiling at Liza's enthusiasm, "You seem very sure of that; I believe you are right."

"Good Mr Turner, we are talking the same language. Where do you live at the moment?" asked Liza.

"I have a couple of rooms in a guest house fairly near here; they are adequate if not salubrious," said Harry.

"Well Mr Turner, I have thought about you a great deal over the past months, and I have wondered whether you would like to live in what was your father's house whilst you are here in Belfast. I will always keep the house as mine, but it sits there with nobody living in it and apart from my bedroom suite, the rest of the house could be yours until such time as you make the change to London or New York or wherever would be best for you to be," said Liza.

Peter was looking at her in surprise, "Uncle James left that to you for your security Liza, are you sure you want to do that?"

"And it will always remain mine. I would move back into it should that need ever arise, but it doesn't mean that Mr Turner can't live there comfortably whilst he is in Belfast. It would be a place that he could call home and I know that it is what his father would have wanted. I always knew that there was a reason why I could not sell it even though I had other homes," said Liza.

"I remember how upset you were when you found that Felicity and Edward lived there without your knowledge or permission," said Peter and Harry realised that there was yet another mystery to uncover about Liza and the Fullers, but now was not the time to go into that.

"It was the only home I had then, and it had been taken away from me. It was a very unhappy time for me, but that was a long while ago and I am not relinquishing my right to live there and own it, I am extending the offer of a place for him to settle in Belfast which was his father's. It will always remain mine but there is no reason why Mr Turner should not have some of the comforts that his father created for his family," said Liza.

"Excuse me," said Harry, "I am here you know."

"My apologies Mr Turner; that was very rude of us, but I would very much like you to take me up on the offer and let the house be used as it should be," said Liza.

"It is very kind of you Lady Edgeworth, but I feel that it could cause difficulties with your housekeeper and gardener. I saw their reaction when I visited with you earlier," said Harry.

"Mrs Edwards, Mr Grouch and his wife were in your father's employ long before I came on the scene. In fact they were there when the first Mrs Marchant was alive. As with all good servants they keep quiet about their employer's business. They were very loyal to him and are also very loyal to me, but you cannot tell me that they did not know of your existence or that of your mother and when they saw you, they most certainly knew who you were. I can see that no problem will be created by you living in that house. They will probably think that it is right and proper, but they would never say so," said Liza.

"Do you really think that they knew, Liza?" asked Peter.

"Your parents knew, you and your brothers knew; there were probably many people who knew and that must have included Mrs Edwards and Mr and Mrs Grouch, and James' valet, whoever he was in those days. Jamie knew that he had a mistress. It seems that the only person who didn't know was me," said Liza.

"James Marchant would not approve of what you are suggesting; he decided to disown me all those years ago and you don't need to have a conscience about

157

it; although it was because of you, it was none of your doing. I am just pleased that you have seen a worth in me for the investment project," said Harry.

"Your father would approve and would know that the decision that he took all those years ago was not a worthy one. I do not know if it was right for your mother, but most certainly it was not a decision that a father should have made regarding his son and that he knows," said Liza.

"I could almost believe that you talk to my father," said Harry and he looked at her closely and suddenly realised that she probably did have that ability. He watched her with concern as she seemed so very far away and then he said, "You do, don't you? I knew that I was drawn here for a reason."

Liza said nothing but Peter said, "It is well known that Liza sees things that others don't, and her son, Matthew, has the same ability. It is nothing to be frightened of; it is very useful, helpful and quite comforting."

"Is she alright, she seems preoccupied," said Harry.

Peter smiled, "She will be back with us shortly; she is probably talking with your father, she does quite often. What you must realise Harry is that she is welcoming you into the family and it will be up to you to take that very large chip off your shoulder and accept her attempt to put right as best she can something that was not of her doing but she sees as a mistake."

"Is that the only reason why I have been offered this promotion?" scowled Harry.

"As you get to know us more, and especially Liza, you will realise that we will always put the best man in a position no matter who they are. We would never consider favours in business and even when Liza was shocked when you arrived on the scene, she told me to employ you if I felt you were the right person," said Peter.

"Shall we go and see Mrs Edwards?" asked Liza suddenly.

"I think I would like that Liza," said Harry and Liza realised that all the fences had come down and Harry was now going to have a better life, even though it would never make up for an unhappy childhood.

Mrs Edwards was delighted to see Liza and even more delighted that she was going to have a gentleman to look after for the foreseeable future.

"And one who is a close relative of the late Mr James," said Mrs Edwards.

Liza looked at Mrs Edwards, but she was unable to look Liza in the eye. "It's alright Mrs Edwards; I am no longer under any illusions."

"That's a relief, Your Ladyship," smiled Mrs Edwards.

Liza smiled knowingly at Harry and when Mrs Edwards had left to arrange refreshments Liza said, "What did I tell you, she has known all along. She had great respect for your father."

"Many people seem to have done; nobody has a bad word to say about him. I wish I could have seen him like that, but of course I really didn't see him at all," said Harry.

"I'll be visiting him tomorrow; would you like to join me?" said Liza.

"I don't think so Liza; I haven't been to his grave since I've been here, I don't think that I want to start now," said Harry.

"He'd be pleased if you did," said Liza. "He wasn't a cruel or unfeeling man, which is why I will never understand how he could have cut you off so completely. Even if he and your mother no longer wanted a relationship, you were the result of that association and you didn't ask to be born; you deserved the love of both your parents. I'm sorry, I should not be moralising; it was something that happened before I came onto the scene. Is your mother still alive?"

"No, she died a few years ago. She was a very foolish woman I'm afraid. James Marchant set us up in a nice home and a local lawyer paid all our bills; also my education was completely undertaken by him. All my schooling was taken care of and followed exactly as he had stipulated. Thankfully my mother had no say in the matter, which was just as well as she had no idea how to handle money," said Harry.

Mrs Edwards came in with tea and cakes and said that she was getting Miss Kate's nice room ready for the young gentleman.

"Thank you, Mrs Edwards," said Liza. "Don't worry Harry, it has been redecorated since Kate lived there; you won't have to live in a room with feminine walls and bows everywhere."

"I'm sure I wouldn't," said Harry. "My mother never really blamed you for my father's leaving her; she blamed him for wanting to be with a child and said that he would regret being with someone who wasn't out of school, probably still sucked her thumb and knew nothing about how to keep a man happy. She felt that you wanted to be married to someone who was well respected in business and had a large social following and money of course."

"James was thirty-years older than me, so she was right that I was still a schoolchild, but she was wrong that I wanted to be married, I wasn't ready, and I had no say in it. My parents sold me to him; they would have sold me to the highest bidder and James knew that. I have always been grateful that he was the one who paid the price and not someone who would be cruel, not that I was aware of that at the time. I grew to love him very much and we had a wonderful life together, although it was only for a very short while. We had some very happy times in this house where he taught me to grow up," said Liza with a smile at the happy memories that she was experiencing.

159

"My mother was wrong about many things. She tried to be a good mother, but she didn't really have the maternal instinct. I think the mistake he made with her was to give her a house; he should have kept it in his name and let us live there. She met someone who she thought loved her; he helped her to sell the house ready for her to move in with him. He suggested that she get her hands on the money for my education but that had been tied up tightly by my father and when he realised that there was no further funds to be had, he ran off with the money from the house sale," said Harry.

"I am sorry Harry; you haven't had an easy life. I know that James would have helped her, why didn't she contact him?" said Liza.

"She had heard that he had died by then otherwise I know that she would have done," said Harry.

"You must have been around ten-years-old then, how did you survive? Or am I asking too many questions?" asked Liza.

"Luckily I was at boarding school thanks to my father; it was only holidays that were difficult, and my mother was discreet at those times. She had rooms by the sea, so my leisure time was quite pleasant. She used to disappear on occasions and it's only since I got older that I realise that she was away earning money. When she was dying she ranted and raved about James Marchant and how he had left us in the lurch. I knew that it wasn't completely true, but I agreed that if he had been more concerned about the mother of his son and his son, she would not have died such a painful, lonely death and I would have had a much nicer worry-free childhood," said Harry.

"You have done extremely well under difficult circumstances. I don't expect you to change your attitude towards us overnight, but perhaps you could get to know us a little and maybe realise that we are not all as selfish as you may have been led to believe," said Liza.

Mrs Edwards knocked and entered informing them that Harry's room was ready and that his supper would be in an hour. She also wondered whether Liza would be staying for supper.

"No Mrs Edwards, thank you. I must leave, I have much to do over the next few days, and I am neglecting my husband," smiled Liza.

"I didn't realise that I would be moving in here now. I must go and collect up my things and give notice to my landlady," said Harry.

"Well you heard what Mrs Edwards said, your room is ready, and she is preparing supper for you but whether you move everything in tonight is up to you," smiled Liza.

The door opened and Jamie came into the room. He saw Liza sitting in the place that she had sat when he had visited years ago, and Harry Turner was sitting in the chair he had used and had previously been James Marchant's. He blinked and could see that it was as it must have been when she was married to James and a feeling of jealousy swept over him.

Liza and Harry looked up in surprise and Liza then said, "Jamie, I'm sorry, I must be very late."

"Peter said that you were probably here. Good afternoon, Mr Turner; I hear that you will be taking up residence here for a while. I hope you will be very happy. I'm sure you will be; I have always found it an extremely happy place to be," said Jamie whose eyes belied his smile.

"I was just about to leave, I'm glad you've come for me," smiled Liza.

"It's snowing a little, so I thought I had better find you before it becomes any worse," said Jamie.

"Of course, thank you Jamie. I'll leave you in peace now Harry and see you tomorrow," said Liza.

"Thank you, Liza, yes, I'll see you tomorrow. We all have a great deal to discuss and organise. It's been a very exciting and informative day today and I believe we have laid a few ghosts to rest," said Harry.

Jamie could see that Harry was far more relaxed than he had been on their last meeting. The day had obviously gone well; Peter had quickly outlined to him what had happened, and it seemed that everyone was pleased with the outcome.

Liza and Jamie walked home, and she presumed that Harry would soon be on his way to collect what belongings he needed for that night. She smiled up at Jamie.

"This is just like old times when you used to come for me and we would walk to Amelia's or go to the park with the boys," said Liza.

"Won't you miss your house, Liza?" asked Jamie.

"I'm not giving up my house Jamie; I'm just letting James' son live there for the time being. I can still come and go as I please and we still have our rooms upstairs, I haven't given those up. You never know when we might need them," said Liza. "I'm happy with the situation and I'm sure James would be also."

"Did you find out if his mother is still alive?" asked Jamie.

"She died a few years ago. James did set her up quite well, but unfortunately, she was hoodwinked by some man and she lost her home to him. Luckily James had left enough money for Harry's education, which was locked away in such a way that it could not be used for anything other than his education or else the man would have had that also. By the time she was virtually destitute James had died, otherwise I'm sure he would have helped her," said Liza.

"Knowing James the way I did, I'm sure he would have done. I hear from Peter that you had a successful day today. He was surprised that you offered him your house, but it is something that you would do. I hope it will be appreciated," said Jamie.

"We have an evening to ourselves; I'm looking forward to that. We so rarely have time alone," said Liza.

***

It snowed very little and by the morning it had cleared. Liza put her warm cloak on and made her way to visit the graveyard. She had no flowers with her at that time of year and she felt that it was one time that she was going when she was not in difficulty, although there was something worrying her, but she could not bring what it was to the fore.

Sitting on the bench opposite James' grave she waited quietly, deep in thought. *"I was wrong Liza,"* said a very gentle male voice. *"I should have kept checking on my boy, but he seems to have turned out well. You are doing right by him now and it is good that you have welcomed him."*

"He is exceptionally bright James. You were right to concentrate on his education, it's serving him well and it is going to make your Company even greater," murmured Liza.

"It's not always about money Liza," said the voice in Liza's head. *"It's about compassion and you have that in abundance."*

"I would not employ him if he was not right for the job," murmured Liza.

"A few years ago you were told that just because somebody looked like Patrick did not mean that he was Patrick. Harry looks like me, but he is not me; just remember that my Liza," whispered the gentle voice and Liza realised what had been worrying her; it was of course that Harry reminded her of her first love and was transporting her back to the happy times that she had experienced with James. No wonder Jamie was so very much on edge; he must also see the similarity. She must make sure that Jamie realised that she was not treating Harry as James.

"I hope I'm not intruding; your husband said that I would find you here," said a voice that startled Liza. She turned and smiled up at Harry and patted the seat beside her.

"Do you talk to him very often?" asked Harry.

"I'm not sure that I really do; I'm not sure that what he says to me isn't really me just thinking it," smiled Liza.

"I wish he had allowed me to know him," said Harry.

"If you were to smooth out the harsh façade that you hide behind and look in a mirror, then you would know him," said Liza quietly.

"Am I so very like him?" asked Harry.

"I can see his character in you, and you have his looks. Luckily you also possess his brain and are putting it to good use," said Liza.

"I see that his son is lying beside him, and his first wife is next to him. Who is at his feet?" asked Harry.

"It is our son, Jonathan. He was born after James died and sadly, he died shortly after his birth," said Liza quietly.

"I'm sorry Liza, I did not know," said Harry.

"It's a long time ago," said Liza. "He would have been nearly twenty-years-old now. Time goes so quickly Harry, please don't waste it in anger."

"When you next speak to him, tell him that the decision that he made was wrong, but I understand why he took it and I forgive him," said Harry.

"You can tell him that yourself; in fact you have just done that because I know you are like me; you see things that others aren't aware of," said Liza.

"I think you are wrong. I don't commune with the dead," said Harry.

"Don't you? I think it does depend on whether they want to commune with you or not but I'm not going to argue with you," said Liza. "I find it comforting to come here to sit and talk to James, he often comes up with answers to problems, but of course all that could just be in my head. However it often makes me feel better."

"Does it not bother Jamie that you spend so much time here?" said Harry.

"I always visit James, Frederick, Jonathan and Martha when I'm in Belfast. I haven't been here since last Easter so I cannot be accused of spending much time here," said Liza. "Jamie often joins me. He knew James and was at one time friends with Frederick."

"Their graves are kept well; I suppose you make sure of that," said Harry.

"Yes, I do. They look nice when there are spring and summer flowers on them," said Liza. "Ah here's Jamie."

She patted the seat on the other side of her and Jamie nodded to Harry and took his place next to Liza.

"Is this the first time that you have visited your father's grave?" asked Jamie of Harry.

"Yes, it is, but I will come again. I have a father, stepmother and two half-brothers lying here. They deserve to be visited regularly by family," said Harry.

Liza turned and smiled up at him and once again he could see why his father had wanted her to the exclusion of all else. Liza stood to leave, and Harry said that he would stay for a while. Jamie smiled at him and nodded his approval.

"No doubt I'll see you back at the office later," said Liza and she and Jamie left Harry sitting and obviously deep in thought.

"He seems to be becoming friendlier towards you and everyone else," said Jamie.

"I don't think that it was just seeing James' grave, I believe realising that he had two step-brothers there has surprised him," said Liza. "Suddenly knowing that you have more family than you expected seems to have affected him deeply, even though they are no longer with us."

Liza and Jamie went home and lunched together before they both went to the offices. They had a meeting that afternoon about the charity and later Liza would continue helping to formulate the plans for the new venture. She smiled as she passed the old Nedbury offices as Harry was there directing the renovations and was at last beginning to smile whilst at work.

They had another evening to themselves, and Jamie happily knew that he was the only man that Liza wanted in her life. He had been momentarily jealous the previous day and he now realised the foolishness of that feeling.

They sat closely together at dinner and Jamie reminded Liza of the time that she had suddenly appeared in his house and asked him not to leave because she loved him.

"You took me to bed Liza, and you enjoyed it, didn't you?" smiled Jamie.

"I remember that you enjoyed it too," laughed Liza. "Do you want me to repeat the exercise tonight?"

"Hmmm, that's a nice idea," smiled Jamie. "I love our family Liza, but it is so nice to have you completely to myself. You made me feel so wanted that night; it was the first time that I had ever felt wanted."

"I have wanted you since that day Jamie, possibly before but I didn't realise it. We have a lovely life but sometimes it becomes a little crowded, so we have to make the most of times like these," said Liza.

***

The new project was progressing well, and Liza found Harry standing outside the old Nedbury offices watching a sign writer putting the name 'MF Investment Consultancy' in gold lettering arched on the glass of the door and underneath it said 'H. R. Turner - Managing Consultant' also in gold lettering.

"That looks very impressive Harry," said Liza. "What does the R stand for; nothing embarrassing I hope."

"No, it's nothing embarrassing. It's Robert, apparently after my mother's father," said Harry.

164

"Did you know him?" asked Liza.

"No, never met him. I have no idea who he was or where he lived. My mother never visited him, nor did he visit us," said Harry.

"Did you have any school friends?" asked Liza.

"Yes, I had a couple that I still keep in touch with, but I always went to their houses, I didn't feel happy inviting them to mine, not that my mother would have liked that anyway," said Harry.

"It sounds as though you had a very similar childhood to Jamie. Anyway you will be able to invite them to your home now," said Liza.

"It's not my home Liza, it's yours," said Harry.

"It may be my house, and I may want to visit whenever I wish, but it is your home for now and you must treat it as such. As long as you do not use my bedrooms, then you may use any other room that you wish, and you may entertain as much as you like. I know that you will not mistreat the house," said Liza. "How are you getting on with Mrs Edwards and Mr Grouch?"

"I may well do that; there are a couple of friends who I would like to meet up with and tell them of my good fortune. They will wonder why I am so familiar with yourself and the Fullers, I suppose that could be awkward," said Harry.

"The truth is always the best course of action if you don't mind the label they may put on you," said Liza.

"I don't think that my friends or their parents were under any illusions. They knew my mother," said Harry as an explanation. "I like Mrs Edwards; she's very efficient and treats me kindly. I have met Mrs Grouch also, both she and her husband talk about you a great deal; they're very fond of you and your boys. It's a very strange name that they have."

"I know; I did wonder whether he had the same nature as his name when I was first here, but he proved to be a very nice and kindly man," said Liza. "Do you need a valet?"

"Good heavens no; I'm quite capable of looking after myself, and Mrs Edwards sees to all my clothing needs and seems to enjoy doing it. I believe she has children from the Charity helping her on occasion, or should I say she's training them in domestic duties. It all seems to work very well," said Harry.

They were dining with Wendell and Amelia that evening; Peter would also be there. Amelia always enjoyed arranging dinner for those she considered close family.

"I'm glad it is just us tonight," said Wendell. "I think we have a decision to make."

Peter, Jamie and Amelia frowned, but Liza thought that she knew what Wendell wanted to say.

"That sounds very serious, Wendell," said Amelia.

"It's not overly serious but is something that should be discussed. I think you know what I am going to say, don't you Liza?" said Wendell.

"I believe I do Wendell; you want to clarify the position with Harry Turner. You want to know how we should treat him socially," said Liza.

"I would like to hear what each of us thinks, but no matter what, the final decision would be yours Liza. You would be the most affected by it," said Wendell.

"Should we not be talking to Edward also about this," said Amelia.

"Edward will always go with his heart and not his head, so I believe we know what he would say," said Wendell.

"I have managed to treat Harry Turner as an employee all the time that he has been with us," said Peter. "I have done that purposely for Liza's sake."

Liza smiled at Peter recognising his concern for her and he knew that she appreciated his thoughtfulness.

"What is your opinion, Liza?" asked Wendell.

"I think I would much rather hear what you all have to say first. I know which way I am leaning, but I may change my mind after hearing what you all think," said Liza.

"There is no denying his family heritage," said Jamie. "He is so like his father that it's uncanny. I would think that there would be no one under any illusions as to his parentage. I don't know whether he will be invited to outside functions, but I do not believe that he should be excluded from family gatherings."

Liza smiled at Jamie; he had said what she was thinking.

"By family gatherings, do you mean Fuller family gatherings or just those of yours when you are here?" asked Peter.

"I can't tell you what to do, but you have asked my opinion and it is that all your family are also ours, so I would hope that you would treat him as family. It is, of course, your decision," said Jamie.

"We have always introduced him as a close relative of James Marchant," said Peter. "There is no reason why we shouldn't continue to do so. Those who didn't know Uncle James wouldn't question that relationship. It probably seems strange that we have yet to include him in our family parties or suggested that he join us when we have been invited elsewhere."

"He seems a very polite young man," said Amelia. "He could be embarrassed by other people's attitudes, and so could we. I would hate to see him put in such a position."

"What do you think Liza?" asked Wendell gently.

166

"I don't wish to open up old wounds but some years ago I had to go through some terrible gossip aimed at me and my marital status and morals. You all stood by me and held my hand when you insisted that I didn't hide away. We knew that the gossip was not true, but there were many who believed it at the time. You made me hold my head up high and ride the storm; you could have let me stay at home and meet nobody," said Liza. "You are the ones who will make him acceptable or otherwise."

"He may not wish to be included in any social gathering. He might just want to be left alone and he could take offence that we were talking about what he should be doing in his leisure time," said Jamie.

"I'm sure he wouldn't appreciate our talking about him this way, but he'll never know," said Wendell. "James Marchant was my greatest friend and business partner; Harry Turner is his son and is Liza's stepson. He's family."

Liza smiled and nodded, *Wendell has spoken,* she thought. It was the right decision and now they just had to make sure that he did not know that they were discussing him in that way.

"I think I will organise a small gathering for the day after tomorrow," said Amelia. "I'll naturally invite Edward and Nicole, also Arthur and Annalise. I believe that David and Anne Benedict are in town, so I'll see them tomorrow and invite them. I'll drop a note to Harry inviting him. That should be a nice gathering and it will be our way of saying goodbye to you before you leave for England."

"I would enjoy seeing David and Anne again; it's been a while since we met up. I would suggest that you don't make the invitation too formal and if you like either Jamie or I could tell him that you are having a small dinner to bid us farewell and we would like him to attend," said Liza.

"I'll leave his invitation to you and Jamie then," said Amelia and Wendell nodded his agreement.

Wendell sat at the head of his table smiling happily at those he considered family, and he was looking forward to welcoming Harry into the fold; James' son deserved to be accepted into the family, but he knew that Harry was still affected by his father's rejection of him, they would have to bring him around very carefully.

Liza went to the office early the next day and Jamie was going to join her in a couple of hours. She worked closely with Peter and Harry until Jamie joined them.

"I've just come from Wendell's and Amelia's, and they are arranging a farewell dinner for us tomorrow," said Jamie.

"That's nice," said Liza. "I suppose Edward and Nicole will be there. Do you think that Arthur and Annalise will be free?"

"I would think so, they are always included in Amelia's gatherings," Jamie turned to Harry and said, "They would also like you to join us." He turned back to Liza and said, "Amelia is going to see Anne and David today and she will invite them also."

"Good, I haven't seen them for a while," said Liza. "I'll look forward to that; I'm glad not too many people will be there. I hope Anne and David can make it."

"Has anyone ever refused my mother?" smiled Peter.

"Will you want us to call for you Harry?" asked Jamie.

"I'm not sure that I can make it," said Harry.

"That will be disappointing," pouted Liza.

"Yes, Wendell and Amelia will also be disappointed, but if you have another engagement then it can't be helped," said Jamie.

"I don't have another engagement; I just don't yet have full evening clothes. I really have never had the need, although I suppose I had better think about that for the future," said Harry.

"I doubt that it will be a formal evening Harry," said Liza. "It's just a few friends to wish us well."

Both Peter and Jamie were studying Harry. "What you are wearing will be exactly the type of outfit that I will be wearing," said Peter.

"I have a few working outfits," smiled Harry. "I'm sure Mrs Edwards will make one of them look presentable."

"I'm sure she will; she won't let you out of the house unless you look respectable," smiled Liza.

"As the Consultancy becomes more established, I dare say there will be a few functions that you will have to attend Harry," said Peter. "I'll put you in touch with our tailor if you would like."

With all that agreed, Liza and Jamie left Harry and Peter to continue with discussing the arrangements for the new consultancy. They called on Wendell and Amelia on their way home to tell them that their dinner the following evening was going to be quite informal.

"I'll have to tell Anne and David and everyone else, but that won't be a problem," said Amelia. "Did he argue about attending tomorrow?"

"Only because he had no formal evening wear," said Jamie. "Peter has suggested that he puts him in touch with your tailor. He feels that Harry may well have to attend formal functions in the future."

"Yes, Peter's right, there will be a number of functions that it would be prudent for Harry to attend. No doubt Peter will be with him to begin with, but I have a feeling that it will not be long before he can attend alone," said Wendell.

Liza and Jamie made their way home and had the afternoon and evening to themselves, apart from Susan and Roberts, both of whom were hurrying around making sure that everything would be ready for the return to Surrey.

"I think that you handled Harry's invitation superbly," said Liza. "I don't believe that he realised that he was being manipulated."

"Oh I'm sure that he did Liza," said Jamie. "He's very astute, but I think that he was looking to be accepted; perhaps he at last feels that he belongs somewhere."

"Have I really gained another son?" said Liza.

Jamie laughed, "So it would appear. Don't forget that Frederick was also your stepson, and he was older than you. You now have one who is a few years younger than you. I wonder if your family relationships are unique."

"My family certainly seems to be growing. I had better find out when his birthday is," said Liza thoughtfully and Jamie just laughed again.

"I'm looking forward to tomorrow evening. I hope that Harry will be able to feel relaxed in everyone's company," said Jamie.

"Well, he knows us and Wendell, Peter and Edward. I presume that he has met Amelia and Nicole before. Anyway Amelia will seat everyone appropriately. He won't feel awkward," said Liza.

***

Liza spent very little time at the office the following day as Amelia had asked her to help with planning the seating for the evening. Jamie decided to go with her to Amelia's and spend the time with Wendell.

Amelia and Liza arranged and rearranged the seating several times but finally settled on Edward and Nicole opposite one another with Wendell at the head of the table; Annalise was next to Edward with Arthur opposite her; David and Anne were next opposite one another, followed by Liza and Jamie also opposite one another and finally Amelia at the foot of the table had Harry and Peter opposite one another with Harry next to Liza and Peter next to Jamie.

"I think that will work well," said Amelia. "We could have done with another couple of ladies."

"I didn't think to ask if he has a lady friend," said Liza. "I just assumed that he doesn't."

"He would probably have mentioned it to Edward if he had; he wouldn't have told Peter as Peter is all business and not leisure," said Amelia.

"I presume everyone knows not to come in dinner suits," said Liza.

"Yes, and all the men seemed quite relieved. They can enjoy their dinner in comfortable jackets. I never thought that the men felt so uncomfortable," said Amelia.

"I don't think they do really; they are just being polite," laughed Liza.

"You are going to collect Harry this evening, aren't you?" said Amelia.

"Yes, we will be arriving with him, so at least he won't have to walk in alone," said Liza. "I'm sure he won't be shy, but I believe this will be his first social gathering. I could be wrong, he may have been invited to every function imaginable where he used to live," said Liza.

"If he did, then he would have had a dinner suit," said Amelia. "I hope he knows how to behave at the dinner table."

"Of course he does Amelia," said Liza sharply. "He knows how to behave; he's certainly not uncouth."

"I know that really; it was just a passing thought," said Amelia smiling at Liza's defence of her newly found stepson.

Shortly after Liza and Jamie left to get ready for the evening. Liza had decided to wear a relatively plain green dress with very little jewellery and Jamie's suit was a fawn colour and he wore a cravat with the small diamond pin that Liza had given him the Christmas that she had returned from America. She looked him up and down and told him how handsome he looked. It was a cold evening and Jamie wore his greatcoat and Liza wrapped herself in a thick cloak.

Their carriage pulled up outside where Harry was living, and he bounded down the steps and Liza drew in her breath; it seemed that James was running towards them. Jamie squeezed her arm reassuringly as he too had seen the similarity.

The door opened and Harry stepped in smiling and looking handsome. He was dressed in a day suit, but he too had a fetching cravat and Liza wondered whether Mrs Edwards had advised him.

Wendell undertook the introductions when they arrived. David and Anne had not met him before, neither had Annalise. Arthur had met him once before and Edward had introduced him to Nicole when she had visited the offices. Amelia had seen him, but this was the first time that they had been officially introduced.

To anyone who knew David and Anne it was obvious that they had been surprised by Harry's looks. He was introduced as a close relative of James Marchant's and after a while Liza noticed that David was talking quietly to Wendell, and she hoped that he was not objecting to Harry's inclusion in the evening.

Liza was talking to Harry and Peter when David and Anne came over to them and David said, "Harry, Anne and I are very pleased to have been included in this very special evening. I know that it is to bid Liza and Jamie farewell on their return to England and also on their trip to America, but I would like you to know that we knew your father well; he was a close friend of our family, and we are delighted to meet you at last. I believe that Liza was the only one not to know of your existence in the past; I am so pleased that she knows now, and we no longer have to keep secrets from her."

"You both knew James Marchant then," said Harry almost with relief.

"Yes, we did. You are very like him Harry and I understand from Wendell that you have inherited his intelligence. I'm looking forward to getting to know you better and trust you won't object to joining us some evenings," said David.

"Thank you, that would be my pleasure," said Harry.

The conversation over dinner was mainly about Liza and Jamie's forthcoming trip to South Carolina and they were asked if they were worried about the talk of war between the Americas.

"There has been talk about such a war for many years now," said Jamie. "Everything seems quiet there at the moment and we are going to take the opportunity to visit whilst it remains so."

"Jamie's right," said Liza. "The whole time that I lived there, the north and the south kept threatening one another and then it would ease for quite some time. I believe that eventually one of the sides will make a stupid mistake and war will break out but hopefully it will be resolved quickly with little damage."

"Do you really think that Liza?" asked Harry.

"The north will win when it happens; they have more resources than the south. The south has land and crops which need to either get to the north or across to England for manufacturing. The factories in England will suffer, but they will probably make up for it with equipment and medication. Our factories in Daltons will probably be converting to uniforms and unfortunately weapons also. The south would eventually be squeezed dry," said Liza.

"Isn't the main problem because the north want the south to free their slaves and isn't the population of the south richer than their counterparts in the north," asked David.

"Many southerners are rich in land, cotton, tobacco and slaves. Take away their slaves and they would be unable to produce their crops. They are mostly rich in commodities and livestock, not money," said Liza.

"I have a sinking feeling that I know what livestock means," said Nicole.

"Horses, cows, pigs, maybe sheep and slaves," said Liza quietly.

"But you don't believe in slavery, do you Liza?" asked Anne.

"I do not; but tell me Anne, what would those slaves do if they were freed? They cannot read or write; they have only ever learned to do what their masters tell them. They would have nowhere to go, no job and no money. They would just roam around and probably die or steal food and be shot. Until they are properly educated and are able to obtain work and somewhere to live, they are probably better off as slaves. It is not a situation that is acceptable, but yet there is no alternative," said Liza.

Jamie was smiling and then said, "And that is exactly what Liza told our Prime Minister a few years ago and the American President."

"Why are you both going to such an unstable place?" asked Arthur.

"We're visiting Charles Enderby. It will be interesting to see his plantation and meet up with old friends," said Liza.

"Ah yes, Charles Enderby. He's knowledgeable on bond servants," said Arthur.

"Yes, he doesn't own slaves; all his workers are bond servants or have been in the past. They still work for him. He was lucky that his family had money, so he has never counted his wealth in the number of slaves owned," said Liza.

"I envy you Liza," said Annalise. "You have been to so many interesting places and now you are going to yet another one. I think I would be a little unnerved by the talk of war, but as you say, it has been talked about for a very long time now."

David was very interested to hear about the new business venture that Harry would be heading up and he asked many questions and finally said that when it was up and running, he hoped to be the first customer.

"It's a very exciting project. I suppose you are spending a lot of time making it legally watertight," said David.

"Arthur has been assigned to study every word for us," said Peter. "We will be very well protected as will our clients."

"I hear you will be spreading your wings; where will you move to next?" asked David.

"London," said Liza. "By the time we are ready to go there we will have become fully fledged Brokers, working closely with our banking section. We will eventually be Brokers as well as Consultants in Belfast, but it is a business that we feel would do very well in London and New York and many other cities in the world. However, we must not run before we can walk."

"Very wise," said David. "Whose idea was this, yours Liza, Wendell's, Peter's or Harry's? Although I seem to think that it smacks of one of your schemes Liza."

"Yes, it was one of Liza's plans but once we started discussing it, the ideas were coming from all directions," said Wendell.

The ladies left the men to their port and cigars at the end of the meal and went to the drawing room.

"Harry and David seem to be getting on well," said Amelia to nobody in particular.

"I'm pleased that you all recognise just who Harry is. It's a shame that he has spent most of his life being ignored by those who knew of him. It doesn't seem to have affected him too badly," said Anne.

"I think that I would disagree with that to an extent," said Liza. "Nobody should grow up not knowing the love of a parent and until now he has had a chip on his shoulder. I believe that it is easing but does something like that ever go away?"

"Well I can see that David likes him and I know that he will now be on our guest list for any functions in the future," said Anne.

"The same will go for us also," said Annalise.

The evening had gone very well and, on the way back Harry smiled and said what an excellent evening it had been and that he had been invited to dinner at David and Anne Benedict's house the next week.

"Mrs Edwards organises some wonderful dinners so you will be able to return the compliment," said Liza. "It's a shame we won't be here to enjoy it with you."

"You are assuming that you would be invited," laughed Harry as they pulled up outside his house. "Goodnight Liza, goodnight Jamie; thank you for making me accepted here in Belfast. I'll see you tomorrow."

"That was a very successful evening," said Jamie. "It was the first step in Harry's road to acceptability. People don't argue with Wendell and Amelia when they introduce someone to certain gatherings."

The next day Susan and Roberts were organising the trunks for their return to Surrey whilst Liza spent time at the office and Jamie was with Wendell and Amelia most of the day. At the end of the day Liza accompanied Harry to his home to say goodbye to Mrs Edwards and Mr Grouch before meeting Jamie at Wendell's.

Amelia was always tearful when Liza was leaving, and she was more so as they would not be meeting up at Easter as Liza and Jamie would be in South Carolina at that time.

"We'll be back by the summer Amelia, so we will make sure we see you as soon as we return. We'll have a great deal to tell you then," said Liza.

"You be careful," said Wendell gruffly, which both Liza and Jamie knew was his way of covering his emotions.

"We will Wendell," said Jamie. "We're looking forward to the voyage on the 'Amelia' and a month with Charles will be an interesting experience."

They left with Wendell saying that he would see them at the dock the next day but as always, Amelia would only say goodbye away from the dockside.

Peter and Harry were waiting for them when they arrived the next morning.

"I thought Wendell said that he would be here this morning," said Liza.

"He is Liza. He's in his office with Sam and will be down shortly," said Peter.

Sailors were helping Susan and Roberts with the luggage, and they went on board leaving Liza and Jamie on the dockside chatting to Peter and Harry.

"I thought that I would spend some time at your place at Easter if you don't mind," said Peter,

"That's perfectly alright," said Jamie. "You know you are always welcome."

"I wondered whether it would be a good idea for Harry to come also as I think we could be approaching a time when it would be prudent to look around London for premises and see if some of our bankers would be useful to the consultancy," said Peter.

"I hope you won't think that it's an imposition as you won't be there," said Harry.

Liza let Jamie handle the situation. "Good heavens it won't be a problem. Liza will sort out a nice room for you with our Mrs Frances."

"It's a shame that we won't be around as I would enjoy looking at premises, but I know that you will be able to manage it wonderfully well without me," laughed Liza.

"You do realise that you will have four young men to contend with, as well as Christopher Pound," said Jamie. "Bella will probably turn up with her two boys, and I have no idea if the Duke will be with her."

"I'm sure you'll both manage to survive their enthusiasms," laughed Liza.

"Are you sure you'll be able to accommodate us," said Harry.

"They have plenty of room, don't worry about that," said Peter.

Wendell and Sam Nedbury came from the offices to bid them farewell.

"I wish you a safe journey," said Sam, "and an even safer one to America. I hear that the south is threatening war yet again. One of these days they will carry out their threat; I hope it isn't while you are there."

Wendell came and kissed Liza on the cheek and put his arm around her. "Please be careful Liza. Jamie, you look after her; we don't want to lose you again Liza, or you Jamie."

Liza frowned. "We'll be alright Wendell. I do have feelings of apprehension as I'm not looking forward to being faced with slaves everywhere, but I'm not planning to interfere with that situation no matter how wrong I believe it to be."

"I said to you once before, a very long time ago, act on your instincts Liza and you didn't and suffered for it. I hope that this is not another of those times," said Peter as he held her closely.

Harry was watching this with a slight frown as it seemed to him that everyone seemed very concerned for Liza.

Finally Liza and Jamie boarded their ship for Liverpool. They would be staying a night at one of the hotels before reaching home.

As they turned and waved, Harry commented to Peter that they all seemed rather worried about Liza and Jamie's forthcoming trip to America.

Wendell replied to him, "We can't lose her again," and he walked off with a troubled look on his face. Harry had no idea what he was talking about, Sam realised this and knew that Peter would probably not enlighten him, and he felt that he would do that when the time was right, and that time could well be later that day.

Chapter 8

It was a very busy time over the following weeks getting ready for their American trip. The 'Amelia' was taking goods on a direct route to South Carolina and would be bringing back cotton, tobacco and many other exports from that area. It would be returning to England as soon as it was loaded but was scheduled to sail back a month or so later when Liza and Jamie would have finished their visit to Charles Enderby's plantation.

Roberts was very composed over his duties, but Susan was becoming rather excited, interspersed with bouts of nervousness. Derek visited her quite often and managed to successfully calm her down. Liza wondered whether April had been that nervous when she had first travelled with them.

The boys were home for the half-term and Liza was pleased that Christopher was with them. Jamie had already sorted out a horse for him to ride. He and Hendry had chosen one which was known to be relatively quiet as he was aware that Christopher may not yet have the full use of his hand.

After greeting their family the boys went straight to the stables to check on their mounts and Christopher was delighted with the one that they had for him and that afternoon he joined the boys on their ride into the village.

Liza watched them leave and they all made a very impressive sight. Miranda was standing with her and said that she knew how much she would miss them, and they would also miss her.

"Well, the next time we travel they can be with us. We'll be back in time for their summer holiday, but I have a feeling that they will be encouraging the villagers to start the cricket season early," said Liza.

"When is Easter this year?" asked Miranda.

"The thirty-first of March is Easter Sunday. It is early this year. We should be in South Carolina by then," said Liza.

"I suppose you will be looking out for business opportunities whilst you are there," said Miranda.

"It isn't my intention to do so, but I am interested in seeing how a plantation is run and there could be something worth looking at, however as I have said, this is not a business trip, it is more for pleasure and to see another part of America," said Liza.

The boys and Christopher had seen Derek that afternoon and while they were visiting Mr and Mrs Rogers, Christopher spent time with Adam and was introduced to some of the children. He then went to see Mrs Price to make sure that she was still happy to have him as a lodger when he had finished his education and began working with Adam and Derek.

The day after the boys returned to Cambridge, Liza and Jamie would be leaving on their American trip. Liza and Jamie made sure that Christopher knew that he was still welcome to spend his Easter holiday at Edgeworth House.

"We should be back by the summer half-term but if by some chance we are a little late, you must spend your time here if you wish," said Jamie to Christopher.

"You really have been very kind to me. I enjoy my time here, but when I go back, I often wonder whether I have taken too much advantage of you both, in fact of your whole family. I feel a little guilty as I can give you nothing for my keep and it does dwell on my conscience," said Christopher.

Liza was about to reassure him, but Jamie beat her to it, "Christopher, we are more than happy that you are here. I wish you had a family of your own, not because we don't like having you around, but because you should have people who are yours. Perhaps one day they will return, and you will be reunited with them. In the meantime we want you to treat this as your home and us as your family."

"Thank you, you know that I appreciate all that you have done. I do make sure that your boys are treated well when they are away. I believe that they will need no prefect with them when I leave. Our Principal is well aware of all their talents and none of them will ever be picked on again," said Christopher.

The day before the boys were due to return to their college Matthew sought Liza out in her study. Grace was with her, and they had been going over last-minute business documents but Grace realised that Matthew needed a private conversation with his mother and she left saying that she would return later.

Liza and Matthew held one another's gaze until Liza finally said, "I will be careful."

Matthew smiled at her. "I know you will, but will others be so careful? I do have an uneasy feeling about your trip, but it is only uneasy; it is not filled with doom, and I know that you will return. However I am not sure when that will be, and that worries me."

"I don't know what to say to you to reassure you Matthew," said Liza. "I have already planned my return trip on the 'Amelia' and short of a massive ship failure I will be back when I have said I will. You know that the talk of war has been

177

going on for years. Even when we lived in Benson it was seriously discussed, but nothing ever came of it. Maybe one day it will happen, but nobody believes that either side would be foolish enough at this time to shoot first."

"There are dangers other than war; the main one being the whole Cherokee nation who are still convinced that you are their special saviour," said Matthew.

"I'm not so sure that you are correct in that. I believe that they think that you are that saviour; it is no longer me," smiled Liza.

"They would like us both, but that is not my main concern. I think that you will be caught up in something that is out of your control, and you will try to help others which will put you in danger," said Matthew.

"I don't believe that I will be in a position to help others Matthew and I am determined not to interfere in the politics of the south," said Liza.

"You will always help others and being in South Carolina will be no exception," said Matthew.

"Please don't worry Matthew; I have Jamie to protect me. You know he will not let any harm come to me," smiled Liza.

"He will do his best, but he is not as daddy Patrick was. He cannot fight like him, he has not been trained that way," said Matthew.

"There will be no need for him to fight, but if it was necessary, he would be able to defend me and anyone else who needed his protection," said Liza with a slight frown.

"I don't mean to upset you and I don't mean to make our father out to be less than brave because I know that he would put himself between you and any danger, but do you need to go to a place that is not as stable as it should be?" asked Matthew.

"I understand your concern, but we are sailing directly to South Carolina, and it is just a short trip to Charles Enderby's plantation; we are going no further and will be returning by the same route. We will not be exploring anywhere else; we will be quite safe," smiled Liza.

"I hope you are right but as I have said before; I have no great feelings of disaster and I know that I will see you again," said Matthew. "A new President has just been elected and will take over shortly; you know that his aim is to abolish slavery which will create tensions in the south. I just feel that this could mean that visiting South Carolina may not be as straightforward as you believe."

"Tensions do not mean disaster; it could become a little awkward, but you know that I am not going there to take sides in any quarrel. I did not know that you had an interest in American politics, have you been studying it long?" asked Liza.

"I was born in America, so I am therefore American as is Simon. John is also interested but he wasn't born there so he is not American although he lived there for a time. James is interested because we are," said Matthew.

"I see," said Liza. "I'm pleased that you take notice of what is going on in the world and especially in your place of birth. Anyway I know that you will care for your brothers whilst we are away. They look to you for leadership, and I know that you accept that responsibility. I believe it is now your supper time."

Matthew smiled realising that his mother wanted to end their conversation. They both knew one another so well that nothing further needed to be said.

The next day the boys and Christopher left for Cambridge. It was the first time that Nicholas and Richard had not been with them during a holiday time as they had family commitments. They all wished Liza and Jamie a safe journey as they drove out with Hendry.

Liza watched them go from the steps of the house and felt that her conversation with Matthew the previous day had unnerved her, but it was soon forgotten with the rushing around in preparation for their long trip the following day.

By mid-afternoon all was arranged and Liza told Susan to visit her mother and brother for the rest of the day. Miranda, Lucinda, David and Grace were joining them for dinner that evening and once again the questions were asked about the possibility of war between the north and south of America.

"Should war break out, which we doubt," said Jamie. "Then we will take the next ship home. It will not be our war so therefore we should not become involved."

The conversation then changed to what they expected to see and do at Charles Enderby's plantation. At the end of the evening it was made clear once again that Christopher would always be welcome to stay with them. David and Miranda said that they would make sure that he knew he had a home with them for however long he needed it.

That night Jamie asked Liza whether she would like him to take all the Edgeworth jewellery with them, apart from the sapphires as he knew that she never wore those.

"No Jamie, let's leave them here; both you and your uncle fought so hard to bring them back into the safekeeping of the family that I don't want to risk their loss. I will take my own diamonds and several other pieces. They look very good and although it would upset me to lose them, it would not upset me as much as if any of the Edgeworth jewels disappeared," said Liza.

"I have a feeling that you are expecting trouble on this trip. Are you sure you want to go on it?" said Jamie.

"I just don't want us to have the responsibility of that amount of jewellery with all its family history when we are going to a place that we are not familiar with. Don't forget what happened to the Edgeworth emeralds when April was accused of stealing them, and that was in a place with people that we knew. I want to enjoy our trip and not have any unnecessary worries," said Liza.

"You are right Liza, it would be a worry for not only us, but also for Roberts and Susan and your jewellery is very attractive and quite expensive. It also has no family history behind it so any loss would be more annoying than hurtful," said Jamie.

***

They settled nicely into the luxury of the owner's quarters on the 'Amelia', where they would be for a few weeks. Roberts' and Susan's quarters were also quite luxurious and nearby. Most of the cabins on board had passengers. Some were disembarking in New York and others going onto Washington, but most were travelling to the Carolinas.

Susan was beginning to adjust to life on board and of course Roberts was used to travelling with Jamie, although this was the first time that he had been further than New York.

They dined with the captain most evenings and enjoyed the enforced rest on board. It seemed very strange to Liza not to disembark when they docked in New York. Henry knew that they would be on board and he and Myra visited whilst they were in port. Bridget and Mary also took the opportunity to see them, and Liza and Jamie showed them around the ship and also introduced them to Susan; they already knew Roberts.

Then they were on their way again with the next port of call being Washington. Liza and Jamie remembered the time that they had been there nearly twenty years before, when Edward and Kate had also been with them. They remembered the theatre where Jamie had rescued Liza from the advances of a drunken, obnoxious man, and it was where Liza realised that Jamie Edgeworth was not as evil as she had first thought. She did not touch on the fact that from there she had gone on to Senor Valdez's hacienda and then had disappeared for two years.

"I wonder if President Lincoln is yet ensconced in the White House. I'm sure it's a far cry from the building site it appeared to be all those years ago," said Liza. "Perhaps on our way back we could see all the improvements."

The weather was warming up as they sailed further south; the seas had been relatively calm for most of the voyage with just one or two days that those with lesser settled stomachs had suffered through.

When they were two days out of Charleston Harbour, they were intercepted by a ship carrying military personnel from South Carolina. They requested permission to board and there was no reason to deny them. After a short while the captain sent for Liza and Jamie, and he introduced a Captain Marlboro and Lieutenant Vance of the South Carolina Militia.

"Unfortunately we will not be able to dock at Charleston Harbour as a couple of ships have sunk in the shipping channel and we will be too large to negotiate the route in. We can anchor offshore, and Captain Marlboro assures me that they will arrange for a more manoeuvrable vessel to take you into port," said the 'Amelia's' captain.

"Is it not unusual for Military personnel to bring this information? I would have thought that a harbour master or some other person in authority at Charleston Harbour would be carrying out that duty," said Jamie.

"The Harbour Master is very busy, and we are able to undertake some of those duties for him," said Lieutenant Vance.

"For some reason these gentlemen want to know what goods we are carrying and who they are destined to reach, and I felt that before I am forced to disclose such details, I should check with you Lady Edgeworth," smiled the captain.

Captain Marlboro and Lieutenant Vance looked confused and slightly annoyed.

"I do not see why our clients' goods should be of interest to the South Carolina Militia, but I would assure you that we are not carrying anything that is illegal or dangerous," said Liza.

"Obviously there is a reason why you are asking permission of Lady Edgeworth, would you mind enlightening us?" asked Captain Marlboro.

"Lady Edgeworth owns this shipping line; she is the Marchant part of Marchant & Fuller, therefore it is her decision to divulge clients' information, not mine. However we do have a manifest that she may allow you to read," said the captain who knew that they really had no alternative if they wished to enter Charleston.

"Tell me Captain," said Jamie. "Is South Carolina under military rule?"

"No Sir; but we do have a slight problem with some personnel who believe that they are in command of Charleston, and we cannot allow goods to reach them where they are hiding in a half-finished fort. They are dangerous people, and we must protect our citizens," said Captain Marlboro.

"All our goods are for diverse plantation owners, apart from some material for ladies' gowns and hundreds of spades, picks and axes for the many hardware outlets in South Carolina. We also have many passengers who wish to disembark in Charleston, and I have no knowledge of their beliefs or military leanings," said Liza. "The 'Amelia' will be returning to England in a few days carrying cotton and tobacco which brings enormous revenue to your State."

"Thank you, ma'am," said Captain Marlboro. "May I ask where you will be staying when you disembark?"

"We are friends and business associates of Charles Enderby, and we will be with him for the duration of our stay in South Carolina," said Jamie. "When the 'Amelia' comes back to South Carolina in around a months' time, we are planning to return to England."

"I know Charles Enderby and I know that he stores goods for many of his neighbours. I hope you will enjoy your stay," said Captain Marlboro. "I will sort out with your captain where he can anchor the ship and arrange for an adequate vessel to take your passengers and goods to shore."

"Thank you, Captain," said Liza and gave him a most charming smile which went from her face as soon as she left the room.

"Has this ever happened before?" Jamie asked Liza.

"I've only heard that it has happened where countries are under military control; not in any American port," said Liza.

"It's a little unsettling; perhaps we should have heeded the warnings that we were being given," said Jamie.

"Well, we're virtually there now, perhaps Charles will have an idea of exactly what is happening," said Liza.

The captain also thought that it was strange that military personnel were querying their goods and ultimate destination.

"I'm sorry that you are going to have to be transferred to another ship to reach port, but I can assure you that you will not have to go in a boson's chair," said the captain. "I did hear what happened to you in the past, but you know that we now have a stairway on the side of the 'Amelia'; the final part of your journey will be quite safe."

When the transfer ship docked in Charleston, Charles was there to greet them. He had carriages waiting for them with the added bonus of Mr O'Rourke and Mr Cavanaugh standing with him. Jamie was surprised to see Liza lifted off her feet in turn by two large working men. Liza then introduced them to Jamie who had heard their story previously from her.

Although Charles' lands were quite extensive, his house was only just over an hours' drive away and Liza and Jamie were pleased to get their feet firmly on the ground. As they approached up the driveway Liza could only admire the beauty of the house with large pillars all around it, keeping the interior cool.

They were greeted by Charles' coloured butler and his housekeeper was also coloured, but Liza knew that they were no longer slaves. They had been at one time when Charles' father had been alive, but they had been free for a great many years and now worked for Charles on a comfortable salary.

They were ushered into a large cool drawing room, and they were no sooner there than a commotion could be heard in the hallway and in burst both Mrs O'Rourke and Mrs Cavanaugh and each in turn engulfed Liza in their arms. Noisy conversations ensued and Charles just stood back and smiled at all the activity. Jamie was a little mystified but eventually gathered that these ladies were the wives of the men who had greeted them at the docks. After a short while Liza managed to extricate herself from them and she introduced Jamie to them. They looked at him closely before deciding to accept him as Liza's husband and Jamie was aware that they had become very close to Patrick in the past.

Mrs O'Rourke's and Mrs Cavanaugh's domain was the kitchen. They both worked hard feeding the household and all the workers, which could be quite extensive in the cropping season. They took great pleasure in informing Liza that they had prepared a very special meal for her that evening. There was a knock on the door and a servant came in with refreshments for them all and Liza asked where Roberts and Susan were.

"They are down in the kitchen and enjoying tea and cakes," said Mrs O'Rourke. "Maggie, the housekeeper, is sorting out your clothes and they will help her when they have finished eating. Their rooms are ready for them as no doubt they will be tired after their long journey."

Liza and Jamie smiled as it appeared that the welfare of Susan and Roberts was being put before their own.

"Joanne and Daisy will be visiting later today. They both worked here for a while, but Joanne showed talents in sewing and dressmaking, so she managed to get a job with the town dressmaker and Daisy has married a young general storekeeper. They have remained the best of friends and they do visit us here often. They are really excited that you are both visiting, and they also remember your man, Roberts, who helped them when they were in New York," said Charles.

Liza smiled at Charles, "It's wonderful that you took such an interest in their welfare Charles and I'm so pleased that they have settled so happily."

Mrs O'Rourke and Mrs Cavanaugh left to make sure that all preparations for their lunch were in place and Maggie knocked to say that their rooms were ready if they wanted to rest before lunch. Then Toby knocked and said that he would show Jamie to his room making them realise that they would be occupying separate rooms.

Charles smiled, knowing that they liked sleeping together and he added that they had adjoining rooms which he hoped would be comfortable for them.

"I'm sure they will," said Jamie and he and Liza allowed themselves to be escorted by Maggie and Toby to their suite.

Susan was waiting for her, and Liza asked if she was happy with her room. "It really is comfortable and I'm really looking forward to our time here. It seems very relaxed," said Susan.

"Apparently two girls that I knew from New York are visiting us this afternoon; I'd like to introduce you to them when they arrive. Roberts has met them before, but I'm sure he'd like to see them again," said Liza.

Liza then stretched out on her bed and before she knew it Jamie had come to find her as it was nearly lunchtime.

"I nodded off also," he said. "We were up very early this morning but I'm sure Charles is waiting for us now."

Over lunch they told Charles of their encounter with the Captain and Lieutenant of the South Carolina Militia and the questioning of the goods that they were carrying. Also that Captain Marlboro seemed to know him.

"I do know him; I can't say that he is a close friend. I have very little to do with the military," said Charles.

"Is there a problem here?" asked Jamie.

"There are some Union soldiers making a stand in a fort and the Southern Militia are trying to talk them out," said Charles. "It is sabre rattling."

The next day was going to be Good Friday and Charles said that he had invited one or two people for dinner on the Saturday and because of the distances they would be staying the night.

"I must warn you that my guests are very excited about meeting a real live English Lord; they don't seem to think that a Lord is just as much a human being as they are. They are also very keen to meet a representative of Marchant & Fuller who they find difficult to believe is a woman. They will probably ask Jamie questions about the business as they would never countenance that a wife could possibly understand the complexities of such a company. It's going to be interesting to observe," said Charles.

"Did you not tell them that Liza is a successful businesswoman," asked Jamie.

"They thought I was joking," said Charles. "They will think differently when they meet you, Liza."

"I'm not here on business Charles. Jamie and I are here to relax and to experience life in South Carolina. I'm looking forward to meeting some of the ladies," smiled Liza.

"I do not wish to belittle the ladies of my State, but I think you may be disappointed in them as our men like their women to be what is commonly known as 'bird brained'. They do not want them to concern themselves with anything other than making sure that their house slaves keep the place clean with good food on the table and the children brought up in their image. Discussions regarding business or the state of the nation would not be tolerated," said Charles.

"Oh," was all Liza could think of saying.

"Liza has said that she has no intention of getting involved with the politics of the area and that includes your way of life," said Jamie not very convincingly.

"I would love to see the reaction if Liza was to give her opinion on the politics of this country. I have always wanted to find a lady who is capable of making an intelligent comment on matters other than entertainment. Why do you think I am not married? To spend my life with a 'bird brain' fills me with horror. Either I bend to the ways of the south, or my blood line ceases with me," said Charles.

"If you can't find such a lady here, why haven't you found one in New York?" said Liza. "You travel there often enough to have met some eligible women."

"That would be worse than marrying a black woman as far as the people around here are concerned; it would take many years for her to be accepted and it would be unfair of me to place anyone in that situation," said Charles.

"The right woman wouldn't worry about that. She would be accepted by the Cavanaughs and the O'Rourkes as well as Joanne and Daisy, so she wouldn't be isolated," said Liza.

"I know that Liza, but she would not be accepted on the social circuit for a long while," said Charles.

"Well that wouldn't worry me. If your neighbours wanted to be that stupid then your wife would be better off without them," said Liza adamantly.

Both Jamie and Charles were smiling at Liza's pouting face.

"You're not going to rock any boats are you, Liza?" said Jamie.

"No, I wouldn't do that. Why are we being accepted if your neighbours are so prejudiced?" asked Liza.

"You are Lord and Lady Edgeworth and you come from England; you are old school nobility and that is very acceptable," said Charles.

"I'm not old school nobility," said Liza. "Will I have to hide my origins from them?"

"No Liza, I doubt that you will be questioned on your origins; they are going to be so in awe of you both that they probably won't be able to speak," said Charles.

"I think you are joking and that we will have a wonderful evening with your friends," smiled Liza.

"I'm afraid that the ladies do not use the brains that they were born with, but perhaps they do when they are without their menfolk," said Charles.

As they finished lunch Joanne and Daisy arrived looking happy and healthy and they spent the afternoon catching up on all their news. Susan was introduced and Roberts was delighted to be asked to join with them. Liza and Jamie promised to visit them during the following week.

Charles then took Liza for a short walk around his perfect garden, and she could almost imagine that she was back in England.

"Your roses are perfect Charles," said Liza with a smile on her face.

"I must admit that when I came to your house in New York all those years ago, I was impressed by your gardens and especially the aroma that your roses gave off. I spoke to your gardeners and they told me which roses to cultivate and they also gave me some cuttings, so you will recognise some of your own roses in my garden," said Charles.

"That really makes me feel at home," smiled Liza.

"Well Liza, there was a time when I had hoped that it would be your home, but that wasn't to be, and I can see that you and Jamie have a very good life together and I'm very happy for you. You haven't always had an easy time, so it is nice to see you so settled now," said Charles.

"Yes, I am settled Charles," said Liza. "I have a large and loving family and my businesses keep me occupied, but most of all Jamie cares for me greatly as I do for him."

Charles refrained from saying that he could see that her love for Jamie was different to that which she had for Patrick. It was not his place to make such a comment as he knew that it could drive a wedge between them, and he had no wish to do that.

They strolled back into the house and Jamie was in the library catching up on reading a newspaper. He dropped his paper down slightly as they walked in, and Liza smiled as Jamie's ritual did not change even in America.

"Charles has cultivated some of his roses from cuttings from our New York garden," said Liza.

Jamie looked over the top of his paper and said that was interesting. "They are obviously surviving well here; your gardens look superb Charles."

"They also smell beautiful," said Liza.

Jamie's newspaper was down a little further. "You are indulging your greatest hobby, Liza. Did you know that she spends what little leisure time she has gardening?" said Jamie to Charles.

"Do you actually get your hands dirty, or do you just give direction?" asked Charles.

"She gets her hands dirty," smiled Jamie, "and enjoys every minute of it."

"Is there anything exciting in the newspaper Jamie?" asked Liza.

"The talk of civil war is very concerning. It seems to be a little more of a certainty than we were led to believe," said Jamie whose newspaper was now down on his lap.

"It would be foolish to say that it would never happen, but we have had this talk before. Sometimes it is genuinely concerning but then it calms down and we all get on with the day to day running of our lives. It has spiked again recently and hopefully it will ease once more," said Charles.

"We know that the abolition of slavery is one reason for the differences between the north and the south, but that isn't all, is it Charles?" asked Liza.

"It appears to be the main reason, but you are right it isn't the only one. We have a strict class society here; one which I hasten to add I do not adhere to, but the north wants to impose their more liberal way of life on the south and southern aristocracy will not put up with that. We broke away from the United States last December because it was felt that they were still insisting that they continued with Federal tariffs being placed on us, but our South Carolinians are determined not to accept that any longer, which is why we have seceded," said Charles. "It does not mean that we are going to start shooting at one another; we are just going to have to learn to negotiate with one another and that is exactly what is happening at the moment."

"It does sound rather serious, but it has been going on for a long time as you say. I promise I will not talk politics on Saturday when your guests are here. You will have to let me know what subjects are of interest to your guests. Are they all plantation owners?" asked Liza.

"They are mostly, but there is one doctor and a lawyer. I thought it would also be quite interesting for you to meet the manager of our local M & F Bank," said Charles.

"Oh! Does he know who I am?" asked Liza.

"Yes, he is aware and is looking forward to meeting you," said Charles.

"I thought you said that nobody would accept a woman in business," said Liza.

"Yes, that is going to be rather interesting, and I am beginning to wonder how you are going to handle the situation," smiled Charles happily.

"I too will be interested to see how the evening turns out," smiled Jamie, but he was used to Liza getting herself out of awkward situations and he suspected that Charles was also.

"Oh well," sighed Liza. "I'm sure that the ladies will be interested in fashion, so I won't have a problem there."

They spent Good Friday relaxing in the morning and Charles drove them around part of his plantation in the afternoon. Once again Mrs O'Rourke and Mrs Cavanaugh excelled with the evening meal. Liza and Jamie began to learn the intricacies of cotton and tobacco growing.

"I didn't see many other crops, Charles; do you not invest in any food items, apart from what you grow for your own consumption?" asked Liza.

"When my guests have left, I'll take you to the rest of the plantation and show you our peach orchard and we do also grow sweet potatoes and yams, which are a similar vegetable, and they are mainly purchased by my neighbours for their slaves. Most of the plantation owners prefer to put their land to tobacco and cotton and only a small amount is cultivated for their own consumption. I also grow corn and wheat and sell that on the local market," said Charles.

Jamie was smiling. "I think you've pleased Liza; she likes to see diversification. I personally call it 'hedging her bets'. I notice that you also have a small number of livestock."

"Yes, Mr O'Rourke has a way with animals, and I am building up that side of my business. His young son also has inherited his talent and will soon be as skilled as his father, but I don't want to rely on that because he may wish to move away from his family at some time in the future. He is a rather restless spirit and will spread his wings as soon as he feels able. It will upset his parents, but everyone should follow their own dreams," said Charles.

"Your warehouses seem quite vast and judging by what I know you purchase through Marchant & Fuller; I am not surprised. It isn't all for your own consumption, is it?" said Liza.

"No, my neighbours order their stocks through me, and I also store their goods for them. They send their slaves to pick up what they need. I have more room than they have for storage. It's something that my father started in a much smaller way, and it has grown quite considerably in my time," said Charles. "Also they know that I have close contacts with your Company and trust my judgement."

Liza elicited a promise from Charles to show them the whole of his plantation over the next week and he told them that they would have to take picnics on some days as it would take them a long way away from the house.

They rested most of the following day as they needed to be alert for the evening entertainment. Whilst Liza was dressing for dinner, Mrs O'Rourke came to see her and it was obvious that she wanted to talk to her alone, so Liza asked Susan to leave for a short while.

"What's the matter Mrs O'Rourke; you seem a little disturbed. What can I do for you?" asked Liza.

"You got our two families out of a great deal of difficulty in the past; you taught us how to read and write and how not to be taken advantage of by anybody. I know that you smoothed our path to our employment here and in time Mr Enderby began acting in the way that he always should have done. We have a great respect for him, and we know that he is often belittled by the very people who will be at his table tonight. He deals in business with them, and I believe that he is under no illusions over their reasons for befriending him," said Mrs O'Rourke.

"What are you really trying to warn me about Mrs O'Rourke?" asked a concerned Liza.

"Most of the men believe that their wives have no thoughts beyond the style of their next dress, but they are wrong. Their women are spiteful and take great pleasure in creating embarrassment for any woman that they decide to pick upon, and I'm afraid that it is your turn tonight. They have got together and learned all they can about you and will enjoy asking questions that you will have no wish to answer. I know you and I therefore know that you will be able to crush them with a look, but your husband and Mr Enderby will be put through torture on your behalf this evening," said Mrs O'Rourke.

"Thank you, Mrs O'Rourke, I will warn my husband, but I will just have to come up with some device to turn the tables on them without upsetting Mr Enderby. He will be mortified if he thinks that I am embarrassed in any way. I presume that they believe that a Lord and Lady of the Realm have very few brains. I might play up to that and create a very amusing evening. Don't worry Mrs O'Rourke; I have yet to come across a situation that I have been unable to handle. One of our guests tonight is an employee of mine, so I doubt that I will have any problems with him or his wife," said Liza.

"I know that it is really not my place to criticise others, but Mrs Cavanaugh and I felt we should say something to you," said Mrs O'Rourke.

"Of course it is your place to say what you feel; we've known one another for a long while and been through some frightening experiences together. We are friends purely and simply," said Liza.

As Mrs O'Rourke left Susan came back into the room. "I'm glad she told you; I couldn't do it although they wanted me to. I don't know who they were talking about, but they were very concerned for you and his Lordship. I believe Roberts is warning His Lordship. He doesn't know them either, but Roberts has an air of authority about him so can handle the problem better than I can."

"Susan, you manage everything beautifully and you must never be frightened to tell me anything," said Liza.

Susan helped her on with her diamonds, they were very expensive, but they were not the Edgeworth diamonds. Jamie came in whilst she was just finishing dressing and he looked concerned. He waited until Susan left and Liza said that obviously he had been warned.

"Do you think that we should say something to Charles?" asked Jamie.

"Charles knows his guests and I have been told that he is under no illusions over their attitude towards him, so I would assume that he is also aware that they will try to belittle us. I would think that he is used to it and that his valet has also warned him," said Liza. "Come on Jamie, let's go and find him and take on the chin all that is thrown at us."

"It is going to annoy me if you are hurt Liza. You've had enough hurt in your life without having people with very little intelligence trying to belittle you and your achievements. You know that I will not stand for it, and I have a feeling that Charles will not also," said Jamie.

Liza grinned at Jamie and said, "Don't forget Jamie that most of them rely on me for their necessary goods. I don't think that the women have even considered that."

"I have a feeling that it is going to be an interesting evening. I think that we must avoid the subject of slavery as I believe most of the guests are serious slave owners and as you have said before, no matter what we think, it is their way of life," said Jamie.

Liza stood up and smoothed her emerald green dress down. Jamie looked at her and told her how beautiful she looked and that her jewellery was absolutely perfect. "The wives are definitely going to be envious of you. Come on let's go and find Charles before the first guests arrive."

Charles was waiting for them in his drawing room, and he looked very handsome and confident. He smiled as they walked in, and he drew in his breath at the sight of Liza. His southern charm came to the fore as he bowed and said that she was definitely going to be the belle of the ball.

The first carriages could be heard arriving and Liza queried why those staying had not arrived earlier to settle in.

"I know that is what you do, and you entertain those perfectly throughout their time with you. Here guests arrive just before the function and all our servants get the rooms organised at that time. We have a duty manager who will call the servants to show guests to their rooms when they wish during the course of the evening," said Charles.

He ushered Liza and Jamie towards the door and as they stood waiting for the first guests to arrive Charles suggested that it may not be a good idea to mention the Daltons project, as any promotion of manufacturing in the north would not be appreciated. Liza nodded and commented that she thought that could be the case.

By that time Toby was announcing the first guests and they in turn were introduced to Liza and Jamie both of whom had always been able to make conversation with everyone, which seemed to surprise the guests, especially the women.

When there was a gap Jamie whispered to Liza, "and so we begin our charm offensive."

"I think it is more playing them at their own game," smiled Liza.

Charles was taking no chances with Liza and Jamie as he had Liza sitting next to him and Jamie next to her; opposite them he had placed the bank manager and his wife which he felt was a sensible move.

Coloured servants had been hired for the night and they performed their duties well.

Charles had been right that most questions on business were aimed towards Jamie, even the bank manager was discussing with him the merits of M & F banking until Jamie just had to say that it was nothing to do with him, which brought silence around the table.

"We were under the impression that amongst other things you were part of Marchant & Fuller which also covers the banking section of M & F," queried one guest.

Charles sat back and let Jamie continue and watched Liza to see her reaction, but she was silent.

"I'm afraid you have been misinformed," smiled Jamie. "I run all the Edgeworth estates in England and Ireland, which are quite extensive. Marchant & Fuller is one of my wife's Companies; I am not involved in the running of any of them. If you have any questions about them then I suggest that you direct them at her."

"No woman would be able to be involved in such a company," said one guest derisively.

"May be that is what you believe, but I'm afraid you are wrong," said Jamie and his attitude was to close the conversation.

Another guest turned to Charles and said that his guest was a great joker.

"Oh, it's no joke. Lady Edgeworth is the Marchant part of Marchant & Fuller and totally owns Bradley & Company. She is a businesswoman through and through and I can assure you that she takes no prisoners where business is concerned. I have dealt with her personally on many occasions and found her to be far more astute than many a man in the same situation. But I mentioned this before, so I do not know why you are all so surprised," said Charles.

"Are you happy with that Lord Edgeworth?" asked one of the guests. "I would not allow my wife to concern herself with any form of business."

"Why should I be unhappy with being married to the most successful, if not the only successful businesswoman in the world?" asked Jamie.

"Do you not find that it interferes with the smooth running of your household?" another guest asked Jamie.

"I have a perfectly smooth-running household, thank you, as Charles will testify to," said Jamie.

"What sort of work does your wife undertake?" asked one of the ladies.

"I would suggest that if you wish to know anything to do with Lady Edgeworth's business, then it would be advisable for you to ask her," said Jamie who was getting increasingly annoyed.

"You must know the type of business that she is involved with," said another male guest.

"My husband is right," said Liza with a smile that did not extend to her eyes. "If it is important for you to know what my business involves it would be best if you ask me and I should be happy to answer any of your questions."

"How did you come to be an owner of Marchant & Fuller?" asked a Mrs Lawrence.

"I am reliably informed that most of you already know the answer to that question, but for those of you who are not so knowledgeable, I would be happy to bore you with the details," said Liza once again smiling.

Mr Knight, the bank manager, came to the rescue. "Of course we know that you were left it by your first husband. I'm sure nobody wishes you to go into any further detail."

"I should like to know a little more about the business," said Mr Godell who was a lawyer.

"I would be delighted to talk to you about my business Mr Godell, but I don't want to bore Mr Enderby's guests," said Liza.

"I don't believe that you would be boring our dinner guests Liza," smiled Charles.

"Well if you think not then I will briefly describe what Marchant & Fuller is all about. I own a little less than fifty percent of the Company and we own ships, offices, warehouses, inns and hotels, not to mention branches of M & F, land, a successful security company as well as diverse means of transport and some manufacturing projects," said Liza to an open-mouthed gathering but wisely did not mention Daltons.

"But what do you do?" asked Mrs Godell not unkindly.

"I help with every aspect of our business, but I am particularly involved with all new enterprises. I do have an assistant who helps me to deal with all my correspondence and Peter Fuller and I discuss in detail all our ongoing projects and of course I attend board meetings," said Liza making it sound very simple.

"Your Company also runs a children's charity, doesn't it Liza," said Charles with a smile.

"Yes, that does take up a great deal of my time, but I do have some wonderful people running the Homes and as you all probably know, Charles organises the correct procedures for any young adults who are suitable as bond servants," said Liza. All eyes turned to Charles and Liza had hoped that she had taken the onus off herself.

"What does your other Company do?" asked a Mr Hamilton.

"Bradley & Company owns property, land, businesses and farms in England, Ireland, Wales, Italy and here in America and we employ many people in all those areas," said Liza.

"Well ladies and gentlemen," smiled Charles. "It would appear to be a very bad idea to upset Lady Edgeworth as she has the power to cut off all our essential supplies, don't you Liza?"

"Indeed I do Charles, but it would be very churlish and unbusinesslike to do such a thing just because somebody says something to upset me," said Liza. "I think that I am above such pettiness."

Liza smiled and noticed that Mr and Mrs Knight, who were sitting opposite her, had amused looks on their faces as did Mr Godell. Mr Hamilton looked slightly confused but Charles and Jamie appeared to be waiting with interest for the next possibly awkward round of questioning.

Sitting next to Mr and Mrs Knight was Brigadier General Beauregard and his wife, Marguerite. He appeared rather stern, and his wife seemed very tight lipped.

"You are not a military man then Lord Edgeworth; have you ever been so," asked the Brigadier.

"Many years ago, when I was first out of university, a friend and I bought our commissions. We saw no action, which at the time disappointed us, but it did teach us a great deal," said Jamie.

"Why did you leave?" asked the Brigadier.

"I have no brothers so I was therefore the only heir to our family estate, and you will appreciate that such an estate is a great responsibility and really has to be run efficiently for it to survive; I therefore left the army and concentrated on learning all that I could about such an operation," said Jamie.

"Your father died then," stated the Brigadier.

"No, he died some years later, but there is no secret to the fact that both he and my grandfather preferred the gaming tables to putting any time or thought into how an estate should be run. They did not realise that they also had a responsibility to the people who worked for them, or indeed all the villagers who relied on the Estate for their welfare," said Jamie. "I am not trying to belittle my family as for a short while I was heading in the same direction; luckily events transpired that brought me to my senses."

"You do not believe in gambling then Lord Edgeworth," said Marguerite Beauregard.

"I do not believe in anyone gambling who cannot afford to do so. In so many cases it is to the serious detriment of their families, as it was in my case," said Jamie.

Liza then tried to steer the conversation in a different direction by asking Marguerite Beauregard what she did in her spare time.

"I have very little spare time Lady Edgeworth. I must make sure that the slaves carry out their duties as they should and that is no easy task. I plan meals and entertainment; it takes up all my time," said Marguerite Beauregard. "I really don't know how you cope with all that you do."

"I told you that I have a very good assistant and I have the help of all the Fuller family, but most of all I have my husband who is not only very understanding but also listens to all my schemes and assists with many of his thoughts on various subjects. He also is a member of the board of the charity, so that helps considerably," said Liza.

"Your jewellery is magnificent Lady Edgeworth," said Mrs Hamilton much to Liza's surprise as it most certainly could not be called magnificent, and she wondered where the conversation was leading. Both Jamie and Charles also looked puzzled.

"I suppose you only wear the Edgeworth jewellery when you attend high class entertainments, not small gatherings with ordinary people like us," said Mrs Hamilton.

"Mrs Hamilton," said Liza. "I would hardly call you ordinary."

"I'm surprised that you are aware of them," said Jamie.

"We do read the newspapers Lord Edgeworth and there are often articles about you attending functions, but mostly they are emphasised when you are in New York.," said Mrs Hamilton.

"We are just custodians of the Edgeworth jewels," said Jamie. "Our voyage was long, and we stopped at many ports where we knew that amongst the decent people there would also be rogues and thieves who would be delighted to relieve us of such pieces, therefore Liza and I decided that the sensible course of action was to leave them in the safekeeping of our family."

"A very wise decision," said Mr Knight and most men nodded their agreement.

"Lady Edgeworth needs no jewellery," said Charles with a smile. "She's beautiful enough without it."

Liza looked at him and gave him a smile which said that he was a flatterer. Jamie also smiled and nodded.

The main interest became Jamie's history, and he went into great detail about his family tree and the diverse marriages which had brought him to this point.

"You have children to carry on your line," said Mr Hamilton.

"Yes, I have three sons, but James is my heir," smiled Jamie.

"They are not all your sons though, are they?" asked Mrs Hamilton.

"They are my sons, they are all Edgeworths," snapped Jamie and Mrs Hamilton knew better than to query further.

The conversation calmed down around the table and covered many generalities until the time came for the ladies to withdraw leaving the men to their cigars and no doubt discuss the possibility of war.

As Liza rose to leave Charles whispered that she was now on her own and one or two ladies delighted in asking awkward questions.

"I thought that they already had done that, but no doubt there will be more," whispered Liza.

The ladies moved into the drawing room and settled themselves whilst being served with coffee by Maggie and her helpers. Liza had been studying the ladies and found that Mrs Godell and Mrs Knight were friendly. She was not too sure about Marguerite Beauregard, although she had no reason to think otherwise, but she was sure that Mrs Hamilton was the ringleader of those who wanted to create embarrassment. The doctor's wife had said nothing over dinner and Liza wondered why she appeared so reticent to join in any conversations.

Liza made her way over to her and said, "It's Mrs Chambers, isn't it?"

"Yes, Lady Edgeworth, I'm Leonora Chambers," she said.

"Well Leonora, my name is Liza, and I would be pleased if you would use it," smiled Liza realising exactly why Leonora had been so quiet. She had a very strong New York accent which would not go down well with these southern ladies or possibly the men also.

"Thank you, Lady Edgeworth," said Leonora and then she corrected herself and said "Liza."

"Have you been in the south long?" asked Liza.

"Just eighteen months," said Leonora.

Liza smiled at her, and they both understood one another as they knew that it could be many years before she was accepted by southerners.

"I knew of you in New York," said Leonora. "I knew about your work. I told my husband, but he also found it hard to believe. I notice you didn't mention Daltons, I suppose it was prudent not to do so."

"Yes, Charles warned me about that," smiled Liza. "Do you live at your husband's surgery?"

"Yes, we have a large premises, and he has a very well-equipped surgery," said Leonora.

"I suppose you help him on occasion," said Liza.

"I helped my father in New York; he is also a doctor. That is how we met. He won't let me help here, so I do find myself at a loose end sometimes," said Leonora.

"When I come into town next, may I call on you? I have friends in a town called Benson and they came from New York, he was also a doctor there, but he now enjoys working in a small close community," said Liza.

"I'd be delighted to entertain you Liza, if you are sure that it would not inconvenience you," said Leonora.

Mrs Godell and Mrs Knight gravitated towards them, and Liza asked if they had been introduced to Leonora, which they had not.

"I shall be visiting Leonora next week," said Liza to Mrs Godell and Mrs Knight.

"I hear that your husband's surgery is very up-to-date; in fact, I am told that it is the most modern in Charleston," said Mrs Knight.

"Yes, my husband is very proud of his surgery, and he is now quite in demand. Whether that is a good or a bad thing is difficult to say as it means that there are many sick people around," said Leonora.

"Perhaps we could also visit Mrs Chambers next week; that is if it is not rude of me to invite myself," said Mrs Godell.

"I'd be delighted to see you all then. What day were you thinking of visiting Liza?" asked Leonora.

"On Monday and Tuesday Charles is showing Jamie and I all over his plantation, so I shall be free on Wednesday early afternoon, if that is convenient to you," said Liza.

"I shall look forward to that," said Leonora who looked happier than she had done all evening. Mrs Godell and Mrs Knight were now sitting next to her.

"Tell us about your children Lady Edgeworth," said Mrs Hamilton in her annoyingly high-pitched southern drawl.

"What would you like to know Mrs Hamilton," smiled Liza as she braced herself for what Mrs Hamilton thought would be an embarrassing onslaught.

"You have three children, don't you?" said Mrs Hamilton. "And they all have different fathers, don't they Lady Edgeworth?"

Liza turned and looked coldly at Mrs Hamilton. "They all also have different mothers Mrs Hamilton, but you knew that already, didn't you? They are all my boys and proud to be Edgeworths and both Jamie and I are proud to be their parents."

Mrs Hamilton seemed to be taken aback by Liza's comments, but a Mrs Wakefield pushed the conversation further. "Your own boy was fathered by an Indian. It was very brave of you to keep him; do you find that a half-breed is accepted in England?"

Liza slowly looked at Mrs Wakefield and her eyes pierced right through the woman, who took a step backwards bumping into Marguerite Beauregard.

"You have been misinformed Mrs Wakefield, I have no son who has been fathered by Indians, but if I had, he would be loved by me just as much as my other boys. I would suggest that you check your facts before you try to amuse yourself by attempting to embarrass others," said Liza as she turned her back on Mrs Wakefield and Mrs Hamilton and resumed her conversation with Leonora.

"Well said, Lady Edgeworth," said Marguerite Beauregard. "We have all been on the receiving end of derogatory comments and personally I would much rather ask questions of an intelligent nature."

Liza smiled at Marguerite and she in turn smiled back which was the first time that Liza had seen anything other than sternness on her face.

"Some of us are meeting at Leonora's home on Wednesday and at that time I would be pleased to answer any questions you may wish to ask, if you would like to join us," smiled Liza.

"I believe I am free on Wednesday, Lady Edgeworth, and I would be delighted to join you all at that time. I do know that you have had an interesting and exciting life, but also realise that there have been times of great fear and unhappiness which you may not wish to relive. I look forward to our meeting," smiled Marguerite.

Liza turned to Leonora and quietly apologised for taking the liberty of inviting people to her home.

"Please do not apologise; this is the first time that I have been able to entertain in my own home. In fact tonight is the first time that I have been invited to a gathering since I have been here. I hope that I don't do anything wrong," said Leonora.

"Don't worry, I'll make sure you have nothing to worry about," said Mrs Knight kindly.

The gentlemen joined the ladies and both Jamie and Charles showed that they wondered how Liza had dealt with any awkward questions that she may have been asked, but from the look on her face they both realised that she had come out of it unscathed.

Dr Chambers joined his wife and he seemed pleased with what she was telling him. He looked up at Liza and smiled and nodded his approval.

It was not long before the Brigadier and Marguerite had to leave. "I would have liked to stay longer," he said. "But duty calls I'm afraid." They bade farewell and Marguerite added that she would meet up with some ladies at Dr Chambers' home on Wednesday afternoon.

The doctor and Leonora also had to leave and soon afterwards Mr and Mrs Knight and Mr and Mrs Godell followed suit, leaving Mr and Mrs Hamilton and Mr and Mrs Wakefield staying the night.

Charles had been the perfect host that evening and as he had no partner Liza stepped into the hostess role which Charles was grateful for.

Finally Maggie and Toby came to show the guests to their rooms and Liza, Jamie and Charles sat down with a nightcap and analysed the evening.

"I think that Leonora Chambers has at last been accepted by some of the ladies of Charleston. She has suffered because she is from New York, but I wasn't going to let the prejudices of some people stop me inviting who I want to dinner," said Charles.

"How was your time with the ladies?" Jamie asked Liza. "Did they upset you at all?"

"It always upsets me when people try to belittle our children; but I don't let them get away with it and in the end, it was not our boys who were in the firing line. Mrs Hamilton and Mrs Wakefield have not been invited to visit Leonora on Wednesday," said Liza with her usual pout.

"Surely you don't mean that Marguerite Beauregard is going to visit someone from the north," said Charles. "If that is the case, then a great deal has been achieved this evening."

When they were alone later that night, Jamie asked what had been said about the boys that had upset her.

"It was the usual half-breed comment and also Mrs Hamilton said that our three sons have different fathers," said Liza.

"Well she wasn't wrong there, but I suppose it sounds as if you have been very immoral," said Jamie.

Liza smiled cheekily. "I told her that they also have different mothers, which rather stunned her. I also said that they were as proud to be Edgeworths as we were proud of them."

"That really must have confused her; she's probably trying to work out who has what father and who has what mother," laughed Jamie.

"How did you get on with the men? Did they try to treat you like an aristocratic idiot?" asked Liza.

"They seemed to be more concerned with what is happening at a place called Fort Sumter than annoying me," said Jamie. "I'm a little worried about what they were saying and wonder whether we should leave sooner than we had planned."

"The 'Amelia' won't be back until the end of April, but I suppose there are other ships that could accommodate us. Is it really becoming serious?" asked Liza.

"According to most of the men this evening, not only would they look forward to war, but they will try to make it so," said Jamie.

"How foolish," said Liza, "What does Charles think?"

"Charles said very little but when he did comment it was to err on the side of caution," said Jamie. "I was asked whether England would support the north or the south. I could only say that I guessed that England would probably remain neutral."

***

The Hamiltons and the Wakefields left soon after breakfast the following morning. They thanked Charles for an entertaining evening and Mrs Hamilton said that she hoped that they would meet up again with Lord and Lady Edgeworth shortly.

"I'd like to arrange a small gathering in a couple of weeks' time, and I would be delighted to welcome you to my humble home," drawled Mrs Hamilton.

Liza smiled sweetly and said, "Thank you Mrs Hamilton."

Charles came back into the room after seeing them off. "I think both Mrs Hamilton and Mrs Wakefield were waiting for you to invite them to your meeting at Leonora's house."

Liza smiled and said, "I can hardly invite guests to somebody else's home. If she wants an invitation, she will have to visit Leonora herself."

"It is going to be an impossible situation for Leonora and her husband if a war does develop between the north and the south," said Jamie.

"It will be for a great many people on both sides," said Charles.

"Of course the doctor will have to treat people no matter which side they are on and that would possibly bring criticism from both sides," said Liza. "War is a terrible thing, but civil war is just about the worst."

"I trust you won't let this talk of war put you off South Carolina and my home in particular," said Charles.

"We have thought of leaving earlier than we had planned, but we don't wish to panic, and we have decided to see how things map out over the next week or so," said Jamie. "However, we had not realised that the ships which are blocking the channels were scuttled purposely and not accidentally. We also now understand why we were asked the content of the goods the 'Amelia' was carrying. It does seem a little more than sabre rattling as we were told."

"I'm sure that there will be ample notice before any shots are fired, if there are any to be fired," said Charles.

"Can we talk about what we are going to do this week," said Liza. "I presume we are putting our feet up today and you promised that you would take us on a tour of your plantation over the next couple of days. You know that I shall be with Leonora on Wednesday."

"I have made no plans for Thursday or Friday, but on Saturday we have been invited to a ball at the Town Hall in Charleston. There will be many people there who you would find interesting to meet," said Charles.

"I suppose those who were here yesterday will also be there," smiled Liza.

"Yes, but nobody would dare to try to embarrass you on that occasion; it would not be tolerated," said Charles.

"We'll look forward to that," said Jamie.

They took picnics with them on the following two days and managed to put to the back of their minds the prospect of war. His plantation was vast with several beautiful places to relax and enjoy the scenery. His peach orchard was expanding, and he had the beginnings of a vineyard. They saw Mr O'Rourke and his son caring for the vines and Liza spent some time talking to them about how they were getting the best from the fruit. She talked to them about her Estate in Italy and what she was growing there and then she mentioned to Charles about all the biproducts that came from Italy.

"When all this silly talk of war is over, will you both return and advise me on the way to get the best out of my Estate?" asked Charles.

"I think that you are already doing that Charles," said Liza. "I think that you will soon be thinking about making something from your produce rather than just shipping it out as it is. You have some vast warehouses that could be converted into manufacturing, but I can see that you are not quite ready for that and of course you are making good use of them at present by storing for other people. Your land is quite vast so with a little expenditure you can build further premises and set up quite a nice little production business."

Jamie was sitting back and enjoying the picnic, but he was also smiling at Liza's enthusiasm at the thought of a business project and wondered whether she would become involved. He looked around and could see that it was a very good cultivating area.

"You have a very great expanse of cotton; doesn't it make enough without diversifying?" asked Jamie.

"All the plantations grow vast amounts of cotton, tobacco and sugar cane. I cannot see that those who import our cotton into their factories can possibly carry on buying at the levels that they have been doing over the past five or six years. It must level out soon, it's as if they have been panic-buying," said Charles.

Liza just sat and did not comment, and Jamie had a memory of a conversation they had had with Lord Palmerston and the Duke of Norfolk some years previously, when Liza had given them the benefit of her thoughts on the possible consequences for England should a civil war in America erupt. Jamie looked at Liza and realised that she was well aware that the textile industry in England had been buying extra stocks just in case they were needed.

That night Jamie asked Liza what she knew about the cotton that was being imported by traders in England.

"I knew that some importers were over buying, I could see that from our company books and realised that the word had gone around for the various textile factories to buy in bulk. I don't think that Charles needs to be given that information," said Liza.

"So your talk to Lord Palmerston and the Duke of Norfolk all those years ago was heeded," smiled Jamie.

"It is something that others must have thought also," said Liza.

"Hmmm," was Jamie's only comment.

* * *

It was the third of April, and that afternoon Liza was to visit Leonora Chambers. She joined Jamie and Charles after breakfast where they had been discussing the possibility of cutting their visit short.

"I think it may be a good idea for you to leave sooner than you had planned," said Charles. "I have no wish to create panic for you Liza, but the more I think

201

about the discussions around my table the other evening, the more I believe that there is a real possibility of war breaking out sooner rather than later."

"It sounds as if you are talking of days rather than weeks, or months and that is a concern, not just for us but also for you and everyone else in America. What are you suggesting that we do?" said Liza. "I suppose we had better see what ships are available to us, but I don't want to worry Susan and Roberts, or anyone else and I don't want it to seem that we are leaving a sinking ship."

"We know that you are visiting Mrs Chambers this afternoon and we thought that we would drive you there and then Charles and I will make enquiries at the docks and then go to his club before collecting you on our way back," said Jamie. "Do you think it a good idea? How long do you think you will be with Mrs Chambers?"

"I should think that I would be with her for a couple of hours," said Liza. "I presume that you will approach our agent at the docks and hope that it doesn't spread panic."

"I thought that you would argue against our leaving so soon," said Jamie.

"I really don't want to leave yet; I like being here, I like seeing Charles and the O'Rourkes and the Cavanaughs as well as Daisy and Joanne. I think that Leonora is a very nice person and I worry that she will soon be in a difficult position. Mrs Godell and Mrs Knight seem to be very caring people and I was really looking forward to the Ball on Saturday," said Liza smiling a little petulantly.

"I'm sure that Jamie and I will not create a panic at the docks and when we have made our enquiries, we will casually make our way to my club and see what's happening there," said Charles with a smile.

"I wonder if Marguerite Beauregard will join you this afternoon," said Jamie.

"She said that she would, and I will not mention anything to do with war, slaves, the north or cotton. I shall remain neutral," said Liza.

After lunch Jamie and Charles took Liza to Leonora's home and carried on their way to the docks. Mrs Godell and Mrs Knight were already there, and they had excelled in helping arrange the afternoon refreshments. Liza smiled and said how wonderful everything looked.

Dr Chambers came in to greet the ladies and as he was welcoming them Marguerite Beauregard arrived apologising for being late, her apology being beautifully brushed aside by Leonora. The doctor said that he would leave them to their afternoon but before he left Liza asked if he would have any objection to her seeing his surgery as she had heard that it was most up-to-date.

"Certainly Lady Edgeworth, it would be a pleasure," said the doctor. "I understand that you have had some experience with medicine in the past."

"I have doctor, but only in emergencies and I'm sure you would frown on some of my methods," smiled Liza.

"Sometimes unusual methods are necessary to save a life," said the doctor and he bowed and left.

"I had some difficulty getting here," said Marguerite. "There seems to be a mob near the docks. I'm not sure whether there are people wanting to leave or people trying to find out where their supplies are. No doubt my husband will enlighten me later."

"So will my husband. He and Charles are visiting our agent at the docks. Perhaps they haven't been able to reach him, so they will be at Charles' club now," said Liza trying not to show concern.

The afternoon was a very pleasant affair and Leonora blossomed in the company and glowed with the compliments on her refreshments.

Marguerite asked if they all were going to the Ball on the coming Saturday. Liza, Mrs Godell and Mrs Knight said that they were, and Marguerite turned to Leonora and said, "Don't tell me that you haven't been invited."

Leonora shook her head unhappily. Liza frowned questioningly but she really knew why. Mrs Knight answered that it had to be because she was from the north.

"Well I'm from even further north so I had better not attend," said Liza.

Both Ruby Godell and Veronica Knight smiled and said that it would not be necessary. Marguerite said that if it was because Leonora was from the north then it was ridiculous, and she would reverse that decision.

"Thank you," said Leonora. "But it would now be embarrassing as I know that others would make it awkward for me."

"You are the wife of a most esteemed doctor in Charleston and should be treated with respect," said Marguerite. "My husband and I will call for you on our way to the Ball; we will arrive together and will tolerate no animosity."

Liza smiled as Marguerite reminded her of Bella and her assuming attitude.

Leonora did not look altogether happy at the prospect of attending the Ball and Liza decided to ignore her reticence. "I'm pleased that you will be going Leonora; I won't feel quite so isolated if you are there."

Veronica Knight raised an eyebrow at Liza and said, "We won't let either of you feel out of place, will we?" she said to the others who agreed that they most certainly would not.

Marguerite then said that she had to leave shortly as once again "Duty calls" and she left telling Leonora that she would see her on Saturday, and she arranged the time to call for them.

The rest of the afternoon was spent discussing what they would be wearing to the Ball and Leonora took them up to her room so that they could help her choose her dress for the evening. Liza was asked what she would be wearing, and she described her silver dress which was edged with red.

"Your diamonds will go well with that," said Ruby Godell. "I thought that it was very sensible of you not to bring the Edgeworth jewels with you. They are not yours but belong to the whole Edgeworth family and it would be heartbreaking if they went missing."

"Yes, it would. My husband and his uncle spent a great deal of time and worked hard for the money to retrieve the jewels from various pawn brokers. He told you of his father's and grandfather's unfortunate gambling habits and the jewels were in and out of a pawn shop on many occasions. In fact it is only in the last four years that we managed to regain the Edgeworth diamonds," said Liza.

When they returned to the drawing room, the doctor said that he would now like to show the ladies his surgery if they were interested, which they all were. Liza was impressed by his equipment, and she asked many questions about the use of some of it. Although interested Ruby and Veronica soon found that it was a little overwhelming and Leonora took them back to the drawing room while Liza stayed and learned as much as she could about the surgery.

"Do you think it wise that Leonora and I attend the Ball on Saturday," the doctor asked Liza.

"Only you can decide that, but Marguerite Beauregard feels that it is important that you do. The north and the south are not yet at war and even if it does come to that, Leonora will be loyal to you no matter what happens," said Liza.

"I know that she will; but she will not have an easy time and it will worry me if I am not able to be here with her on occasion," said the doctor.

"It seems that Mrs Godell and Mrs Knight have taken your wife under their wings," said Liza. "Mrs Beauregard is also keen not to discriminate against anyone from the north. You are acting as if war is inevitable; do you know something that I do not."

"No I don't Lady Edgeworth, but I know most of those in the militia and others in authority and they are all desperate for a fight. Keeping the Union soldiers holed up in the fort is not enough for them," said Dr Chambers.

"I suppose if it comes to a conflict, it will all seem so glamorous to the youth of the south and most of them will not know why they are fighting. The same will happen in the north; it's all very depressing," said Liza.

"You're lucky, it isn't your fight," said Dr Chambers.

"I have many business commitments in both the north and the south, although fewer in the south, so it is my fight, but not in the same way that you may have to be involved," said Liza. "I also am fortunate to have close friends in your country and if they are affected then so am I."

A servant came in and said that Mr Enderby and Lord Edgeworth were there and that they were also showing an interest in the doctor's surgery which delighted Dr Chambers.

Liza went back to the ladies leaving Jamie and Charles with the doctor. Leonora was still concerned about the Ball on the Saturday, but they managed to persuade her that it was a good idea and how disappointed Marguerite would be if her kind offer to transport them to the Ball was refused.

On their way back both Jamie and Charles were very quiet until Liza said that they might as well tell her what had happened as she would find out eventually.

"Is it anything to do with the number of people clambering at the dockside?" asked Liza.

"How did you know that?" asked Jamie.

"Marguerite said that she had difficulty getting through the throng at the docks," said Liza. "What were most of them trying to do?"

"They were trying to leave, but no ships are leaving and none and arriving. They have reinforced the blockage by scuttling more ships and they are not allowing any to get near us just in case they are bringing supplies to the men in the fort," said Charles.

"So we have two choices. Either we go overland up the coast to the nearest port and hope that a ship will be able to take us, or we wait and hope that all the talk of war dies down and the channel will be cleared in time for our return," said Liza.

"I'm surprised that everyone is still looking forward to the Ball on Saturday," said Jamie. "I would have thought that the event would have been cancelled."

"It is taking people's minds off the situation," said Charles. "Do you feel that you don't want to attend?"

"I don't think that there will be any danger for anyone at such an event," said Jamie.

"Marguerite and her husband are going to call for Leonora and the doctor and take them to the Ball," said Liza.

"That's very kind of them," said Charles. "It has been very upsetting for the Chambers. I wondered whether they had been invited."

"They had not but Marguerite has changed all that. She was annoyed that they were being ostracised. I said that if they were not invited because Leonora was from the north, then we should not have been invited as we were from even further north," said Liza.

"I believe that as it is going to be difficult to leave immediately then we should stay as planned and see how the situation develops," said Jamie. "In fact I don't think that we have very much choice. As you say Liza, we could go up the coast but there is no guarantee that we would be able to get passage on any ship and from what we have been told today there are negotiations going on between those holed up at the fort and the local militia, so let's try to relax and enjoy the rest of our stay with Charles."

"The Company will realise what is happening and I'm sure they will also come up with a plan to get us home safely; it just might take a little longer than we anticipated," said Liza. "We may have to prevail on your hospitality past the date that we originally agreed."

"You know that it is not a problem to me; I enjoy having company and I know that the O'Rourkes and the Cavanaughs are very happy to have you here. I also believe that your Roberts and Susan are enjoying what they are experiencing here," said Charles.

"I must call on Daisy and Joanne soon, I did promise that I would," said Liza. "I think you are right Jamie; we should carry on as if nothing is happening, especially as nothing may indeed happen. I believe our problem will be being able to get passage rather than war."

Liza was not too sure that she really meant that, but that was how she was going to carry on.

They spent the next two days at the house but each day either Mr O'Rourke or Mr Cavanaugh made the trip into Charleston to find out what was happening, and it appeared that all was quiet, and plans were being made to try to clear some of the scuttled ships; the feeling being that they had been a little hasty in completely blocking the channel.

"That seems wise," said Charles. "In their rush they appeared to have forgotten that we also need to ship our own goods out of Charleston. They were so concerned with not getting any supplies to the Union soldiers that they didn't think that we would soon need supplies as well."

"I suppose that will take some weeks," said Jamie. "It does seem that the situation has eased somewhat and maybe our ship will arrive on time and we won't outstay our welcome."

Charles just smiled at the comment. He enjoyed their company; he rarely entertained as his thoughts and way of life were very different to other plantation owners and they viewed him with scepticism. He despaired at the way that they treated their wives and their slaves; he was much happier in the

206

company of the O'Rourkes, the Cavanaughs, Daisy and Joanne. When he had to meet with other owners he would smile and nod and listen to their chatter; he would then return to the sanity of his own life.

He realised that Liza and Jamie were staring at him.

"I'm sorry, I was deep in thought," said Charles. "I shall be sorry when you leave; you have brought some normality to an otherwise insane world. I envy you both your way of life; I know that it's very busy, but I have met many of the people that you associate with, and you can be yourselves in their company and not put on the façade that I must show to those around me. I would really like to meet someone like you Liza; someone that I could talk to and get a sensible answer from; relax with and not appear to be someone that I am not."

"You sound so very sad Charles; do you really hate your life so very much?" asked Liza gently.

"I don't hate it, but when I see a couple like you communicating together, laughing together and just enjoying being together, I know exactly what is lacking in my life. It's close companionship that I would like and much as I appreciate my friendship with the O'Rourkes and the Cavanaughs it isn't the same as the love of someone who would also be my best friend," said Charles.

"Well Charles," said Jamie, "you have everything here that you could possibly want, except someone to share it with. If you are so discontented with the eligible ladies around you, then you will have to look further. Dr Chambers did it, so perhaps you could also. It isn't easy for Leonora Chambers or the good doctor, but they have not let that stop them. You may not even have to go north to find the woman of your dreams; there are many other southern states, or even another country."

Charles smiled again, "I'm getting a little long in the tooth to go racing around America or any other country to find someone to suit my age and my need for intelligent conversation on occasion."

"Only on occasion Charles?" queried Liza.

"Of course Liza; there should also be fun in a relationship," laughed Charles.

"Yes, there should, and we are very lucky to have the sort of relationship that you would like," said Jamie. "Keep looking Charles; it took me a long time to find what Liza and I have."

"I know that you spent many years chasing your dream Jamie; you wanted Liza since the first moment you saw her; it must have been very hard for you to have to wait that long but it was worth the wait," said Charles.

Liza did not show that she was uneasy with what Charles had said as it had taken two deaths for Jamie to achieve what he had wanted.

"I hope that you do find someone to love and be a true companion to you Charles," said Liza. "When all this silliness is over, you must start looking in earnest and part of that should be to visit New York again and come to England and we will take you to Belfast as well. You never know, you may find some wonderful Irish girl to appreciate you."

"Liza likes happy endings, and she will do her best to make sure that they happen," smiled Jamie.

"If you'll excuse me," said Liza, "I want to find Susan and try to calm her fears whilst I also sort out what I shall be wearing tomorrow evening for the Ball. She has obviously been a little unnerved by all the talk of war and although Roberts has been very caring of her, he can be too honest on occasion; he does tend to call a spade a spade."

She found Susan sorting out Liza's underclothes and told her about how some of the scuttled ships were going to be removed, although it would take a while. Susan asked if that meant that there would be no war and Liza was honest enough to say that she could not say for sure, but it did mean that there was a considerable easing of tensions.

"Tomorrow's Ball hasn't been cancelled, so I can only assume that war is no longer on their minds. They still have some Union soldiers blockaded in Fort Sumter, but they have been there for a while and they are again negotiating terms for them to leave," said Liza. "It's all been very silly really."

They then sorted out what Liza would be wearing for the Ball and discussed the accessories to go with her silver and red dress.

Dinner that evening was a little more relaxed than it had been on recent days, and they retired relatively early as the next days' Ball was going to be quite tiring and they would be late home afterwards.

***

Liza enjoyed getting ready that evening; she was looking forward to seeing Leonora again as well as Veronica and Ruby. Marguerite fascinated her and she wondered how surprised the other guests were going to be when she and her husband arrived with Leonora and the doctor. It was going to be an interesting evening.

Susan brought her jewel box to her, and Liza chose the diamonds that she had worn before, but she was also going to wear her tiara. Susan had worked miracles with her hair and her tiara sat beautifully on her head. Jamie and Charles were waiting for her in the drawing room, and they smiled as she came in and Jamie could see that seventeen-year-old again.

208

The venue was already crowded when they arrived and they were greeted by many people, most of whom neither Jamie nor Liza had met before. Veronica and Ruby and their husbands were there, and they gravitated towards them, and Liza asked if Leonora and the doctor had yet arrived.

There seemed to be a bristling amongst the guests and Liza assumed that Marguerite and Brigadier General Beauregard had arrived with Leonora and the doctor. After they were announced Ruby and Mr Godell were the first to join them and at last Leonora smiled. Charles was an absolute gentleman and bowed to Marguerite, Leonora and Ruby making conversation with them and their husbands.

Liza and Jamie finished talking to one of the plantation owners and his wife and they then moved towards where Charles was talking and at the same time Veronica and Mr Knight joined them. Leonora was beginning to get over her nervousness and although there were one or two glances in her direction, overall they seemed to be accepted.

Mr and Mrs Wakefield and Mr and Mrs Hamilton treated Liza and Jamie as if they had known them all their lives, but they totally ignored Leonora and Dr Chambers and merely nodded towards Marguerite and the Brigadier and just a sharp verbal greeting to the Knights and the Godells. They were cordial towards Charles which did not worry him.

There was so much noise and laughter that Liza wondered whether they were trying to cover the fact that they were worried at the prospect of war.

Many of the guests wanted to be introduced to Liza and Jamie and Charles spent a large part of the evening undertaking that task. The dancing had begun, and Jamie led Liza onto the dance floor and whispered that their every move was being watched and analysed.

"It's not going to stop me enjoying being held by my husband," retorted Liza as Jamie smiled at her happily.

They noticed that quite often the men would talk together with serious looks on their faces and Jamie commented that perhaps the tension was not yet over.

Mr Knight asked Liza if he could visit her during the following week as he had one or two business problems that he would like to discuss with her and he hoped that it would not disrupt her holiday too much.

"Mr Knight, these have been very worrying times for everyone here and I'm sure that M & F Bank could be put in a difficult position should the tensions escalate," said Liza. "If I can help you to resolve any problems before they arise, then it is sensible for us to have discussions. Jamie and I are enjoying our time with Charles, but we are under no illusions about what may happen and I'm sure

Charles would be happy to accommodate a meeting between us. We have nothing planned for next week; perhaps Tuesday if that would suit you."

"Thank you, Lady Edgeworth, as you say these are indeed worrying times and I hope that they do not become even more disturbing. However I do understand that negotiations may well ease the situation and I do know that it would be a sensible outcome. There is no need for war," said Mr Knight.

During the evening, Mrs Hamilton extended invitations to Liza, Jamie and Charles for dinner the following Saturday.

"I believe that we have a planned engagement with Dr and Mrs Chambers," said Charles. "That's right, isn't it Liza?"

"I think that it has been mentioned," said Liza. "If it is the case then I'm afraid that regrettably we will not be able to accept your very kind invitation."

Mrs Hamilton gulped and said, "I was going to ask the doctor and his wife to join us also."

Liza smiled and excused herself and made her way towards Leonora and her husband. She told them what Charles had said to Mrs Hamilton and the fact that she in turn had said that they would also be invited to her home.

Dr Chambers smiled and said that he supposed it was because Charles did not like the way his wife had been treated by Mrs Hamilton and some of her friends.

"We do not want to get in the way of your enjoyment of your stay in South Carolina," said Leonora.

"You are not Leonora, in fact you have both enhanced it," said Liza.

They could see Mr and Mrs Hamilton making their way towards them and Leonora asked Liza what she wanted her to say to them.

"I'd listen to what they have to say first of all," smiled Liza.

"Dr and Mrs Chambers," said Mrs Hamilton. "I was going to invite you to a small dinner party on Saturday, but I understand that you already have an engagement on that day; would you be free on the following Wednesday? I am just organising it for Mr Enderby, Lord and Lady Edgeworth, Mr and Mrs Wakefield and the two of you of course."

"I will have to check my appointment book and let you know Mrs Hamilton," smiled Dr Chambers. "Thank you for the invitation."

Mrs Hamilton turned towards Liza and raised her eyebrow questioningly. "Thank you, Mrs Hamilton; I will of course also have to check if Charles has made any arrangements for that day and will let you know by tomorrow," said Liza.

"If that turns out to be a difficult day for you then I can make it on another day," said Mrs Hamilton.

"That's very sweet of you Mrs Hamilton, thank you," smiled Leonora who was obviously enjoying Mrs Hamilton's desperation to entertain Lord and Lady Edgeworth and realised that she would do anything to achieve it.

Mr and Mrs Hamilton smiled and moved away, and Dr Chambers turned to Liza and asked if it meant that he and Leonora would be entertaining them on the following Saturday.

"Don't worry doctor, I'm sure that Charles just said that because he wanted to punish Mrs Hamilton; I don't believe that he thought further than enjoying seeing Mrs Hamilton squirming," said Liza.

"I think that it's a nice idea and I wish I had thought of it myself," said Leonora. "Will you be able to join us next week for dinner?"

"You don't have to do that Leonora; Charles would be mortified if he felt that he had imposed us on you," said Liza.

"If you are free next Saturday, I know that Leonora would love to entertain you at our home, and we would be delighted if you accept; besides it will not make a liar out of Charles," laughed Jackson Chambers.

"I will tell Charles and I'm sure he'll accept and make arrangements for next week," said Liza.

Liza went over and briefly told Charles what had been said and he was indeed appalled that his comment to Mrs Hamilton had resulted in an invitation to the doctor's house and he immediately went to talk to them, but the outcome was the same and he returned saying that he was looking forward to an evening with Leonora and Jackson Chambers.

"I ought to lie more often," he said to Liza and Jamie. "I could get a great many more invitations to dinner than I am used to."

The rest of the evening was enjoyable, and Liza and Jamie were much in demand. They tiredly made their way home shortly after midnight and it took just over an hour for them to reach the plantation. On the way they decided that they would also accept Mrs Hamilton's invitation as Charles said that there would be people there who would be understanding of the doctor's and Leonora's difficulties.

Sunday was very restful, and Mrs Cavanaugh prepared a wonderful traditional Sunday lunch for them after which they all went for a walk and felt better for it.

"I need to do some shopping," announced Liza sometime later. "I'll take Susan with me and see if Leonora would also like to accompany us. Would one of your grooms be able to take us tomorrow?" she asked Charles.

"And what do you need to buy?" smiled Jamie.

"I need to buy presents for the boys and for your mother and uncle; also for Lucinda, Grace and Christopher. I mustn't forget Adam, April and Derek. I suppose I should think about Mr and Mrs Lambert and Mrs Frances and Harper," said Liza.

Charles and Jamie were smiling, and Jamie said, "What about Hendry and Davis and young Ernie and of course Mrs Price and Mr and Mrs Rogers. And you mustn't forget Ken Wallace and all his girls, and then there are the Fullers and Harry as well as the Major and Jennifer and all the children in the Homes."

"I know you're laughing at me," smiled Liza.

"I'm surprised that you haven't thought about Myra and Henry and Hector and Estelle and everyone in Daltons, not to mention Anthony, Diana, Rose and young Thomas," laughed Jamie.

Liza pouted at him, and he said, "Don't worry, I'm not really laughing at you."

"I think that's a few too many to buy for," said Liza.

"I'll get young Donal O'Rourke to take you tomorrow; he has friends in Charleston so he will be occupied whilst you are shopping but I'll make sure that he knows to look after you also," said Charles.

"Are you sure that he is responsible enough to be taking Liza and Susan? He seems rather young," said Jamie.

"He must now be seventeen or eighteen-years-old," said Liza. "He was such a little boy when I first knew him."

"He has never forgotten what you did for him and his family and the Cavanaughs," said Charles.

"What did you do?" asked Jamie.

Liza smiled at Charles and said to Jamie, "I just taught them to read and write."

"You found them somewhere to live and you made sure that their terms of employment were correct," smiled Charles. Jamie raised an eyebrow; he had felt before that Charles and Liza shared a secret that had not shown Charles in a very good light.

***

Liza was awake very early the next morning and Susan was excited about her trip into town. Liza was going to help her buy some presents for her mother and Derek; she was also interested to see Dr and Mrs Chambers house as she had been told that they were very up to date with their furnishings.

Donal O'Rourke was a very pleasant young man and he seemed to take a fancy to Susan, who Liza had to admit was getting prettier by the day.

Liza commented to Donal that she remembered him from when he was a small boy and he said that he remembered her also. "You and your husband then were very kind to us," said Donal. "I was sorry to hear that he had died."

"Yes, that was some years ago now. You have grown so much Donal; I think you are taking after your father," said Liza.

"Maybe I am in looks, but not in any other way. I know he would like me to become a farmer, but I don't have the talent for that," said Donal.

"What would you like to do?" asked Liza.

"I would like to see a bit of the world; when I'm a little older I may join the army," said Donal.

"That would upset your parents," said Liza.

"I know it would and now is probably not the right time to approach them on the subject," said Donal.

They reached Leonora's house, and she was delighted to join them in their shopping expedition, and she arranged lunch for them at her house for when they had finished. Liza turned to Donal and told him to return for them at three o'clock. He agreed and said that he had one or two friends to see whilst he was in Charleston.

Shopping was fun and lunch at Leonora's was delightful. Susan was included at the table much to her surprise.

Three o'clock came and went and by four o'clock Liza was getting both worried and annoyed. Another half an hour passed, and Leonora suggested that they send out a search party for Donal. Unfortunately Jackson was out on a call which was some distance away and he would not be back until late that night and just as Liza was about to ask if one of Leonora's neighbours could lend them a buggy, Donal turned up driving their small carriage. Liza was about to give him a piece of her mind when she noticed that he was wearing a uniform.

"Donal, what have you done?" asked a distraught Liza. "Please don't tell me that you have enlisted."

"Yes, I have; I shall be with all my friends. The Militia needs all the young men that they can find to fight for the rights of the south," said Donal.

"And what rights might they be, Donal?" said a furious Liza.

"Well, they shouldn't tell us what to do," said Donal.

"Who are 'they'? You haven't even thought about it properly, have you? You don't know what the argument is all about. By rights you should be joining the north if you have the same views as your family and Charles Enderby," shouted Liza.

"I live in the south so I should fight with the south," said an equally adamant Donal.

"So you believe in owning slaves, do you? How many do you own?" shouted Liza.

"Well I've never owned any and don't want to," said Donal rather sheepishly.

"So what you will be fighting for is something that is of no concern of yours. I suppose you are going to tell me that you understand the south's concern regarding the Federal tariffs," said Liza.

Donal blinked not understanding what Liza was saying.

"You don't even know what I am talking about, do you?" said Liza through gritted teeth.

"Those Union soldiers have to be got out of the fort and they need men to do it," said Donal lamely.

"Those Union soldiers are already negotiating terms to leave; so when they do, what else will you have to fight over?" said Liza.

"I don't know, but all my friends have joined. I didn't think clearly, but it's too late; I've signed up and I must get back or I will be in serious trouble. Will you tell my parents?" said Donal.

"I have no choice as I think that they might notice that you are missing. They are going to be so upset and so will the Cavanaughs and Charles," said Liza.

Donal climbed down from the carriage, handing Liza the reins. "I'm sorry; I'm sure somebody will be able to take you home. I must go now."

He walked away and Liza could see that there were people waiting for him a little way down the street, and he joined them, looked back and raised his hand in farewell.

Leonora, Liza and Susan were staring after them as they rode away.

"I don't know anyone who can take you back Liza," said Leonora.

"Don't worry; I'm quite capable of driving a carriage such as this. Can you load it with our goods please Susan, and we had better leave as soon as possible so that we get back before it gets too dark? It gets dark earlier here than where I am used to," said Liza.

"Are you sure you will be alright, it's quite a long journey for you," said Leonora.

"We will be fine. I'll just see that the horses have been looked after well," said Liza as she checked their harnesses and made sure they had water and generally got to know them. They would have to wait for their feed until she got them back.

Susan loaded the carriage and Liza helped her up and then climbed aboard herself and was thankful that she had learned to drive a carriage successfully when she was in Benson. Hopefully she would remember all that was necessary as it was a long drive home.

"Don't worry Susan; it may be a while since I did this, but I haven't forgotten how. I used to drive daily when I was in America, so you are quite safe with me," said Liza trying to put Susan's mind at rest.

She drove slowly out of town but picked up pace when they were in the countryside. It was now gone six o'clock and they still had at least an hour before they reached home; it would be dark by around seven o'clock and they would stop and hopefully be able to light the lantern well before darkness.

It was beginning to get dark, and Liza stopped and after several attempts they managed to light the lantern. It threw a little light for them, but Liza felt that it was more useful for someone else to see them. She slowed down as it became darker although she could see fairly well, she wanted to take no chances.

Susan was very quiet but was peering ahead through the darkness.

"That's good Susan; two pairs of eyes are better than one," said Liza trying to make light of the fact that the surroundings looked very different at night, and she hoped that she had not taken a wrong turn, but the horses did seem to know where they were going.

"I can see lights moving towards us," said Susan.

"Good, hopefully they're from our place," said Liza and she was right it was Jamie, Charles, Mr Cavanaugh and Mr O'Rourke who were on their way to find them.

Even in the darkness Liza could see the look of relief on Jamie's face. Charles looked just as relieved, but Mr O'Rourke and Mr Cavanaugh looked puzzled.

"Where's Donal?" asked Mr O'Rourke with panic in his voice.

"I'm sorry Mr O'Rourke, but he has joined the militia and seems to think that he is going to war, although I'm afraid that he doesn't know why."

"You mean that he left you to find your own way home alone," said Jamie. "Why didn't Jackson help you? He has a driver."

"He was called away to an outlying place so there was nobody to help. Leonora suggested that we stay the night, but that would have worried you even more. I have driven a carriage before; I was just a little concerned in case I took a wrong turn, but obviously I didn't," smiled Liza.

Mr O'Rourke was sitting silently on his horse, trying to digest the information that Liza had given him. "How am I going to tell his mother?" he muttered.

"Let's get home and try to sort this mess out there," said Charles whose usual smile was not in place.

Jamie climbed up beside Liza and took the reins and drove the last mile to the house. A groom took the carriage after it had been emptied of their purchases and Liza, Jamie and Charles made their way to the drawing room. It was not long before they heard Mrs O'Rourke cry out and Mrs Cavanaugh try to pacify her.

"I never thought that Donal would be foolish enough to enlist. I knew that he was a little restless but to do this on a whim seems so unlike him," said Charles.

"He is convinced that he is needed to fight; it hasn't occurred to him that there may not be a battle and he has no idea what it is all about. I asked him if he believed in slavery, which he said he didn't and I asked him if he thought the Federal tariffs were worth fighting against and he had no idea what they were, so I told him that he had therefore joined the wrong side, he should enlist for the north with his beliefs. Of course his friends have all enlisted, so I suppose it made it easy for him to follow without thinking," said Liza.

"Whether he enlisted or not, he should never have left you to find your own way home; he was charged with your safety and to leave you high and dry is unforgivable," said Charles.

"I always thought that a militia was a group of men who had everyday jobs until they were needed to fight for their country; I didn't know that they enlisted and had to stay away from home, just like being in the army," said Liza.

"I'm afraid that Brigadier Beauregard is treating it like a full-scale war, but there are still negotiations going on with Major Anderson so hopefully something positive will come out of them," said Charles.

"That isn't Major Robert Anderson, is it?" asked Liza.

"Yes, I believe so," said Charles. "Do you know him?"

"I do, but it was a while ago. I met him many years ago in New York. You did also Jamie at the first function I held in New York, he came with General Winfield Scott. I also saw him again when he visited the fort at Benson about a year or so before I had to leave," said Liza.

"I'm afraid that I don't remember him or Winfield Scott," said Jamie, "and probably it would be just as well if you don't shout about that around town at the moment."

"I suppose you're right, but I wonder how some of the people I know in the north would react to my knowing Brigadier Beauregard. We are English and the policy of England will be to stay neutral, and we have to remain the same," said Liza.

"Unfortunately many people around here know who you are Liza," said Charles, "although I don't believe that many know that you are involved in the Daltons project which would be manufacturing goods that could enhance the north's means of success should a war break out."

"Anyone who knows Marchant & Fuller will know that Liza is a partner in the Company, and they have not hidden the fact that they have an enormous input in Daltons, as has the American government, which now I presume is the Union government," said Jamie. "Are you worried that someone might take revenge on her because of it?"

"We are not at war yet Jamie and from what I know of the people of Charleston, they would not hold one person responsible for the success or otherwise of such a conflict," said Charles. "I must go and see the O'Rourkes; they will be very upset because of Donal."

"I do feel quite responsible; if I hadn't decided to go shopping then he would never have been in Charleston and met up with his friends," said Liza.

"It's not your fault, he's been unsettled for quite some time now and the militia became a means for him to break away. However I have a feeling that he probably regrets his decision now," said Charles. "I'll see what I can do to get him out of it; I do hope that he hasn't signed up for years."

"Could he do it without his parents' permission? He isn't yet twenty-one," said Jamie.

"Well, that's what I'll find out tomorrow," said Charles. He left to see how he could help the O'Rourkes.

Dinner was late and very subdued that evening and a very despondent Liza went to her bed that night. Jamie came to her and tried to cheer her up.

"I know it's difficult at the moment, but I think we should leave as soon as we can," said Liza.

"Are you frightened Liza?" asked Jamie.

"No, just a little concerned," said Liza. "We may have to travel overland to North Carolina or even Virginia?"

"I'll look into it, Liza," said Jamie. "You know that I'll look after you. We will get home somehow, but we may have to let the negotiations at Fort Sumter blow over. It would upset Charles if we were to leave early, but he would understand that we are looking for alternative routes home if it becomes necessary."

"I don't like the thought that we could be used as pawns in a game of war," said Liza.

"I don't think it will come to that," said Jamie. He yawned and put his arms around her and said, "I won't let anything happen to you Liza, you know that don't you."

***

The next day Jamie and Charles went into Charleston with Mr O'Rourke to find out what they could do to help get Donal out of the militia.

Mr Knight came to visit as planned. He was concerned as several clients were pulling their money from the bank.

"If things get more serious and more people demand their money, our bank could be in serious difficulties," said Mr Knight.

"Your branch and many branches may get into difficulties, but M & F Bank will easily survive the pressure. We will have to be very careful if a conflict escalates across America. If it does, we will have to limit the amounts that any one person can withdraw. We do have more than enough funds to make sure our clients are covered, but we do have a great deal of that money invested and we won't be able to reimburse them overnight," said Liza.

"If we go into full scale war, we will have to do something more drastic than limiting the amount that a person can withdraw," said Mr Knight.

"We will do our best to pay out everyone eventually and keep securely any valuables that they have left in our safekeeping. Should the worst come to the worst, we will have to find the relatives of those who have died. We must make sure that our records are above reproach and kept safely. You had better keep two sets of books in two different places. Banks can often be in the firing line in conflicts," said Liza.

"With any luck I'll try not to get in the firing line; hopefully I will survive," smiled Mr Knight.

"We will also have to keep the records and deeds safely of those people who owe us money. We are covered for any premises which are destroyed. I do not wish to be harsh, but we will give people time to pay before we foreclose on any properties still standing," said Liza.

"I wish I could give you a more definite answer to any problems which may arise, but where war is concerned there is no definitive answer. You will just have to manage each problem as it arises; what could be the answer in one area could be totally different in another. All you can do is continue to be the honest person that you are and hope that your clients will understand that. I will discuss the situation with Wendell and Peter Fuller and our investment consultant, Harry Turner. I do hope that we are worrying unnecessarily," said Liza.

"As I said to you the other day, it seems as if those in authority are desperate for a war. They should know better, but they haven't learned from their past mistakes," said Mr Knight.

"I note from our records that you are a Louisiana man; does your wife also come from that State?" asked Liza.

"No, she's from North Carolina," said Mr Knight.

"You had no wish to move to the northern States then?" asked Liza.

"We did move to New York where I trained for my current occupation; but we are both southerners and were very content to move here and even more delighted when I was made the manager of the bank. We have settled happily and hope that everything will get back to normal as soon as possible. The fact that South Carolina broke away from the Union last December has caused one or two difficulties, but nothing that we have not been able to sort satisfactorily," said Mr Knight.

"Yes, we did see that Mr Knight. It was a matter of good negotiations on your part. Let us hope that the negotiations that are currently happening between the Union soldiers and the southern army are just as successful," said Liza.

"Thank you, Lady Edgeworth, you've put my mind at rest to an extent, although as you say we will just have to manage any situation as it arises, but at least I feel more confident having spoken to you," said Mr Knight.

"I'm sorry that I can do no more, we must just hope that we are worrying for no reason," said Liza.

Charles, Jamie and Mr O'Rourke arrived back just as Mr Knight was leaving. None of them looked very happy. They had gone to the recruiting office and were told that all yesterday's recruits had already been sent to a post in Alabama. The Recruiting Officer was not very helpful so they went to see Brigadier General Beauregard who said that he would do what he could, but they all knew that he had greater things on his mind than getting a wayward boy out of the newly formed Confederate Army.

Mr O'Rourke went to his home to break the news to his wife and once again it was hoped that no serious conflicts would take place before they could bring Donal home.

Jamie asked how Liza's meeting had gone with Mr Knight.

"Naturally there are concerns should a war break out. People are already taking their money out of the bank, but really there will be nothing that we can do if that time comes as we have most people's money in sound investments, but they won't see it that way. We will have to restrict the amount which any one person can withdraw and when all the ready cash has gone, we will just have to close the doors and make sure that we keep the records safely in at least two places. Hopefully people will want to empty their safety deposit boxes, so that not too many will be our responsibility. The same would be throughout the nation. M & F can ride the storm but will have to re-establish in many areas if and when any conflict is over. I really could not give Mr Knight any great words of wisdom, it will just have to be handled as best it can if we are plunged into this unnecessary war," said Liza.

"There are people who owe the Bank money, have you made any plans for them?" asked Jamie.

"Unfortunately they will still owe the money; we do have a certain amount of insurance against destroyed properties, but we will give people time to pay once any conflict is over," said Liza.

"What if they die?" asked Charles.

"We will still have their collateral, but we are not monsters, we will look at every case as it arises," said Liza.

Jamie and Charles stared at her as she had been rather casual about her remarks.

"It's business Jamie, purely and simply," said Liza.

"I know Liza, and I know that you will always be firm but fair," said Jamie.

Liza then said that she must visit Mrs O'Rourke shortly; although she did not feel that there was much she could do to help.

"She knows that Liza, but you do have a way of calming situations and listening to peoples' problems which makes them feel better," said Jamie.

"From what we gleaned from Brigadier Beauregard, it seems that he and Major Anderson have almost reached an agreement, so we all may look forward to a peaceful time ahead," said Charles.

"I suppose that won't make it any easier to get Donal out of the army," commented Liza, Jamie and Charles just shook their heads.

Liza's visit to a tearful Mrs O'Rourke could only be an attempt to comfort her. Mr O'Rourke had told her about the prospect of an agreement over the Union soldiers leaving Fort Sumter and she seemed hopeful that it would bring her boy back. Liza did not say that it seemed unlikely, but she put her arm around her and said that both Jamie and Charles were doing all they could, and that she would also speak to Mrs Beauregard to see if there was any way that she could help.

"We can but hope," said Mrs O'Rourke, "and I know that you will all do your best to help Donal. He is such a silly boy; I know that he was a little restless and we had planned to train him like his father, and he could then get a job anywhere. I know that you have interests up north and I had suggested that we contact you to see if you could find a place for him. We were so excited that you were coming to visit but we didn't have the chance to talk to you about it."

"Mrs O'Rourke, when he comes back, even if I am not still here, I will find a position for him, possibly at our Daltons project; we always need good dependable workers and our manager would put him in the best situation that suits him, but first we must get him back here," said Liza.

"Thank you, Lady Edgeworth," said Mrs O'Rourke as she dabbed her eyes with her handkerchief.

"I was Liza to you all those years ago and I'm still the same person. I don't need a title when I'm with friends. You and Mrs Cavanaugh looked after me when I was knocked unconscious, and you and your husbands protected me when I was in danger. We went through too much together for you to treat me as anyone other than the Liza that you knew then," said Liza.

Mrs O'Rourke smiled, "Do you remember the house that you put us up in? The French and the Spanish families also stayed with us. It was so much better than on the ship even though we were a little overcrowded. Have you heard from them? I remember that you gave them something to keep them safe from the Indians."

"Yes, and it did. I have heard from them, and they are doing well. I'll give you their address if you like," said Liza.

"Well you taught us to read and write, so it would be good to use it. You also taught them English, didn't you?" said Mrs O'Rourke and Liza nodded.

"It was a long voyage and it kept me occupied," smiled Liza.

"You and Patrick were very happy together," said Mrs O'Rourke.

"Yes, we were, and we were happy up until the day he died," said Liza quietly. "But that was over eight years ago, and life has to go on. Jamie and I are also very happy."

"I can see that you are, but not in the same way. How are those two boys of yours?" said Mrs O'Rourke changing the subject.

"They are now at University and my family has expanded. Jamie's son is now my son and I also have a boy from Benson, who I always considered as a son, living with us and is also at University with our boys," said Liza. "I definitely have a house full now."

"You haven't had any more of your own then," said Mrs O'Rourke.

"Patrick and I had a girl, but she found it difficult to come into the world and when she was there, she found it easy to leave it, little Meg was her name. She's buried with her father and Matthew's godfather in Benson," said Liza.

"I'm so sorry Liza; life hasn't been too kind to you," said Mrs O'Rourke.

"It was all a very long time ago and my life is settled now. Jamie looks after me and cares for me so well, as I do for him," said Liza.

Mrs O'Rourke put her arms around Liza and for a moment Liza found it difficult not to shed a tear; she pulled herself together as she was the one who was meant to be comforting Mrs O'Rourke, not the other way around.

They walked back to the main house together. Mrs O'Rourke wanted to get back to the kitchen to occupy her mind although her thoughts would never be far from Donal.

Liza went up to her room to rest for a short while before dressing for dinner. Her mind went back to the voyage across to New York all those years ago, and how happy she had been with Patrick and the boys. How excited she had been to be returning to her home in Benson. A terrible wave of pain and sadness washed over her, and she had to admit once again that she missed her life in Benson. She missed the fun, the excitement and the freedom that it had given her, but most of all she still missed Patrick and it was only when she met up with people like Mrs O'Rourke that she realised it.

Why do people always say that they could see that she loved Jamie, but it was different to the way that she had loved Patrick? she thought. She then smiled because the way she had loved Patrick was totally different to the way that she had loved James Marchant, so nothing was wrong with loving people in different ways, it was still love and she knew that she would be lost without Jamie.

She brushed the tears from her eyes but not before Jamie had entered and caught sight of her doing it.

"What's the matter Liza, has something upset you?" asked Jamie gently.

"Mrs O'Rourke reminded me of when the boys were young, and we all travelled across to New York on that fateful voyage when our ship was damaged by a storm. You remember it Jamie because the ship you were on came to our rescue," said Liza.

"I remember that a sailor tried to kill you and Matthew because he thought that you were a Jonah," said Jamie. "I also remember that my heart was in my mouth when I saw what was happening."

"Really Jamie, when I was finally brought on board your ship you were so casual about it. You didn't seem to be at all concerned," smiled Liza.

"I always found it difficult to show my feelings in the past, but I was beside myself when I saw that sailor trying to cut your rope and there was nothing that I could do about it. You were so sick when you came aboard and I vividly remember Matthew peering into your sick bucket and taking great pleasure in it," laughed Jamie.

"You looked after me even then, didn't you Jamie?" said Liza.

"That is because I loved you even then. You were married but it didn't stop me loving you. You can't stop feelings like that no matter that you were with somebody else and had a life that was totally different to the one that I would have liked you to have had," said Jamie. "You are right, people like Mrs O'Rourke bring back to life the memories and there's nothing wrong with that. We all have memories Liza, some we enjoy and some we want to forget, but we have come through it all and made a good life for ourselves. I am happy; I do hope that you are."

"I am Jamie," said Liza. "But I have made no secret of the fact that the freedom that living in Benson gave me is something that I do miss. However it is only on occasions like today that I remember it."

"I'm saddened that you don't feel free Liza," said Jamie with concern.

"Of course I feel free; I am talking about the freedom that I used to experience by running across a road to see friends, by visiting the fort to see other friends. That type of freedom is when I did not need to make arrangements to go anywhere. You must admit that I have to organise Hendry, Davis or Ernie to take me to the village. I cannot just jump into a buggy on a whim and meet with people. I'm not unhappy about it Jamie, it's just something that I have had to get used to," said Liza. "I know that I am not the only one to have made adjustments. You have also; you are surrounded by people now. You have three sons, one mother, one uncle, one cousin and Lucinda."

"In any marriage there are adjustments, but I wouldn't have it any other way. I love all the people who are now with me; my life was very lonely before. I can honestly say that it is no longer lonely. It is fun and exciting, and I never know what I am going to be faced with on any day. Our boys and Simon keep me constantly amused, as does Lucinda. I have a mothers' love as well as an uncles' and cousins' but most of all I have yours and I do understand that you had previously happy lives. They have made you what you are, and I wouldn't change you for the world, you make me very happy Liza," said Jamie. "I really can't wait to get back to that madhouse."

"From what you have said today, it would seem that an agreement is being reached and if that is the case then our only problem in getting back to that madhouse is how to get round the scuttled ships in the harbour, so we may well have to go up the coast a little way," said Liza. "We had better get ready for dinner or we'll be late."

"Mrs O'Rourke seemed a little better after you had spoken to her today, Liza," said Charles when they joined him for dinner.

"She started talking about when we had met in the past and it seemed to cheer her up; also she believes that something may be done to help as an agreement has nearly been reached. It is unfortunate that Donal has been sent to Alabama, but we'll have to see what can be done. How long did he sign up for?" asked Liza.

"Five years," said Charles. "All his friends signed up for that time. It really is more of an army enlistment than a militia agreement, which is rather worrying. I hope that his age will negate his signature."

Liza said nothing but she doubted that they would be able to retrieve Donal as she was well aware of army regulations, and she was certain that the new Confederate Army had the same rules as the army that she knew in Benson.

"What would you like to do tomorrow?" Charles asked them.

"I would feel guilty if we went off to enjoy ourselves when Mr and Mrs O'Rourke are going through such an unhappy time," said Liza.

"I think that we should go into Charleston and once again try to make sure that our request to release Donal from his enlistment is being processed correctly and also highlight the reasons why he should not have been accepted in the first place," said Jamie.

"I believe that it would be good for you to try but I also believe that you will be wasting your time," said Liza. "Having realised that he has enlisted in the new Confederate Army and not a militia then he will not be released, especially if they have the same rules as the army that I knew in Benson. Donal is eighteen years old, not thirteen, fourteen or fifteen. Although they should have had his parents' consent, he probably lied and looking at him he could be taken for twenty-one. If he hadn't been immediately sent to Alabama, which is currently the Confederate headquarters, then there could have been a chance, but he has now been absorbed into the Army and I don't think there will be a way out for him."

"That sounds very depressing; I presume you didn't tell Mrs O'Rourke of your thoughts," said Charles.

"No, I would never hurt the O'Rourkes," said Liza. "You did say that Donal was restless, perhaps the army life will suit him. It could be exactly what he needs and what will do him a great deal of good. If he's bright enough he could work his way up the ladder; the only problem that I can see with it is that he has enlisted in the wrong army."

"That's not a very tactful thing to tell Charles, after all it is his army," said Jamie.

"No Jamie, Liza's right. I'm a southerner through and through, but what is happening at present is wrong. To threaten civil war is very foolish and as everyone with any sense would know, civil war is the most disastrous of wars. All I can see is that most of the aggression is coming from the Confederate side; they have already commandeered the Federal forts and premises, although I believe they are now offering to pay for them. They do not believe that the Federal tariffs are fair, and they certainly don't want to abolish slavery," said Charles.

"What do you think that the North wants?" asked Jamie.

"I believe that they need to impose the tariffs on all States, and they want to end slavery, but they do not understand that for many plantation owners their slaves are their wealth," said Charles.

"That is basically what Liza told Lord Palmerston and the Duke of Norfolk some years ago," said Jamie. "Shall we all go into Charleston tomorrow and see what we can do to help the O'Rourkes. I would also like to see what is happening at the harbour."

"I don't think that you will be leaving when you had planned," said Charles. "Hopefully the tensions will have eased but it is going to take some time to clear the harbour ready to receive large shipping, but I enjoy your company, so you are welcome to stay as long as you feel it is necessary. We are going to the Chambers' on Saturday and to the Hamilton's on Wednesday. Normally the Beauregards would be entertaining, but under the current circumstances they are probably quite busy."

"I would like to visit both Daisy and Joanne, after all they are from the north and I wonder if they are having any difficulties, but they do still have the remnants of a soft Irish accent. They don't sound as obviously from New York as Leonora does."

"Everyone is on edge at present, and I dare say that Daisy and Joanne are feeling a little more vulnerable than most. At least Daisy has a husband to protect her, and the general store's customers are very fond of her. Joanne only has herself to count on. If things get difficult, I will suggest that she moves back here. Hopefully it won't be necessary," said Charles.

"You are very caring Charles," smiled Liza.

"I did promise to look after them, so it's the least that I can do. If you think that I am caring, then it is only what you have made me Liza. There was a time when I thought differently," said Charles. "Did you know that Liza blackmailed me, Jamie? We crossed swords and she won."

"I always had a feeling that she had something on you Charles, but she has never said what it was and knowing her, she never will," said Jamie. "I have to say that I am intrigued."

Liza grinned and said nothing, but Charles told Jamie that in the past he had not been as open with the detail of his bond servant agreements as he should have been. "They are now one hundred percent correct and I make sure that all others are also."

"I know that Liza has a philosophy of 'set a thief to catch a thief;' don't tell me that you are one of those?" said Jamie.

"Well I didn't steal, but I did manipulate the terms of the agreement so that they had to work longer than they should and I'm not proud of it. I have never believed in slavery, but really what I was doing was placing people in situations where they were virtual slaves. I thought that I was so clever at the time, but Liza showed me the error of my ways and besides, she blackmailed me and did it so beautifully," grinned Charles.

Liza raised her eyebrows and smiled in an attempt to look innocent.

"Were the Cavanaughs and the O'Rourkes involved?" asked Jamie.

"Yes, they were, but they have never mentioned it and they are as loyal to me and this plantation as any family member would be. That is why I feel that something is missing with Donal not being here; he has been a part of my life for a long while now. I've watched him grow." said Charles.

"Well, we'll try again tomorrow," said Liza.

***

The feeling in Charleston was one of suspense as no agreement had yet been reached.

"I think I'll arrange a party for the Saturday after next," said Charles. "It will be either a celebration or commiseration and let us hope that we can sort out the problem with young Donal. It would be nice to see Mrs O'Rourke smiling again; she normally has an infectious smile."

"I don't suppose it would be possible to have the O'Rourkes and the Cavanaughs as well as Joanne and Daisy and her husband also, or is that not the 'done' thing," asked Liza.

"I have always thought differently to others so I can't see that there would be a problem, just as long as they feel comfortable joining us," said Charles.

"What about Toby and Maggie? Is it right to leave them out?" said Liza.

"It isn't right to leave them out, but I can tell you with certainty that they would not accept as they would most definitely not be comfortable in such a situation," said Charles.

Whilst Jamie and Charles went once again to see the Recruiting Officer and then probably on to try to see Brigadier Beauregard, Liza went to find the general store and was greeted by Daisy as she entered. Her husband, Connor, seemed very young and was from Irish descent. She was ushered through to their back room which was used as their dining and sitting room. It was clean and comfortable, and Liza felt that it was reminiscent of Kathy and Joe's small room at the back of their general store, although they did have larger rooms on the first floor where everyone had gathered for Christmas lunch and other occasions.

Connor said how pleased he was to meet Liza as he had heard a great deal about her. "We did hear that you were attacked as Daisy and Joanne left New York. Were your friends very badly hurt?"

"Luckily their wounds were all relatively light, but none the less it was very brave of them both. They saved my life," said Liza.

"We had heard that the woman was aiming for you and your friend jumped between you, and your security man also was stabbed," said Connor.

226

"Yes, he was but not seriously so; the woman who did it was deranged," was all Liza was saying.

"I do know Daisy's past Lady Edgeworth, and I know that she and Joanne helped many little ones to safety, and I also know that you run a charity for abused children. I'm very proud of Daisy for what she did to help others and I know that both she and Joanne had no choice about their pasts. It's wonderful that they had the chance of a better life and they both have taken full advantage of the opportunity," said Connor.

"You don't know how pleased I am to see you so settled. Your store reminds me of one in a place where I used to live in America. Do you bake for your customers?" asked Liza.

"Yes, we do, and Daisy is getting quite adventurous with her cake making," said Connor. "I do hope that life gets back to normal soon as we are beginning to run out of stores."

"It must be becoming a worry for you," said Liza. "How are you being treated Daisy; do people know that you are from New York?"

"I am the same as Connor. I was very young when I came from Ireland. I have no idea who my parents were; I don't think that the people who brought me to America were my parents. I hope that they weren't as I don't like to believe that my parents would sell me to that awful place," said Daisy.

"I don't suppose you will have the same problems as some other people from New York," said Liza.

"Yes, I have heard that anyone from the north is being treated in a bad way," said Connor. "It's rather silly really as where you were born shouldn't make a difference, it's what you believe that dictates which side you are on. But it may all disappear as I understand that negotiations are going quite well."

From the general store Liza made her way to the dressmakers where Joanne worked. A Mrs Perry owned the establishment and Liza could see that Joanne went up in the woman's estimation when Lady Edgeworth was introduced as her friend. Joanne was working on some very delicate embroidery on an evening dress and Liza commented how beautiful it was.

When the opportunity arose for Liza to be alone with Joanne, she told her that Charles was offering her a roof over her head should she feel threatened in any way. "He is very concerned for your welfare especially as the circumstances are rather worrying at present."

"That's very kind of him and should it be necessary I will take him up on his offer, but I have heard that the negotiations are going well," said Joanne.

Mrs Perry brought coffee and biscuits for them and took pleasure in showing Liza what they were working on and the future orders that were on her books.

"I may have to come to you for some dresses Mrs Perry. We are unable to leave when we had originally planned as our ship cannot negotiate the channel. I know it is being cleared but that could take some time. We could go overland if necessary, however we will see what is happening over the next week or so," said Liza.

"It would be our pleasure Lady Edgeworth, just call in at any time," said Mrs Perry. She left Liza and Joanne to talk for a short while and Joanne agreed that she would seriously think about moving back to the plantation should life become difficult for her.

Liza left and found Jamie and Charles waiting for her in their carriage. Unfortunately the news was not good; Donal O'Rourke was definitely in the new Confederate Army, but Brigadier General Beauregard said that when he had time he would write to Donal's unit commander to see what could be done to release him from the army, if indeed he wanted to be released.

Jamie and Charles knew that they were the words of someone who had much greater matters on his mind, and they were just to placate them.

Liza asked how the clearance of the shipping channel was coming along and was disappointed to hear that it was going very slowly.

"I think that we will just have to settle down and impose ourselves on Charles until our ship arrives. We will try not to take over your life whilst we are with you," said Liza. "I presume that our agent will let us know when a suitable ship manages to dock."

"Yes, I went to see him again today and he will book us all on the first available sailing," said Jamie.

"Well that's all we can do, so we might as well enjoy the rest of our stay, however long that may be," said Liza. "Mr and Mrs O'Rourke are not going to be happy with the result of your visit today."

***

They spent the rest of that day and the following day relaxing although Liza devoted some time writing letters to the boys, the family and Wendell letting them know what was happening and that because of the events in South Carolina they had no choice but to extend their time with Charles. She hoped that there was a means for her letters to reach England and Ireland.

Mr and Mrs O'Rourke were naturally still upset about Donal, and they lived in the hope that he could come back to them soon.

It was a warm evening and Liza and Jamie were sleeping that night with the windows open. They were woken at around four thirty in the morning by the sound of explosions; the noise obviously being carried on the wind. They knew instinctively that the negotiations between Major Anderson and Brigadier General Beauregard had not been successful.

They could hear movement within the house as well as coming towards the house from the O'Rourke's and the Cavanaugh's homes. Jamie donned his dressing gown and went to see if he could find out what had happened, although it did seem obvious that Fort Sumter had been either fired upon or been fired from.

Liza also made herself respectable and went down to join those who were in the drawing room. Charles said that he would ride into Charleston to find out what was happening, but they all really knew that the war had started no matter who had fired the first shot. Jamie offered to go with him, but Mr Cavanaugh said that he would go instead.

They did not return until nearly eleven o'clock and the news was not good. Major Anderson had offered to leave Fort Sumter with his troops on the fifteenth of April, but after consultation, this had not been accepted, and the first shot was therefore fired at the Fort within the hour.

The noise of the continuing bombardment could still be heard at the plantation, and everyone tried to go about their usual tasks. Roberts was staying close to Susan and Toby and Maggie were keeping one another well within their sights. Mrs O'Rourke was wearing her fingers to the bone in the kitchen trying to keep occupied and Mrs Cavanaugh was cleaning up after her as she was not being her usual tidy self. Liza, Jamie and Charles were keeping up an unconcerned appearance, which was far from how they really felt.

Liza decided to study some figures that she had from Mr Knight, she wanted to work on the number of customers the M & F Bank had who were investors and try to analyse how much each could be allowed to withdraw and somehow she would have to make arrangements to have enough cash in the vault. If she and Mr Knight could establish a standard, then it would help all the other branches both in the north and the south.

Jamie wandered in to where she was working, and she looked up and could see that he was very concerned.

"There's no point in my asking you what is wrong, we all know what that is," said Liza.

"I've been talking to Charles, and we think that our best route home is up the coastline to a port in North Carolina. North Carolina have not seceded and are therefore still part of the Union, so once we cross the State line, we should be safe," said Jamie.

"We are safe here Jamie, unless we get hit by a cannon ball. We have no argument with anyone here, or anyone from the north," said Liza. "I also think that we should turn up at Leonora's tomorrow for dinner, unless we hear that it has been cancelled."

"Are you really as calm as you sound?" asked Jamie.

"I'm not calm, I just don't want to panic others, also I do have one or two problems to think about concerning the bank," said Liza.

Charles joined them and Jamie said that Liza thought they should continue with their plans for dinner at the Chambers' the following day.

"I doubt that they will be continuing with their dinner plans now," said Charles.

"I hope that they do as it would help everyone here to see us carrying on as normal and going out to dinner in Charleston would give them confidence," said Liza.

"I don't suppose any of them have experienced a conflict before. Have either of you?" asked Charles.

"I was in the army for a while, but I never saw active service, much to my disappointment at the time," said Jamie.

"I have been in the middle of a couple of battles, but they did not involve cannons. They were pistols, rifles and arrows; I learned to duck quite successfully," said Liza.

"You have both experienced more than I have. I have not seen any action whatsoever. What a sheltered life I have led!" exclaimed Charles.

"Unfortunately, I think that you are now going to see much more than either Jamie or I," said Liza.

"It has been going on now for nearly twelve hours; I wonder which side is going to run out of gunpowder first," said Charles.

"Do you think that you will have to fight, Charles? Will all eligible men have to join the army?" asked Jamie.

"I hope it won't come to that, but everyone should fight for their country," said Charles.

"And what country might that be Charles?" asked Liza frowning.

"I take your point Liza; it is all my country, but I suppose I will have to fight for South Carolina," said Charles.

"You should fight for what your conscious tells you in any war but especially in a civil war," said Liza.

"I hope that I will be able to sit on the fence and I also hope that what has happened today will be recognised as foolish by the powers that be, and they will get together and sort out their differences before it escalates into something that becomes uncontrollable," said Charles.

"Shall we go into Charleston tomorrow?" Jamie asked Charles. "We will be able to judge the situation and we can call on Leonora and Jackson just to establish whether we will still be welcome there tomorrow evening. I think that Liza is right that we should try to keep some form of normality for the sake of our staff."

"I believe that should our dinner at the Chambers' still be scheduled, it would be advisable to ask Mr O'Rourke and Mr Cavanaugh to stay at the house until our return. We will not make it a very late night," said Charles.

"I know that it is Saturday tomorrow, but if possible, I would like to call on Mr Knight as I have been studying some figures and will have to put a plan in place in case there is a run on the bank," said Liza.

"I would not be happy with you venturing into the centre of Charleston," said a worried Jamie.

"I knew you would feel that way," said Liza. "I also worry about you both going into town."

"I understand how you feel and that you need to talk to Mr Knight but tomorrow could still be the middle of a bombardment and I'm sure that Mr Knight would come here to discuss your plans," said Jamie. "I'll get a message to him."

"What's the difference between going to Leonora's and Mr Knight's?" asked Liza.

"We can take the back roads to Leonora's, but Mr Knight's house is in the centre of town, near the bank," said Charles.

Nobody got much sleep that night and they were all down early for breakfast. The noise from Charleston was becoming more intense and Jamie and Charles were ready to leave by ten o'clock.

"Be careful," was all Liza could think of saying.

Roberts decided that he would accompany them, and it raised a smile when he could be heard telling Toby how to make sure that Susan was not worried. "She's very young you know," he was saying, "she needs to be protected from all this nastiness."

They got to the outskirts of town by eleven-thirty and made their way to the main thoroughfare and Charles asked one or two people what was happening, but nobody seemed to know, apart from the fact that the bombardment was continuing which was obvious as they could hear the noise.

Charles decided that he would visit Leonora and Jackson Chambers and Roberts asked to be pointed in the right direction for the general store and he would see what Daisy and her husband knew. Jamie went off to find Mr Knight to give him Liza's message and ask if he had any idea of how the conflict was progressing.

As Jamie passed the bank, he saw a number of people loitering outside and then found that there were several waiting at Mr Knight's front door. He pushed his way through and banged loudly on their front door shouting his name out to anyone inside. The door opened quickly, and a hand grabbed him, and he was yanked unceremoniously inside.

"I was hoping to see Lady Edgeworth, but I was going to ride out to you later today. What we thought might happen has happened. People want to draw all their money out and they are not happy that I have not opened the bank today," said a concerned Mr Knight.

"She has been working on some ideas to help with the situation. She wanted to come into town today, but I was not happy exposing her to the dangers here, so she asked me to make arrangements for you to visit her. Perhaps you would like to go now. Take your wife with you. Do you have children?" asked Jamie.

"Yes, just one girl. She is five-years-old," said Mr Knight.

"Take her with you, and anyone else you feel you would like to get away from Charleston at present," said Jamie. "Bring a change of clothes with you just in case they are needed; I know Charles won't mind."

"Thank you, yes I'll do that," said Mr Knight. "I can leave by our back way."

"I'll see you there later," said Jamie and he left also by the back way and found Charles and Roberts waiting for him outside the general store. He told Charles what he had suggested that Mr Knight did that afternoon.

"Yes, there is rather a large gathering at the bank, and I can see that they are making their way to his house, I hope they don't do any damage," said Charles.

"I would like to see Joanne," said Roberts. "I would like to make sure that she is not frightened."

Charles showed him where she worked. "I'm afraid I don't know where she lives, but I'm sure Daisy would know."

Roberts found Joanne and he knew that she was nervous being in Charleston, so he told her to pack a bag and go with him. Charles and Jamie were surprised to see them riding double, but they were told to catch up with Mr Knight and his family who were on their way also to Charles' plantation and he was sure that there would be room for Joanne in their carriage.

It was difficult for both Jamie and Charles not to smile at Roberts' enthusiasm to keep Joanne safe. When they were on their way Jamie commented that Roberts had also made sure that Daisy was being looked after.

"If you remember, Roberts helped both girls when they were staying at Liza's house in New York. I believe he feels that he has a responsibility towards them," said Jamie. "Are we dining at the Chambers' tonight?"

"Yes, but we have brought the time forward to six-thirty," said Charles. "We had better start to make our way home."

As they were about to leave a shout went up that the soldiers in Fort Sumter had agreed a truce, so Jamie and Charles waited to watch what was happening. It was with relief that they learned that the Union garrison surrendered to the Confederate army; however it did mean that the north and the south were now on a collision course.

They quickly rode home and found Liza organising rooms for Mr Knight's family and their servant as well as one for Joanne. Toby and Maggie seemed a little confused, but Liza had summoned Mrs Cavanaugh from the kitchen, and she took control of the situation.

"It's good and bad news," Charles announced to everyone. "There is a truce, and the Union soldiers are leaving Fort Sumter; they've called it an evacuation but really they've surrendered."

"I suppose we don't need to impose on you then Charles," said Mr Knight.

"I'm afraid that it means that the first shots have been fired in a civil war Mr Knight," said Jamie. "I would remain here for a couple of days as there are quite a few people wanting to withdraw their money from the bank and the crowd outside your house is growing."

"All monies and valuables are quite secure in the bank vault, and we have brought anything that we care about with us," said Mr Knight. "It might be sensible to let the atmosphere cool before I open the bank and Lady Edgeworth assures me that we will be able to accommodate our customers, although not to the tune of all their monetary assets immediately."

Maggie and Mrs Cavanaugh came to say that their rooms were ready, and that Joanne was in the room that she had used when she had lived there. Mrs Cavanaugh went with Joanne and Liza accompanied Veronica and her daughter, Fern, to their rooms.

"This is very good of you, Liza," said Veronica.

"Please Veronica this isn't my home; it's just that Charles has no one to act as the lady of the house, so I seem to have fallen into that role," smiled Liza.

An evening meal was arranged for the house guests and Liza excused herself as she had to get ready for their dinner with Leonora and Jackson. Charles assured everyone that they would be returning early, and Mr Cavanaugh and Mr O'Rourke would be keeping guard on the house in their absence.

Before they left for the evening, Liza gave Gus Knight the figures that she had been working on just to give him an idea of her thoughts.

They arrived at the Chambers' house early that evening, but Jackson was not there. Leonora said that an accident had occurred during the formal handover of the fort and one man had been killed, another seriously wounded and four more hurt and the doctor had been called to assist.

Within half an hour Jackson came rushing in and said that he had done everything that he could.

"The rest of the Union soldiers are on a steamer out of Charleston, apart from the seriously wounded man, he's still here," said Jackson.

"That means that there is now a channel out of here, so we may be able to leave as we had planned," said Jamie.

"You may be able to take a steamer up the coast to get on a larger ship, but your ship still won't be able to get into Charleston Harbour, or you could go overland to Wilmington and get a ship from there," said Jackson.

"North Carolina hasn't seceded, so it's still part of the Union," said Charles.

"I wouldn't guarantee that it will stay that way," said Jackson. He excused himself and went off to change for dinner.

All through dinner they could hear a great deal of movement and shouts from outside, but the occurrences of the day had relieved some of the tensions in Charleston.

The men stayed in the dining room for their port and cigars, while Liza and Leonora moved into the sitting room.

"Jackson may have to go away if this conflict escalates; he joined the militia many years ago and now he could be called upon to be an army doctor. I dread the prospect of that; there are very few people here who would be tolerant towards me. I would be very frightened to be here alone; I know how I would be treated. I dare say that any southerners in the north would be treated the same," said Leonora.

"It may be advisable for you to travel north, should Jackson not be around to protect you. I presume that he would have the opportunity to make arrangements for you, but you could be worrying unnecessarily," said Liza.

"I don't think that I am Liza; the word around is that it has all become very serious," said Leonora.

"We'll just have to see how the situation turns out," said Liza but she was more concerned than she was showing.

The men came through to join them and they were all looking uneasy.

"What's the matter?" asked Liza.

"Jackson has been telling us that he may well be sent away as he is a Captain in the Confederate militia," said Jamie.

"If that is the case then I am very concerned about leaving Leonora here alone," said Jackson. "Charles has been kind enough to offer for her to stay at his plantation; she would be welcome as I know that there would be no prejudices in his household."

"That's very kind of you Charles," said Leonora. "I was in fact saying to Liza that I was worried should Jackson have to leave. I would feel safer there than here."

"I would really prefer to get her to her father in New York, she should be safe there. Nobody would worry that she was married to a southerner," said Jackson.

"How soon would you know whether or not you could be called up?" asked Liza.

"I should think that I would know the worst in a week or possibly two," said Jackson. "I believe that Leonora should start packing immediately, just in case."

"I am not sure when we will be leaving but we could take Leonora with us. I know that we will stop in New York so we could see her safely to her father's house," said Jamie.

"Would you like that, Leonora?" asked Jackson.

"My loyalties are with you Jackson, but I would feel safer in New York with my father if you have to go away," said Leonora.

"So we have a plan," smiled Liza.

"Unfortunately we must leave shortly; we have the Knight family staying with us tonight, they are also a little on edge. You have probably seen the people gathering outside the bank and outside Mr Knight's house. It was a little intimidating for them," said Charles.

"I suppose Mr O'Rourke and Mr Cavanaugh are keeping guard at your home, Charles," smiled Jackson.

"Yes, nobody will get past them," said Charles.

As they left the Chambers', there were people milling around and one or two Charles knew. They called to him, and Liza and Jamie could hear him saying that he had just had a wonderful dinner with friends, and he would be carrying on as normal from then onwards.

Veronica and Gus were still up when they arrived home. Mr O'Rourke and Mr Cavanaugh reported that all had been quiet that evening.

Liza and Gus Knight spent some time going through figures, but tiredness overtook them all and they retired to their rooms before midnight.

A note was delivered the next day from Mrs Hamilton apologising as she felt it prudent to cancel her planned gathering the following Wednesday due to the present circumstances. She trusted that they would understand and hoped to meet again in the not-too-distant future.

Jamie, Liza and Charles were polite enough not to show that they were quite relieved at the cancellation, although they had to appreciate that nobody really knew what would be happening in the immediate future.

On the Monday the Knights and Joanne said that they would return home and Gus said that he would open the bank later that day.

Each day over the following week somebody went to the docks to see what movements there were out of Charleston. The day that Liza and Jamie were due to leave came and went. Another week followed and still they were unable to get passage away from South Carolina.

All clambering at the bank had stopped; they had paid between one hundred and two hundred dollars to each client, and most had understood that their money was soundly invested elsewhere, but Mr Knight was awaiting further funds which he hoped would arrive shortly. Some clients had removed their valuables from the vaults which meant that there was less of a responsibility for Gus Knight.

Jackson drove up one day with Leonora and her luggage. He was in a Confederate Captain's uniform with a medical insignia and there was no hiding the fact that Leonora had been crying bitterly. Charles helped her down and Liza put her arm around her and ushered her inside.

The news was that North Carolina had joined the Confederacy along with several other States.

"That doesn't mean that we can't get to Wilmington and get a passage from there," said Liza. "I own most of the ships, so I shouldn't have any difficulty getting us on board some vessel."

"When are you leaving?" Charles asked Jackson.

"Later today; I have to be at the docks by six o'clock and we'll be sailing by nine o'clock," said Jackson.

"I wonder why we are unable to get a passage out; there are steamers and ships leaving every day, but each time we try they tell us that nothing is sailing, or they are full, or they are only for army personnel. We are not being told the truth," said Jamie.

"No you are not," said Jackson. "They do not want you to leave. You and Liza are from the English aristocracy, and they want England to side with the Southern States."

"We would have no influence over which side England supports; besides England would not want to take sides, it would want to stay neutral," said Jamie.

"It has also been mentioned that Liza's Companies would make her a useful bargaining chip. They know that both her Companies work closely with the American government in Daltons. The factories there could turn out armaments and because of where it is it must support the northern cause. Apart from all that there is one thing that the Confederacy is desperate for and that is money, and they know that Liza has a great deal of that, and they are talking about holding her to ransom," said Jackson. "I should not be telling you all this, but what they are discussing is not what an upstanding government should be contemplating."

All eyes were on Liza's shocked face.

"If they are being serious and not just throwing up ideas without any real foundation, then we must make plans to leave overland before they decide to take you into custody," said Jamie to Liza.

"They can't do that; we are British subjects. There are people from many countries who have business interests in America, are they going to stop all those people from leaving," said Liza.

"You also have a banking system in place throughout America which can influence either one or the other side," said Jackson. "You are both very desirable to the Confederacy cause as you would be to the Union government."

"How do you know all this Jackson? With all due respect, you are a Captain in the medical corps and not someone who makes lofty decisions," said Charles.

"I had somebody who is in the know come to me because they were aware that I would be bringing Leonora here. I cannot say who it is; I cannot jeopardise them, but they do not agree with this type of situation," said Jackson. "They know that you have no control over how this war will evolve and what they are trying to do is bordering on illegal."

"It now seems obvious why we have been unable to leave Charleston, we will have to make plans to leave by some other route," said Jamie.

"Don't tell me what your plans are going to be, but I would be grateful if you would take Leonora with you as I don't believe that she will be safe even here," said Jackson. "I must now make my farewells to Leonora, so excuse me for now and I will see you in a short while."

With that he took Leonora's hand, and they went into the hall, but Charles guided them into his study so that they could have some privacy.

"Well we are certainly going to have to make some careful plans," said Jamie. "Have you a map?"

They could hear the study door open and Leonora crying. Jackson came back into the room and bade them farewell. He shook hands with Charles and Jamie and kissed Liza.

"Thank you for taking care of Leonora and I wish you well on your journey home," said Jackson.

"We wish you well Jackson; you are going into a conflict not of your choosing and we know that sadly you will have a very necessary task ahead of you," said Jamie.

Charles and Jamie saw him off and Liza went into Leonora and gently guided her up to the room that had been prepared for her. Liza knew how she felt as she had experienced loss like that on a few occasions and it was difficult to describe the emptiness that comes with having to say goodbye to your loved one.

Mrs Cavanaugh knocked and entered with a tea tray for them both. Liza smiled and thanked her, and she could see the sympathy on her face. Leonora sipped a little of the tea and managed to control her tears; Liza handed her a damp cloth to wipe her face.

"You are amongst friends here Leonora. I know it doesn't make up for having your husband with you or your own home around you, but we will do our best to make you feel comfortable. You must also help us to make our plans for getting to New York as I think that it is going to be a long journey," said Liza.

"I suppose you will have to keep a low profile until you leave here. We are both in a similar situation; yours is because you are wanted and mine is because I am not," smiled a watery eyed Leonora.

"That is one way of putting it," said Liza. "I was a little shocked that Jamie and I seem to be so desirable to the Confederacy. They are wrong in what they surmise; we will not be considered bargaining chips by either the British government or the Union, so it is best that we remove ourselves from America as soon as possible."

Liza then said that she must join the men as they had a great deal to discuss.

"Of course, you must think about your own future," said Leonora.

"It is your future also Leonora, so if you feel up to it, please join us," said Liza.

They went down and joined Jamie and Charles who were in the dining room studying maps.

"I think that Roberts and Susan should also be here," said Liza. "And the Cavanaughs and O'Rourkes also as their input could be invaluable."

"I'll find them," said Charles and he left the room and made his way down to the kitchens.

Susan and Roberts entered the room cautiously and Liza told them to sit at the table. They looked uneasy and even more so when Toby and Maggie also arrived; they were also guided to chairs around the table. Mrs Cavanaugh and Mrs O'Rourke came in, both wiping their hands on their aprons. Charles then walked in telling them that Mr O'Rourke would find Mr Cavanaugh and they would be there shortly.

Charles joined Jamie who was looking closely at a map; everyone was quiet with concerned looks on their faces.

Mr O'Rourke and Mr Cavanaugh looked into the dining room and Charles beckoned them in and told them to sit down.

He looked around at everyone and said, "We have been informed of a very serious concern relating to Lord and Lady Edgeworth. I know that those of you who live here may well have loyalties towards the Confederacy and if those loyalties transcend those that you have for me and this house, then I would ask you to leave the room now and I will respect your decision."

Nobody moved. "I will also ask that whatever we discuss here today goes no further; it is important that confidence is kept."

Everyone nodded. Charles then outlined the reasons why alternative routes had to be found for Liza, Jamie, Leonora, Roberts and Susan to get to New York and then on to England.

"That's outrageous," exclaimed Mrs Cavanaugh.

"I gather that making our way up the coast to another port is out of the question," said Roberts.

"I'm sure they will have thought of that and will be looking out for us," said Jamie. "They know that most of the ships at places like Wilmington are Marchant & Fuller ships and they will be under constant surveillance as will the route up the coast. We believe that our best option is to travel inland to Kentucky and find a port back across land which comes under northern control."

"Sir, both Maggie and I have spent very little time away from here, so there is really nothing that we would be able to add which could assist you," said Toby.

"Toby," said Charles. "Although Lord and Lady Edgeworth have every right to leave here whenever they wish, it will be obvious that we have helped them and there may be repercussions so you will be involved regardless of whether or not you have been able to assist."

"If we can leave before it becomes officially known that they want us to stay, then there should be no repercussions," said Liza. "We must therefore make plans for our departure, hopefully within the next couple of days."

Mr Cavanaugh and Mr O'Rourke began studying the maps with Charles and Jamie and they discussed the best route to be taken. Mrs Cavanaugh and Mrs O'Rourke concentrated on the food and drink which would be useful to take, and Roberts and Susan started planning the clothes needed.

"We won't be able to take many clothes," said Liza. "And any that we do take must be functional or adapted to be so."

"I can help you with that," said Maggie to Susan.

"I can guide you out of the plantation the back way," said Mr Cavanaugh, "and head you in the right direction for Kentucky, but I'm afraid you will be on your own after that, so you will have to plan your route very carefully."

"Have any of you ever driven a wagon before?" asked Charles.

Everyone but Liza was shaking their heads. "I did drive one many years ago, however it was with oxen and not horses. I haven't driven anything over two horses recently."

All eyes had turned to Liza when she said that.

"Oxen" muttered Jamie. "Did you say oxen? Aren't they difficult to control?"

"No, they were very slow and lumbering but very strong and reliable. Horses are faster but can be a little unpredictable," said Liza.

"Well, I didn't know you had done that Liza," said Jamie with a smile which relieved the tension around the table.

"I've driven a carriage and four," said Roberts. "I am sure I could handle a wagon. Would that also have four horses?"

"It could have six, but I think that four would be adequate and easier to manage," said Mr Cavanaugh.

"Would one wagon be enough?" asked Mrs O'Rourke.

"It will have to be," said Liza. "There are going to be five of us, so we will have to have two riders. I presume you will be riding Jamie; Roberts and I can take it in turns to drive the wagon and ride."

"I'll be able to take my turn in driving the wagon," said Jamie. "I'm sure I will soon get used to four horses rather than the two that I am used to."

"Of course you will," smiled Liza.

"I've driven two horses also," said Leonora, "so I'm sure I will be able to take a turn at driving."

"It's good that you are all used to handling horses, although slightly differently to what we are planning," said Charles. "Everyone's input is necessary regarding food, clothing, sleeping arrangements, horse handling and anything else you might think of."

"I believe that we should all think about what we have discussed and meet again at dinner time around this table. We can all say what we have come up with whilst we eat," said Charles and he noticed Toby and Maggie's strange look. "You too Toby and Maggie, you must also be with us, after all it does affect you."

Sitting around the table that evening brought forth many positive ideas and as they talked the question of armaments was touched upon.

"You will need at least a couple of rifles as well as a couple of pistols," said Charles. "I presume that as you were in the army at one time Jamie, you do know how to use a rifle and pistol."

"Yes, I was trained in both, but I have never fired a shot in anger," said Jamie. Liza knew that it was not true as he had at one time attempted to shoot her and he was prepared to kill Patrick in a duel, but she said nothing.

"I have used both in the past," said Roberts and both Jamie and Liza were not surprised as they knew that Roberts had had a chequered past.

"I did have quite some lessons when I was in Benson," said Liza quietly.

Jamie looked at her and realised that it was something else that he had not known about his wife. Charles continued, ignoring the surprise on Jamie's face, "In that case you will need three of each. Does anyone else know how to use a weapon?"

Leonora and Susan shook their heads.

Mrs Cavanaugh and Mrs O'Rourke discussed what food could be needed and Maggie was going to help Susan to sort out the clothes for the ladies.

"My jewellery will have to be sewn into my clothes, as will any that Leonora has," said Liza.

Toby was going to help Roberts to sort out what Jamie would need, as travelling in either a wagon or on horseback needed far more serviceable clothes than Jamie's usual attire.

With dinner over, the table was cleared and maps were laid out which were studied in minute detail.

Their discussions went on until late into the night and finally when Liza and Jamie were alone it was difficult for them not to show the concern that they felt.

"This has been a very unsettling day for us," said Jamie. "I had no idea that you had driven a wagon before. I also did not know that you knew anything about firearms.

"I drove a wagon for about half a day around twenty years ago and learned how to shoot when I was in Benson. It was essential to have that knowledge when I was there, although I never had a chance to use it, but I wish that I had," said Liza bitterly.

"There are still so many things that I don't know about you," said Jamie slightly coldly.

Liza looked at him and frowned. "I know how to light a fire with a stick, and I know how to cook on an open fire, not very successfully admittedly. I know how to sew with a bone needle and cut thread with my teeth. I know how to ride without a saddle. What else would you like to know?"

"Do you remember the times that I was always apologising to you; Amelia commented on it," said Jamie and Liza nodded. "Well, I'm just about to do it again."

"There's no need Jamie and if I remember correctly Amelia said that we were both forever apologising to one another, so let's not do that," said Liza. "By the way, you told a lie this evening."

"I know, I saw your face when I did. I said that I had never fired a shot in anger," said Jamie, "and I was so angry with you the day that I did that," Jamie was kissing her and fondling her, "but I'm certainly not angry with you now," he whispered as he started making love to her.

***

"I think that we should go to the docks again and bother the shipping agent one more time as it will seem that we are not planning to leave by any means other than sailing," said Jamie over breakfast.

Roberts volunteered to go with him as Mr O'Rourke and Mr Cavanaugh were needed to get the wagon ready and sort out the horses for it. Charles wanted to make sure that all was being managed correctly and out of sight of anyone who may visit unexpectedly.

Liza, Leonora and Susan were organising the clothes that they were to take, and Maggie was making pockets that would take the valuables that they needed to hide. When they had finished, they were going to sort out the bedding that would be useful.

Just before lunch they heard horses arriving and they all assumed that Jamie and Roberts had returned until it became obvious that the noise was coming from more than two riders. Looking out of her window Liza could see that it was a contingent of Confederate soldiers and she told Susan and Leonora to hide the clothes that they had been working on and told Maggie to tidy the two rooms that they had been working in, but hopefully the soldiers would not be going upstairs anyway.

She smiled at them and told them to keep calm and remain where they were unless they were called. With that she slowly walked down the stairs and into Charles' study leaving the door open and taking a book she sat and pretended to read. It was not long before she heard raised voices, one being Charles'. A shiver went up her spine as she had lived through this experience before.

Liza sighed and decided that there was only one way to face the situation and that was head on, so she stood up and still carrying her book she made her way out into the hall where Toby was standing looking very worried.

"Don't go out there Miss Liza; stay here with me, Mr Charles will handle it," said Toby.

Liza put a hand on his arm and said, "I have to go, Toby; I must try to diffuse the situation."

Still carrying her book Liza quickly made her way to the front door and started to run down the steps to where Charles was standing face to face with a Confederate lieutenant.

"Did you call me Charles? I heard my name mentioned," she said.

Charles turned and came face to face with an impossibly innocent looking Liza.

He said, "No Liza, I didn't call you, perhaps it would be better for you to go back inside," but he knew her well enough to know that she was playing for time and that she was going to twist this lieutenant around her little finger.

"Oh I thought that you had called me," and she turned to leave.

"Just a minute," said the lieutenant gruffly and Liza turned with a frown on her brow.

"I'm sorry, were you talking to me?" said Liza.

"Yes, I was," said the lieutenant.

"You haven't introduced me to the lieutenant, Charles," said Liza still with a frown and also having emphasised the English pronunciation of 'leftenant'. Charles knew that she was trying to distract the soldiers so that anything in the house to do with her leaving was tidied away and giving Mr O'Rourke and Mr Cavanaugh time to disguise what they were doing with a wagon.

"There is no need Liza, the lieutenant and his men are just leaving," said Charles although he knew that they had no intention of leaving.

"You are to come with us," said the lieutenant.

"Is he talking to me Charles?" asked a mystified looking Liza.

Oh Liza, thought Charles, *you are playing this game so well*. He then said, "I believe he is, but his social graces are sadly lacking."

"Oh," said Liza as she started walking back up the steps towards the door.

"Hey," shouted the lieutenant.

Liza carried on walking and Charles said, "Her name is Lady Edgeworth, not 'Hey'."

The lieutenant pursed his lips and nearly choked as he called, "Lady Edgeworth; I'd like a word with you."

Liza stopped and turned and waited with a questioning eyebrow raised.

"Lady Edgeworth, I have been commanded to bring you and your husband to our headquarters in Charleston," said the lieutenant.

"I am sorry Lieutenant, but you have had a wasted journey. My husband is already in Charleston trying to secure our passage home and I have no plans to visit there until we are able to leave," said Liza.

"My orders are to bring you into town to talk to our Colonel," said the lieutenant.

"Your orders may be that Lieutenant, but I do not know your Colonel and I have no wish to talk to him. I shall go into town when I wish to and not when it pleases your Colonel. Good day Lieutenant," said Liza and she turned again and walked up the steps and through the front door.

Mr O'Rourke and Mr Cavanaugh sauntered towards Charles and at the same time Jamie and Roberts rode up. Jamie quickly dismounted and asked Charles if there was a problem.

"Not as far as I am concerned," said Charles. "The lieutenant was trying to persuade your wife to go into town with him, but she refused."

"I should think so," said Jamie, carrying on with the game of words that Liza had started. "She has no reason to go into town. Why did you want her to go into town Lieutenant?"

"My Colonel Morrison wants to question you both," said the lieutenant.

"About what, Lieutenant?" asked Jamie.

"It's not my place to tell you that," said the lieutenant.

"Well, if that's the case then I suggest you tell your Colonel if he wants to talk to us, he knows where we are," said Jamie and he also made his way up the steps leaving the lieutenant not knowing what to say or do.

Charles looked at the lieutenant and said, "You have your answer, Lieutenant. Good day to you."

Charles also walked up the steps and closed the door firmly, with the lieutenant silently staring after him. He suddenly made a decision and snapped at two of his men telling them to guard the house and make sure that the Edgeworths did not leave. With that he rode off to face the wrath of Colonel Morrison.

Inside the house Jamie found Liza standing in the study still clasping the book that she had been pretending to read. "Are you alright Liza? I didn't think that they would come to find us so soon."

Charles joined them. "Unfortunately the lieutenant has left two soldiers to guard the house. We will have to think carefully about what we can do."

"At least they are outside the house; we can carry on with our preparations, but when we can leave is anyone's guess," said Liza.

Leonora was in her bedroom and Susan was with her and they both looked up expectantly when Liza came in.

"I'm afraid that two soldiers have been left here to guard us," said Liza. She told them about the lieutenant insisting that she go into town.

"How have you managed to stay then?" asked Leonora.

"I told him that I didn't want to go into town," said Liza.

"That must have annoyed him," said Leonora.

"He had no right to demand anything of me. I am not a subject of this country; I am a British citizen, and they cannot tell me what to do," said Liza.

They continued preparing for their departure but were dismayed to see that the two soldiers had been replaced by six dispersed around the house. Mrs Cavanaugh wanted to know if they were supposed to feed the soldiers and Charles was adamant that they should not.

"We have not asked them to be here and quite honestly, I'm sure that they have better things to do with their time and they probably feel that way themselves. If they haven't brought food and water with them, then more fool them. When they are tired, hot, hungry and thirsty then they won't be so observant. I'm sure that when some time has passed, they will be recalled to more important duties," said Charles.

"I know you're right Charles," said Liza, "but it does seem a little harsh."

"I presume you can let the smell of your excellent cooking waft from your kitchen out to the soldiers," smiled Charles at Mrs Cavanaugh.

"I'm sure I can, but sometimes you can win people over through their stomachs," said Mrs Cavanaugh.

"Well, we'll try both ways; first of all my way and then yours," smiled Charles.

Unfortunately neither plan appeared to be working as the number of soldiers increased over the following days.

To carry on with the subterfuge they decided to send either Mr Cavanaugh or Mr O'Rourke to the docks with Roberts each day to enquire about sailings, but everything was ready for them to leave at a moment's notice.

Chapter 9

The weeks were passing, and they were now well into May. They could only imagine the concern that was being felt both in Ireland and England over their continued absence.

There were reports of fierce battles taking place between the Union and Confederate soldiers but still they were being guarded by soldiers who would be better employed elsewhere.

Both Liza and Jamie were concerned that if they did manage to leave, serious reprisals would be taken against Charles, the Cavanaughs and the O'Rourkes.

When Roberts returned from one of his trips to Charleston, he had Joanne with him as although she was not being treated as an enemy, she was a woman alone and now her employment had all but disappeared and an unruly element had appeared in town.

Charles, Jamie and Liza were pleased that she felt that she could rely on them; however she was another person who would have to keep their secret and they were now responsible for her safety.

On the same day Mr O'Rourke came back with the information that millions of bales of cotton were being burned on the dockside and all plantation owners were asked to burn their own stocks.

"Why?" was Liza's question.

"Because for some strange reason they believe that England will support the Southern cause if they burn all the cotton," said Mr O'Rourke.

"Of course they think that it will damage the British textile industry severely, if not irreparably, but they are wrong. Do not burn yours Charles; it will make absolutely no difference to how Britain will act. It is insane and those who are ordering it have not done their homework," said Liza passionately.

Charles was looking curiously at Liza and Jamie put his hand on her shoulder. "Liza, I don't believe that you will be breaking any confidences by telling Charles what you know."

Liza was finding it difficult to say anything, she felt disloyal, but she did not know why. Charles was her friend and there was really nothing secret about her business knowledge of the cotton and textile trade.

"For the past five or six years the English textile industry has been stock piling cotton. They were warned that if a civil war broke out in this country it could disastrously affect not only their income but that of those who relied on them to keep their families in food and a roof over their heads," said Liza.

Charles sat down and said, "I see. When I came to England for your charity function nearly six years ago, I remember Lord Palmerston and the Duke of Norfolk being very anxious to talk to you and I also remember their interest in both the views that Henry and I held on the subject of the differences between the north and south of my country. Could that be the time when your textile industry began with their contingency plans to keep their mills in business?"

"I have no idea Charles," said Liza. "All I do know is that my Company began shipping vast amounts of cotton; much more than was needed at the time. If you want to put that down to me then I cannot stop you, but you must also appreciate that I am not the only one to foresee what could occur should a civil war erupt between the two factions in your country."

Charles thought about it for a while and then said, "Of course you wouldn't be the only one to read the future situation, but you are one of the few people who would see what is being imported into your country and work out why. I will take your advice and hold onto my cotton as long as possible and you are right, somebody has not done their homework correctly."

"I do not divulge business matters to anyone, not even to Jamie, but I must change some of my thoughts on that as long as it is not deemed as insider trading. Today is a case in point as should I not have been here you would have sent up in smoke something that could eventually keep you alive, although that may not be until the war is over," said Liza.

"No wonder the army of the south are anxious to keep you here," said Charles. "You know many things that could be useful to them; we really must take the chance and get you out of this situation as soon as possible."

"If you really think that Charles, then we must leave but we must appear to steal horses and go with nothing other than what we stand up in," said Jamie. "You will have to report to the soldiers some hours after we have left that we are missing; that should keep you and all else in this household safe."

"I know that the soldiers surrounding this house are getting very bored, but they are still very vigilant. I suppose we could tempt them with alcohol," said Charles.

"I'm not sure that Susan can ride," said Jamie. "I know Roberts can, but can Leonora?"

"All the plans that we made nearly a month ago have come to nothing, the only advantage is that we have preparations in place that we can adjust for a quick exit," said Liza. "I suppose it will take us a couple of days to be ready."

"Mr O'Rourke tells me that the fighting is getting nearer, and many residents are leaving, mostly by ship, so there is no reason why you should not travel by sea, but you will of course be stopped. Perhaps we could pretend that you have left that way and they will be sent on a wild goose chase," said Charles.

"It's a possibility, although we may be clutching at straws," said Liza.

They were disturbed that night by the constant sound of rifle fire. At five o'clock in the morning everyone was awake as they knew that the war had been brought to them.

"That is so close," said Charles, "that it must be on my land. I've looked out and the soldiers around the house seem to be unsure of themselves. I wonder what is happening. I suppose I should find out."

"No, don't Charles," said Liza. "It would be best if you did not. You will know soon enough."

"What are you thinking, Liza?" asked Jamie.

"Nothing Jamie, but I do know how the army works and if we get in the way we could be in serious trouble, even though it is your land Charles," said Liza.

The O'Rourkes and the Cavanaughs made their way to them. "We didn't want to be alone in our own homes," said Mrs Cavanaugh. "We felt that there is safety in numbers. The soldiers that we passed really don't know what's happening, but the shots are getting very close."

"I think that the opportunity may be presenting itself for us to leave," said Jamie. "While all this is going on we may be able to slip away unnoticed."

"You could be right," said Charles. "The wagon has been ready for weeks; we will just have to put some food and water in it. Perhaps you should get dressed now."

Joanne was looking puzzled however it was slowly dawning on her that the plantation may not be as safe a place to be as she had assumed, but she just accepted the situation and asked what she could do to help.

By six o'clock they were all dressed, but the fighting was now so near the house that the soldiers guarding the house were preparing to retaliate. Some bullets came through the windows, and they all had to take cover behind various pieces of furniture. It was now too dangerous for any of them to consider leaving.

For the next half hour the battle became more ferocious, and nobody could move. They were all lying on the floor; Jamie was protecting Liza and Charles was doing his best to cover both Leonora and Joanne. Roberts had a protective arm around Susan. Toby and Maggie were huddled together in a corner and the O'Rourkes and the Cavanaughs were under the large dining table.

Suddenly it became very quiet. Liza had not realised that Jamie and Charles were holding pistols. Mr O'Rourke and Mr Cavanaugh had rifles. There were shouts all around the house followed by the crashing sound of the front door being kicked in. Liza could feel Jamie stiffen and clasp his gun tightly aiming it towards the door.

A voice that stirred old memories for Liza shouted but it was indistinct. The voice called out again.

"Liza, are you there? Where are you hiding?" shouted Bart Shaw.

Liza gasped and tried to stand up, but Jamie pulled her back down.

"It's alright Jamie, it's Bart and he's obviously come to help us," said Liza and before Jamie could stop her, she was rushing out into the hallway and into Bart's arms.

"Well, that's one of the best greetings I've ever had," smiled Bart.

"I'm so pleased to see you, Bart; what are you doing here?" asked Liza.

"Apart from the fact that there is a war on; we've come to rescue you," smiled Bart. The sergeant with him was also smiling.

"Really? How did you know I was here?" asked Liza.

"You're always headline news Liza. We've known that you were being held here for some time; there are a lot of people worrying about you," said Bart.

"I've been well looked after, but we were not able to leave," said Liza.

Bart looked at Jamie and saluted him and then at Charles and did the same.

"We'll get you all underway as soon as we can; Confederate reinforcements could be here in a while, although we did take them by surprise."

There was another noise at the front door and Bart smiled and said that there was somebody else there who was an old friend, and she instinctively knew who that was. She rushed through the dining room door and straight into the arms of Sean who whispered "Got'cha" as he had done when he had rescued her from the Cherokees after Patrick had died.

The relief that Jamie and Charles felt was plain to see. Sean looked over the top of Liza's head and nodded to Jamie and then said that he presumed that it was Charles Enderby with him.

"Yes, Captain," said Charles. "We are pleased to see you, although I won't be shouting about that when you have gone."

"How soon can you be ready to leave," asked Sean still holding Liza in his arms.

"We have a wagon which has been ready for some weeks," said Jamie. "We need to organise the horses and some food and water. We already changed for the journey hoping to take the opportunity to leave whilst the fighting was going on. However we must ensure that no reprisals are taken on those who are remaining here."

"We'll leave within the hour," said Sean who still had his arms around Liza.

"I gather you are pleased to see my wife, Captain," said Jamie laughing.

Sean also laughed and said, "Liza has always made me feel that normality has returned to my life, but I had better let her go so that she can prepare to leave with us."

"How are we going to protect Charles and everyone else here?" Liza asked Sean.

"Our instructions are a scorched earth policy; so we will have to set light to this place," said Sean.

A look of horror crossed all their faces.

"You will not," said Liza with conviction.

"No, you are right, I will not. It is a senseless policy, but just let me know which barns and warehouses will cause the least damage and we will set light to those as we leave. Also we have some prisoners and some who are wounded and if you drive them into town for treatment when we have left, then I'm sure you will not be blamed for tonight's events," said Sean.

"I'll arrange that those getting the wagon and horses ready will be seen to be carrying out instruction with our guns pointed at them," said Bart. "Don't worry Liza, we know that your friends need protection. Of course before they take our prisoners into town, they will have to try to put out the flames, so that will give us some time."

"So you are finally going to leave us," said Charles. "I want you to know Captain that in this house we have loyalties neither to the north nor to the south. I suppose that one day we may be forced to take sides and because of where we are, our loyalties will have to be to the south. I told Liza that I may well have to fight for my country and her response was to ask where that might be. She was right, America is my country, but I am a southerner and I hope that I do not meet you in battle, Captain; I hope that I do not have to meet anyone that I know in such circumstances. It will be bad enough meeting fellow Americans at such a time."

"What about your slaves?" asked Sean indicating Toby and Maggie. "Another order that we are given is to free all slaves as we go."

"There are no slaves here, Captain," said Charles. "I have never agreed with owning another human being. Toby and Maggie are as free as you and I and have always been free to leave whenever they wish."

"It would seem that you have gone against the local trend, which cannot have made you very popular with your fellow southerners," commented Sean.

"I work well with my neighbours, Captain," smiled Charles.

"Having seen what you do here and what you store here, I would say that it's a case of them needing you rather than you needing them," said Sean.

Liza smiled and left them so that she could complete her arrangements for leaving. Leonora and Susan were packed and waiting for their final instructions. Roberts had everything ready for his departure and Jamie came along the corridor dressed as she had seen him many years before when he and Edward had come for her when Patrick had died. He looked striking in very casual clothes.

Charles was in the dining room with Sean and Bart, and he was showing them the route to take through his property which was relatively obscure.

"We will see you outside in a short while," said Sean who could see that Liza wanted a private word with Charles.

"Take care, Liza," said Charles. "None of us realised just how important you are to your country; I don't think that you even realised it."

Liza handed him her diamond tiara. "Take this Charles. Remove each diamond when you need it; they will keep you and everyone here in food for quite a while."

"I don't need it, Liza; I have money; you know that I have," said Charles.

"Yes, I know that you have, but I also know that no further cash has arrived at our bank for some weeks now, and you will shortly have a Confederate currency, which will be valued at much less than normal currency. You may well be able to draw a little cash, but shortly you will have no means of bargaining. This trinket of mine should keep you, the O'Rourkes, Cavanaughs, Joanne, Toby and Maggie in food for quite some time," said Liza.

"I can't take your jewellery; you will need it yourself. It has sentimental meaning for you," said Charles.

"It has no sentimental meaning for me. It is something that I bought for myself some years ago. I have enough jewellery with me to keep us out of trouble if necessary. Hopefully you won't need it and when we next meet, you will be able to place it on my head in readiness for a magnificent ball," said Liza.

Charles put his arms around her and held her closely; she was crying silently, and she could not be sure that Charles was not also. Jamie came into the room and saw Charles holding Liza's tiara and nodded his approval.

"I hope you won't need it Charles, but I have a sinking feeling that you will," said Jamie.

The food and water had been packed as had the pistols and rifles. Most of Jamie's and Liza's clothes were left and Liza told Charles to get what he could for them. Charles was about to protest again but Mrs Cavanaugh stepped in and said that she would see to it should it become necessary.

They said their goodbyes in the privacy of the house and then went outside and Liza, Susan and Leonora climbed into the wagon with Jamie and Roberts mounting their horses. Bart climbed up into the driving seat and he grinned at her and said that he did not expect her to drive as he knew that she had become used to the soft life in England.

As they drove off, they could see Mr O'Rourke and Mr Cavanaugh helping the prisoners and the wounded men into carts, but then a shout went up and two barns and a warehouse were set alight, but Sean played his part well and yelled that there was no time for that, and they all raced away without the opportunity for a backward glance.

They went at a fast pace for the first hour, and then slowed to conserve the horses. Liza asked Bart about Laurie and Greg and all else in Benson. He said that it had been a while since he was there, but they were all well when he had last seen them.

Some of the soldiers had left to join the south, but most of them fought under the Union flag. The fort at Benson was now manned by a few soldiers as most were away on the battle fronts. The Colonel had come out of retirement to cover for Marshall who was normally in charge of the fort but was also away.

As far as he knew nobody from the town had joined the army, but he felt that it was only a matter of time, and most would become Union soldiers. It was early days of the war, and they were still hoping that it could all be settled amicably shortly.

Jamie and Roberts were riding with Sean and a sergeant, and Susan and Leonora were resting in the wagon and listening to Liza and Bart's conversation. They had not realised that Liza had led such an exciting life in the past. Leonora suddenly realised that it was not in the past that her life had been exciting, it still was.

"How did you know where we were?" asked Liza.

"Our information was that you were visiting friends in Charleston and when the Confederate generals started negotiating with Britain to join their cause and said that one or two of their citizens would be under their protection until it was established exactly who England would be supporting, it didn't take long for it to be worked out exactly who they were talking about. Also it was known that you had not returned when you had planned. I believe that the British government confronted the representatives of the Confederacy who admitted that you and your husband were their bargaining chips," said Bart.

"I would think that it was like a red rag to a bull; Britain will not be blackmailed into joining in a war," said Liza.

"No, you're right; so our Union government told us to come and get you and not to return without you," said Bart.

"Really? I don't know many in your government. I haven't yet met Abraham Lincoln; I'm surprised that they were concerned," said Liza.

Bart laughed. "I seem to recollect that it has been mentioned that you are naïve in many ways, and very bright in others. Obviously your comment is one of your naïve moments. Your Companies make you important and being a member of the British aristocracy makes you high on the list of those who must be protected at all costs."

They travelled for some hours and as evening approached, they camped in a clearing and guards were posted. A fire was lit, and Liza came to help with cooking some food, but there was a chorus from Sean, Bart and Jamie to leave well enough alone with Bart adding that they wanted to survive this trip.

"I've made a few good meals in my time," muttered Liza scowling.

Sean and Jamie were sitting together, and Liza sauntered over to them, and they made room between them for her. Susan handed her a plate and she looked up and thanked her. Roberts and Sergeant Rowe seemed to be communicating well, which did not surprise Liza as she was no longer amazed by anything that Roberts did or had done in the past. Bart was keeping an amused eye on Liza; she had always entertained him and no matter how lofty her title might be, to him she had not changed, and he realised that he missed her and especially her sense of fun. Laurie would be pleased that he had met up with her; she had been instrumental in not only his promotion but in helping to get Laurie accepted by the people of Benson.

Leonora was beginning to yawn, and Liza realised how tired she was also. Susan was getting their bedding organised in the wagon and Leonora commented that it was going to be cosy for the three of them in the wagon.

"I won't be sleeping in the wagon," announced Liza. "So there'll be plenty of room for you both."

"Where will you be?" asked Jamie.

"Wherever you are," said Liza. "I've slept on the ground before."

Sean smiled at her, and he thought that she had not really changed. He had been watching the way she and Jamie talked together and he could see that she loved him, but it was not the way that she and Patrick had loved one another. She and Jamie had a gentle, caring love and not the passion that had been between Liza and Patrick. He was pleased that she had made a good life for herself and for her boys. He knew that Jamie had loved her for a very long time and his patience had been rewarded, sadly through the death of Patrick, his dearest friend.

Liza jumped up and grabbed her bedding as Jamie was rolling his blankets out. She placed hers next to his and lay down covering herself with her blanket. Jamie looked down and smiled at her and then settled himself next to her. He whispered that they were going to have to control their urges over the next days and she laughed with him.

Sean, Bart and Sergeant Rowe were discussing plans for the next day and making sure that fresh guards were on duty for the following few hours and then Sean made his way to where Liza and Jamie were lying, and he unrolled his bedding and placed it next to Liza which was just naturally accepted by her. She turned and smiled at him, happy to be between these two men.

Bart was relaxing leaning up against a tree and he looked towards Liza and smiled as she was sleeping between the two men that she cared the most about in this world and who cared the most for her.

Roberts had made his bed under the wagon and Sergeant Rowe was nearby. Bart realised that although this man was a posh valet, he had a past which made him a great deal more worldly than he appeared and he had made the ladies his responsibility.

One of Bart's talents was to analyse people, and many times it had meant that he was one step ahead of those who were threatening. Now he was thinking about the two women who were travelling with them. The young one was apparently Liza's maid. She was nervous, which was understandable, but she would have a wonderful story to tell when she returned home. The other woman, Leonora, was a sad lady, either she had lost her husband, or he was in the war. She sounded like someone from New York, and he supposed that was why she was travelling with them. A northerner would not have a very comfortable life in a place like Charleston, so it was best that she was with them.

He once again checked around the area and then settled down for the night with his last thoughts being of Laurie and wishing that he was with her.

At some time during the night Liza turned and ended up with her head comfortably on Jamie's chest; he woke slightly and remembered her doing that some years ago when he had come to find her. He put his arm around her and heard her sigh and he thought that she was not the only one to feel contentment, he felt the same.

***

Leonora and Susan climbed down from the wagon early the next morning and were surprised to find that they were the last to rise. Roberts handed them a plate of food each and poured them some coffee.

Liza looked up and asked them if they had slept well. Susan said that she had slept surprisingly well.

"I did also," said Leonora. "I suppose it's because it was such a long day yesterday."

"I think we'll have another long day again today," said Liza. "We've crossed into North Carolina, and we have to head a short way through Tennessee before we reach Kentucky, and both North Carolina and Tennessee have now seceded. Kentucky is trying to remain neutral and once we reach there, we won't have to look over our shoulders quite so much."

"Unfortunately it doesn't mean that we won't come across Confederate soldiers wherever we travel, even in neutral Kentucky," said Sean

They were on their way again soon after breakfast and this time Sergeant Rowe was driving the wagon. Liza noticed that Jamie looked a little uncomfortable, but as he had not spent all day in the saddle for a very long time, it was understandable. She wondered whether Roberts was also feeling the same way. She would offer to change with him in an hour or so.

They stopped to rest at midday and Liza told Roberts that she felt that she would like to ride for a while, and he could take her place in the wagon. He looked at her gratefully whilst asking if she was sure that she could manage.

"It's been a while since I rode but I was an adequate horsewoman in the past," smiled Liza, talking more confidently than she felt.

Liza mounted the horse and rode up to Jamie and they rode off side by side, chatting as they went. Sean and Bart watched as they went, making sure that Liza was riding safely.

It did not take her long to get back into the rhythm of riding and it perked Jamie up by having her ride next to him. Leonora offered to let Jamie rest in the wagon, but he said that he would like to take her up on her offer the next morning, if she still felt able.

By the evening both Liza and Jamie were so tired that they could hardly eat their supper. A stew was served and as Liza ate, she managed to dribble a little down her chin; Jamie took out a handkerchief and absentmindedly wiped her chin much to the amusement of Sean who had seen Patrick do the same thing on so many occasions. *She most definitely hasn't changed*, thought Sean.

She felt warm sitting in front of the fire. Her eyes kept closing and she put her head on Jamie's shoulder and went to sleep. Bart laid out her sleeping blankets and Jamie carefully lifted her and laid her down, covering her with a blanket. She hardly moved throughout the night and was surprised to find that it was daylight when she awoke.

Jamie decided that he would attempt to drive the wagon that day, so Leonora mounted his horse and Roberts accompanied her on his. Susan stretched out in the back of the wagon with Liza sitting next to Jamie. Bart decided to ride next to the wagon just in case Jamie experienced any trouble with the horses.

They crossed into Tennessee near lunchtime that day and so far they had managed to avoid contact with any other person, but they would be passing through farmland and near a town and even if they were spotted, it was imperative that nobody discovered who the soldiers were guiding and protecting.

Sean rode up and suggested that Liza hide in the wagon whilst they neared the town.

"Nobody knows me here Sean; I shouldn't think that I would be known anywhere along our route. I'm sure I haven't been here before," smiled Liza.

"Anyone with southern sympathies could know as much as we do, especially those in authority in the town," said Sean.

"They don't know what we look like," said Liza. "And they can't possibly yet know that we have left Charleston."

"Maybe not, but you are travelling with Union soldiers so they will think that you are northern sympathisers which will not be healthy for you in a southern state," said Sean. "I have always found it surprising how quickly the word spreads from one town to another. Lieutenant Shaw is going into the town to see what the mood is and if there are any Confederate soldiers in the area."

Bart appeared out of uniform, and he had Sergeant Rowe with him, also in civilian clothes. They rode off towards the town and Sean ordered the wagon and the soldiers to slowly go on their way. Roberts took the reins with Jamie next to him and Liza, Leonora and Susan stayed out of sight in the wagon.

They carried on slowly for a couple of hours and then finally heard horses catching them up. It was Bart and Sergeant Rowe and they reported directly to Sean.

"Well," said Sean. "The town is not friendly, and we could expect to come face to face with a few Confederate soldiers, but it doesn't appear that they know anything about you. We'll just carry on until dark and see where we end up for the night. The horses will need resting soon."

They travelled until the light faded and made camp in a small clearing. They lit no fire that evening and just ate biscuits for their meal. Liza was advised to sleep in the wagon that night which she was not happy about. If there was going to be a fight she wanted to be with Jamie.

"I will be under the wagon," Jamie said to Liza. "Roberts and I will be guarding you all and it will be safe for us under there. Sean has posted double guards tonight, and we will have to take our turn later tonight. I want to know where you are should anything happen."

Sean came over and said, "You know the drill, Liza; if you hear shooting lie flat and hopefully the wagon base will stop anything hitting you. Please don't try to run anywhere as we won't be able to look after you; we will have a hard enough time looking after ourselves. Pack whatever you can against the edges; that should stop the bullets."

Liza nodded, she had been in that situation before but then she had been avoiding arrows, not bullets. She looked at Susan and Leonora and they looked concerned but started padding the edges of the wagon with whatever they could find.

"Nothing may happen," said Liza reassuringly.

They managed to get relatively comfortable for the night and Liza slept fitfully. She could hear Jamie and Roberts talking for a while and then all was quiet. Just before dawn the horses started nickering and Liza realised that either they were being harnessed or there were intruders around. Unfortunately it was the latter, and it was not long before shots were being fired. Liza prayed that all would be safe, and she lay as flat as she could in the wagon, as did Leonora and Susan.

The fight only lasted around ten minutes and Liza heard Jamie calling her name and telling her that it was safe for them to come out. One or two of their soldiers had slight wounds but there were three dead Confederate soldiers and two wounded. Only five had taken on Sean's much larger troop. Sean was shaking his head sadly and he ordered his men to put the dead soldiers over their horses and made sure that the wounded were capable of going back to the town for treatment.

"It's not easy fighting your own countrymen. Unfortunately we are going to have to do a great deal of it in the future. Are you ladies alright? I trust that you two haven't been wounded?" said Sean directing his question to Jamie and Roberts.

"We have come away unscathed," said Roberts. "We did get in one or two shots."

"We had better get underway," said Sean. "We can't stop for breakfast, so we'll have to eat on the way. Biscuits again I'm afraid."

Sergeant Rowe came to drive the wagon, he said that it would be quicker if he did and told Jamie and Roberts to stay close to the wagon. With the horses harnessed and the Confederate soldiers sent on their way, they set off quickly and made good time.

"We should reach Kentucky either late tonight or early tomorrow morning," said Sergeant Rowe. "We will have to rest the horses in an hour or so."

When they pulled up, Bart rode in. Liza had not realised that he had not been with them and then Sean came to them.

"We are being followed by about half a dozen men, but they don't appear to be in uniform but this is a southern state so we must assume that their allegiance is to the Confederacy," said Sean.

"What are we going to do?" asked Jamie.

"We'll have to face them head on here," said Sean. "Our horses are tired so we wouldn't be able to get much further. I don't think that they realise that we know they are there. Better keep your head down Liza and tell your ladies to do the same."

"I have a gun Sean and am quite capable of using it," said Liza.

"I know you are Liza; you were taught by the best, as was I, but you have never shot at anyone, would you be able to do that?" said Sean.

"If my family or friends are threatened then I wouldn't hesitate," said Liza adamantly.

Susan and Leonora climbed down from the wagon to stretch their legs. "We'll soon be in Kentucky," Sean said to them.

Jamie put his arm around Liza. "Will you really be able to shoot a person?"

"Yes, Jamie I will. We must take sides unfortunately and that means helping to protect Susan, Leonora, Roberts and all those who are protecting us," said Liza.

"I gather that Patrick was a very good shot," said Jamie.

"He always hit what he aimed for. He taught many in the army; they always called him their sharpshooter," said Liza smiling at a memory.

"So when I called him out, I didn't stand a chance of winning," said Jamie thoughtfully. "You saved my life then, Liza."

"You could have killed him, and you would have been in more trouble than you were," said Liza.

"I wasn't that good a shot," said Jamie.

"No you weren't, thank goodness, because if you were I wouldn't be here now," smiled Liza. "But you have improved since then."

"You don't seem frightened by what may soon be happening," said Jamie.

"I've been in many frightening situations over the years Jamie, and I've learned not to show my fear," said Liza. "I will admit to you that I am very frightened, but I must try to reassure Susan and Leonora, they haven't been in a situation like this before."

"Neither have I, Liza," said Jamie. "Have you really been here before?"

"Yes, I have, but as I said before it was with bows and arrows pointing at me. It took me a long while to learn not to show fear. There have been times when I forgot how to do that, but today is a day when I mustn't show what I feel," said Liza.

"Neither of us must," said Jamie. "I'll talk to Roberts, although I think he may have seen more action than I have. When I've seen him, I'll come and give you some support with Susan and Leonora."

Leonora asked Liza what was happening, and she was told that they were being followed by about six men but although they were not in uniform, they had to assume that they were southern sympathisers.

"Can't we get away from them? There are more of us," said Leonora.

"The horses are tired, and they won't be able to go much further, so I'm afraid that we will have to stay here and find out exactly who they are," said Liza. "You will probably see that although these men will think that they will be surrounding us, we shall in fact be surrounding them and we will probably find out who they are without firing a shot."

Susan and Leonora climbed back into the wagon and Liza went to Jamie and sat next to him. She had her pistol hidden in her dress. Roberts sauntered over to the wagon and leaned against it with his rifle resting against the wheel. Sean and Bart were checking that everyone was aware of their role in the coming confrontation. Sergeant Rowe was nowhere to be seen and neither were at least half the soldiers.

"Don't you think that you ought to take cover Liza?" said Jamie.

"I know that I should, but I don't want to. If this is going to be a battle that we both must fight, then I want to fight it next to you. I want you to promise me that you will take care of yourself and not worry about me, and I will take care of myself. We will both have enough to do without watching out for one another," said Liza.

"I can't promise you that Liza; you know that I will always watch out for you, and I know that you would put yourself between an enemy and myself without a second thought; so you will never practice what you are preaching," said Jamie. "We had just better accept that we will look after one another."

Liza nodded and smiled up at him and at the same time shots were heard from not too far away. She and Jamie clasped their weapons, but Liza said that they sounded like warning shots. There were no further sounds and everyone in the clearing held their breath.

They could then hear Bart shouting for the intruders to get off their horses and then six men were ushered into the clearing with Bart, Sergeant Rowe and some soldiers holding guns on them whilst their guns had already been taken from them.

Everyone in the camp held onto their weapons tightly and watched as the men walked towards Sean. One was middle aged and had a military demeanour, the rest ranged from possibly eighteen years to mid-twenties.

Sean could be heard asking why they had been following them. Liza wanted to hear their answer, so she moved nearer, as did Jamie.

"We are Tennesseans, Sir and proud of it, but there are many of us who do not believe that we should have seceded and as far as we are concerned, we are Americans with one government and wish to help to get back to being one country. None of us believe in owning another human being, in fact I am the only one who has ever come across a slave," said the older man.

"That doesn't explain why you are following us," said Sean.

"We are following you Sir, because we know that you will reach one of your military units and we wish to enlist in the Union army. We saw the result of the fight you had with the Confederate soldiers and therefore knew that you were in the area and took advantage of the opportunity," said the older man.

"I suppose there will be many who feel that way, and possibly many northerners who believe in what the south are doing," said Sean. "If what you are saying is true Sir, you are welcome to travel with us, but we will only return your weapons when we reach the next military post. Have you brought food and water with you?"

"I believe we have enough. I should introduce myself. I am Major Conrad Belling late of the United States Army, and I have my son and nephew with me and three young men from the town. I understand that we have yet to earn your trust; you are right to be cautious," said Major Belling.

"We are resting the horses at the moment," said Sean. "Be ready to leave in an hour."

"By the way Captain, word had reached our town of who you were taking north, and it may well have already gone ahead of us," said Major Belling.

Liza looked at Jamie and said, "Does he mean us?"

"He must do; we are the only ones travelling with an escort," said Jamie.

"I don't wish to appear naïve but why are we so important? There must be many other either businesspeople or those of the aristocracy caught up in this conflict," said Liza.

"But not many of them own the largest shipping company, or vast swathes of valuable land and of course there's the Daltons project," said Jamie. "All these things make you a very desirable captive."

"I don't feel very desirable; I keep dreaming of a bath," said Liza. "If we get to Kentucky tomorrow, I'm hoping that we will find a stream that I can jump into and stay there for hours."

"That does sound good. Do you remember when we did that in Italy? It was a happy time for us, but we have too many people around to do what we did then," laughed Jamie.

Roberts was helping Leonora and Susan down from the wagon and they were eyeing the newcomers with suspicion and Roberts was explaining who they were.

A fire was lit, and Liza said that they may not have to suffer biscuits again for their meal and Susan climbed back into the wagon and brought out some cured bacon and the last of their eggs as well as a stale loaf followed by a large frying pan.

"We don't have enough for everyone, but we do for ourselves and a few others," said Susan.

"Who's going to cook it?" asked Jamie.

"I'll help," said Liza happily.

"No you won't," said Jamie. "I'd like the last of our bacon to be edible."

Sean and Bart smiled, having heard what Jamie had said and they also saw the pout that Liza was displaying and that they had seen before.

"I think there will be enough for you," Leonora said to Sean and Bart, "and probably Sergeant Rowe. That will save some of your supplies," she added not realising that they would have to get the rest of their food from the soldiers' rations or wildlife.

Still pouting Liza arranged their own fire and showed with triumph just how to light it with sticks, a rock and some dry undergrowth. She then left them to it with her nose in the air, much to the amusement of her companions.

Leaning against the wagon Liza watched as Roberts sliced the bacon and Susan placed it carefully in the frying pan. Leonora had sliced the bread as best she could and was toasting it using a stick and Roberts was mixing the eggs to make them go further. The smell of bacon was wafting around the clearing and Liza thought that if anyone was looking for them, they only had to follow their noses.

Susan brought Liza her plate and Sean came to sit next to her with Bart joining her on the other side. Jamie was sitting opposite with Sergeant Rowe and Roberts with Susan and Leonora sitting next to him.

A stray morsel of egg landed on Liza's chin and both Sean and Bart took their kerchiefs and mopped it away, who actually got it could not be seen, but it was so natural for them to do it that Liza did not notice. Jamie did and he burst out laughing. "So I'm not the only one to try to keep Liza clean."

"No, I'm afraid she hasn't changed," said Bart laughing, with Sean joining in and Liza wondering what they were laughing at.

The newcomers were sitting nearby eating food that had obviously been brought from their home kitchens and the soldiers were cooking some chickens that they had found on their travels. It was best not to ask them where they had come across them, but soldiers were very resourceful. They did not have much water to wash their dishes, but they managed to get them relatively clean.

"We should reach water tomorrow," said Liza. "We'll be in Kentucky then and there's a wonderful stream there."

Sean and Jamie looked at her questioningly and she said quietly, "I've been here before."

"Yes, of course you have," said Sean equally quietly.

Major Belling came over to them and said to Liza, "You don't remember me, do you?"

"Well Sir," said Liza, "your face is somewhat familiar."

"I was visiting with Colonel Western at Benson when you came back from the dead," said Major Belling.

There was a stunned silence from everyone within earshot. Susan and Leonora knew nothing of that part of Liza's past.

"I'm sorry, have I spoken out of turn," said the Major.

"Of course not Major;" smiled Liza. "It's just such a long while ago that I'm surprised that you remember."

"It was a difficult day to forget. We had all looked for you for so long that we thought that you had to be dead, and you walked into the Colonel's office under your own steam. You had that young lad with you, and he didn't even know who you really were. The word went around from fort to fort that a miracle had happened and here you are now once again trying to get back to where you belong," said the Major.

Many would not have known from the smile on Liza's face that she was not pleased to hear what was being said, but three people did and all three were cringing inside knowing how Liza felt.

"As I said Major, it's a very long time ago," smiled Liza.

"Nobody should have to go through what you have done, and not only have you done it once, but you are going through it all again," said Major Belling. "I want to apologise to you for the unbelievably crass and illegal behaviour of my fellow countrymen. I think you realise why we need to fight for a regime with a conscience."

"There is no need for you to apologise Major; we are all only responsible for our own misdeeds," smiled Liza and she swiftly changed the subject. "I hear that you have your son and nephew with you."

"And some close friends of theirs," said the Major. "There are many who think as we do, but they have families to worry about; we have none to concern ourselves with. My wife died five years ago, and my nephew has always lived with us. Their friends have spent more time with us than anywhere else; we all want to do the right thing."

"You could be right Major, but I have tried not to take sides, although it has been somewhat difficult by not being allowed to leave when we wanted," said Liza. "I wish you all well and hope that this conflict will be over before too long and will not cost too many lives."

"Thank you," said Major Belling and he bowed and moved back to the other newcomers.

"That was something that you did not wish to be reminded of," said Bart.

"I suppose it was a large talking point at the time, but it is something that I prefer to leave in the past," said Liza.

Leonora made a mental note to ask Roberts what he knew about Liza's past as it sounded rather intriguing.

Jamie laid his hand on Liza's shoulder and said that it was rather unfortunate that the Major had a long memory. Sean said that no matter how hard anyone tries, the past never goes away.

"I know you don't like to talk about it, Liza," said Bart, "but I believe that your past is something to be proud of."

"I prefer to live in the now and the future," smiled Liza. She took her bedding and placed it near the fire and Jamie smiled and put his next to it.

Sean was discussing the plans for the next day with Bart and Sergeant Rowe; he turned to Liza and asked if she was sure that they would reach water the following day, and did she remember the route to it.

"Yes, I travelled there often, so unless it has dried up in the last twenty years, we are in for lots of drinking water as well as being able to bathe and wash our clothes," said Liza.

"We'll get an early start tomorrow and we'll let you lead us Liza," said Sean.

"I'm sure Bart knows the way, but I'll be happy to ride up front," said Liza.

"I know there is a stream nearby, but not exactly where. I don't think I've been there before. I know I would have eventually found it, but it will take less time if you know the way," said Bart.

Liza got into her bedding and wriggled to get comfortable; she would be pleased to get back into a bed again. Jamie lay down beside her and held her closely; they did not care if others noticed as Liza needed the security of Jamie that night.

***

They crossed into Kentucky the next day and after travelling for a couple of hours, Liza led them to the stream that she remembered from the past.

After they had watered the horses and filled barrels and water bottles, Sean arranged that the ladies went into the water first. There was a small inlet that was relatively private. Susan and Leonora stripped down to their shifts, but Liza went naked, which was how she was used to bathing in streams. She scoured the edges and found the root that made soap, much to Leonora and Susan's surprise.

They washed their clothes and Liza got out of the water to hang them all on bushes.

"It's just as well that I have been given the job of watching over you," said Jamie. "I did have my back turned but realised that it was you and couldn't resist the temptation to look."

Liza laughed. "I wish you could be in here with me." She jumped back into the water and squealed.

With their hair, bodies and clothes washed the ladies finally climbed out of the stream and wrapped blankets around themselves. Leonora and Susan wriggled out of their shifts and hung them over bushes. Liza giggled and walked back to the wagon with Jamie. He helped Leonora and Susan into the wagon and with a great deal of laughter they managed to get some clothes out of a trunk and get dressed. Liza sat outside the wagon and waited until they had finished.

"Go on Jamie, go and join the men in the water. You'll feel so much better," said Liza.

She handed Jamie what was left of the soap root and told him to find others on the waters' edge and the men would feel cleaner. He grinned at her and asked her if she was going to peep at the men.

"Don't let the men rummage through our underclothes," smiled Liza.

She sat against the wagon drying her hair in the sun and the unruly curls that she had managed to train over the years had returned. It was something that he had remembered in the exceedingly long time that he had been unable to be with her. He smiled and pushed some of them out of her eyes and whispered that he loved her, and he always had done so. He left to take advantage of the cool stream water.

When her hair was virtually dry, she struggled up into the wagon and dressed in her alternative travel clothes. Leonora and Susan were waiting for her when she climbed down; they had looks on their faces which said that they wanted to ask some questions.

Liza looked from one to the other and asked them what they wanted to know.

"Liza, you know so much more than even the soldiers, you know where to go and what we will find, and that Major said that you had returned from the dead. Is it only the Confederate soldiers who are looking for you? Or do we have to protect you from others?" asked Leonora.

"It's only the Confederacy who seemed to want me, but I think they have more on their minds now. Any others I will not need protecting from, but they may well know where I am," said Liza.

"Liza, who are you really?" asked Leonora.

"I am exactly who you know me as. I married Jamie some years ago hence my title. I have been married twice before, both died in tragic accidents, one at sea and the other murdered. I lived in America for some years, two of which were not of my choosing and once again I have been held here against my will. I have companies that seem to be attractive to both the north and south of America, which is why everyone wants me, but I feel that I am safer with those of the north as I believe that I know them better and that they will not hold me to ransom," said Liza. "Does that put your mind at rest?"

"Where were you held before?" asked Leonora. Susan was asking nothing and suddenly she decided that she did not want to join in the conversation, and she walked slowly away.

Liza looked at Leonora and asked, "Why is that important to you?"

"It isn't, I'm so very curious," said Leonora. "And I have a feeling that it could be hostiles who held you before. Am I right?"

"The original natives of America are never hostile unless they are acted against," said Liza. "I do not wish to be rude Leonora, but I would prefer not to talk about that time in my life. My nightmares have passed, and I do not wish them to return."

"I'm sorry Liza; I understand that it must have been a very frightening time for you, and I apologise for trying to elicit information to salve my curiosity," said Leonora. "Please forgive me."

"There's nothing to forgive," smiled Liza and she changed the subject by asking what they would be eating that evening.

"I don't know. We've eaten everything that we brought with us," said Leonora.

"So we'll have to beg and see what we come up with," said Liza.

Bart came sauntering across looking scrubbed and clean.

"Do you want to join us for dinner Bart?" called Liza. Leonora looked surprised and Bart laughed.

"Have you run out of food Liza?" he asked.

Liza smiled and nodded.

"I'd love to join you for dinner," he smiled. "What time?"

"What time do you suggest?" laughed Liza.

"I'll let you know," he said and went off laughing.

"What was that all about?" asked Leonora.

"You want to eat tonight, don't you? It will be interesting to see what Bart brings back for our dinner," smiled Liza. "I hope you'll be able to cook whatever it is."

"It might be snake or rat," exclaimed Leonora with a horrified look on her face.

"Yes, it might," laughed Liza. She saw Jamie coming towards them and she went to join him, passing Sean on the way.

"Am I invited tonight, Liza?" Sean called out.

"That depends on how big Bart's offering is," she shouted back.

"Fair enough," called Sean.

Jamie looked confused and Liza explained that Bart was organising dinner.

"What's it going to be?" asked Jamie.

"Don't know, but Leonora is cooking it," said Liza as they came into earshot of Leonora.

"Is that fair on Leonora?" asked Jamie.

"Yes, she gave all our food away yesterday and nobody will allow me to cook anyway," said a triumphant Liza.

Susan and Roberts were sitting and waiting to see what was going to happen, and Leonora was looking worried. Sean was also leaning back and seemed to be waiting confidently.

It only took another half an hour for Bart to stagger in with a deer across his shoulders.

"There you are Leonora; it's not snake or rat. You'll know how to cook deer won't you?" smiled Liza. "You'll know how to butcher it and clean it, won't you?"

"You're very cruel to your friends Liza," said Bart. "Don't worry Mrs Chambers; I know how to butcher it. Can I trust you to prepare the right fire for this Liza?"

"I can help you with the deer," said one of the young men with the Major and he and Bart got on with preparing the animal. When they had finished, they went and washed in the stream, leaving others to worry about how to cook it.

Leonora had a look of panic on her face, but she need not have worried as there were many there who knew how to deal with it.

Liza had made an excellent fire and had arranged various spikes for the meat and then stood back and let everyone else take over. Jamie was sitting with Roberts and Susan while Liza and Bart were admiring her fire. He looked clean, smart, and happy.

"You did very well Bart and you look very happy," said Liza.

"You knew that I would get dinner, but I'm happy because it seems that we will be travelling very near to Benson, so I may be able to see Laurie," said Bart.

"Are we?" and Liza turned to Sean for confirmation, and he told her that they seemed to be heading in that direction. "Our military unit is camped near Harris. You'll be able to catch up with old friends."

"I thought that we might be able to take a route across land to pick up a ship from one of the northern ports," said Liza.

"I understand that it will be bringing back memories for you," said Sean. "It would for me also."

"Bart's very happy about it and it will be nice to see all my old friends. I keep in touch with them regularly, so I know what has been happening there. I have met up with Gabriel, Kate and Zelma and I have Simon living with us whilst he's studying," said Liza.

"Being confronted head on with the past is going to be difficult," said Sean. "I haven't been back since you left, but I requested that Bart was assigned to me to help find you and Jamie. I needed the best for that, and you have to admit that he is the best."

"He is the best of soldiers and the best of friends," said Liza.

"Apparently he didn't need any persuasion to come on this assignment. He has a great deal of respect for you Liza, as do I and I know that you will handle seeing all your friends in Benson well. You'll be able to visit Patrick and little Meg; that will be hard for you, but it will be tempered by seeing everyone else. We'll be at Harris first and I know you have friends there also, as well as business ventures. I hope this war won't interfere with those," said Sean.

"How are you going to deal with being back in Benson?" Liza asked Sean.

"I probably won't go into town. The fort is virtually deserted so there is no reason for me to be there," said Sean.

"Patrick is still there Sean," said Liza quietly.

"That's what concerns me," said Sean.

"It's been eight and a half years and every now and again it still hurts, and this is one of those moments. Jamie and I have a very good and happy life together. I love having our boys around us and the past disappears from my thoughts, but there are times when my memories of the past become so painful that I don't know how to bear them," said Liza. "But bear them I do, and it passes; I get on with my life and Jamie looks after me so well and he does make me very happy."

"Patrick played a very large part in both of our lives, and it is right that we don't forget him. You are right to have made another life for yourself and your boys; unfortunately I haven't managed to do that no matter how I have tried. I think of him every day and I also think of you often and how you made him so happy," said Sean.

"He made me happy; he was all that I wanted in life, but I had the boys to consider and had to carry on. It took me a while to realise that I wanted and needed Jamie; the boys adore him, but they have never forgotten Patrick and they keep a picture of him in their room and talk about him frequently, as do Jamie and I," said Liza. "Come on Sean, we have a great deal to be thankful for and one of those things is the deer that Bart got for us, so let's join the others and see how our dinner is getting on."

Leonora and Susan were not doing very well cooking over an open fire, but Roberts and Sergeant Rowe were showing them how it should be done. Once again Liza realised that Roberts had led a very different life to the one he had now which was really very fortunate for them all.

They could see Liza and Sean approaching and Bart could be heard telling everyone not to let Liza anywhere near the cooking.

"I trust you'll allow me to eat some of it," said Liza.

"Only if you stay well away from the fire and don't interfere with what the cooks are doing. Your two ladies are having a quick lesson in the finer points of cooking over an open fire, which I'm sure they will put to good use when they return home," said Bart.

***

It took five days for them to reach the Harris area and a camp was set up in the farmland that Alice, Jim and Hal Barrows worked. They were surprised and alarmed to see so many soldiers milling around, but when the wagon drew up and Liza stepped down their alarm turned to pleasure.

Through the tears and the hugs Jim managed to say, "Ah Liza, you've been found again at last."

They remembered Jamie, Sean and Bart from the past and they were ushered into the house.

Hal came bounding in and clasped Liza so tightly that she felt that she could not breathe. "Oh Liza, thank God that you're here."

Liza introduced Leonora, Susan and Roberts.

"You have so many soldiers with you and that's just as well as there is a group of Confederate soldiers nearby, but I don't think that there are enough of them to take all your people on," said Jim.

"Which direction were they heading?" asked Sean.

"West," said Hal. "They were near here yesterday. Are they looking for you Liza?"

"I hope not," said Liza.

Sean and Bart looked concerned, and Jamie asked them why.

"We will be heading Northwest once we've been into Harris town. How many were there?"

"Ten and they were rather unruly. Their captain was having difficulty keeping order, and he had a sergeant with him who was marginally better," said Hal.

"Did they do much damage?" asked Liza.

"They took food, and then started to kill the animals, but the captain stopped them; so they tried to set fire to the smoke house. They were not very intelligent, just aggressive. The smoke house was hardly damaged as you would expect, hence the name," said Jim.

"We managed to salvage food from the pigs that they killed; the rest are fine. We are a little lacking in hens and eggs, but we will manage. They didn't find our storeroom for the cured hams and bacon. I think that the word must have reached them that a much larger Union force was on its way, so they left in a hurry," said Alice.

"Are you thinking of enlisting?" Jamie asked Hal.

"I'm hoping that it won't be necessary," said Hal. "We've already lost some of our workers to whichever side they support, which leaves this farm grossly undermanned. I haven't the time to leave, even if I wanted to, which I don't."

"Right Liza," said Alice. "What would you like now?"

"I would like a hot bath," said Liza. "As I am sure we all would."

The men were ushered out and two baths were brought in and filled. Liza and Leonora jumped in before Susan had a chance. "Don't worry Susan; you'll have it all to yourself soon."

Alice came in and gathered up all their clothes and had found their clean ones in the wagon. Liza was stepping out of the bath and Susan did not wait for her to get out of the way before she was lowering herself into it. Alice laughed and brought more hot water for her; Susan sighed with contentment.

When the ladies had finished, Jamie and Roberts were next, followed by Sean and Sergeant Rowe. Bart was keeping order amongst the men, and finally he too stripped off and sunk into the warm water.

Leonora, Susan and Liza were sitting at the large table dressed in an assortment of mismatched night clothes and there was a wonderful smell of pork cooking coming from the big oven.

"I've put you, Leonora and Susan in Angela's room," Alice smiled at Liza. "Your husband, Roberts and Sean will be on mattresses in the sitting room. I don't know if Bart and the sergeant need to be in with us, but if they don't, then our barn is very comfortable."

Liza tried not to show her disappointment at not being able to be in bed with Jamie, but the thought of sleeping in a bed that night far outweighed the comfort of lying next to Jamie.

Sitting around the large table that evening was just as it had been when Liza had first met the Barrows' family and she asked if they had seen Ambrose recently.

"Not for some years now," said Jim. "He did come by once since you were here, but that was around six years ago. I know he's still alive as one of his friendly Indians collects goods and his post from the town. I believe he also visits the Indian encampment when they are nearby."

"Are they nearby?" asked Sean who suddenly realised that Bart was saying nothing. Liza also noticed Bart's change of expression, or more to the point his non-expression.

"I don't know if they are," said Hal. "They no longer bother us. There have been no further spears or arrows in your grave Liza since you were last here."

Liza smiled whilst Roberts, Leonora and Susan stared at her in astonishment.

Leonora stammered, "Your grave?"

"It's a long and complicated story," said Liza. "But I had to die to live and on our long trip to Benson I'll tell you all about it, unless somebody does that before me."

Leonora suddenly felt very guilty; she had not thought about her husband for a while. Her life had been so exciting since leaving Charleston. She had experienced fear, curiosity, companionship, fun and laughter and rarely had she felt the longing that she should have for Jackson. She was travelling with soldiers who would be fighting her husband, but it did not seem that way. They did not seem like enemies, they appeared to be friends.

Everywhere they went people seemed to know Liza. She could see that Sean and Bart loved her in their own way. Roberts and Susan were devoted to her and the whole Barrows family pampered her; her association with them seemed to go back a very long way. Tomorrow they would be on their way again and would pass through a town called Harris and Leonora had no doubt that Liza would be known there also. After that they would be travelling to a town called Benson where Liza had lived for a number of years, she would probably be welcomed there with open arms.

When Liza, Leonora and Susan had gone to bed, Jamie asked if they were now going to have to fight two enemies.

"I would think that the Confederate soldiers will be joining with others; I just hope that it's not before we get to our larger unit, but I don't think that we have anyone else to worry about. What do you think Bart?" asked Sean.

"Bandor has already made contact with us," said Bart. "His people know that Liza is here, and they will make sure that she is safe."

"So the Indians will be friendly, but we may have to defend ourselves against this small band of Confederates or larger if they join with others," said Jamie.

"My only worry about the Indians is that they may think that she would be safer with them; as you know they have done that before," said Sean.

"If Matthew was with her then I believe that they would definitely want to have them both under their care," said Bart thoughtfully.

Jamie looked at him curiously. "Why," he asked.

"I'm sure you know that he is the chief's grandson and could be in line to be the next leader of the people. Although his young son's health has improved, if anything happens to him, Matthew is next," said Bart quietly.

The memory stirred in Jamie, "Of course," he said, "I had forgotten."

"They may still think that she needs their protection," said Sean.

"Instead of just taking her as they did last time, they would ask her first and act on her answer," said Bart. "They will watch over her until she is safe."

"You know a great deal about them," said Jamie. "I remember that you pretended to be Zelma's husband when Liza was taken before. That was very brave of you."

"Not really," said Bart. "They are my people, or should I say partly so."

"Of course, I should have realised. Liza never said and there's no reason why she should," said Jamie.

Both Bart and Sean nodded.

***

They all had an excellent nights' sleep and were up early enjoying Alice's tasty breakfast.

Jim, Hal and Liza discussed business for a short while.

"We won't be able to feed all the troops who happen to come by," said Jim. "We don't want to see anyone starve, but we have to think of ourselves and our neighbours first."

271

"I know we've been expanding nicely and were planning a great deal more, but it's going to be difficult to maintain what we have until this war is over," said Liza. "Whatever help you can give to the people of Harris should firstly be for those with children and the elderly. It's going to be hard for you to act as God but that's what you will have to do. I dare say there will be a market for some of our products; take what you can for them which will help you to replenish your supplies. I'm not looking for a profit, I just want everyone to survive and when this war is over, we will get back to making money. The land we will always have, so we will never lose everything."

"I think that our biggest problem is going to be unruly soldiers, like those we saw the other day. Their only thought was taking and destroying and there aren't enough of us to defend as we would like," said Hal.

"Nothing is worth losing your life for," said Liza. "I'm not without funds and if it seems that you have lost everything just remember that you haven't. I can always reinvest, but my problem could be not being able to do it until the war is over and that could be years."

"We've lived through difficult times before," said Jim. "You know that we have and if we end up with nothing to eat, we will go out and catch something. If we have no roof, then we will build a shack of some sort and survive. We are luckier than most as we know that we are part of a very large company."

"I think that I will give more concentration to growing, firstly for us and anything that is surplus can go into the general store. There are not too many men left to help with harvesting anything that is too large," said Hal.

"Women and children could help with that Hal; their payment could be part of that harvest, or other food," said Liza.

"They would have to stay over several nights and we do have the facilities for that," said Jim. "Of course they could bring their own sleeping blankets. It could work quite well; we have several huts that we use when we need extra help. I don't know what our school master will say about it."

"I would think that the school master will be one of the first to join in, after all he also has to eat and much as the town has at last managed to pay his salary, under the current circumstances he probably won't be getting his full payment for quite some time," said Liza. "It could become just like a co-operative society."

"If we all pull together the town will survive. It is actually quite an exciting prospect, we won't be concentrating on profits and losses, we'll be concentrating on keeping one another alive," said Hal.

Liza laughed and said that she hoped that it would not be too long before he could go back to looking at profits, but lives were more important.

"I'll call in to see the school master and the general store when we get into town," said Liza. "I'll also see all those at the hotel."

"I'll come into town with you," said Jim. "They'll be pleased to see you there."

"I'd like to go with you also, but I'm not happy leaving my mother alone, although I think the other soldiers are long gone. It's difficult for me to be impartial as the Confederate soldiers did not treat us well. There could be a time when Union soldiers act just as unruly, but from what I have seen here they do seem to be more conscious of others," said Hal.

"Most of the soldiers who are here are trained Hal; they are not ones who have just enlisted because there is a war, so they know how to act correctly, but you are right, who knows what will happen when they have been fighting for a while and have seen things that nobody should see. There will be some Confederate soldiers who have also been trained correctly and that will be when you will find the situation difficult," said Liza.

People had been coming and going all the time that Liza had been talking to Jim and Hal. Jamie, Roberts, Leonora and Susan had packed and organised their wagon. They had enough food to last until they reached Benson, which Liza was grateful for as she remembered the tasteless meat stews at each stopping place on the way.

"I gather that this is one of your businesses," said Leonora with a smile.

Liza laughed and nodded.

"I think you will find that there is also one or two in the town," said Jamie also with a smile.

Alice gave them all a hug and she was shedding a tear, she also handed Liza a letter for Wes and Enid and then they were all on their way to Harris.

Jim was riding beside the wagon and Liza said that he must be careful on his way back alone.

"I know Liza," said Jim. "I have my rifle and pistol with me. I normally carry my rifle just in case I have problems with any wild animals, but the wild animals could well be humans now. I will be careful, I promise you."

It was decided that the soldiers and newcomers would camp outside town whilst Liza, Jamie and the rest went in. Sean and Sergeant Rowe would also be with them, but they did not want to create too much of a presence in town.

Sadly many of the stores had been damaged and if anyone there had originally thought to join the Confederates, they had now changed their minds.

Jamie said that whoever was in charge of the Confederate unit had no control over them and that it was a shame because all those that he had met in Charleston were totally respectful and careful of the property of others.

The windows of the general store were broken and most of the goods had either been taken or damaged.

The storekeeper said, "I'm sorry Liza but I couldn't stop them. There was no need to damage what they didn't want, but I think liquor had a lot to do with it. Their captain was furious, but it was too late for him to do anything about it."

"I'll see if I can get more stocks for you, but it may well be difficult," said Liza.

The hotel and bar had been well used and also damaged, but only surface damage.

Liza and Jamie then made their way up to the school and tiptoed in so that they did not create too much of a disturbance, but several of the older children saw Liza and called out to her which made their teacher stop what he was doing and when he realised who she was, a grin spread across his face.

He told the children to carry on with their reading and then greeted Liza and Jamie happily.

"I'm so pleased that you have managed to get away. I presume you are making your way home. I suppose the ports were being watched," he said.

"Yes, we've had to come overland, and we might as well continue to do so having got this far," said Jamie.

"I see that the school remained undamaged," said Liza.

"They were heading in this direction, but their captain fired over their heads and that calmed them down. I believe they had been drinking. There seemed to be one soldier who controlled the others, and it wasn't the captain or the sergeant. They had a hard time keeping them in order and you could see that the captain was getting very frustrated with them," said the teacher.

"I hope we don't meet up with them," said Liza and she then proceeded to tell him about everyone, including women and children, helping with the Barrows' farm at harvest time.

"It could be a very good idea, and perhaps there could also be other times, such as planting times, when we could all pull together. Much as I don't agree with child labour, we are in very difficult times and several of our young men have enlisted and I can see that food stocks could run very low," he said.

"There are huts there where people could stay; they would have to bring their own bed linen, but that's all," said Liza.

"It could be a life saver for many," said the teacher. "I could hold lessons for say an hour in the morning before everyone sets to work. They would be too tired later in the day. I'd be able to help too."

"Jim's in town now. He'll come up and see you before he leaves," said Liza.

Having spoken to everyone in town, Liza said goodbye to Jim and climbed up onto her wagon. She was sad to be leaving Harris, but she wanted to be on her way and more than that she wanted to see her boys and all the family. She had been away too long, and she was also nervous of arriving in Benson, there were too many memories. She cheered up at the thought of seeing Zelma, Kate and Gabriel. She would probably cry when she saw Kathy and Joe and no doubt the same would happen when confronted by Ada, Bea and the Colonel. There were so many there to see but she had around four days to get used to the thought of seeing them all.

***

They followed the stagecoach trail out of town and continued until nightfall. They set up camp away from the track and ate their evening meal. Liza rested her head on Jamie's shoulder and just as she was nodding off a shout came from the soldiers on guard.

Sean and Bart were on their feet with pistols in their hands before the shout had ended. Jamie was also on his feet and standing between whoever was entering their camp and Liza. Susan and Leonora were being pushed to one side by Roberts and Sergeant Rowe. Liza hoped that she knew who it was and that it was not the larger unit of the Confederacy.

Bandor slowly came into the clearing leading his pony. Sean and Bart could be seen to relax a little. Bandor looked around and saw Jamie protecting Liza. He nodded his approval and Bart approached him, after a short conversation Bart came to Liza and said that yo-nv-a-di-si and di-da-nv-wi-s-gi would like to visit with i-tse di-ka-ta. It had been many years since she had been called by that name.

"Are they here?" Liza asked Bart.

"Yes, they didn't want our soldiers to shoot first and ask questions later, so they sent Bandor because he is known to them," smiled Bart.

"I would like to see them, it's been a long while, would you have any objections to their coming into camp?" Liza asked Sean.

"They have been near us for some time now; a few of them coming into camp will not be a problem," said Sean.

"Is it wise of you to see them Liza?" said Jamie.

"I really don't have a choice. If I don't see them here when I am surrounded by armed soldiers, then they will find some time when we have no protection," smiled Liza. "However I'm sure that if we had no protection from the soldiers, then we would have protection from my Indian friends."

Liza nodded to Bandor, and he left and when he returned, he had Running Bear and the traditional healer with him. They entered the clearing and made their way towards the fire; they stood and waited with expressionless faces.

"Liza, don't go," said a very frightened Leonora.

"There's nothing to be frightened of Leonora. Stay with Susan and Roberts and relax. We are in no danger," said Liza.

"You can't know that," said Leonora.

"But I can, and you are quite safe," smiled Liza.

Liza walked towards them, and Jamie was about to follow her, but both Bandor and Bart stopped him. He turned on them and was about to tell them to let him go.

"She's in no danger Jamie," said Bart. "They want to see her and talk to her. They want her to know that they will watch over her until she reaches safety. They want nothing to happen to her because she is the mother of the one who will bring them back to greatness. They thought that was her at one time, but they now know that it is her son, White Hawk."

Liza was giving them the usual Cherokee greeting which was also expressionless. It was all coming back to her.

"It is good to see you Green Eyes; the world is treating you well. You look as you did when you were with us," said Running Bear.

"You seem as strong as you always did," replied Liza. "How has your son fared. I trust he is well."

"He is Green Eyes. His mother found what was hurting him and he has grown strong. He will make a fine chief when I am no longer here," said the Chief.

"I hope that will be a long way off," said Liza.

"You know that White Wolf died, although he really died many years before. Brave Eagle also died, it took him a long while, which was what he deserved. He gave White Wolf the blow to the head; he said so in one of his times of pain. One of his sons is following his father's path, which is not that of the Cherokee. His other son is not strong, he will not be with us long," said the Chief.

"I'm sorry to hear that. Is there nothing that can be done; is he eating the wrong food?" asked Liza.

"If he is, his mother has not found what it is," said the medicine man.

"How is my grandson?" asked Running Bear.

"He is very well and growing tall like his father," said Liza.

"We will see him one day when he is ready to take his place with us. It is good that he is learning all the white man's ways as we will then have the best of both our worlds," said the Chief.

"We have heard that the ones with the light coats want to keep you here and use you in their war with the blue coats. We hope that the blue coats do not have the same thoughts; we will watch over you until you reach your destination," said the medicine man.

"You have a new protector," stated Running Bear. "We have seen him before. He came for you after your soldier died. He is a good man; he will try to protect you, but he is not a warrior like your other protector. He is brave and will put himself between you and any danger, but he is not skilled. He would die protecting you but that would leave you alone and in danger. We will not allow that to happen, we will keep you both safe."

"I thank you for your concern," said Liza. "How are all the people faring? Are they fit and keeping warm and healthy?"

"We grow food and hunt well. The food and clothing that you send to us before each winter keeps us warm and healthy. We would not accept it from anyone who is not one of us; you are still one of us," said the Chief.

"I am hoping that this war between the white men will not interfere with what I send you. I will try to get another supply to you before the winter, but sadly I cannot guarantee that it will reach you. You may have a few lean years ahead. I know that you are very careful with your food stocks; you may have to be even more cautious in the future," said Liza.

"This white man's war seems very foolish. They are fighting for no good reason. Many will die and nothing will have been gained. We will try to stay out of it, and we will be cautious," said Running Bear.

They talked for an hour and then they left as quickly and as quietly as they had arrived. Bandor followed them and once again nodded to Liza as he left.

The worried look left Jamie's face; he had not liked seeing Liza sitting and talking with the Indians. He remembered them from the past and he still did not trust that they would not try to take Liza back with them.

Sean asked if there was anything that he needed to know.

"They will make sure that we reach our destination; Bandor will be guarding us from afar and he will let them know if we are in any danger. They think that the white man's war is foolish, and they knew that the Confederates wanted to hold us to ransom," said Liza.

Sean nodded knowing that a great deal more had been talked about, but he was confident that Liza would have told him if it was going to affect him and his troops in any way. He left her with Jamie; he knew that she wanted to talk to him privately.

"What did they say Liza?" asked Jamie. "Obviously a great deal more than you told Sean."

"They talked of the past a great deal. They are convinced that Matthew will return and lead them and that it's his rightful place. I didn't disillusion them. They think that you are very brave because you have not been trained to kill but you would put yourself between me and any enemy. If you died doing that, I would be unprotected so they would then have to step in to save me," said Liza. "They are right Jamie; you are very brave. You do put yourself between me and any danger."

"I would not want to be without you Liza, so I do everything I can to keep you alive," said Jamie.

"It could cost you your life Jamie and I wouldn't want that. I don't want to live without you, so you've got to be more careful and think of yourself," said Liza with a pout.

Jamie put his arm around her and pulled her even closer to him. He smiled and told her that he promised that he would be careful and that she must be the same.

"Is everything alright Liza," asked Leonora. "They're not going to hurt us, are they?"

"Quite the contrary Leonora," said Liza. "They are going to protect us."

Susan was looking relieved. "So we have the soldiers and the Indian's guarding us. We are very lucky," she said, and Roberts was agreeing with her, although Leonora still needed some convincing.

They settled for the night with Liza putting her head on Jamie's chest and she was asleep almost immediately. Jamie could hear Leonora, Susan and Roberts talking.

"She was speaking their language," said Leonora. "How could she know that?"

Roberts could be heard replying that Lady Edgeworth spoke several languages fluently and that was obviously just one of them. Jamie smiled at the indignation in Roberts' voice as he did not feel that anyone should be amazed at Lady Edgeworth's intelligence. Roberts did not think that it had to be questioned or pointed out to anyone.

"That's right," said Susan. "She's very clever; so are all the boys."

Jamie stroked Liza's head as he felt contented having heard the pride in both Roberts' and Susan's voices. Even under these difficult circumstances they were devoted to the family and would hear no criticism of anyone.

He knew that they were being watched over not only by the soldiers but also by Bandor; he had no need to stay awake, so he closed his eyes and went into a deep sleep only waking when it was daylight and the sound of men moving around roused him.

They were on their way again and Sean had said that they should be meeting up with the rest of the unit and that Liza would see a few old faces, one being Marshall Graves and others being Ben Webber and Paul Southern.

"Bart told me that they were with this larger unit; I haven't seen any of them in years," said Sean.

"It's going to be quite a reunion," said Liza not too happily.

"I thought you would be pleased," said Sean quietly.

"It will bring back too many memories," was all that Liza would say and Sean nodded in agreement.

"Sometimes we just have to face these things," said Sean also not very happily.

Soon after midday the guards of the main unit stopped them. Bart rode forward and was known to those guarding the encampment. Liza and Jamie were riding that day, Roberts was driving the wagon with Susan next to him. Leonora could not be persuaded to sit with them; she reminded them that her husband was in the Confederate army and that those in the camp were his enemies.

"Well, we're not going to shout about it," said Liza. "You have been travelling with your husband's so-called enemies for the past weeks, so what's the difference now?"

"I find it difficult Liza. I feel disloyal to Jackson, and I also feel disloyal to the men who have rescued us," said Leonora.

"You will not be the only one to feel that way. There will be many families and friends in America who will feel how you do. I do also; you must remember that we met at Charles' house deep in the south. He is a wonderful friend of mine, and I got to know Jackson and saw how well his surgery was equipped. Donal O'Rourke is now in the Confederate army and his parents and the Cavanaughs are people that I love dearly. I have many friends in the north and that is because I have lived in Benson, and I also have a house in New York. I have many painful thoughts over this war and feel very disloyal to each side," said Liza. "However I am not going to hide myself away from either side."

They continued to the main encampment and Bart led the way to the largest tent. Before they reached it Ben came rushing towards them and as Liza dismounted, she was swept up into his arms and a large kiss was placed squarely on her forehead. All Jamie could do was smile at Ben's enthusiasm and he could not be sure that Ben was not crying.

It seemed that word was spreading, and soldiers were appearing from various tents, and many were calling out to Liza.

Another lieutenant came smartly towards them, and Liza turned and smiled, "It's good to see you Paul," she said, and he too put his arms around her and kissed her fervently.

"Ah Liza, you've been rescued, thank God. We knew that Sean and Bart would manage it," said Paul. He turned and smiled at Jamie. "I'm pleased to see you again Sir. You've all had a very difficult time. I believe that Major Graves is anxious to see you."

"It's Major Graves now, that's good," said Liza.

Jamie introduced Leonora, Roberts and Susan to both Ben and Paul, and they were all ushered into the large tent and there was Marshall standing and smiling down at Liza. He too then clasped her to him and muttered that it was such a relief to know that she was safe and well. He then shook Jamie's hand and looked at Leonora, Roberts and Susan who Liza then introduced to him.

"Mrs Chambers is travelling to New York, which is where she is originally from. It was not very healthy for her to remain in Charleston," said Liza.

"I dare say that there are many northerners in the south who feel the same way, as well as those from the south in the north," said Marshall. "I am afraid we're moving out tomorrow morning and Sean has been ordered back to his unit. I can allocate a couple of men to show you safely to Benson, after that I'm afraid you're on your own."

"Thank you, Marshall, but we will be quite safe getting to Benson," said Liza. "We already have an escort, although we would not know it."

"Ah, your native friends are keeping an eye on you, and this time they don't want to abduct you," said Marshall.

"I'm no longer number one on their list of desirable people. Matthew is," said Liza.

"That's understandable," said Marshall. "You'll all join me for dinner tonight, I hope."

"Thank you Major, that will be very nice," said Jamie. "Is there somewhere that we can wash? We are all a little travel weary."

"We have some makeshift showers," said Marshall and he called to a young orderly and told him to show them to the facilities and to make sure that their wagon was placed nearby.

They made their way to the showers, which consisted of buckets of water placed precariously on shelves. They all looked at them with dismay.

"There's a stream nearby; I'm going to that," said Liza.

"Is it very far?" asked Leonora.

"About five minutes away, that's all. You and Roberts can make sure nobody peeps at us and we'll do the same for you afterwards," said Liza. Leonora looked shocked but Susan giggled and said she could not wait.

"There are so many men around, they'll see us," said Leonora.

"I'm sure they've seen women before, but you'll probably wear your shift anyway, so nothing will show," smiled Liza.

The stream was cool and flowing gently. It was not very deep but even Leonora had to admit that it was a wonderful idea. Men were walking past, possibly more than usual, but Jamie and Roberts were keeping watch over them. Liza did wear her shift as she appreciated that there was very little opportunity for privacy.

When they came out of the water and stretched their clothes over bushes to dry, Jamie and Roberts jumped in having stripped down to their underclothes. Finally they were all lying back drying in the sun and when they were dry, they made their way back to the wagon and dressed as best they could for dinner with Marshall.

Both Sean and Bart joined them for dinner. Paul and Ben were on duty that evening, but they had said that they would catch up with them before they left the next day.

"I'm sending Bart back to Benson with you; I'm afraid I can't afford to send any more and I know that he is wily enough to see any danger before it happens. You will also have Bandor watching out for you, and he would get help quickly if it became necessary," said Marshall.

"Are you sure that Bandor and Bart will be enough?" asked Sean. "I know how efficient they both are, but there is a large contingent of Confederates roaming around; hopefully they are not too near yet. There was a small unit in Harris who carried out a certain amount of damage and I know that the people there were told that they would be meeting up with others. Their captain seemed not to have a great deal of control over his men."

"That's the group that we are ordered to engage, and we are to intercept them, but it isn't near Benson, so you should be fine," said Marshall. "There are several of the men who would like you to take letters for them to their families in Benson. I am one of them and Ben is also, although I believe Brigeta decided to take her children to be with her family whilst Ben is away."

Liza and Jamie were allocated a tent together and when they entered there were two very uncomfortable looking beds for them. Susan and Leonora also had a tent with the same sleeping facilities and Roberts was in with Sergeant Rowe.

"I think I prefer the ground," said Liza.

Jamie grinned at her and said, "Oh, I think we'll manage quite well."

It had been the first time in weeks that they had experienced any privacy and Jamie was going to make the most of it.

"Those beds don't look terribly strong Jamie," said Liza with a sly smile.

"I think I would prefer the ground also," whispered Jamie and Liza nodded.

***

Soon after dawn the camp was being packed up and Liza and Jamie staggered up from the floor and stretched out on their beds which they hoped would take away the aches and pains of their night-time activities.

"They really are moving out early," muttered Jamie. "Even these beds are beginning to feel comfortable. I hope they don't expect us to get up quite so early."

"They probably will," mumbled Liza. "They'll need the tent and the beds probably. My back aches."

"So does mine," whispered Jamie and they both went to sleep for a short while and were woken by Roberts calling out to them.

"Some of the men have already moved out," said Roberts. "I think they want to get everything moved within the hour, so I'm afraid you'll have to get up now."

Liza and Jamie looked at one another and they both thought that their exertions of the night on the ground had not been such a clever idea, enjoyable as they had been at the time.

"Alright," said Liza and she moved and promptly fell onto the ground, letting out a cry as she went.

Jamie started laughing and found it difficult to stop.

"Are you alright," called Roberts.

"Yes, thank you Roberts. I've just fallen out of bed," muttered Liza.

"I'm going down to the stream to freshen up," said Jamie sleepily and Liza agreed to join him. They both staggered out of their tent and made their way to the stream. Jamie quickly washed whilst Liza just sat in the water in her nightdress.

"Oh Jamie," she said. "I'm so tired."

"Come on Liza," said Jamie. "Once we set off again you can rest in the back of the wagon and sleep for as long as you like."

"That's not fair on everyone else," she mumbled as she walked back to the wagon in her wet nightdress.

"Just look at you Liza," exclaimed Leonora. "You're soaking wet and half asleep. Susan, you'd better help her get ready for the day."

282

Liza looked at her like a naughty schoolgirl which sent Leonora into peals of laughter. "Seriously Liza, there are a lot of people who want to see you before they leave."

"Yes, I'll be ready shortly," said Liza and as she climbed down from the wagon after dressing, she was handed several letters from the various soldiers from Benson. She promised to deliver them personally to their wives, girlfriends and in some cases children and parents.

When the throng had eased a little, Marshall came over and asked her to deliver a letter to Bea and he had also written one to each of his girls. Ben was standing behind him and he also had letters for Brigeta, and one for each of his children.

Paul came over and said, "I still don't have anyone Liza, but I've written to both Kathy and Joe, and the Colonel and Ada. They have acted like both parents and exceptional friends to me all the time that I have been in Benson."

"I'll make sure they get them; I know they will appreciate the sentiment and will probably write to you. As you know at times like these, letters don't always reach where they should. When Patrick was away, I used to write anyway and even if he didn't receive all my letters, he knew that I had written which meant a great deal to him. So if you receive the odd letter at least you know there were more and that they were thinking of you," said Liza.

Sean and his unit were ready to leave. "Well Liza," he said, "seeing you again gave me the will to carry on. I'm delighted that we could get you out of that awkward situation and hopefully you will have no further trouble reaching your home. Remember me to young Matthew and John; of course Simon is also with you in England. I've written to Gabriel and Kate and a short note to Zelma, but if I may, when I get the opportunity, I would like to write to you. I have your address, but with this war any letters may not reach you."

"But I will know that you have written," said Liza. "I'll do my best to keep in contact with you Sean, and when this war is over, I'll return to New York and wait for you to join me."

"That's a deal Liza," said Sean and he held her and kissed her.

"Stay safe Sean; I'll be thinking of you and praying for you; God Bless you," said Liza tearfully and Sean then quickly left without looking back.

Sergeant Rowe waved and then he, Sean and his men rode out. Jamie came across to her and said that he knew that it was never easy to say goodbye to old friends. "You're doing a lot of that this morning," he commented. "I think we ought to get on our way and leave these men to get organised for their mission."

Liza nodded and climbed aboard the wagon. Bart was at the reins with Susan next to him; his horse was tied to the back of the wagon. Jamie and Roberts mounted their horses, and they were then all ready for the next part of their journey to Benson and then on to either a port which would take them to New York, or a means to get there across land.

There were shouts and waves from the soldiers as they left and soon they had reached the stagecoach route and on their way to Benson. It was going to take at least two days, but they felt that they had already been through the worst of the journey. How they were going to get to New York was another matter. If the stagecoaches were still running, then that would be the best way to go until they reached the start of the railway. The alternative was to continue by taking the wagon across to the nearest port and get passage to New York; they would have to make the decision when they arrived in Benson.

"You're very thoughtful Liza," said Leonora. "Is it because you've just left many of those that you know?"

"Yes, I suppose so," said Liza. "And I will soon be seeing many more people that I know and I'm not sure that I'm looking forward to it."

"Really, I would have thought that you would have been pleased," said Leonora.

"It will bring back too many memories, many of which I had blocked from my mind, but they are all coming back now," said Liza.

"Were they all unhappy ones?" asked Leonora. "Surely there were some good ones."

"Plenty of good ones, but they ultimately became very sad ones," said Liza.

"When you are there perhaps you'll just remember the good times," said Leonora.

"I hope you're right. The place won't be the same without all the people at the fort; it's all part of Benson," said Liza as she stretched out and made herself as comfortable as possible.

"Are you tired Liza?" asked Leonora. "I heard that you fell out of bed; those beds weren't very comfortable, but I suppose they were better than the ground."

Liza looked up at her and wondered whether she was being sarcastic and knew that she and Jamie had spent the night on the ground, but the look on Leonora's face told her that she knew nothing. Liza yawned and soon nodded off despite the rocking of the wagon.

They stopped at lunchtime and Liza felt rested and was back to her normal happy self.

"Bandor is travelling with us," said Bart.

Leonora, Susan and Roberts looked around and Bart smiled. "No you won't see him, but he will have a very good view of us. He's ready to ride back to his camp for help if necessary."

When they were on their way again Bart rode his horse, Leonora decided to ride also, and Susan sat with Roberts whilst he drove. Liza and Jamie stretched out in the wagon and enjoyed the rest.

They made camp that night and Bandor rode into the clearing. He spoke to Bart and then came to Liza and Jamie.

"You're being followed," said Bandor. "It's just a small band of men. At the moment they have camped nearby, and they don't know that I am here. I will watch them tonight as will Bart. Just carry on as you normally would, they may not bother you and you may reach Benson safely. If the soldiers are still there tomorrow, I will find my people and bring them to you. Keep your weapons handy but we will be watching you."

They spent a very uneasy night. Leonora and Susan slept in the wagon and Liza, Jamie and Roberts lay down by the fire, each had their weapons at the ready. Soon after daylight Bandor crept into their camp and said that a larger group had joined the soldiers, but he did not know whether they were heading in their direction.

"There is one piece of bad news; the captain is someone that Bart knows well so he would not get away with being a civilian travelling with you," said Bandor.

Bart suddenly appeared and said, "If they are just following us then I could stay in the wagon until we reach Benson. I'll watch from there and keep my weapons aimed at any intruders. We'll just hope that they don't approach and want to search the wagon."

"Who is it?" Liza asked Bart.

"Rufus Denton," said Bart.

"You'll have to leave us Bart, and you too Bandor. You're both very well known to him and you're both too valuable to be taken prisoner or worse. If they know who we are, they will not hurt us, they will want us alive and well," said Liza.

Bandor started speaking in the Cherokee language to Liza.

"They will want you alive and well i-tse di-ka-ta; the others will mean nothing to them," he said.

Liza frowned and said, "I know Rufus Denton; I knew him well and he has a temper, but he isn't that ruthless. Has he changed much in the years since I was there?"

"Yes, he is an intolerant man. He has no love in his heart now. He is a good soldier but only sees in front of him, he sees nothing either side; there is only right and wrong and if he feels that his way is right and the orders that he is given are right, nothing will get in his way. He is now quite dangerous," said Bandor.

"I did not know he was a southerner," said Liza.

"He's from the place you call Virginia," said Bandor.

"Of course, they didn't join the Confederacy until May, it must have been a hard decision for him having lived, trained and worked with those who have remained in the Union," said Liza. "Do you really think that he would allow everyone but me to be killed?"

"He will not disobey his orders not to take prisoners; Bart knows that, but he will do his duty to protect you and if there is a choice of who he must protect, then it is you and no one else. My duty is the same," said Bandor.

"Your duty is to get back to your people and bring help to us and Bart must go with you; you must not risk yourselves; you will be needed. I will deal with Rufus as best I can," said a worried Liza.

"We cannot let you do that i-tse di-ka-ta," said Bart who had joined in the conversation.

"You must," said Liza. "We need help and only you can bring it to us. If you stay with us, you will be sacrificing yourselves and we will have no help. You must go before they know you are here and get help for us."

"Liza what are you saying," said Jamie who had joined them.

"The captain of the unit that's following us is well known to both Bart and Bandor. In fact they have served together for many years, and he is someone who will follow orders and his orders could well be not to take prisoners. We should be safe enough, but they will not," said Liza.

"Then they must leave us and bring help. They cannot sacrifice themselves to keep us from being taken," said Jamie.

"I've told them that because they are the only ones who can get help to us. They are arguing but I think they are beginning to see the merit in it," said Liza.

Jamie looked closely at Liza and said, "What aren't you telling me Liza?"

"Bandor thinks that the only prisoner to be taken will be me," said Liza quietly.

"By that you mean that the rest of us have no value to them and would only get in the way," said Jamie.

"Liza is the valuable one, but you could also be considered worth keeping. If you are able to talk to them then Leonora's husband being in the Confederacy could help her, but I'm afraid the other two have no value to them," said Bart.

"I didn't think you knew about her husband," said Liza. "Would you be able to take Susan and Roberts with you?"

"We could not travel fast enough with them, and we might be too late to help you. I think one of us should stay and help you. Bandor should go and I'll stay," said Bart.

286

"No," said Jamie. "You must also go, and we'll not stop until we reach Benson."

"It will take longer than a day to reach Benson and the horses must be rested," said Liza. "We'll have to stop at a staging post and take our chances there. I presume there will be people there, but I suppose they won't want to get involved and we will be putting them at risk."

"The more we talk the less time you will have to get help and reach us. We won't tell the others our concerns but will tell them that you are getting help which will reach us shortly, and that we must get on our way as soon as we can. It will worry them, but they won't know exactly what we have discussed," said Jamie.

"I know that I will be able to talk to Rufus and I know that if given the opportunity I will be able to make him think before anything terrible happens to the others; I just have to be given that opportunity," said Liza. "But we must all now get on our way, and I wish good luck to you both. At least there are two of you to get our message safely to your people."

"I do not like leaving you, but you are right. You need help and only we can do that. We cannot do that if we are dead, and we would be if we stay with you. You do stand a better chance without us, we will not fail you and we will see you in Benson, if not before you reach it," said Bart. "Take care with Rufus Denton; don't forget the black eye he gave you. He lashes out before he thinks, so tell everyone to be careful."

Jamie was staring in horror at Liza and would ask her later about what had happened in the past and then with a last look at them Bart and Bandor quietly led their horses away from the clearing and Liza and Jamie told the others to quickly pack everything away. Liza took the reins with Jamie and Roberts riding beside the wagon and keeping a watchful eye on the surrounding area.

"Are we in trouble," Leonora asked Liza.

"Well we are being followed and they are catching up with us, but Bart and Bandor will be bringing a great deal of help for us. We must travel without stopping until we reach a staging post. It would be better if we could get to the town, but the horses will need resting before we reach it," said Liza.

"They want you don't they Liza? What will they do with us?" asked Leonora.

"They'll probably let you go as your husband is in their army. Susan and Roberts, they will probably ignore. They are English and have allegiances to neither side. I know the captain from the past," said Liza and she hoped that she sounded convincing.

They travelled at quite a pace only stopping for a short while to rest the horses before they were off again. Jamie knew that they were not making good time and wondered whether they would reach the staging post before nightfall.

Jamie took over the reins and Leonora rode his horse. "What happened between you and this Rufus person in the past?"

"It was an accident, he didn't mean to hit me, but he did mean to hit someone else, but that person was better at ducking than I was, and I happened to be standing behind him; unfortunately I felt the full force of the blow," Liza smiled at the memory.

"It seems to amuse you, Liza; I would have thought that it would have been an unhappy time," said Jamie.

"The town and the fort had a joint picnic the following Sunday and Andreas and Patrick had identical bruises on their chins, and I had a black eye, all courtesy of Rufus. The Colonel just looked at the three of us with disbelief and he thought it best not to ask," smiled Liza.

"Andreas? Is that the Andreas that I know? What was he doing in Benson? And why did Rufus hit him and Patrick?" asked Jamie.

"Andreas brought his daughter to live with her grandparents. Christina is Felicity's daughter, and she is also my responsibility should anything happen to them. He stopped at my place in New York on the way and his nurse did not want to go any further, so he brought Mary with him to help. Rufus fell in love with Mary but didn't know how to handle the situation. He upset her terribly and there were times when he was insisting that she went with him against her will. The first time Patrick stepped in and received a blow to the chin, and the second time Andreas felt the blow, the third blow was meant for Andreas, but I got it instead," said Liza with a smile.

"Not many people would smile at such a memory," said Jamie. "Most people in Belfast believe that Felicity's child is living with her father and stepmother in Greece. I saw the child when I was last in Benson, and I couldn't mistake who her father was; her red hair gave her away."

"She was a very pretty child when last I saw her; I wonder if she has changed much," said Liza.

"Andreas said that he had been with you when you came to Belfast all that time ago and I know I upset him when I laughed at him. I knew you hadn't because you had spent the time with me, and I knew that you wouldn't anyway. I think he just said it to annoy me," said Jamie.

"He thought that he had been with me; Felicity pretended that she was me. He had called at my house before she and Edward had moved out and she acted as if she was me. He told us what had happened when he came to Benson. He thought that he had confused the description that he had been given; you will remember that his English was not particularly good then. He was more than astounded when I was announced at a function, and he realised who Felicity was. He had cuckolded the son of the owner of the business that his family had agreed an association with. It was all very embarrassing at the time. He was very sad having to leave his daughter, but his wife couldn't cope with her; she had thought that she would be able to, but she just couldn't. Her grandparents love her dearly and she's doing very well with them."

"Well you've told me why Rufus is bad tempered; it's unrequited love," said Jamie.

"I think he's always been like that, he just managed to keep it under control until he didn't get what he wanted, and that was Mary," said Liza.

"We'll have to make up a story about Roberts and Susan; they'll have to become part of the English aristocracy. Roberts will be able to carry it off, but will Susan be able to?" asked Jamie.

"She's too young to be his wife; she'll have to be his daughter. She's young enough to be scared and it will be no surprise if she shows it," said Liza.

They stopped for a very short while so that they could arrange what they were going to say to Rufus when he caught up with them. Roberts was to be Lord Robert Langston and Susan, Lady Susan also Langston.

"If you have to describe where you live, think of Langston House; you both have spent some time there so it should be easy," said Jamie. "We don't have much time; they will be catching us up shortly."

"What about me?" asked Leonora.

"You are the wife of a Confederate doctor and as long as we can get that message across then you have nothing to worry about. We just must think of a reason why you are travelling with us," said Liza.

"My father has been unwell for a while, so it would be natural for me to try to see him," said Leonora.

"Yes, it is natural for you to want to see him, but there is a war, and you are travelling to enemy territory," said Liza. "They will just have to believe it."

"We had better get on; I believe they will be on us within the hour," said Jamie.

Susan was looking frightened, and Liza suggested that they sat together as she drove the wagon, Jamie and Roberts would be riding.

As they set off Susan asked if she really needed to become Lady Susan and Liza wondered how she was going to convince her without frightening her even more.

"The Confederate army want the British government to side with them and their way of trying to ensure that they do is to hold to ransom any aristocrats who are currently in America. If you are an aristocrat you will be treated well and looked after, if you are not, I wouldn't like to say what would happen to you. I promised your mother that I would look after you and I haven't done a very good job so far. By taking part in this little charade should guarantee your safety," said Liza. "You had better start calling me Liza, or if it helps you could call me Aunt Liza and Lord Edgeworth will become Uncle Jamie. Start getting that into your mind."

Liza called out to Roberts and said that he was to call her Liza and Jamie also by his first name. "Please remember it."

They could now hear horses approaching and they had decided that they were going to act innocently and appear to think that the troops were on their way somewhere and that they had nothing to do with them being there.

A shout went up and two horsemen passed them and caught the bridles of their lead horses pulling them to a halt.

"What do you want?" Roberts called out in his best English voice and Liza hoped that he would not become too aristocratic to be believable.

"Get off your horse, and you get out of the wagon," said one of the soldiers gruffly.

"I beg your pardon," said Roberts acting out his part a little too well. "Do you hear that, Jamie? They want us to get down. I don't think so my man."

"I think we should Robert, they do have guns aimed at us. I feel it would be foolish to refuse," said Jamie.

"Which one of you is Liza?" asked the gruff soldier.

"I am Lord Robert Langston and my daughter, Lady Susan, is up there," said Roberts pointing at Susan. "Here are Lord and Lady Edgeworth and this lady is Mrs Jackson Chambers. Who are you Sir?"

"Never mind who I am, I said get down and which of you is Liza?" said the soldier.

Nobody said anything.

"Alright," said the soldier. "I know she's not a man, so I'm going to shoot this mouthy one, and then the other one and I would think that before I do that Liza will come forward."

"You know who I am, Corporal," said Liza. "Why are you acting so aggressively? What do you want with me?"

"You are needed back in Charleston or somewhere in the other southern States," said the Corporal.

"I don't think so Corporal; I have no business in Charleston, or anywhere else," smiled Liza. "I think you have your facts wrong."

Then Rufus rode up and his men were surprised to see the smile on his face, it was a look that they had never seen before.

"Liza, are you giving my men a hard time?" he smiled. "It's good to see you. It's been a long time."

He dismounted and came across to her and he was another man who put his arms around her and held her tightly. This was a sight that his men were astonished by; they had never experienced a soft side to his nature. By then Jamie was used to his wife being hugged by various soldiers and he thought how sad it was that these soldiers, who had obviously been friends, would be fighting and possibly killing one another in the not-too-distant future.

"Well Liza, you've brightened my day as you always did. Are you going to introduce me to your travelling companions?" said Rufus.

Roberts immediately answered, "I am Lord Robert Langston, and this is my daughter Susan. Lord and Lady Edgeworth you already know, and this lady is Mrs Jackson Chambers whose husband is a surgeon in your Confederate Army."

Rufus raised his eyebrows and said, "Indeed. Well I'm glad it wasn't you introducing these people Liza, as I know you are a useless liar, but if you want to play it that way then I won't argue. It's good to see you again Lord Edgeworth, it's been some years since you were here."

"Yes, it has been," said Jamie. "I'm afraid that we got caught up in your war and were unable to leave for home from Charleston, so we had to come overland instead."

"Shall we get on our way; there's a stage stop a few miles up the road; we'll go there and spend the night. We're very near Benson and my orders are to see how many Union soldiers are there and take them into custody. Then I'm afraid I must return you into the care of the Confederacy" said Rufus, "but you knew that didn't you?"

"You have no right to do that; it will not persuade the British government to side with the south, in fact it will probably make them go the opposite way, that is if they go any way at all and I know that they don't wish to take sides in this war," said Liza.

"I'm afraid you'll have to tell that to my superior when he catches up with us," said Rufus, "but in the meantime let's enjoy one another's company and talk about the past and try to forget the present and the future. Of course Mrs Chambers may go on her way to wherever it is she wants to be."

"Well Rufus, we are on our way to the stage stop and then onto Benson, so it will be a pleasure to have you with us," smiled Liza and Rufus just laughed at her as he helped her back on to the wagon. His gruff sergeant indicated that the others get back onto their horses and onto the wagon.

"Where are we going Liza?" asked Leonora.

"We're continuing on to the stage stop and then onto Benson, just as we planned," said Liza calmly.

"You were very friendly with that officer. I don't know how you could show such friendship to the enemy," said Leonora.

"Have you forgotten which army your husband is serving with?" said Liza sharply. Leonora gasped at the realisation that she had called Jackson's army the enemy.

"Of course, you are right. I suppose it was seeing you so friendly with the Union soldiers and how good they were to us and then you are showing such friendship to a Confederate officer, it seems disloyal," said Leonora.

"Yes, I can see that it could be confusing for you, but it's not confusing for me. It's sad that they may well kill one another on the battlefield but I have no allegiances to either side. It is not my fight and when I get back to my home in England, I shall pray for all my friends on both sides and when this war is over, they will all still be my friends; at least those who are still alive will be," said Liza. "All we have to do is get out of this situation and make it to New York without getting too many people hurt."

"When do you think your Indian friends will reach us?" asked Leonora.

Liza frowned at her and said, "I just hope that nobody heard you ask that."

"I'm sorry Liza, I just keep saying the wrong thing," said Leonora.

"You're nervous which makes you talk too much," said Liza. "It happens in some people. Susan is nervous but she knows not to ask too much just in case somebody hears her. She also trusts us because she knows that no matter what we must do we will get her out of this situation and back home."

"I'll keep quiet from now onwards," said Leonora.

"That will probably be best," and then Liza laughed saying that it would not really be necessary and that it would be much better if they talked about normal things. "Do you like living in Charleston?" Liza asked.

"I love the place and my house is getting more and more as I like it. Jackson's surgery is really quite the best in Charleston and the number of patients were increasing. It started to become awkward as soon as South Carolina seceded last December and I experienced subtle animosity at first which then turned into open hostility from some quarters," said Leonora. From that point onwards she carried on talking about the whole of her life and Liza knew that it was the only way that Leonora could control her fear.

Liza was no longer listening, and it gave her the chance to think and plan. Rufus was riding next to Jamie and making conversation with him, but Liza could see that Jamie was not being very communicative and she assumed that Rufus would understand that Jamie would not appreciate being held against his will.

They arrived at the place where the stagecoaches stopped, and the sergeant ordered them to get down and into the post and he was about to manhandle Liza.

"Stop that," shouted Rufus. "They are all quite capable of walking; they don't need your assistance."

"We've been told to make sure she doesn't get away," grumbled the sergeant.

"She's not going to get away, Sergeant," said Rufus.

Liza made her way to Jamie, and they sat together with Roberts sitting between Leonora and Susan. It was getting dark, and they could hear the soldiers walking around outside. The sergeant had grudgingly gone outside having been told by Rufus to make himself scarce.

Rufus made his way over to Jamie and Liza and said that they would rest for a few hours and make their way early to Benson. He was expecting Major Teague's arrival and he did not look happy about it.

"You seem worried about his arrival Rufus; do you have a problem with him?" asked Liza.

"You wouldn't expect me to answer that, Liza. He is my superior officer and I take orders from him," said Rufus.

"And would you carry out orders that should never be given?" asked Liza.

"You know me better than that Liza," said Rufus quietly.

"I hope so," said Liza also quietly.

The door burst open, and the sergeant and a couple of men threw someone into the room. He landed at Rufus' feet and the sergeant gave the man a hefty kick. Liza frowned and pretended to be surprised but she knew that it was either Bandor or Bart. Jamie pulled her closer to him as he knew that she would want to help whoever it was. Rufus moved to one side, and they could then see that it was Bandor, and he had been hurt.

"He's been trailing them," said the sergeant indicating Liza and Jamie, "and our scouts saw him ride off towards the Union troops to get help. Well he'll be helping nobody now." The sergeant lifted his rifle and was about to smash the butt of it into Bandor's head. Rufus shouted at him to stop as Liza was already diving towards Bandor. The sergeant looked as if he was about to smash his rifle into Liza's head as Jamie threw himself at the man and Rufus pulled the rifle out of his hands.

"How dare you do that to another human being," shouted Liza at the sergeant.

Jamie pulled Liza to one side as Rufus started to deal with his man.

"He's just a dirty breed," said the sergeant.

"That dirty breed, as you call him, has saved more soldiers' lives than you've had hot dinners," said Rufus to the sergeant. "He has worked with the army for many years and warned us of untold dangers. It is not your decision to treat him that way and if you had killed him, you have no idea what you would have brought down on us. It may not have just been Union soldiers that we had to deal with; it could well have been the whole of the Cherokee nation also."

Rufus turned and looked at Liza and she could see that realisation was dawning on him. "No wonder you were so calm Liza. Where was Bandor going, was he going for the soldiers or the Cherokees?"

Liza said nothing. Rufus looked at Jamie and then at Roberts, Leonora and Susan. "Surely you knew Mrs Chambers," said Rufus.

"No Captain I wouldn't know. I saw that Indian, but Liza spoke to him in his language, so none of us could understand what they were talking about, could we?" said Leonora referring to Roberts and Susan and they both shook their heads.

Rufus turned back to Liza and said, "No matter, he didn't make it, so help won't be coming for you."

"Bandor needs help. I presume you have no objection to my seeing to him," said Liza.

"What do you need?" said Rufus.

"My medical bag from the wagon and plenty of water," said Liza.

"Mrs Chambers can get it for you," said Rufus, which she did.

Jamie and Roberts helped to turn him on his back and Liza, Leonora and Susan washed away the dirt and blood from various parts of his body. Bandor started to revive, and Liza could see that he was in a great deal of pain. She started talking to him in the Cherokee language but before he could answer Rufus stopped her.

"If you are going to talk to him, speak in English please Liza," said Rufus.

"What are you going to do about it Rufus? Hit me? I seem to recollect that you were always very good at that," said Liza scathingly.

The familiar look of fury came onto his face, and he clenched his fists. Jamie stepped between them and said, "Don't goad him, Liza."

Bandor had taken a severe beating and he was covered in cuts and bruises. He had been kicked a few times and both Liza and Leonora felt that some of his ribs were broken.

"We need some bandages," said Leonora. Liza nodded and asked the people who lived at the post if they had anything to bandage Bandor with. They brought out an old but clean cloth which Jamie and Roberts tore into strips and when they had helped Bandor to his feet they tightly wrapped the bandages around him.

"Do you feel more comfortable now," Liza asked him, and he nodded his thanks.

"I'm surprised you got caught," said Liza in Cherokee.

"One of us had to be sacrificed," said Bandor.

"I'll see if I can find you something to eat," said Liza quickly to avoid Rufus asking what they were saying. There was some weak soup on the fire and Susan organised a bowl for him. Liza was going to feed him, but he said that he felt that he would be able to lift a spoon and if he could not, he would drink from the bowl.

They all then made themselves as comfortable as possible and slept fitfully for an hour or so until there was the sound of horses, followed by the noise of three people entering the room and Rufus was confronted by a very stern looking major, a lieutenant and a sergeant.

"Where is she?" demanded the Major and Rufus indicated where Liza was sitting.

"Who are the others?" the Major hissed.

"The tall one is her husband, Lord Jamie Edgeworth. The other man is Lord Robert Langston, and the girl is his daughter," said Rufus not letting the Major know that it was not the case. "This lady is the wife of a surgeon in our Confederate army."

"Who's the Indian?" asked the Major.

"He's a scout and has been injured," said Rufus and he did not go into any further detail.

"We need none of the others; get rid of them," said the Major.

"What do you mean, 'get rid of them'?" said a worried Rufus and the lieutenant and the sergeant looked shocked.

"What do you think I mean? They are of no use to us, and we don't want to leave anyone to say where we have taken her. We will take no prisoners, only her. She is needed," said the Major.

"I don't think you realise the implications of such an action Sir. These people are British subjects and are not part of our war; it's irregular enough keeping her against her will, but to do away with the others is foolhardy. Mrs Chambers' husband is fighting on our side, you cannot seriously mean to kill his wife in cold blood," said Rufus.

"Captain Denton," shouted the Major. "You will do as I say, and you will carry it out immediately."

"No Sir, I will not, and I will not allow you to do that either," said Rufus.

"You are relieved of your duty Captain," shouted the Major. "Sergeant" he called, "Carry out my instructions."

"No Sir, I did not join this army to murder civilians," said the Sergeant.

"Lieutenant," snapped the Major.

"Oh no Sir! Not me," said the Lieutenant.

"I'll deal with you all later. I will have to do it myself," said the Major.

"You will not," said Liza. "You will do no such thing."

"You have no say in this," said the Major to Liza.

"Indeed I do," said Liza and she pulled out a pistol which she had hidden in a pocket of her skirt. It was heavy but she had already cocked it ready and put it to her temple. "You take all of us, or you take none. And don't even think of trying to stop me. I am not going to be a widow just to be a pawn in your stupid war games. You are a disgrace to your army Sir. I also seriously believe you are mentally deranged and should be removed from your position."

She had given Rufus the excuse that he needed. "You are indeed not in control of your senses, and I am relieving you of your duties and placing you in custody."

Rufus nodded to the lieutenant and sergeant who disarmed the major as he struggled and objected strongly.

Liza was still standing with the gun to her head and Jamie gently took it from her. Rufus moved over and took it from Jamie. "I'll take that, thank you," he said. He looked at Liza and added. "You would have done it, wouldn't you?"

"Yes, she would," answered Jamie quietly. "And she was right to say that it was all or nothing. It was brave but it was all that was left for her to do. I take it that you will not be carrying out his orders; if you had I would not have liked to have known what his superiors would do to both him and you. But I would not have known it as I would have been dead, as would we all, including Liza."

Liza sat down; she looked very pale, and Jamie recognised the signs; she was going to be sick, and he grabbed the bowl that she had used for Bandor and got it to her in time. She retched pitifully as Jamie held her closely until finally her stomach settled. Leonora wiped her face; Susan took the bowl away and Jamie kissed her head.

"She still does that then," said Rufus.

"Rarely now; only when idiots threaten her," said Jamie bitterly.

"We should get on our way now," said Rufus.

"I am not going to be used to bring trouble to Benson. You can't expect me to do that. They are also your people Rufus. You have worked with them, played with them; been welcomed into their homes. How can you go there knowing that you are going to fight and possibly kill the men that are your friends? How can you do that? I'm not going as I don't want to see any of my friends hurt and I don't want to see you stoop that low," said Liza and she sat down and folded her arms determinedly.

Jamie sat down and folded his arms also and Roberts, Susan and Leonora followed suit. Bandor tried to fold his arms but could only hold them across his stomach. They all looked defiantly at Rufus asking him what he was going to do about it without using words.

Rufus looked thoughtfully at them. "I can't fight you all," he said. "I have heard that there are hardly any soldiers left in Benson and that Colonel Western has come out of retirement to take charge of the fort."

"So you think you are going to walk in there and take them prisoner, you know that Colonel Western would never survive that. The people in the town would fight you over that and they are not trained soldiers, so it would be very unfair of you to bring the war to them, and it would be tantamount to murder on your part," said Liza.

"I have my orders Liza, and I must secure Benson for the Confederacy and I must take you back to Charleston," said Rufus. "However my orders don't say when I must do it; so it is half a day to Benson, and I'll give you another day and a half to do whatever you have to for the people. If I allow you to do that, will you agree that you will stay there until I arrive and then go back to Charleston and remain there as long as necessary?"

"Think of our boys Liza, and the rest of our family. Remember all the Fullers and all the children that you have given a better life to. You don't have to think of me because no matter what you decide, I'll be with you," said Jamie.

"I could stay here and do nothing, but I would still be forced to go back to Charleston, or wherever else they decide. I could go into Benson and help to warn that these soldiers are coming and then try to make my way to New York. How far do you think I would get before they found me?" said Liza. "I might as well agree as the ultimate outcome would be the same, it will just be with less of a fuss and at least the people of Benson will know what their options are."

"I suppose you do really have very little choice," said Jamie.

"If I agree, I want your word that my friends will be allowed to go on their way to New York without interference from any of your men," said Liza.

"Agreed," said Rufus.

"Alright then," said Liza and Jamie noticed that she neither promised nor said the words that she agreed, but Rufus had not realised.

"Right," said Rufus, "We'll stop a few miles outside Benson and give you time to organise whatever it is that is needed. You'll have what is left of today and all day tomorrow and I hope that we don't have to fight to take over the fort."

They helped Bandor into the wagon and tied his pony onto the back. Leonora and Susan got in with him and Jamie and Liza were in the front with Jamie driving. Jamie's horse was also tied onto the back and Roberts was riding beside them.

Chapter 10

As they drove into Benson the sun danced off the gravestones as they passed the churchyard and Liza purposely looked away. She would visit Patrick and little Meg privately; it was not the time to look for them. They drove past Mrs Long's cottage and then past Dr Tom Marsden's practice. Next to the surgery it was the Boarding House where Angela lived and then Gabriel and Kate's home. Then slowly they went past the home that she had shared with Patrick, the boys and Zelma. Liza could not look at it. She knew that they had then passed the driveway up to the stables and she breathed a sigh of relief when Charlie Penn's carpentry shop and home came into view.

"Where shall we stop Liza?" asked Jamie. "Do you want to go straight to the fort?"

"That could be the best thing to do," said Liza, but that was not going to happen as Jake Smith came walking towards them with a look on his face which was showing that he was finding it difficult to believe what he was seeing.

"Liza, that can't possibly be you. It's wonderful to see you. You haven't changed a bit," said Jake. "Hey Joe, Kathy, look who's here," he shouted.

"I think we'll have to stop here," said Liza and she then turned and gave Jake her most disarming smile. "Jake you always were a flatterer."

Jamie started to help her down and Jake took over and lifted her to the ground where she was nearly knocked over by Joe and an amazingly fast-moving Kathy.

"Oh Liza, you got away from them; we've been so worried about you," said Kathy as she engulfed Liza in her arms and cried all over her. Joe also had tears running down his cheeks.

Jake was rushing off towards Gabriel's office and he could be heard shouting that Liza was back in town. The door to the upstairs flat banged open and Zelma appeared running down the steps and launching herself at Liza, knocking Kathy to one side.

Jamie climbed down from the wagon leaving Leonora and Susan looking out from the front of the wagon. Once again they were treated to the sight of Liza being clasped in yet another person's arms. Gabriel was marching towards them, shouting at Jake to find Kate and see if Ada was at home.

"Liza, it's wonderful to see you but somewhat surprising. Are the Confederates chasing you or have they realised their stupidity?" said Gabriel.

"No they're not chasing me," said Liza honestly.

Gabriel looked at her and she knew that he was thinking that she was not lying but also she was not exactly telling the truth. He turned to Jamie for confirmation, but Jamie would not look him in the eye and as he looked around he noticed that none of Liza's travelling companions would hold his gaze either.

Kate and Ada were running towards the wagon with Kate carrying little Liza, although she was quite capable of walking. "What are you doing here Liza," mumbled Ada as she held Liza tightly.

"I'm travelling to try to sort out what has been happening over the past months and I couldn't miss the opportunity to see you all," said Liza. "We have Bandor with us; he's been hurt."

"Are you staying a while?" asked Ada.

"A few days only," replied Liza.

"You can stay at your old house, if you like," said Ada quietly but she knew from the looks on both Liza's and Jamie's faces that it was not an option. Kathy also noticed and said that she had plenty of room and she would go and organise beds for them all.

"You and Jamie can have Danny's old room, and your two lady friends can have the spare room, and if your man doesn't mind, we have a small box room," said Kathy and off she went with Joe to arrange the sleeping accommodation.

Dr Tom arrived and Bandor was helped from the wagon, and it was decided that Zelma would take care of him at her place. After Dr Tom had warmly greeted Liza and Jamie, he helped Zelma to take Bandor to her home.

"I must see the Colonel," said Liza quietly to Ada.

"I'll take your friends across to Kathy and Joe's to freshen up," said Ada. "The Colonel is in his old office at the fort. There's a problem, isn't there Liza?"

"Yes, there is Ada, but I'd prefer to talk to the Colonel first and see what we can come up with," said Liza.

There were many willing hands, and the wagon was taken to Kathy and Joe's yard, whilst Ada went to get her buggy so that Liza and Jamie could go to the fort.

As they drove through the gates of the fort one of the guards was a corporal who Liza knew.

"What are you doing here Mrs Kelly?" he asked. It was a name that she had not heard in a long while and she just smiled and hoped that Jamie would not be too upset.

"I'm here to see the Colonel," she smiled at him, and she was told that he was in his office. Jamie knew where the Colonel's office was and he drove over to it, pulled up outside and helped Liza down. In the Colonel's outer office sat a young corporal and as he looked up, the Colonel's door burst open and there he stood staring in disbelief.

He mouthed her name, and the corporal was treated to the surprising sight of his Colonel clasping the woman tightly and crying, all the while mumbling unintelligible words into her head. Jamie had a smile on his face as he was becoming used to seeing his wife held by so many people and cried over not just by women but also by the hardest of men.

The people of Benson loved his Liza and she in turn loved them; he could see what she had meant by the freedom of living in the town; he hoped that he would be able to persuade her that she was just as loved with him and their family in Surrey. He wondered whether her heart was still really in this place; he was going to have to tread carefully and hope that he could win her back. She had not wanted to come to Benson, and he now understood why, but he knew that she could not turn her back on the people here when she knew that they were in danger, and he would not have been able to live with himself if he had persuaded her otherwise.

The Colonel took out a handkerchief and mopped his eyes and blew his nose. "I am sorry," he said, "that was unforgivable of me. Jamie, I'm pleased to see you also. Come, let's go into my office."

He pulled out a chair for Liza and indicated that Jamie sat in the other one.

"What are you doing here Liza? I thought that you would be well on your way to New York, or even on to England. Where are your escorts? Sean should have been with you and Bart and several others who were meant to get you to safety."

"They did get us to what they thought was safety, but Sean had to re-join his Unit and Marshall had orders to engage a large Confederate army and he left us in the capable hands of Bart and Bandor, only I'm afraid it didn't work out that way," said Liza.

The Colonel frowned and looked from Liza to Jamie and back again. Jamie continued telling him that the Confederate section that Marshall was looking for was not where he had been told but was in fact directly where they had been heading. When Bandor had realised that, they then knew that they were going to be intercepted but Rufus was in command of a smaller Unit which they would meet before encountering the larger section. Bandor and Bart had to leave them as they were both known to Rufus, but also they had to get help and inform Marshall where the enemy was.

"They both left you," exclaimed the Colonel. "That's very unlike them. They would die rather than leave you in danger."

"They couldn't get help for us if they were dead, and they would have been if Rufus' superior had had his way," said Liza.

Jamie then told him the whole story, including Bandor sacrificing himself and Rufus not knowing that Bart was still going for help and why Liza held a gun to her head and threatened to pull the trigger.

"How did you get away?" asked a shocked Colonel.

"We didn't Colonel," said Liza. "The Confederate army are a few miles out of town, but Rufus has given us the opportunity to warn the people of the town and also for you and your men to leave."

"We can't leave Liza. We must stay and defend what we have here," said the Colonel.

"You can't stay Colonel. The Confederate force is enormous, and I don't know how many men you have, but I have only seen around ten. You cannot defend with that number of soldiers, and you also have the families of those men and the men that are already out in the field to consider. You also will be creating a conflict which will spill over into the town, but there is one thing that Rufus doesn't know and that is that Bart is getting help not only from Marshall's unit, but also we are to be guarded by Liza's Indian friends," said Jamie.

"So you are saying that Rufus' large Unit have an even larger Unit to contend with and they have no idea that they are going to have to engage them," smiled the Colonel.

"You and your men can ride out of here with the help of Bandor, who I'm sure will brave the pain that he is in and guide you to join Marshall and the rest of your men. It may seem that you are abandoning your post, but really you are going to help with a greater battle which will push the Confederates away from this area," said Jamie. "I believe that it's the sensible thing to do."

"You could be right, but I will stay at the fort and take the consequences. I have been here since before it was built and I cannot leave it to an undignified abandonment," said the Colonel.

"I understand how you feel," said Liza. "Perhaps I can persuade Rufus that you have become senile as Dr Bridges was."

"Don't you dare try that," said the Colonel with force. "Tell me, why is Rufus allowing you time to help us?"

302

"Because he still has a love for Benson," said Liza. "It's a place that gave him respect; it's where he made friends and was welcomed into many homes. He doesn't want to hurt anyone in Benson."

"And if you expect me to believe that they are the only reasons, then you must think that I have indeed gone senile. What's the real story?" said the Colonel.

Liza pursed her lips and Jamie decided that he had better tell the Colonel exactly why the town was being protected. "Rufus gave us until tomorrow afternoon to do whatever was necessary to help the families in the fort and warn the people of the town that they were going to take over. The agreement was that Liza is taken back to Charleston, or wherever they decide she should be held."

"No Liza, you can't do that. It's not fair on you or on Jamie, nor is it fair on your family in England. How will young Matthew and John feel if you are away from them for years? It's not right. You've already done enough for the people of Benson," said the Colonel.

"It's already done Colonel and besides it may never happen because Marshall's Unit will be here shortly as I'm sure Bart will have reached them by now," said Liza. "Now, it seems that we have to organise the families at the fort and find them safe places to stay while their men are away and the Confederates are nearby. Shall we call a meeting for later this afternoon at the school?"

"The ladies will not wish to leave their homes Liza, even if their men are away," said the Colonel.

"Then they must be persuaded Colonel. You had better tell the men who are left that their wives and children must move for their own safety and Ada and Bea must persuade the others. If there are still some who argue then we'll have to give them no choice, as for the hopefully short time that Rufus and his men are here, it will not be safe for them to be unprotected in the fort," said Liza.

"I'll get young Corporal Raines to fetch Bea and then go into town for Ada. I think Laurie is in her quarters," said the Colonel and as he went to the door it opened and Bart appeared slightly dishevelled. He saluted the Colonel and nodded to Liza and Jamie.

"Lieutenant Shaw we are delighted and relieved to see you," said the Colonel. "Did you reach Major Graves and is the Unit on its way here?"

"Yes Colonel, they will be nearby in about three days. I don't think that the Confederates realise yet, but if their scouts are any good, they may well know by tomorrow or the day after," said Bart. "I also reached your friends Liza, and they will be here tomorrow, but nobody will know that unless there is trouble, then they will know. Was Bandor very badly hurt?"

303

"Very many bruises and a couple of broken ribs, Zelma and Dr Tom are looking after him. He's at Zelma's home," said Liza. "I'm sorry Colonel; I seem to have taken over your report from the Lieutenant. I'll leave you to make arrangements for the people in the fort and let them know about the meeting."

Liza and Jamie found Bea sitting in the outer office with Rachel and Judith and Liza found it difficult to believe that they were now around fifteen and nine years old. Rachel was first to throw herself at Liza, but her first words were to ask how Simon was in England and then she followed on with Matthew and John. Bea was holding Judith to her and crying on her.

"I didn't come here to make people cry, but I seem to have done that to everyone," said Liza and she went over to her and put her arms around Bea. Liza told her all about her meeting with Marshall and after a short while she asked her to help arrange a full town meeting for later that afternoon. "It's important Bea, everyone must be there."

"Isn't Ada here?" asked Bea.

"No, we took her buggy, so she has no transport," said Jamie.

"It's good to see you, Liza; we'll catch up either later or tomorrow, but I'll go into town and organise the meeting. It sounds very serious Liza," said Bea.

Bart came out of the Colonel's office, "I'll take the men to Major Graves tomorrow afternoon. I'm sorry that the Colonel's not joining us, but I understand. That young corporal wants to stay with the Colonel, and I couldn't persuade him otherwise, but I admire his dedication. The Colonel told me what you had to agree to so that the people in Benson can prepare for their own safety. I'll see you at the meeting Liza, but I'm off to see Laurie now."

"She'll be pleased to see you. I suppose Laurie will go to Wes and Enid's for a while," said Liza.

"That will probably be the best place," said Bart and he made his way to his quarters with a smile on his face.

"Shall we get some rest?" said Jamie and they drove back to the town and Liza went into Kathy and Joe's leaving Jamie to deal with the horse and buggy. She was not yet able to face putting it in the stable that had been hers.

"I hear you are holding a meeting tonight," said Joe. "That's just like old times Liza. Caroline has been here, and she's left some clothes for you, Susan and Leonora."

"That's very kind of her. I hope they aren't evening gowns," smiled Liza.

"No, they're everyday wear," said Kathy strutting into the shop. "She knew you wouldn't be going to any balls for a while."

"I'll see her later," said Liza and she made her way up to the room that she and Jamie would be using and lay down on the bed. She could hear Susan,

Leonora and Roberts talking about whether they should attend the meeting that evening. Liza called out that she felt that they should. She then closed her eyes and nodded off and was not aware that Jamie had joined her. She woke up a while later in his arms.

"I see you have some new dresses," smiled Jamie.

"I could do with something new and clean. Caroline brought it over; she also brought some for Susan and Leonora. You and Roberts haven't done so well," said Liza.

"Yes we have, the dressmaker also had some men's clothes, so Roberts and I will look quite smart for the meeting," smiled Jamie. "What if we find that the Confederacy wins the battle? Do you think that your Cherokee friends will be able to help?"

"Probably not until we are on our way back to South Carolina, but they will help," said Liza.

Within the hour Kathy arranged hot water for them and told them that supper would be ready in a short while. Liza washed and put on one of Caroline's dresses, which was the green colour that Caroline knew Liza loved. She wondered whether Caroline kept such a dress in stock just in case she visited, but then brushed that thought to one side.

Jamie also washed and changed into a very handsome beige suit with a lighter beige shirt and brown cravat. Roberts knocked and entered with his clothes brush which was never far from him. He had polished Jamie's brown boots and helped Jamie on with them.

"I must find some scissors," said Roberts as he eyed Jamie's longer than usual hair.

"We've plenty of time for that later," said Jamie.

"You have to admit, Roberts, that he does look casually handsome with his hair that length," said Liza which elicited a rather loud sniff from Roberts.

They walked out of their room to find Susan and Leonora admiring their new clothes; Liza smiled and did not like to remind Susan that it was really her job to make sure that Liza always looked her best.

Supper was necessarily fast, and Liza said that hopefully the next time they sat around the table it would be more convivial. The table was quickly cleared, and Joe and Jamie went outside to take the afternoon air and sat on two seats at the front of the shop. Kathy would not let Liza help and told her to relax before the meeting and so she decided to join the men. Jamie stood to let her have his chair, but she brushed his offer to one side as she had seen Caroline leaving her shop and said that she would cross the road and thank her for her kindness.

With a hop, skip and a jump Liza was with Caroline and Joe and Jamie sat in their chairs and watched the unfolding scene. People were making their way to the school for the meeting and as they passed Liza she was hugged and kissed and introduced to new additions to various families. Laurie and Bart drove into town and Laurie jumped down and went to Liza and she was joined by a couple and two children, who Joe said were Wes and Enid. Kathy came from the shop with Susan, Leonora and Roberts and said that they had better make their way to the schoolhouse.

"I see that she's surrounded by her friends; Jamie you had better go and rescue her," said Kathy.

Bea drove into town, flanked by the Colonel and his corporal, and Ada came from her home and waited for Gabriel and Kate to join her.

Jamie got up and made his way across the road and put an arm around Liza, he smiled at the people around her and said that they had better go to the meeting and that they could all meet up later.

"You must be so pleased to see all your friends," said Jamie as they walked back across the road to join Kathy and Joe to make their way to the schoolhouse.

As they entered the schoolhouse Angela and George came up to greet them warmly. Joe guided Liza and Jamie to the front row with Kathy. Leonora, Susan and Roberts were shown to seats nearer the back. Liza noticed that nine seats were set out at the top table, and she wondered who was now on the town council.

The Colonel took his place at the table, followed by Joe, Gabriel, Angela and George. Leonard Pembroke rushed in and made sure his wife was seated before going to the top table. Dr Tom and Hannah arrived with Ellen and the twins who were now attractive youngsters. Tom went to the top table and was closely followed by Jake Smith. The seat in the middle was vacant and Liza knew that it was her seat, but she would not presume to take it immediately.

Jamie whispered to her, "Who's missing; who are we waiting for?"

Kathy answered, "Our Town Council Chairman." Jamie nodded, understanding exactly what she meant.

The Colonel called the meeting to order and slowly the room became silent.

"Nearly ten years ago our Benson Town Council was formed and at each meeting either Joe, or Gabriel and sometimes I act as Chairman, but tonight we have our original Chairman with us, and I would like to ask Liza to come up and take her rightful seat at this table."

Jamie stood and took Liza's hand and led her up to the table, smiling as he went. He was not surprised but he was saddened that it had to be because of such a worrying occurrence. He returned to his seat and Liza took hers.

The Colonel smiled at Liza and sat down. She stood and looked around the room and saw faces that in her mind seemed not to have changed over the years. There were also many new faces, but all the faces were looking at her expectantly.

"The Colonel is right," started Liza. "It is nearly ten years since we formed this Town Council and over eight years since I have been able to attend a meeting such as this. I am so happy to see you all, but I wish I was not the bearer of worrying news."

She looked at the Colonel and her eyes were questioning whether she should carry on or whether he wanted to speak. He indicated that she should continue.

"There is no easy way to tell you this," said Liza. "By this time tomorrow this town and the fort will be under the control of the Confederate Army."

There were many intakes of breath and audible cries of fear and confusion. "How do you know this?" was one of the many questions shouted out.

Liza waited for the room to quieten and said, "I know it because they are camped a few miles outside the town, and we had the advantage of knowing the captain in charge. He is someone that you also know, it's Rufus Denton. He has assured me that he will give us the opportunity to organise ourselves before they come into the town."

She continued, "It is imperative that we arrange for the wives and families at the fort to move into town for their own safety as we have so very few soldiers at the fort to protect them. In fact they would never be able to repel the Confederate soldiers. I think that the Colonel should take over for the moment as he will inform you of what can be done in the short term."

The Colonel stood. "Sadly, I must tell my men to leave the fort and find a way to join with our other troops who are not so very far away. I have just ten soldiers in the fort, and it was deemed that they would be more than enough to look after the fifteen families who live in our married quarters. The town will be the safest place for these families."

The Colonel let this information sink in.

Somebody commented that they thought that the Confederate army would not be interested in a place like Benson. "Does it mean that they followed you here?"

"No they didn't follow me. I would not have led them here but unfortunately they are here, and we have to deal with the situation," said Liza. "I would like to add that our ten soldiers will be joining others who will regain Benson for the Union army as soon as possible. The Colonel and Corporal Raines have however refused to leave the fort and the town, and they will hand over with dignity, no matter what the outcome will be for them."

"Why are they allowing us time to make plans; it seems very unlike what we have been told of the Confederacy," commented Charlie Penn.

"I think that we must be grateful that it is Rufus Denton who is waiting outside town. Personally, I believe that he chose the wrong uniform because he has a great affinity to this town and he doesn't want to see anyone hurt or any of it destroyed," said Liza. "He also has a great respect for the Colonel, and I hope that he just places him under house arrest rather than sending him to prison."

"If anyone can persuade him then you can Liza," said George.

The Colonel stood and said, "Before we get to the serious business of finding rooms for our fifteen families; I want you all to know the real reason why we are being treated with leniency." He paused, looked at Liza and then looked slowly around the room, making sure that he had everyone's attention.

"The reason is because Liza has agreed to return to one of the Southern States to be held captive until the British Government agrees to support the Confederacy. Also part of that agreement was on condition that her travelling companions are free to continue on their journey home."

There was silence as this information was being digested and finally a horrified Gabriel said, "But that's illegal. Liza is a British subject and cannot be held by either side on such a whim. Besides, the British Government will never be blackmailed into such an agreement. Anyone with a modicum of intelligence would know that. It means that you could be incarcerated for years."

The place seemed to erupt with indignation and many people advised Liza to get in her wagon and run.

"That's a wonderful idea but in practise it would be futile. It wouldn't take long for them to catch up with me and I wouldn't like to guarantee what revenge would be taken on the townspeople," said Liza. "It may not happen as there are those who are working behind the scenes to assist, but I'm not going to say more. What I want to help to organise is how the fifteen army families are to be accommodated in the town. Can those fifteen families indicate who they are please?" said Liza.

"I'm sorry Liza, I want to say something first," said Joe. "Many years ago you left us as the town was in danger because the Cherokees wanted you and your sons. They were likely to fight us for you. In fact that is exactly what they did, and they took you. When you were finally rescued you did what was necessary for our sakes by leaving us. You are now going to give up your freedom for us. You could have run to your Indian friends who we know would move heaven and earth to keep you safe, but you haven't, you have remained so that we have the opportunity to safeguard ourselves. A few years ago we gave you the key to our town and I would like to say that nobody deserves it more."

Liza sat with her head down whilst there was clapping and cheers. *This is not what I want,* she thought. *We have got to organise the people from the fort, not sing my praises.*

Finally she stood and smiled and thanked everyone. "However, our main objective tonight is to get families housed in town and it must be done by lunchtime tomorrow. So much as I appreciate your thoughts, we must concentrate on our army families," said Liza.

"I can take in a family," said Mrs Henshaw. "I have two spare rooms, so I can take a family of four or so."

"That's wonderful Mrs Henshaw," said Liza. A family of a mother, a daughter and two boys were allocated to her, and Angela made the necessary note of it.

Mrs Long was next, "I can move my boys in together, so I have a spare room." A mother and small child were allocated to Mrs Long and once again Angela recorded it.

Liza looked up and asked Laurie if she was moving in with Wes and Enid and they all answered in unison that she was, so Angela made a note of that.

"I have two small rooms available," said the Boarding House owner. Two older ladies were happy to be going there.

"That's five down and ten to go," smiled Liza.

"My place can get a little raucous Liza," said the bar and hotel owner. "I do have two rooms, but they aren't suitable for families. If you bear them in mind should you not be able to house everyone, then you are more than welcome."

"Thank you. We understand that and we will only use them if necessary," smiled Liza.

"Sam can move in with me," said Archie Trower. "That leaves a room for two and a small room for one." A lady with two teenage sons volunteered for the Blacksmiths and Liza noticed that it was the teenage sons who seemed quite enthusiastic.

"Bea and the girls will be with me," said Ada.

"Of course," said Liza. "Well, we're nearly halfway there. Who else has room?"

Jake elicited a laugh by saying that he had two places that could be used, if they were not needed by any criminals.

Caroline had room for a family, as did Mr Pembroke.

"I can take two families," said Charlie Penn. Liza remembered that his house had many more rooms than most.

"We just have to find room for four more families," said Liza.

"We can move little Liza in with us," said Gabriel. "That leaves two spare bedrooms."

309

Two younger married ladies without children were allocated to Gabriel.

"We could take a family," said Tom.

"I'm afraid that you may need all the space that you have because I believe there will soon be many injuries for you to treat Tom," said Liza sadly.

There were just two middle aged ladies left and Liza said, "I believe we may have to take you up on your offer of rooms at the hotel. I'm sure you ladies can cope with a bit of raucous behaviour."

"When you have left us Liza, Joe and I will have room to take the ladies. It may not be necessary, and everyone could be back in their own homes by then," said Kathy.

"That's what we can hope for," said Liza. "At the end of this meeting it would be a good idea if you all go to where you will be staying and see what you will need to take with you. There will be plenty of people to help you all tomorrow morning."

The Colonel stood and said, "We're all going to have a difficult day tomorrow; so I would just like to say that all those moving from the fort need to get organised as quickly as possible and be ready tomorrow morning. As Liza says, go with those who you will be staying with and see what you need to take with you."

"Sadly you won't be able to take all your possessions so just concentrate on clothes, bed linen and any food. Toys for the children and of course anything that is valuable. I would like to give our troops my best wishes and I know that we will all be praying for them," said Liza.

Jake stood up; he was not one who normally spoke to a crowd, "Before this meeting breaks up, I want to say that when Rufus and his army arrive, I will be standing with the Colonel and Corporal Raines as representative of the law in this town and also to give them moral support if nothing else."

"Thank you, Jake, I appreciate that, but please don't put yourself in danger," said the Colonel. "I know that Liza has to be with us, and I believe that Jamie will also be there."

"I shall be with you Colonel," said Angela and George said that he would also.

"Yes," said Gabriel, "I shall be there." The rest of the Council were nodding, and Joe said that they all would be there when the time came.

Liza stood, "The Colonel has already said it; please don't put yourselves in danger. They are not going to shoot us; they need us. If you do want to be with us, it would be better if you don't appear threatening. I know that Rufus will understand that you are members of the Benson Town Council, but I have no idea who he will have with him and if any superior officer is like the insane major that we have already met then I beg you all to show restraint."

310

Roberts suddenly jumped up and shouted, "Lady Edgeworth is right." His very English accent surprised those in the room. "I and my colleagues and Lord Edgeworth would be dead now if that Major had had his way. It was only when Lady Edgeworth put a gun to her head and told him that he takes all or no one that we were not taken outside and murdered. You must all be very cautious in your dealings with those other than that Rufus person."

Liza and Jamie were looking with surprise at Roberts whereas the rest of the room were staring at Liza. It was taking a while for people understand what had been said. Gabriel was the first, "Oh Liza; were they going to take you and get rid of Jamie and the rest?" Liza just nodded. "How many lives have you used up now?" said Gabriel sadly.

"Too many Gabriel," said Liza. "My luck is bound to run out soon."

There were people now questioning Roberts, Susan and Leonora and they were giving details of the meeting with the Confederate Major and looks of horror were appearing on many faces.

Liza conferred with the Colonel and Joe, and they agreed that the meeting must once again be called to order and then closed so that the necessary arrangements could be made for the safety of all the people of Benson.

Liza banged the table loudly and gradually silence prevailed. "You must all carry on with the arrangements that you have to make. Time is of the essence."

People were nodding in agreement. Wes stood up and said, "I think that we now all understand why it is necessary for us to not only take in the wives and families from the fort, but also to closely watch out for the welfare of all the people of Benson. Liza, you have seen an army superior at his worst, and you are not sure that others aren't the same. We know Rufus Denton and much as he is in a different army, I am confident that he will do his best not to allow any violence, but he is not totally in charge so we must act with caution and look after one another."

Everyone was nodding and Liza said, "I would expect nothing less from the people of Benson. You must all now start organising yourselves and I would like to thank you all for your love and concern."

Kathy was sitting next to Jamie, and she asked him if Liza was really going to blow her brains out.

"Yes Kathy, she would have done that. Rufus refused to murder us and so did a lieutenant and sergeant, so the major said that he would do it himself, which was when Liza put the gun to her head. She had it ready to use and she would have done it. The major hesitated and Rufus relieved him of his duty. I believe he was taken to the person in charge of the larger unit who I hope agreed with Rufus' decision," said Jamie.

It was still daylight as they left the schoolhouse and people could be seen going to the various houses where they would be staying for however long it was felt necessary. Others were going to make sure that their homes were secure.

Liza and Jamie made their way back to Kathy's and sat quietly at the large table. They could hear people talking and there was a great deal of movement. It seemed that the people of Benson were preparing for war.

"You look tired Liza," said Jamie.

"We're both tired Jamie," said Liza. "I can't recall the number of times I've sat at this table for Sunday lunch, Christmas dinner, afternoon tea. We used to sit at the small table downstairs and have coffee and cake in the morning or afternoon."

"I always thought that your house was the main meeting place," smiled Jamie.

"Yes, it was but only when we weren't here," smiled Liza.

"Is that all you did in the days?" smiled Jamie.

"I saw Kathy nearly every day. In fact I seem to remember that I saw everybody nearly every day," Liza was smiling at the memory.

"When did you find the time to look after your family and work?" asked Jamie.

"Yes, it's a mystery, isn't it?" said Liza. "Jamie I'm beginning to feel frightened. I really want to be home now; I want to be with our boys and Miranda, Lucinda, David and Grace. I want to see Mrs Frances, Mr and Mrs Lambert, in fact I want to be with everyone at home; I don't want to be here, I never wanted to be here."

"Everybody seems to want you here and you looked happy enough running across the road to see the dressmaker. I watched you and I understood what you meant by the freedom that you had living here. I can't see you lifting your skirt and leaping across the Edgeworth village road to sit at Mrs Price's table for coffee and cakes, or at the Inn with Mr and Mrs Rogers. You probably would be able to, but they would be on edge the whole time you were there. I know that they admire and respect you but sitting with your feet up at their table would embarrass them. Here is a free life and you must miss it," said Jamie.

"Yes, I miss how things were, but I have a different life now and I'm desperate to get back to it. I want to go home Jamie and I'm not able to. I want to see our boys and Simon and deal with whatever antics they have been getting up to. I want to laugh with our villagers at our cricket matches. I want to see Adam and April and see how their school is progressing. I wonder how Christopher is getting on because by now he should be with Adam. I want to be home and in your bed at night and I don't know how I am going to get there," said Liza and by now she was softly crying.

"We'll get there Liza; I promise you we'll get there," said Jamie. He mopped her eyes and kissed her. "Kathy and Joe will be back soon; they won't want to see you upset like this because if they do, they may do something silly tomorrow."

"Yes, of course you're right. I wonder where Roberts, Susan and Leonora have got to. It was surprising of Roberts to address the meeting. I wasn't too pleased with what he said, but I know that he did it because he could see that some were not taking the situation as seriously as they should. He certainly got everyone taking notice," said Liza.

Liza knew that they would all be back shortly, and probably more than those in the household, so she got the table set and found ham, cheese and tomatoes as well as several loaves of bread. Jamie was smiling at her.

"You know where everything is here then Liza. You look as though you live here," said Jamie.

"You're right, I do know as nothing has changed," laughed Liza and with that the shop door opened and several people came in. Roberts was first and he apologised profusely for speaking at the meeting.

"It got everyone moving Roberts, so it proved necessary," smiled Liza.

Gabriel and Kate arrived. "I hope you don't mind, but I've left little Liza with your Susan for a while," said Kate. "She's already helped me move little Liza's bed and clothes into our room ready for our guests tomorrow. She's a little apprehensive about leaving here without you but I know that Roberts and Leonora will be with her and I'm sure that some of your Indian friends will make sure that they are safe."

"Possibly," was all that Liza would say on the subject.

Kathy came in, "good you've got supper ready," she said to Liza. "I don't know who will be calling this evening. Bea has already moved in with Ada; the Colonel may be staying at the fort tonight although Ada would prefer him to rest at home, but he is saying that the families are his responsibility."

Zelma joined them saying that Bandor was much better, and she whispered to Liza that he would leave the next day after the Confederates had arrived so that he could report back to his people.

The evening was full of people coming and going. Kathy and Joe's had become the hub for the people of Benson, and it was well after midnight when Liza and Jamie finally went to bed, but noises of wagons and carts could be heard for some hours; the people of Benson were looking after one another.

***

The ladies who were staying at the Hotel and the Boarding House had got together and completed their move in the early hours of the morning. They were then free to help those with families and they could be seen squashed into one buggy going towards the fort at a dangerous speed at seven o'clock in the morning.

Liza was watching them from the bedroom window and commented that she hoped that they would take more care if they were going to drive any of the children to town.

All the men in town made their way to and from the fort and by midday all the families were ensconced in the houses that would become their homes for however long it was found to be necessary.

Ada slowly drove back into town and stopped at Kathy's. She made her way up to the large dining room where Liza was sitting trying to calm her nerves before she made her way to the fort. Jamie would be back shortly as he was helping with the move. Liza looked up and the fear and sadness on Ada's face made it difficult to hold back any tears. They both put their arms around one another and sobbed.

"He came to Benson before the fort was here and saw it built piece by piece. He has fought in several battles and waged war on the Indians. He has commanded the men under him with strength and compassion and has never been defeated, but he is defeated now, and they will probably imprison him, and I know that he won't survive that. For the first time in our lives together we are unable to help one another or give each other strength. At least you will be with him, although that is no comfort to you because you are going to be in the same position as he is. I shouldn't be bothering you with my worries, you have enough of your own," said Ada.

"You're not bothering me Ada and you haven't added to the worries that I already have. I will try to look after him and I'm going to suggest that he's placed under house arrest, especially as he's no longer in the army. He's retired and therefore he should not be treated as army personnel," said Liza.

"Do you think they would agree to that?" said Ada looking hopeful.

"If the commander is anything like Rufus, then yes, it is a distinct possibility. The only person we would have to worry about is Corporal Raines and I'll see what I can think of for him," said Liza. "Has Bart set off with the soldiers yet?"

"They were just about to leave when I left the fort, so I suppose they will be on their way now," said Ada. "I must get back to the house and Christina. She knows that there is a problem, but of course she and Judith keep one another occupied. Bea is trying to make life comfortable for the girls, so she and Rachel are concocting a special meal for us tonight."

"You never know, perhaps the Colonel will also be able to enjoy the offerings. Bart is taking Ben's letter for Brigeta. I know that his route will be passing near the Dornberg's farms. You got a few letters from the men, didn't you?" said Liza.

"Yes, they were very touching. It was nice to be considered family to those who have no family. Both Eugene and I took it as a very great compliment," said Ada. "Goodbye Liza, you know I wish you well and pray that you will be able to get out of this difficulty. You know that I love you." Ada kissed her and quickly left before she could show just how upset she was.

Jamie, Kathy and Joe appeared, and it seemed that they had been giving Ada the time she needed with Liza.

"Will you have some lunch, Liza?" asked Kathy.

"I'm really not very hungry," said Liza. "And if you don't mind, I have one call to make before we set out for the fort."

"I'll come with you Liza," said Jamie and Liza looked as though she wanted to be alone, but then she smiled and told him that she would appreciate his thoughts.

"Where are we going?" he asked when they had left the general store.

"We're going to visit Zelma and Bandor," said Liza.

"What are you cooking up?" asked Jamie.

"A way to get the Colonel and Corporal Raines out of the fort and away to join the troops," said Liza.

"Is there one?" asked Jamie.

"Oh yes, there's always a way," smiled Liza.

Zelma looked up and smiled her lop sided smile as Liza and Jamie went into her home. Bandor was sitting with his eyes closed and meditating; he slowly opened his eyes and nodded.

"What is it that you need me to do i-tse di-ka-ta?" he said in Cherokee.

"I need you to help the Colonel and Corporal Raines if you can," replied Liza.

"It is you that I have to help and keep safe, not the Colonel or the corporal," said Bandor.

Jamie was looking puzzled, and Liza said that they would now speak in English so that Jamie would know what they may be able to plan.

After some discussion Bandor said that it would be easy to take the Colonel to his men if they just put him under house arrest; he could be spirited from his home, but they would not be able to take his own horse as that would be immediately noticed, so he was going to arrange to get one waiting for him on the outskirts of town.

"What about the corporal?" asked Liza.

"We can get him out of the prison if that is where he is held and out of the fort without too much difficulty. He'll need a horse also. I'll be able to guide them to where his troops are. If the Colonel is under house arrest, he will be safer here than where he would want to be," said Bandor.

"Even though he has retired, all of the Benson soldiers have served with him and he has a responsibility towards them. In his way he loves them and their families, he feels that Benson has been one big family and he wants to be with them in this awful conflict no matter how it turns out," said Liza.

"The Colonel is an honourable man and deserves to be treated with dignity and so does the young corporal," said Bandor. "I must make arrangements; I'll be back before the other soldiers get here. Make sure the Colonel knows that he must do exactly as he is told as must the Corporal."

He then said in Cherokee. "You know that the Colonel will then know how his daughter's killer escaped and that you had to be behind it."

"I believe that he has known for a long time but preferred not to acknowledge it. He is now in trouble and needs help. I can't abandon him no matter what the consequences," said Liza also in Cherokee.

"Hmm," said Bandor gruffly.

"Please be careful Liza," said a very concerned Zelma. "You have had so many scrapes with death in your life and I don't trust the soldiers who are coming. Don't forget how Rufus used his fists on people; I don't suppose that he's changed."

Bandor had disappeared and Liza and Jamie got up to leave. "I promise that I will see you later Zelma; stay safely in your home no matter what you hear. Or perhaps you would prefer to go to Ada's or Kathy's?" asked Liza.

"I'll go to Kathy's," said Zelma. "She'll make room for me. I'll get my things."

It didn't take her long to pack everything that she needed, and they carried her bedding and clothes over to Kathy's. She carefully took her medicinal herbs and any food that she had, although as she was going to Kathy's it was unnecessary to take anything.

Joe was waiting for them with his buggy. Gabriel came over and climbed in with them and they slowly made their way to the fort. Many of the townspeople were standing outside their houses to watch them go. Angela and George joined Leonard Pembroke who drove them on their way. Tom had decided to ride out as did Jake Smith and it was a rather subdued procession that the townspeople watched until they were out of sight.

They all managed to fit into the Colonel's office and outer office with Corporal Raines.

"I need to speak to you Colonel," said Liza.

He ushered her into his office and closed the door, which did not surprise anyone there.

"I am attempting to make arrangements to get you and Corporal Raines to your troops if you are agreeable. Bandor and my Indian friends will be helping in this and in fact Bandor has already started organising what is needed. I am hoping that you will just be placed under house arrest as we are going to make it clear that you are no longer army personnel and therefore should be treated in a civilian manner," said Liza.

"I am a little puzzled that you are thinking that way Liza; I believe that your position is far more concerning than that of mine and Corporal Raines," said the Colonel.

"Would you not prefer to join your unit and fight to regain Benson for your army?" said Liza.

"Of course I would, but I cannot believe that it will be possible. It's good of you to try to give me hope, but for once you haven't succeeded," smiled the Colonel.

"Oh for heaven's sake Colonel, I'm not placating you; it is going to be more than possible. It will be a little difficult for Corporal Raines, who I believe will be placed in the prison, but there are ways around that. If you are at home, it will be easy, but if you are in the prison, it will just be a little more difficult," said Liza.

"So you know how to break out of the prison then Liza," said the Colonel.

"Where do you keep the spare set of keys? I bet it's also in the prison. It would be prudent to remove them now and give them to Jake who will in turn let Bandor have them," said Liza and the Colonel called Corporal Raines in and instructed him to find the spare keys to the prison.

"Well Liza, that could get us out of prison but getting out of the fort will be more difficult," smiled the Colonel.

"Colonel, do you honestly think that the way out that you found all those years ago was the only way out. I have no idea where it is but I'm sure Bandor does. He will have horses for you both as you will not be able to take your own; that would be too noticeable if they were missing, and it is imperative that you do exactly what Bandor, or any other Indian tells you to. You must make it clear to Corporal Raines that he must also not question his instructions. We will get you to your men Colonel and we will see you coming back to Benson under a Union flag," said Liza.

"How will your Indian friends know where we are Liza?" asked the Colonel.

"They will know Colonel; there is no doubt about that," smiled Liza.

The Colonel sat and stared at Liza for a short while and she could see that what he had previously suspected about her involvement in getting Mark Kendal away from the prison was indeed the case, but he decided to say nothing on the subject, all he did say was that he knew that she always had good reasons for everything.

"I do want to join my men Liza and I do want to return to Benson triumphant and be able to leave it safely in our army's hands. I will see Corporal Raines and strongly impress on him that he must take advantage of the opportunity and that it is imperative that he questions nothing that he is instructed to do by Bandor and his friends," said the Colonel.

There was a knock on the door and Corporal Raines entered with the spare keys and the Colonel asked that Jake come in and when he did, he placed the keys in his hands for safekeeping until either Bandor or his friends needed them. Jake raised his eyebrows questioningly and the Colonel told him that it was best if he did not know. Jake nodded and left the room.

The Corporal was about to leave but the Colonel called him back and said to Liza that he would now instruct him and that perhaps she would like to join the others and try to relax a little before Rufus and whoever else arrived. She nodded and left Corporal Raines to be given his instructions.

Everyone knew that Liza had been concocting an escape plan for the Colonel and Corporal Raines but realised that the less they knew the better it would be for them.

Liza looked around the outer office where she had fond memories of Ben working and noticed that it was particularly empty of documentation. She presumed that it had all been spirited away. *Why give them a present of all the men's records*, she thought. She wondered where they had gone and thought that the most secure places were the bank and Gabriel's lawyers' offices.

The Corporal emerged from the Colonel's office and nodded to Liza which let everyone know that a plan was definitely in place.

"I believe that our visitors are arriving," said the Colonel and he brushed himself down; he was wearing his best army uniform, complete with his sword. Corporal Raines also looked presentable, and he slowly saluted the Colonel, and they walked out of the offices and onto the parade ground with great dignity.

"This is it, Liza; are you ready for this?" asked Jamie.

"No, but I have no choice," muttered Liza and she and Jamie also walked with dignity to the parade ground.

Rufus and a Colonel rode into the fort followed by at least thirty soldiers who slowly surrounded the Colonel, the Corporal, Liza and Jamie. The rest of the town council moved into the parade ground and stood quietly.

Rufus dismounted and held the Colonel's horse whilst he also dismounted. They both saluted Colonel Western and Rufus introduced the Colonel and Corporal Raines to his Colonel Knowles.

"I was given to understand that you were no longer in the army Colonel," said Colonel Knowles.

"I have retired Sir but felt that I could do some good by ensuring the safety of the soldiers' families within these walls whilst their menfolk were away defending their country," said Colonel Western.

"I'm surprised to see you in uniform Sir," said Colonel Knowles.

Colonel Western did not dignify the comment with an answer.

"Are the families still within the fort?" asked Colonel Knowles.

"No Sir, they are now housed with friends in the town, but it has been necessary for them to leave some of their belongings, and I trust that your men will not damage or take them until they are able to be retrieved," said Colonel Western.

"We will ensure that they are taken care of. I see that you have a corporal with you. Is he part of the regular army?" asked the Confederate colonel.

"He bravely remained to ensure that all families were safely removed and to look out for me. I trust you will appreciate that, although an army man, his sole task was to assist with keeping records in order," said Colonel Western.

"I will bear that in mind," said Colonel Knowles. "I presume that the lady standing with you is Lady Edgeworth."

"Yes, and the gentleman is her husband Lord Jamie Edgeworth," said Colonel Western. "The rest of those here consist of members of our town council. I can introduce them to you now."

"That will not be necessary Sir; we have no intention of disrupting the smooth running of the town and no doubt in the fullness of time we will get to know one another, but I thank them for their courteous thought," said Colonel Knowles.

A prison wagon trundled into the fort and Rufus looked decidedly uncomfortable. That was something that Liza had not bargained for. It appeared that they were going to transport the Colonel and Corporal away immediately. She had no doubt that her friends would eventually deal with the situation, but it was not going to be easy.

"That seems rather unnecessary Colonel Knowles," said Liza. "Neither Colonel Western nor Corporal Raines need such incarceration."

"No Lady Edgeworth, you are right. I have decided that as the Colonel is now a civilian then he should be returned to his home and stay there under house arrest. The Corporal is a different story, he is a member of the opposing forces and therefore he must remain behind bars until he is removed to a southern prison," said Colonel Knowles. "The wagon is for you Lady Edgeworth, as you will be immediately transported to our headquarters in Alabama, where you will remain until we have an agreement with the British Government. Your husband will be taken to another area; we cannot allow you to remain together."

"You will not Sir," said Liza. "I have voluntarily agreed to return to one of the southern states. I do not need to be transported in a prison wagon."

"My wife is not a prisoner, and we stay together," said Jamie adamantly.

"That is not your decision to make. I am charged with the task of delivering your wife to Alabama. I will not fail in that duty, and it will be undertaken as I see fit," said Colonel Knowles. "However, you will also be useful to us, but it is too much of a risk keeping you together."

Liza turned to Jamie with panic in her eyes, "I'm not going in that thing, Jamie; please do something. I can't be caged."

Colonel Western recognised panic in Liza, as did Rufus, but neither of them were fooled. Jamie knew that she had no fear of small, closed in places but he played along with the deception, and he said, "It's alright Liza, I won't let that happen. I promised you that I would look after you."

But the appearance of panic was not easing. Jamie turned to Colonel Knowles and said, "My wife is not going to be transported like a common criminal and I am telling you that I will be with her every step of the way. However as you have broken your word we are no longer required to abide by the agreement."

The Town Council, led by Colonel Western moved forward and surrounded Liza and Jamie. There was a noticeable sound from the Confederate soldiers of rifles cocking, but the Council held their ground. Rufus could be heard voicing his opinion to his Colonel.

"Sir, this is a mistake," he said. "I know this Council and this town, and they will not allow Liza to be taken this way. The outcome will be a blood bath throughout this town, and I don't believe that you would really want that."

"Captain," said Colonel Knowles, "you are advocating that we pander to the whims of overly pampered English aristocrats who have never had a days' deprivation in their lives, so it's about time that they learned what it's like to eat humble pie. No, she will be transported that way and that's an end to it."

The Town Council moved even closer to Liza and Jamie as Rufus turned and physically pulled Colonel Knowles to one side.

"Do you really know who Liza Edgeworth is, Sir?" said Rufus, to which the Colonel frowned. "She's Liza Marchant and she has known the worst kind of deprivation that you could ever imagine. I tell you Sir, neither her husband nor this town will allow her to be taken in this way and quite frankly you could end up with somebody who would have to be placed in care for the rest of her life, that is if she didn't find the means to end it herself beforehand."

Colonel Knowles was still frowning, and it was obvious that he had the stirrings of a memory and as it came to him, he closed his eyes and nodded. He stood for a minute and signalled for his soldiers to lower their weapons.

"Lord and Lady Edgeworth," said Colonel Knowles, "Captain Denton has convinced me that there is no need to keep you under lock and key. Your word is your bond, and I am prepared to accept that, but will you please make preparations to leave for Alabama the day after tomorrow. Your travelling companions are free to leave whenever they wish."

Jamie nodded his assent and Liza said that it gave her time to make a visit or two. Once again Colonel Knowles frowned with his lack of understanding and Rufus whispered to him that she had family to visit in the graveyard and who they were.

"Ah," said Colonel Knowles nodding, "I understand. I knew Lieutenant Kelly; he was a good and dedicated soldier. Captain Denton, will you arrange for the Corporal to be placed in the prison and make sure that Colonel Western is escorted to his home. All the others are free to return to their homes or places of work, but I trust that you will make sure that Lord and Lady Edgeworth are watched over."

"Sir," said Gabriel bravely. "As Lord and Lady Edgeworth's legal representation in this town, I feel that it is my duty to point out to you that what you are doing is totally illegal. Lord and Lady Edgeworth are British citizens and are therefore not subject to incarceration by either army within any states in America. What you are doing Sir can only be classed as a war crime."

"And you are Sir?" asked Colonel Knowles.

"I am Gabriel Sanderson, advocate of this town of Benson," said Gabriel.

"Ah yes, of course, you are General Sanderson's son," said Colonel Knowles. "I have no idea whether you are right or whether you are wrong; all I do know is that my orders are to bring Lady Edgeworth to Alabama. It has been intimated that her husband could also be useful. I follow orders Mr Sanderson. My duty concerning the Edgeworths is complete when we reach Alabama. Good day gentlemen and ladies, you can rest assured that we have no intention of disrupting the smooth running of your town."

Colonel Knowles turned to Rufus and asked him to direct him to the Colonel's office. Colonel Western was the only person not to bristle with indignation. Corporal Raines was marched off to the prison and Rufus returned and was about to escort Colonel Western to his home when Liza looked at him and said that she and Jamie were quite capable of making sure that the Colonel joined his wife, and they would wait for him to retrieve his horse.

"You know that the Colonel has made it my duty to make sure we know where you are Liza," said Rufus. "I'll ride into town with you and Colonel Western."

"I hope you are not expecting to watch us every second of every day as that would be most embarrassing for all of us," said Jamie. Rufus just shrugged and both Jamie and Gabriel moved around to help Liza into Joe's buggy. Rufus moved off towards Colonel Western and Gabriel whispered, "You played that one well Liza. I presume you got exactly what you wanted."

"I don't know what you mean Gabriel," grinned Liza. "But if I had exactly what I wanted, I would be well on my way to New York having spent a happy couple of days with you all."

As they drove into town they watched as Rufus escorted the Colonel towards his house and Liza could only imagine the sense of relief that Ada must be feeling seeing her husband safely home.

Kathy was also breathing a sigh of relief as they all arrived back, and she wanted to know what had happened. Joe said that he would tell her as he knew that Zelma needed to talk quietly to Liza. Gabriel left for his home saying that the less he knew about anything the better it would be.

Everyone seemed overly occupied and when Liza followed Zelma it was to find Bandor sitting quietly in the small downstairs dining room.

"The Colonel and his Corporal will be leaving us tonight. It is arranged and I hope that you have ensured that they do exactly as instructed," he said in Cherokee.

"Yes, they know that Bandor," said Liza also in Cherokee. "Are you taking them?"

"I am taking the Colonel. He will be leaving as soon as it is dark. I'm taking him to Little Dove's brother and friend on the outskirts of town. I must return to you then; you are who I must guard," said Bandor.

Liza nodded. "What about the Corporal?" she asked.

"After midnight we are moving him. We already have the keys from your lawman. With luck he will catch up with the Colonel before he reaches his forces, but if not, he will be with them in the early hours of the morning," said Bandor.

"You know the way out of the fort then," said Liza.

"It wouldn't matter if we didn't. We always find ways to go where we want," said Bandor.

"Rufus Denton may well know the way out of the fort," said Liza. "He was there long enough, and he may have used it himself on occasion."

"I've told you; it doesn't matter," said Bandor.

"I presume you have horses ready for them," said Liza and Bandor looked at her as if she was asking stupid questions. "I'm sorry Bandor but I find it difficult not to have been involved in this arrangement and I worry that you and our friends will get caught and are hurt or worse."

"Worry about yourself i-tse di-ka-ta and let us worry about ourselves and your Colonel and Corporal. I am not leaving you for long, probably only an hour. You will not have to go back to the south, but we think that it will not be us who stops you; it will be the ones wearing the blue coats. You have many people working to help you, but we are watching over you," said Bandor.

"I have tried very hard not to take sides in this conflict, but I have found it difficult not to lean towards the north. They do not appear to want to use me and being with them means that I may at last return to my home and my family," said Liza.

Bandor nodded, "Yes you must return to u-ne-ga ta-wa-di-u-s-di. He is our future, and you need to be with him for now. He will return to us and guide us one day. You will teach him what is necessary. It's getting dark, I must leave now but I will be watching over you later."

"Take care Bandor; you know you mean a great deal to me. Your life is important," said Liza.

"It is not as important as yours," said Bandor as he left.

Liza turned towards Zelma and asked her if she knew how they were going to get the Colonel and Corporal Raines away.

"I do not, but even if I did, I wouldn't say as it is best that you do not know. Let's go back and join the others. I know that they are concerned, and it is obvious to them that you have arranged to help the Colonel and Corporal Raines. Rufus will also know when they cannot be found tomorrow. Did the Colonel realise that you had helped his daughter's killer to get away?" asked Zelma.

"I'm sure he has always known but he said nothing today. He just went along with what I told him he had to do if he wanted to join his men," said Liza.

They joined all the others and there were looks of concern from everyone. "Are you going to be in trouble Liza?" asked Kathy.

"I'm already in trouble Kathy," said Liza. She turned to Leonora, Susan, and Roberts. "I presume you have been told that you can leave whenever you wish. It may be better for you to go by stagecoach rather than using the wagon. I believe that one is due to leave tomorrow afternoon; I'm sure you can be ready by then."

"I have already told them that we will arrange for their passage, but Roberts has refused to leave until he knows either we are also free to leave, or we have no alternative but to return to the south. And if we are returned to the south, he says that he will also be with us," said Jamie.

"That's very loyal of you Roberts, but you know that we need you to get Susan and Leonora to safety because we will be unable to do so," said Liza. "We are relying on you to do this for us."

"I don't want to go on without you," said Susan and it was obvious that she had been crying.

"We need you to get back home to reassure everyone that we are alive and well," said Liza. "This country is at war, and we have already seen a little of what that entails. It is only going to get worse, much worse and Jamie and I will have enough to worry about without wondering what is happening to you."

Leonora looked from Jamie to Liza and back again. "I have every confidence that you will not be going back to the south, so I'm going to wait and see what happens. A few days will make no difference to our getting to New York safely."

Liza and Jamie smiled. "Let's have a compromise then," said Jamie. "If we do have to leave and we are not back within three days, you must all promise that you will make your way to New York and then arrange with Henry Mahoney for your passage home to England."

"Leonora, I presume your father will be delighted to see you safely back with him. I know that Roberts will make sure that you reach your family in New York," said Liza.

"You don't need to worry," said Joe. "We will make sure that they are looked after and help them on their way if you don't return. I think Leonora is right and that you won't be going back to the south, but we had better keep quiet about that."

"I wonder where Rufus is," said Liza. "He's meant to be watching us."

"I think that he has delegated that to a couple of unfortunate privates. One is across the road and the other is lurking behind our store. They are not going to be very happy by the morning as it looks like rain," said Joe.

As they sat down to their evening meal the rain started. It was not heavy but it must have been miserable for the soldiers who were watching the store. Liza noticed that Zelma had disappeared and when she returned later, she just nodded to Liza which meant that the Colonel was on his way to join his troops. She knew that she would not be made aware of when and how the Corporal had been freed; she just knew that it would happen.

Not only would Rufus be furious, but he would also have to face his Colonel who would blame him for losing not only Colonel Western but Corporal Raines also. Liza had no doubt that she would be the first person he called on when it was realised that the Colonel and Corporal Raines were no longer in Benson.

Tiredness was overcoming them all and after clearing up, Liza made her way to their room. She was lying back in bed when Jamie came in and she could see that he was unhappy, and she knew that he was finding it difficult being in the town where Patrick had played such a large part in her life. He seemed reluctant to join her and she felt that she had to allay his fears and so she called to him gently.

"It's been a very difficult day today; I was so proud when you stepped forward to defend me. I may not have shown it, but I was very frightened. That Colonel was not a very nice person, and I thought that I would have to be caged in that terrible wagon, but I knew that you would not let that happen. I really don't know what I would do without you and even worse than the prison wagon was that they were going to separate us. I don't ever want that to happen, I want to be with you always. I really need you to hold me and love me tonight, Jamie," said Liza. "You mean the world to me."

"Do I Liza?" said Jamie. "For a while I thought that your past was clouding our future."

"I can understand why you thought that, but no, we have a close relationship that the past will never interfere with," said Liza. "I love you Jamie Edgeworth and it's wonderfully comforting to know that you love me."

***

Liza and Jamie were sitting at the breakfast table the following morning when Rufus burst in with a look of fury on his face. Kathy and Joe frowned at the uncalled for intrusion and Joe asked him what he meant by coming into their home without an invitation.

He brushed aside their indignation and headed straight for Liza who frowned up at him and asked what he was doing there.

"You know exactly what I'm doing here Liza," he said through gritted teeth.

"Well I presume that it's your way of keeping an eye on us," said Liza. "Although you look rather annoyed; has something happened?"

Rufus banged the table with his hand and told Liza not to treat him like an idiot. Jamie stepped between him and Liza and told him to step back and kindly explain his actions.

"You cannot possibly try to convince me that you did not have a hand in Corporal Raines' escape. Who did you get to help him; not one of my men, I'm sure? Tell me who was it?" shouted Rufus.

Liza stayed seated and looked at Rufus with what she hoped was puzzlement and Joe came forward and said, "How dare you come into my home and start creating a scene. Get out and calm down; you are not welcome here."

Jamie was standing between Liza and Rufus and everyone else was showing that they were protecting Liza.

"Well Liza," said Rufus, "It's your fault now. I'm going to get Colonel Western and transport him in the wagon to our nearest prison and it will be a miracle if he survives that."

"Why are you doing that?" asked Liza innocently. "You know perfectly well that the fort prison is rather insecure. I'm sure Corporal Raines knew how to get out of it, so why blame everyone but yourself for his escape. You knew the failings of the prison block; you should have checked it. Don't blame me or the Colonel for you not doing your job properly."

"Get out Rufus and leave us in peace. You are no longer welcome in this household," said Joe.

Rufus stared at Liza for a moment and then retreated down to the roadway. He could be heard barking orders to a couple of his men to go across the road and arrest Colonel Western.

Liza turned to Jamie with concern and said that there were no men in Ada's house to protect the women. Joe immediately reached for his rifle and Jamie and Roberts followed him out of the room, down to the roadway and across to Ada's home.

Rufus was on his horse waiting for his men to bring the Colonel out. The two soldiers emerged from the house and Joe, Jamie and Roberts took up positions in the front garden and Gabriel came out of his house and joined them.

"He's not there, Sir," said one of the men.

Rufus jumped from his horse and marched into Ada's home. Jake Smith walked across and joined the men in the front garden.

Liza and Kathy came across and Liza said that they were going in to make sure Ada was handling the situation.

"I'm going with you," said Jamie and Joe said the same and they walked into the house only to hear Rufus shouting at Ada demanding to know the whereabouts of Colonel Western.

"How dare you march into my home demanding where my husband is," said Ada. "You should have more respect for me than that. It is none of your business where my husband has gone, but if you really want to know I will tell you that he has gone to join his men, which is where any good soldier should be."

Rufus' face was a picture of fury and he said, "He was under house arrest and was honour bound not to leave."

326

"Did you ever hear him say that he would remain here; just because you said that he was under house arrest did not mean that he or anyone else agreed that he should not leave," said Ada. "He has been in charge of men for many years, and although he has retired, it does not mean that he does not take his loyalties and duties seriously. He is not here, so what are you going to do about it? Arrest me?"

Rufus turned, clenching his fists he stared down at Liza. For a moment she thought that he was going to hit her, and Jamie and Joe thought the same and both stepped between her and Rufus.

"I know you did this Liza," said Rufus between clenched teeth. "I'm going to lock you up until we can take you to Alabama. I'm not going to have you meddling in our affairs any further."

"You are not sir," said Jamie. "You will not lay a finger on her or incarcerate her in any way. Tell me what were your men doing last night? Were they asleep on duty? They were not Sir. They watched where we were all night. We went nowhere and spoke to no one other than those within the household. If you want to blame somebody, blame yourself for not guarding your prisoners well enough. You know this town and the fort sufficiently to have realised that there must be many ways out of it. I would have assumed that you would have made sure such ways were guarded. Now get out of our way, we are returning to the store, and we need no help to get there."

Jamie put his arm around Liza and guided her towards the door; Joe took up a position on her other side and they pushed their way past Rufus who seemed unable to make any decision. Ada then demanded that Rufus leave her house immediately as he was no longer welcome there.

Roberts, Gabriel and Jake were in the front garden and in the street outside stood Wes, Sam and Archie Trower, Leonard Pembroke and Greg Long, with Dr Tom and George also making their way towards them. There were also many Confederate soldiers loitering around town and they seemed not to know what was happening, but the men of the town were making it obvious that they were in charge and that Liza was in their care.

Jamie smiled down at Liza and commented that she had better keep a low profile from now onwards.

"I have some visits to make in a little while; once I have done that I will stay within the store until we know what is happening," said Liza.

"I know that you would like to be alone for your visits but I'm not sure that it is safe for you to do so," said Jamie.

"I won't be alone," said Liza quietly. "There are many there who will keep me company."

"But nobody who could protect you," said Jamie.

"I don't mind if you would like to be with me," said Liza.

"No, it's your time to be alone with your past. You have family and friends to visit. There is only one that I would know, and I think he would prefer to see you alone," said Jamie gently. "The only other one would be Felicity and I don't think that she would want to see either of us."

Tears welled up in Liza's eyes. "I very much appreciate how understanding you are Jamie."

Kathy and Ada caught up with them and Liza asked if Ada was feeling all right.

"Yes, I am Liza," said Ada. "I was so relieved to see Eugene when he returned yesterday. I understand that he wanted to be with his men. He still thinks of them as his and although Marshall is now in charge, he knows the respect that Eugene is held in with all at the fort."

"And in the town also Ada," said Liza.

They went into the store and made their way up to the dining room.

"When you have a minute, I'd like to talk to you Liza," said Ada quietly and Liza nodded and said that she would call on her later, but firstly she had to visit her family and friends in the graveyard.

"If you want some flowers, take some from the garden," said Ada.

"I'll do that, thank you Ada," said Liza and she turned and smiled at Hannah and the twins who had just come to visit. Ellen was also with them, and Tom was checking that they were all unharmed.

"We have some flowers that you can have Liza," said Hannah. "The twins will help you pick them."

Liza laughed and said that she remembered a time when the twins had helped themselves to every flower in every garden just for her.

"That's a long time ago Liza," smiled Hannah.

"Yes, it's almost ten years now," said Liza.

The room seemed to be filling as Kate and Gabriel arrived with little Liza. "You can take what you want from our garden also," said Kate and Liza could see that Gabriel was remembering the devastation that the twins had created in his garden all those years ago.

"Don't worry Gabriel," said Liza. "I'll supervise what we take; your garden won't be trampled this time."

Kathy, Zelma, and Susan were organising coffee for everyone. "I understand that the Colonel is no longer in town," said Tom without any surprise in his voice.

"He's gone to join the men," said Ada.

"And I also hear that the Corporal Raines has also disappeared," carried on Tom.

All eyes were on Liza waiting for her to say something or show some emotion, but nothing was forthcoming from her.

"When I've had my coffee, shall we go and pick some flowers, Laura and Benjy?" said Liza changing the subject.

"I'll help you," said Ellen. "The twins can still be a little messy in everything that they do. I can help to control them, although it's not easy." She smiled and Liza could see that she had now become a very pretty woman and she wondered if she and Greg still kept one another company.

After a short while Kathy handed them baskets and scissors for their flowers and while they made their way to the various gardens, Jamie and Joe sat outside the store and Jake came to join them to watch over Liza, Ellen and the twins.

There was a great deal of noise coming from the saloon and the bar keeper could be heard telling them to leave as he was not opening that day. Jake slowly moved across to see if he could help and at the same time Rufus rode back into town with a couple of men, and the bar was soon cleared of the disruptive element.

Jake moved back to Jamie and Joe, and they all continued watching Liza, Ellen and the twins who were now helping Liza sort the flowers in the baskets. When they had finished, they helped to carry the baskets up to the graveyard and then tactfully Ellen took the twins home, leaving Liza to visit alone.

They watched her until she disappeared from sight as she went to lay some flowers on Angus Campbell's grave. Dr Bridges' grave was nearby, and she told him that she hoped that he was resting peacefully as he had worked so hard in the past for the town. The town drunk, Wilf Cody, was also there, whose attempted duel with Angus had resulted in Danny's death. Liza said a prayer for him and knew that he was finally at peace.

Jamie moved up towards the graveyard; he did not want to intrude on Liza's time with her past family, but he wanted to make sure that she was safe. Rufus rode up, dismounted, and walked towards him. Jamie had no desire to talk to him, but Rufus seemed to want to say something to him.

"There's an unruly element in town Lord Edgeworth. I just want to make sure that the townsfolk are aware that they are around. They have been ordered back to the fort, but they are only recently enlisted men and have yet to realise the consequences of disobeying orders. I see that Liza is visiting her family and friends," said Rufus.

Jamie found it difficult to be civil to Rufus, but he made the effort just saying that she needed time to have her memories. They both watched as she laid flowers on Danny's grave, and they could see that she was talking to him. She then moved to her daughter's grave and placed flowers there also. Finally she moved to Patrick's grave having saved roses for him. Jamie turned away from watching her; he felt that she should not be watched at this time.

"Well Patrick," she said, "I didn't expect to be visiting you now, but I'm pleased that I can talk to you. I have felt your presence on many occasions, and I know that Matthew has also. John hasn't been so lucky, but he accepts that he is not like us. They still love you and talk about you often, as does James who remembers you with great affection. He often talks about the time that he stayed with us in Belfast all those years ago and being allowed by you to eat with his fingers."

"I'm sure that you know that Jamie and I are now married, and he has adopted our boys. He is a very good father to them, but they only agreed to be adopted as long as they could still think of you as their daddy and talk about you as much as they wanted to. I have adopted James; Evelyn refused at first, but James told her that it was what he wanted and then Matthew decided that he would tell her also, much to Jamie's and my horror at the time. But it worked and we now have a large family of boys. Simon is staying with us whilst he finishes his education, so I am very much outnumbered in our household."

"It is difficult for me being back in Benson. Much as I have always loved the town, it brings back so many memories which remind me of how happy we were here and how much I still love you, which does, of course, make me feel very disloyal to Jamie. He loves me very much, but you know that; he had made that quite clear when you were still alive. I love him but it is different to the way that I love you. It is difficult to explain it, so I won't even try."

"Sean came to rescue me from Charleston and Bart was with him but I'm afraid that Rufus and the Confederate army found me again although I know that it won't be long before I'm on my way to New York and then onto England where our boys are waiting for us. But I am so sad that this country is now split in two and families are fighting families and friends are fighting friends. I think I know which side you would be on but there will be many who you would know on the opposing side. Their Colonel knew you; he probably knows Sean and perhaps others."

"I still miss you Patrick, and every New Year's Day is purgatory for me, but I have made a good life for myself and for our boys. I'll say goodbye for now; I have visited our daughter and I know that you are resting with her and with Danny. I'll try to visit you again before I leave for home. Thank you for allowing me to talk to you and for listening to me. Stay resting peacefully Patrick and I will love you forever."

Liza stayed kneeling as she carried on arranging the roses neatly on Patrick's grave. She heard a noise coming from the church which sounded unusual, and she looked up over Patrick's headstone and saw George arguing with a couple of soldiers. They knocked him over and much to Liza's horror he did not get up. She slowly stood up as she saw them using their bayonets to damage the gravestones and as they came towards her, they stopped and grinned. One of them lifted his rifle with its bayonet and was about to damage Danny's grave as she shouted at him.

"Don't you dare desecrate that grave, or that of my husband, or my daughter. Don't you touch any of the graves of the people of this town! How dare you even think of doing so," she shouted.

One of the soldiers held back but the other slowly came towards her with his bayonet levelled at her chest and as he drew it back ready to plunge it into her, she could hear Jamie shout "No! Oh my God Liza, no!" At the same time a shot rang out and the soldier fell forward with a bullet between his eyes and an arrow in his back.

Jamie reached her in seconds and clasped her tightly to him as Rufus appeared holding the rifle that he had used on the man. He looked down at the soldier and then at Liza and said, "So you have your own protection, Liza. Did you know that they were there?"

Liza just shook her head. Rufus went over to the body and turned it over; his bullet had been perfectly placed between the man's eyes and Jamie commented that it had been an exceptional shot.

"I had an exceptional teacher," was all Rufus said.

Jamie thought for a moment and then said, "I suppose you mean Patrick," and Rufus just nodded.

Suddenly Liza remembered George and she broke away from Jamie and went running towards where she had seen him fall. Jamie followed her and they found George unconscious and bleeding heavily from a cut on the head and a wound to his left hand.

Joe and Tom quickly made their way up towards them and they lifted George and helped him down to Tom's surgery.

"Are you all right Liza," asked Tom as they went. "You weren't injured, were you?"

"I'm just a little shaken. I'll be over to see how George is later," she said as she desperately fought the sickness that was rising in her.

"Take deep breaths Liza," whispered Jamie as he knew from the slight green tinge to her face that she was feeling nauseous.

Rufus had disappeared and they presumed that he was organising the removal of the body and then reporting to his colonel. He was having a very difficult time in Benson, but nobody was feeling sorry for him.

Liza glanced back at Patrick's and little Meg's graves whilst taking the deep breaths that Jamie had suggested and then she leaned against him until she managed to control her stomach.

"Do you feel up to walking back to the store now Liza?" asked Jamie gently and she nodded. As they walked Jamie asked if she knew that she was being protected by her Indian friends.

"I knew that Bandor was around, but I had no idea that he was so close. I didn't think about that when I stupidly challenged that soldier. It seemed so important to me that he didn't damage the gravestones, but I was wrong; gravestones can be replaced, lives can't, and now somebody else has lost their life," said Liza.

"If he hadn't lost his life then you would have done, so I feel no sympathy for the dead man. I think that the reverend is lucky to have got away with just his injuries, I believe that you distracted them before they could kill him," said Jamie.

"I wish we were at home Jamie. I love the people here, but I love our family more and I desperately want to be back with our boys and the rest of the family but most of all I want to be home with you," said Liza and tears of frustration spilled down her cheeks.

Jamie smiled at her as it was exactly what he wanted to hear. "I would think that it won't be too long before we are on our way to New York, and then on to home. The Confederate scouts must soon come across the main Union force and report back. I think we should now keep a very low profile, or we may get caught up in it and be used as pawns in their game again."

"Ada wants to see me, and I think I know what she wants. If the Colonel was here, he would also want to see me. The time has come for me to explain my previous actions. I think you know what I am talking about, don't you Jamie?" said Liza.

"Yes, I believe I do. It has to do with Felicity's killer, and I would think that they have always really known that you were behind his escape, but because you arranged to spirit the Colonel and Corporal Raines away from Benson, they now want to know why you did it," said Jamie. "I would also like to know why, but you don't have to tell me. You don't have to tell Ada and the Colonel either; you will though, won't you?"

"I will but whether Ada will believe me is doubtful," said Liza sadly.

"It may upset Ada, but she knows you well enough to accept that you had a very good reason for doing so," said Jamie. "I met him when you took Evelyn to Wales, didn't I?"

"Yes, that was him," said Liza.

"Do any of the Fullers know that he is working for them?" asked Jamie.

"I doubt it, but Wendell and Peter aren't stupid; they may have realised that he was a friend of mine and suspected who he was," said Liza.

"You didn't mention Edward and Joseph. Surely it was difficult for him to work for the man whose wife he had killed. I would have thought that he would have found employment elsewhere," said Jamie.

"He has implemented many safety and security measures within the Company. I believe it is his way of trying to make amends, although he has never forgiven himself for his actions and sadly, I know that one day he will ensure that he pays for what he has done," said Liza.

"I will come with you if you wish, but I have a feeling that it is something that you have to do alone," said Jamie.

"Thank you, Jamie, but I need to see Ada alone. It is just as well that the Colonel is not here as Ada is the only one who will ever be able to fully understand," said Liza.

"You're looking better now," said Jamie as they entered the store. Ada and Bea were there with Christina and Judith; Rachel was with Ellen and the twins at Dr Tom's house. Liza looked at Ada who knew that the time had come for their private conversation.

They left the store and went to what was now Ada's home. Liza walked in and the past hit her like a physical blow. She stood at the foot of the stairs and could see Matthew crawling up them trying to tell her that he was going to get some toys. She turned and saw Simon following him and talking to him in the language that both little boys understood. Liza shook her head to bring herself back to the present but as she walked into the main room, she saw Patrick sitting in his rocking chair and looking at her with his piercing blue eyes; he started rocking and as he did Ada jumped because she could see the chair moving but nobody was in it.

Liza just stood and stared at Patrick, and she could not stop the tears from cascading down her cheeks and sobs shook her whole body.

Ada said something and as she did Patrick disappeared, and Liza knew that he had never really been there; it was her mind playing tricks on her.

Ada repeated herself, gently saying, "You have never stopped loving him have you Liza?"

"No, you are right, I still do and being here has brought it all back to me, but I do love Jamie and it is possible to love more than one person. Patrick was the passion of my life and Jamie is the love of my life. But I know that there are matters that you want to talk to me about Ada. There are things that you feel that you must understand, and I will try to be honest with you. The time has come for us to talk. What do you want to know?" asked Liza.

"I have always trusted you Liza and I know that whatever you have done it has never been to hurt anyone, but I do find it difficult to understand why you helped Mark Kendal avoid justice. He was determined to take the consequences of his actions, but you intervened, and he completely disappeared. Eugene and I have always suspected that you were behind his escape, but it is only now that we realise exactly how it was achieved. We need to know why," said Ada.

The chair had stopped rocking and Liza knew that she could now call on other powers to help explain to Ada exactly why Mark Kendal was living when he had been responsible for the deaths of Ada's daughter, Felicity, and that of Lieutenant Crown.

"Sit down Ada," said Liza and when she had Liza sat also and held her hand. She was silent for a short while and closed her eyes. Ada frowned as she watched but then she too closed her eyes and Liza started talking gently.

"There are things that I see," said Liza. "They may be just in my imagination but even if they are I cannot take the chance and I must act on them."

Ada remained quiet with her eyes closed and in her mind Liza called on James to help her explain her reasons to her dear friend Ada.

Images were coming to her, and she held Ada's hand even more tightly. "I saw something in Mark's future that would affect many people if he were to have died ten years ago. I saw a pretty lady with Mark and a child – no, children – who were important to the long-term future of Britain."

Liza was getting the images again as she had done ten years before and she heard Ada gasp and knew that she was also seeing the same.

Liza carried on, "but it is not his children, it is not only his children's children who help to alter the way that Ireland is governed and bring some peace to the land, but his great, great, great grandchildren are the ones who finally assist in the negotiation of a lasting peace agreement in that country. Without his future offspring, for many years hence England and Ireland will be in everlasting conflict. By sacrificing his life he would have denied life to many necessary people."

Ada was still holding Liza's hand and she was making small grunting sounds and strange images were passing from Liza to Ada. For many minutes nothing further needed to be said until finally the images faded, and Ada opened her eyes, but Liza's were still closed, and she had a frown across her brow. Ada realised that Liza was seeing something that was concerning her.

Ada could sense Liza's unrest and as she pulled her hand away Liza opened her eyes and all the images faded.

"I'm not sure what I have been seeing, Liza," said Ada quietly.

"It has been the same for me Ada. All I can tell you is that I have met the pretty woman that we have both now seen and she and Mark are married and have children. I often wondered whether what I saw ten years ago was just my imagination, but his wife is surprisingly real, although a day does not go by when Mark does not regret his actions of the past. You know that it was a moment of madness on his part and totally out of character. I have experienced the hatred that comes when someone loves you so much that it turns to hate with rejection. I don't know if you have ever heard Amelia's great thought on the matter which is that love and hate are strange bedfellows, and she is absolutely right. There is very little control when somebody realises that who they thought loved them had no feelings for them at all," said Liza.

"Do the Fullers know where he is?" asked Ada.

"It's best if all else I keep to myself. Mark has a new name and career. He has a new life and a family. Nobody but his wife and I know of his past. However I will say this to you, I have the strangest feeling that he will eventually feel that he must pay for his crime," said Liza with concern.

"You've seen something else, haven't you?" said Ada. "And what you have seen concerns you."

"I often have dreams and thoughts and they mean nothing," smiled Liza reassuringly.

"I must tell Eugene what I have seen and why you helped Mark; I know that he will understand as he knows that you always have reasons for everything that you do. He also knows that you believe that a punishment should fit a crime and that murder is one crime that does warrant the death penalty. We can couch it in manslaughter whilst he was unhinged, but my daughter is dead and so is the lieutenant and Mark Kendal killed them and he has yet to pay for that," said Ada.

"You're wrong Ada, Mark Kendal pays for it every minute of every day and at some time in the future he will answer for it. At present he has a wife and children that he loves and who need him," said Liza and Ada realised that she would say no more.

There was a great deal of noise outside and both Ada and Liza looked out of the window only to see Confederate soldiers riding swiftly in all directions out of town. The foot soldiers were being hastily lined up and marched out.

Ada and Liza looked at one another, "so they have discovered that the Union army is nearby. Well at least they do not appear to want to fight their battle in town," said Ada and then she looked concerned as Rufus approached the house. Jamie and Joe were rushing across the road to reach them.

Gabriel appeared through the back entrance and Jake was joining Jamie and Joe, but Rufus just knocked on the door. Ada looked at Liza and all Liza could do was nod to let him in.

He came slowly into the main room. Jamie, Joe and Jake followed him in; Gabriel was standing with his arms folded and a determined look on his face.

Rufus stood looking at Liza and seemed to be trying to make up his mind what to say.

"You knew that the Union army were coming, didn't you Liza?" said Rufus. "For all your maintaining that you have not taken sides; I believe that you have, otherwise you would have warned me that they were close."

"I have not taken sides; I have just kept quiet about everything that I know, but the way I have been treated by your so-called army it would not be surprising if I did become a Union sympathiser," said Liza.

"My colonel wants me to seize you and take you to the front line; foolishly he is hoping that by showing you to your friends from the opposing side that we will win the battle. Well, I have tried to be loyal to my chosen side, but what is being proposed is ludicrous, so I will just say that I have been unable to find you," said Rufus with a sigh. "I also know that your Indian friends would never allow you to be taken by us."

"I have no idea whether you have chosen the right side to fight with; all I do know is that you have chosen a side that has the wrong leaders. I'm sorry that you are now going to battle against your friends and former colleagues, and I do sincerely wish you well and pray that you come out of this in one piece. Good luck Rufus, try not to take too many chances," said Liza.

Rufus came over and put his arms around Liza and kissed her on the head. "I know you mean what you say Liza. I do hope that I will see you later. Goodbye Mrs Western, gentlemen," said Rufus and he bowed and left leaving everyone silent and saddened.

"Do you have a plan for the wounded," Liza asked suddenly.

"No, we did not think that it would come that close to us," said Ada, "but I suppose we could see Dr Tom and see what he is going to do. Whatever he does he will need Hannah and Ellen with him, and Bea and I have experience and Liza, I know that you have also."

"Well we men can carry the wounded wherever necessary," said Jamie. "I suppose a relatively safe area will be set up for a hospital and I know that it will be useless for me to try to persuade you ladies not to leave town and stay where it is safe."

"We'll see what Dr Tom says," said Ada. "I'll find Bea and let you know what's happening."

They went back to the store leaving Ada to find Bea and talk to Dr Tom.

"It's starting then," said Kathy. "I suppose we'll all be needed to help the doctors. I presume Dr Tom will be going and both sides will probably also have doctors, although I didn't see one with the Confederates. I wonder how many of the young men from our fort are fighting on opposite sides. It's so depressing and I'm glad my Danny isn't here to see this."

Liza had to agree with her, it truly was very depressing.

"Ada is finding out what Dr Tom is planning, and she'll let us know," said Liza. "I think I'll go to our room for a while, but I'll be ready whenever Ada tells us what is happening."

Up in their room Jamie said that he realised that they could all leave now, but he knew that there were people who would probably need help and who were friends.

Liza lay down on the bed, she felt exhausted, but she would have to carry on when called to help.

"How did you get on with Ada? Did she understand your reasons for helping Mark Kendal?" asked Jamie.

"It is always difficult for others to understand, but she knows that I did what had to be done and she accepts that. She will tell the Colonel and I know that he will say nothing," said Liza.

"Does anyone know that Leonora also has nursing experience?" asked Jamie.

"I have said nothing; she may have mentioned it to somebody," said Liza.

"I believe that the good doctor is going to need all the help he can get," said Jamie. "I don't suppose that any battle will take place until tomorrow. They have to reach one another, and I would say that it is going to take the rest of the day for that to happen."

"Perhaps we will be able to get some rest tonight; we'll have to be up early tomorrow, but we'll have to see Dr Tom in a little while to find out what he thinks we will need," said Liza. "Seeing Rufus off today has made me feel so sad. I remember back to when all the young lieutenants worked together and watched out for one another and now they will be fighting one another."

"There's only one who will be on the opposite side," said Jamie gently.

"I don't know if that's really the case Jamie," said Liza. "Who knows who is on which side now?"

"Try and get some sleep Liza," said Jamie. "I'll call you when Ada wants to see you."

"Will you stay with me please Jamie," said Liza.

"Of course I will Liza," said Jamie and he lay down beside her and stroked her head gently until she was asleep. Jamie enjoyed the feeling of closeness that he had but he really wished that all this was behind them and that they were back at home in Surrey.

He was concerned for his family in England and knew how worried they must all be. Kathy knocked and called out that Ada and Dr Tom were there and would like to see them both. Liza stirred and opened her eyes.

"I gather that we are wanted," said Liza sleepily and Jamie nodded.

Tom was there with Ada and Bea. Kathy, Joe, Leonora and Roberts were sitting at the large table.

"I hope you don't mind Liza, but Susan is with Rachel, Judith and Christina and I believe Kate is going to leave little Liza with her," said Bea. "We also thought that it would be a good idea if she stayed with them tomorrow. She is very young; not much older than Rachel and doesn't need to be exposed to some of the sights we may have to deal with."

"That's very sensible," said Liza.

Kate, Gabriel and Zelma arrived with Jake and then Wes, Enid and Laurie knocked and entered and were quickly followed by Greg Long and Archie and Sam Trower.

Dr Tom started without ceremony. "I have no idea what will happen tomorrow, but all I do know is that first thing tomorrow morning I will be heading towards where any fighting may take place. Ada and Bea have agreed to go with me; Hannah and Ellen will be on duty at my surgery ready to deal with any wounded brought here. This evening I will be going to the hospital at the fort to see how it can be arranged also to take any wounded; I would ask Liza to come with me to help in this; who else would be able to help?"

"I'll do whatever is needed," said Jamie and Roberts also said that he would help.

Then Leonora spoke up, "Doctor, I am the wife of a doctor and the daughter of one. I have had much experience in helping the sick and I would like to volunteer to go with you tomorrow morning. I have seen many things in my life and will be able to be useful in the field. I am not frightened by the sight of blood."

"That's wonderful," said Dr Tom. "You are Mrs Chambers, aren't you?"

"Yes, I am, but I would prefer it if you called me Leonora; everyone in Benson is on first name terms and I would like to be the same," said Leonora. "However I would like to tell you all that I was born in New York, but my husband is a southerner and is a doctor in the Confederate army. If that makes you all uncomfortable then I will step back but I would like to add that I believe in the Hippocratic Oath, as do my husband and father and I will help to treat soldiers from either side without prejudice or favouritism."

There was silence for a moment whilst everyone digested the information and as Liza was about to move towards Leonora, Kathy reached her first and put an arm around her shoulder.

"I would expect nothing less from the wife and daughter of doctors," said Dr Tom. "I would be pleased for you to join me tomorrow morning Leonora, as I hope would Ada and Bea."

"Of course we would," said Bea. "We have no idea where any of our allegiances lie, but what we are proposing to do tomorrow is to help those who need our help. We also will show no prejudice or favouritism, so you are not alone in that Leonora."

"All I would say," said Ada. "Is that if I see my husband wounded, I will find it difficult not to show favouritism towards him, as I presume would you also Bea if it were your husband."

"I believe that it would be understandable," said Dr Tom.

"Where would you like me, Tom?" asked Liza quietly, although she had a feeling that she knew the answer to her question.

"Liza," said Tom. "I think that it is well known that you have talents that others don't possess. I have seen you work, and I know that you will work well with Zelma."

Several people were looking puzzled, including Jamie. Liza was looking down and troubled.

Tom carried on, "I would like you to help the dying as only you can, and Zelma will have her means of assisting you in that. Perhaps you could clear out your wagon and use that to get you where you are needed. I pray that there will not be too many for you to see through to the other side. Maybe you will not be needed at all."

Liza looked up and gave a weak smile, "I think that is a faint hope, Tom."

"Kate, Enid and Laurie," said Tom. "Will you remain on duty at the fort hospital?"

All three nodded.

"I have no idea what may be set up near the battlefield for the wounded and I do not know if there will be another doctor there from either side. I am hoping that Dr Steele is travelling with the Union force, but I will find that out tomorrow. Now for the men of the town. Can you all get a means of transport to bring any wounded here? Or they may just have to be moved to a hospital tent which is already there. I am hoping that both sides respect that we are civilians doing a necessary task and if anyone wishes to back out, nobody will think the worse of you," said Tom.

339

Nobody said anything so Tom continued, "Jamie and Roberts. This is not your fight; this is not your country. You really should not be involving yourselves. It is the same for Liza."

"The Confederate government have made it our fight and if they get their way then Liza and I will be incarcerated in some southern state for the foreseeable future, so I do not feel that we have any other choice but to assist in whatever way we can. But I feel as Liza does, and that is that we want to do what we can to help anyone who is hurt," said Jamie. "Roberts has already told you how he feels, and he knows that what we are attempting is essential work."

"Where would you like me, Tom?" asked Kathy.

Tom smiled and said, "This is your town, Kathy; you must choose wherever you think you will be needed."

"Well Tom," said Kathy. "Unless otherwise called upon, I think I will spend my time in my kitchen and keep everyone well fed and that includes all the workers and all the wounded, no matter which side they come from. If there is a hospital tent out there then Joe can take food to that, so I shall be very busy tomorrow and I think I'll ask Mrs Long to help me."

Everyone was smiling at Kathy as they all knew that her answer to all problems was food.

The meeting broke up and Liza, Jamie, Roberts and Tom made their way to the fort and Ada and Bea said that they would follow them there as they knew where spare beds and bedding were kept. They managed to set up five more beds in the hospital bringing the total to nine and then Ada suggested that they use the small Assembly Room should it be necessary, and eight more beds were placed there.

"I hate to mention this," said Ada. "But there is a room where we could place any bodies."

"I know the room," said Liza. "That's where Rachel and Judith's family were placed, isn't it?"

Bea just nodded.

Finally they made their way back to the store and Kathy and Joe had prepared a meal for them and although tired they realised that they were hungry, and they enjoyed their food and sat around the table discussing the plans for the following day.

They all then went to their beds, but understandably, nobody got much sleep that night.

Chapter 11

Liza and Jamie were washed and dressed soon after dawn and they could hear Kathy working in her kitchen and Joe was getting the horses ready for his carriage and Sam was helping him with the horses for both Liza's wagon and the large buggy that Jamie and Roberts would be using.

Leonora was also dressed, and she had a very large apron that she would be wearing over her clothes that day. Susan was helping Kathy get breakfast for everyone and she was also helping with the bread that Kathy was baking for others. There were pies ready to go in the oven and several large pots of stew were prepared and would shortly be placed on the oven top to slowly cook.

"Rachel and I will be looking after as many children as necessary at the Sanderson's house, and I know that several ladies, as well as the schoolteacher, will be popping in to make sure that we are alright," said Susan.

"Yes, it's a very necessary job that you will be doing," said Liza.

They all sat down to breakfast and surprisingly they all ate well. When they had finished Jamie escorted Leonora to Dr Tom's house and Ada and Bea were already waiting there. As he returned, the sound of gunfire could be heard followed by the louder sound of cannon fire and they all then knew that the battle had begun.

Tom ushered Ada, Bea and Leonora into his carriage, which left Ada's buggy for someone else to use. Hannah and Ellen saw them off and then took Laura and Benjy to Kate's house just as Susan was arriving. Angela walked across to the store and said that she did not believe that any children would be in school that day, but she would have to wait to make sure that no one turned up, but then she would go where she was needed and that could be where the greatest number of children were which was at Kate's and Ada's houses.

Jamie said that he was not happy with Liza driving the wagon with just Zelma and as he was about to suggest that he took the reins, Bandor appeared and climbed up into the driving seat.

"I know you are i-tse di-ka-ta's protector," said Bandor to Jamie, "but it is what I do best and what I have been commanded to do. You are needed elsewhere, and you know that I will protect her with my life, as will Little Dove. I have eyes in places that you would never dream of; she will be safer with me than with anyone else."

"I know what you are saying Bandor," said Jamie quietly. "I am not a warrior as you are, or as Patrick was, but I will always protect her with my life. She is more important to me than all else in my life including my own life."

"Jamie can drive me," said Liza.

"No Liza, Bandor is right. I may not be able to protect you as he can, and if you were attacked and I was to lose such a fight, then you would have no one to keep you safe. Bandor will never lose such a fight," said Jamie.

"Everyone is talking as if I am a target in this war. I am just someone who will be attending to the wounded along with many others," said Liza.

"Don't worry Liza, I'm not upset. I'm pleased that I don't have to be concerned about you whilst I help others," smiled Jamie. "Go on, get on your way and I'll get on mine."

"I do love you Jamie Edgeworth," said Liza. "Please be careful. I'll see you later."

Bandor drove off and as they were passing the graveyard and church George ran towards them. He still had a bandage around his head and his arm was in a sling. "I need to get to the battlefield. There will be those who need me there," he said.

They stopped for him, and he clambered aboard with difficulty. Liza enquired after his health and wondered whether it was wise of him to go with them.

"You know that it is what I must do. I have my instructions from a higher body than those foolishly fighting ahead of us," said George and Bandor nodded wisely.

"I hope that they have organised something for the wounded," said George.

"If they haven't, I know that the town has," said Liza. "It will just take longer for any wounded to get help."

"Several carts and carriages are following us," said George.

"That's the men who will bring any wounded to us," said Liza.

"That's very brave of them," said George. "They could get caught in the middle of the gunfire."

The sound was getting louder and by the time they had been travelling for half an hour it was becoming deafening. They came into a small clearing and Liza was relieved to see an adequately sized tent and she saw Tom's carriage parked there.

They came to a halt and Liza and George were first to enter. Inside Liza was delighted to see Dr Steele who was setting out operating equipment with the help of Tom. Ada and Bea were arranging canvas beds with a couple of Confederate soldiers and Leonora was making sure all cloths and bandages were in place.

Dr Steele looked up and said, "I was told that you would be here Liza; we have no patients yet. This is a Confederate tent and all they have so far are two orderlies. I've commandeered it and hope that if their doctor arrives, he will have the good sense to join us rather than shoot us. I have a couple of orderlies also, but I understand that many of the men from town will be helping us."

"It's good to see you again doctor," said Liza. "I hope that you won't be needed too much today."

"I hear that they caught you again," said Dr Steele. "And that Lieutenant Denton saved you from killing yourself."

"He's Captain Denton in the Confederate army and he seems to have more common sense than any of his superiors; but of course he has been well trained during his time at Benson," said Liza.

A noticeably young man walked into the hospital tent and stopped short, surprised to see the number of people there and even more surprised to see a man in the Union uniform sorting out medical equipment.

"Who are you?" asked Dr Steele.

"I'm Dr Fernleigh," stammered the young man. "Who are you?"

"I'm Dr Steele and this is Dr Marsden. We also have Mrs Western, Mrs Graves and Mrs Chapman to assist in whatever is necessary as they are experienced in nursing and over there is Lady Liza Edgeworth, Bandor and Zelma who will be easing any patient's pain. Do you have a speciality Dr Fernleigh?"

"I really should not be called doctor yet as I had no time to gain my diploma before being conscripted into the army. I am relieved that you are all here," said Dr Fernleigh.

"By the end of today you will be a hardened, fully fledged doctor," said Dr Steele and they all then continued with their preparations.

"What would you like me to do?" asked Dr Fernleigh.

Dr Steele and Dr Tom stared at him, and Dr Tom then said that perhaps he could differentiate between those who were not able to be saved and those who stood a chance of survival.

"Why?" he asked cautiously.

"Because we will be unable to waste our time on those who will eventually die regardless of any treatment that we can give them," said Dr Tom.

"You don't want me to kill them, do you?" asked a horrified Dr Fernleigh.

Dr Steele sighed with resignation, "No doctor, we don't want you to kill them; we want you to just bring us those who you feel we are able to save and let Liza and the reverend take care of the dying."

Dr Steele's orderlies arrived with another tent, and it was placed next to the main one. A few camp beds were placed in it and Liza took up her position there. It was going to be used for the dying.

Dr Tom came in to see her. "I know this is not what you wanted to do Liza, but I have seen how you make the dying have no fear and a great deal of that talent will be needed today, although I don't think that you will be able to help the number who will be brought here and there will also be those that we can't reach in the field."

There were shouts and cries of pain nearing the hospital tents and Dr Fernleigh was sending all the wounded into Dr Steele as he found it difficult to make the decision between life and death. Liza went into the hospital tent and looked at those waiting for treatment and asked for two of the men to be brought to her tent.

George sat with one whilst Liza talked quietly to the other until he died peacefully. She turned to the other man, smiled at him, and held his hand whilst also talking to him quietly and he gently passed away. More were brought in, and Liza and George worked their miracles on them.

Zelma used some of her concoctions to ease the pain of many of the dying. Bandor watched silently as Liza worked and he thought that no matter how much she denied that she had any special powers, he knew that she had and as he continued watching her, in his own way he was praying for the souls of those who were dying.

By then the less badly wounded were being taken to either Hannah at the doctor's surgery or to the fort hospital where Kate and Laurie were treating them.

Liza had lost track of the number of soldiers she had helped when the big guns stopped, there was still sporadic firing but overall the battle was over. In the hospital tents they had no idea who had come out on top, they were too busy to ask.

It was with great relief that Liza looked up and saw Jamie entering her tent. He looked exhausted and was covered in mud and blood and she did not realise that she looked just as tired and bloody.

"What's left of the Confederate army are on their way back to the southern states," said Jamie but he did not look pleased, and Liza raised an eyebrow for him to say what he had on his mind.

"Paul Southern is badly wounded Liza," said Jamie. "It appears that there is nothing that the doctors can do for him. Shall I arrange for him to be brought here?"

She asked where he was, and Jamie said that he was lying outside, and Liza went with Jamie to see him. She smiled beautifully at Paul and asked where he was wounded. She could see that he had a large hole in his chest, and he was finding it difficult to breathe, but she estimated that they would be able to get him back to Benson so that he could die in comfortable surroundings. Jamie and Bandor gently lifted the stretcher onto Liza's wagon and as she was walking past those she thought had already died, a familiar voice called her name and when she looked, she saw that it was Rufus. He had an evil wound to his stomach and Liza knew that he would not survive such an injury.

"We lost the battle Liza," said Rufus, "and now I'm going to lose my life out here on the ground amongst the dead."

"No you're not Rufus, you're coming back to Benson where you belong. We are taking Paul back so you can keep one another company," said Liza.

"Is he badly hurt?" asked Rufus.

"Yes, you both are. The journey back may be a little uncomfortable, but you will be better when we get you both home," said Liza.

Jamie and Bandor came and lifted Rufus into the wagon with Paul and Liza climbed up with them. Bandor took the reins and Jamie sat with him. Zelma and George would be travelling back with Roberts when they were ready.

Bandor skilfully and gently drove the wagon into Benson and then went directly to the fort.

"They always shared a room so I think that they could go there and be comfortable," said Liza and she showed Jamie and Bandor the room that they had used. Laurie saw them arrive and was surprised that they were going to the living quarters, but when she saw who they had brought and the condition they were in she understood exactly why Liza wanted them both to be in familiar surroundings. She helped to light the lamps as it was now getting late and then went to find some bandages and water so that the wounds could at least be cleaned a little.

Kate came back with Laurie and they both washed Rufus and Paul as best they could.

"Ben has been hurt," said Kate, "luckily not seriously. A bullet clipped his arm but it's not going to permanently damage him."

"Have you heard from Bart?" Liza asked Laurie and she shook her head.

"Knowing Bart I'm sure he is going to come out of this unscathed," said Liza.

Paul's breathing was becoming increasingly laboured and after checking on Rufus, Liza sat with Paul and bathed his head and then held him tightly and talked quietly to him. He gasped that he was pleased that Rufus was back with them, and Liza said that it was indeed good that he was there. He could hardly speak but his eyes told her that he was frightened, and she whispered to him not to be frightened as she was going to keep him company for as long as necessary. She continued holding him and kissed him gently on his forehead and the shadow passed over him and he was peacefully taken from her. She carried on holding him for a while and rocked him backwards and forwards but then she knew that she had to concentrate on Rufus.

Jamie asked if he had gone, and Liza nodded and covered him with a sheet.

Rufus was looking towards Paul and realised that he had passed away; a tear trickled down his cheek.

"Have I time to write a letter Liza?" he asked.

"Yes, Rufus, you have plenty of time for that," smiled Liza.

"Will you write it for me? I don't think I can manage it myself," said Rufus.

Liza went to the desk in the room knowing that there would be paper and ink there. There was an assortment of pens, and she chose the most suitable. Jamie lit another lamp for her and then said that he would see if there was anything he could do to help around the fort, and if not, he would go to the store and change and be back later.

"Your husband is being very discreet. He knows that there will be things that I will be saying that are private. You chose well Liza," said Rufus.

"He chose me many years ago, but it took me a long while to realise that I wanted him," said Liza.

"It cannot have been easy for you to get over Patrick; but you seem to have made a good life for yourself and your boys," said Rufus.

"You never totally get over a loss like that; but you do realise that life has to continue and with that realisation comes an acceptance that you are loved by someone and in time you can return that love," said Liza. "But that isn't getting your letter written. Who is it to? Your mother?"

"No Liza, my mother is dead. She was killed by my father," said Rufus.

"Oh!" said Liza.

"And before you decide to be diplomatic and ask nothing else; my father was hanged for her murder," said Rufus. "I want to write to Mary; I have never stopped loving her, but it would have been a disastrous marriage. I am too much like my father."

Liza smiled at him and said that she was ready to write.

My darling Mary,

Liza is writing this letter for me as I am no longer able to, but I want to tell you exactly how I feel and hope that it will not upset you or disrupt any part of your life.

I still love you; I have tried to find love elsewhere but have never found anyone to compare with you. However you were right to refuse me as I know that you had already come out of an abusive situation, and you would have ended up in another.

Over the years I tried to change and managed to control my temper on many occasions, but there were times when it came to the fore and I realised that I was just like my father who, although he loved my mother dearly, killed her in a fit of temper and he paid the ultimate price for that.

When I was with you, I managed to forget my past and felt that I was a different person, but if you disagreed with me even slightly, I felt a rage that I so desperately tried to control.

I am so sorry that I belittled your sister who I know worked so hard to bring you safely to America, but my theory was that I wanted to have you all to myself. I did not want anyone else to have any influence over you, which is just as my father acted towards my mother.

My friends and colleagues here in Benson helped to keep me on the straight and narrow over the years, but many have now gone. Patrick was lost to us some years ago and Sean left soon after. Liza also had to leave when Patrick died and my greatest friend Paul is now lying dead in this room, but I will be joining him shortly; Liza will help me through this last ordeal.

There is so much I would like to say to you, but I am running out of time. I truly wish you a happy life and hope that you meet someone who will love you as much as I do but will treat you with the kindness that you deserve.

Goodbye my darling Mary, I wish I could have been different,
Rufus

"I know you will make sure she gets it," said Rufus to Liza, and she nodded.

Over the next hour they talked about the past and even laughed at some of the funny times that they had both experienced.

Zelma came in and gave him more pain-relieving medicine and the Colonel knocked and came to see what was happening. He shook his head and left but was shortly followed by Marshall who asked if they wanted Paul moved elsewhere, but Rufus was adamant that he wanted to be with him until the end.

"I chose the wrong uniform Liza," said Rufus quietly.

"You chose the uniform where you were born," said Liza.

"Does it mean that Paul and I will have to be buried in different places?" he asked.

"No, you are just as much a Benson soldier as Paul was; I won't let anyone separate you, I promise," said Liza.

Dr Steele came in to make sure that there was nothing that he could do, and he commented that Zelma's concoction was working well. "Are you alright with this Liza?" he asked.

"Of course I am doctor," said Liza.

"It's been a difficult day for you," said the doctor.

"It's been a difficult day for everyone," said Liza quietly.

Rufus moaned a little and Dr Steele remained but moved into the shadows, he knew that it would not be long now.

Liza moved closer to him and held his hand. She quietly talked to him about all the good times that he had experienced. She smiled at him and smoothed his brow and told him not to be frightened when a worried look crossed his face. "Thank you, Liza," he muttered as he closed his eyes, and the shadow came and took him to join Paul.

Dr Steele came and put his hand on her shoulder as she cried and said that Patrick had more friends with him now.

"Your husband is waiting outside. I'll arrange to have them moved," said Dr Steele.

"Oh no, don't do that. Leave them together tonight. I'll be back tomorrow morning to make the arrangements with Marshall and the Colonel," said Liza and she pulled the sheet over Rufus and said that she would see them both tomorrow.

Dr Steele led her out of the room and carefully closed the door behind them. Jamie got down from the buggy and helped Liza into it; he noticed that Bandor was quietly standing in the shadows, and he had watched over Liza all day. Jamie wondered whether he would sleep now that she was safely with him. *Probably not,* he thought, *he takes his duties more seriously than any white man would.*

As they drove back to town Jamie commented that Liza never got the easy jobs.

"Has anyone had an easy job today?" said Liza.

"No, you're right. I must admit that I have seen things today that I never want to see again, as I am sure has everyone else. At least we kept it away from Susan and the children. Your friend Angela really helped to keep all the children occupied and Kathy fed them well," smiled Jamie.

The store seemed crowded when they arrived back, and Kathy rushed up to Liza and said that she had heard that she had done a wonderful job that day.

"You need to get out of those clothes Liza," said Kathy. "Joe will bring some hot water up for you, the bath is set up in your room and when you've done that there'll be some supper ready for you. I suppose you haven't eaten all day."

"I'm not hungry," muttered Liza.

"I'm sure you're not, but you must try to have something. We've all managed to eat a little," said Kathy and she added, "Have both Paul and Rufus gone?"

Liza nodded and then she could not control her tears any longer and she made the most terrible sobbing sounds which Zelma recognised as the noise she had made when Patrick had died. Jamie lifted her up and carried her up to their room and then held her until the sobbing eased. Joe knocked and put more water in the bath whilst asking if she was alright or should he fetch Tom to see her.

"I think she will be alright thank you Joe," said Jamie. "I'll help her bathe and then see if she can eat something."

Jamie helped her off with her blood-stained clothes and she felt better when she was lying in the hot water. Zelma surprised him by bustling into the room and grabbing all her dirty clothes saying that she would try to get them clean the next day.

Liza smiled and said that it was just like old times as Zelma's answer to everything was a hot bath and clean clothes.

Jamie came over and looked down on Liza who smiled up at him and asked if he was going to make sure she was clean.

"Would you like me to do that Liza?" he asked, and she continued smiling and nodded. "You know somebody is bound to come in."

"Well, that shouldn't stop you washing me," she smiled and when he had made sure she was clean he helped her into her nightdress and dressing gown and they both went down to the large dining room which was still full of people.

Dr Tom had come to make sure that Liza was alright as he knew that she had had a difficult task that day.

"I am fine thank you Tom. It is a day that I really would not want to experience again, but everyone has had a difficult day and tomorrow will also be difficult, especially for you and Dr Steele," said Liza.

"I gather that both Rufus and Paul have gone," said Tom and Liza just nodded once again; she found it difficult to talk about.

"So have many others," said Liza. "How are Hannah and Ellen?"

"They dealt with many wounded today, luckily none were too badly hurt. Ben had a bullet in his arm and Corporal Raines will be limping for a while," said Tom.

"Is there any news of Sean and Bart?" asked Liza.

"They are both fine," said Tom. "Laurie was very relieved to see Bart, and Sean is camped outside town. He doesn't seem to want to join us."

"I can understand that," said Liza. "I'll make sure I see him tomorrow."

A bowl of soup was placed in front of Liza, and she picked up her spoon and immediately dribbled soup down her chin; she tut-tutted herself but before she could mop it up several hands with napkins came forward to wipe her chin. Jamie laughed, which set several people off laughing.

"I see that you haven't changed, Liza," said Gabriel.

"What happened to the young Confederate doctor?" asked Liza.

"He's a much older doctor now," said Tom. "Marshall told him to join his forces as they retreated. He was quite surprised as he thought that he would be spending the rest of the war in a northern prison. I think that he would have preferred to do that but as Marshall said, really there are no facilities to keep anyone here. When their wounded have healed, we will have to make arrangements to send them somewhere."

"Have all the opposing forces left the area?" asked Roberts.

"I believe so," said Tom. "There may be one or two deserters who could be hanging around, so we had better be vigilant for a while, but there are many of our soldiers who will take care of that."

Leonora came over to Liza and asked to speak to her privately, so Liza finished her soup and then went to a quiet corner.

"When you leave here, I would like to stay," said Leonora. "Do you think that the people of the town would accept me?"

"I think they already have," said Liza. "What would you do here because unless you have unlimited money you would have to work at something."

"I haven't thought that far ahead," said Leonora. "It's just an idea at the moment. I can see why you love this town so much. There are no prejudices here."

"Won't your father be worried when you don't arrive in New York? I suppose I could see him and tell him where you are," said Liza.

"He doesn't know that I was planning to join him, so he won't be worried, but I will write to him and also to Jackson to let them know where I am," said Leonora.

"It seems like a good plan; I know you'll be happy here, but we'll have to think about your finances. I have some important arrangements to make first thing tomorrow morning, but I'll see what we can come up with after that," said Liza.

The store door opened and Greg Long and Sam Trower called and asked to come up. The large dining room was getting even more crowded.

"Sam and I have been to see Major Graves this evening and we have both enlisted. We saw what happened today and we want to do our bit to protect our people," said Greg. "The Major has explained that it will not be easy, and this conflict could go on for years. Many from the south have said that it will be all over by Christmas, but nobody here thinks that it will be."

"What does your mother think, Greg, and your brother, Sam?" asked Joe.

"They are not happy about it, but they know that it is something that we feel we must do," said Greg.

"You both must be careful and look after one another," said Liza. "I hope you know why this country is at war and what you are really fighting for, but I wish you well and feel very proud of you both."

They stayed for a while, and everyone discussed the situation and when they left Liza commented that Kathy and Joe would have to find someone to help them in the store and she would have to find someone to help Laurie in the print shop.

She smiled at Leonora and said, "I think that you will have to be interviewed for two positions. Do you know anything about printing?"

"No, absolutely nothing, but I'm sure I could learn. I know I could help in the store," said Leonora.

"And you also have your uses medically," said Liza. "I'll talk to Kathy and Joe tomorrow and see Laurie also. I'm sorry that Sam and Greg are enlisting, it's all so very dangerous, but if you can fill in whilst they are away then it will suit everyone. If Kathy and Joe and Laurie agree, I must emphasise that it will only be until Sam and Greg return home."

"You mean if they return home," whispered Leonora.

"I don't want to think that way," said Liza quietly.

**

The following morning Liza could be seen visiting the undertakers where she arranged for two decent coffins to be delivered to the fort. They had several in stock but mostly they were hurriedly making dozens for the number of dead that they had to deal with, and Charlie Penn was doing the same. The undertaker agreed to go out to the fort and help Liza to get Paul and Rufus laid out. Liza wanted them buried in their dress uniforms and she was going to request that Rufus wore his Union outfit; she would have to discuss it with Marshall and possibly the Colonel also.

Liza slowly made her way back to the store; she was going to borrow Joe's buggy to go out to the fort. Jamie and Roberts were going to see what help they could give to Tom and possibly to Dr Steele at the fort and Liza planned to meet with them later. She was surprised to see a smartly uniformed Greg smiling happily with Ellen on his arm.

"We're getting married Liza," Greg blurted out suddenly.

"Oh," said Liza as she breathed a sigh of relief. "What wonderful news. I'm so pleased for you and the rest of the town. Benson needs some good news and what could be better than your marriage. When is it taking place?"

"We're going to see Reverend Prior now and hopefully he can work miracles and we can be married at the weekend," said Greg.

"You'll have to ask him, but we are in exceptional times so hopefully he will be able to make exceptional arrangements. It's been a long time coming and I know that you have loved one another since you first met. I wish you every happiness, I know you are well suited," said Liza.

"We wanted you to be one of the first people to know. You have helped both of us in so many ways, we will never forget your kindness," said Ellen.

Liza gulped back her tears as that day was not a day that she could accept kind words.

"I didn't mean to upset you," said a distraught Ellen.

"You haven't," said Liza. "Tears can mean sadness, but they also can mean happiness and I am truly happy for you both."

"We'll leave now and find the reverend, he may be with the wounded, and we know that you have another difficult task today," said Greg with understanding.

When they had left Jamie came into the room and said that it was the best piece of news that they could have. "Is Ellen the girl that April knows?"

Liza nodded and Jamie said that he therefore understood why it had taken them so long to make their decision and he asked if Greg knew of her background.

"Yes, she told him many years ago and made it the reason why she could not marry him. I know Greg will treat her gently with great care," said Liza.

Jamie then helped organise the buggy for Liza. "I know that this is something that you want to organise yourself Liza, but I am quite willing to go with you if you are worried at all."

"Thank you, Jamie; I do appreciate your care and concern, but this I have to deal with myself and there are also things that I have to discuss with Marshall, after all both Paul and Rufus were military men," said Liza.

He kissed her and helped her into the buggy and off she went to the fort. She drove into the stable area and the stable lad took her pony and buggy leaving her to walk into the fort.

The Colonel watched her walking across the parade ground and Marshall joined him at the window.

"That's a sight that we haven't seen for many years," said the Colonel. "I keep expecting Patrick to appear and catch her up. He would say something to her, and she would look up and her eyes would sparkle with fun, and he would grin down at her and walk her over to either Bea's or Ada's quarters. They were such a happy couple and I believe she still hurts, but she has done the best thing for herself and the boys. I'll miss her when she leaves, so will Ada."

"I think we all will," said Marshall. "I wonder if she'll stay for the wedding. I hope so."

"Of course, that's young Greg and Ellen. This town needs something to look forward to," said the Colonel and he continued watching Liza talking to the undertaker and his assistant who then went into the room where Paul and Rufus lay. She left shortly after and made her way over to what had been the colonel's office and was now Marshall's.

Liza was delighted to see Ben sitting at his desk. His arm was bandaged and in a sling, but he was managing to sort out some of the paperwork that the Colonel had secreted in the bank and at Gabriel's office for safekeeping.

"Ben how wonderful to see you," she exclaimed "You are managing to work. Is Brigeta here?"

"Yes, Brigeta and the children are here to keep me company. They are back here for a while," said Ben happily.

"I'll try to call in later," said Liza. "Is the Major in his office?"

"Yes, and so is the Colonel. This is just like old times Liza," smiled Ben as he got up and knocked on the office door, which was immediately opened, and Liza was ushered in quickly.

Both Marshall and the Colonel smiled and pulled out a chair for her.

"I need to discuss something with you both," said Liza. "Rufus and Paul trained together, worked together and died together; I would like to think that they could be buried next to one another."

"I can see nothing wrong with that," said Marshall. "We will be burying several Confederate soldiers in the same graveyard as our own dead. I'm sure that's not all that you want to talk about."

"No, you're right," said Liza. "One of the last things that Rufus said was that he was wearing the wrong uniform. I would like to ask that he is buried in his Union dress uniform. It is something that he seemed very concerned about. I also think that he would like his rank in your army on his headstone rather than his Confederate rank. I need your agreement to all this."

"You were with him at the end, so I bow to your judgement Liza. I know that you have a way of making the dead happy, so go ahead and do what you think is best," said Marshall. "When are you planning their burial?"

"I'll see George later, but I think the sooner the better, so hopefully tomorrow would be a good day," said Liza. "I presume it will be acceptable to leave both Paul and Rufus in their quarters until they are buried. Perhaps some people would like to pay their respects to them."

"Ben has checked their files and he can find no relatives listed for either of them," said Marshall.

"Rufus' parents are dead," was all that Liza could say.

"I think we have to assume that Paul also has no relatives and if he did then he didn't want us to know about them," said the Colonel.

"Both of them considered Benson their family. I know that Paul wrote to you and Ada and to Kathy and Joe when we met up earlier and he knew that I was travelling back here. He wrote to nobody else. Rufus tried to protect the people from the worst excesses of his soldiers; his loyalties were to Benson rather than anywhere else," said Liza as she desperately tried to control her emotions.

"Will we have to find a uniform for Rufus?" asked Marshall.

"No, his uniform is still hanging in the closet," said Liza quietly. "I'll go and make the necessary arrangements with the undertaker and then with George."

"I'll walk you over," said the Colonel and Liza realised that he wanted to talk to her privately.

When they left the office, the Colonel said that Ada had told him what she had seen, which he did find difficult to believe, but he knew that Liza had often seen what others had not.

"Are you going to arrest me?" asked Liza.

"Of course not Liza," smiled the Colonel. "Ada and I understand that you could do nothing other than what you did but you did take a tremendous risk. I always knew that you helped him, but I knew you well enough to realise that you had a very good reason for doing so. You used the flaws in our fort to spirit him away and you used similar flaws to release Corporal Raines and your Indian friends to get me to my men."

They stopped outside Paul and Rufus' quarters and the Colonel continued talking. "Ada tells me that Mark is married and has children now and your concern was always that his descendants are important, so I understand your actions. I can believe that he lives with his guilt; he was always an honourable man. You also feel that one day he will answer for his crime; well Liza, only time will tell over that."

"Sadly, he will," said Liza.

"We've lost so many good men in recent years," said the Colonel. "There was Lieutenant Crown, if indeed he was a good man! Then of course Mark disappeared. Dear Patrick died; Sean left and now both Paul Southern and Rufus Denton have gone. At least Ben was only wounded, and Bart Shaw has come back unscathed, but I would expect nothing less from him."

"At least we have a wedding to look forward to," said Liza.

"Ada and I need to talk to you about Christina. Will you be able to visit us later today?" asked the Colonel.

Liza looked up at him and read his mind. "You want to discuss her leaving Benson for a safer place, don't you?"

"It will break our hearts, but we want what is best for her and we have also heard from her father, and he is very concerned about the situation here," said the Colonel.

"When I have finished here and seen George, I'll come and see you both. I presume you will be home this afternoon," said Liza.

"Yes, we'll be there," said the Colonel and Liza went into the quarters and could be heard telling the undertaker that both men should be dressed in their best lieutenant's uniforms. She stayed until the undertaker said that it would be better if she left, but she should return in around two hours to visit her departed friends.

She saw Bea drive into the fort with some of her possessions and spent an hour helping her settle back into her quarters and then she went to visit Brigeta and her children and finally she went back to see Paul and Rufus as the undertakers had completed their work. They looked as Patrick had done; handsome and as if they were just asleep.

She sat between them and told them that she was arranging for them to be buried side by side and that Rufus was accepted back in the army where he belonged. She told him how handsome he looked in his dress uniform. She then turned to Paul and said that he always looked handsome but even more so now that he was in his best uniform. She also said that she hoped that they approved of her arrangements for them, and she knew that the people of Benson would always look after them.

The door opened and Marshall stood there saying that he had come to pay his respects and that Liza had been correct to put Rufus in his rightful place. He continued telling her that Bea would be across shortly to watch over his men and that Brigeta was coming later and so would Ada visit.

"I think one or two people from town would also like to come," said Liza.

"Go home Liza, you look tired. I'll watch over them until Bea get here," said Marshall.

"I have to see George before I can rest," said Liza.

"I know that you have to see Ada and the Colonel this afternoon, but perhaps you will be able to spend a little time with Jamie before you see them," said Marshall.

"Thank you, Marshall. You're right, I'll find Jamie after I've seen George. I'm tired but I don't think I'll be able to sleep. I suppose there are many who feel that way today," said Liza. She left, made her way to the stable and then went on to see George at the church where she arranged for Rufus and Paul's funeral.

She noticed that several enlisted men were digging in the graveyard, preparing for the burial of soldiers from both sides. Liza went and chose the place for Rufus and Paul and made sure that George knew where they were to be placed.

"Go and rest Liza," said George. "You look exhausted."

Liza smiled and said that he looked just as exhausted, and he had a great deal to do in the next few days.

"Are you going to be able to marry Greg and Ellen quickly?" asked Liza.

"Rules are made to be broken, especially in war time," smiled George.

"That's good news. It will cheer everyone up," said Liza.

She drove down to the store and Jamie saw her coming and helped her down whilst Joe put the pony and buggy away.

"You look tired Liza," said Jamie. "Why don't you rest before lunch?"

"I think I will," said Liza. "Are you able to join me?"

"No my darling, I'm helping Tom and Dr Steele move their equipment back from the hospital tent. One or the other must stay where the patients are just in case they are needed," said Jamie.

"I have been asked by the Colonel to visit him and Ada this afternoon. I think they are going to ask me to take Christina. You know that I am one of her legal guardians and they are worried that this war is going to get much worse. Also her father has written to them and has expressed concern about the situation in America and he is right to do so," said Liza.

"I've spent a little while with Ada and she was looking after Bea's girls and Christina who seems to be a very intelligent and kindly girl. It's difficult to believe that she's Felicity's child. What are you going to do if they do ask you to look after her?" asked Jamie.

"I have a duty to do so Jamie, but how would you feel about it? It would mean her living with us and she would be bound to be upset at leaving the only happy life that she has known. She was pushed from pillar to post for the first years of her life, and she has been happily settled for some years now," said Liza.

"It will be a very difficult decision to make," said Jamie.

"When I became a guardian to Christina my life was very different to the life that I have now, and really it was because Ada and the Colonel are her grandparents and therefore their life expectancy was less than a parents would be. I lived here so if the worst came to the worst, she would still be in familiar surroundings with her friends. I don't believe anyone thought that my life would change so dramatically or that this country would embark on this terrible civil war," said Liza.

"Ada and the Colonel love that girl; it is going to break their hearts to hand her over to you. How do you think Christina would react to leaving here?" asked Jamie.

"We would be able to honestly tell her that it would only be until the war is over and that she would enjoy travelling and seeing Simon again. I'm not sure that she would remember Matthew or John, but they will remember her," said Liza.

"If they ask, then I don't think that we have a choice and you do have a duty towards her. How do you think that Edward will react, and the rest of the Fullers for that matter?" said Jamie.

"Well, that's another problem that we would have to face, but I know that they realise that the circumstances of her birth are not her fault. Her father tried to do the right thing for her, but it's understandable that his wife found it difficult to warm to the child. He was very happy that she was here in Benson amongst caring people," said Liza.

"I know that he thought that Felicity was you and I realise that I had treated him with such contempt that he wanted to parade you in front of me, making it clear that he had slept with you," smiled Jamie.

"Well you know that his English was appalling then, and he thought that the description he had been given had lost a great deal in translation," said Liza.

"You may be asked by others to take their children to safety," said Jamie.

"I doubt it; all the other parents are of an age to stay alive a great deal longer than Ada and the Colonel, but you never know," said Liza.

Jamie left her to return to helping the doctors and Ellen was waiting to see her as she was delighted to tell her that she and Greg would be marrying on Sunday and that Caroline Browne was altering a beautiful cream dress for her to wear. Angela and the children would be picking flowers for her bouquet and to decorate the church. Sam was to be Greg's best man and Laura was her bridesmaid with Benjy as usher.

"Kathy, Mrs Tolany and the Dornberg ladies are arranging food and a cake for us, and Major Graves has said that we can use the fort's assembly room for our reception," said Ellen. "Everybody is being so kind to us, and it is at such short notice."

"It's going to be a wonderful day for you and for everyone in Benson. I presume that you will be returning to Dr Tom's when Greg goes with his unit," said Liza.

"The choice is mine as I could move into married quarters but I don't know how long he will be away so it would be better for me to remain with my family," said Ellen. "You look tired Liza."

"Everyone keeps telling me that," smiled Liza. "I'm going to rest for a while. I have one or two appointments this afternoon so I must wake up for them."

Kathy bustled through and also said how tired Liza looked, at which she just smiled at Ellen, who left to return to Caroline's to see how her dress was coming along.

"I think Leonora will work out well helping us in the store," said Kathy. "I understand that she may also help Laurie at the print shop now that Greg is in the army. She seems very happy here and she's probably right that it would be difficult for her in New York, and it has already been difficult for her in Charleston, and that was before there was a war."

"Will she be able to live with you? Or would you prefer her to stay somewhere else?" asked Liza.

"I've discussed it with Joe and Leonora, and we would be happy for her to live with us; she can have Danny's old room when you leave. She's also a very skilled nurse so she will be very useful in our town," said Kathy.

"She knows that it is only until Greg and Sam return, but by that time her husband will be free, and they can take up where they left off, although I am not sure that she is altogether happy in Charleston; but that is their problem, not ours," said Liza.

"Go up and rest Liza, I'll call you when lunch is ready," said Kathy.

***

Liza was not looking forward to the meeting with Ada and the Colonel. She knew that it was going to be upsetting for them all. She agreed with Jamie that Christina appeared to be a well-balanced and happy child and she wondered whether taking her out of this environment would alter her personality.

Ada and the Colonel were waiting for her in the sitting room. Christina was with Judith at Bea's quarters at the fort.

"Eugene tells me that you know what we are going to ask of you," said Ada.

"I understand your concern regarding Christina, but surely that is the same fear that everyone here has for their children, and no one is suggesting that they send them away," said Liza.

"But there is nobody of our age with a child of Christina's age, they are all much younger and you know that it was only because you and Rufus intervened that I was not sent to a southern prison, and I know that I would not have survived that. The same situation may occur again. Marshall and the troops will be leaving again shortly and I will only have a handful of men to guard the fort. The Confederate leaders may well still want to take this fort as it is very strategically placed and I will not be able to stop them," said the Colonel.

"If this area is so important, why won't you be given more men to protect it?" asked Liza.

"I don't know Liza, but it seems to me that orders are given without anyone looking at the overall picture," said the Colonel.

"You know that the people in this town would fight to stop you being taken anywhere, and there are others who would protect you if I were to ask them," said Liza.

"I would not allow myself to be the cause of any fight that the townspeople would create. They are not soldiers and must not sacrifice themselves on my account and you must not use your influence to get your Indian friends to protect me. They have enough to worry about to keep themselves alive in this day and age," said the Colonel.

"And I will not allow you to end your days languishing in some disgusting southern prison and neither will anyone else in this town, so you will just have to accept that you will be rescued no matter where they try to send you," smiled Liza. "I do however wish that you would be allocated more soldiers to defend what you term a strategic position."

"We really want to talk to you about Christina and ask you to look after her until we feel it is safe for her to return," said Ada. "However we do appreciate that this war could go on for years and we may not be around at the end of it."

"I can't bear the thought that you won't be around," said Liza.

"If the fight that we experienced the other day was a few miles nearer this town, then many of us could have been killed, so nobody can guarantee that they are going to survive for any length of time," said the Colonel.

"I know that you will miss her terribly, but you know that I will look after her as if she were my own and I will make sure that she realises that Benson is her home and you both will be anxiously waiting for the day when she can return," said Liza.

"We appreciate that you have to discuss it with Jamie," said the Colonel.

"I already have done so, and he is happy that we will be extending our family for as long as necessary," said Liza, "but he knows how sad you will both be not having her with you. Does she know that she will be leaving you?"

"Not yet, we decided that we would not tell her until we knew that you had agreed," said Ada. "We'll tell her later today; she knows that Simon is with you and she has recollections of Matthew and John, and she does remember you, Liza."

"That's surprising as it's around eight years since we were here," said Liza.

"Yes, but you were always kind to her, and she saw a great deal of you because you used to visit me nearly every day," said Ada.

"She's going to miss Judith; they are such good friends," said Liza.

"I can see that you are not happy about taking her Liza," said the Colonel. "Is it because it could create an awkward situation with Edward and possibly the rest of the Fuller family?"

"I'm very happy to have her as part of my family Colonel," said Liza. "I'm just not happy for you and Ada. She has been such a wonderful part of your life for so long now and you have brought her up so well. She is a credit to you both. As far as Edward and the Fullers are concerned, they have always recognised that Christina had no control over her parentage, and they have all been so pleased that she has been well loved and cared for by you both."

The Colonel cleared his throat and gruffly said that there were one or two things that he had to attend to at the fort, but he would be home in time to be with Ada to tell Christina that she would be going on an exciting holiday with Aunt Liza.

Ada was dabbing her eyes and Liza was trying not to become too emotional.

"Before you take on the responsibility for Christina, there are matters that you should be told Liza," said Ada.

Liza frowned and said that she already knew about Christina's origins and Ada did not need to go over any history which would be upsetting for her.

"I have to tell you Liza, as you could be taking on more than you think you are," said Ada quietly.

Liza realised that Ada needed to tell her something important, so she sat quietly waiting for Ada to continue.

"I know what you do with abused children. I know how you care for them, and I know that your John has suffered in the past. I also could see it in Ellen's eyes when she first came to Benson and so I realised that the twins had also been hurt," said Ada.

Liza looked shocked that Ada had been so accurate in her assessments.

"Don't look so surprised Liza. What you must realise is that it takes an abused person to recognise the signs in others. You must also be aware that abuse doesn't only happen in the homes of the poor, it happens in wealthy homes also," said Ada.

"Oh Ada, not you also! It must have been purgatory for you when I talked about what was happening with the charity," said Liza.

"I know that you were aware that Felicity was not Eugene's daughter; no doubt you often wondered who and what her father was," said Ada.

"I knew you well enough to know that you had not been promiscuous; I thought that the father could have been dead. As Eugene and you have such a happy marriage, I knew that it was not a situation where forgiveness was necessary," said Liza.

"I'm afraid that Felicity's father was also her grandfather. The abuse went on for years and my mother either did not believe me or didn't want to know. I had already met Eugene when I became pregnant and although I was hardly allowed out, there was an instant attraction between us. When we did meet one day my father was so angry that he hit out at Eugene and dragged me back home. Eugene recognised that my father's attitude was not normal or healthy and of course it concerned him."

"A few weeks went by, and Eugene made up his mind that he was going to call on me and for once I was home alone and he was shown in, much to my surprise and fear as I was beginning to put on weight by then. Both my parents were ignoring my condition and I believe they were planning to hide me away and deal with the birth themselves."

"Eugene looked at me and took in the situation immediately. The look of fury on his face was something to see and of course I thought he was annoyed at me. I tried to run out of the room, but he stopped me in my tracks by telling me to go and pack a bag as he would be taking me somewhere safe and when we got there, we would discuss our marriage."

"My father returned at that moment, and I cringed with fear, and I really don't remember what was being shouted by either Eugene or my father, but the result was my father being knocked to the ground and Eugene kicking him mercilessly; I believe he was telling him that he was going to make sure that he never abused anyone ever again. He then turned to me and said that I was to forget about packing a bag as there was nothing that I needed from that house."

"We married at the first opportunity and Eugene was posted to a fort on the edge of the Indian territories where we stayed for a few years, but it was dangerous, and we wives were hardly able to leave the fort. I had Felicity there and there were some complications which is why we had no more children. But Eugene loved her as if she were his own."

"From being a young lieutenant he was promoted many times until finally he became a colonel soon after moving to Benson. There was very little here. Kathy and Joe were here, and they had Danny. The fort was hardly built but gradually it became habitable, and people started settling here and it has been our home ever since."

Liza sat quietly, digesting what Ada had told her until finally she said, "It answers a great deal about why Felicity was as she was. I see none of Felicity's traits in Christina, so it would seem that any incestuous problems have passed her by."

Ada frowned and Liza said, "I know that sounded rather hurtful, but you know that mental and health problems do occur in such relationships, otherwise you would not have told me, and I know that you told me as a warning of what I could possibly expect by taking Christina with me."

"I know what you are thinking Liza," said Ada. "Why did we let Felicity marry Edward and you are right, we should not have done, but when she returned from finishing school, she seemed so happy and normal. All her little strange ways seemed to have disappeared and she and Edward seemed very much in love. We had no idea how badly she had treated you or how her mind had worked trying to take what was yours and both Eugene and I regret that we said nothing. We are so sorry that you and Edward went through such a terrible time with her."

"There is no need to feel sorry Ada," said Liza. "It is all in the past and we must all look after Christina as best we can. Thank you for telling me, it makes no difference to how I feel about you. I love you just as much as I always have done, and I will look after and love your granddaughter to the best of my ability and return her safely to you when this stupid war is over. Did Eugene know that you would be telling me of Felicity's origins?"

"Yes, we both felt it best that you should know," said Ada.

"It doesn't have to be mentioned again. It's over and we must all now look to the future and do what is best for Christina," said Liza gently as she noticed that Ada was now crying bitterly, and all Liza could do was to put her arms around her and wait for her to calm down.

"Come on Ada, let's go and put the coffee pot on and I'd like to see what cake you have. It wouldn't be a proper visit here without cake," said Liza brightly, which was certainly not how she was feeling.

"I suppose you will have to tell Jamie," said Ada.

"Jamie and I have no secrets," said Liza. "He will understand."

There was no need for Liza to tell Jamie as the Colonel had made a point of finding him and telling him of Felicity's parentage. The Colonel knew that Liza would still be with Ada so he brought Jamie to the house and when he arrived, he went straight to Ada and put his arms around her and told her that he totally understood how she must feel and that she need have no worries about Christina as he and Liza would look after her with care until she could return to their loving home.

Liza looked up questioningly at the Colonel and he said that he felt that he should tell Jamie about Felicity as he knew that Liza would think with her heart and take Christina regardless of any problems which may arise, whereas Jamie would act with his head.

Liza then looked at Jamie and grinned as she knew that he had acted not with his head but with his heart, and she knew also that he had taken on John without a second thought knowing his background and he loved him dearly and treated him with a great deal of care because of his past.

They talked for a while until Jamie said, "Well, you both now have the most difficult task of your lives. You must tell Christina that she will be leaving you. I presume you are going to say that it is a holiday. Does she realise that there is a war going on?"

"Yes, she does, and she knows that we are worried for her welfare because of it," said Ada.

"She's going to wonder why she is the only one to leave the town because of it," said Jamie.

"She writes to her father regularly and she knows that he can't visit her here because of the war, so she may feel that she is going somewhere that he can be with her for a while," said Ada.

"Has he visited her often?" asked Liza.

"He has been to see her several times in the last few years. He loves this town, although he said that he could feel how everyone felt that something was missing because you weren't here," said the Colonel. "Our last letter from him said that he was going to try to get to New York and perhaps we could get Christina to him there, but so much has happened since then that we don't know if he has got there or if he was stopped on the way, but it doesn't matter as if you cross on the way you will eventually all meet up whether it is in New York or back in England. Even if you do miss one another at least he will know that Christina is safely with you."

"So really you are pre-empting her father's request," said Liza. "I know that he will be happy that she will live with us in England. He can get there relatively easily and visit whenever he wants. That does not mean that he would not prefer her to be with you, but I can understand his concern regarding her welfare at this difficult time, and the fact that this town could be in the firing line of opposing forces."

"It is a worrying time for all parents," said Ada.

"I think it might be an idea to have a town meeting as some parents may wish to make the sacrifice of allowing their children to evacuate with us when we leave next week," said Liza.

"That's quite a responsibility for us Liza," said a concerned Jamie.

"It is, but it's the least we can do, however I believe that there would be very few who would take us up on the option, but I feel that we should make arrangements for them to take advantage of the opportunity even if we are no longer here. My friends will get them safely to the nearest railway station to New York, so we would only need a couple of people to see them to my house there. From there Henry Mahoney would make arrangements for them to travel to us in England. It probably won't be necessary, but parents would know that they have the option to make their children safe should they feel the need, hard as it would be for them," said Liza.

"I presume that you mean your Indian friends," said the Colonel. "Would the people of this town feel happy about that I wonder?"

"They trust you Colonel and they trust Ada; they also trust Zelma and I know that you trust Bandor and so do several people from the town. It would be up to you to convince them that they are in safe hands. You know that they would be," said Liza.

"We'll call a meeting for Friday," said the Colonel. "We have many funerals tomorrow and the following day, so Friday would be a good day. I hope that it won't distract from the wedding on Sunday. Do you know when you are leaving?"

"We haven't discussed it but probably a week today which will be next Wednesday," said Liza. "So you have a week to prepare Christina, and yourselves."

"We'll leave you now," said Jamie. "As I know you have a great deal to think about."

"I must go to the fort to collect Christina; we'll talk to her as soon as she is home," said the Colonel sadly.

Back in their room at the store Jamie asked Liza if she really thought that nobody would take up their offer of taking their children to safety.

"It's not dangerous at present, so they won't think it would be necessary, but they have seen a little of what it could be like; the burials are showing them that. I believe that if they can be sure that their children can safely reach New York in the future should there be the slightest possibility that this town becomes a battle ground, then they will have no choice but to do what we are suggesting," said Liza.

"I was wondering if the Colonel and Ada would like to come with us to England," said Jamie. "It would solve their sadness at parting with Christina."

"We can suggest it to them, but I think you really know the answer. The Colonel will be placed in charge of Benson once again and he will take that duty very seriously and Ada will never leave him," said Liza.

"You had no idea about Felicity's father, did you?" said Jamie and Liza shook her head. "It does explain a great deal about why she had so many strange ideas and acted in such peculiar ways. Such parentage can lead to so many problems. I think we have been lucky with young John; his only problem is that he can be a little unsure of himself, but his brothers help him with that."

"John will be worried about us, but I know that Matthew will calm him down," said Liza. "Did you know that Matthew told me that we would get back safely but not when we planned? He will also make James understand that we are alright, as well as the rest of the family."

"I'm glad that the Colonel told me about Ada's past because I know you would have a dilemma over whether you should tell me or not. He also knew that," said Jamie.

"I had no dilemma over that Jamie," said Liza. "I told Ada that you and I had no secrets."

"That's nice to hear," said Jamie. "The Colonel also realises that you may have to tell Edward and possibly Wendell and Amelia as it will help them to understand why Felicity acted as she did and perhaps they won't feel any antagonism towards Christina. Although I don't think that any of the Fullers would show negative feelings towards a child, regardless of the difficulties that they had with her mother."

As they sat down to dinner that evening Kathy said, "I hear you are taking young Christina back with you to England."

"That's going to upset young Judith," commented Joe.

"I know it will, but it's what the Colonel and Ada want," said Liza.

"Her father is worried about her also," said Kathy. "The Colonel is calling a town meeting for Friday; do you know what it's about?"

"I think there are many things that need to be discussed," said Liza.

***

The next morning it seemed that the whole of Benson was up early, and all were dressed in sombre clothes. Jamie took Liza to the fort so that she could say goodbye to her friends Rufus and Paul before the undertaker closed their coffins. They were going to be interred at around midday; other burials were taking place throughout the morning. George was going to be very busy, and he was still suffering from the attack that he had received.

Ben had been meticulous in finding the names of most of the dead. There were one or two from the Confederate side that had to remain nameless, but he had arranged descriptions, and these were going to be sent on to Alabama with the names and ranks of the rest and details of where they were buried. The Union dead were easier to deal with as they were known to their commanding officers.

Liza had arranged small headstones for each with their names and ranks and date of death, but these would take some time. She also stipulated that the unknown ones had whatever limited information available carved on them.

Finally at midday Paul and Rufus were brought to the graveyard and most of the townspeople turned up to see them laid to rest side by side. It was a very moving event and even some of the men could be seen to shed a tear. Most of the people had raided their gardens for flowers for all the soldiers but they knew that they had to save some as they had more burials the following day. Liza hoped that there would still be enough flowers for Ellen and Greg's wedding.

George looked tired and ill, and Kathy insisted that he went back with her when she would feed him and make sure that he rested.

Liza made her way to her family's graves and Jamie said that he would see her later. She went immediately to Patrick's grave.

"Well Patrick, you have a great deal of company now. I tried to take the fear away from most of them and I spent time with Paul and Rufus. I arranged for them to wear their best uniforms and Rufus wanted to revert to the uniform that he should have worn all the time. He knew that he had chosen the wrong side and that choice was only because of where he had been born. He really didn't believe in most of the southern policies. He tried to protect the people of Benson and if it hadn't been for him, I would have been put in a prison wagon and paraded back to Alabama. They wanted to use me as a pawn in their stupid game."

"I know that you will look after them, as you do our daughter and Danny. This is such a sad time for this country, and I will shortly be leaving it for my home in England and back to our boys. We are taking Christina with us as Ada and the Colonel want her safely with us, and so does her father. By now you will know of Felicity's origins and realise that she was not really in control of herself. It was so sad and none of us realised just how mentally unsound she was, and why."

"I'll visit you again tomorrow when we have buried the rest of the soldiers. You'll be pleased to hear that Ellen and Greg are getting married on Sunday. It's a quick marriage but George has bent the rules as Greg is now in the army, so is young Sam and they will be going away soon. It's all very depressing; I shall be pleased to get back to our boys, they will always make me feel better. Goodbye for now my Patrick."

Ada called Liza as she passed her house and asked her to come and see Christina.

"My grandmother says that I am to go on a long trip with you to England," said Christina.

"Yes, it will be quite exciting for you and when we get to England, you'll see Simon and Matthew and John again," said Liza.

"Will I be anywhere near where my mother lived?" asked Christina.

"Your mother stayed in my house in New York for a short while, but she then lived in Belfast not in England," said Liza.

"How long can I stay with you?" asked Christina.

"As long as you like, but you know that your grandparents and your father are worried about you because of the war that is going on at the moment, so you will be with me until it is over," said Liza who realised that Christina was a great deal older than her years.

"My father will find it easier to visit me in England. Do you think that Judith will be able to visit me also?" asked Christina.

"You'll have to ask her mother about that," said Liza.

"Would you have the room for her to stay if she says yes?" asked Christina.

"I would always make room for any of your friends if their parents agreed to their visiting you," said Liza.

"It would be better if my grandparents could come with me, but I know that my grandfather has to stay to look after the people at the fort and in the town and my grandmother needs to stay with him until they can bring me home," said Christina.

"Yes, it is essential that your grandfather stays until he can hand over his duties to someone else, which probably won't happen until after this war. We will stay in New York for a couple of weeks, and if we find that there is a truce then there will be no need for you to travel to England, but if not then we will make the journey across the sea and be settled there well before Christmas," said Liza.

A tear started trickling down Christina's cheek and Liza could see that Ada was also about to cry. Liza could not be sure that she would not follow suit.

"I do remember you and Matthew and John and the nice soldier that you were married to then, he was very kind. I remember him dying and everyone being so sad. I don't know your new husband. Is he kind?" said Christina.

"Yes Christina, he is very kind. I would not be with somebody who wasn't. He has become father to Matthew and John, and he also has a son called James and he is now also my son. You will meet him when we get to England. Simon lives with us while he finishes his education, so there will be people there who you already know. They will all be very pleased to see you. It will just be like old times," said Liza.

"It's a long way from here," said Christina. "It's going to take a long while to get there."

"The worst part of the journey will be from here to the rail station outside New York and from there it will be easy. Do you remember being at my house in New York? Do you remember coming here with your father and Mary?" asked Liza.

"I remember Mary," said Christina. "Is she still in New York?"

"Yes, she's still there. You know Susan also; she'll be with us all the way; so the journey should go quite quickly for us. We'll be travelling across the sea in a very large luxury liner, so we can relax for that part of the journey, and it's only a short drive from the docks to our house in England," said Liza.

"What can I take with me?" asked Christina.

"We'll have plenty of room for your clothes and your favourite toys and books. Shall I send Susan over to help you with that?" asked Liza.

Ada was very quiet, and Liza thought it best to leave them alone and all she added was that Christina could come over to the store at any time and if she had any worries then they could talk about them.

Jamie and Joe were sitting outside the store and Jake was standing with them. Liza smiled and thought that the three Js were very diligent in watching over her. She wondered where Bandor was and knew that he was around somewhere also keeping watch.

Jamie came over to see her safely across the road. "How was Christina?" he asked.

"She was a little upset, but asked if you were kind," said Liza. "I said that you were."

"Does she remember much of the past?" asked Jamie.

"She remembered Matthew and John and also Mary, and of course she knows Simon well. She told me that she understood that her grandfather had to stay to look after all the people and that her grandmother had to stay with him. She also asked if Judith could visit her in England. I said that if her mother let her then we could do that," said Liza.

"She sounds quite intelligent," said Jamie.

"She seems to be," said Liza. "I cannot see any of her mother's traits in her. I hope that it stays that way. She didn't ask if I knew her mother but no doubt she will do that during our time together."

George was resting with Angela watching over him. Susan was helping Leonora set the table and she smiled at Liza and told her that she had been helping Joe in the store and after the funerals the next day she would be visiting Laurie at the print shop to see how she could help there.

"I must also introduce you properly to Wes Barrows who looks after my business interests in this area along with Gabriel," said Liza. "Although I would think that business will not be thriving for the duration of the war, but we will all do what we can."

Over dinner George asked if everyone had got the message that there was a town meeting.

"I believe so," said Liza. "I trust you are all going to it."

"It's not really to do with us," said Roberts.

"It has Roberts," said Liza. "Whilst you are in Benson you are one of its inhabitants, and that also goes for Susan and especially for Leonora as she will be living here for a while."

Liza wanted to visit Zelma that evening, so she and Jamie set out knowing that Bandor would realise that she wanted to speak to him.

"I've been expecting you," said Zelma as they arrived.

"You've always known me so well," smiled Liza.

It was not long before Bandor silently entered the room. "What is it that you want of me i-tse di-ka-ta?"

"I want to know if I can rely on my friends to help the children of Benson if it becomes necessary," said Liza.

"Whatever you want done, it will be done," said Bandor.

"We are leaving next week, but some parents may wish to send their children to me after that time," said Liza. "It would be wonderful if this war is over before we leave here, or even before we leave New York, but I doubt it. It is going to get more and more difficult for the ordinary people to survive and the danger from the fighting could become very close to the town's people. At that time parents will try to protect their children and they may see that the only way to do so is to evacuate them to somewhere that they think is safe and they know that such a place is with me, either in New York or better still, in England."

"You would want us to make sure that they reach safety," said Bandor and Liza nodded. "You are right, this foolishness is not the children's fault, and it is right that they are taken somewhere safe should it be necessary. I'll leave now and will be back before your meeting."

"The people of this town know you and trust you," Liza said to Bandor. "You have done so much for their safety, and I feel that you should also be at the meeting. It will reassure them that their children will be in safe hands if they decide to send them to me, although I think there will be very few who make that decision."

"What of your people's children?" Jamie asked Bandor.

"We are not involved with this war and the food and goods that i-tse di-ka-ta sends us each year gives us extra, but if the goods can't reach us, we will survive. We did so in the past and may have to in the future," said Bandor. "But if the situation changes, I will find a way of letting you know."

"If any child needs to come with me now, make it clear to Running Bear that it will be looked after as my own," said Liza.

"I will tell him," said Bandor and he left to make his way to the Cherokee encampment.

"Do you really think that they will send their children to you?" asked Jamie.

"If they were starving or sick then yes, they would, but failing that they would not want them to be taken away from their culture; but I have to give them the option," said Liza.

"We could have a problem if all your Indian friends decide to bring their children to us," smiled Jamie.

"I doubt that they would; they are more likely to move the whole of their tribe to somewhere out of danger; unfortunately such a place would probably have very little food to sustain them," said Liza. "Zelma and Bandor will find a way to let me know and I would see what I could do to help. Hopefully I could get some wagons to them with the bare essentials."

***

The whole of the following morning was taken up with the final funerals for soldiers from both sides, after which Liza not only visited her family and Danny, but she also spent time with Rufus and Paul.

George was going to stay with Gabriel and Kate for a few days as he had not yet recovered fully from the attack on him, and he wanted to be fit for the services on Sunday and Greg and Ellen's wedding. He would normally have stayed with Kathy and Joe, but there was very little room left for anyone else at the store.

Jamie saw Liza coming down from the churchyard and walked up to meet her.

"They all have been laid to rest," he said. "We can now look forward to the wedding and then we will be on our way home a couple of days later. I believe we are going to have an army escort all the way to New York."

"I didn't think that they could afford to lose any men from their unit," said Liza.

Jamie smiled, "No, Marshall can't, but Sean can. He and his unit, including Sergeant Rowe, will be escorting us all the way."

Liza smiled happily at the thought that she would have some time with Sean.

Joe and Jake were sitting outside the store and they both waved as Liza and Jamie came into sight. Kate was crossing the road to the store and Liza was going to follow her in and see how Leonora was coping and then go with her to see Wes and Enid.

Somebody rode up behind Liza and she could see the looks of surprise on Joe, Jake, and Kate's faces. She and Jamie turned and could see that it was Bandor and he had a very pretty little girl sitting in front of him, who could be no more than three years old.

Bandor jumped down and lifted the little girl to the ground. She was holding a buckskin bag and Liza knew that it contained everything that she possessed in the world.

"Her name is tsu-lv-sa-da no-qui-si; in your language it is Bright Star, and she is now yours," said Bandor without emotion.

There was a stunned silence but both Liza and Kate were not surprised.

"Won't her mother be sad?" asked Liza.

"Her mother is no longer with us, but even if she was, she would know that this is best for her," said Bandor.

Liza slowly looked from the little girl to Bandor, and realisation set in. "She's yours, isn't she?" said Liza.

Bandor nodded. "She needs to learn how to live in both worlds, you will teach her that, as you have done for your son. Your man is a good and kind man, and he will keep her safe. She will be fed and warmly dressed. Soon we will not be able to do that."

Liza looked at Jamie and she could tell from his expression and the way he was nodding that he was not going to turn the girl away.

"She will also be loved Bandor, I can guarantee that," said Liza quietly and he nodded his approval.

"Bright Star is a very pretty name," said Jamie. "Perhaps soon she will be shining happily because she is not looking too happy at the moment."

"It's very strange for her and it must be rather frightening, although she is not showing any fear, but they are taught that from the day they are born," said Liza.

"The people will help if your town children have to be moved," said Bandor starkly and he walked away leading his pony. His daughter watched him leave but said nothing and stayed where she was.

Liza and Jamie looked at one another, and Jamie asked if she spoke English. Liza shrugged her shoulders and then crouched down to the little girl and discovered that she only knew the Cherokee language.

Kathy moved near and said that she will have to find Danny's old cot. Liza replied that there was no need as the little girl would only be used to sleeping on skins on the floor, so Kathy went off to find some blankets.

"She'll have to sleep in with us," said Liza to Jamie. "I wonder how she will react to being kissed and cuddled."

"Well you might as well find out now," said Jamie. "Everyone in England will be surprised at the increase in our family."

"You are being very understanding Jamie; not many men would have accepted the situation so readily," said Liza.

"I could see that there was no arguing with Bandor. I could also see behind his façade. He wants what is best for his daughter and what is best is not leaving her in the Indian encampment without a mother. He was paying you the greatest compliment by entrusting you with his flesh and blood and he also paid me a compliment by knowing that I would not turn her away. I think that she is going to be easy to love," said Jamie.

Liza bent down and picked Bright Star up and spoke to her in Cherokee asking her what she had in her special bag which she then held out for Liza to look inside. There was a carved wooden doll, a talisman to keep her safe, a beaded armband and three American dollars.

The beaded clothes that she was dressed in were probably the finest that she possessed, and her dark hair was tied in charming little bunches. Liza carried her into the store and Jamie followed.

"We'll have to find some clothes for her," said Kathy and Kate said that she would bring some of the clothes that little Liza had grown out of.

"You'll be able to get her some new ones when you get to New York," said Kate.

Ada and Christina appeared. "I heard that you have been given a little girl. Oh! She's beautiful," exclaimed Ada.

Christina was smiling at Bright Star, "I'll help you look after her Aunt Liza. She's very little and will need someone to be with her all the time. I'll play with her on our journey."

"That's really kind of you Christina but it could be a little difficult as she doesn't speak English yet. You can help me to teach her if you would like to do that. Hopefully by the time we reach New York she will be able to talk to us a little. Playing with her will also help her learn," said Liza.

"Can I bring Judith over to see her?" asked Christina.

"Of course you can, but you must realise that she isn't a doll, she's a little girl who is now in a place that is very strange to her, and she must be feeling rather frightened. I know you and Judith will try to make her feel comfortable," said Liza.

"Why don't you go and find some toys that you think she might enjoy playing with," said Ada to Christina.

"I know why Bandor wants us to take care of his daughter, but I would never be able to give up one of my children," said Jamie.

"The Indian culture is very different to ours Jamie," said Liza. "A brave will give away his favourite wife to show his regard for another man. Giving away a child is not as big a sacrifice as giving away a wife. I do however believe that Bandor has done this for the sake of his child, and I think that he has found it very difficult. He would hate to know that we can see through his apparent harshness."

Christina returned with a doll and a spinning top which she showed to Bright Star and in turn the little girl pulled out her carved wooden doll and showed it to Christina. It was a good start to their relationship and both Liza and Ada realised that Christina felt that she was needed by the little girl and that was going to make her leaving Benson much easier than it would have otherwise been.

Susan appeared saying that she had heard that they had a small child to look after and by that time Kate had returned with some clothes which Susan said she would take up to the bedroom.

Christina was talking to Bright Star and showing her how the spinning top worked. The little girl had no idea what she was talking about but for the first time she showed pleasure and smiled up at Christina.

"That's the best way for her to learn our language. I have seen how playing together breaks down all barriers. That was how the Tolany and the Dornberg children learned to speak our language," said Liza.

"Don't be so modest Liza, you had a great deal to do with their understanding and speaking English," said Ada.

"I wonder if she's hungry," said Kathy.

"I suppose we had better find out," said Liza. "Christina, would you like to eat with her?"

Christina looked at her grandmother who said that it would be a good idea for her to help the little girl to eat.

"I think you'll have to eat sitting on the floor. Bright Star won't yet know how to sit at a table," said Liza.

So they both sat on the floor and Christina showed that she was enjoying eating what she had been given and Bright Star followed suit and slowly ate her meal. Liza smiled and felt that Christina was going to be a great asset to them, especially on their journey to England.

Susan came and Liza said that it would be a good idea if she joined in eating sitting on the floor as it would make Bright Star feel comfortable. There would be time enough for her to be taught how to sit at a table.

When Christina and Ada had left Liza decided that they should set up a bath for the little girl and she was no trouble to undress, and she enjoyed playing in the warm water. Susan was happy to be helping with the little girl and when she was dried and wearing a warm nightdress, she was once again given food for her supper and then both Liza and Susan took her up to bed. Kathy had arranged a feather mattress covered in blankets on the floor in Liza and Jamie's room and Bright Star was clever enough to know that it was her bed and she settled down comfortably. She had both her carved doll and the one that Christina had given her to comfort her in her bed. Liza stayed with her for a while, but Susan was insistent that she would stay until she was asleep. It was obvious that Bright Star was going to be a great favourite with everyone.

"Well Liza," said Jamie as she came into the dining room, "today has been a strange day. It started very sadly with all the remainder of the soldiers' funerals and is ending with having a beautiful child joining our family."

"We mustn't push Christina into the background. She will be very sad at leaving Ada and the Colonel, so we must make her feel very wanted," said Liza.

"I believe that both Christina and Susan are going to enjoy looking after Bright Star which is going to make our journey much easier. It is a blessing that you speak her language," said Jamie.

"Someone that young will soon learn English, but I won't let her forget her own language or culture. She must not also forget her father and when she is old enough, I will tell her of the sacrifice that he made for her," said Liza.

***

The next day it seemed that the whole town wanted to see Bright Star and in the end Liza just allowed Christina and Judith to spend time with her, with Susan and Zelma watching over them.

Leonora was spending the day with Laurie at the print shop and Liza wondered whether she would return covered in ink as Laurie and Greg had done when they had first worked with the printing press.

George was looking much better, although he had a huge bruise on his forehead and his hand was still bandaged but being cared for by Kate obviously suited him.

Angela was at the school as a number of children had returned to classes as their parents felt that it was safe for them to leave their homes.

The Colonel was at the fort with Marshall and Bea was spending time with Ada.

Tom and Dr Steele were still caring for the wounded and Marshall had the dilemma of not knowing what to do with the wounded Confederate soldiers.

Sean had not ventured into town; he had his own unit camped on the outskirts of Benson and Liza wondered whether she would see him before he joined them on their trip to New York.

The Tolanys and the Dornbergs came into town late that afternoon so that they could attend the meeting that evening. The meeting was going to be well attended.

Hannah and Mrs Long were with Kathy and all three were preparing for Greg and Ellen's wedding reception whilst Ellen was with Caroline having a final fitting of her wedding dress.

Jamie was visiting Gabriel as he wanted to know if there were going to be any problems with them taking Bright Star with them to England, but Gabriel knew that Bandor had given his daughter to Liza and even though there was no formal adoption, it was what her only parent wanted for her.

The day was passing quickly and soon the time had come for them all to go to the meeting and Liza was surprised to see Sean and Sergeant Rowe making their way towards the schoolhouse and she could see that there would be no vacant seats that evening. Susan decided that she would stay and look after Bright Star with Christina and Judith.

Bandor was standing quietly at the back of the room and when Zelma noticed him, she moved over and stood by him.

The Colonel called the meeting to order and invited Liza to join the committee.

"This town showed compassion for all the soldiers no matter which side they were fighting for. You all helped with getting me and Corporal Raines back to our army but none more so than our Cherokee friends and especially Bandor, who we all know," said the Colonel.

"We now have people who we thought of as enemies lying in our graveyard and I know that you will all care for them just as you will do for our own dead soldiers. Liza spent her time easing men from both armies out of this life and you all know that our dear friend Rufus Denton wanted to be laid to rest next to his good friend Paul Southern. It just shows you how terribly sad this war is," he said.

"Benson is a very strategically placed town and fort but even though it is an important place, our army is not yet large enough to stay and defend it with a vast number of soldiers. We will have more than previously allocated to us, but it is still not enough to take all our worries away. I know that the people of this town will try to defend me and my men and you will put your lives at risk, which you must not do. You have not been trained as our soldiers have been and you are needed by your families. If you must fight, then it is best that you fight in the defence of your wives and children."

"It is hoped that this war will be short lived, but I believe we all realise that the way things are going, this could last for years, and we will all go through a time of great deprivation. I want to be wrong, but only time will tell," said the Colonel. "We are lucky that we have a town full of people who have always pulled together and looked out for one another. I know that Liza would like to talk to you all."

Liza stood and said, "As you all know it was under very difficult conditions that I arrived back in Benson recently, and without Rufus Denton's intervention and the help of everyone in this town, both Jamie and I would have been escorted back to one of the southern states and imprisoned there for the duration of this war. I thank you all for your care and concern. We will be leaving on Wednesday to return to New York and onto our home and our family in England. You all also know that we will be taking young Christina with us as well as dear little Bright Star. They will be treated as our own and cared for in a safe environment."

"This war could go on for a very long while and during that time there could be dangers that we are not yet aware of, as well as the difficulty of finding enough food for you all. There may be a time when you feel that you will have to make some tough decisions, and if you do, then for your children I want to put at your disposal my house in New York, followed by passage to my home in England. You may think that it would be risky to travel at that time, but I want to assure you that should you feel that you would like to place your children somewhere safer than here, then they will be guarded every step of the way by Bandor and my Cherokee friends who you all know you can trust with your children's lives. They will guard them and make sure they reach their destination safely. Someone from town must travel with them but once they reach New York my agent, Henry Mahoney, can be contacted at the Marchant & Fuller offices at the docks, and he will not only make arrangements for them to stay in that city, but he will also arrange their passage to me in England, where they can stay until the war is over."

"I am not suggesting that you make such a decision before we leave next week; I am suggesting that you think about such a scheme and act on how you see this war progressing, after all it could be over in a very short while, or you all manage to have enough food to see you through without difficulty, or nobody from the Confederacy approaches Benson. There could be many reasons why you are all spared in this town, but if at any time you feel that you would like to protect your children, then please take Jamie and I up on our offer. You know that we will look after your children and make sure they are clothed, warm, well fed and loved by us."

"It is very much food for thought but I really hope and pray that you will never have to make such a decision."

Liza sat down to a very quiet and thoughtful room and the Colonel stood again.

"Liza's right that we hope that none of you have to make such a decision, but I think you will agree with me that it is a very generous offer and I know that you will also agree that you can trust Bandor and his friends to guard your children and see them safely to New York," said the Colonel. "Our children are our future, and we must protect them in whatever way we can. Ada and I are doing that now with our beloved granddaughter, and believe me it is very hard for us, but we know that she will be safe and happy with Liza and Jamie until her return at the end of this senseless conflict."

"I'd like to say something," said Joe. "There is so much that we have Liza to thank for and sometimes I think that we take a great deal of what she does for granted, but also we take for granted what Bandor and his friends are prepared to do for us and indeed what he has already done for us. I for one would like to say how much I appreciate his help in the many ways that he has watched over not only our soldiers but also the people of this town."

There was agreement from those in the room and the Colonel said that Joe was right, and he wished he had thought of saying that himself. Bandor just stood stony faced but those who knew him realised that he was content that the people of Benson trusted him and his people.

The meeting broke up and several people came up to both Liza and Jamie. Mostly they wanted to make sure that should they part with their children that they would not be placed in an orphanage.

"They will be with me," said Liza. "I can assure you that we will not let them go to any orphanage, but should our house become full to overflowing, we will arrange for them to stay within other families, and I will make sure that they are safe and happy. We really hope that it will not come to that, and I will attempt to get food and goods through to you as much as I possibly can."

The consensus of opinion was that the time was not yet right to make such decisions, but the future was looking rather bleak so they may have to send their children away for their own good and they had faith that both Liza and Jamie would do all they could for them. Most of the people said that it was a great relief to them to know that if the situation became dire, they would have somewhere safe to send their children.

Bright Star was sound asleep when they returned, and she once again had with her in bed her own carved doll and the one given to her by Christina.

"What are we going to call her?" asked Jamie.

"I like her name as it is," said Liza.

"It won't sound right in England," said Jamie. "I know Bright Star is a very pretty name and it does suit her, but she needs to be able to answer to a normal name. Stella means star; it's not as attractive as Star but we could call her Star as a nickname but register her as Stella."

"Unless we can think of anything else, then we will have to go with that idea," said Liza.

**

Saturday was a very busy day with everyone rushing around and preparing for Greg and Ellen's wedding the following day.

There was a feeling of euphoria throughout Benson as the last week had been such a frightening and sad time that the thought of a wedding was raising everyone's spirits.

"I have some pretty dresses that little Liza had which Bright Star could wear for the wedding," said Kate.

"That's very kind of you Kate, but the beaded clothes that her father dressed her in to come here were very pretty and suited her so well. She will have very little opportunity to wear them in the future, so tomorrow will be a good day for her to show them off," said Liza. "They are part of her heritage, and I will make sure that she keeps them safely even when they no longer fit her."

"Yes, I think you are right; especially while she is here she should be what she is, when you get her to England she will have to become someone else," said Kate starkly.

Leonora joined them and she was ready to go to the print shop with Liza, who was also going to show Christina and Judith how the press worked. She also decided that she would take Bright Star with her, and they all made quite a sight going on their way to meet up with Laurie at the shop.

Much to Liza's delight Greg was spending a while there. He had the day away from the fort and would be returning later that afternoon and the next time anyone would see him would be at the church the following day for his wedding.

Christina and Judith were to be flower girls throwing petals at the happy couple as they left the church and Judith suggested that Bright Star might like to also be a flower girl and she would arrange a small basket of petals for her.

"I think that's a wonderful idea," said Liza. "I will make sure that she understands what she has to do."

Leonora was beginning to come to terms with how the press worked and Laurie was explaining to the girls the way pamphlets were printed. Greg was showing Leonora how to set the letters and when she stood up Liza noticed that she was in exactly the same ink covered state that Greg and Laurie had been in when they first started. Christina and Judith were amused at the sight of an adult getting so dirty.

"Leonora is doing quite well here," said Greg with a worried look on his face.

"Don't worry Greg, your job will be waiting for you when you get back, and so will Sam's," said Liza.

"That's good to know," said Greg.

Liza then left with the children, leaving Leonora in Greg's and Laurie's capable hands and they made their way to Ada's for afternoon tea. Liza was pleased to find that Bea was also there, and they all spent a lovely time chatting whilst the children played together; it felt like old times to Liza.

The whole town seemed to be awake very early the next morning and there was an air of excitement around. Liza and Susan helped dress Bright Star in her immaculate beaded Indian clothes and her hair was combed loosely and not in bunches. She had a matching beaded headband and she looked absolutely charming.

They all made their way to the church and saw Greg waiting nervously with Sam, and when Ellen arrived, Tom proudly walked her down the aisle. It was a very moving ceremony as they all knew that within a few days Greg would be leaving with his unit, and nobody knew when he would return.

Christina and Judith quietly left the church with their baskets of petals and Liza took Bright Star to join them and they waited for Greg end Ellen to emerge and as they did, they threw their petals over them. Bright Star happily took a handful of her petals and threw them at the happy couple; they landed nowhere near them, but she smiled happily and continued throwing them until all the petals in her basket were gone. She looked up at Liza with triumph written all over her face.

Bandor stood in the shadows and was pleased to see his daughter dressed in her own beaded clothes and was also pleased to see her smiling and joining in throwing petals with the other girls. He could see how happy she looked, and he knew that he had made the right choice for her. Green Eyes would look after her and make sure that she knew her heritage, but most of all she would love her as her own mother would have done. He felt a pang of loss, not only for his daughter but for the wife that he had so recently lost. He had not found it easy living in two worlds and some years before he had made a difficult choice as he had felt that he was more white than Indian; the town of Benson had done that for him. He knew that Liza and her husband and friends were to be escorted on their way, but he would also make sure that they reached their destination safely. He silently left the churchyard and made his way to a place where he could sit quietly and meditate.

Everyone was letting their hair down at the reception; they appeared to be trying to forget the events of the previous week and most were succeeding. Bright Star was a little in awe of the number of people who could not resist talking to her and in the end she hid her face in Liza's skirt and Liza then lifted her onto her lap and put her arms around her. Jamie looked across and it took him back to a time when he had seen Liza with a very young Matthew on her lap and knew that she was at her most contented when she was with children.

The revelries were still going on when Liza and Jamie carried a sleeping Bright Star back to the store. Susan offered to help them, but Liza told her to carry on enjoying herself; she would be back to her duties soon enough.

The town was very quiet, but they could see Bandor waiting in the shadows. "Do you have something to tell us Bandor?" asked Liza.

"I thought there might be something that you wished to ask," he replied.

Liza carried Bright Star up to her bed and just took a short while to put her in her nightdress before she went down to see Bandor.

He and Jamie were talking rather stiltedly when she returned.

"Bright Star is a lovely little girl," said Liza. "She is indeed a bright star. When was she born?"

Bandor had to think about that and finally he said, "it was halfway through the month that is called September, and this will be her third year."

"So if we say that her birthday is the fifteenth of September, we will celebrate that date with her every year. When did she lose her mother?" asked Liza.

"Just two months ago," said Bandor.

Both Liza and Jamie were quiet for a moment and Jamie then said, "That was when you were chasing after us. I'm so sorry that we were the reason why you could not be there for her."

Bandor just nodded whilst his features gave away no emotion.

"You know that we will do our best for her; we will treat her as our own and when the time is right, we will make sure that she knows the sacrifice that you have made for her; she will not be allowed to forget her heritage, but she will also be well educated in our ways," said Liza. "I hope that she will want to return to the land of her birth when she is old enough to make that decision."

"She will have a better life with you. Being the motherless child of someone who is neither Cherokee nor white would not help with her treatment in the encampment. There is no one who would spend much time with her; she would be treated little better than an outcast. If her mother had survived it would have been different for her as she was full Cherokee although she was an orphan. One of her cousins took care of Bright Star but she was not treated as her own. Your offer to take care of any children was more than I could have wished for her."

"I thought that children were taken in and adopted quite easily within the tribe," said Liza.

"If you are talking about the chief adopting White Wolf, you must remember that he was a male child. Male children are wanted, females are not considered important and especially those who are not full Cherokee," said Bandor.

"Women are the mothers of all children," said Jamie. "They should be equally important, if not more so."

Bandor just shrugged.

"What did she die of?" asked Liza.

"A fever; that's all I know," said Bandor. "Why, are you worried that her daughter might have the same?"

"No, that didn't occur to me. She must have been young, it's so sad," said Liza.

Once again Bandor just nodded.

"I will be riding with you until you reach the railway to New York. I know that you will be protected by soldiers, but I want to make sure that you get there safely," said Bandor.

"Thank you Bandor," said Jamie. "You have been more than a friend to us, and we promise you that we will give Bright Star the best start in life with so much love that she will never want for affection."

"I think that she and White Hawk will have a great deal in common," said Bandor.

Jamie frowned questioningly. Liza said that Bandor was referring to Matthew whose Cherokee name was White Hawk.

"Of course, I had momentarily forgotten that," smiled Jamie.

"I'll leave you now; others will be returning soon," said Bandor.

"You don't have to leave just because others are returning. You know you are always welcome in all households in Benson," said Liza.

"I like to be alone," said Bandor and this time Liza just nodded.

When he had left Jamie also commented that he liked to be alone with Liza. "We have had such little time to ourselves over the past weeks. It's nice for just the two of us to sit here quietly. I know that soon everyone will descend on us and this will become the hub of the town."

"It's been very hard on you Jamie; I do realise that. This is part of my past which I thought I had left behind, but somehow it has all come back. The memories have engulfed me on occasion, but I want you to know that I do love you Jamie, and I can't wait to return to our normal life. I want to see our boys and the rest of our family and friends. It's going to be interesting when we introduce Christina and Bright Star to them. I know we have said that we will have to tell Wendell and Amelia about Felicity's parentage, do you think we should do that sooner rather than later?" asked Liza.

"I suppose the sooner we do that then I believe the more easily Christina will be accepted by them; they will then understand some of why Felicity was as unbalanced as she became. I know that they will feel that Ada and the Colonel should have stopped her marriage to Edward, but she didn't show much sign of how her mind worked in the early days of her association with him," said Jamie.

"I hope they don't think that I have betrayed them by bringing her with us, but I am sure that they know that I was made her guardian should the need arise, although I think that her father was worried about Ada's and the Colonel's ages and should anything happen to them, he wanted to be sure that she was cared for," said Liza.

They could hear people returning from the wedding reception. There was lots of laughter and a great many voices could be heard coming up the stairs to the dining room where Liza and Jamie were sitting. It seemed that the party was going to continue there, and Liza smiled as there always seemed to be impromptu parties whenever she was about to leave a place.

Susan checked on Bright Star who was sleeping peacefully despite the noise from the dining room. Many people were calling in to see Liza and Jamie before they left on Tuesday morning. They did not have too many clothes to pack, so the next day could be used to call on everyone at the fort as well as those in the town. One of the main places that Liza wanted to go was to say a final farewell to Patrick, little Meg and Danny and then on to Rufus and Paul. There were also others that she wanted to visit in the churchyard, so the following day would be very busy for her. She needed to say a special goodbye to Ada and once again reassure her that Christina would be loved and cared for until she could return to her.

Roberts had made many friends in the town and at the fort. The people had appreciated how he had helped and kept calm when many had panicked during the fighting. They also realised that Jamie was not as pompous as he had first appeared.

They finally got to bed well after midnight. "I'm going to miss Benson and I'm very worried about what is going to happen here. With young Greg and Sam going off to war, who knows if they will return, and if they do, will they be in one piece? The same goes for all those already in the army and if another fight comes to this town, how many will survive that? I feel that I am deserting my friends in their time of need," said Liza.

"You are doing the finest thing that you can for the town; you are providing a home for Christina and have offered to take as many of their children as they need to send to you. You will also be making sure that they receive as much food as possible, and you will also be doing that for your Cherokee friends. You know that Bandor trusts you otherwise he would not have given you Bright Star," said Jamie. "Come on Liza, get some rest. You know we are not going to get much sleep until we get to New York."

Their last day in Benson was exactly as Liza had planned. She was firstly seen driving out to the fort and once again the Colonel stood at the window and watched her head towards the office where she chatted to Ben before he showed her into the office that he was sharing with Marshall.

"Well Liza, have you come to say goodbye to us?" asked Marshall.

"Yes, I have, although I will probably see you as we go tomorrow," said Liza. "I'll miss you both. I will look after your granddaughter, Colonel. I will try to make her as happy as I can, but she will find it hard to be completely happy without you and Ada."

"We'll miss her too," said Marshall. "Judith will be really upset when Christina leaves. Bea is with her at Ada's now."

"Yes, I'll call in there later, but I wanted to see everyone here before I left," said Liza.

"Sean hasn't come into the fort or into town, but I suppose you'll be seeing him a great deal on your way to New York," said Marshall.

"Is Bart on duty?" asked Liza.

"I'm afraid he's out on patrol at present, but he'll be back in a while. No doubt you'll meet up later," said Marshall.

"It's not the same here. The town hasn't changed, but here has. There are so many that I knew who are missing. I suppose when this war is over it will get back to some normality. You'll have some new lieutenants by then; probably some will be from the south and everyone will realise just how senseless it has all been," said Liza.

"I'm afraid that the powers that be don't think that it's senseless," said Marshall. "They know the reasons behind it all; unfortunately not many others know what they are fighting for."

"I'd better leave before I make a fool of myself," said Liza who was near to tears.

"We've seen you in tears before Liza and we understand your sadness now. You've seen some terrible sights since you arrived here and helped many through their final ordeal. If anyone has a reason to cry it's you," said the Colonel.

Liza looked down and then turned on her heel and left the room without another word; she quickly moved through Ben's outer office waving to him as she went much to his surprise as she had always spent time asking about his family. He did however realise that she appeared close to tears, and he felt that she must be upset at having to leave the next day.

She quickly collected her buggy from the stable and drove back into town hoping that her tears would end before she reached her destination.

Jamie saw her coming; he was finalising what he would need with Roberts, but he could see that Liza was not her normal bright self and he followed her round to the back of the store to help her unhitch the pony.

"What's upset you, Liza?" he asked.

"Nothing in particular, it's just that everything is so different. It's all changed and so many are going into a fight, and they really don't know why. I'm glad to be leaving as I don't want to see the damage that is going to be caused to the people here, or anywhere else for that matter," said Liza.

"Have you said goodbye to everyone yet?" asked Jamie.

"I really have not said goodbye to anyone," said Liza. "But it will happen, it always does. I'll check that Susan is organised and see that Bright Star has everything that she needs; then I must visit the rest of my family."

It was after lunch when Liza went to the churchyard, and she was surprised but pleased to see Sean there visiting Patrick's grave. He looked up and said that he hoped that he was not intruding on her time with Patrick.

"No Sean, I've visited him several times since I've been here. I'll leave you to spend time with him; I have others to visit," said Liza.

"I've been here for some time; I think I've said all I needed to. I see that Rufus and Paul are together; that's how they should be. I suppose you organised that for them," said Sean and Liza just nodded.

"I'll see you tomorrow, Liza. We'll be spending some time together and my instructions are to see you safely to New York so I will be with you all the way. I dare say you'll find a room for me to sleep in," said Sean and he smiled.

"I'm pleased it's you Sean, although it is taking you away from more important duties," said Liza.

"There's nothing more important than seeing you safely out of harm's way. You know that you are still wanted by the Confederate leaders," said Sean.

"I didn't know that; I thought they had given up on me," said Liza.

"No, you are considered a prize possession, although I don't think they know that you are leaving tomorrow or if you are still here. This time we won't leave you to fend for yourself," smiled Sean.

He bent over and kissed her on the head and left her to visit her family and friends.

"I'm pleased that Sean has visited you, Patrick. It has been hard for him to come to terms with your loss, but you know that. I'm leaving tomorrow and I don't know that I will ever be back, but it doesn't mean that I won't think of you or talk to you. I know that you will probably meet up with others that you know if this war carries on for much longer. It's all so sad and all I can see are young lives being lost. I'm sure that the vast majority don't know what they are fighting for."

"Sean is taking us back to New York. We have Bandor's daughter with us now. He has given her to me for safekeeping. She is beautiful and her name is Bright Star. Her mother died recently, and she needs a great deal of love. So we have Christina and Bright Star as additions to our family. Everyone is going to be so surprised in England."

"Now I must leave Patrick; I'm sorry I couldn't bring you any flowers today, but there are none left since Greg and Ellen married, they used them all up. Goodbye my darling Patrick, please take care of all those who will now be following you. God Bless You."

She went down directly to see Ada and Bea and spent an hour reassuring Ada that Christina would be well loved by everyone in her household. Christina's case was already packed, and Liza took it so that they would be able to organise where everything would be stacked on the coach the next day. She left so that they had time to themselves.

Kate called her and she spent some time with her, and Gabriel joined them for a while and said that he would see them when they left the following day. He and Kate had letters for Liza to take to Simon.

She had seen Wes and Enid, and all was in hand for running her various local businesses. She had already arranged that the wagon and horses which Charles Enderby had loaned to them be used by whoever needed them and should be returned to him when the war was over.

It was late in the afternoon when Liza finally returned to the store. She was pleased to find that their packing for the next day had been virtually finished. Bright Star smiled and put her arms out for Liza to pick her up, which pleased her as the little girl was at last acting as a child should.

Liza sat her on her lap and told her what was happening the next day and that she was going to enjoy all the places she would see on the way and that they would all be looking after her from now onwards. She held up her carved doll and Liza realised that she was asking if she could take that with her and Liza told her that she could take that and her new doll also.

Bright Star said "doll," which was the first word she had spoken in English. She was beginning to learn their language.

Chapter 12

The coach that Liza had hired was ready and waiting just before midday the next day. Two soldiers were at the reins, and it was loaded with their cases and most of the town and the fort were there to wave them off. Bart was checking that all was in order, although he really wanted to make sure that he said goodbye to Liza. Zelma was telling Liza to give her love to the boys and everyone else she had met in the past. Ada and Christina were nowhere to be seen and Liza assumed that they were saying their farewells in the privacy of their home.

Kathy was handing them enough food to last them some days and Liza was saying that they would not need that much but her objections were falling on deaf ears. Jamie finally made the decision for them to board as he realised that too many people were showing signs of distress, including Liza.

Jamie helped Susan aboard and told Roberts to lift Bright Star into her seat. The Colonel and Ada appeared from their home leading a reluctant Christina between them. Liza kissed Kate, Gabriel, Zelma and Bea and finally she waited for Ada and the Colonel to bring Christina to her and when they did Jamie lifted her into the coach and Liza turned and kissed Ada and then the Colonel and quickly took her seat, followed by Jamie. The door was closed, and the coach moved forward, and the next stage of their journey had started.

Firstly they had to stop at the fort to be joined by Sean and his escort unit and at that time both Ben and Marshall came to bid them farewell and hope that they had a safe and comfortable journey. Sean barked his orders to his men, and they surrounded the carriage and left the fort without a backward glance.

Christina was crying bitterly and before Liza could do anything to help her Bright Star took her hand and gave her the carved doll for her to hold. Christina smiled through her tears and took it while Bright Star climbed up next to her and put her arm around her as far as she could, which was really not very far at all.

The adults looked at each other recognising that children had their own way of comforting one another. Susan picked up a book and started reading to them as Liza wiped Christina's tears away. Bright Star smiled but she understood nothing of what Susan was reading although she appeared to be listening.

"This part of the journey is going to be the worst," said Liza. "When we stop at the various posts, we will be tempted with the delights of indeterminate meat stew; it's just as well that Kathy supplied us with various goodies to eat, although they won't last us for the whole journey."

"You've been on this journey before then," said Roberts and both Jamie and Liza nodded with resigned looks on their faces.

Susan carried on reading for a while, but the swaying of the coach had lulled Bright Star to sleep lying on Christina whose eyes were also beginning to close and they both slept for two hours.

They stopped to rest the horses for a while and Sean came and joined them and they shared some of Kathy's food with him.

"We'll reach the staging post in a couple of hours. I notice that Bandor and Zelma's brother are keeping watch over you," said Sean.

"Yes, well he has his daughter to protect," said Liza.

"He may be doing that, but his main reason is you, Liza. He's not going to let anything happen to you," said Sean.

Sean had been right; it did just take a couple of hours to reach their first staging post. There were just two rooms available for their overnight stay. The largest had a double bed and one single but Liza arranged for a mattress and covers for herself. The other room would have to be shared by Jamie and Roberts. The meal was as predicted, meat stew which they all ate very little of and when they had finished, Susan and Liza got the two children ready for bed and they looked quite comfortable together in the double bed. Susan said that she would take the mattress, but Liza said that she had been used to sleeping on the floor, so the mattress would be just right for her.

Sean and Sergeant Rowe would be bedding down in the main room with the rest of his unit outside. Where Bandor and Zelma's brother were nobody knew but they were bound to be close by.

Liza was aroused the next morning by the smell of ham and eggs cooking and when she opened her eyes, she came face to face with Bright Star smiling at her. She was already dressed, as were Christina and Susan.

"We thought we'd let you sleep in for a while," said Susan. "I'll take Christina and Bright Star down to breakfast and then come back and help you dress."

"No need Susan," said Liza. "You stay and have breakfast with them, I'll get myself ready."

Jamie knocked and entered as Liza was washing. "I peeped in earlier, and you were sound asleep. I'll help you get ready. I missed being with you last night, my Liza."

Liza smiled and said, "Not much longer, my Jamie."

Jamie could see that she was getting back to being the Liza that he knew and loved. She had not wanted to go to Benson, and she certainly had not wanted to be caught up in the battle around it or helping with the dead and dying. Even though they had a long journey ahead of them she was beginning to relax and enjoy her time with him.

When she was ready, they went down to breakfast together. Roberts was also returning to his normal demanding self. He was being critical of how the ham had been cooked as he felt that it should be crispier than was being served, although nobody was taking any notice of him.

Sean was sitting with Sergeant Rowe, and he asked if they had slept well and said that they must be on their way as soon as possible after breakfast.

"Susan has done a good job with the children so we will all be ready whenever you say," said Liza. "I trust you slept well also."

"The sergeant and I have slept in some very uncomfortable places so last night was luxury for us," said Sean as he got up to leave the room and organise the rest of his men.

"Are you coming with us all the way to New York?" Jamie asked the sergeant.

"Apparently so," replied Sergeant Rowe. "It's a good many years since I was there. It will be interesting to see the changes."

He smiled and also left the room and could be heard barking orders to the men, who appeared to be tardy in saddling their horses.

Their bags were once again placed on the coach and after thanking the people at the staging post, they all climbed aboard for that days' journey to the next post.

They met several Union patrols over the next days; each one stopping them and asking their destination before being sent on their way. The information that they were being given was that there was a small Confederate unit in the area, but they seemed to be trying to make their way back to a main unit somewhere further south.

"They can't be looking for you Liza or they would be following us rather than trying to avoid us," said Sean. "But we will take no chances. We'll be at the train station the day after tomorrow, but I think we'll take a small detour and stay the night at the nearest army post. I'm sure they'll make room for us all."

They drove into the fort later that day, much to the surprise of the major in charge. There were quarters that they could use for the night and Liza and Jamie were invited to join the major for dinner that evening.

"We'd be delighted to Major," said Jamie. "But first we must settle the children and the rest of our fellow travellers and make sure they have food for the evening."

"Don't worry," said the Major smiling. "They won't be subjected to meat stews."

"That will be a relief to them. Obviously you have travelled on our route Major," smiled Jamie.

"I believe that it's the staple diet on all routes," smiled the Major. "Captain Byrne and Sergeant Rowe will be joining us, if you have no objection."

"It will be a pleasure to see them in a relaxed atmosphere, Major," said Liza. "They have been on duty twenty-four hours a day since taking on the responsibility of getting us safely to New York."

"From what I hear, you are very much wanted by the Confederate hierarchy; although I don't believe they have infiltrated this far north. A small unit has got lost and is making its way back and we are watching them closely," said Major Simpson. "However, Captain Byrne was right to seek safety for you here, just in case there was anything untoward."

"Thank you Major," said Jamie. "We'll see you later for dinner. I trust you will excuse our attire; we only have travelling clothes with us."

"Of course," said the Major and they left to find where they would be staying the night.

Roberts was to be sharing with Sergeant Rowe and quarters were made ready for Susan with Christina and Bright Star, and Jamie and Liza had the luxury of a room of their own.

"Wonderful," said Jamie as he prized off his boots and lay back on the bed. "We're nearly there Liza. We've nearly reached civilisation."

"I wouldn't let Major Simpson hear you say that; what he is doing tonight is civilised," said Liza.

Roberts knocked to see if there was anything that he could do for them, and Jamie said that all he needed was one of his better outfits for this evening and if he could find that then he would not be needed later as he would dress himself. An audible sniff came from Roberts and Liza laughed and told him that he was going to have his work cut out when they reached New York as none of them had very much other than travelling clothes.

"If the tailors and dressmakers are still in business there, then we are all going to have to smarten ourselves up, you included Roberts," smiled Liza.

"Of course we are," smiled a placated Roberts and as he found the clothes that Jamie needed that evening both Liza and Jamie could see a look on Roberts' face which told them that he had all sorts of clothing plans coming into his mind.

Susan then knocked to see if she was needed, and Liza told her to look after the children and that the major had said that they would not be subjected to meat stew that evening and somebody would call for them when their meal was ready.

"And you too Roberts, I trust you won't mind eating with Susan and the children this evening," said Liza.

"I'd eat with the whole Confederate army if I had the promise of not another meat stew," mumbled Roberts.

"Only one more tomorrow evening, Roberts, and then we'll be on our way by train to New York. We'll be staying at a hotel before we leave, so I'm sure there will be something else on the menu," said Liza.

Both Roberts and Susan left, each savouring the prospect of a decent meal that evening, leaving Jamie and Liza smiling at the conversation they had just had.

"I noticed that Bright Star didn't complain about any of the food," said Jamie. "Christina turned up her nose, and I don't blame her."

"Bright Star has been taught to eat what she was given as sometimes they never knew where the next meal was coming from. I remember times like that," said Liza thoughtfully as a memory from the distant past came into her mind.

Jamie nodded his understanding. He frowned with concern as he knew that a memory could trigger a nightmare in Liza but at least he would be able to hold her that night.

They could hear movement outside and when they looked a soldier was leading Roberts, Susan, Christina and Bright Star presumably to where they would be eating their meal and they both smiled as Roberts was holding Bright Star's hand and talking to her.

"She doesn't know what he's saying," smiled Jamie.

"She's learning very quickly and that is the best way to learn. Just being spoken to in someone as young as she is will bring its own understanding. I've seen it happen before," said Liza.

"You wrote to Henry and Myra, didn't you?" said Jamie.

"If they received my letter then they know that we are safe and will be making our way to New York, but they don't know when we will be arriving or the number of people we will be arriving with. But that doesn't matter; I'm sure all will soon be made ready for us. I wonder how the war has affected New York; it's still early days so I suppose there will not yet be shortages," said Liza.

They rested for a while and then slowly got ready for their dinner with Major Simpson but before they went, they checked on the children and found Susan and Roberts sitting outside their quarters taking in the evening air. Christina and Bright Star were sound asleep having enjoyed a roast chicken meal.

"Both children were pleased to see chicken for their dinner," said Roberts. "And so were we."

"I'm sure you were," smiled Jamie and they then made their way to the Major's quarters where they arrived at the same time as Sean and Sergeant Rowe.

They were also treated to roast chicken as a main course and the Major smiled at the looks of relief on all their faces.

"The menus en route leave a great deal to be desired," said the Major.

"Yes, but we've managed to survive," said Liza.

"We had heard that you were being held in Charleston and then again later on. I had been informed that you were being escorted by our soldiers at that time, what went wrong?" asked the Major.

"We received orders to return to our units and Liza and Jamie were very near safety. Our information was that there were no opposing forces nearby," said Sean.

"We had Lieutenant Shaw and Bandor with us and when it was obvious that they were outnumbered they left to get help, which they did successfully," said Liza.

"I'm surprised that they left you," said the Major.

"They were both known to the commanding officer, as was I," said Liza. "They were no use to us captured, or worse. We knew that we would not be harmed by their captain, but we needed help and only they could get it for us. Bandor got to my Cherokee friends and Lieutenant Shaw reached the Union forces."

Both Liza and Jamie kept quiet about the fact that when the Confederate Major had arrived, he was going to execute everyone but Liza. Sean and Sergeant Rowe took their lead and said nothing.

The evening was pleasant and at the end Sean and Sergeant Rowe saw Liza and Jamie back to their quarters.

"I noticed that you chose not to say anything about the insane Confederate Major," said Sean.

"Why create more hatred than necessary. Even the Confederates would not have approved of what that Major wanted to do," said Jamie. "You are right in the fact that he was insane. He certainly had no orders to execute everyone but Liza. I just hope that he has not been set free to continue in his unbalanced manner."

They said goodnight and it was remarked that there was only one full day left for them to endure in the coach.

Liza was asleep as her head touched the pillow; Jamie smiled as he climbed in beside her. He would have liked to have made love to her, but he was happy just being in bed with her and feeling her warm body next to his. It seemed that the nearer they got to New York the more she became the Liza that he knew so well.

Once again they were up early the next morning and having said farewell to the Major, they left the fort for their last full day travelling by coach and just one more stop with the inevitable meat stew.

Christina and Susan were doing a wonderful job teaching Bright Star various items in English and she seemed to revel in learning. It made the day go quickly for them and when they reached the final staging post there was only one room available which was made ready for Susan, Christina and Bright Star. Liza and Jamie would have to sleep on the floor of the main room along with Roberts and Sean and Sergeant Rowe.

"Are you sure there's no room for you in with the girls?" said Jamie to Liza.

"There's really not room for the three girls, they're not going to have a very comfortable night," said Liza.

"And neither are we," commented Jamie and he was right. It was no hardship for them to be up early the next morning and they were all looking forward to just a few more hours of coach riding. When they reached the train station they would spend the rest of that day at a hotel and Sean and his men would be at the garrison which was nearby.

"Don't worry Liza, I will have some men guarding the hotel whilst you are there and you will be escorted onto the train, after which it will be just Sergeant Rowe and myself who are in charge of your safety," said Sean.

"Surely you don't think that they will come into New York. That would be very dangerous for them," said Liza.

"Until you are back in England you can't be sure that you will be one hundred per cent safe," said Sean.

"You're not filling me with confidence Sean," said Liza.

"Don't forget that Sergeant Rowe and I will only be with you for a couple of days," said Sean.

"That's a shame; it would be nice if you could stay longer, although I'm sure I don't need your protection once we reach New York, in fact I don't think that we have needed it on this journey, but it was nice having you with us," said Liza.

They drove into the town and pulled up outside the hotel. Arrangements were hastily made for the Company suite to be made ready for them and they all breathed a collective sigh of relief as they went to their rooms. Christina and Bright Star were sharing, Susan had her own room, as did Roberts, and Liza and Jamie had the best room in the hotel, and they eyed the bed longingly. Unfortunately the children needed their attention and Susan and Roberts needed to rearrange the luggage which seemed to be in some disarray.

"Will you be joining us for dinner tonight, Sean?" asked Jamie.

"Not tonight I'm afraid. I have some reports to make, and I will see you first thing tomorrow morning, and then we'll have a few days to relax together. I've arranged for a couple of men to guard the hotel tonight although I do think you are right that this is going to be too far for anyone to try to abduct you," said Sean.

Jamie and Liza enjoyed their dinner alone that night and their time in bed even more so.

Sean appeared soon after breakfast and Liza asked if he knew where Bandor was as she needed to see him before they left; also she needed to make a quick visit to the bank in the town.

"Sergeant Rowe saw him this morning just outside the garrison; I'll send him to find him. Do you really need to go into town?" asked Sean and Jamie also queried if that journey was necessary.

"I'll go with her," said Jamie.

"So will I," said Sean and they both looked slightly annoyed at the disruption that Liza was creating.

It did not take her long to establish with the bank manager who she was and to withdraw money from her account, which she secreted carefully in a pocket in her skirt. She smiled up at Jamie and Sean as she emerged from the bank and said that all she now had to do was write a couple of short notes and they all made their way back to the hotel.

"What are you doing Liza?" asked Jamie when they arrived back at the hotel.

"I'm repaying a debt," said Liza. "I'll tell you about it later when I've finished these letters."

Jamie left her to her task, and it was not long before she emerged from their room with four letters in her hand.

"Bandor is waiting for you outside," said Sean and off she ran down the stairs to find him.

"Thank you for caring for us Bandor," said Liza when she found him. He was waiting for her with Zelma's brother. She had rolled up five hundred dollars into two bundles and she handed them to Bandor. "This may be needed by my friends in the future. These letters all say that you are entitled to have this money should anyone query why people from your tribe have such currency."

"We will not need this," said Zelma's brother. "And we do not accept charity. Our chief will not accept this."

Liza smiled at this as each year she sent wagons of goods to them, which they accepted.

"Many years ago Running Bear gave me money to help me. That was an act of charity on his part; I am just repaying that debt," said Liza.

"Running Bear and our medicine man know that this war between the white men could create many problems for our people. The soldiers will not worry if their battles come to our lands and destroy what we have built. We may have to move to a place of safety that will be barren. They will not worry if the buffalo get in their way, they will not worry if we get in their way. If your wagons cannot get through to us and if we cannot hunt, the people will starve. This money will keep many from dying. I will thank you i-tse di-ka-ta and I know that the people will appreciate what you are doing as they know that you can see into the future, and that future is not good," said Bandor.

Zelma's brother appeared to finally understand that the money could be necessary, and he nodded and grunted his grudging approval and both he and Bandor placed a bundle of money carefully on their person together with the letters.

"It might be a good idea to have Ambrose Cutler with you when you first try to use the money; he is trustworthy in both worlds," said Liza.

Bandor and Zelma's brother both nodded in agreement.

"Do you want to say goodbye to your daughter?" Liza asked Bandor.

"I have already said that to her; she is now your daughter i-tse di-ka-ta and I have seen that she is happy with you and your husband. I know she will return one day, as will you. Goodbye i-tse di-ka-ta, we will leave you. You are safe now," said Bandor and they both mounted their ponies and rode off.

***

The train was due to leave at eleven o'clock that morning and everyone was aboard well in time for departure.

It was the first time that Bright Star had seen a train and she was a little frightened when being helped into it. Christina was also in awe as she had no recollection of her journey to Benson as she had been too young. They all settled into their seats with Roberts grumbling that there were no first-class carriages and that was barbaric. Sean and Sergeant Rowe had never seen a first-class carriage, so they had no idea what he was mumbling about. Liza and Jamie just smiled at his indignation.

They pulled out of the station and started getting up steam and as they passed some trees, they could see Bandor watching the train. Bright Star saw him and frowned; Liza told her to wave to him and she did and although he did not wave back, he nodded that he had seen and then turned his pony and rode away.

Liza knew that he felt Bright Star's leaving more than he liked to show; his white side had come to the fore on occasion, and this was one of them.

There would only be one overnight stop before reaching New York and much as the train ride was quite exciting to the youngsters, the adults had had their fill of travelling and all were dreaming of the luxury that arriving in New York would bring.

The stop was just after the turn off for Daltons and Liza could see the hustle and bustle of the workers and tradesmen travelling to the area. The hotel was busy, but the company rooms were soon made ready for the travellers. Sergeant Rowe was mesmerised by the speed that they were all ushered into the sitting room and refreshments brought.

"Is there going to be a room for me also?" he asked, and Liza smiled and said that there were always perks to owning a hotel, which the sergeant had not realised.

The children's room was the first to be made ready and they were fed their evening meal. Both were very tired, and Liza and Susan took them to their room, and they happily went to bed with Christina asking if they would be in New York the next day and Liza said that they would. There was also a bed there for Susan, but she would not be going to her bed for a while.

It was a very cosy meal in the small dining room which they all enjoyed after which tiredness seemed to engulf them all.

Sean had a small room alone and Roberts and Sergeant Rowe were once again sharing, Susan was in with the girls and Jamie and Liza had the best room in the hotel.

As they settled into their bed Jamie commented that Liza was right in that there were advantages to owning a hotel.

"Tomorrow, Jamie," said Liza. "We will be in our own bed in New York. I can't wait to get back to some normality. I presume that everything will still be the same there; everything else has been sadly different."

Everyone had slept well that night and they were all up early and breakfasting well in time for them to catch the train for the final leg of their journey. They would not be arriving until after dark and Liza and Jamie decided that they would probably have to make their own way to the house as it would be past working hours.

As it got later the children went to sleep and when they arrived at New York station Jamie carried Christina and Sean held Bright Star, whilst Roberts and Sergeant Rowe organised carriages to take them all to Liza's house. One of the cab drivers recognised Liza and soon they were all ushered into the cabs and were on their way up to the house on the hill.

The sound of the cabs making their way up the drive roused the staff, and it was with a great deal of concern that the front door was opened by a startled Bridget and Stephen, the chef. As Bridget realised who the visitors were, and before Liza could climb the steps to the front door, she was engulfed in Bridget's arms, showered with kisses and unintelligible words of welcome.

The girls had woken up as they were carried into the house. The fire was hastily lit in the drawing room and the chef disappeared to his kitchen to make a light supper for the girls and prepare a larger meal for the adults. A bleary-eyed Mary appeared, and Liza said she was sorry to have woken her.

"I'm so pleased to see you back safely with us," said Mary. "I'll take the children down for their supper and then help get them ready for bed. Their room should be ready by then. I presume they'll be sleeping together."

Christina seemed to remember Mary, but Bright Star was reluctant to leave the people that she had come to know. Susan said that she would go with them and help with getting them to bed.

"Do you want to eat with them also?" asked Liza and Susan nodded. "I'll come and see them when they are in bed. Can you make sure that the room the other side of the children is made up for Susan? They are lucky as they'll have you on one side and Susan on the other."

Bridget knocked and entered and said that Liza and Jamie's room was ready for them and asked where she would like her to put the other guests.

"Roberts can be in the room he had before, and do you remember where Captain Byrne was last time he was here?" asked Liza.

Bridget said that she did and then Liza suggested that Sergeant Rowe had the room next to the Captain's.

"I think I'll go down to the kitchen for my supper," said Roberts, "and by that time I'll be able to unpack His Lordship's cases."

Liza smiled and said that he must do what he felt happiest doing, but there was really very little to unpack for His Lordship and he deserved his rest as tomorrow there was a great deal that he would have to help to organise.

"Shall I eat down in the kitchen?" asked Sergeant Rowe.

"You are a guest in this house, Sergeant. You are not staff," said Jamie.

Liza smiled and said, "It's about time that we knew your name, Sergeant."

"It's Arnold," said the sergeant.

Liza smiled again and said that it was good that they could all now relax on first name terms.

"I have been a little taken aback by the size of your house. I knew that we would be coming to somewhere that we could all just about sleep in, but as we drove up here it took my breath away," said Arnold.

"It does that to a great many people; but it is just a house, it's the people who make it a home and I hope that we do that," said Liza.

Once again Bridget knocked and entered to say that all the other rooms were now ready if they would all like to freshen up before dinner. Sean and Arnold were looking around for their bags and Bridget informed them that their spare uniforms were already unpacked and hanging in their wardrobes and if they would like to leave what they were wearing now she would arrange to have them cleaned.

One of the footmen was waiting to show them to their rooms and Liza and Jamie made their way up to their room. They quickly washed and could only dress in their slightly better travelling clothes for their dinner and by that time they could hear Susan and Mary helping the girls up to their room.

Liza walked into their room and found Bright Star laughing and pointing to the dolls that had been laid out on her bed and she said "bed, doll."

When they were in bed Liza sat down and read a short story to them; it was probably too young for Christina, but it was all that Liza could find that had been left by the boys when they were last there.

Bright Star was asleep, and she was obviously getting used to sleeping in a bed and Liza kissed her on the head and then turned to Christina and kissed her also. Christina then put her arms around Liza's neck and cried. Liza then sat on her bed and said that she knew that she missed her grandparents, but she would see them again as soon as it was possible to do so and that she knew that her father would be coming to visit her and spend some time with her when they were settled back in England.

"Christina, whilst you are with us we feel that you are one of our children and we love you as if you were. You are in our care, and we will care for you with all our hearts. I know it's been a very difficult time for you, but you have dealt with it wonderfully well and the way you have cared for Bright Star will always be remembered not only by us, but she will never forget your love and kindness. You really are a very caring person and I'm proud that you are now part of our family. Wipe away your tears and think of all the nice things that we will all be doing in the future. Goodnight, Christina, never forget that we love you."

She kissed her once again and smiled and left the room. Susan was hovering around outside and said that she was going to get ready for bed, but she would listen out for the girls and she was only a short way from them.

Liza went back to Jamie in their room, and he said that he had heard what she had said to Christina, and he felt sure that it would have calmed her.

"You will have a difficult task to undertake with Mary," he said. "I presume you will do that tomorrow."

Liza nodded, "I want Bridget to be near her when I tell her, because I know that she still felt a great deal for Rufus, and you know that he had never stopped loving her. The sooner I do it the better, but tonight is not the right time."

As they made their way down the stairs they were joined by Sean and Arnold, and they went into the drawing room to wait to be called in for dinner.

Stephen knocked and entered and said that he hoped that they would not be too disappointed in their meal tonight, but he had to improvise on one or two dishes.

"Stephen, when you have people descending on you with no notice, it's surprising that you have managed to feed us at all, and I want to thank you in advance for the effort you have put in to feeding us all tonight. I know that the children enjoyed what they had and I'm sure we will do the same," said Liza.

They moved into the dining room and as always in her own house Liza sat at the head of the table with Jamie to her left, Sean to her right and Arnold next to him.

A light vegetable soup was served to start with, and this was followed by slightly thin but tender steaks with sauté potatoes, green beans and carrots. It was washed down with a choice of either white or red wine. For dessert there was a fruit tart with the chef's special sweet white sauce. Cheese, biscuits and a selection of fruit followed and as the men did not want cigars, Liza decided to stay at the table and joined them in finishing with a glass of port.

"Well," said Arnold. "If that was a cobbled together meal, then it must be amazing what he can do when he has notice of guests."

"Stephen is a miracle worker where food is concerned," said Liza.

Roberts was waiting for Jamie in the dressing room and Mary was in the bedroom to help Liza get ready for bed.

"This is just like old times," said Liza to Mary.

"I told Susan to go to bed, she looked exhausted," said Mary.

"It has been a tiring time for her. It was her first trip abroad and it turned into a disaster for her, but I think she has grown up considerably in the last few months," said Liza.

Liza was already in bed by the time Roberts had left. Jamie came through to the bedroom and smiled at her.

"It's good to be here Liza," said Jamie. "I'd much rather be at our home in Surrey but being here is a great relief and it's very comfortable. That bed looks very inviting."

"Well, you don't need to be invited to join me; the bed is yours just as much as mine," grinned Liza.

***

Liza was in her dressing gown and sitting in her study before breakfast the following morning. She was writing notes to the men's outfitters, to Henry and to Myra, but as she was writing Myra pushed her way into the study before Bridget could announce her.

"Oh Liza, thank God you've made it here; we have all been so worried about you. We thought you could be incarcerated for years," said Myra with a sob in her voice.

"How did you know we were here; I was just writing to let you know," said a surprised Liza.

"It's the talk of New York. You were seen arriving last night. I think you had better get dressed as you are going to be inundated with people calling to make sure that it really is you," said Myra.

"It's good that you're here Myra; I was going to ask for your help as the children and I have very little to wear," smiled Liza knowing that Myra was a genius at organising whatever was needed.

"Ah yes, I heard that you had children with you, both girls I gather. I presume you are writing to arrange for the tailors to call for Jamie," said Myra.

"And for Roberts," said Liza. "We had to leave nearly all our clothes behind in Charleston. The way things are I know that Charles will be able to get a good price for them."

"Is it that bad there?" asked Myra.

"Not yet, but it will be soon," said Liza. "I want to take the children and Susan to the dressmakers this morning. I presume you would like to join us."

"I would indeed," smiled Myra. "Go and get yourself ready; I'll arrange to have your note delivered to the tailors. Henry has sent a letter to England on a ship that was leaving this morning. No doubt you will be writing to them later."

Liza ran up the stairs and was pleased to see that a bath was ready for her; she stripped off and climbed in slowly relaxing for ten minutes. She closed her eyes and when she opened them, she found Jamie smiling down at her. He was fully dressed and about to go down for breakfast.

"I hear that Myra is here. How did she know that we were here?" asked Jamie.

"She tells me that the whole of New York knows. Apparently we were seen arriving last night. I've arranged for a tailor to call round today for you and for Roberts. Myra and I will be taking the children and Susan to the dressmakers. I don't think that Sean and Arnold are in need of anything, but perhaps you could check with them before the tailor arrives," said Liza. "I had better get dressed now and go down to breakfast. I suppose the children are still asleep."

"No, I could hear them talking to Susan and Mary, no doubt they'll be going down to breakfast shortly," said Jamie. "When are you going to talk to Mary?"

400

"After breakfast and before we go to the dressmakers," said Liza. "I don't want her to hear from anyone else. Susan and Roberts might say something, or Sean or Arnold could also. Sean knew the situation between Mary and Rufus."

Jamie left her to get dressed and Mary came in to help her and she was shortly making her way down to the dining room for breakfast where Sean and Arnold were already eating and Jamie was asking them if they needed anything from the tailors, which they said they did not.

Susan could be heard coming back from the kitchen with Christina and Bright Star and Liza called to her telling her that they would be going to the dressmakers shortly.

Myra was fending off callers, saying that Lord and Lady Edgeworth would be available later that day and that she would tell them that they had called and that they would appreciate the concern that was being shown.

Liza went into her study after breakfast and Myra asked if there was anything that she could do.

"I'm afraid that I have a difficult task to perform now Myra and I would ask you to make sure that I am not disturbed. I have to tell Mary some bad news," said Liza and Myra nodded although she had no idea what that bad news could be.

Liza called for Bridget to come to her and when she did, she asked her to send for Mary. "I'm afraid that I have something to tell Mary and I believe that she will need you to be with her," said Liza.

"Oh dear," was all that a distressed Bridget could say and as Mary came in Liza told her to sit down.

"When I was in Benson I saw some terrible things and to the best of my ability I comforted and eased many of the soldiers out of this life. Sadly two of those were well known to me and also to you Mary," said Liza.

All the colour had drained from Mary's face as Liza continued.

"One of those was our dear Paul Southern and I'm sorry to tell you that the other one was Rufus," said Liza.

Tears were now cascading down both Mary's and Bridget's faces.

"I was with him to the end and before he died, he asked me to write a letter to you for him. There was nobody else that he wanted to write to, only you Mary," said Liza and she handed the letter to Mary who clasped it to her.

"Was he in pain?" sobbed Mary.

"No, I took his pain away; both he and Paul died peacefully together, and I had them buried side by side. They were the best of friends in life, and I felt it right that they be buried as friends in Benson. The people of Benson will watch over them. Rufus' last thoughts were of you Mary. I wrote that letter for him, but

I can assure you that the words are his alone and throughout the time that we were with him he acted honourably and with great courage. I was proud to have known him and glad that I could help him at the end," said Liza.

"I'm glad that he had someone like you with him," said a very tearful Mary.

Liza was also in tears as she once again remembered two such lively young lieutenants who were now dead and it brought to the fore how senseless it all was and such a waste of life.

"I'll take Mary up to her room," said Bridget.

"Both of you take as much time as you need. We can look after ourselves. Bridget, you need to look after Mary," said Liza.

When they left, Liza sat for quite some time as she found it difficult to compose herself and luckily it was Jamie who came to find her. He put his arms around her as she cried on his shirtfront.

"How did she take it?" he asked.

"As you would expect; she obviously still had strong feelings for him. I believe they are just as strong as the feelings that he still had for her. Bridget is with her. I suppose that the only good thing that will eventually come out of this is that in time Mary can finally have closure on her association with Rufus and perhaps look towards a future with someone else," said Liza.

"It has been a lot of years that they both had those feelings; it could take some years for Mary to get over it. She probably thought that one day he would turn up and his temper would have totally disappeared. We must appreciate that her dreams have probably now been crushed. It's a blessing that she has her sister with her," said Jamie.

"Life goes on and I must see that Christina, Bright Star and Susan are ready to go to the dressmakers. Myra is looking forward to it also," said Liza. "Later today I want to see Henry and introduce Sean and Arnold to Walter as I know they want to meet him and hand over their duties to him."

"I suppose they think we are still in danger, and they could be right, although I doubt it," said Jamie.

"I also want to visit Leonora's father," said Liza.

The tailor was arriving, and he was shown up to the dressing room where Jamie joined him. Roberts was already there, and Liza had no doubt that he had many ideas on the attire that was needed.

Liza noticed that Mary's door was firmly shut, and she went into the girls' room where Susan had Christina and Bright Star ready for their visit to the dressmakers. Christina knew what was happening, but it was left to Liza to tell Bright Star exactly what they were about to do, and she asked if she could take one of her dolls with her and Liza said that of course she could.

Myra was waiting in the hall for them, and she had their carriage ready at the front of the house. It was with an air of excitement that they set off on their shopping spree.

Myra asked how Mary was and Liza said that obviously she was sad, but Bridget was looking after her. Nothing else was said about it and they arrived at the dressmakers and spent nearly three hours trying on various outfits; all of which were attractive but most needed alteration. The assistants enjoyed dressing the girls and they ended up with some very pretty dresses. They also were going to make elegant cloaks edged in fur which would be needed as the weather was turning a little cold. Susan was enjoying being fitted for some new but necessary clothes and she also needed a warm cloak.

All this time Liza was having fittings in a private room. She needed both day clothes and evening dresses as there were one or two functions that they had already been invited to and she also needed a warm cloak or two. Underclothes and night clothes were also needed by everyone and some of the outfits would be ready later that day, but most would take a day or two to complete.

They arrived back at the house in time for lunch which they took together with the girls in the dining room. Sean and Arnold were looking forward to meeting Walter and Liza had no doubt that they would be giving him chapter and verse on how to safeguard Lord and Lady Edgeworth. Liza hoped that Walter would not take offence at being instructed on how to do his job.

Bright Star was very tired after lunch and Susan took her to her room for a rest and Christina wanted to look at the items that had been bought that morning and when they had left Sean rounded on Liza and Jamie much to their surprise.

"The Sergeant and I and many in the Union army have spent time and taken countless risks just to keep you both safe. Twice we have had to rescue you from Confederate forces who would incarcerate you for the duration of the war, and what do you do at the first opportunity Liza? You go out and about with no thought for your own safety. What makes you think that there aren't those out there who would be happy to kidnap you? There is a price on your head Liza. The Confederates would pay a great deal of money to have you in their clutches again. You know that they think you are a bargaining chip with the British Government, wrong as that may be. Why should New York be safer than anywhere else? It could be more dangerous because of the number of people here and the number of strangers that a large city always has passing through. You really are your own worst enemy Liza; you are naïve beyond belief," said a very annoyed Sean.

Myra was looking shocked at the ferocity of Sean's words as were both Liza and Jamie. Arnold was looking quite embarrassed.

Jamie was first to be able to speak.

"You are absolutely right Sean. You all have taken great risks to get us here and once we arrived, we felt that we had reached safety, but I must admit that none of us know who is lurking around the corner just waiting to pounce. People will do anything for money, and I now realise that I have failed in my own duty towards Liza as I did not have any thought that she might be in danger. I apologise for my error of judgement, and I will make sure that she is guarded wherever she goes until we reach the safety of our home in England. Thank you for pointing it out," said Jamie.

"I'm just as much to blame. It did not occur to me that a trip to the dressmakers could be dangerous, but I can see what you mean and in the future I will go nowhere without an adequate escort, and you know that I do appreciate all that has been done to get me this far. I can only apologise for my total thoughtlessness and thank you for all that you have already done for me," said Liza.

"I have not said this to receive thanks Liza, I have said it to make you aware of how unsafe even New York could be for you. I don't need thanks as it has been a pleasure rather than a duty to guard you and apart from having to look behind every bush on our journey, until now you have both acted impeccably and I know you have been appreciative of our concerns and followed instructions to the letter. It has been commented in the past that you are naïve Liza; you are very bright in so many ways, but you are known to be too trusting of others," said Sean.

"You are right Sean, she is too trusting but I do try to protect her from such people," smiled Jamie.

"It may be what you like to do Jamie, but although it is a pleasure for us to take care of Liza, the Sergeant and I are instructed to do so, and if anything untoward happens to her whilst under our care, our lives would be made a misery by our superiors and incarceration could well be part of any punishment handed out to us, which is something that neither the Sergeant nor I wish to contemplate," said Sean.

A tear trickled down Liza's cheek. "I seem to have upset everybody. I never want to do that, but I often manage to do so. I am so sorry; I can't bear the thought that you and Arnold could go to prison because of me."

Another tear trickled down Liza's other cheek followed by an audible sniff, much to the amusement of everyone around the table.

"They're not going to prison Liza," sighed Jamie patiently.

Sean looked at Liza's quivering lips and smiled. "You have survived your trip this morning, so there's no reason for the Sergeant and I to be blamed for anything. All we must do is make sure that it stays that way. I need to meet your security man sooner rather than later and if I am not happy with the arrangements for your safety, then Arnold and I will have to stay until you leave for England."

Liza's tears turned to a look of pleasure at the prospect of having Sean with them for more than just a couple of days.

"From the look on Liza's face it is going to be unfortunate that our man Walter is totally efficient," smiled Myra.

"We have been ordered not to leave until we can guarantee your complete safety," said Sean.

"Good," said Liza. "You'll never be able to guarantee my safety whilst I'm here, so you'll have to stay until we leave for England. That's good, isn't it?"

"I think you'll find that Sean and Arnold have a war to deal with and that over the next day or so Walter will show them just how dedicated he is to you, me, our family and the business," said Jamie.

"I know that really," said Liza. "It was just a nice thought that we could have Sean and Arnold with us until we left New York."

It was decided that Sean and Arnold would go with Liza to meet Walter and Jamie felt that he would like to accompany them. Myra was to stay and take delivery of any clothes that would be arriving from the dressmakers. She would help Susan to try them on the children, which she was looking forward to.

Sean was ready to leave for the Marchant & Fuller offices at the dockside and he was waiting in the drawing room when Liza came in.

"You know that Patrick often called you naïve," said Sean. "It was just one of the reasons why he loved you and why the rest of us wanted to look after you. Today I could see that Jamie also loves that side of you. You made a good choice in him Liza. It is obvious to everyone that he loves you and that you love him, although it was different with you and Patrick."

"That was a different life Sean," said Liza. "When this war is over, would you consider visiting us in England and spending some time with us and the boys?"

"That would be something to look forward to. Would you mind if I wrote to you? I won't have much time to do that, but I have no one else in my life, only you and your family," said Sean.

"It would be wonderful to hear from you. Where can I address any letters to you?" asked Liza.

Sean gave her the name and general area that his unit was normally based, and Liza said that even if he missed out on some letters at least he would know that she had written.

"That's what Patrick said when he was away from Benson, and it would be a comfort to me to know that someone cares enough to write," said Sean.

Their conversation was halted by Arnold joining them and shortly after Jamie was ready and they left in the carriage for the dockside where Walter was there to greet them. There were also several other men standing guard which meant that Walter was taking no chances with security for Liza and Jamie.

Walter came straight over to Liza and before he could be introduced to anyone he said, "Well Liza, I hear you've been in trouble again, but they weren't strong enough to keep you away from us."

"That's right Walter, there was no way that they would keep me where I didn't want to be," said Liza with a smile and she then introduced him to Sean and Arnold.

"I presume you want to discuss arrangements for Liza's safety both here and at her home," said Walter and he led them up to his office. Liza decided that she would leave the men to their discussions, and she went to see Henry who was delighted to see her.

"I'm afraid that we are getting very few shipments from the south and most shipments to them are searched and confiscated, so we now refuse to accept any orders from any of the southern states. There's no point in their spending what little money they have on goods that they will never receive. We have some of their goods stored in our warehouses. I'm at a loss to know what to do with them; do you have any suggestions?" asked Henry.

"My only suggestion is that you sell the goods where possible and put the money in a specially set up account which eventually can be repaid to the buyers and if that is not possible then when the war is over it can be put to some good use in the south, no doubt there will be some orphans who will need to be cared for," said Liza.

"I have some goods ready to go to Benson, they should get through alright, and I can incorporate a couple of wagons for Bandor's people, and at the moment there seems to be no problem going that far," said Henry.

"Do you think we could take a chance and add some wagons and let them go further to Charles? How do you feel about that Henry?" asked Liza. "Do you consider it being disloyal to our northern friends?"

"We have many southern friends also Liza, and we are in the business of freight. I have tried not to take sides, but I think the time will come when I have to and where I live will dictate that. You are more fortunate, you don't have to stay in America so you can keep sitting on the fence," said Henry.

"I have loyalties to friends Henry, not to sides in a war, so I do find myself in a difficult situation. Unfortunately the Confederate leaders wish to incarcerate me and use me as a bargaining chip in a game they wanted to play with the British government. One Major even wanted to kill everyone in my party apart from me, so I have not found it easy to be impartial. I saw two close friends die, one from the Union forces and one from the Confederate side and they are buried side by side, so you can see why I try not to take sides, but I would not call it 'sitting on the fence'," said Liza.

"I apologise Liza, it was a silly comment," said Henry. "I'll manage to get some wagons to Benson and the encampment, and I'll see if Cole and Jack will have a way of getting through to Charles, but if they do, I feel that it will be the last that I will be able to organise until this war is over."

"I think the sooner that I leave here the better as I have had to rely on my Union friends to protect me and Jamie and the rest of those with us from Confederate forces," said Liza. "I also had to keep quiet when I knew where the Union forces were and not let my Confederate friend know. It's all very confusing."

"The last thing that Myra and I would want is for you to leave, but I understand what you are saying," said Henry. "You will not be a worry to anyone when you are back in England, and you could probably do more good from there. Who are the children that you have with you?"

"One is Andraes' daughter, Christina, and the other is Bandor's daughter, Bright Star," said Liza. "I am legal guardian to Christina and Bandor gave me Bright Star."

"Of course, Indians do that sort of thing, don't they?" said Henry.

"Bandor's wife died a couple of months ago and what are termed 'half breeds' can be just as unacceptable to the tribe as they can be to white people. He wanted what he felt was best for his daughter, and it was difficult for him to give her to me, but he would have hated anyone to know that. I have to say that I had no choice in the matter, he brought her to me and left," said Liza with a smile.

"He is therefore giving her the best start in life. They don't normally care much for their women, Bandor must have more white in him than anyone realises," said Henry.

The meeting with Walter was over and Jamie came to find Liza and he was greeted warmly by Henry.

"You've both had a very difficult time getting here," said Henry. "No doubt we'll be meeting up again in the next day or so. Myra will probably have arranged something for us all."

"No doubt," said Jamie. "I'll look forward to it."

"I have to call in to see Leonora's father. It shouldn't take me too long," said Liza.

"Now you don't think that either Sean or Walter are going to let you do that alone, do you?" smiled Jamie.

"Surely you are safe enough here in New York," said Henry.

"As Sean pointed out to us, New York has a great many strangers coming and going and some people will do anything for money," said Jamie.

"I suppose he's right," said Henry. "And I have heard that you are very much wanted by some in the southern army."

Liza smiled and said that she would see what Myra had arranged and no doubt see him at that time unless he needed her for anything else.

Walter and his cousin were waiting in the hallway with Sean and Arnold, and they all groaned when Jamie told them that Liza wanted to visit Leonora's father.

"I must put his mind at rest about his daughter. He may think that she is still in Charleston which is not a place that is necessarily healthy for a northern lady whose husband is away in the war. He will wonder why she is not with us under the circumstances, and I do hope that her letter explains it all," said Liza.

"I'll come with you," said Jamie.

"And so will I," said Sean.

"I suppose it would be a little excessive for you to have five men guarding you when you visit someone to deliver a letter," said Walter. "I'll go up to the house with your sergeant and my cousin and start making plans."

The doctor's house was fairly large, and it appeared to have a surgery to the left of the front door. It was beginning to get dark, and lamps could be seen burning in the hallway and to the right of the house.

"I'll take the letter to him," said Sean.

"There may be questions that only Jamie or I can answer," said Liza.

The coach driver stepped down and knocked at the door and when it was answered by a housekeeper, he said that Lord and Lady Edgeworth were there to see a Doctor Busby.

There could be seen a sudden flurry in the lounge room and the housekeeper came back to the door and approached the carriage saying that Dr Busby would be delighted to see them.

Sean said that he would wait outside the carriage and watch the house whilst Liza and Jamie were ushered into the doctor's lounge and the surprised doctor asked what he could do for them.

"We have a letter for you from your daughter," said Jamie.

"How do you know my daughter? You obviously met her when you were in Charleston. I'm pleased that you have both managed to get out of trouble and make your way to New York," the doctor was rambling a little.

Liza smiled and said, "Thank you Doctor; it has not been an easy journey. We travelled out of Charleston with Leonora; she was not having a very good time there, especially so when the first shots were fired and then Jackson was called up. Jackson brought her to Charles Enderby's house for safety and asked us to take her with us when we left. Unfortunately nobody realised how dangerous that was going to be. We'll leave you to read your letter doctor."

"She isn't with you now then?" questioned the doctor.

"No, we know she was also worried about returning here. She was made to feel out of place in the south and being married to a southerner she was concerned that she would be made to feel the same back in New York," said Jamie.

"Where is she now?" asked a very concerned Dr Busby.

"I presume it is all explained in her letter to you, but I will tell you that she is safely in a town called Benson, and the people have taken to her and made her one of their own. She spends her time at the local store, and she is learning to operate a printing press. She also helps with the sick and wounded when needed," said Liza.

"She could have come back here. I would have looked after her until this war is over. She would not have had to meet anybody; I would make sure that she stayed out of sight for her own good," said a very disturbed Dr Busby.

"I see," said Liza. "Well, she doesn't have to stay out of sight in Benson; she has become a very important and helpful part of the town's community. As I said Doctor, we'll leave you to read your letter and if you would like to know anything further, please do call on us at any time. I take it you do know where we live, and we will be in New York for at least another ten days. Goodbye Doctor."

"Indeed Doctor, if you have any queries, please let us know and we will try to help you," said a rather tight-lipped Jamie.

"Thank you both for calling and for helping my daughter. I wish you a safe journey back to England," said Dr Busby.

They left and thankfully got back into their carriage with Sean climbing up after them.

"I take it that the meeting did not go too well. He either expected her to be back with him or thought that she should be waiting at her home for her husband's return," said Sean.

"He would have preferred her to be with him and hidden from sight," said Liza with annoyance.

"He said that he would have kept her out of sight for her own good," said Jamie shaking his head in despair. "No wonder she preferred to stay in Benson and take her chances with a war that might surround her. It would have been worse than being in a Confederate prison. She made the right choice."

"I suppose it would have been difficult for her staying in Charleston. She would probably have had to stay out of sight there. So she knew that her alternatives were to stay hidden in Charleston or stay hidden in New York," said Sean. "You're right; she did make the right choice."

Liza smiled again and said that she could just imagine Leonora happily going from one job to another: calling on various people for coffee and cake. "She was very much at home there; perhaps her husband will think about moving there when the war is over, although they don't need another doctor at the moment, but who knows what the future will bring, especially if the town keeps growing the way it has over the past few years."

By that time they were nearing the house and Sean was pleased to see that Walter and his cousin were going over the grounds with Arnold, and Walter was making notes.

As they came in the front door the girls were making their way down to the kitchen for their supper with Susan, and Bright Star stopped and pointed to her feet and said "shoes."

"Isn't she clever Aunt Liza," said a proud Christina. "She can also say 'dress'; I'm sure she'll soon be able to speak properly. I'm teaching her how to use a knife and fork; she's finding it a little difficult but she's managing."

"You are so good with her Christina," said Liza. "Can you see how she is looking at you; you know that she really loves and trusts you. We are all going to have such a happy time together. Go and get your supper now and I'll be along to see you when you've finished."

Walter, his cousin and two security guards were with Sean and Arnold in the drawing room, they were waiting for Jamie and Liza to join them. They had pinpointed one or two areas that needed to be more adequately secured.

"When the Captain and Sergeant have left, I would suggest that I move in here in their place until you are safely aboard the ship to England," said Walter.

"Well if you think that is necessary, then of course you are welcome to stay," said Liza.

"I will have two men patrolling the grounds day and night and my cousin will carry out a full security check each day. Of course it would be easier if you didn't leave the house because if you do, I will need to allocate someone to be with you wherever you go," said Walter.

"I truly think that there is no need for such drastic action," said Liza.

"And you thought that there was no need for drastic action when Zelma was stabbed by that woman aiming for you, and I don't forget that I was also stabbed by her at that time," said Walter sarcastically.

"Am I hearing this correctly?" said a shocked Sean. "Someone tried to stab you before."

"Yes, but that was because of the charity," said Liza as if it explained it all to Sean, who was looking both puzzled and horrified.

"So somebody got close enough to do harm," said Sean. "Now you have the whole of the Confederate army on the lookout for you and you think there is no need for drastic action. I think naïve is the correct word to describe you, Liza."

"Sean, you seem to forget that I am with her at all times, and I will never let anything happen to her," said Jamie with some annoyance.

"You are one man, Jamie," said Sean. "Walter has many men at his disposal, and all are trained to guard not only goods but people also. It is their job as it is mine and I will not leave here until Walter has all in place and I am sure that it is adequate, and I mean no offence by that Walter."

"No offence taken, we are all here to make sure that everyone within this household is kept safe and secure," said Walter.

"I suppose I had better tell you that I must make a trip to Daltons. I have business commitments there as well as family, friends and associates who I want to take the opportunity to visit," said Liza.

A groan came from Sean and Walter stared in disbelief.

"Is that really necessary Liza?" asked Jamie.

"It is the biggest business investment that Bradley & Co has, and I need to see Brendan, Hector and Estelle. Daltons will unfortunately do very well during this war; I need to make sure that it is being handled correctly and hopefully staying impartial; although it will be difficult as it is situated in the north," said Liza.

"Liza, if we had not been caught up in the problems of this war then we would be home by now and would not feel the need to go to Daltons," said Jamie.

"You're wrong Jamie. I know that we would have been home by the summer, but I had plans to visit Daltons in the autumn because there are matters that need my attention. Hector does a very good job, but there are expansions that only I can approve, and they have been put on hold because of the circumstances in which we found ourselves," said Liza.

411

"You haven't been to Daltons for some time, have you Liza?" said Walter.

"No, but Brendan and Hector give me regular updates and I know that it is growing by leaps and bounds but there are several manufacturers who want to rent premises; some are genuine, but others could be looking to hide behind an honest façade, but you know that Walter, as you are the one finding out who the proprietor is of every business applying to operate in Daltons," said Liza.

"Well you therefore know that everything is under control and in very good hands," said Walter. "You don't need to go there. I have been there recently, and it is full of people from all areas and countries. You would never know if there was someone willing to take you and hand you back to the Confederates. The up-and-coming town is quite orderly, but the campsite areas are full of itinerant workers and often become quite unruly. If we weren't in a war situation, I would say that your safety could be guaranteed because of the number of security people there, but people come and go, and we have no idea where their allegiances lie. They are all there to earn money and you must not forget that there is a large price on your head Liza. You are a wanted person."

"Really?" said Liza. "How much?"

"Last time I heard it was three thousand dollars," said Walter. "It could have risen by now."

"I could pay them more not to take me," smiled Liza.

Sean was looking shocked as was Jamie and Arnold was scratching his head.

"I didn't realise that Liza had created such a stir," said Jamie. "I truly believed that we had reached safety here, although since earlier today it has dawned on me that there could be a few people who would like to benefit by dealing with the Confederates."

"I would really like to see all that is going on in Daltons, but I also had not realised that we had not reached safety here and I must therefore bow to everyone's better judgement," said a concerned looking Liza.

"From that I gather that you will not be going to Daltons," said Sean.

"I will not be going anywhere until the day comes that I have to get on a ship to England," said Liza. "It's disappointing but there is no point endangering myself and Jamie and we also have children to consider as well as staff. All are vulnerable, not just me."

"You are right Liza; whoever they are could take the children to get you. You know you would give yourself to them to safeguard the children and anyone else," said Sean. "When are you leaving for England?"

"I believe the 'Amelia' is arriving here in just over a week, so give it a couple of days and we will be on board in around ten days' time," said Liza. "I have yet to finalise it with Henry."

"I did not know that there was such a high price being offered. My superiors will not want to have to deal with rescuing Liza again; in fact they may not be in a position to do it," said Sean. "I don't think that it would go down too well with them if Arnold and I were to stay here for the next ten days, but I think that another two to three days would be quite acceptable to them. Walter will definitely have everything well in order by then," said Sean.

"It's virtually in order now," said Walter, "but I realise that I will need more men here than I had first thought."

"I'll leave you to it; I'm going to see the girls now;" and Liza left the room as she did not want to continue with the conversation or be bothered with the arrangements that were being made, most of which she considered unnecessary.

Christina was sitting with Bright Star, and she was showing her pictures in a book and telling her what they were. Bright Star appeared to understand what was being said and was attempting to repeat what Christina was saying. It was Bright Star's bedtime but as she seemed to be enjoying her time with Christina, Liza decided to leave them a little longer and she went to find Susan.

Susan was in her room trying on her new clothes and she was delighted to show them to Liza.

"Have you seen Mary today?" Liza asked Susan.

"Yes, she has been very upset today; is it about Rufus Denton?" asked Susan.

"Yes, they were very close at one time, and they both felt a great deal for one another," said Liza.

"Why didn't they get married then?" asked Susan.

"There were many reasons, but it's best not to ask about them," said Liza.

"I suppose it was because of his temper; I know he tried to control it, but he found it hard, didn't he?" said Susan.

"You're very astute Susan, but it's very sad that someone has to die like that," said Liza. "We'll be leaving New York in about ten days' time so you will have time to go shopping, but you must not go alone, you must take someone responsible with you."

"I've seen that there are some people who seem to be checking the security of the house; are they worried about you?" asked Susan.

"Everybody always seems to worry about me," said Liza. "It's very caring of them really. I think it's Bright Star's bedtime now. I'll be in to see her in a short while."

Liza went to her room to get ready for dinner and she was surprised to find Mary waiting to help her. She looked pale and very sad, and Liza decided to let her talk if she wanted to, but she would ask her nothing.

"Have you decided what you are going to wear this evening?" asked Mary.

"Yes, as at this moment I only have one dress that's suitable," smiled Liza trying to lighten the atmosphere. "The rest will be ready tomorrow; not that I will be able to show them off as I will be going nowhere whilst I'm here."

"The talk is that there could be people who could make a lot of money by kidnapping you," said Mary.

"So I've also heard," said Liza. "I was just one dissenting voice amongst four panicking men, so I had to give in to their concerns."

"We're all worried about what could happen to you; we were all very worried when we heard that you had been captured by the southerners. Was Rufus in the southern army?" Mary suddenly asked.

"For a while, yes, he was. He was born in Virginia so therefore he was a southerner. Many people felt that they had to have allegiances to where they were born. He told me that he was in the wrong uniform, so I put it right for him in the end. I must say that we were lucky that he was the one guarding us when the Confederates recaptured us because, if it had not been for him, we would all be dead. He protected us from his superior who was intent on taking no prisoners; he disobeyed his order and bravely relieved him of his command. He also helped to protect the people of Benson. He always considered Benson his home which is why he should never have joined the army of where he was born," said Liza quietly. "He and Paul were injured together, and they died together in the same room that they had shared in life, and the people of Benson buried them side by side, both in their proper northern uniforms. Regardless of which side they were on, they remained the best of friends, so it was only right that friends stay together forever. Patrick is watching over them and the people of Benson are taking care of them."

"I'm glad you were with him. I'm sorry that Paul is also dead, but it helps to think that they are together," said Mary. "You also know what was in his letter. It explained a great deal of why he was as he was. We would never have been happy together; we both knew that a long time ago, but I never knew why until now. I made the right decision at the time. I do have some happy memories of him and the short time that we spent together. Some people never experience love, I'm lucky that I have."

Liza could say nothing in reply and Mary just got Liza's dress from the wardrobe and quietly helped to get her ready for the evening.

"Would you like to come with us to England for a while?" Liza asked her.

"I'd like to think about that; it's very kind of you to offer," said Mary. "I know that it would be stepping on Susan's toes if I did, and I also have my sister to think about. I would have been lost without her over the years."

"I know you are very close to her and I'm sure Susan would understand if you wanted a change of scenery for a while but think about it. We're not leaving for about ten days, so there's plenty of time," said Liza.

They could hear Roberts in the dressing room getting Jamie's clothes ready for the evening and Liza thought it strange that with everything that was happening around the house, and what had happened to them on their way there, that the evening was going to be so normal.

Jamie came bounding into the room and acknowledged Mary before going into the dressing room, but Liza realised that he had wanted to tell her something. However that would have to wait until they were both ready for dinner.

Liza could hear Roberts asking Jamie if all was well within the household, which was his way of asking what all the security men were doing around the house. Jamie answered that it appeared that there was quite a high price on Liza's head and there were some unscrupulous people who might take advantage of the offer no matter which side their allegiances were.

Jamie could then be heard telling Roberts that it had been decided that no one should leave the house without an escort as they could be used as leverage to get to Liza.

"He's right," said Mary. "There are some very funny people in New York and of course this war has made everyone on edge. There will be some who will do anything for money. I'll go and see Susan now; she seems a really nice girl."

"She is. Why don't you ask her about her family; she's very proud of her mother and brother. Her father's dead, and I really shouldn't say so, but it's unfortunate that he didn't die earlier than he did, but she may tell you about that," said Liza trying to get Mary's mind off Rufus even though it would be making her think about what had been a disaster in Susan's family.

Jamie came through to Liza when he was dressed for dinner and Liza said that she had heard what he had discussed with Roberts. "I suppose that being here is a better prison than I would have had in Alabama, or wherever they thought I should be," said Liza.

"This is no prison, Liza; it's large enough for you not to feel restricted and the grounds are beautiful, although winter is approaching and the flowers are not as pretty, but the autumn colours are magnificent. It isn't too cold to walk in the gardens and in around ten days' time we will be on our way to England where you can go where you please, when you please."

"I know Jamie; I just don't like not being able to go visiting or to the docks to see Henry. I enjoy going to the various merchants and shops in New York and I remember taking the boys to the park and I would have liked to have gone with

Christina and Bright Star also to the park, but we can't even let them go with Susan or Mary," said Liza.

"I can understand that you feel hemmed in, but it is for your own good," said Jamie.

Liza smiled, "There's nobody that I would rather be hemmed in with than you Jamie. We'll make the best of it, and I'll make sure it's an enjoyable time for everyone. I'll just check on the children and then go down to dinner."

"I'd like to go with you Liza, especially as they are now my children also. It's going to be really interesting to see how the boys are going to react to them," said Jamie.

"All the boys are very thoughtful of others. They'll be interested to know why they are with us, and they'll then just accept that they are there; after all they are only girls," smiled Liza.

"I think that soon their attitude towards girls will change, if it hasn't already," laughed Jamie.

Bright Star was sound asleep, and Christina was in her bed and smiling happily. "I'm looking forward to going to England," she said. "I miss my grandparents and I know that they miss me, but I'm going to be safe with you and I'm pleased that I shall be seeing Simon again soon, and I do just about remember Matthew and John. What's James like?"

"He's kind like the others and I know that he will make sure that you and Bright Star settle in happily with us, as will Matthew, John and Simon also. We will all be very happy together," said Liza. She kissed her goodnight, checked Bright Star and then she and Jamie made their way down to dinner.

"Has Walter gone home?" asked Liza.

"Yes, his cousin and five men are here," said Sean. "Walter will be back later, and he and I will go around the house and check all the entrances. You know that he will be staying when Arnold and I leave."

When they were halfway through their meal they heard a carriage draw up at the door and a few voices demanding 'who was there.' Jamie, Sean and Arnold were immediately on their feet but there was no need to worry as Henry was ushered into the dining room by Walter's cousin, Bertram. Much to everyone's surprise they were followed in by Christina's father, Andraes.

"I'm sorry to intrude on your mealtime, but I thought it best to bring Andraes here immediately," said Henry.

Once they had all got over the surprise, Andraes was greeted by everyone and introduced to Arnold, who was the only person not to have already met him. Jamie had seen him on occasion over the years and Sean remembered him from the past and Liza had also not seen him for many years.

"Henry has put my mind at rest. You have Christina with you, I am so relieved. I have been trying to get to Benson for weeks, but I was travelling in South Africa when I got the news that war had broken out in America. Those from the north thought that I was a blockade runner and kept searching my ship at every port until finally it was requisitioned by the army. I did start out overland but was stopped on so many occasions that I was getting nowhere. Eventually I managed to return to New York on one of your ships and was ready to start out again for Benson," said Andraes in a rather garbled manner.

"Sit down both of you," said Liza.

"If you don't mind Liza, I'll get back to Myra. We are entertaining one of my cousins. I presume Andraes will be able to stay with you," said Henry.

"Of course he'll be staying with us. Thank you, Henry, I'll see you tomorrow," said Liza and Jamie got up and showed him out.

"Obviously if I had known you were in New York I would have come here first and not bothered Myra and Henry. I was so pleased when I heard that you were here and that you had Christina with you," said Andraes.

"Would you like to see her? She may still be awake, but even if she isn't it would be good for you to look in on her," said Liza. "I'll just organise a room for you and I'm sure you must be hungry."

Liza rang for Bridget and made the necessary arrangements, and also asked that a meal be organised for Andraes. She excused herself from the dining room and left Jamie to entertain Sean and Arnold until her return and went up to Christina's room with Andraes.

Christina was asleep and Andraes just stood and looked at her, smiled and nodded his contentment and relief. They quietly left the room and Bridget whispered that she had water in his room, and he could quickly wash up before they made up his room. Liza waited in the hall for him to finish and made all the alternative arrangements necessary with Bridget to accommodate another guest. He looked slightly refreshed when he emerged, and they went down to the dining room together.

Food was placed in front of Andraes, and everyone waited whilst he caught up with them. He took a long drink of wine and Jamie refilled his glass and they talked amongst themselves until Andraes finished his main course. He sat back and said that he was now feeling much better.

"I am not only relieved that Christina is safely with you but also that you are here. The last I heard was that you had disappeared and were being held to ransom somewhere in the south," said Andraes.

"That was the case Andraes, but with the help of our northern friends and Liza's Indian friends we managed to gain our freedom," said Jamie. "We came here via Benson and in fact have only been here for a couple of days. It has been a very stressful time for us, but the good side of having to travel overland was that Ada and the Colonel could place Christina safely in our care."

"She was very sad at leaving her grandparents and also all her friends in Benson, but she has taken a little girl under her wing, and it has taken the edge off her sadness," said Liza.

"I noticed that there was a young child in with her. Are you also looking after her?" said Andraes.

"She is the daughter of a friend of mine and unfortunately she lost her mother a couple of months ago. Her father has placed her in our care, and we were pleased to take on the responsibility," said Liza.

Andraes' plate was cleared away and dessert arrived after which it was once again decided that a glass of port would be good, but cigars would not, so Liza stayed at the table with them. They discussed the state of the war and also referred back to when they had last met and then Liza admitted that security around the house had been stepped up as there was apparently a three-thousand-dollar reward for her recapture.

"I thought that the men who greeted us were a little abrupt," said Andraes with a smile.

"Arnold and I are staying longer than first planned, but Liza's head of security will be moving in when we leave and there are guards on duty day and night. Liza has also promised not to leave the house and no chances are being taken with the children. There's plenty for them to do here and the grounds are extensive, and they will not be out of sight of guards at any time. It is not an ideal situation, but once they leave here, they will be safe enough and have as much freedom as they would like," said Sean.

"It's good to know that you are being so thorough," said Andraes.

"I do wonder if we are being over cautious," said Liza, "but we are taking no chances where the children are concerned. We will be leaving in just over a week and once the 'Amelia' sets sail and leaves the New York dock we will be able to relax. I do have one or two small gatherings arranged so we will meet some of our New York friends, but we will not be attending any gatherings outside. The friends have been selected very carefully; they are friends and not acquaintances."

"Liza was saying earlier that it is a shame that she can't take the girls to the local park, but it's not worth the risk. When we get back to our home in England, they will be able to go where they please. However it is all new to the girls and they seem to enjoy being here. I don't think that they will have any desire to go to the park, there is plenty for them to do here and they are doted on by all the staff," said Jamie.

"If it's not an inconvenience to you, I wonder if I could travel to England and stay with you for a while. I could then make my way back to my homeland from there. I know what I am asking is an imposition, so please say if it would not be possible," said Andraes.

Liza smiled but let Jamie answer. "It would be our pleasure Andraes, and you would have the opportunity of spending more time with Christina."

"I would like to take Christina home with me, but she would not have a happy life in my house," said Andraes.

"Would you like us to leave so that you could discuss this privately?" Sean asked of Andraes.

"No, all I am doing is making a general comment. I know that I can go into further detail with Liza and Jamie at some other time. Liza is a guardian to Christina, my thoughts on that when it was drawn up were because her grandparents were just that, grandparents. Their life expectancy was naturally less than a parent, so I asked Liza to take some responsibility should the worst happen. None of us envisioned that a serious war would break out and I presume that you were asked to take her to safety," said Andraes.

"Yes, it was a very hard decision for them to make," said Liza. "But all going well she can be back with them when the war is over. Until that time she will become part of our family and we will treat her as our own; in fact we already do."

"I want to thank you both for taking her in and especially you Jamie, as the guardianship was arranged before your marriage to Liza, but I am extremely grateful that you have also taken that responsibility. You know that she will never want for anything as far as I am concerned but that is financial. I do love her, but I am unable to have her living with me unfortunately, so I did the next best thing and placed her with her loving grandparents, and now she is with loving guardians," said Andraes. "And now we should talk about other things. This house is magnificent; it has changed slightly since I was last here."

"I didn't realise that you had been here before," said Jamie.

"Yes, Liza kindly placed it at my disposal when I brought Christina to her grandparents. We stayed here for a few days before travelling on to Benson. Is Mary still with you?" asked Andraes.

Liza acknowledged that she was, and he then asked about the young soldier who was smitten with her and who found it difficult to keep his fists to himself.

"Sadly he was killed in a battle a couple of weeks ago," said Jamie, "along with his friend Paul Southern. The battle was just outside Benson and apparently it is a very strategic area, which is one of the reasons why it was felt that Christina should come with us. The Colonel has come out of retirement to look after those in the fort, so he is very vulnerable. If things get very serious there, either with battles or difficulties in feeding the people, Liza has said that they can bring their children to us, firstly here in New York and then on to England if the war continues. But it was felt that the time had not yet come for such drastic action."

"Civil wars are the worst types of war," said Sean and Arnold nodded in agreement. "We have already found ourselves fighting friends and that has been very difficult, but we have to close our minds to the people we are fighting and just follow orders to the best of our ability."

"I don't think that any of us envy you your task and I pray that it will be over in a very short time," said Andraes.

They moved into the drawing room, and it was noticed that Andraes had difficulty keeping his eyes open and Liza said that she knew that he had had a very tiring time. His sense of relief must also have given him a relaxed feeling and that nobody would be offended if he wanted to go to his room and take advantage of an early night.

"Yes, thank you. I have a few things to unpack before I can relax, so I will leave you now and see you all tomorrow. Once again thank you for your hospitality," said Andraes.

"I think you'll find that Roberts has organised whatever you need," said Jamie. "Goodnight Andraes. We look forward to seeing you tomorrow."

When he had left, they sat quietly for a while and then Jamie said that it had been a surprising evening.

"It will be nice that Christina will have her father with her for a while. It's a pity that his home life stops him from having her with him, or seeing her more often, but he does do the best he can for her," said Liza.

Sean understood the difficult situation that Andraes was in as he knew the background to Christina's birth, but Arnold had no idea of her origin and just assumed correctly that her mother was dead and Andraes lived a long way from her grandparents who had taken responsibility for their granddaughter.

Walter knocked and entered. "I'm taking over from Bertram, so I'll be here for the night. I understand that you have another houseguest and that Mr Mahoney brought him here. I take it that he is well known to you and not someone that is just a casual acquaintance," said Walter.

"He's Christina's father," said Jamie. "He will be staying here and travelling to England with us. I understand that it is necessary for you to know who is in the house, although it does seem strange to us to have to answer to you for any who are in this household."

"I'm glad you understand as I do realise that it must seem intrusive," said Walter.

"Thank you, Walter, we do feel very safe with you around. Sean and Arnold will be able to have a good nights' rest as I know they have been guarding us throughout the day and then take it in turns to watch over us at night," said Liza.

"I didn't think you realised that Liza," said Sean.

"I know that you take your duties towards us seriously and you know that we very much appreciate it," said Liza.

***

Liza could hear Susan taking the girls down to the kitchen for their breakfast the next morning. It reminded her of her boys, and she felt sad that she had not been able to see them for such a long time. She comforted herself with the thought that in just over three weeks' time she would at last be back with them and they would all be getting ready for Christmas. It was going to be Bright Star's first Christmas and Liza wondered how she was going to react to all the festivities that occurred.

Mary came in with Liza's breakfast and Jamie followed her. Liza was surprised as she normally had breakfast in the dining room, but Mary was obviously keeping herself very busy and she had taken it upon herself to wait on Liza that morning. Jamie smiled and sat on the bed and waited patiently with a serviette ready to wipe Liza's chin.

"You're bound to dribble down your chin so I thought I would pre-empt your problem," smiled Jamie. "What are your plans for the day?"

"Henry will be calling around and so will Myra. I think all our new clothes are being delivered later. I also want to spend some time with the girls. I know that Myra has organised dinner for a few friends tomorrow evening, so I must make sure that we have an interesting menu. It's very extravagant really when you think that there are some food shortages, but while we are feeding our guests, they don't have to feed themselves," said Liza.

"I'm not sure that's logical, but never mind, I suppose it will all work out for everyone," smiled Jamie as he mopped marmalade from Liza's chin.

Christina had been surprised but very happy to see her father and she delighted in introducing him to Bright Star, telling him that she was helping to teach her English.

Later that day when all deliveries had been received and meetings were completed, Liza, Jamie and Andraes decided to take a walk in the garden. Christina and Susan were showing Bright Star how to play hide and seek. It was a little confusing for her, but she was beginning to understand how to play the game.

As they walked in the garden, they could hear laughter and Bright Star being called by Christina to go and find her. Bright Star gave a delighted cry and ran around a corner and straight into Andraes who managed to catch her as she tripped. They were all surprised to see the look of fear on her face and then even more shocked to see her move away and lay face down on the ground and cover her head with her hands.

"What's she doing?" asked Andraes.

Liza was horrified to realise that Bright Star had prepared herself to take a beating. Jamie was blinking as the same thought was dawning on him. Liza ran forward and picked the little girl up, cradling her in her arms as she moved to a seat and sat down with her on her lap.

Jamie was quietly talking to Andraes who could be heard to say that it was barbaric. Meanwhile Liza was talking to her in her own language.

"You have done nothing wrong Bright Star; I'm so sad that you thought that we were going to punish you. We do not believe in beating anyone, we will never do that to you. You bumped into somebody and that is not wrong, it was just an accident, and nobody was hurt. Have you been beaten in the past?" asked Liza.

Bright Star nodded as she stayed contentedly in Liza's arms.

"I would find it difficult to believe that your father ever did that to you," said Liza. "He didn't, did he?"

Bright Star shook her head and Liza heard her mumble something about her aunt.

"We will look after you Bright Star, you are now part of our family, and you need never fear that you will be hurt by us. We love you and want you to be happy and part of being happy is being able to play and have fun and nothing gives us greater pleasure than to see you enjoying yourself. When you are ready you can carry on playing with Christina and Susan and if you run and bump into somebody then there is no sin in that," said Liza.

Bright Star relaxed in Liza's arms and stayed with her head pressed into Liza's chest. Christina came over and asked what was wrong and Liza said that she thought that she had done something wrong, but she had not. All she had done was bump into Christina's father, which had hurt nobody.

"We all have accidents," said Christina. "I've done that before. My father would know that she didn't mean to do it; it was just that she was having fun. What was she doing lying on the ground?"

"Sadly she thought she was going to get beaten," said Liza. "You have to appreciate that she has come from a place where life is very serious, even in the very young and sometimes making a noise could mean that an enemy could know where you were. Children are taught to keep quiet and there are those in the tribe who think that beating is the only answer. They do not think that reasoning with a child would do any good."

"That's silly," said Christina. "I know that she's beginning to understand our language, but will you tell her that I'll look after her from now onwards. I won't let anything happen to her; she's my little sister now."

"I'll tell her that, but you do know that none of us will let anything happen to her," said Liza and she proceeded to tell Bright Star what Christina had said. Bright Star turned her face and looked at Christina and gave her a beautiful smile.

Susan came over realising that there had been a problem and Liza told her what had happened.

"I think it would be a good idea if Christina and I took her back to the house and we'll see if supper is ready and if it isn't I'll get a book and read to them for a while. She certainly doesn't need to have any fear in this household," said a determined Susan.

Liza kissed Bright Star and told her that Christina and Susan were going to take her into supper, and she climbed from Liza's lap and Susan took one of her hands and Christina the other and they went off to the house.

Jamie and Andraes came over. "She thought she was going to be beaten, didn't she?" said Jamie.

"Yes, she did but I have assured her that we would never do that. She's alright now and Christina and Susan have taken her in to supper," said Liza.

"Who's beaten her?" asked Andraes.

"Apparently it was her aunt. Her father never did; I knew that he would not have done that to one so small," said Liza. "It's just another adjustment for her. She seemed happy enough as she went off to supper."

They made their way back to the house and Liza decided to rest for a short while before dinner. Jamie came to join her.

"Christina is really doing a good job with Bright Star. I felt so sorry for the little girl when I realised what she was getting herself ready for. She is so small for anyone to consider punishing her in that way. You handled it very well and so did Christina," said Jamie.

"I'm sure she will soon forget all about any punishments that she may have had in her previous life and I'm also sure that she is going to become a very happy member of our family," said Liza.

Just before dinner, as they were in the drawing room, they could hear a carriage draw up and a slight commotion in the hallway. Jamie and Sean were making their way towards the door as they heard Walter telling his men that there was nothing to worry about and once again they had a surprise visitor. As Jamie got to the door it opened and Brendan walked in.

There was a gasp of surprise and pleasure from Liza, "Brendan how wonderful to see you. You seem to have arrived in a hurry. Is there a problem?"

Brendan acknowledged everyone in the room and came over to Liza and clasped her to him in relief. "The only problem that we have is you, Liza. I'm so pleased that you are here and have not attempted to go to Daltons."

"Sit down Brendan and tell us what you mean," said Jamie. "Is it because of the price that's on Liza's head?"

"Yes, it is," said Brendan.

"I think that Walter should hear what Brendan has to say," said Sean and he went to the door and called Walter in to join them.

"As you know Daltons is full of all types of workers, some are from the north, some are from the south and some are from various countries but most of them have no allegiance to anyone but themselves. Three thousand dollars is a vast amount of money and could tempt the most loyal of people, but it has now gone up to five thousand dollars and there are considerable murmurings amongst many of the men. They can be heard making weird and wonderful plans on how they can achieve getting you. They know that you are nearby, and most are convinced that you will visit your holdings in Daltons," said Brendan.

Liza was sitting quietly and listening. She realised just how right everyone had been that she should not go to Daltons and that she should stay hidden in her home.

Sean was looking at her as if to say, 'I told you so.'

"Do you think that any of them have already made their way here?" asked Walter.

"I'm afraid I wouldn't know that, but most seem convinced that Liza will travel to Daltons," said Brendan.

"Why would anyone think that?" asked Jamie. "Are there many there who know Liza well enough to know her attitude towards business?"

"There are a few and obviously she has been the subject of many conversations throughout the time that you have been trying to get to safety in New York. When word of the reward went around several of the workmen disappeared. Hector and I discussed that we felt that one of us should come here to make sure that you don't go to Daltons and the other should stay just in case you were to turn up there," said Brendan.

"I had been thinking that we were being overly cautious, but I have changed my mind. Putting up rewards for people is a very dangerous thing. I wonder how many poor ladies will be grabbed and offered up as me by the more

424

unscrupulous elements in our society," said Liza. "It's such a shame because I wanted to see how Daltons is progressing and I especially wanted to see Hector and Estelle. At least I've managed to see you Brendan, so that has made me happy."

"If I don't arrive back in Daltons on the evening train tomorrow, they will know that you have not left for Daltons, and they are ready to get on the next train to here. They won't get here until the following day, so you will be seeing them," said Brendan.

"That's wonderful; Jamie and I will look forward to it," said Liza.

"Who will be looking after Daltons if you are all away from it?" asked Walter.

"We have a wonderful overseer in Carl Fairburn," said Brendan. "You remember him and his wife, Gwen, don't you Liza? We also have Garth Jones who looks after several of the building projects and commands some considerable respect."

"I do seem to remember the Fairburns; they had several children if my memory serves me correctly," said Liza. "I don't seem to recall the other person, but no doubt he will come to me."

"Let me see," said a thoughtful Brendan. "His wife is Tess. She helps Estelle with teaching some of the children."

Jamie had a look of assumed non-recollection on his face and Walter just raised an eyebrow. Sean looked closely at Liza because he had seen slight signs of both surprise and annoyance on Liza's face. Liza nodded but, in her mind, she wondered whether she would ever be able to be rid of Gareth and Theresa Jones.

Bridget knocked and asked if Mr Brendan would be staying the night, and if so, she would get his room ready and water for him to freshen up before dinner.

"Yes Bridget, thank you," said Liza. "Mr and Mrs Ffoulks will also be arriving in the next couple of days."

"I think we ought to discuss our next move," said Jamie.

"Yes, you're right," said a very determined Liza. "Brendan, go and get yourself cleaned up and Walter, if you and Bertram can join us for dinner, we may be able to sort out what we should do next."

Stephen, the chef, was a miracle worker where catering for extra dinner guests was concerned and within half an hour, they were all sitting down to dinner.

Many suggestions were put forward, but the two main ones were that Liza goes into hiding for the duration of her stay in New York and the second was that she leaves on the next ship to another port, possibly in Canada and then onto England.

"I'm already in hiding," said Liza.

"No you're not Liza. Everyone knows where you are," said Brendan.

"I am, Brendan," said Liza. "I'm hiding behind the walls of this house. I can go nowhere, and all my guests must be vetted before they are allowed to see me. Whenever anyone new comes here they marvel at the size of the place. It is large and until just two days ago, I considered it airy, roomy, and comfortable; I now find that the walls are closing in on me, but I am not going to be turned out of my own home to go to some strange place. At least Walter and his men know this house and its grounds; they know which areas need more concentration than others. They know the staff and they mostly know my friends and I am confident that nobody will be able to use me as a pawn in this stupid game of war."

"Liza is right," said Walter. "We know every part of this house and its grounds, and we know those who can be trusted to visit. To go somewhere else would mean that we must learn all the vulnerable places and it takes time to know them, and we don't have that sort of time. I know it must be annoying for you to turn every corner and come face to face with one of our security men."

"Well, I'd much rather come face to face with one of your security men than some complete stranger who is determined to use me as a means to collect a vast amount of money," said Liza.

"I think that it would be more dangerous for Liza to travel to another port and then onto England. She would not only have to get to the docks here but would be waiting elsewhere for passage on another ship and there would be no knowing who is working at those docks and if the sailors are honest," said Jamie. "At least we know the docks here and the majority of those who should be working there."

"We will be leaving in a week and once we board the 'Amelia' our problems will be over. It would be better if we board the ship just before it leaves port," said Liza. "It does weigh on my conscience that I have kept Sean and Arnold from more important duties, but I wish I could keep them with us forever and away from the terrible battles that they will have to become involved with. Will you be able to stay here until we leave, or would that be asking too much of your superiors?"

Sean smiled at Liza and said, "It is inevitable that we will be caught up in some serious battles and who knows what the outcome of those will be. We are soldiers Liza, and we carry out our orders to the best of our ability and those orders were to get you safely here and make sure that you are well guarded. It was not expected that the Confederates would continue in their efforts to imprison you the way they have, therefore we have already extended our stay to make sure you are safe. It is also doubtful that they truly have the money to pay such an amount to anyone who helps with your capture."

"If that's the case it would be even more dangerous for Liza if she were to be taken and there's no money at the end of it," said Brendan.

"We are going round in circles," said Walter. "We have talked ourselves into Liza going into hiding, and then out of it again. We have discussed leaving from a different port, and immediately dismissed that. We've brought forth many other ideas, all of which had flaws; so I suppose what we will have to do is carry on as we are but possibly bring in even more men who we know are trustworthy. Bertram and I will move in when you leave Sean, in fact I think we should do that before you leave. I presume you have the room," and he laughed at his comment.

"You know we have a large dinner party here tomorrow evening, which will be a welcome change for me as I will not be the only female sitting at my table. Walter and Bertram, it would be wonderful if you could also attend with your wives. That way you can keep your eyes on me and enjoy yourselves at the same time," said Liza.

"That's a very good idea," said Jamie. "It would mean that you could meet our friends in a relaxed atmosphere, so that you would know who could be allowed into the house over the next week. We would find that your company would enhance the atmosphere. You know Myra and Henry and you probably know one or two of our guests. Everyone here this evening will also be there, so you will also be surrounded by friends."

Walter smiled and said, "It's a long while since I attended one of your functions as a guest." Nobody knew what he and Liza were smiling at. Jamie had his suspicions about Walter's past as he knew Liza believed in setting a thief to catch a thief.

"At least we have attended functions with our wives when we wanted to blend in with the guests, so our wives are used to dressing for such evenings," said Bertram.

"I know that Bertram, otherwise I would not have invited you. I know that you and your families are quite capable of blending in with all walks of life which is a great asset to you," said Liza. "I can make arrangements for you all to stay the night if that would suit you."

"Yes, that would add to the security, although I have a feeling that it won't be needed tomorrow; unless somebody decides to climb the fences," said Walter. "No doubt I have met all your guests previously."

"It will be interesting to hear what our guests think of the situation as they are bound to have heard what happened to us, and they probably have also heard of the price on Liza's head," said Jamie.

427

"I'll make sure your rooms are ready early so that you can all take advantage of them whenever you like," said Liza who seemed more concerned with organising the next evening's function than worrying about her safety.

"I think that if I feel that all is well here, Arnold and I should leave on Monday. We have a long journey ahead of us and who knows what we are going to find at the end of it," said Sean. "Don't look like that Liza, you know that as soldiers we have orders to follow, and we have to leave as soon as we are sure that you are not going to be used to try to persuade the British government to support the south. I do wonder why we know that the British government would not bow to blackmail, but the Confederate leaders still insist that they will."

"You're very quiet Andraes," said Jamie. "Do you have any thoughts on what we have been discussing?"

"You seem to have tried to cover all eventualities," he said. "I obviously will keep my eyes open, but I think that I will concentrate on watching the children closely, and that includes Susan; she's not much more than a child."

"That's a very caring thing to do Andraes, and you're right Susan is not much more than a child; although over these past months she has seen and experienced things that it would have been better not to have done. She has had to grow up quickly," said Liza. "This was her first trip abroad, and she was so looking forward to it and both Jamie and I thought that she would really enjoy it. The fear that she has gone through will not be easy for her to forget."

"As she is young she will be able to forget, given time," said Andraes.

"I'm not so sure that's true Andraes," said Liza thoughtfully. "Some things you never forget no matter how many years pass."

All around the table knew that Liza was referring to herself; they had either experienced her nightmares or had heard about them and Andraes said quietly, "Of course."

***

All preparations were in hand for the dinner party that evening. Myra and Henry had arrived early and were shown to their usual room. Walter and Bertram's wives, Barbara and Winifred, showed a confidence that they really did not feel. Liza and Jamie welcomed them like old friends, and they quickly introduced them to the other members of the household and were then ushered into the drawing room so that they could become familiar with all else there. They would naturally be introduced to the other guests when they arrived.

Stephen was in his element in his kitchen creating extravagant dishes for the guests. Liza thought that he had better make the most of it for she felt that in time there would be food shortages and his creativity would be needed to feed everyone else in the household.

Liza was going through documents in her study with Myra. The orphanages had settled to numbers which were easily handled, but Liza was worried about what may happen if the war went on too long.

"We won't be able to rely on the generosity of those who donate towards the Homes and people will not want to adopt in these unsettled times," said Liza. "How self-sufficient are the Homes now?"

"You know that many of the children enjoy growing various crops and there are a few chickens and one or two goats, but they would not be able to keep themselves in food," said Myra.

"Well, instead of it being a game to them they will have to increase what they do, and it would be worth investing in animals and animal feed now as well as crops. If we start now then when supplies become short, they will hopefully be able to survive on their own produce," said Liza. "Have you someone who can advise on getting the grounds in order and pens ready for animals. I can supply enough money for feed and seed, hopefully such items will be able to reach you."

"I'm sure that I will be able to find someone reliable," said Myra.

"We'll have a word with Brendan tomorrow, as you know he was brought up in farming, so he should be able to advise us," said Liza.

"I think you've also had some experience in such things Liza," smiled Myra.

"I've never really got my hands dirty; I just buy them and get someone to run them for me. I do have some idea how they should be farmed, but that's all," said Liza. "I also realise what would sell well in certain areas. My interest has always been in the profits that they could make, that is up until now."

They were all ready early for dinner and were waiting in the drawing room for their other guests to arrive. Philip and Pricilla Sheldon arrived at the same time as Clarissa Prentiss and her sisters Joan and Amanda Drake. All donated to the charity and Pricilla, Clarissa, Joan and Amanda gave up time to help the children in the Homes. Clarissa was a relatively young widow and her sisters had never been married. They knew everyone but Sean, Arnold and Andraes. Walter, Bertram and their wives had met them at other functions and Brendan had met them one evening at Myra and Henry's.

Next to arrive were Drew and Paula Darnley. Drew owned a construction company based in New York and he was assisting on many projects in Daltons. They had a boy and a girl who had often met up with Matthew and John and then with James on their visits.

Last to arrive were Errol Gardner, his wife Patricia and his sister Hattie. Errol was the manager of the largest branch of the M & F bank in New York.

Liza was pleased that she had managed to invite enough ladies to make the seating arrangements even. The initial conversation was all the new arrivals showing concern about Liza and Jamie's difficulties in reaching New York and outrage at why they had been held against their will. This led onto the exorbitant price that was being offered to take Liza back to the southern states.

"Such a price is going to attract all the unscrupulous elements in our society. Even if they have allegiances to the north, that sort of money could tempt even the most loyal of northerners," said Errol.

"I understand why you and Jamie are not accepting any invitations to gatherings outside your home," said Clarissa. "It's a shame as I would have loved to have you all to dinner at my house. I notice that we had to be questioned by your men at the door. Walter and Bertram really do make excellent arrangements for your safety. They have kept my house well-guarded whenever I have held a large function; I'm pleased to see them enjoying a relaxing evening with us tonight."

"When are you leaving Liza?" asked Drew.

"I'm not altogether sure Drew," said Liza. "But I can't wait to get back to my family. We have been away far too long. We were meant to be back before the summer. Henry sent a message as soon as we arrived here, so they know that we are safe."

"But you're not really safe, are you Liza?" said Errol. "Until you are on a ship that has put some miles between you and New York, you will be quite vulnerable, and I can understand why you are not saying when you are leaving. I know that around this table nobody would take advantage of what is being offered, but any one of us could say something by mistake. We could mention in passing when you are going to the docks and who knows who could be listening."

Myra now came to the rescue and asked Sean if he was going to find it difficult getting back to the discipline of army life.

"It has been very pleasant spending time here with Liza and Jamie, but duty does call. It is a life that I am used to and unfortunately it is one that is now very necessary," said Sean.

"It is a shame that this country has reached this point," said Drew. "If the war goes on for any length of time, we will not have the pleasure of sitting around a table like this. We will be lucky to have any food on our table. However we will probably be better off than those in towns such as the one you have come from Liza."

"Yes, it is very worrying," said Jamie, "and I know that both Liza and I feel that we are deserting America in its time of need, but really there is nothing that we can do about the situation, and I know that Liza is arranging to help in various ways, especially the children in the Homes that are here."

The courses were served, and wine consumed and the conversations around the table took on a lighter note. Liza and Jamie breathed a sigh of relief and settled down to enjoying the company of their friends. At the end of the meal the ladies withdrew leaving the men to their port and cigars. Liza had no doubt that the state of the country would be discussed by the men whilst the ladies asked Liza about the two young girls that she had acquired on her travels.

"Their families asked that I take them safely into my care for the duration of the war, and I was very pleased to do so," said Liza and then she laughed and said that it was such a change from being surrounded only by boys for the last few years. "Others may follow if the situation worsens considerably."

"You might become inundated with children Liza," said Amanda. "Will you be able to accommodate them all?"

"If I do get overwhelmed then I will make arrangements for some to be looked after within family units nearby," said Liza.

"Wouldn't you put them in one of your Homes," asked Hattie.

"No they would need to be in a family environment; they would not be orphans or abused. Those who run the Homes do try to make them as friendly and comfortable as possible, but these children would come from loving families and I would try to place them in loving families, including my own home," said Liza. "But it's not happening yet; they haven't reached that point yet; hopefully for their sakes they never will."

"How will they get to you?" asked Joan.

"I have some good friends who will make sure they reach New York safely and they will have at least one responsible adult with them. Myra and Henry will arrange passage for them and who knows, in the meantime the war could be over," said Liza.

Eventually the men joined the ladies and coffee was served. Sadly the evening was over and those who were leaving bade farewell to Liza and Jamie, all of them saying that they would probably not see them again until after the war was over and wishing them a safe journey.

"That evening went well," said Myra. "Are you sure you won't be able to hold another one whilst you are here?"

"There is nothing to stop these friends calling around, but we are putting a great deal of pressure on Walter, Bertram and their staff," said Liza.

"It was very wise of you not saying when you were leaving," said Walter, "but once the 'Amelia' is seen docking it won't take a genius to know that you and

Jamie will be on it. That is going to be the most dangerous time for you all. We may well have to create a diversion."

"What are you suggesting Walter?" asked Jamie.

"I'm not sure yet, but Bertram and I will work something out," said Walter.

"I don't want anyone taking any chances on my behalf and what you seem to be suggesting is somebody pretending to be me and leaving themselves wide open to being kidnapped and when the perpetrators find that it isn't me, who knows what they would do to that person. No I'm not having that," said Liza.

"No, Liza's right. It's too dangerous for somebody to take Liza's place but some form of diversion could work, although like Walter, I haven't thought of what yet," said Jamie.

"None of this may be necessary. I should be able to get from here in a closed carriage and I won't be alone reaching our cabin on the 'Amelia'. Andraes can take Susan and the children a little earlier and get them settled, and if I know Roberts, he is not going to let me out of his sight," smiled Liza.

"Neither will Bertram and I," said Walter.

"I'm the same height as Liza," said Barbara. "I could head off into town a little earlier. I could borrow one of your cloaks and cover my head and everyone would think that I was you."

"That's too dangerous," said Liza. "Walter has already been stabbed by a deranged woman who wanted to stab me. I'm not going to have another member of your family taking risks because of me. And that's final."

Jamie was smiling, so were Sean and Brendan. They had all seen that look on Liza's face before; the pouting lips and the determined frown; it was a look that said, 'don't argue with me.'

Liza could see that Barbara and Winifred wanted to go and enjoy their night in the luxury of their rooms and Liza said that the evening had been a great success, but she was feeling a little tired and would soon like to go to her bed. She noticed that Barbara and Winifred were nodding in agreement.

"I want to thank you all for making this a lovely evening for me, especially you Walter and Bertram and of course Barbara and Winifred. I had a very relaxing, worry-free time and that was down to you," said Liza and everyone began to organise moving up to their rooms with Barbara and Winifred leading the way.

Liza made her way up the stairs and onto the girls' room and found that Andraes was also there, checking on his daughter as well as Bright Star.

"You really are a very good father Andraes," whispered Liza. "It is a pity that you can't have her in your care, but we all understand why. You know that you can visit her whenever you wish. There will always be a place for you in our home whilst she is with us."

"Thank you, Liza, I know that you would do that for me, and I know that she will be very happy with you," said Andraes as they walked away from the room.

"I'm looking forward to getting the two girls settled with us in England where they won't be as restricted as they are here. How long do you think you will be able to stay with us once we reach our home?" asked Liza.

"I have been away a long time; however I think that I could manage another two weeks, but that is all I'm afraid," said Andraes.

"You'll have plenty of time with Christina now and when we are on the 'Amelia'," said Liza.

"You and Jamie are very understanding, especially considering how Christina was conceived," said Andraes. "Does Jamie know that I thought that Felicity was you?"

Liza smiled and said, "Yes, he does. You didn't know me then and you thought you knew who you were with. After all it was only a name that you wanted to be with. Mistakes do happen but the result of yours is a very beautiful girl who obviously has your very nice nature. I have to say that your English has improved immensely since that time."

"I was trying to get one over on Jamie then," said Andraes. "Instead I hurt Edward Fuller and all the Fuller family."

"Yes, Jamie was rather pompous in those days," smiled Liza. "The Fullers have forgiven you; they knew how it had happened and they no longer hold you responsible. They know that you do your best for your daughter, and they admire that."

Roberts was just leaving their room and Liza found Susan waiting for her. "You're looking a little sad Susan," commented Liza.

"I'm alright, but I will be pleased to get back home," said Susan.

"Yes, it has been a difficult time for us all. Your mother and brother will be relieved to see you. They do know that you are now safe; Mr Mahoney sent word by the first ship leaving as we arrived. You will deserve a great deal of time off when you get home."

"My mother and Derek must have been very worried about me. I thought that we were coming to safety when we got here, but we're not really are we?" said Susan and tears could be seen on her cheeks. Liza put her arms around her and let her cry on her shoulder.

"We are safe Susan. You've seen how Walter and his men guard us," said Liza. "I know that this has not worked out as we had all hoped, but none of us could have imagined that we would get caught up in a civil war, and we certainly could not have envisioned that we would be used as pawns in their war games. In years to come you will be able to tell your children of the adventurous time you had on

433

your first visit to America. Hopefully it will not be your last one, but we will not be travelling here for some time to come."

"I'm sorry, I should be braver than I am," said Susan.

"I think you've been very brave. You have experienced things that most people three times your age would not be able to handle and I'm sorry that we put you in that situation. We had hoped that your first trip abroad would have been more enjoyable for you," said Liza. "Our next trip will probably be to Italy; I don't think that they have a war starting there."

Susan started helping Liza out of her dress and Liza told her just to hang it up and then get to her bed as she looked tired and needed her sleep; she would be able to manage by herself and she would see her the next morning.

Jamie came through from the dressing room. "I heard what Susan was saying, it has been very stressful for her, and she is very young. I do hope that we have no difficulties getting to the ship. Has Henry said when it's due in port?"

"He believes it should be Friday, but it won't be leaving port until Sunday lunchtime," said Liza.

"So we have another week here and much as it is very comfortable I would much rather that we were already on our way home," said Jamie. "Do you have much to do this week as far as business is concerned?"

"The charity must take priority as the children could find themselves without food. I need Brendan to go to both orphanages with Myra to see how they could be set up to be self-sufficient. Unfortunately I won't be able to go," said Liza.

Liza was undressing slowly and absentmindedly with Jamie watching her with a grin on his face.

"You know Liza, people would pay a lot of money to see a woman stripping the way you are now, and very enjoyable it is too," smiled Jamie. "You're not going to bother putting your nightdress on, are you?"

Liza grinned and said that it would be a waste of energy.

***

Hector and Estelle would be arriving later on Sunday and Myra was up early questioning Brendan on how he thought the Homes could help to increase their food supply. He said that until he could see what they were like, he could not advise on anything, so Myra and he decided to make a trip to both Homes shortly after breakfast.

The day seemed to be passing slowly. Brendan and Myra returned from the Homes, and they were listing the changes which would enable them to become self-sufficient. A groundsman was employed by the charity to keep each Home in order, and he realised that he would now have a much more important job and he would have to get help from the older children.

Andraes was spending time with Christina and Bright Star and as the day had turned wet and cold, they were enjoying a game in the library with Susan and Mary joining in.

Barbara and Winifred had left after breakfast and Myra and Henry stayed for lunch and left early afternoon. Sean and Arnold were spending some time getting ready for their departure the following day. Liza had tried to encourage them to stay a little longer, but she knew that they really had to get back to their duties.

Knowing that Hector and Estelle would be arriving later that day, Liza knew that she would have very little opportunity to speak privately to Sean before he left so she went to his room and found him organising his clothes neatly as many soldiers were capable of doing.

"I'm glad we'll be keeping in touch Sean," said Liza. "I'll be waiting and praying until I receive each letter. I know you won't be able to write that regularly, but I will be able to, and you know that I'll send them to where your unit is normally based. Whether you will receive them I will never know, but at least you know that they have been written. I wish you could come home with me Sean; however I know that isn't possible."

"When this war is over, I promise that I will come and visit you Liza," said Sean. "I will probably have had enough of army life by then, although I have no idea what else I would be able to do. I will be owed plenty of leave so I could use that time to see what other life I could have."

Suddenly it all got too much for Liza and she started sobbing and when Sean put his arms around her to comfort her it was just as if Patrick was there with her and consoling her and this only made her sob even harder. Sean was also finding it difficult to control his emotions.

"We both still love him, don't we Liza?" said Sean quietly. "It's been very difficult for both of us, but you have done what is right for you and for your boys, and I can see that Jamie loves you very much, he always has done, and it's obvious that you love him but in a very different way. I have never found anyone to compare with him. I envy Rufus and Paul, at least they died together; I was not so fortunate."

"I told you that we had to stick together as we were the two people who loved him the most, but I was endangering the people of Benson if I had stayed at that time. Of course Matthew and John were also in danger, and I had to protect them. You then decided to pack up and move to the Badlands and I didn't know where you were. I had lost you, and Patrick would have been sorry about that, I know he would," said Liza.

"I always knew where you were Liza," said Sean. "I don't mean every second of every day, but I knew that you stayed in Ireland for some time and also that you went to Italy for a short while. I was a little shocked and saddened when I learned that you had married Jamie, but I understood that the boys needed a father figure, and I knew that Jamie would be kind to you. It's only now that I realise that you do have deep feelings for Jamie; I should have known that really because I know that you would not marry without love as you know that would not be fair on your husband."

"I found it very difficult to be in Benson. I felt the overpowering presence of Patrick and it created a great feeling of disloyalty not only to him but also to Jamie," said Liza. "I had a conversation with Ada and in that conversation I realised exactly what I was experiencing, and I explained that Patrick was the passion of my life and Jamie is the love of my life. It does leave a question over what my first husband was. I was so young when I married him and he had the patience to allow me to grow up with him, and I visit him whenever I go to Belfast, as well as my son and stepson."

"Oh Liza, you have not had an easy life," said Sean.

"No, but I now have a great deal of love from Jamie, and stability for me and my boys and we now have to create a happy home for two girls who need love and care," said Liza.

"You'll make sure that they get that Liza; I can see that you already love them, and they think the world of you. Jamie is also very good to take them in. When I first met him, he was so aloof that nobody could get on with him, but he has mellowed, which I am sure is down to you," said Sean.

"He has never been aloof with me, and I have known him for many years. He lets the boys run rings around him; he knows they do it, but they don't know that he knows. He prefers being at home in England as it is his family home; I know that he is not as comfortable here, but normally he does enjoy the space and freedom that New York offers," said Liza.

"You will have a great deal to tell me in your letters. The boys will keep me amused and I know you will let me know how the girls are settling in. I will want chapter and verse on the functions that you attend and the people you meet as well as how the charity is faring. There is so much that happens in your life that I want to know about. When your letters reach me, they will take my mind off the devastation that will be surrounding me and then you will see me when the war is over," said Sean. "Your friends will be arriving shortly. You have so many people who care for you Liza and I'm one of them."

"I care for you very much Sean. I would give anything to keep you safe, but I know I can't do that," said Liza.

"I will try to stay safe as I now have something to look forward to," smiled Sean.

Liza wiped her eyes and smiled back at him as they heard a carriage drive up to the door and Liza made her way down the stairs and was met at the bottom by Jamie who was heading towards the door to greet Hector and Estelle. Jamie looked at Liza and realised that she had been crying and he took out his handkerchief and dabbed her face, looked at her closely and said, "You'll do."

"I know I've been silly, but I may never see Sean again. He has promised that he will visit us when the war is over and he has told me that it has given him something to look forward to, so perhaps he won't go headlong into any dangerous situations," said Liza.

Hector marched into the house, almost knocking over the two security men who were on duty. He lifted Liza up and swung her around and planted a huge kiss on her head. "Well Liza, you're worth a great deal of money to everyone in America but it's good to see that Jamie hasn't been swayed by the reward money. I, on the other hand, might take advantage of what they are offering."

"Oh Hector, it's wonderful to see that you haven't changed. Where's Estelle; you haven't left her to carry your bags in, have you?" smiled Liza.

"No, she's here somewhere. You'll probably find that your security men have arrested her as an undesirable. As long as she stays undesirable to them then I will be happy," said Hector. "Jamie, it's good to see you."

Liza extricated herself from Hector's grip to greet Estelle who was trying to tell the security men that she still had to arrange for their bags to be brought in.

"It's alright Estelle, I'll get somebody to deal with that," said Liza. "Welcome Estelle; I am so very pleased to see you."

Liza ushered them both into the drawing room and arranged for refreshments to be brought into them.

"I had to make sure that you were both alive and well after your ordeal down south," said Hector. "But I also hear that you were caught up in a battle around the town that you used to live in. That must have been quite frightening for you both."

"It was frightening for a lot of people, not least Roberts and Susan as well as all the people of Benson," said Jamie.

"We have several people staying with us at the moment, so dinner this evening should be quite lively, as I know you don't like to be bored," smiled Liza. "I'm afraid that we will be outnumbered Estelle, but I'm sure we'll manage to amuse ourselves."

"That's alright Liza, I'm used to being surrounded by men," smiled Estelle.

"You may have noticed that I'm going to be a father," announced Hector unceremoniously.

"No I hadn't noticed, but I've hardly had a chance to look at you," said Liza to Estelle. "That is wonderful news. I'm so pleased for you both. When is the baby due?"

"At some time in early April," said Estelle.

"Does Adam know that he's going to be an uncle?" asked Liza.

"No, not yet," said Estelle. "I'm hoping that you'll take a letter to him for us."

"And one for my mother; I'm sure she'll be delighted to know that she is going to be a grandmother again," said Hector.

"Yes, I'm sure she will be," said Liza without conviction.

Hector laughed knowing his mother as he did. "Well at least Anthony and Diana will be pleased."

"I dare say you'd like to rest for a while; it's been a long journey for you both," said Liza.

"Thank you, Liza, but I'm not tired, although I'm sure Estelle would like to put her feet up," said Hector.

"Yes, I do feel a little tired," said Estelle.

Liza went up with her, having first arranged refreshments to be brought up.

"How are you enjoying Daltons?" asked Liza.

"I love it, Liza. It's dusty, dirty and bustling with life. We have a house now and I teach every day. I have children eager to learn and I also have adults who feel the same. Workers are arriving all the time and Hector is in his element, as is Brendan. It's such a shame that you can't see it, you would be impressed by what has been achieved," said Estelle.

"I had every intention of visiting and seeing what is happening, but it wasn't to be. I did think that everyone was making too much of a fuss, however I have since realised that I was wrong, especially when I was told that I had a price on my head. Hopefully it won't be too long before I will be able to spend some time with you there," said Liza.

"I have a great deal of help from Tess Jones; she was still learning to read and write when I first met her, but she was so enthusiastic and receptive that she is now able to teach the younger children. She says that she was encouraged to learn by the only person who was kind to her before she met Garth," said Estelle. "Do you remember her? She and Garth came out on the first wagon train to Daltons."

"There was a great deal going on at that time; I do remember the Fairburns. How are they all getting on? There seemed to be a great many children in their

438

wagon," said Liza trying to move the conversation away from Tess and Garth Jones.

"Gwen has had another child since we arrived in Daltons. They do have a house now, but I don't know that it is going to be big enough for them if they keep having children the way that they do," smiled Estelle.

"I'll leave you to rest now Estelle," said Liza. "Mary will be in to help you dress before dinner. I'm so pleased that you are here."

Meanwhile Jamie was in the library with Hector and Walter. Liza hesitated before entering but realised that they were probably discussing her welfare and so she felt she should be in on the conversation.

"Are you talking about me behind my back?" smiled Liza.

"Of course we are Liza," said Hector jokingly.

Jamie knew that Liza did not want to be kept in the dark and so he told Hector to let her know what he had been telling them.

"Brendan has probably told you that several men have been talking about how to get their hands on the reward which is being offered for you," said Hector. "Initially we took no notice of it as most of what they were discussing was ludicrous and therefore seemed just as if they were joking. When the reward increased it seemed as if there was a change in attitude and there were small gatherings and we noticed that whenever anyone in authority approached, they looked guilty and either moved away or started talking loudly about work, which in itself was unusual."

"Were there any particular ring leaders?" asked Walter.

"Yes, we noticed that the loudest mouths in the bars were those who looked like the leaders of groups, or some just stayed by themselves and went around with pursed lips. Carl Fairburn came to me and said that it appeared that something was creating unease in many of the workers. Garth was telling me the same thing and it was then that we felt that we had to warn you not to visit us," said Hector.

"You did the right thing Hector and hopefully most will still be waiting for me to turn up at Daltons," smiled Liza.

Hector carried on, "Unfortunately on the train on our way here we have seen several of our own workers who should really still be in Daltons and also we have noticed one individual in particular walking near the driveway up to the house, so at least one person knows where you live."

"That's a little unsettling," said Liza. "There are also those who nobody recognises that we have to worry about."

"I am not going to let you out of my sight," said Jamie with determination. "It is so annoying that we still have a week to go before we can leave this place, and we also have responsibility for others in our care."

"I have many responsibilities that I have been unable to fulfil over the past months. I'm pleased that you will have me in your sights Jamie, but I'm sure that we will not have unwelcome visitors within this house. I must now see Brendan who is advising on how our orphanages can become self-sufficient," said Liza and she left the room much to the surprise of everyone there.

Brendan was sitting at Liza's desk in the study going through lists of items that he felt could make the lives of the orphans better should food supplies become difficult in times to come. He stood and Liza waved him back down and they spent the next hour discussing what was necessary, until the time came to change for dinner.

When she was dressed, Jamie came through to their bedroom to escort her down to dinner.

"I thought you said that you were not going to let me out of your sight," smiled Liza.

"I could tell that you didn't think it necessary whilst we were within the house," smiled Jamie. "I also feel that you are planning to go visiting despite all the warnings that you have been given."

"I feel that I must spend some time with the children in the two Homes that are here. I started them and talked people into giving money to them. You know that the then President did a great deal to try to stop the abuses that were being perpetrated against children and some of those children went through heart stopping fear and horrendous dangers to get to safety and away from evil. The least I can do is put my own fears to one side and make sure that they are still happy and that they will be able to survive during this war," said Liza.

"You know that what you are suggesting is not wise and it will be putting Walter and his men under a great deal of pressure," said Jamie. "I would prefer that you stayed here, but whatever you decide I will be with you, and I do understand your reasons. I do however believe that those running the Homes and the children would realise the difficult position that you are in and would not expect you to put yourself in danger for their sakes."

"I don't want to put anyone else in danger and certainly not you Jamie, but I do need to see those running the Homes and I would like to see the children. Their future is worrying me considerably," said Liza.

"We have two children with us who need you to worry about them," said Jamie. "Myra is visiting tomorrow, isn't she? Perhaps she could arrange for those in charge of the Homes to come here, and I'm sure a few children could also visit during the course of the week. I know it is not ideal, but it could be one solution and would perhaps put your mind at rest that all is being done that can be done."

Liza smiled up at Jamie and said that they should go down to dinner and that she would think about his suggestion.

Dinner was lively, as it would be with Hector leading the conversation. Jamie was quiet as he was concerned that Liza would decide to visit the orphanages. Sean was watching both Liza and Jamie closely, he could see that they both had something on their minds and if Liza was contemplating endangering herself then he would have to stay and guard her, even if it meant locking her up.

Liza and Estelle went into the drawing room after dinner, leaving the men to talk over their port.

"What has Liza decided to do that you don't approve of Jamie?" said Sean. "I suppose she is going to visit one of her orphanages."

"She was Sean, but I have suggested that they come to visit her, and she is thinking about it. She is so concerned that they will suffer badly throughout this war. As you are all aware many of the children risked life and limb to get not only themselves but also little ones to safety and she feels that the least she can do is be brave enough to see them and do everything she can to make sure they are prepared for what may be to come," said Jamie. "I do understand how she feels but I have pointed out to her that we also have people here who need her just as much."

"I can arrange to see Myra tomorrow morning and we can bring anyone you wish here," said Brendan. "As you know I've visited the Homes and made a few suggestions on how they can help themselves to survive if the worst comes to the worst."

"Of course," said Hector, "I had forgotten that you were in farming previously."

"Walter will have his work cut out if she does venture out," said Andraes.

"I won't insult you Jamie, by saying that I will talk to her and persuade her otherwise because I know you have done all that you can already, but if she does get taken by someone who eventually manages to take her to the Confederates, she will have to be rescued again which will put at risk a number of our soldiers. I really cannot afford to spend any more time here, but I will if I have to, and I know that my superiors will not feel kindly towards her for putting herself back in that situation," said Sean.

The men went to the drawing room to join Liza and Estelle.

Liza looked up and smiled, "I think that once again you have been talking about me behind my back. Don't worry I have bowed to Jamie's concerns and

441

decided that his idea is the best one. I do feel that I should at least see those who run the Homes and I am not going to endanger others by endangering myself."

Jamie breathed a sigh of relief, as did many others in the room.

"Well Liza, you have a week to sort out all the problems at your two orphanages which I am confident you will do with your eyes closed," said Hector. "I am sure that with your organising skills you will have those Homes selling food to everyone in the neighbourhood."

"If only that were to be the case, but sadly I think that they will just about have enough to feed themselves and really it will be Brendan's ideas that will help to keep them fed, not mine," said Liza.

"Thank you for your confidence, Liza, but if the war goes on for any length of time it will take more than what I'm suggesting to keep them well fed," said Brendan.

"They won't be the only ones to go hungry; I hope that you are all looking to the future," said Liza.

"You know that you've already done that with the supplies and animals that you have had delivered to us," said Hector.

"Even they won't last you for years; but I know you will be able to afford to buy what you want, after all owning and running factories will mean that you will be able to supply certain commodities to those who can afford to pay, sad as it is," said Liza.

"Well, that's business, isn't it?" said Hector.

***

Sean and Arnold left the following day and Liza found it difficult to keep her emotions in check. Sean reiterated that he would keep in touch as much as possible, and he would look forward to hearing all the news of Liza's family and friends.

"I promised you that I would come to see you when this war is over, and I always keep my promises," said Sean as he kissed Liza goodbye. She found it difficult to let him go, but she knew how she should react having been an army wife in her previous married life.

As they drove away Liza immediately turned and went back into the house as she could not bear to watch them leave. Back in the house she went to find Christina and Bright Star and spent some time with them until Myra arrived with those who ran the orphanages, and that meeting went on for a couple of hours.

Each day Liza kept herself busy in meetings with Myra, the carers at the orphanages as well as some of the children that they cared for. Also there was a great deal to discuss with Hector and Brendan. Estelle brought her up to date on all that was happening in Daltons as far as the education of the children and others who wanted to learn.

Hector, Estelle and Brendan left on the Friday and soon after the 'Amelia' docked and began to unload and then make ready for departure late on the Sunday.

The house seemed depleted. By the Saturday all their trunks and cases were packed and ready to be taken to the ship.

Myra and Henry dined with them that evening and everyone was subdued and when they were leaving, Liza reiterated to Henry that there could be children from Benson who may need to travel to England.

"I know Liza; I won't let them down," said Henry.

"Whatever you need to do to keep yourselves fit and healthy you must do, no matter what the cost," said Liza. "I am very worried about you both; we've known one another for a very long time, and I hate the thought that the current circumstances may put you in great difficulty."

"We'll be there to see you off tomorrow," said Henry. "I know that Walter will get you there safely; he's done an exceptional job these last weeks, so has Bertram and all the men."

When they had left Andraes made his way up to bed and Liza and Jamie sat in the drawing room for a while.

"I hope we get to the ship tomorrow without difficulty," said Jamie. "I shall be pleased to be on our way home, it's been a very turbulent time for us all."

"We seem to have been embroiled in many types of battles since we arrived in America all those months ago; starting with our ship being stopped before we even reached Charleston. I do hope that Charles and his people survive what was started whilst we were with him," said Liza.

"Shall we get some rest now, you are looking tired. I dare say we won't be back here for some time. It's a shame as normally we have a nice time when we are here, but this became very unsettling and until that ship leaves port it will remain so," said Jamie.

"Thank you for looking after me Jamie," said Liza. "I would have been even more frightened than I was without you."

"I try to Liza. Sometimes you don't make it very easy for me, but I will always try to," said Jamie.

Chapter 13

Sunday was the start of another phase in their lives. The girls and Susan went to the kitchen for their breakfast as usual. Liza and Jamie came to the dining room that morning and Andraes was already there. Bridget brought various dishes in and out, and all the time she was sniffing and occasionally mopping her face on her apron. Mary was helping her, and she too was not looking happy. She had decided not to leave New York with them, having thanked them for their offer but she felt that she wanted to stay with her sister, especially as it could be a difficult time and they were a comfort to one another.

Liza and Jamie had emphasised to all the staff that if they were in any danger or had any problems whatsoever, they were to see Henry and Myra and Walter also. She was leaving more than enough money to keep them well cared for over a number of years. She could not advise on what to do if supplies ran out; she could only suggest that they think about converting some of the garden for their own produce. She had already spoken to the groundsmen about possible sites to expand what was already grown in the kitchen garden and they had already bought in seed and chicks could be heard in one of the pens.

She had also warned them that some children from Benson may visit on their way to her in England.

The 'Amelia' was not setting sail until the evening tide. Andraes was to take Christina, Bright Star and Susan to the ship after lunch that day; Bertram and a couple of security men were to accompany them and see them safely settled, staying with them until the last minute. It would be just before it sailed that Liza and Jamie would join the ship. Walter and another couple of security guards would be with them. Henry and Myra would be aboard to greet them and would not leave until just before the gangway was removed.

Their trunks and cases were already on board and Liza and Jamie went to see the staff again.

"If the situation gets really serious for you all, please just close the house and get on a ship over to us in England. We will make room for everyone. Henry will arrange passage for you should you need it, and we would be delighted to see you and know that you are safely with us. Walter will be keeping a very close eye on you all, as there could be those undesirables still around who won't know that we have left here. So be careful and stay safe. You know that we both care for you all a great deal and we would hate for anything to happen to any of you."

Of course this set Bridget crying again and mumbling unintelligibly whilst wiping her eyes on her apron. Mary was also crying but with very good reason, she had been sad for the whole time that they had been in New York. Stephen had pursed lips and was nodding his agreement with what was being said.

Liza took a final look around the house that she knew she would not see for some time, if at all. She remembered being there with Edward and Kate before her disastrous trip to the Valdez hacienda and then she remembered her sad return when she thought that Patrick was married to someone else before she went to Belfast to lick her wounds. She had happily returned having sorted out her problems with Patrick before travelling back to what she had considered her home in Benson. Once again she had returned after Patrick's death and spent some time trying to come to terms with it. Throughout all her traumas Jamie had been there to comfort her, and she had treated him so badly, not realising how much she needed him and how true he had been to her.

As she continued to look around, she nodded her contentment at how she had changed the house and it had become a home for her and Jamie. They had spent some happy times there and held some sparkling entertainments. It was certainly now her's and Jamie's; there was no trace of her previous life and that was how she wanted it. It was a shame that they had to leave it now under such difficult circumstances.

Walter and his men were waiting for them in the hallway along with the staff who all wanted that final farewell before ushering Liza and Jamie into their closed carriage. Walter was riding with the driver and there was also a security man inside with them.

They drove at a normal rate to the docks and Walter would not let them get out of the carriage until he was sure that there were no undesirables waiting for them. He had already checked the passenger list and as far as he could tell there was nobody that he thought could hurt them, but he had emphasised that they should still be vigilant.

When they got to their cabin Myra and Henry were waiting for them.

"I'd forgotten how comfortable the owner's suite was," said Henry. "You should have a very relaxing trip."

Andraes knocked and entered. He had a large cabin which he was sharing with Roberts and between them, and Liza and Jamie, was another large cabin which was occupied by the children and Susan. The owner's cabin also had a sitting room which was to be used by their party and there was a door which cut them off from the rest of the passengers.

Liza went to see Susan and the children and found them at their evening meal. Bright Star smiled up at her and showed her that she was using a knife and fork.

"She's really doing very well now," said Susan. "Christina is helping her so much."

Christina also smiled up at her and said that she was looking forward to the trip and then getting to England and seeing the house where she would be living.

"Yes, I'm looking forward to the trip and it will be such a relief to reach home and see all my family. At least you will know Simon and Matthew and John. I know Susan is looking forward to seeing her mother and brother," said Liza.

"And everyone else at Edgeworth House," added Susan.

Liza went back to the sitting room where Henry, Myra and Walter were getting ready to leave. "The ship is full," said Henry. "I suppose there are many people who want to leave America should the war become much worse."

"I know how they feel, but I am worried about those I'm leaving behind. I'm sure I've said it all, but you must promise me that you will not put yourselves in danger and you will come to us if it becomes unbearable," said Liza.

"We've said that we would Liza and we will look after your interests for as long as we can," said Henry.

There was a knock at the door and Bertram came in to say that they were waiting for those who were not passengers to leave as they wanted to remove the gangway and cast off.

"Well this is it," said Jamie. He shook hands with Henry and Walter and kissed Myra on the cheek; Andraes followed suit and then it was left to Liza to say goodbye, which she did by kissing everyone, crying, and then wishing them good luck. They left and Liza, Jamie and Andraes stood looking at the door where they had left, each deep in thought.

There were lots of shouts and they heard the gangway being removed and then the small boats were guiding the ship away from the dock and into the main waterway. They were finally on their way home.

They watched through their portholes as the New York skyline disappeared and with a choke in her voice Liza said that she wondered when they would see that again, in fact she wondered whether they would ever see it or America again.

"I have spent many years of my life in America; it's Matthew's place of birth and John spent much of his young life here, as has Christina, and of course Bright Star was also born here. We are leaving it to its own devices; we are abandoning it as we have no choice. We were more of a burden to it than an asset. I wonder why the other passengers are leaving; perhaps they have the same reasons as we do," said Liza with her lips still quivering with emotion.

Roberts knocked and when he entered, he took in the situation and suggested that he poured them all a drink to settle their stomachs before their dinner.

Jamie smiled at him and said, "And yours too Roberts. I seem to remember that it does take you a couple of days to get your sea legs."

"I will be surprised if I suffer with mal de mar after all the stomach jerking events that we have experienced over the past months," said Roberts haughtily to the amused listeners but they noticed that he poured himself a small whiskey.

"Have you eaten yet, Roberts?" asked Liza.

"No your Ladyship," said Roberts. "I'm not very hungry tonight." Which also amused his listeners and Liza knew that he would be indisposed over the next day or so.

Roberts then bowed and hastily left the sitting room. Liza turned to Andraes and said that if Roberts' indisposition became too much then Andraes could have his bed moved into the sitting room for a while.

"Don't worry Liza, I'm used to dealing with people whose stomachs rebel against the ships movements, but if it does get too bad, I will take you up on your offer," said a smiling Andraes.

"Susan was alright on the way out," said Liza. "I hope that the children don't suffer that way."

"Christina didn't all those years ago, and she went from Ireland to England and then onto Greece. A while later we had to make our way to New York. She was only three then, but I presume she will be able to cope now. We'll soon find out whether Bright Star has sea legs," said Andraes.

"It's going to be embarrassing for Roberts if he is the only one who suffers from 'mal de mar' as he puts it," smiled Jamie.

There was another knock on the door and a rather pale faced Roberts ushered a steward into the sitting room.

"This is Jefferies who will be on duty at mealtimes. Excuse me," said Roberts as he beat another hasty retreat from the sitting room.

They all watched him leave and then Jefferies said, "I have been informed of your situation and Walter Anderson and I had a long discussion concerning your safety and I will be serving all your meals. I will introduce you to your housekeeper and her assistant tomorrow; they also have been vetted by Mr Anderson. You will be able to rely on our complete tact and loyalty whilst you are on this voyage. I will be serving your meal in half an hour; I hope that will be acceptable to you."

"Thank you, Jefferies, I'm sure that we will all get on together very well," said Liza.

"Haven't you got something in your medicine case that would help Roberts?" asked Jamie.

"Most of my cures make you feel sick before you feel better. I'm not sure that he would appreciate being made to feel even worse than he does now," said Liza. "You know that it only takes him a day or so to feel better."

"I suppose you're right," said Jamie.

They were well under way by the time dinner was served and the sadness at leaving everyone in New York was tempered by a sense of relief that they no longer had to worry about being taken hostage by the Confederacy. They slept well that night; even Roberts' stomach seemed to settle remarkably well over night although in the morning he was unable to face breakfast.

The Captain invited Liza, Jamie and Andraes to dinner on many occasions throughout the voyage, and on most days Liza spent time with Christina and Bright Star playing with them and reading to them. Bright Star's command of the English language was improving; she was recognising items and attempting to say what they were. She was a little young to learn how to read, but as either Christina or Liza read a particular word, she wanted them to point to it and she would then say it. Liza was quite impressed with her efforts. It was obvious that Christina loved Bright Star like a sister, and they were becoming inseparable.

It did take Roberts only two days to recover from seasickness, after which he spent a great deal of time brushing and generally keeping Jamie's and Andraes' clothes neat and clean. He also took a daily walk around the deck just in case he heard any conversations which could be of interest.

The excitement of the voyage was palling, but they all managed to keep Christina and Bright Star occupied and in doing so they took the boredom out of their own situation.

England appeared in the distance, and it was interesting to see the coastlines emerging through the mist. By the time they docked in London it was raining heavily but that did not stop family and friends waiting to greet them. Before they left their cabin, four young men burst through the door and engulfed them both, all of them talking at once and not allowing either Jamie or Liza time to answer.

Finally, between Liza's tears and all the hugs and words of welcome, Jamie told them that they also had others with them and who they were. As they left their cabin Andraes and Roberts were emerging from theirs and hands were shaken and greetings given and then Susan ushered Christina and Bright Star from their cabin and Simon immediately went over to Christina and said how pleased he was that she was safely with them. Matthew, John and James were welcoming Susan, and Bright Star was looking confused and a little fearful. Liza went to her and picked her up and said to them: "This is Bright Star and she's Bandor's daughter, but she will now be living with us."

Matthew went to her and spoke his welcome to her in Cherokee, and she smiled at him, and he immediately loved her. John and James also welcomed her, and Simon turned and smiled warmly at her.

Jamie's mother, Miranda and his uncle David found their way to the cabin and Jamie clasped his mother closely to him whilst David hugged Liza.

"We have been so worried about you. The only news we had was from official channels and that was not very informative; we were so relieved to hear from your overseer in New York that you had at last reached safety," said David.

"It is such a relief to be back," said Liza. "It has been rather an ordeal and at one stage we wondered whether we would ever get back."

"I presume we have some carriages waiting for us," said Jamie.

"Yes, we have plenty of them and Uncle Wendell and Aunt Amelia are waiting in one of them," said Matthew.

"Good heavens, they must be cold. Come on Jamie we must go and see them," said an excited Liza.

They had already thanked Jefferies and the rest of those who had looked after them so well and all they had to do was thank the Captain and First Mate, both of whom were waiting for them at the gangway. At the same time Andraes arrived there and he was introduced to Miranda and David as an old friend.

It was still raining but they could see both Wendell and Amelia waving from a carriage, and they quickly made their way over to them and climbed in. Amelia was in danger of becoming as unintelligible as Bridget and Wendell was beaming from ear to ear.

"We have Andraes and Christina with us," said Jamie carefully and he waited for their response.

"Oh, of course," said Wendell. "You are guardian to her aren't you, Liza? Is Andraes going to take her to his home?"

"No, Wendell, she will stay with us until she can return to Ada and the Colonel. It isn't practical for her to go to Andraes' home," said Liza quietly as David helped Miranda into the carriage and climbed up afterwards.

Andraes came across to greet Wendell and Amelia and to say that he was going to travel in the carriage with Roberts, Susan and the children and he would see them at the house.

The third carriage was to carry Matthew, John, James and Simon and the fourth had the luggage.

"What did Andraes mean 'the children'?" asked Wendell.

"We also have a little girl with us," said Liza. "You will remember that we told you about Bandor and how he has helped me in the past. The little girl is his daughter, and he has asked me to take care of her as if she was my own and of course I will do that."

"Of course you will Liza," said Amelia, "and I know you will do the same for Christina. Edward would have liked to have been here to greet you, but Nicole has been a little unwell recently because they are to become parents again."

"That's wonderful news to come home to," said Liza. "We have a great deal to tell you all about; so much that we don't know where to start, so I'm just going to sit back and enjoy your company. I have looked forward to this moment for so long."

It was a little crowded in their carriage, but nobody was complaining. Questions were asked about many things but mostly Jamie and Liza wanted to know how everyone was at home, especially Mrs Price and Derek.

"They must have been really concerned for Susan," said Liza.

"We kept in touch with them every day, even if we had nothing to tell them, but they appreciated our visits," said David. "I must tell you that although worried, they had great confidence in you both that you would get her home safely and they were right as it turned out. We arranged that they would be waiting at the house for our return."

"I presume that Christopher is now working with Adam and living with Derek and Mrs Price," said Liza.

"Yes, he's been with them since the summer, which has been quite good for Mrs Price as she had two men to care for, although it didn't stop her worrying about Susan," said Miranda.

"How is Lucinda?" asked Jamie.

"She has been so worried, as we all have been, but you know that Lucinda shows her emotions and on many occasions she stayed in our home as she knew that she was in danger of upsetting the household. I'm sure you are all going to be covered in tears when you get home," said Miranda.

Both Liza and Jamie asked numerous questions about everyone at Edgeworth House and in the village as well as in Belfast.

Wendell had been quiet for some time and finally said, "Well Liza and Jamie, so far you have managed to avoid telling us anything about your time away; was it so very horrendous that you find it difficult to talk about?"

It took time for them to answer but finally Jamie said that there were some good times, but for the last few months they had to look over their shoulders every moment of the day and latterly they were unable to venture out of the

New York house for fear of being taken by those who wanted to gain the reward that had been posted for Liza.

"The Confederates should have known that our government would not give in to blackmail; they are not going to take sides in that war no matter what tactics are tried to persuade them. Obviously the Union hierarchy knew better otherwise they would have tried the same trick rather than getting you to safety," said Wendell.

"We heard that you were caught up in the battle around Benson," said David. "Did you see much of it?"

"Yes, we saw some terrible things and lost some close friends," said Liza and Jamie took her hand and squeezed it. Everyone in the carriage knew that neither Liza nor Jamie were ready to go into detail of what had happened in Benson.

"No doubt the time will come when you feel able to talk about it, but I see that now is not the time," said Wendell.

The carriages trundled through the village and there were calls of "Welcome home" from many of the villagers and Mr Rogers' voice could be heard above all else.

It was with great relief that Liza and Jamie saw their home come into view; it was still light but dusk would soon be upon them. The door was thrown open as their carriages drew up and Harper was standing in the doorway; for once he was beaming from ear to ear. Mrs Frances came into sight closely followed by Lucinda who was already crying.

As Jamie helped Liza down from the carriage, followed by Wendell and Amelia, Liza quietly said that she and Jamie needed to see them privately and they were both astute enough to know that it had to be some information about Felicity and therefore Christina. They both nodded and smiled their acknowledgement.

Once inside the house Liza organised rooms for Andraes, Christina and Bright Star. Liza then told Susan to go and find her mother and brother. Lucinda was another one to be sobbing and muttering unintelligibly and Grace hugged Liza and Jamie in turn. Liza looked around and saw that Bright Star was holding tightly on to Christina who was in turn leaning against Andraes, she smiled and went over to them and crouched down to their level.

"Mrs Frances is making up rooms for you both and soon you can have your supper and make yourselves comfortable as this is now your home. There are a lot of people here who are all pleased to see us back safely, it won't be so confusing shortly," said Liza and she told Bright Star the same in her own language.

"We'll be in the same room, won't we?" said Christina. "I think she could be frightened if she is on her own."

"I'll arrange that with Mrs Frances," said Liza and Miranda, who was standing nearby, said that she would see Mrs Frances and tell her to make up just one room.

"Shouldn't you boys be at your university?" said Jamie suddenly.

"We were given time off because they knew you were arriving today," said a beaming Matthew. "Richard and Nicholas wanted to be here too, but they were told that it was not their parents who had been kidnapped so they had to stay. They argued that you weren't Simon's parents either, but the professor said that you were Simon's guardians and that was the same as being a parent. We have to go back on Monday, but Richard and Nicholas will be here at the weekend so we can all go back together."

"Well, I see that you have it all organised Matthew," said Jamie. "I would have expected nothing less of you."

Harper ushered in maids carrying tea trays and cups were handed around to everyone. Liza and Jamie smiled at their sips of decent tea for the first time in months; Amelia grinned at their contented faces and commented that there was nothing like a good cup of tea to welcome somebody home.

Mrs Frances announced that the rooms were now ready, and Liza suggested that she takes Christina and Bright Star up to show them where they would be. "Where are Bright Star's dolls?" asked Liza.

"They are already in her room," said Mrs Frances and Liza took Bright Star's hand and put her arm around Christina and took them to see their room. Their clothes were already hanging in their wardrobe and their nightclothes were laid out on their beds. Bright Star's dolls were on her pillow. It was a very pretty room, but Liza could see that it could be made more comfortable for children than it already was. She would see to that the next day. She stayed and talked to them both for quite some time and by doing that she had settled them in well.

Mrs Frances came to find them saying that their supper was ready for them in the kitchen and that Susan and Mrs Price and Derek were there and were also going to have supper with them.

"I'll bring them down Mrs Frances, and introduce them to everyone down there," said Liza and nervously Christina and Bright Star went down to the kitchen with Liza and Mrs Frances.

"Thank you for bringing Susan back safely," said a relieved looking Mrs Price.

"We knew you would," said Derek. "It just took longer than expected. Matthew told everyone that you would get back safely; he seemed to know that it would not be when you had planned."

"Yes, he does seem to know these things," said Liza and then she introduced Christina and Bright Star to everyone in the kitchen. "Have you seen Matthew and the others yet, Derek?"

"I saw them this morning before they left to meet you; I'll see them again before I leave," said Derek.

"Susan you must spend as much time as you need with your family; we'll be able to look after ourselves for the next few days. I don't suppose you have room for Susan to stay at your house Mrs Price, now that Christopher is there. I'll get her brought to you each day when she is ready," said Liza. "Or you can spend as much time as you like with her here."

Mrs Lambert smiled and pulled out chairs for the girls next to Susan as she realised that both the girls were nervous of their new surroundings. Liza settled them down as their food was put in front of them and Susan kindly helped them. Liza told them that she would be back when they had finished, but Susan said that she would look after them.

"You are meant to be taking some time off, Susan," said Liza and Susan smiled and said that she would start the next day.

Liza left the kitchen and went back to the drawing room where everyone was still chatting and relaxing. They all would be dining together that evening, so David and Grace left to change for dinner and Miranda and Lucinda went with them for the same reason. Andraes was shown to his room where Roberts had unpacked for him. This left Liza and Jamie with Amelia and Wendell.

"You have something to tell us," said Wendell.

Jamie poured them all a drink as Harper discreetly closed the door behind him.

"I see," continued Wendell. "It must be something private about Christina or Felicity.

"It may be that we will have Christina with us forever, although Ada and the Colonel would really like her to return when it is safe for her to do so, but who knows when that could be," said Liza. "I'm sorry if it makes things difficult for you and especially Edward, but she is a lovely girl and has a very sweet nature."

"So what you are really saying is that she is nothing like her mother," said Amelia.

"Yes, that's exactly what Liza is saying," said Jamie

"It might be a little awkward for Edward, but he will get over it," said Amelia. "After all her birth was not her fault."

"What is it that is so important that even Andraes cannot be told?" asked Wendell.

"We may well have to tell him, but firstly we wanted to talk to you and ask your advice on the subject. We are not breaking any confidences as Ada and the Colonel know that we must tell you the true parentage of Felicity," said Jamie.

"Ada put it so delicately when she told me," said Liza. "She said that abuse did not just happen in poor homes, it also happened in those which were well off and that she could recognise those who had been abused as she had also been one of them."

Amelia had her hand to her mouth in shock and Wendell just looked very sad.

Jamie carried on. "The Colonel, who was then a young lieutenant, met Ada and was quite taken with her but her father was adamant that there would never be any form of association between them, so much so that it seemed an unusually harsh and unnatural refusal. Apparently a few weeks went by and he took the bull by the horns and called at Ada's house and luckily she was alone. She was shocked and embarrassed to see him, and he could not help noticing that she was pregnant. He understood the situation immediately and told her to pack a bag and he would look after her and marry her. Her parents arrived home and naturally a fight broke out. Luckily the Colonel came out on top and told Ada to forget about packing a bag as she needed nothing from that house."

Amelia continued to look shocked, but Wendell just shook his head as he was a man of the world.

"He must have loved Ada very much as that was a great responsibility for any man to take on," said Wendell. "So they married, and Felicity was born. It does answer a great deal about why Felicity was mentally unstable. These children rarely come out of such a situation unscathed."

"It may be something that Edward should be told; it could help him to understand why he had to go through such unhappiness when he was with her and why she made his life such a misery," said Liza.

"As we said, we may have a duty to tell Andraes as we don't believe that he has been told," said Jamie. "He has mentioned nothing about that to us and we have said nothing to him. Andraes has not seen the Colonel and Ada for some time; he arrived at our house in New York the day after we got there. He had been trying to reach Benson to ensure his daughters' safety but was stopped every step of the way. After his ship was turned away from many ports, it was finally requisitioned, and he made his way back to New York to start his journey to Benson again. Naturally he made contact with Henry, and he was delighted to learn that Christina was with us in New York."

"Felicity should never have been allowed to marry," said Amelia.

"You are probably right, but when I first met her, she appeared to have the sweetest of natures. Soon after she and Edward married, I did notice her dislike of me, but I put that down to a little jealousy on her part as Edward made no secret of the fact that we had a very close relationship. She had been away to finishing school and returned a very elegant lady who seemed to care a great deal not only for Edward, but her parents and friends also," said Liza.

"Were there no signs of her instability when she was a child?" asked Wendell.

"Apparently she used to play with Danny quite happily most times, but she could stop talking to him for no obvious reason on occasion," said Liza. "I don't think that it bothered Danny too much or was it very noticeable to others."

"No doubt you will have Christina with you for some time to come, so Edward will have to meet up with her on occasion and if he doesn't know that there were reasons why her mother was the way that she was, then it could be very awkward for him. When I see him, I will tell him, I think it would be better coming from me," said Wendell.

"No matter what her parentage, you know that we would make Christina as welcome as we will do for the other little girl. What was her name?" asked Amelia.

"She's called Bright Star. We had thought of calling her Stella to the outside world, but Bright Star suits her so well," said Liza. "She's a beautiful child and Christina has taken her under her wing. She says that she now has a sister."

"What a terrible young life Ada must have had. How lucky she was to meet the Colonel otherwise I don't know what would have happened to her," said Amelia.

"From what we were told, her parents were going to take her away and deal with the birth themselves; whatever that meant, but we can only surmise that the child may not have been allowed to survive and whether Ada would have done also is doubtful," said Liza.

"Her mother must have known what was going on and she did nothing to help," said an incensed Wendell.

"Wendell, our charity deals with children like that every day and in many cases, we know that mothers can be just as frightened of their husbands as their children are. Who knows how we would react to an abusive husband? I hope that I would be as strong as I feel now, but I'm not in that situation. My instincts are to protect my children and I do feel that all mothers should feel that way, but as I say, who knows what any of us would do given such a situation," said Liza.

"I know exactly what you would do Liza," said Jamie. "You would die in the attempt to protect your children and it's not only a mother who would do that, I would do that also."

"Yes, I am confident that you both would, as would Amelia and I. It is difficult to understand how anyone could want to abuse their own child, it is distasteful, but unfortunately it happens quite often," said Wendell. "I'll think about whether Andraes should be told as I'm sure you both will also."

"I have to say that I will feel easier with Christina now that I know the true facts about her mother's instability and you are right, she does appear to be very sweet natured. I'm sure that the Colonel and Ada had a great deal to do with that and now that she will be under your influence, she will end up a very charming young lady," said Amelia.

They all then left to get changed for dinner and Liza was surprised to find Susan waiting to help her get ready.

"I didn't expect to see you this evening Susan," smiled Liza.

"I like to be busy and besides I'll start my time off tomorrow," said Susan. "Derek is up with the boys whilst they are getting ready for dinner, I'll see him tomorrow when I visit my mother. Christopher will also be there; I understand that he and Derek are getting on really well, but they both have been so concerned about us all, as have Mr Reece and April. In fact it seems that all the villagers have been worried."

"I'm glad that Christopher is getting on so well, no doubt I'll see him tomorrow. It's been such a long time since I saw everybody," said Liza.

Matthew knocked and looked in to tell her that he had arranged for Ernie to take Derek and Mrs Price home. Liza smiled at him and as always, they understood one another without speaking; he showed that he was delighted that she was home and that he had always known that she would be back.

Liza would have liked to soak in a hot bath, but she had no time, so she just washed, and Susan helped her dress for dinner and when she was ready, she found Mrs Frances bringing Christina and Bright Star up to their room. Susan said that she would help get them organised for bed, but Liza wanted to make sure that they were happily settled, so she went to their room with Susan.

Christina was not yet ready for bed, but Bright Star was smiling happily lying under her bedclothes whilst holding her two dolls. She looked contented and warm.

"It's a little early for you to be in bed Christina; what do you want to do now?" asked Liza.

"I think I will get into bed and read for a while," said Christina.

Andraes was ready for dinner, and he had come to say goodnight to his daughter. Liza left the room so that they could have some time together and Susan said that she would return to make sure Christina was settled. Liza saw that Jamie was ready and he was looking in her room for her and then he saw her and made his way to her so that they went down to the drawing room together, where they waited for everyone else to arrive.

The boys were dining with them that evening and really they were now old enough to join them for dinner every evening that they were home, but Liza had a feeling that they enjoyed eating down in the kitchen with Mrs Lambert surprising them with what their meal would be.

David and Grace were already there, and they were shortly joined by Miranda and Lucinda. The four boys walked in, and Liza and Jamie stared at their sons and Simon. They were immaculately groomed, and they all grinned at them knowing that they had gone to a great deal of bother to make their parents proud of them. They did not realise that Liza and Jamie were proud of them no matter how they were dressed.

Andraes joined them and last to arrive were Wendell and Amelia. Luckily nobody was superstitious as thirteen sat down to dinner.

The discussion over dinner came around to Bright Star and what she should now be called.

"I like her name as it is, but it won't be practical for her now that she lives here," said Liza. "We have thought of Stella which does actually mean Star in Italian."

"It's not as pretty a name as Bright Star," said Miranda.

Surprisingly David came up with the name Zara telling them that it meant Star in Arabic and he believed that going even further back in time it was also Hebrew for Star.

"I believe that it also means Princess in Russian," said Liza.

"That's quite a possibility," said Jamie. "It sounds nicer than Stella; we'll think about that, won't we Liza?"

Liza nodded and then continued asking the boys if they had meant that Richard and Nicholas were coming to stay for the weekend, and therefore so was Bella.

"Yes," said John, "and I believe the Duke has also said that he will be coming to see you."

"Anthony and Diana are calling tomorrow as are the Major and Jennifer, and I have a feeling that Joseph and Lily will also be visiting," said Miranda. "You are going to have a house full tomorrow, but I don't think that they will be staying. I know you would probably prefer to have some time to yourselves, but everyone is so pleased that you have at last returned safely that they want to see you."

"It's very kind of them all," said Liza. "So we don't have to make arrangements for anyone to stay tomorrow. I presume that Bella and the Duke will be arriving on Saturday.

"Well knowing both Bella and the Duke, it would probably be just as well to get their rooms ready tomorrow as they do tend to turn up without warning," said Miranda. "They have both visited on many occasions whilst you were away."

"Peter and Harry Turner are travelling over from Belfast and will be here sometime at the weekend," said Wendell.

"I presume that business is going well, Wendell," said Liza. "But we can discuss all that when hopefully I will have some time tomorrow."

"Yes Liza," said Wendell. "All is going well, but it will be good to be able to go through some documents with you; we've all missed talking to you about business."

"I have a lot to catch up on, not only for business but also for the household," said Liza. "Have you read your letters from home yet Simon?"

"No I thought I would do that later when I go to bed," smiled Simon and Liza thought that he would not be so happy when he read some of the content as she presumed that it would have been mentioned what had happened in the battle around Benson. She and Jamie had made light of it to the boys, but it was not up to them to tell others what to write in their letters.

The boys made it a very lively time for everyone. Andraes commented how he found it difficult to believe how grown-up Matthew, Simon and John were as the last time he had seen them had to be ten years ago and they were very little boys then.

The men stayed in the dining room whilst the ladies retired to the drawing room after dinner. Simon said that he would like to read his letters but before he left Liza gently said, "I'm afraid that both Paul Southern and Rufus Denton were killed in the battle around Benson. I know that they were both friends to all of us and even though James didn't know them, I'm sure that you all will appreciate his support."

"Of course," said James. "Simon has spoken of them both in the past, as have Matthew and John. I'll go up with them."

"Thank you, James," said Liza. "I don't want to intrude on you all, but if you need to ask me anything, I'll do my best to answer you. I'm sure that it will be mentioned in your letters Simon, but I felt it best to tell you so that it will not be too great a shock for you when you read them."

Matthew and John were already on their way to be with Simon, and James told Liza not to worry as he would make sure that they were alright, but he would come and get her if she was needed.

"It must have been a very difficult time for you Liza," said Amelia when the boys had left the room.

"Yes, it wasn't easy," said Liza and then she immediately changed the subject and asked if Amelia knew when Peter and Harry Turner would be arriving.

"I believe that they were aiming to arrive late tomorrow, and I know that during next week they are going to see how their London offices are progressing," said Amelia.

"That's interesting; I hope I can join them next week. Will Wendell also be inspecting it?" asked Liza.

"If he feels up to it then yes, he would like to see how it's getting along," said Amelia, who was well aware that Liza had changed the subject and so were Miranda and Grace.

The men came to join the ladies and Liza quietly told Jamie that Simon was reading his letters and she felt it prudent to tell the boys about Rufus and Paul.

"Yes, I suppose his letters will have that news, but even if they don't, they had to be told at some time," said Jamie.

"Although James didn't know them, he wanted to be with Simon and his brothers," said Liza.

Wendell and Amelia were the first to make their way to bed, followed shortly by Miranda, Lucinda, David and Grace going to their homes. Andraes said that he would look in on Christina and Bright Star, or Zara, if that is what she was going to be named.

As Liza and Jamie were preparing to go to their rooms, James led the other boys back into the drawing room. "We would all like to know what happened to Rufus and Paul and everyone else in the battle."

"Weren't you told what happened in your letters from home?" asked Jamie.

"My parents have said about Rufus and Paul, but Rachel says that you were with them both and that Rufus was a Confederate and Paul a Union soldier. Rachel says that you had them buried side by side," said Simon.

"That's what they wanted," said Liza. "Rufus was only a Confederate because of his place of birth and just before he died, he told me that he was in the wrong uniform, so I had him buried in his proper uniform. He and Paul died in their old quarters together. Paul died first and Rufus refused to allow his body to be taken away, so I stayed with them until Rufus finally went, and many people came to pay their respects to them both. There were many things that Rufus could have carried out, but he went against orders to save our lives. We would not be here if he had not stepped in and countermanded his superior's orders. He was right; he was wearing the wrong uniform, but he's not now and he and Paul are keeping one another company."

"Are they near our Daddy and little Meg?" asked Matthew.

"Yes, not too far away. Near enough to be looking after one another," said Liza quietly.

The boys were sitting silently, deep in thought.

"Nobody from town was hurt; they all looked after one another and they also looked after the wives and families from the fort," said Jamie. "Ben Webber was hurt, but not too badly. Your Uncle Sean was not hurt, neither was Bart Shaw. Greg Long and Sam Trower joined up after the battle, and Greg married Ellen. But I presume you have been told all that."

"Some of it," said Simon. "My father said that Colonel Western was looking after the fort; I thought he had retired."

"He had, but he came out of retirement to take care of the families at the fort as most of the men had orders to leave. When all the men had to finally join forces with others, he refused to abandon the post when the Confederate soldiers came to take over. His assistant also refused to leave but our friend Bandor arranged to have them spirited away to join the men, which infuriated the Confederate Colonel," smiled Liza.

"What your mother isn't saying is that she arranged for the Colonel and the Private to be spirited away and the Confederates seemed to think that it was the case, and they were not best pleased," smiled Jamie. "Is there anything else that you need to know now because if not we are very tired and would like to get some rest."

"We are really sorry about Rufus and Paul," said Matthew. "I hope nobody else that we know dies. There are some things that we would like to ask you, but tomorrow will be fine. I think it will take us a while to sleep tonight."

"Yes, it has been a strange day for us all. Try not to dwell too much on those who have died; they are very much at peace now. What we must do is concentrate on the living and now we have two little girls that we must take care of," said Liza.

"They'll need to be looked after. It must have been quite frightening for them leaving their homes and coming all this way to a strange country," said John. "Christina will be alright as she's older and she does have her father with her at the moment, but it must have been terrifying for Bright Star."

"Yes, it has been very strange for Bright Star, but she is smiling a great deal now," said Liza, pleased that they were talking about something other than the battle at Benson. "What do you all think of the name Zara for her? We can't really keep calling her Bright Star now that she is with us in England, although I think that name suits her."

"I think that it's a nicer name than Stella," commented Matthew and the others seemed to agree with him. Matthew smiled at his mother and nodded as he realised that there was much that she found difficult to talk about regarding her time in America. "We'll see you tomorrow," he said. "Goodnight and we're really pleased that you are both back with us safely."

The boys went back to their room leaving Liza and Jamie in the drawing room, where they stayed for a while enjoying the quietness as well as the closeness of one another.

"I doubt our boys will sleep well tonight," said Jamie. "Were Matthew and John very close to Rufus and Paul?"

"They both used to visit us on many occasions, as did Ben and Bart. They enjoyed going to the fort and playing cricket with the men. They were part of the Benson family, because that's what Benson was; it was a family and we all looked out for one another. We were all close," said Liza.

"I could see that when we were there," said Jamie. "I suppose Simon will be affected the most."

"I think that Matthew and John will be just as affected; Paul and Rufus were part of their happy childhood. James is very caring, and he will help them all a great deal," said Liza. "Hopefully when they go back to Cambridge on Monday, they will push their sadness to the backs of their minds. I daresay Nicholas and Richard will also help them this weekend."

"It seems that we will have a very busy time tomorrow and also at the weekend. I know it's very kind of everyone to want to visit us to welcome us back, but it would have been nice to settle back home without having to worry about guests," said Jamie.

"I know what you mean, but we'll survive and as you say, it is kind of everyone," said Liza. "I gather that the house has been full of guests since we left, so they don't need us to entertain them, they seem to do that quite well themselves."

"You look very tired Liza," said Jamie. "I think we should get some rest now."

"I'm afraid you look exactly the same," said Liza. "It's been a very tiring few months."

Susan was waiting for her when she got to her room; Liza said nothing about her not working because she knew that it would fall on deaf ears. She could hear Roberts in Jamie's room and Liza thought that he should also take time off and she knew that Jamie had told him that, but his attitude was probably the same as Susan's.

When Liza was ready and Susan had left, she listened for Roberts to leave Jamie's room and when he did, she picked up her lamp and made her way towards his bedroom and as she approached, the door opened, and Jamie welcomed her into his room and then into his bed.

461

"Did you hear me coming across?" asked Liza.

"No, I just guessed that you would be there and it's wonderful to get back to how we like our lives to be. There was a time when you seemed to be away from me, but I know you were just preoccupied and as concerned as I was at the situation we found ourselves in," said Jamie.

Liza was lying back with a contented grin on her face. "Your bed is so comfortable; I've missed it so much. Come on Jamie, let's enjoy being home."

***

Jamie awoke very early the following morning; he was warm and comfortable with Liza asleep with her head on his chest. Her shoulders were uncovered, and he pulled the bedclothes over her and lay back happy that they were home and his Liza was as she had been before the turmoil of the past months.

He thought about all the people who would be visiting that day and knew that they needed to see that they had returned safely. Liza moved slightly and he stroked her head and thought that although they would have a very busy day, they could stay as they were for at least another hour. He relaxed, closed his eyes, and contentedly went back to sleep.

They were both still asleep when Roberts knocked and entered; he drew back the curtains and only then realised that Liza was still in His Lordship's bed. He knew that they spent their nights together, but normally she had returned to her own room by that time. He decided to leave the room and return in half an hour.

To see two such people so happy with one another inspired Roberts and he knew that he never wanted to leave the household. It had been a different story when the previous Lady Edgeworth had been in residence. Roberts had never been aware of Lady Evelyn enjoying his Lordship's bed, but he knew that there had to be a time when they had got together as there was no doubt over young master James' parentage as he was looking more like his father every day.

Liza stirred again and woke Jamie who realised that Roberts had been in and opened the curtains. Jamie looked down and was relieved to see that Liza was well covered with the bedclothes. He called her gently and said that it would be a good idea if she put her nightdress on and if he put his nightshirt on.

"Roberts has already been in and has obviously left discreetly; no doubt he will be back shortly," said Jamie.

"That's a shame, I feel very comfortable and could stay like this all day," yawned Liza.

"We have a great many people visiting today and tomorrow and all want to make sure that we are really here," said Jamie.

"Yes, I had better get up and start the day," said Liza. "I wonder who will be here for lunch and who will be here for dinner. I also would like to see Adam, April and Christopher at some time today."

Reluctantly Liza climbed out of bed, donned her nightdress and dressing gown; she kissed Jamie on the cheek and made her way to the door where she turned and grinned at Jamie, who was smiling as he watched her leave.

Her room was warm as the fire had already been made up that morning. She sat in a chair next to it, enjoying the warmth as Susan came in with her breakfast tray. So her busy day was starting as she heard the water being brought up for her bath, which she would have liked to have spent a great deal of time in, but she could not afford more than a short while in it. She sighed and moved to her table for her breakfast.

"You told me that you would be starting your time off today," Liza smiled at Susan.

"I'll be going just before lunchtime," said Susan. "Derek will also be there then." Liza nodded and concentrated on eating her breakfast.

Within the hour she could be found making her way down to see Mrs Lambert and Mrs Frances as she had to be sure that they were able to cater for an unknown number of people who could be with them at lunchtime, and perhaps also at dinner.

"I know that Mr Peter and Mr Harry will be with us this evening for a few days," said Mrs Frances.

"Apparently the Ffoulks family are visiting today, but I don't believe that they are staying, although I'm not sure about that," said Liza. "The Major and Mrs Styles and Mr and Mrs Joseph Fuller will also be here at some time today."

"When are the Duke and Duchess of Berkshire arriving?" asked Mrs Frances and Liza just stared at her and slightly shrugged her shoulders.

"I know that Mr Nicholas and Mr Richard won't be with us until tomorrow, but I can only assume that the Duke and Duchess will be with them then, although I have known them to arrive at any time," said Liza.

"I'll get all their rooms ready now and that will leave time for us to make up other rooms should the Ffoulks family decide that they are also staying," said Mrs Frances and she went to make her arrangements.

Liza looked at Mrs Lambert. "I'm afraid that I have no idea how many you may be catering for at lunch today, Mrs Lambert."

"I already have an enormous beef stew on the go, and I can make as many dumplings as necessary when we know the number who will be here lunchtime. It may not be very elegant, but it will most certainly be tasty. We're in the

463

process of making several fruit pies and all we will have to do is roll out the pastry when we know how many will be here," said Mrs Lambert.

"I wish I could tell you who will be here for dinner, but I have absolutely no idea," said Liza. "Definitely there will be fifteen, but there could be as many as twenty-five."

"We'll have to sacrifice some of our poultry which will be easy to cook and if we cook too much, we can do a great deal with cold chicken tomorrow," said Mrs Lambert. "I'll get Mr Lambert to organise that. We have plenty of potatoes which I'll do something interesting with. We will have to have some carrots and I am going to use some white cabbage which I will lightly cook with some vinegar so that it stays crunchy and of course the stuffing for the chicken will make it all very tasty."

"What shall we start with?" asked Liza.

"I'll make a very thin consommé with all the usual trimmings," said Mrs Lambert. "For dessert I have plenty of plums which I will cook and sit on a cake base soaked in juice in individual dishes and I'll drizzle a sweet white sauce over them. I'm afraid most of it will have to be hastily arranged, but nobody will starve."

"I'm sure it will all be excellent Mrs Lambert," said Liza. "And we'll have to do it all again tomorrow."

"Tomorrow we will know exactly who we are catering for, and I have a spit roast already organised for that, but I'll speak to you later about what else we need," said Mrs Lambert. Liza smiled and nodded and for once felt that she was not up to the tasks that were being asked of her; she would have loved being home with just her family. She wondered why she felt tired as she had slept well that night and she supposed it was the strain of the past few months.

Liza went to find Jamie who was catching up on the news of the past months in the library with Wendell and Andraes, all of whom were concentrating on reading the newspapers. Liza smiled recognising that happily nothing had changed.

"Good morning gentlemen," said Liza.

"Morning Liza," they choroused.

"I shall be away from home for the day," said Liza. "You'll be able to deal with all our guests, won't you Jamie?"

"Yes," mumbled Jamie.

Wendell and Andraes were now looking over the top of their papers.

"That's good," said Liza. "I'll be back in time for lunch tomorrow."

There was silence for a moment and then Jamie's newspaper dropped to his lap. "What?" he said.

464

Andraes was looking puzzled, but Wendell was smiling broadly. "I've missed your humour Liza," said Wendell.

By now Jamie was also smiling, "What is it that you really want to say Liza?"

"I want to go into the village for a short while before our guests arrive. I want to see April and hopefully Adam and Christopher also. Do you want to come with me?" asked Liza.

"Yes, I'd like to do that, but do we have the time?" said Jamie.

"If we leave within the next half hour we should manage it," said Liza.

"I'll organise the carriage," said Jamie.

"I've already done that," smiled Liza. "Hendry's waiting at the front."

They were on their way in a very short time and Jamie was happy to have Liza to himself in their carriage.

"Is there a reason that you wish to see Adam, apart from just enjoying his company?" asked Jamie.

"Yes, I want to discuss sending Christina to school in the New Year," said Liza. "I can deal with Zara's education until she's old enough to attend school."

"Don't you want to employ a governess for Christina?" asked Jamie.

"No, I don't want to isolate her from other children," said Liza. "She's used to attending school in Benson, and I would like her to make friends with children of her own age. Our boys used to attend school until they came back from America, but they were lucky to have one another when they moved here with James, and they also had Derek. Christina will only have Zara and there's quite a difference in their ages."

"I suppose it could be a little frightening for her going to a strange school," said Jamie.

"I'll make sure that she meets up with other children on many occasions before she starts," said Liza.

Adam was making his way to the headmaster's study when they arrived to visit him. He ushered them in and said how delighted he was to see them now that they were safely home.

"Have you seen April yet?" he asked.

"She's next on our list to visit," said Liza.

They discussed a little of what had gone on in America and Adam told them how worried everyone had been, and he reiterated what they all had thought of the stupidity of trying to get Britain to take sides in the American conflict by stopping them from leaving the country.

"I suppose it became very disturbing for you both," said Adam.

"It has become very disturbing for many on both sides of the war in America, and it's going to get worse, sadly," said Liza.

Adam said that he had heard that they had brought some children safely away from the conflict.

"Yes," said Jamie. "We have two girls with us, but it is the eldest who we would like to enrol in your school."

"You're not going to employ a governess for her then?" asked Adam.

"She's used to going to school and mixing with other children," said Liza. "I'm also going to make sure that she meets some of those she will be learning with."

"Well, you could start with the Wallace girls. The two elder ones have just started school. Ken has managed to find someone to look after the two younger ones during the day," said Adam.

"They'll enjoy being with others. I noticed that they do talk to the village children," said Liza. "It will be nice that they will already be there when Christina starts. I'll make sure that they meet before then."

"They will probably be at the staff Christmas lunch which isn't so very far off now," said Adam.

"Of course they will, but it would be better if they meet before that," said Liza.

They then gave Adam her name and age and Liza said that she appeared to be quite bright, but she would leave that for her teachers to find out.

"How's young Christopher doing?" asked Jamie.

"He's fitted in very well and the children like him, as they do Derek, but the way things are going I will have to soon employ another teacher as the lists for those attending next September are growing," said Adam.

They then made their way to April's house and were surprised to find that all the boys' horses were tied up outside and they could be heard all talking at once in her kitchen. It took two knocks for her to hear them above the noise and when they finally were invited in, they found their four boys munching their way through cakes that April had obviously made for Adam.

"We were telling April that we have Christina and Zara now living with us," said Matthew.

"Your cakes were lovely thank you April," said James.

"We have to visit Mr and Mrs Rogers now," said John, "then the bakers and finally Mrs Price. We're having a very busy morning."

"Bye April, we'll see you soon," said Simon and they all left and headed for the Inn.

Liza and Jamie watched them go, both thinking that this was their way of working through the sadness that they had felt over Rufus and Paul's deaths.

"Do you think that their stomachs ever feel full?" commented Jamie to nobody in particular.

"I'm sorry, but I'm afraid I have no cakes to offer you," said a resigned April.

"We should have come to you first, before going to Adam and then we might have beaten the boys to all your cakes," smiled Jamie.

April asked about everyone she knew in New York and after a while Jamie and Liza left to visit Mrs Price, and they managed to get there before the boys arrived. Mrs Price was going to look after Ken Wallace's two younger children whilst the older ones went to school. She didn't have to go out to work any longer; she worked at various tasks from home and now that Christopher paid her some rent and Derek and Susan were working, she did not have to work every second of the day, she therefore had time to make sure that Cora and Libby Wallace were cared for, and all the Wallace children would have their evening meal with her. What Ken Wallace was going to do for his meal Liza thought it best not to ask?

"You're still going to be very busy Mrs Price," said Liza.

"Yes, but it's much easier work. I no longer have to worry about where the next meal is coming from. Things have been getting easier for me over the last few years and now I can sleep well every night, and that's thanks to you both," said Mrs Price.

"We can't take credit for that Mrs Price," said Jamie. "You have worked your way up to this point and you are still working hard, but it's much more pleasurable work for you. Any task that you enjoy won't seem like work."

"Christopher is a really nice young man and he and Derek get on very well; they are both a pleasure to have around," said Mrs Price.

They left to call in on Mr and Mrs Rogers and they could see Susan coming to visit her mother and the boys leaving the bakers obviously having sampled their wares, and they called out to Susan and then shouted to Liza and Jamie saying that they were now on their way home.

"We must get back soon," said Jamie but they still managed to spend a little time with Mr and Mrs Rogers.

On their way back Jamie observed that their family seemed to have taken over the village for a while.

"I know," said Liza. "But I wanted to see and be seen by those who have been worried about us. They have been very supportive to the family whilst we've been away, and I do appreciate their concern."

"Well no doubt you'll plan something for them," said Jamie.

"I'll try to organise something for New Year's Eve and see the New Year in with family and friends," said Liza.

Jamie looked at her and asked her if she was sure she was up to that. He did not mention his concern because it was the anniversary of Patrick's death, but he knew that she was well aware of what he was thinking.

"Yes, we will probably be busy at Christmas again. I have no idea who will be with us this year, but I know it won't just be our family; it never is. Our guests will presumably stay until after the New Year, so they will already be here and those from the village don't have far to travel. I'd better see what Harper, Mrs Frances and Mrs Lambert think about it, hopefully they will be able to cope."

"Don't wear yourself out Liza, you've had a very difficult time recently," said Jamie.

"We've both had a difficult time recently, and so has everyone else who have been sitting at home waiting and worrying. It will give everyone something to look forward to," said Liza. "So we can have a family and close friends Christmas, and New Year will be with absolutely everybody. We have a few weeks to rest before Christmas."

"If this weekend is anything to go by; we will not have any time to rest until well into the New Year," said Jamie.

They turned into their drive and were followed by Anthony's carriage; so their weekend entertaining had begun.

***

There was a whirl of activity throughout Friday; it felt to Liza as if everyone was talking at the same time. Peter and Harry Turner arrived, and Liza was delighted to see that Edward had also made the journey. Annalise and Arthur had agreed to stay with Nicole and little Edward whilst Edward was away. Mrs Frances quickly made up a room for him.

Liza still found it surprising how much Harry Turner looked like James Marchant, but both Wendell and Amelia now seemed to be used to his appearance. They had obviously seen him on many occasions whilst Liza and Jamie were away.

Lily and Joseph spent some hours with them, and Liza thought how wonderful it was to see all the Fuller boys together again, and Wendell and Amelia smiled throughout the afternoon.

The Major and Jennifer were also in their element and Liza felt that it was such a happy gathering of people who were very much like family to her, and the boys were delighted to see Edward, Peter and Joseph, although John was immediately drawn towards Peter.

Anthony's family left in time to reach their home for Thomas' bedtime and the Major and Jennifer, and Lily and Joseph, needed to return to their Children's

Homes before nightfall, which meant that the only extra guests that evening were Edward, Peter and Harry Turner.

Although the Berkshires would be arriving the following day, Wendell and Peter requested a Company meeting and it was to include Harry Turner, however Wendell wanted to see Liza privately prior to the meeting.

After dinner Wendell quietly asked if he could use Liza's study so that he could talk to Edward and both she and Jamie assumed that he was going to tell Edward about Felicity's parentage.

Liza sat next to Amelia who confirmed that Wendell had decided that telling Edward sooner rather than later was the best course of action, especially as he had already been surprised to find that Andraes was with them. He had yet to meet Christina and they hoped that this knowledge would allay any awkward situations.

"I hope that Edward truly understands what his father is telling him; he's really led a very sheltered life. He is not what could be considered a man of the world like his father and Peter," said Amelia.

"Oh I think he will immediately understand and realise what a sad situation was created by a very evil man all those years ago," said Liza. "It has had such a knock-on effect on many people."

Liza then asked Harry how Mrs Edwards, and Mr and Mrs Grouch were.

"They have been very worried about you," said Harry. "They seemed to think that America has never been the safest of places for you. They were so pleased when I could give them the news that you were safely in New York and when I followed that up with when you were travelling back to England, Mrs Edwards and Mrs Grouch shed a tear, and I can't be sure that Mr Grouch didn't also."

Wendell and Edward finally joined everyone again and Liza noticed that Edward's normally jovial demeanour was missing.

"You're looking very tired Liza," said Grace. "It's been a very busy day for you, and tomorrow is going to be just as busy. I'll come over in the morning and see what I can do to help you. We don't want you getting ill, especially with Christmas looming."

"Thank you, Grace. I have a meeting tomorrow morning, but I would be grateful if you could sort out all the letters we have received welcoming us back home," said Liza.

"Do we have many?" asked Jamie.

"Yes, and I have a feeling that many more will be arriving shortly," said Liza. "People have been so kind and thoughtful."

The boys were about to make their way to bed and Liza wished that she was doing the same.

"I think I will go up too," said Edward. "That is if you will excuse me."

"Of course Edward," said Liza. "We can catch up with one another tomorrow and all the time that you are with us."

Edward came over to her and put his arms around her and kissed her. Slowly and thoughtfully he made his way to his room.

"Is Edward alright?" asked Miranda.

"Yes, he has a great deal on his mind and of course is a little worried about Nicole and the birth of his second child. You know that he does worry unnecessarily about many things," smiled Liza. "He'll be right as rain tomorrow when he's had a good night's sleep."

Gradually everyone left either for their homes or to their rooms, but it was noticed by Liza and Jamie that Wendell and Amelia made no move to leave.

"Have you something that you wish us to know, Wendell?" asked Jamie.

"I wanted to tell you about my meeting with Edward," said Wendell. "It took him a short while to understand what I was telling him, even though he has come across situations like that during the course of his involvement with our charity. I think that he never believed that it could have happened to someone that he knew and that the result of that unseemly association he had married. He didn't blame either Ada or the Colonel, although he did say, as we all have done, that Felicity should never have been allowed to marry."

"It would have been difficult to have stopped such a marriage, and I truly believe that Ada and the Colonel felt that Felicity was quite normal. She had a few strange habits but nothing that could have made them think that she was mentally unstable," said Liza. "Edward did truly love her at that time, and it seemed as though she felt the same for him. I believe that she did love him, and I can tell you that she mostly acted quite normally and happily until just before they both left for New York. She seemed a little disturbed after the wedding."

"Until now Edward had never been able to understand why Felicity had acted in the manner that she had, not only to him but also to you Liza, and to many others. He did realise that she had strange thoughts on occasion, but he put that down to being influenced by Evelyn. He often thought that she was led astray by Evelyn as he realised that Felicity was not very bright," said Wendell.

"Does he feel that Andraes should be told of Felicity's parentage?" asked Jamie.

"I'm afraid Edward has left that decision to us," said Wendell. "He did comment that if he is told then he will always be looking for instability in his daughter, possibly where there is none."

"He's right," said Liza. "I think that as Andraes is leaving her in our care and we already know the truth, then why add to his worries, especially as he loves his daughter, and it is going to be difficult for him returning to his homeland without her."

"There's no point in worrying him unnecessarily," said Amelia. "You are her guardian Liza, so the decision should really be yours."

"I believe that it would be right to keep such information to ourselves and only tell Andraes should Christina show signs of instability in the future and seeing how she is at the moment, I'm not envisioning any difficulties. She cares for Bright Star in such a way that she is only showing a nice side to her nature," said Liza.

"I'll tell Edward of our decision first thing tomorrow morning," said Wendell.

"We'd better let you two get to your beds," said Amelia. "You have a busy weekend ahead of you."

Later when Liza and Jamie were alone, Jamie commented that he thought that the decision not to tell Andraes was the correct one.

"She is perfectly stable and Andraes could treat her as different if he thought that there was a mental problem within the family. She is definitely not showing any signs of abnormality and I believe that if we treat her as any other child then she will never have a problem," said Jamie. "I do wonder why we seem to always have to take such responsibilities on our shoulders."

"It does seem that way, doesn't it," said Liza. "We must now put all this out of our minds and make a happy home for Christina until such time as she can return to Ada and the Colonel."

***

Amelia was right; they had a very busy weekend. Liza was awake early and sought out Wendell so that they could have their meeting.

"I wanted to talk to you about the future Liza," said a very serious Wendell.

"I have a feeling that this is something that I would prefer not to hear," said Liza.

Wendell gave her a smile which he hoped would allay her fears. "I have not been told that I am yet dying but I have to consider what will happen to the Company when the time comes when I am no longer around. I have reached an age when I must be practical about such things, and as you know I have already had one stroke and am therefore susceptible to another."

"I don't want to think about a time without you," said Liza and she felt tears welling up within her.

"Well I'm not planning to go just yet, but I want to be sure that the Company will continue to succeed without me and that my family will benefit from everything that I have worked for throughout my life. I know you have said that your shares will go to Edward, Peter and Joseph when your time comes; are you still contemplating carrying that out?" asked Wendell.

Liza frowned at the question but answered that it was still the case and was written into her Will.

"What I want to do is give a few of my shares to each of my sons, but I want to bequeath the bulk of my shares to you Liza as I believe that you should have the casting vote. There will always be major decisions to make, and I can see that both Edward and Joseph have difficulty in making such decisions, and Peter would want someone to bounce his ideas off, but he's not ready to take total control," said Wendell.

"But Peter does already take control of Marchant & Fuller," said Liza.

"He does on the day to day running of the Company, but on major decisions he always defers to me," said Wendell. "The fact that you will eventually be leaving your shares to my boys makes what I am arranging the correct thing to do."

"Do they know what you are thinking of?" asked Liza.

"No, that will be up to you to sort out," smiled Wendell.

"Thank you, Wendell. I always get the worst jobs," smiled Liza. "Shall we talk about happier things?"

"What's on your mind Liza?" asked Wendell.

"How is Harry Turner getting on? I have glanced at some of his documentation and he appears to be very much his father's son. Is he settling into the Company without that chip on his shoulder?" asked Liza.

"I suppose Peter is the best one to answer that, but I have seen him at work and Peter does keep me well informed regarding his work. He has done some surprisingly clever deals with some very influential people. The chip on his shoulder never shows in business, but it must still be there as one never forgets an unhappy childhood," said Wendell. "His concern for you was genuine; I think I would have seen if it were otherwise. He is an asset to the Company, and I feel that Peter must have seen something unique in him which was why he was so insistent that we employ him."

"So it is felt that he is completely trustworthy and loyal to the Company and if, as you say, he was concerned for our welfare, then he seems to also have loyalties to our families," said Liza.

"You have something in mind don't you Liza," said Wendell, "and I think I know what it is."

"A long time ago I gave Edward, Peter and Joseph each one share in the Company. I also gave Kate two shares as she would have been married to a

Marchant if Frederick had not perished with James. I feel that it is only fair to give one share in the Company to the son of a Marchant."

"I can't tell you what to do with your shares; I can only advise," said Wendell.

"You can tell me Wendell as you know that it has been written that no shares can be sold without your permission," said Liza.

"I'm afraid that it hasn't been written anywhere that you have to defer to me regarding your shares; you had it written into the boys' shares and Kate's shares, but it was never written that I have to give you permission on what you do with yours," said Wendell.

"Then it should have been, and I would suggest that we rectify that situation immediately," said Liza. "What if I were to become insane and sign my shares over to totally unsuitable money grabbers? You must be protected from such an eventuality. And when the time comes that I inherit your shares, I will ensure that the other shareholders must be consulted should I decided to sell or give away my shares to an outsider."

"I think that will secure the Company for my family, and you know I consider you my family. Are you still not going to leave any of it to your family?" asked Wendell.

"None of them are either Marchants or Fullers, so I don't feel that they are entitled to any of it. If they want to work in the Company, and there is a genuine position for them, then they will earn a salary from that, but they will be well provided for with all else that I have," said Liza.

"I believe that they could be entitled to a part of the Company, but I bow to your judgement especially as I know that you have created a company that has just about eclipsed the wealth of Marchant & Fuller," said Wendell. "In answer to your query about a share for Harry Turner; I believe that he would appreciate it, although I don't think that he would immediately accept it as he would feel that you could be trying to buy his loyalty, which is unnecessary as he already has far more loyalty to us than even he realises."

"So I will have to be subtle when I organise it," smiled Liza.

Before they started their meeting with Edward, Peter and Harry more arrivals could be heard in the hallway and Liza assumed that it was Bella and her boys.

"You had better greet your other guests before we start our meeting," said Wendell. "We have plenty of time, but it would be useful to get business out of the way so that the rest of the weekend can be more relaxing for you."

Liza just smiled at him knowing that her weekend was going to be anything but relaxing. Jamie was already greeting Bella, Nicholas and Richard and when Liza joined him, she realised that the Duke and Douglas Carlton were also with them. The Duke's room was ready as she and Mrs Frances had thought that he may wish to spend the weekend with his family, but they had not realised that Douglas Carlton would also visit.

"I trust my arrival is not an imposition on you Liza," said Douglas, "but I really wanted to make sure that you had indeed arrived back safely."

"It's no imposition Douglas," said Liza. "It will just take a minute to get your room ready. We had wondered whether you would be joining us this weekend."

"You're always such a good hostess Liza; we really have missed you all these months," said Douglas. "Lady Redfern will be arriving shortly. She is coming directly from the Palace as she is not on duty this weekend and I know that she was anxious to see you both. I also know that the Queen and Prince Albert have shown concern regarding your problems in America, but she will tell you all about that herself."

Jamie came to the rescue by ushering all their guests into the drawing room which allowed Liza to organise refreshments for everyone and to arrange with Mrs Frances that rooms were made ready for Douglas Carlton and Lady Redfern. She also needed to make sure that Mrs Lambert knew the number of people she was now catering for.

She then joined them all in the drawing room for a while before excusing herself so that she could have her business meeting. Wendell, Edward, Peter and Harry also joined Liza in her study.

"Have you the time to go through some figures with us Liza?" asked Wendell.

"I have Wendell. We have planned this meeting for this morning. I shall enjoy my guests later, but I had not planned for several of them to be staying. However they all know that I have business commitments and they also know that our staff are superb and know how to make everyone comfortable without my standing over them all the time," said Liza.

They spent time going over figures and discussing the London premises that Peter and Harry had in mind for the investment brokerage business. It was decided that Liza would visit it after the weekend. The next topic was how Marchant & Fuller were going to survive the war in America.

"The shipping side of our company cannot take sides," said Wendell, "although we will have to take care that any shipments to either side will have to be prepaid. I believe that we could find that goods going to the south could be stopped and taken by the north; in fact that has already happened. I have heard that the southern states' navy are sailing nearer to our shores to create their own blockade. We must also be well aware that our vessels could be requisitioned as was Andraes' ship."

"Daltons is beginning to reap the rewards of war, unfortunately," said Liza. "But we always knew that would happen if the threatened war ever started. We are in partnership with the American government and that government is the Northern Union government; so I'm afraid we are unable to sit on the fence as far as that enterprise is concerned. Daltons has become even more profitable for us at this moment. Obviously if the war ends up in favour of the south then we could lose everything in that area, although they would need people who know how to run such a vast enterprise, so we could retain some input there."

"I'm concerned about the American banking outlets," said Peter. "I'm getting very little feedback on them at present. Do you know anything Liza?"

"I naturally was in touch with Mr Pembroke in Benson and there were one or two people panicking and requesting cash withdrawals. Also I arranged for the manager of our New York head office, Mr Hodges, to visit me several times whilst I was in New York. He has had the same requests from diverse people, but what he has also noticed is that there are clients that you would think would be southern sympathisers who are depositing goods and cash money in safety deposit boxes. They are not opening accounts; they are just using the security of the strong room before they return to their homes in the south. Many northerners are doing the same as they feel that their homes could be destroyed, and they want to know that they have some security for the future. It would appear that many people believe that the north will prevail. Whatever happens we will still own the premises. I can only tell you what is surmised in the south and that is that the plantation owners are using up money to keep going. They have warehouses full of cotton, tobacco and sugar that they are unable to get to factories either in the north or across to us here in England," said Liza.

"Our southern M & F banks will become like pawn brokers until they run out of money; they'll have a great deal of valuable goods that will eventually become useful, but I wouldn't like to guarantee that we will not be robbed should this war go on for any length of time and people become desperate," continued Liza.

"It is all sounding very worrying for us," said Edward.

"It is worrying Edward," said Liza. "But there are always winners in every war, and I think you will find that Daltons will allow us to keep our heads above water. We made a great deal of money shipping vast amounts of cotton to our mills in England. It was a clever move for the factories to stockpile. Whilst I was in Charleston I heard that the plantation owners were told to burn their cotton on the dockside because the generals thought that England would support the south when the factories were desperate for the raw material. They had not done their sums correctly and if they had they would have known that it will be years before our factories run out of stocks. I'm afraid I broke my own rule on confidentiality and told Charles Enderby to keep his stocks intact and the reason why."

"Our charity is going to suffer, as we normally get a great deal of support from America, not only in money but also in sending children to be cared for there," said Edward.

"You're right," said Peter. "Somehow we will have to make our Homes more self-sufficient than they are already and also focus on attempting to get the older children trained and placed in apprenticeships. Hard as it sounds, we will have to take fewer children, but how we are going to do that, I do not have the answer to that."

"You must remember that we have a great deal of support from the English aristocracy; some of whom are here today. America takes many of our children and gives them the opportunity of a better life; it would be difficult to now give them that opportunity in a hostile environment. So we will all have to think again to come up with an alternative solution," said Liza.

"I know that all your Bradley & Company holdings here and in Italy are working well Liza," said Wendell, "but what is happening to them in America?"

"The land and premises that I bought in and around Daltons is producing well and I don't think that I am going to have a problem there. The other areas around and in Benson and Harris Town are a different story, although whilst I was there I arranged that the people from the towns form a co-operative and work the land so that they can at least feed themselves. The schoolteacher from Harris was going to hold classes in the mornings and then help to farm with the children and their parents later in the day. There are some old houses that they could stay at whilst they were working. They were all quite enthusiastic about it. Benson is already a little more self-sufficient and their need will not be as great, although that could change. The land and the properties which are owned by Bradley & Company are relatively secure, unless they are burned to the ground, but they will need further investment when the war is over. Let us hope that it doesn't go on too long. I'm lucky that my investments are greater in other parts of the world, so I can ride the storm for some time to come and of course we do know the people who should be able to get limited supplies to those who need them."

"May I ask what goods are being manufactured in Daltons?" asked Harry. "Although I suppose that is none of my business, but I am curious."

Liza let Wendell answer that. "You work for the Company Harry, so you have every right to know what that Company deals in. At present Daltons is concerned with all that has to do with railway links in America, but also one of the factories is producing armaments and another is taking business away from our factories in England by producing the material for uniforms. Also leather is required for saddles and bricks for buildings. Tents to keep the armed forces at least a little dry. All forms of revolutionary machinery are being invented and I can say that whatever is needed we can arrange it. But Daltons is still growing, and we are continuing to build the factories."

"So what you are really saying is that we could lose out considerably on our main shipping industry and our banking section could eventually suffer, but it seems that we may well make up that shortfall with the Daltons enterprise," said Harry.

"As we have already said, there are always winners in every war, and I am not referring to the opposing sides," said Liza. "Unfortunately there are also those who will act unscrupulously and take from those who can least afford it. I saw a little of that when I was over there and as I have also said, I am concerned about the security of our banks."

Harry gave a small smile and said, "Well I suppose it is down to me to help recoup any losses with our Brokerage business."

"Indeed it is Harry," smiled Liza. "And I believe that by you studying what is happening in America and having some insight into how the war is progressing will give you the ammunition you need to invest or not at the right time."

"There are places worthy of studying other than America," smiled Harry.

"But every war creates wealth for those who are prepared to take a chance, especially if they are able get the best advice available," said Liza.

"One day I would like to see Daltons. I would also like to discuss the various aspects of all the factories. You say that you have land there. What are you using it for?" asked Harry.

"Beef and agriculture; we do have some other animals, but it is mainly cattle," said Liza. "We'll see how the London office takes shape and of course how volatile America is and perhaps you could look at travelling there in the spring."

"That would be interesting," said Harry. "At least I am not well known enough to be kidnapped and held to ransom."

"You had better get to your guests now, we can finish here. Will you be free to go to the new London offices next week Liza?" asked Wendell.

"Yes, the boys will be going back to university on Monday and most of my house guests will be leaving on that day also, except Bella. I never know when she is leaving, but she knows I have commitments," said Liza.

Lady Redfern arrived as the meeting broke up and Liza joined Jamie in welcoming her. She kissed Liza warmly expressing how pleased she was to see her home safely. She was ushered into the drawing room where everyone else was relaxing. She was introduced to Andraes who was the only person that she had not previously met. Liza therefore assumed that she had visited on occasion during their absence.

It was lunchtime and Liza had arranged that everyone was to help themselves and sit where they liked; she had also insisted that Christina and Zara joined them.

"Do you think that they will both be a little shy?" Jamie had asked.

"Yes, they probably will be, but they will have to get used to such gatherings in the future. I'll make sure that Zara is sitting next to me with Christina on her other side and Andraes next to his daughter. I know the boys will make sure that they feel happy," said Liza.

Liza brought the two girls into the dining room with Zara still clasping her wooden doll. Liza led them to the table with the food and she handed Christina a plate and took one for Zara. Mrs Frances helped Christina to what she wanted, and Liza spent time asking Zara what she would like to eat, but she was too shy to choose, so Liza made suggestions and put food on her plate as she nodded to what she would like. Andraes walked back to the table with his daughter, and Liza led Zara to the chair next to Christina and lifted her onto it whilst Mrs Frances brought some food for Liza.

It was a happy carefree lunchtime, and some were surprised to see Liza helping Zara to cut up her food and gently talking to her, sometimes in English and sometimes in Cherokee when she felt it was too difficult for Zara to understand what was happening.

Matthew and Simon made a point of sitting opposite them and talked to both Christina and Zara, putting them both at ease. Liza smiled and nodded her appreciation to them both.

Lady Redfern appeared to be watching closely and Liza assumed that it was because she had never heard the Cherokee language spoken before. Edward smiled at Liza and sat next to Andraes, so it was assumed that they had buried their differences. Edward had always understood how Christina had come about, but up until that point they had always kept a distance between one another.

"I always enjoy these relaxed lunchtimes," said Douglas Carlton and the Duke nodded his agreement. "You both know how to make people feel very welcome," he said to Liza and Jamie.

As always Peter made his way towards Grace and John followed him and made sure he sat with him; Richard, Nicholas and James entertained Wendell, Amelia and Harry. Bella was deep in conversation with David, Miranda and Lucinda. Jamie sat at the head of his table and smiled as he watched everyone enjoying themselves as he also welcomed these lunchtimes.

It was a question-and-answer time in the drawing room after lunch and Liza let Jamie answer most of them. When the questions got around to the battle outside Benson, Liza excused herself saying that she wanted to check on the girls and make sure that all was in order for their evening meal. All eyes were on her as she left the room and when she had left, the eyes turned towards Jamie.

"There are some things that are just too difficult and upsetting to talk about. We both experienced things that nobody should see and Liza more so than me," said Jamie.

"Sometimes it helps to talk about them," said Lady Redfern.

"I looked after the wounded," said Jamie. "And some of those wounds are too difficult to describe."

"Our mother looked after the dying," said Matthew starkly.

"I had no idea that she had told you that Matthew," said a slightly annoyed Jamie.

"She didn't, and she wouldn't," he said. "But I know my mother and I know that she has ways of taking the fear away from the dying. She did it for our daddy, and I know that she did it for my godfather. She also did it for Rachel's brother and I'm sure she did it for Uncle Paul and Uncle Rufus, and probably many others during the Benson battle. She will not talk about it, but they were all lucky that she was with them, they were no longer afraid of dying."

Everyone was silently staring at Matthew, apart from John and Simon who were nodding in agreement as they had seen it happen in the past.

Suddenly David broke the silence. "She therefore has a unique talent, but it is too much of a pressure for one person. No wonder she does not want to talk about it. You are right Jamie; you have both seen things that nobody should have done and probably the best way to deal with it is to get back to a normal life in a loving household such as this one."

"Is it true that Liza threatened to kill herself," asked Lucinda. "I heard that Roberts and Susan were talking to our butler about it."

"I really don't want to talk about this Lucinda," said Jamie. "All I will say is that anything that Liza threatened was to save the lives of the rest of us. She would not contemplate suicide for any other reason."

"What are we all doing for Christmas?" asked Amelia skilfully changing the subject.

"I hope that you and Wendell will be with us again this year," said Jamie.

"You know that we love spending Christmas with you Jamie, but we have been away from Belfast for most of this year. We spent our time here whilst you were away and I know that Edward, Nicole and little Edward would like us to be with them," said Amelia.

"That's a shame; you know that we will miss you. You are our family, the boys will miss you," said Jamie.

"Perhaps you could come to Belfast for Christmas," said Wendell. "It's a while since you spent the holiday there."

"We'll see what Liza thinks," said Jamie. "We have a number of people to take with us if we do decide to go."

"We'll miss you if you do go," said Douglas.

"Well you can always join us," said Jamie and then thought that perhaps he should not have said it as it would be nice just to have family with them for Christmas.

The rest of the weekend went smoothly with everyone enjoying the company and whatever happened in America was not mentioned again.

On the Monday Jamie and the Duke took the boys back to their university, Douglas and Lady Redfern left and Bella had a couple of appointments that she needed to keep.

Wendell and Amelia decided that they would return to Belfast with Edward and Peter at the end of the week; Harry would be staying for a further week when he felt that all the work on the offices would be completed, he had staff lined up to begin the London enterprise after the New Year. Andraes still had ten days before he was leaving for Greece and Liza knew that he was not looking forward to leaving Christina, and she was sure that the feeling would be mutual.

Liza still had to view the new offices and they set out to see them early on the Tuesday morning. The premises were quite impressive, and Harry told her that he had created an office especially for her whenever she needed it. He had a couple of people to interview that day, so Wendell, Edward, Peter and Liza left him and called on a couple of businesses that they had contacts with and also visited the London docks where their shipping offices were. Liza also called on the Company lawyer.

When they returned home Liza had some correspondence to attend to and when Grace had left for her home, Harry sought her out.

"You haven't said what you thought of the offices Liza," said Harry.

"I'm sorry, I thought I had shown my approval and I will find my office very useful on occasion. I suppose you will be spending more time in London than in Belfast when everything is up and running," said Liza. "You know you can live here with us when that time comes."

"I realise that you have more than enough room for me, but it would be more convenient to get rooms nearer the offices and perhaps I may come here for weekends. I will of course also have to travel back to Belfast regularly," said Harry.

"I presume you have a reliable deputy already in Belfast, and I assume you will also have one in London. Do you have someone in mind?" asked Liza.

"Yes, I have very good cover in Belfast, but I have yet to find someone for London, however I'm sure that will come with time," said Harry.

"It would be better if we had a Marchant & Fuller shareholder in charge of the London operation, it would make our Bankers have more respect for what we are doing," said Liza to a shocked looking Harry.

Liza continued, "Some years ago, just after your father died, I gave the Fuller boys each a share in Marchant & Fuller and also two shares to Frederick's fiancé. I was left some shares in James' Will and his son, Frederick, was to have the bulk of them but Wendell's shares had to be increased so that he would have the controlling interest. It was also written that should Frederick predecease James or die without issue, all shares allocated to him were to revert to me."

"Wendell did not think that I should divest myself of any of them, but I felt that I was not entitled to such a bequest. James had already made adequate provision for me. I do not feel that James ever made adequate provision for you or your mother. He may have ensured your education, but he did not ensure that your mother kept a roof over your head. He should also have acknowledged that he had you as a son. It may sound strange to you, but I know that he is well aware that he was wrong. Therefore I want to treat you as I treated the Fuller boys; they are the sons of a founder of the Company, as are you."

"Are you making me a shareholder?" asked an astonished Harry.

"I already have done so," said Liza as she handed the documentation to him. "I trust you have no problem in accepting this."

He took the share documentation and stared at it. "When I came for my interview, you told me that there was never a possibility that I would have a share in Marchant & Fuller. What made you change your mind?"

"I haven't had the opportunity to study your work for the past months, but I had seen your dedication prior to that, and it is obvious that that dedication is still there. I had a chance to review many decisions that I have made over the years and yours was one of them," said Liza.

"Does Wendell approve of your decision?" asked Harry.

"Whereas you would have to get his approval if you ever wished to divest yourself of your share, I do not, but he was not against my decision. In fact I believe he thinks that it is very fair, and he is looking forward to working with you on that level, as am I," said Liza.

"I can normally think of something to say, but I am lost for words, apart from thank you," said Harry.

"Well it's only one share, but it does give you a voice at board meetings which, as you are running an important section of the Company, is quite essential," said Liza.

"Do Edward, Peter and Joseph know that you have done this?" asked Harry.

"Yes, Wendell informed them over the weekend; they are quite good at keeping a confidence," smiled Liza.

"I think I'll go to my room for a while; I'll see you at dinner. I'm not sure how I feel, all I know is that I feel different and that's better," said Harry.

"Good," said Liza. "I'll see you at dinner."

Chapter 14

The house seemed very quiet. Andraes, who was their final guest, had left that morning for his journey to Greece as he needed to be there in time for Christmas. Christina was very upset, and Liza was spending a great deal of time with her and Zara.

Jamie was taking the opportunity to visit the various farms on his Estate with his overseer. Grace was working her way through the various invitations that had been received as well as the letters from well-wishers regarding their safe return.

Liza had managed to calm Christina down and it was wonderful to see Zara trying to comfort her by offering her the treasured wooden doll. Christina smiled through her tears and recognised that by accepting it made Zara feel happy that she was helping to cheer Christina up.

Susan suggested that she took them to see her mother in the village as she was looking after the two younger Wallace children and she was sure that Zara would enjoy their company, whereas Christina would probably enjoy the change of scenery. Liza thought that it would be a good idea that they left the house for a while, and they arranged for Ernie to take them and organised a time to bring them back.

Liza waved them off and returned to the study where Grace was working. "What's the matter Liza?" she asked.

"It's a long time since I have been in a house this quiet. I should be enjoying the silence, but it doesn't seem right," said Liza.

"Enjoy it, Liza; you'll soon have to organise Christmas for everyone, because even if you decide to go to Belfast, you know that everyone will follow you there," said Grace.

"Hmmm," said Liza. "Yes, I'll have to make up my mind shortly."

Miranda knocked and entered the study and she looked concerned.

"What's wrong Miranda, you look worried," asked Liza as she realised that Miranda wanted to talk to her privately.

Liza got up and ushered Miranda into the library.

"Mr Rogers came to the house earlier looking for Ken Wallace but was told that he was out with Jamie at one of the farms, so he came to see me," said Miranda.

"What did he want?" asked Liza.

"Somebody has been asking around the village about Ken. Mr Rogers thinks that it was a private investigator, most people will say nothing, but it's not easy for some people to recognise when to say something and when not to and Mr Rogers thinks that he got some information from a child," said Miranda.

"I know Ken is out with Jamie and the overseer today," said Liza. "He may be back shortly. I'll make sure I warn him of what has happened. I don't know his background, but I do know that he has been used to a better life than he has now."

"Yes, I could see that at one of the gatherings, he was quite confident in Penny Langston's company," said Miranda. "But his past is his affair, and he seems quite content now that he can feed his family adequately and put a roof over their heads."

"Thank you for telling me, Miranda. I'll make sure that I have a quiet word with Ken today. He's just got his family organised with Mrs Price. She is looking after the younger two so that the older ones can attend school. He's a very good father to them. Susan has taken Christina and Zara to visit them this afternoon," said Liza.

"I'll leave it in your very capable hands then Liza," smiled Miranda.

Liza went back to Grace and the correspondence until she heard Jamie arriving home. At the same time Ernie was driving up with Susan and the girls, so Liza took advantage of everyone arriving at the same time to find Ken who was with them. They all came in through the kitchen; the men because their boots were covered in mud and the girls because it was their supper time.

Liza welcomed the girls and asked them if they had enjoyed their afternoon and then she turned to Ken and told him that the girls had spent the afternoon with his daughters and then she pulled him to one side to ask him how his two oldest girls were settling into school, and that Christina would soon be joining them.

He told her that they were enjoying the regular lessons and the opportunity they had to join with others especially at play time. She then carried on saying how good the arrangement was with Mrs Price, and by that time nobody was listening to their conversation.

Quietly she said, "I've been informed that an apparent private investigator has been asking after you Ken and I believe that he gleaned some information from a child. Nobody in the village would ever give away any information about anybody but they wanted you to know. As you weren't around today one of our friends made sure that I was told so that I could let you know."

He had a look which was a mixture of resignation and concern. "I did not think that I would still be of interest to anyone but thank you for letting me know. I have an idea what it is all about and I would assure you that I am not a wanted person and that neither I nor my girls are in any danger. I enjoy my life here and I have no wish to return to my old life."

"I am well aware that you have been used to a better life than this, but if you are happy here, then I'm pleased for you. Your business is precisely that and I can assure you that you are very important to us here. No information will be given to anyone about your whereabouts. Whatever happens is up to you and I know you will make your own decisions regarding your life and the lives of your daughters," said Liza. "If you are in need of any help, just let us know."

"Thank you," said Ken. "I know you have already done a great deal to help us. I hope that I won't have to ask for any more."

Christina and Zara were enjoying their supper and Liza noticed that a plate was ready for a man's sized portion so she smiled at the girls and said that she would leave them to enjoy their meal and then suggested to Ken that he ate his meal before it became cold so that he could then get home to his girls in good time.

So that was the new arrangement for Ken's evening meal now that his daughters went to school and Mrs Price fed them their main meal of the day. *How very sensible*, thought Liza.

Liza then ran up the stairs to find Jamie. Grace had left for her home and Liza was looking forward to dining just with Jamie that evening. She found him in his room soaking in a hot bath and asked him how his day had been. He explained that most of the tenant farmers were dedicated to their work, but there was one who appeared to be letting the land go to waste.

"I have laid down the law to him and if he doesn't comply then he will have to go. I don't like doing this, but all the farms must be worked correctly, however I want to find the reason why the farm is not being worked; I couldn't get a sensible answer today. The tenant has been with us for a number of years and was always a good worker in the past," said Jamie.

"If he has been with you for some time, perhaps he is just getting too old to handle what is necessary. How old is he?" asked Liza.

"You're right; he is probably around seventy years old, and he doesn't have family to take over from him. His wife is still around but is rarely seen," said Jamie.

"Sadly he will have to be retired and a new tenant found, which shouldn't be difficult," said Liza.

"That sounds very harsh of you Liza. Normally you are thoughtful of people's situations," said Jamie.

"We're talking business Jamie," said Liza. "You need your tenant farmers to work well, otherwise you will go back to the old days when as long as your father gained enough to play the tables, there was no concern for more than that, so the farms went to rack and ruin. They all run well now but they need to for your sake."

"What you are advocating is putting a man and his wife out of their home," said a surprised Jamie.

"No I'm not Jamie. He obviously has become unable to work his land correctly, so neither he nor you are gaining anything. He will be starving before you do, if he isn't already. There is an alternative and that is to divide his land between the nearest farms and let them bring it back to the way it should be. The main problem would then be leaving an elderly couple in a farmhouse which should really be earning you money. How big is the farmhouse?" asked Liza.

"It's one of the larger ones; it's too big for two people. I suppose it could be used to house some of the farm workers. There are quite a number who have to travel in from the village and it would be more convenient for them to be nearer their work, especially in the winter," said Jamie.

"Do you think that the old couple would be capable of running the farmhouse as a boarding house for farm workers? Would they be able to keep the place clean and prepare meals for the men and how many could they accommodate?" asked Liza.

"That could work Liza, but they also have large outbuildings which are not being used correctly," said Jamie.

"What does your overseer think should be done?" asked Liza.

"The same as you," said Jamie. "That they should not remain on their farm, but I am reluctant to remove them. He has spent his whole life there and his father before him."

"You say that they have no children to carry on the tradition." asked Liza.

"No, they only have each other," said Jamie.

"Then you had better find some for them," said Liza to Jamie's surprise.

He frowned thoughtfully as he stepped out of his bath and wrapped a towel around himself.

"What would you have done if you didn't have James?" asked Liza. "You have no brothers, or male cousins. In fact the only relatives you have are your uncle and Grace, and unless you have a deadly accident, your uncle is of an age where you will outlive him, so what would you do?"

"I suppose Grace would then inherit, although she is older than me," said Jamie.

"Now you are being literal, I really meant, what if you had absolutely nobody to call your own, just like your tenant farmers?" asked Liza.

"Hmmm, I see what you mean," said Jamie. "I suppose the best course of action would be to take a young man into my home and train him to take over the responsibilities of the Estate. If it all worked out well, then I would leave the Estate to him in my Will."

"That could work, but it would be better if you adopted him, and he would therefore be legally your son and entitled to all that is yours. However, that won't necessarily apply to your tenant farmers. You are the one who allocates the lease so they would not have to adopt, but it would be essential that they have someone with them that they like, who knows the basics of farming and is willing to learn more. It would be nice if the farmer feels that he is imparting all his knowledge on to someone worthy of it," said Liza.

"A young couple would be better. I'll have a word with my overseer and find out the background of some of our workers from the village and see if he thinks that anyone would be suitable. The farmer and his wife may not like the idea," said Jamie.

"It seems to me that there are only two options, one is what we have just discussed, and the other is not a happy outcome for the farmer," said Liza. "What's his name by the way?"

"Jeb Wickes, I believe," said Jamie. "The same as his father."

"Just like your family," smiled Liza. "What is Jeb short for?"

"Jebediah, I suppose," said Jamie. He smiled at her realising that she had given him an idea of how to solve the problem of Mr and Mrs Jebediah Wickes.

"I'll quickly change for dinner, although it's just us but I would like to dress just for you," laughed Liza as she left his room to go to her own where Susan was waiting for her, but it didn't take long for her to be ready for dinner. Jamie came to see if she was dressed and she was, so they went to say goodnight to the girls and then made their way down to the dining room.

"Christina and Zara seemed to have enjoyed their afternoon with Mrs Price," said Jamie. "They were laughing as they arrived back; it seems to have helped Christina get over missing her father. I presume Ken's girls were there, is that what you were talking to him about?"

Liza realised that Jamie knew that she had spoken to Ken about things other than his girls and he continued to look at her questioningly.

"Yes, I asked him how his girls were settling in at school, but I think you realise that I had another reason to talk to him," said Liza and she told Jamie about his mother's visit and that a private investigator was asking about Ken in the village.

"Did Ken seem worried when you told him?" asked Jamie.

"He didn't seem surprised; he appeared to have been expecting it at some time, but he has assured me that he is not a wanted man. I know that we have discussed before that it would appear that he has been used to a more luxurious life," said Liza.

"Yes, I like him, and he does a good job. He gets on well with everyone. I hope he has no problems," said Jamie, "but no doubt if he has you will attempt to help him."

"It does depend on what his problem may be," said Liza and they then got on with enjoying their time together.

On several occasions over the following days Liza discussed with Jamie whether they spent Christmas in Surrey or in Belfast.

"There would be at least fifteen of us travelling," said Jamie. "I know that Bella and her boys will probably also join us, as will the Duke and Douglas. If Lady Redfern is not on duty at the Palace, she will want to be with her family. Then there are all the Fullers and Harry as well as Anthony, Diana, Rose and little Thomas."

"We'll be catering for a number of people if we stay here. It will seem strange not having Wendell and Amelia with us for Christmas. Perhaps we can spend Easter in Belfast instead. I wanted to give everyone a party at the New Year, so it's probably a good idea if we stay here this year. The boys would probably prefer it as they don't like leaving their horses for too long," said Liza.

"So we have decided to stay then," said Jamie.

Liza laughed and said, "Until I change my mind again."

Harper knocked and said that there was a person to see them, and he brought a visiting card over to Jamie.

"Do you know a Mr Oscar Logan who appears to be a Private Investigator?" Jamie asked Liza who shook her head. "I suppose you had better show him in Harper."

Harper nodded with a definite look of distain on his face.

Liza looked at Jamie and said, "I wonder if this is about Ken."

"What can we do for you Mr Logan," asked Jamie as Harper showed the man into the room. Liza leaned back in her chair and Jamie stared at the man imperiously.

"I understand that you have a person who calls himself Wallace working for you," said Mr Logan bluntly.

"I have many people working for me Mr Logan," said Jamie evasively.

"He's a man in his thirties and has four children," said Mr Logan.

"That describes many in my employ," said Jamie and Liza was proud of the way he was confusing Mr Logan.

"He originated from Hertfordshire. My Company has traced him on many occasions, and he has always moved to another location," said Mr Logan.

"Why do you want him, Mr Logan?" asked Jamie.

"He leaves a trail of destruction behind him, and things go missing," said Mr Logan.

"Are his children that unruly, Mr Logan?" asked Liza.

"It's not his children," said Mr Logan gruffly.

"Are you saying that he is a thief, Mr Logan?" asked Jamie.

"I am saying that it has never been proved," said Mr Logan.

"That's very wise Mr Logan, because accusing without proof is a very dangerous thing," said Liza. "Is this man moving from place to place because he is being hounded by you?"

"Certainly not," snapped Mr Logan.

"We have no thieves in our employ Mr Logan and if we do find that we have, then we will go to the proper authorities, but thank you for calling by," said Jamie and he rang for Harper who appeared extremely quickly and showed a very disgruntled Oscar Logan out.

"Ken is no thief," said Jamie. "He has obviously upset somebody at some time."

"I presume that every time he settles somewhere, somebody like Mr Oscar Logan turns up and he has to move on with his daughters; probably also with his wife before she died. I suppose we will have to tell him that he has been found again," said Liza.

"When he comes in for his supper he will have been told; Harper seemed to be listening and I don't blame him," smiled Jamie.

They could hear Susan taking Christina and Zara down for their supper, and they knew that Ken would soon be in for his. He would then know that the private investigator had visited that afternoon.

"I suppose we will have to send for him," said Jamie.

"I would think that won't be necessary as I'm sure he will ask to see us as soon as he is told what has happened," said Liza and she was right. Harper knocked and said that Ken would like to have a word with them.

Both Liza and Jamie smiled as he came in.

"I understand that you have seen a private investigator this afternoon. I am sorry that you have been bothered with my problems and I would like to tender my resignation. You have been very kind to me and my girls, but I must now move on," said Ken.

"We would be very sorry to see you leave Ken," said Jamie, "and if you are doing it because of the gentleman who called on us this afternoon, as far as we are concerned there is no need for you to move on. We are very happy for you to stay."

"We do not take notice of what others say," said Liza. "We go by our own experience of a person, and we have always found you to be honest and trustworthy and are quite content for you to continue as you are. Of course the choice is yours, but we would be very sorry to see you go."

"It would appear that somebody does not want you to have a settled life as it would seem that you have been hounded from place to place, but I hope that this time you will not have to move your family on anywhere else," said Jamie.

Ken was quiet for a while and Liza told him to sit down as she realised that he was wrestling with the decision to tell them the reasons behind his problems.

"You don't need to tell us anything Ken," said Liza. "Your private life is your affair. All we would say is that if there is anything that we can do to help you, then all you have to do is ask."

"I said to you before that you have done more than enough to assist me and my family, but I think that the time has come for me to tell you a little of my previous life," said Ken. "Firstly I would like to say that I am no thief and I know that has been said to my previous employers."

"It was not really said to us, but it was definitely intimated, but we told Mr Logan to be careful of what he said as it was dangerous to accuse of such a misdemeanour without proof and if it has been said then I would suggest that you use the law to put a stop to such accusations," said Liza.

"I have been sacked from many places because of such an accusation and I had no alternative but to move to a new place. I had hoped that I had at last found a new life where I was able to give my daughters a little better life than they previously had," said Ken. "My father is a vindictive man, and he did not approve of my marriage. I am the second son of the Earl of Graystead and for my sins I fell in love with the daughter of one of his grooms. My father sacked him, but he was lucky enough to find employment elsewhere and I married his daughter and we lived with him in the Company accommodation. I worked around the grounds and we settled into a very happy life. The people who employed us were like you and took no notice of the lies that were told about me."

"It was there that we had two of our girls, but our employers fell on hard times, and we had to find new employment and accommodation, which my

490

father-in-law did quite easily as he was an excellent groom. I managed to find work nearby and once again we settled, and our third girl was born. Word was spreading that I was dishonest, and my father-in-law's employer became concerned and suggested that we did not live in the accommodation, so my wife and I moved on and found somewhere to live and I found work. We received a letter that my father-in-law was ill but by the time my wife could go to him he had died. She was at the time carrying our fourth child and when she returned, she was very ill and it was doubtful that the child that she was carrying would survive, but little Libby lived, although my wife never fully recovered."

"Once again we had to move on and the accommodation that we found was very poor but by that time we had no choice but to live in what I can only describe as squaller. I found work digging ditches and a woman kindly came to our home each day and helped, but the strain was too much for my wife who died quite suddenly one day whilst I was at work."

"I have since that time moved from place to place, always with the word being spread that I was not honest enough to employ, until two years ago when I came here and as time went by I thought that my father had given up the vendetta, but I was wrong and here I am again facing the result of his vindictiveness."

"Thank you for telling us Ken," said Jamie, "but I want to assure you that you have a home and employment here as long as you want it. We have absolutely no reason to make you move onto somewhere else. I would however suggest that you try to put a stop to your father's strange behaviour against you and perhaps we can help you with that."

"As your father has an older son, why is he so adamant that you were wrong in your choice of wife? I would have thought that you were not as necessary to the bloodline of his Earldom as your brother. I presume that he is carrying out the duties of a first son, but of course that is none of my business," said Liza. "I have one or two contacts in investigative areas, and they could perhaps be useful. I will contact them if I have your permission to do so."

"I don't want to put you to any bother or expense; you have both already done enough for me and my girls," said Ken.

"It's no bother Ken," said Liza. "And it won't be any expense for me as I own a security company which handles diverse aspects of life."

"Then, yes, I would be grateful for any help you can give to put us back to the peaceful life that we have managed to enjoy over the past two years," said Ken.

"You're not away from that peaceful life Ken," said Liza. "I know that everyone around here speaks as they find, and they like you and your girls and will take no notice of any malicious gossip. So if you are happy to continue as if nothing had been mentioned, then we are just as happy for you to do so. I will of course let you know if I hear anything further, but you must not worry about it."

Jamie nodded, smiled and said, "I think your supper could be cold by now, but I'm sure Mrs Lambert will get something warm for you."

"It's a pleasure to work for people who are not frightened of my father; he does seem to create fear in many," said Ken and he smiled, thanked them and left.

"Do you know Earl Graystead?" Liza asked Jamie.

"I know of him, but I have never met him. I have heard that he is a little temperamental," said Jamie.

"Have you met Ken's brother?" asked Liza.

"Not to my knowledge," said Jamie. "But who knows, I have met many people and not necessarily been introduced properly to them."

"Christopher knows the family," said Liza. "He comes from the same area as Ken. It has been puzzling him since he first saw him. I suppose it will now put his mind at rest, if it hasn't done already. I'll write to Cyril Andrews and get the letter off to him tomorrow."

"So you are going to take on the might of the Graysteads," smiled Jamie.

"A lawyer should really be consulted, but that is up to Ken and not us. The most I will do is ask Cyril's advice and see if there are any measures that can be taken without too much trouble. It is very wrong that Ken's father is maligning his son in that manner. It can't have been a very loving family. I wonder if his mother is still alive, he didn't make any mention of her," said Liza.

Two days later Cyril Andrews rode up, much to Liza's delight. She had been in touch with him on numerous occasions but had not seen him since April's problem with the accusation of theft just prior to her wedding to Adam.

"How is young April," asked Cyril and Liza told him that Adam was now headmaster of the local school and he and April were happily living in the schoolhouse and that she visited them regularly.

"When the boys are home, their first port of call is on April and they eat her out of house and home; as they do with most of the villagers," smiled Liza. "Will you be staying the night, Cyril?"

"If it would be no trouble to you, I would be grateful," said Cyril.

"Ken won't be back for another couple of hours, but I will tell you what I know already," said Liza, which she did.

"From what you are telling me, Ken Wallace should really consult a lawyer, but that may not be practical. When I have gone into more detail with him, I may suggest that I make certain arrangements, which will mean that no investigator will take instruction from the Earl," said Cyril.

"Do you have the power to do that Cyril?" asked Liza.

"No, but you do," smiled Cyril. "I can see from your expression that you did not know that. You are far more powerful than you know; many people rely on you for their livelihoods, even if it is only indirectly. As I say, I'll talk to Ken Wallace and get as much detail as possible from him. He does know that whatever he divulges will go no further, doesn't he?"

"I believe so, but it will do no harm for you to reassure him," said Liza. "I'll arrange for your room to be made ready and also for Ken to see you as soon as he returns from work."

***

Whilst Cyril and Ken were having their discussions, word came to Liza that there had been a severe problem on the high seas. Luckily it was not a Marchant & Fuller vessel, but it put all shipping lines on alert. Two American Confederate agents had been taken from the 'Trent', which was a British West Indies Mail Packet, by agents from the North. They had been on their way to gain support for the South from various places in Europe. The British government were outraged over the incident as it breached the neutrality of Britain.

Peter arrived soon after the news had reached Liza of the incident. "We felt that we needed to talk to you Liza, especially as you have so recently been in America and have seen both sides of the conflict at first hand. This is a very serious incident. We carry goods for both the north and south and it means that at any time our vessels could be boarded and both goods and personnel seized."

"I said that this could happen, and it could mean that Britain must take sides. With this incident it could mean that we begin supporting the south and if that is the case then not only does it jeopardise our shipping line, but it could mean disaster for the Daltons project. The whole of that project is run by our British people, and we have a vast investment in it. I know that the American government also have a large investment there, but it will not go down well with them if our country sides with what they term their enemy," said Liza.

"Father is very concerned; he can see his life's work being destroyed overnight. I have managed to reassure him that with all else that we do, Marchant & Fuller will not collapse. We may have to adapt, but we will not lose the Company," said Peter.

"I hope that Wendell is remaining calm; he's already had one stroke, I know your mother and Edward will do their best to reassure him," said Liza. "We'll have to study some new routes which avoid the risk of requisition as happened to Andraes' ship. We'll study the maps tomorrow and see what routes and areas we can open up. We may have to adapt some of our ships to purely passenger lines. There are many families who are being encouraged to emigrate to Australia and if it is planned properly, we could make our ships a little more comfortable than those already transporting such people, and I am not talking about criminals, many areas are opening to those looking for a new start. That market has yet to be seriously tapped for both goods and passengers."

"We could also increase our shipments to Mexico, and those routes could mean that goods could be transported overland to some of the southern states," said Peter.

"Yes, there's nothing illegal in that and also if Britain does unfortunately support the south, then it would be one way of carrying out our country's wishes," said Liza. "However, I do know that Prince Albert is attempting to calm the situation. I believe he is trying to take the fire out of Lord Palmerston's indignation over the seizure of these Southerners. I know that the Queen's leanings are towards supporting the south and she also has been quite vocal on the situation. I hope that the Prince's wisdom will prevail."

"He's not too well, is he?" said Peter.

"So I've heard, although we are told that it is not serious, but it seems to have been going on for quite a while," said Liza. "Anyway, we'll put our heads together tomorrow when we can study our maps."

"I think we have already come up with some useful ideas to combat any losses that we may have, but I am more concerned about Daltons than anything else. We are making good profits there now, but if Britain sides with the south both Marchant & Fuller and Bradley & Company could lose the whole of their investment in Daltons. Even with what we could plan for Australia and Mexico, we are going to lose a serious amount and much as we believed that at the end of the conflict, we would still have properties and land, if we support the south, we could immediately lose all that as well," said Peter. "This is the most serious situation that our Companies have ever been in and really no matter how we have tried to reassure my father, he is not a stupid man; he may be getting old, but he is not senile, and he knows that we must take some sensible steps quickly to ward off disaster."

"I wish Wendell was here so that he could see that we have thought of a few alternatives for the Company," said Liza.

"He brightened up when I said that I would come to see you Liza," said Peter. "He has great faith in you and knows that you will come up with some ideas to alleviate the situation."

"Peter, you also come up with good ideas. It is just so much easier when you can bounce them off someone else and Wendell knows that and that is why he seemed happier. It was because you and I have always been able to work together well," smiled Liza.

Jamie came rushing in to greet Peter and said that he had heard just how serious the situation was and he hoped that Britain could retain its neutrality.

"I suppose you have both come up with some ideas on how to protect your Companies," said Jamie.

"Yes, we have but we are going to have to work on them in detail tomorrow, so I shall be very busy," said Liza. "How are Ken and Cyril getting on?"

"I believe that Ken is going to let Cyril deal with the situation rather than going to the law, but no doubt they will both tell you what action they will be taking," said Jamie.

Peter raised an eyebrow, "Is that the Cyril that I know?"

Liza nodded and said that one of their employees had a problem that Cyril was attempting to sort out.

"Just another little problem for you to solve then Liza," said Peter.

"No, all I've done is to introduce our employee to Cyril and they can sort it out from there," said Liza.

They discussed the situation a little more and then Peter went to his room to wash and change for dinner.

Cyril looked into the drawing room and said that Ken would like to see them both, so Liza and Jamie told them to come in.

"I just wanted you to know the outcome of our discussions, as at some time it may be that another individual could come looking for Ken," said Cyril. "Although I believe that could now be unlikely. I have advised him that he could take legal proceedings against his family, but he doesn't feel that it is an option."

Ken then said, "I have spent many years moving from place to place, always having been put in the situation of not knowing where the next meal would be coming from. I know that I could take matters to a legal conclusion, but that would be expensive, and I do not really have that kind of money. All I want is to look after my girls in an environment where I do not have to look over my shoulder every second of the day. We are very happy here; I have a job that I enjoy, and my girls have become part of the village. Mr Andrews has intimated that there are ways of putting a stop to my father's vindictiveness but that does involve the use of your name and your Company."

"What do you have in mind Cyril?" asked Liza.

"Some years ago our Company was approached by the Earl of Graystead's secretary to look for his son. That in itself was not a difficult or distasteful assignment, but the letter that accompanied the request showed signs of paranoia. We refused the request as it was not the type of business that we

495

normally undertook. We are solely concerned with the security of people, houses, goods and businesses; we do not search for anyone who is missing unless they are linked in some way to family or our own businesses," said Cyril.

"You are right, it is not the type of business that we have ever undertaken," said Liza.

"I know those who do undertake such assignments and most of them have goods and services provided by Marchant & Fuller; they bank with M & F. None would want to upset your Companies, and neither would the Earl, because he also uses your services," said Cyril.

"Are you suggesting that we blackmail all these people including the Earl of Graystead?" said Liza. "I cannot say that I am happy with that prospect. I would not make such a decision, it is not up to me to sanction such an action, I am only part of Marchant & Fuller."

"I am suggesting that we inform all private investigators that you are extremely unhappy because one of your essential employees and his family are being unfairly harassed by the Earl and that if it continues, a warrant claiming defamation of character will be issued to any who continue perpetrating such lies. I am sure that they believe that Ken does not have the finances or the will to undertake such a course of action; they would however believe that you have the means for such an undertaking, and you are known to champion the downtrodden," said Cyril.

"Why don't you try talking to your father," Jamie asked Ken.

"I have tried to on a couple of occasions, but I have been lucky to stay alive. My father has a temper that has not eased over the years. There is no talking to him; my brother has found the same. Both my mother and brother always agree with my father, it is the easiest way to deal with him and to stay alive under his roof," said Ken. "I do not wish to put this pressure on you and perhaps the best course of action is if I move to another location."

"It will be the same wherever you go. Cyril, if you can convince others to leave Ken and his family alone then that seems a satisfactory solution, although it's doubtful that anyone will be sent to find him as he has now been found; however if all this could be sorted out directly with the Earl, then that would really be the best outcome," said Liza.

"Ken," said Jamie. "I believe the time has come for you to stand up to your father. Enough is enough and I think that no matter what can be done to stop investigators looking for you and spreading lies, it will always be an unresolved situation. If something were to happen to you, how vulnerable would your girls be? They must be your priority."

"With all due respect Sir, I have stood up to him on many occasions, but he does not use fists; he uses whatever he can get his hands on. We have all had broken bones, including my mother. I married with a broken arm and facial injuries," said Ken.

"Do you think that now that he knows where you are, you could be in danger and your daughters also?" asked Liza. "Is that one of the reasons why you have moved on so frequently?"

"The reason that I moved on so much is precisely the reason I told you the other day. I had been accused of theft and therefore any trust that I had built up with my employers had gone," said Ken. "I am wary of coming face to face with my father as I could be damaged enough to be unable to work and my first responsibility must be to my daughters."

"You must be concerned for your mother and brother," said Liza.

"Of course I think about them, but my daughters are my concern, and my livelihood is important to their welfare. Sadly my mother and brother must look after their own welfare," said Ken. "I know that I have had to divulge to you my reasons for being in your employ and why I have been chased from pillar to post, but I believe you will appreciate that for two years I kept my past to myself and only spoke to you about it because I had no other choice. I enjoy working here and my daughters enjoy the community spirit of both here and the village. Thanks to you I have a very adequate roof over our heads and enough food to keep us healthy. We have become part of Edgeworth and all that would really make it perfect would be if my wife were still with us. She would have been so happy with this life."

"I think that she probably knows that you are now settled and that your girls are being well educated and cared for not only by you but by the whole community," said Liza.

"I am quite prepared to accompany you to see your father, if you think that it would be of use, but in the meantime, I'll arrange that no private investigator is employed by your father," said Cyril. "You can rest assured that this is the last time that you will have to think about moving away."

"I have burdened you with a problem which you should not have been concerned with, but I am so grateful for your help and support. I will think about making one last trip to see my father, although I have no real desire to do so, but if I do, I would be grateful to have somebody else with me for, as I say, my priority is to stay fit so that I can provide for my family," said Ken. "I'll leave you in peace now and once again, thank you for all your help."

When he had left, they were all silent for a while until Jamie said, "He has been carrying a great deal on his shoulders for a number of years. He must have a very strong character to come through all the problems that have been thrown at him. I can see why the life that he has now is so much better than the one he had in the past."

"His father must have exploded when he realised that he wanted to marry his groom's daughter; it's a wonder he didn't have an apoplexy and collapse and die, which I suppose would have solved a lot of problems," said Liza.

"Hmm," grunted Jamie. "I had better change for dinner now."

"Yes, I had as well," said Liza and she followed Jamie and Cyril out of the drawing room and up to her room where Susan was waiting for her.

"Is Ken alright," asked Susan. "He has been on edge for the past few days."

"Yes, he is alright now Susan. It was just a small difficulty from his past, but it is all sorted now. There is no need for you to worry," said Liza.

At dinner Peter said that he realised that they were sorting out a problem with Ken, who he had spent some time with on many occasions recently whilst they were away. The discussion around the table was mainly concerning the situation with the Confederate agents removed forcibly from the Trent.

"Does it mean that you are concerned for some of your ships?" asked Cyril.

"Yes, it means that they could be vulnerable to anyone boarding them and removing personnel; they could also take goods and go so far as to requisition our ships," said Liza. "Not only that but Britain could side with the south and therefore we would no longer keep our neutrality which would jeopardise much of what we operate in both the north and the south, but mainly in the north, we have very large investments there."

"All we can hope for now is that Prince Albert can intervene and calm the situation down. He knows that taking sides would be a costly disaster for this country," said Peter.

Cyril left the next morning and for the rest of that day Liza and Peter could be found pouring over maps and drawing up alternative shipping routes.

"We have very little difficulty shipping to New York, although I have heard that the confederates are attempting to blockade fairly near the port, but they have been chased away frequently," said Liza.

"Our main problem is getting to the southern states," said Peter and they looked at their maps again.

"We have goods that often go to France, Spain, Portugal and Morocco. If we also take the goods bought by the south, if necessary, we can cut across to Mexico from Morocco and get them transported overland from there. We will be hugging the European coast and then across to Morocco. Looking at the map we should then be past the northern blockades but even so we are quite within our rights to sail to Mexico and as we are neutral, we really should be at liberty to deliver to anybody we wish to, including any port in the southern states," said Liza.

"It's going to add quite some time onto how long it takes us to deliver, but I suppose they will be so pleased to receive what we have for them that late delivery is a small price to pay," said Peter.

Peter was staying with them for a couple of days and during that time word was received that British troops were being sent to Canada and that Britain was planning to attack the fleet which was blockading the south and they would also put measures in place to blockade northern ports; surprisingly France would be assisting in the undertaking.

"It would appear that we will soon be at war with America," said Peter. "This is getting very serious, Liza. We have ships already on their way to North America as well as to the Southern States; we are in danger of losing a great deal as we are carrying goods and personnel for both sides in their own conflict, although we are adhering to the neutral rule that we carry no armaments to either side. What is going to happen in Daltons now that we are so near all-out war, I have no idea."

"Our own personnel are now in danger," said Liza. "We may have to make arrangements to bring Hector, Estelle and Brendan back and there are many others from Britain who are working there. I truly hope that any British workers will be allowed to leave and not be imprisoned. My country will be at war with my friends in Benson. I thought that the civil war was bad, but I feel as if I am in the middle of my own civil war."

"The Prince is still advising caution," said Jamie. "I hope that his efforts will come to fruition. The Queen does listen to his advice, and I believe that at the moment he has calmed the situation, although there is still a great deal of indignation amongst the members of Parliament."

"Well Peter, we will just have to continue as before as we are not yet at war with America. We must contact Henry personally and ask him to make arrangements to get our people out of Daltons should it become necessary. Did I tell you that Estelle is pregnant, so it could be difficult for her to leave the place? It seems strange to think that Henry and Myra could be on opposing sides to us, as could Walter and his family, and all the people I know in the northern army and Ada and Bea. I could go on, but I'm only depressing myself with all these thoughts," said Liza.

"We'll carry on making contingency plans for the new routes and I am going to study trading in Australia and New Zealand," said Peter. "This situation did not come as a complete surprise to Harry. I know that he hedged his bets and those of his customers; they will be winning either way, but one way will win more than the other and I think you know which way the high rate will be."

Liza smiled and nodded, "but as you say, they all win to a greater or lesser extent. Harry is proving to be a very shrewd analyst."

"We still have a great deal going for us," said Peter. "Our only problems could be with the north of America. We don't have a problem with the south as there are ways to reach it avoiding the blockade, and if Britain comes out in sympathy with the south, then we will manage a clear route to them. We will lose a great deal of investment in Daltons, but we will stop putting money into it and unfortunately stop making money from it. We ship to and from many other parts of the world, admittedly not as large as America. We have a banking division also in many parts of the world and our security section is getting stronger. Harry's department is gaining recognition and it has yet to be set up in America, so we don't have to worry about that."

"Our profitability will probably drop but we will not lose the Company," said Liza. "I hope you will be able to reassure your father of that and prove to him that we are moving into a different but more exciting phase of business. We could become blockade runners which sounds very much like privateering."

"How is this going to affect Bradley & Company," asked Jamie.

"Unfortunately Bradley & Company owns a great deal in the northern states. I know that the farms and farmers will keep them safely for the Company, but for the duration of the war they will earn nothing for the Company, and I'm concerned that I may not be able to pay salaries, especially to those people like Bridget and Mary and Kathy, Joe, Zelma and Leonora in Benson. Wes looks after my interests there, along with Gabriel, and Wes has a family to provide for. Angela's parents are the same, but at least they can keep themselves alive by farming. I'm lucky that I have interests in other places. Italy is my biggest investment and that is paying dividends as are my properties in Wales and Ireland. I have a few in England and they are beginning to pay off, so Bradley & Company will survive and still make a profit although not as much as in previous years," said Liza.

"The charity will survive," said Jamie. "We get a great deal of funding from the British aristocracy, but we will probably get nothing further from America for the duration of the war and of course many of our children go to America for adoption or some form of work, so our Homes will become overcrowded. We cannot send them away with nowhere to go. We will have to look to other parts of the world."

"I would suggest Australia, but that has a stigma of criminal transportation, and I wouldn't like to guarantee that the children would not be used as slave labour; we can't check up on them as easily as we can in America," said Liza.

"Overall, what we are really saying is that even if we go to war with America, we will still be profitable, although not as we have previously been and the charity can run with adequate funds, but we will have problems placing some of the children," said Peter. "We have new routes to consider, which I know will give my father something to think about. I know that I can reassure him that our two companies are not going to become bankrupt, we may have to tighten our belts a little and study the markets, but we have Harry to do that for us."

"It's nothing that you could not have sorted out with your father. As much as I am always delighted to see you, you really were quite capable of thinking of our various solutions without me," said Liza.

"Quite possibly, but you know that you and I have a way of bouncing ideas off one another and we come up with the right answers. You know that my father has great faith in both you and I together and it put his mind at rest that we were going to spend some time thinking of ideas and creating something innovative to make up for what we could be losing in America," said Peter. "And he's right, we do work well together and take one another's thoughts and hone them into something workable."

"If the situation in America wasn't so serious, it would have been more of an enjoyable exercise," said Liza.

***

Over the following days Liza and Jamie just had their close family with them. Peter had left with all their plans to counter any disasters that could occur should Britain side with the confederacy rather than remain neutral. Unfortunately the two Confederate agents taken by the northern forces from the British West Indies Mail ship remained imprisoned and Britain was discussing the options.

Both Liza and Jamie decided that as there was absolutely nothing that they could do to alleviate the situation they would concentrate on preparations for Christmas which was looming fast and they also began to organise their New Year's Eve party for all their guests as well as the staff, villagers and farmers and everyone was looking forward to that.

Liza had no idea exactly who would be staying with them at Christmas. She would miss all the Fullers from Belfast, but Joseph and Lily would join them at some time on that day as would the Major and Jennifer. Lady Redfern was not on duty at the Palace that year so she would probably spend her time there. It went without saying that Bella and her boys would visit for a number of days and no doubt if Lady Redfern was with them then Douglas Carlton would also be a guest. The Duke normally turned up invited or otherwise so Liza would have a room ready for him. Anthony and Diana had yet to decide whether they took their family to Belfast, but if they did not, they could also be staying with them.

This was going to be Christina's and Zara's first Christmas in England and they were getting quite excited about it. Christina had carefully told Zara what Christmas was all about. She had gone into great detail about how she had spent Christmas with her grandparents in Benson, and about the wonderful times she had had with them and her friends. Liza hoped that she would enjoy her time with them just as much.

Liza was looking forward to the boys being home. She still thought of them as her boys even though they were now handsome young men. They would be home in just over a weeks' time. She remembered that Christopher had been with them the previous year when he had stayed after the operation on his hand, and she made a mental note to see him and ask how his hand was progressing. She wondered whether he had realised who Ken was; he probably had by now.

As Liza had spent so little time at home that year through no fault of her own, it seemed as if she had only just celebrated the previous Christmas and now it was on her again and she did not feel as organised as she normally did, and her enthusiasm was sorely lacking.

Gradually over the course of the following days, Liza received letters from both Lady Redfern and Douglas Carlton each mentioning that Bella had informed them that she was spending Christmas with the Edgeworths and asked whether they would be welcome to join them at that time. So she knew that she would be having house guests for Christmas, and she asked Jamie whether they should also invite Anthony and Diana to join them that year.

"I believe Anthony was contemplating travelling to Ireland this year and I know he was hoping that we would be spending Christmas there," said Jamie. "I would suggest that you write to them and say that they would be welcome here should they decide to remain in England."

It did not take long for Liza to receive a reply to her note to Anthony and Diana which accepted her invitation for them to spend Christmas with them.

"We will be quite busy again this year," said Jamie. "I will miss Wendell and Amelia. It's a long time since we haven't seen them at this time of year."

"Yes, but I hope we can go over to Belfast for Easter," said Liza.

"I suppose you are assuming that the Duke will be joining us also," said Jamie.

"Yes, I've arranged with Mrs Frances to have his room made ready and that of his valet," said Liza. "I presume that he will only be bringing his valet with him and not the rest of his household."

"I'm afraid that he is very unpredictable so not only do you not know if he is coming, but you won't know who will be with him until he arrives," said Jamie. "It is a time of year when I never feel that I am in charge of my own household."

Liza smiled at him and said, "You are more in charge of your own household than you know. You'll enjoy having Anthony here. I suppose Rose will be with them; I hope she is not still harbouring a grudge against me over Hector."

"Anthony wouldn't stand for that Liza, and neither would I," said Jamie.

It was very early on Sunday morning just ten days before Christmas and Liza was surprised to hear the church bell tolling as for a funeral and at the same time she received a message from Lady Redfern stating the horrendous news that Prince Albert had died the previous night and naturally her time would now be totally with Her Majesty. A shocked Liza went to find Jamie and was told that he was talking to Hendry in the stables, and she asked Roberts to ask him to join her in the library as soon as possible.

Jamie came rushing in with a concerned look on his face, "What on earth's the matter Liza, you look quite shocked. The church bell is tolling."

"I've heard from Lady Redfern that Prince Albert died last night," said Liza.

"Good heavens. I thought he was getting better. I don't know what to say," said Jamie. Liza handed him Lady Redfern's letter to read, which he did.

"We had better let your mother and Lucinda know; as well as your uncle and Grace," said Liza.

"Yes, I'll do that now," said Jamie. "Will you tell the staff?"

Jamie went off to see his mother and uncle and Liza rang for Harper and asked him to gather all the staff together, including any gardeners and stable hands and she wanted to see them all in the kitchen in ten minutes and when they were all there Liza told them the sad news and tears were shed by some. It was commented that they had heard that although ill, the Prince was in no danger and that his health was improving.

"Yes, we all believed that," said Liza. "Hendry perhaps you could arrange for someone to go into the village and inform Mr and Mrs Rogers and Adam and April, although they may well know as the church bell has been tolling for a while now. On your way please see the vicar and let him know that I have been officially informed by one of the Queen's ladies in waiting."

The meeting broke up and Hendry and Ernie went on their way to the village, and Susan went up to Christina and Zara.

"It will still be just six of us for lunch as well as the two girls Mrs Lambert, although probably none of us will feel hungry," said Liza and she left to go back to her study where she sat and contemplated what this news meant to everyone. *The country will be in mourning for quite some time*, thought Liza. *The Queen is going to be devastated; it's well known that she and Prince Albert adored one another. I know how she's feeling; it will take her a long while to get over this, but she is not only a mother, but she is also mother to our nation, so she will have to get on with life no matter how she feels.*

Jamie returned whilst Liza was still sitting and contemplating the future, "How are your mother and Lucinda?"

"They're very upset and of course Lucinda is in floods of tears. David and Grace were shocked as they had heard that his health was not of great concern at present. They all wondered whether to still come over for lunch, but I told them that it was already organised, and we would like them to join us," said Jamie.

"Yes, we must try to make life as normal and as happy as we can for the sake of the girls," said Liza. "They will not understand just how devastating this is for the country. Prince Albert was a calming influence not only on the Queen but also on many members of Parliament and without that steady hand who knows what will happen. However I believe that it will be right to cancel the large New Year's Eve party that I was planning, but instead I shall organise something special for all the children from the village and the farms, as it's not right that they should be plunged into mourning as undoubtedly it will be expected of us and all adults."

"No doubt I will be receiving notification of the funeral details which I will have to attend," said Jamie. "Anthony and I will probably travel together when we know where it is going to be held. I suppose Diana and little Thomas will come and stay here; it will just mean that they will be here earlier than they would normally have been for Christmas. I think that you're right; Christmas is a time for children to enjoy and much as we adults may not feel like celebrating, we must make the effort for the children. It's Christina's and Zara's first Christmas in England and I would like to see them enjoy it."

"I must see the Major and Joseph as I feel that all the children in the Homes should also have as good a time as possible for Christmas. I'm not saying that everyone must leap up and down with joy as a little decorum would be appreciated, but children are children and should be treated as such. I'm sure that both the Major and Joseph will be emphasising the sadness of the situation and offer prayers for the Prince each day, but those children have had little happiness in their lives, and they don't need to become even more depressed than they are already," said Liza.

"We must attend church this morning, but perhaps we should leave Christina and Zara behind today," said Jamie.

"Yes, and we had better find something sombre to wear," said Liza. "I had better sort out at least a black cloak and hat; I think I have a black skirt. I believe that my full mourning clothes need some attention before I can wear them."

"I suppose that Bella and the boys will still be staying this year, but I wouldn't think that Douglas will come now that Lady Redfern will be elsewhere," said Jamie. "The Duke has always made it difficult for us to know what his plans are. Anthony and Diana will probably still be joining us. I feel a little guilty discussing this under the circumstances."

"I know what you mean but I must now try to judge how it will affect business," said Liza. "The Prince was a steadying influence on both the Queen and some members of Parliament. I now doubt that any decisions will be made regarding America this side of Christmas, nobody will want to commit to war and certainly not the Queen. At this moment she will be unable to think of anything but her grief."

"Yes, she did seem to rely on him for many things not least sound counsel," said Jamie.

"They had more than sound counsel; if they didn't then there would not have been nine children to the marriage," smiled Liza. "She would have had the power to stop after securing the crown for the next generation."

Liza then went up to sort out her attire but firstly she spent some time with Christina and Zara, who were sitting a little dejectedly in their room. Liza went in smiling and told them to stop looking so sad as although the Prince Albert's death was a sad event and they must say some prayers for his soul, they could still play with their toys and read their books as well as think about what they would be doing at Christmas. They were not to forget that the boys would be home within the week, and they would also visit the Wallace girls and one or two others from the village during the next week.

The girls brightened up a little and Liza said, "We all feel very sad for the Queen and her children and in our quieter moments we will think about them, but we all have things that we must get on with. We still must eat, drink, get washed and dressed and sleep and we also all love one another and look after one another."

"Yes, it's always very sad when somebody dies," said Christina. "I feel sorry for the children. Both Zara and I have lost our mothers. I never really knew mine and Zara doesn't remember hers. I am lucky because my grandparents love me, and I was very happy with them. Zara never had anyone to cuddle her, but she does now. You cuddle her and so do I. Susan does also. You cuddle me every day, so we are both very lucky. Do you think that the Queen cuddles her children?"

"All mothers cuddle their children, so I'm sure that the Queen cuddles hers. They also have people like Susan to look after them, so they are well loved," said Liza not really knowing what the situation was like at the Palace. "You haven't had your breakfast yet, have you?"

"No we were about to go down when Susan was called away," said Christina.

Liza asked Susan to take them down and then come back and help her find suitable clothing for church.

Of course it was all that was talked about at church that morning and as always prayers were said for the Royal family and sadly Prince Albert's name was omitted from the list for prayers. Everyone attending the service was either dressed in black or had at least a black armband.

Lucinda had decided that she would not attend the service, and nobody was surprised as they knew that she would not be able to keep her tears at bay; it was of course the reason why everyone loved her. She also decided that she would not join them for lunch and when Miranda said that she would stay with her she was adamant that she should not and that she would calm down by the time Miranda returned.

Lunch was a little sombre, but everyone made an effort to smile and talk of everything but the Prince's death in front of the girls who enjoyed their lunch and smiled happily at everyone, especially little Zara who seemed to feel triumphant using cutlery. David was sitting on one side of her with Christina on the other and he was charmingly helping her with her food. *This is a far cry from when we first met David,* thought Liza. *He was bad tempered then and appeared to hate children.*

Susan came and said that she was going to visit her mother and brother that afternoon and would Liza like her to take Christina and Zara with her and they would probably also be able to visit Ken's girls.

"Would you like to do that?" Liza asked the girls and they both said that they would like to, so they were excused from the table and went with Susan to get ready for their visit.

"Those two girls seem very happy here Liza," said David. "They've both had a very upsetting time recently, but they seem to have settled well.

"Yes, it has been very upsetting for them, which is why I am hoping that I won't have to concentrate on the Prince's death too much with them and also with the children at the Homes. As I said to Jamie earlier, those children have already had such unhappy lives that to depress them even further will do no good," said Liza. "I'm sure that there must be a compromise where they sadly acknowledge the situation but still enjoy their Christmas."

***

Over the course of the next few days the boys arrived home for the holidays and details of the funeral emerged and it was to take place at Windsor on the twenty-third of December. Jamie was going to attend with Anthony, and they were going to stay at their Club the day before. Jamie had not been there since the serious problems that were created between them a few years before and Liza was not happy that he would be away but realised that it was essential and at least Anthony would be with him the whole time, as would Roberts.

On the morning he was leaving he looked at Liza's pouting face and smiled, "I will be good, I promise you Liza. I will be back either very late after the funeral on the twenty-third, or early on Christmas Eve. You have no need to worry as I would never do anything to hurt you. Besides, I have Anthony and Roberts to keep me in order," he joked.

"You know that I'll miss you," said Liza. "Bella and her boys will be here when you return."

"Well, you already have our boys back, and the girls are very excited, so you will have your hands full whilst I'm away," said Jamie. "Diana and little Thomas will be arriving this afternoon. You are going to be busy, but I do feel that it is going to be a strange Christmas this year."

"The tree is being brought in tomorrow, but somehow I don't feel that we should decorate it until Christmas Eve. It seems wrong to be doing it on the day of the Prince's funeral," said Liza.

"I know what you mean, but we have the girls and little Thomas to think about and the staff will be having their Christmas dinner later on the day. I presume that Ken and his girls and Adam and April will also be joining them. What about Mrs Price, Derek and Christopher?" said Jamie.

"Yes, I believe they are also coming. Last year Christopher ate with us. It's always difficult. It's such a 'them and us' situation," said Liza.

Jamie then left with Roberts. Hendry was to take them to Anthony's and then wait for Diana, little Thomas and their nurse and bring them to Liza. Jamie and Anthony would return together after the funeral.

Liza went about completing all the arrangements for a Christmas that was going to be very different to previous years. Mrs Frances came to find her as she had received word that Mrs Price, Derek and Christopher would not be joining the staff that year for their Christmas lunch.

"That's a pity Mrs Frances," said Liza. "Is it because they don't feel that they should enjoy the day this year?"

"Yes, I believe so," said Mrs Frances. "They will dine quietly at home."

"I can understand how they feel. Do you think that they want Susan with them?" asked Liza.

"Mrs Price didn't say if she would. I suppose if you can do without Susan, you could give her the option of spending her time there," said Mrs Frances. "Adam and April are thinking of doing the same, but Ken and his girls have confirmed that they will be with us."

"It is difficult to become enthusiastic about Christmas this year, but I really want Christina and Zara to have a good and happy day," said Liza. "It will help if Ken's girls are here as they get on well with Christina and Zara. Our boys will miss Derek and Christopher, but they can see them any time."

"I think that they are planning to come here to visit this afternoon," said Mrs Frances. "They now have a pony and buggy between them."

"It's good that life is working out so well for them both," said Liza. "Your Christmas celebrations are going to be somewhat depleted this year and I'm not sure exactly how many will be with us, but I should know by later today. As you know I was planning a large New Year's Eve party for our friends, your friends and all from the village and the farms as his Lordship and I wanted to thank everyone for their care and concern for our welfare whilst we were held in America, but I feel that it is no longer appropriate. However I would like to do something on New Year's Day for the children from the area and their parents can join them if they so wish. It could start at around three o'clock and last until say seven o'clock."

"What age group are you thinking of?" asked Mrs Frances.

"It could be from any age. I know our boys will probably join in, which means that Derek and Christopher will also, as will some parents," said Liza. "This year has not been a very good year for us, and it is ending very sadly, I would like to start the next year with a little happiness and children should be allowed to be happy and not worried by depressing events."

"I think that most parents would agree with you," said Mrs Frances.

"Well, the choice will be theirs," said Liza. "I believe I can hear a buggy coming down the drive, and I can also hear four people running down the stairs. I think we are in for some noise for a while."

Liza also went to greet Derek and Christopher; especially has she had not had the opportunity to see Christopher since her return and he proudly showed her his hand. There was a scar, but all the fingers were flexing well, and the rest of the hand and the wrist were moving well.

508

"He's started drawing now," said Derek, "and his pictures are looking very good; in fact, he's giving some art classes at the school."

"That's really a very good improvement in just a year. I look forward to seeing what you've done. I hear you'll be having your Christmas lunch at home this year, but it's understandable under the circumstances," said Liza. "I'll see you all over the holiday though. Anyway I can see that my boys are anxious to spend time with you now, so I'll let you get on. No doubt there'll be something for you in the kitchen when you're ready."

As they all moved up to what had been the boys' schoolroom and was now used by them as a sitting room, Diana, little Thomas and their nurse arrived.

"You're looking much better now Liza," said Diana. "You really looked very unwell when you arrived back from America."

"Thomas is getting quite big now. He must be looking forward to Christmas and I'm determined that the children are going to have a nice time despite the sad circumstances," said Liza.

"I'm glad you've said that, because even though I feel extremely sad and very sorry for the Queen and her family, our children should have a happy Christmas. They don't really understand how serious the Prince dying is and why should they, they'll be adults soon enough," said Diana.

"It's a relief you are saying that because I felt that I was the only one to think that way. They have been told the reason why we all have been shocked and upset and we will keep saying prayers for his soul. This is Christina's and Zara's first Christmas in this country, and I want them to enjoy it. Now that you and little Thomas are here, I'm sure that they will," said Liza.

"Who else is joining us this year?" asked Diana.

"I have no idea if Douglas and the Duke are coming but I know that Bella and the boys will be with us tomorrow," said Liza. "Where's Rose; she did come with you, didn't she?"

"Yes, but we dropped her off at Miranda and Lucinda's; she could see that your boy's friends had just arrived and thought it best to let them get their enthusiasm out of the way. She knows that you would not be offended, and she'll see you shortly," said Diana.

Derek and Christopher were dining with the boys later that afternoon and then spending the evening in their sitting room. They were being allowed to use the dining room early and much to Liza's amusement she saw Derek sliding down the banisters with Matthew at the top of the stairs, James in the middle and John ready to catch him at the bottom; Christopher was shaking his head and Simon was laughing.

Liza turned to Diana and said that she hoped that little Thomas had not seen what Derek had just done, or Christina and Zara.

Diana laughed and said that it was just some harmless fun and that it was good to see somebody having some enjoyment.

"It's wonderful that all our young men are such good friends," said Liza. "They have all gone through diverse traumas to a greater or lesser extent but have always come out the other side smiling. I'm very proud of them all."

"They care for one another and will protect each other with their lives," said Diana. "It must be a wonderful comfort to you to know that."

Liza smiled and nodded. "It's Christina's and Zara's supper time. I presume you would like Thomas to join them."

"Yes, that would be fine, but really I know that Thomas would have preferred to be in the dining room, sitting next to Matthew," said Diana.

The next day Ken and Mr Lambert brought in the Christmas tree and put it securely in its normal place, but as previously decided it would not be decorated until the following day.

Bella, Nicholas and Richard arrived later that day, but Bella had no idea whether the Duke and Douglas Carlton would be spending Christmas with them.

"Their rooms are ready should they decide to join us," smiled Liza.

"It's going to be a very strange Christmas," commented Bella.

"That's what everyone is saying, but we will make it the best we can for the sake of the children," said Liza.

All the boys joined them for dinner that evening which relieved David of the pressure of being the only man at the table as Jamie had not managed to return home that day.

Liza spent a second night alone in her bed; she missed Jamie terribly and could not wait for his return. *He'll be back tomorrow,* she thought. *I wonder if the Duke and Douglas will also be with him. I wish it wasn't Christmas as I really don't know how I am expected to react.*

She finally went to sleep having already worried that she could upset some of her guests by not being sad enough, but she was not going to make the girls' Christmas unhappy for them.

Liza was up early the next morning, and she was surrounded by her boys, the girls and Nicholas and Richard in the dining room for breakfast and they were all discussing the decoration of the tree. The door opened and little Thomas was standing there asking if he could have his breakfast with them. It reminded Liza of Matthew and then also James struggling into the room with their breakfasts dripping off their plates and then being allowed by Patrick to eat with their fingers.

Her heart missed a beat, and she was afraid that the tears that she felt at the back of her eyes would spill over. Matthew looked at her and knew instinctively how she felt; he also knew that to show any sympathy towards her would open the flood gates. He got up and guided Thomas over to the table and helped him to some breakfast. The look on Thomas' face was ecstatic. His nurse looked into the room and Liza told her that everything was under control and that Thomas was behaving beautifully.

"When are we going to decorate the tree?" asked Christina.

"Matthew, James and John know where the decorations are, so as soon as we've finished breakfast then you can start," said Liza.

Mr Lambert and Ken helped the boys and Christina, whilst Zara sat on the floor and watched it all happen. She was coaxed once or twice to place something pretty on the lower branches, but she was fascinated by what was happening. She disappeared up to her room for a short while and when she returned she was carrying her wooden doll and she handed it to Matthew to put on the tree, which he did, placing it right at the front so that it was in full view of everyone. She turned to Liza and smiled up at her triumphantly. Liza did wonder whether she would be happy leaving it there as she had never gone to bed without it, but if that was a problem it had been placed where it could easily be reached.

Just after lunch Jamie and Anthony arrived; they were both very tired and after greeting everyone they made their way to their rooms to change and rest for a while. Liza followed Jamie to his room to make sure that he was alright. Roberts was there sorting out his clothes for later in the day, but he discreetly left as Liza arrived.

She asked him how the funeral had gone, and he said that obviously it was a very sombre affair which the Queen was unable to attend as she was so distraught, in fact there were no women there at all; it was a men only funeral. He went into a few more details and said that he would be down to see their guests shortly when he had rested for a while.

Liza said that she would leave him in peace and made her way to the door.

"Come here Liza," said Jamie. "You look as if you could do with a cuddle."

"Yes, I could Jamie. I really missed you these last couple of days," said Liza. "This Christmas is so difficult, and I am trying so hard to make it a happy time for everyone, especially Christina and Zara and I don't feel that I am making a very good job of it. I wish that all this hadn't happened at this time of year. Then every night I felt so alone without you."

Jamie put his arms around her and kissed her on the head saying, "Well, I'm here now Liza and we'll handle Christmas together. Everyone will enjoy it, especially the girls; we'll make sure of it. I forgot to tell you, the Duke and Douglas will be joining us later today. They know that you had arranged that they could spend the time here if they wished."

Liza smiled happily as she stayed in Jamie's arms. "I should let you rest now; I know you're very tired."

"Ah Liza, holding you like this has taken much of my tiredness away and it's nice to know that you missed me so much. I missed you too," said Jamie. "When we get Christmas and the New Year over, we can have some time just with our family, unless we get snowed in before all our guests have left, as we have done in previous years."

They stayed together for a while until a carriage could be heard making its way up the drive and Liza had to leave to welcome the last of their guests and she wondered how many members of staff they had brought with them.

Liza ran down the stairs in time to greet the Duke and Douglas. They had only brought the Dukes' valet and their driver. The driver would be comfortably housed in the stable block and there was plenty of room for the Dukes' valet in the staff quarters.

After ushering the Duke and Douglas into the drawing room and arranging refreshments for them, Liza apologised for Jamie not being there to greet them as he too had not long arrived, and he was taking the opportunity rest for a while.

"It's been a difficult few days for everyone," said the Duke. "I know that Douglas and I are also very tired and if you don't mind, I would like to rest for a while."

"I would also, Liza, if you have no objection," said Douglas.

"Of course," said Liza. "Harper and Mrs Frances will arrange anything that you need with your valet. Dinner will be at eight o'clock this evening, so you have plenty of time to rest, and I look forward to seeing you later."

The boys joined them for dinner that evening; Christina and Zara had their supper earlier and Liza and Jamie had seen them settled in their beds. Both were looking forward to the following day with Zara being particularly excited.

On occasion it was a little sombre around the table as some of the talk was about the funeral the previous day.

"I don't know how the Queen is going to manage without the Prince," said the Duke. "She relied on him for a great many things; in fact there appears to be little that she did without consulting with him."

"Do you think that this problem with America is going to be resolved?" Anthony asked of the Duke.

"It is no secret that the Queen is in favour of the Confederate states, although your difficulties with them did sway her somewhat," said the Duke to Liza and Jamie. "But now with our neutrality being challenged she was once again leaning towards supporting them. However Palmerston also needed cooling down and the Prince did manage to calm him in that respect. Going to war with the Union is certainly not a wise move, but they did overstep the mark by taking those two southern representatives from one of our British vessels."

"It's going to affect your business, isn't it Liza?" said Douglas.

"If we go to war with the north, it will seriously affect everything that we have there. If we keep our neutrality, we will still be affected but not to the same extent," said Liza. "All we can do is to wait and see."

"I understand that your man Harry Turner has given some good advice to many investors," grinned Douglas.

"He does seem to have the ability to read the markets. No matter what the outcome of this particular problem, those taking his advice will either gain considerably or to a lesser extent, but they will all gain," said Liza.

"Well he certainly appears to give sound advice," said Douglas.

The ladies left the men to their port and cigars and moved to the drawing room. The boys decided to go to their sitting room.

"I'm so pleased to be here with you again this year Liza," said Bella. "I know it's not going to be the same as other years, but I'm glad that we are going to make an effort for the sake of the children; it will help us to stop being so morbid."

"I'm afraid that it has rather blighted Christmas this year," said Grace. "It does make us realise just how important the Prince was to this country. I feel really sorry for the Queen, I know how my father was when my mother died; he found Christmas a very difficult time, especially the first one without her."

Liza was quiet as she was remembering that she had already been through that sadness twice in her life. She was well aware of how the Queen felt, and how Grace's father felt and probably still did. Miranda was always sensitive of Liza's feelings, and she moved next to her and patted her hand reassuringly. Liza smiled and nodded to her and hoped that it conveyed to Miranda that she was alright and coping with the conversation.

The men came and joined the ladies, and it was not long before Miranda, Lucinda and Rose decided to go to their home and David and Grace said that they would also leave and see everyone the next morning.

"You normally have many of the Fuller family with you at Christmas," said Douglas. "It seems strange not to see them this year."

"Yes, I do miss them, but they did spend a great deal of time here whilst we were away. They helped to keep the family calm and the household running smoothly in our absence," said Liza.

"We will still enjoy the day tomorrow, after all we have our closest friends with us," said Jamie. "Is Bernard Collins joining us tomorrow, Liza?"

"No he seems to think that he should stay at his home and contemplate all that has happened recently. I have made sure that he has plenty of food though. You know what he's like; he never thinks to make sure that his food cupboards have anything in them," smiled Liza.

James came into the room and made his way over to Liza. "Zara's sitting in front of the Christmas tree, Mother," said James. "I cannot coax her back to bed and neither can Susan. I think you are needed."

"Does she want her doll back?" asked Liza.

"I've asked her that, but she just shakes her head," said James. "She's not sad; in fact she's smiling quite happily."

Liza excused herself from the room and went to find Zara and found her sitting on the floor watching the Christmas tree. Liza sat down on the floor next to her and asked her what she was doing.

"I'm waiting for Father Christmas," whispered Zara. "Christina says that he visits children tonight, so I'm waiting for him."

James and Susan could be heard muttering their realisation of what Zara was doing and Liza pulled Zara onto her lap. "Father Christmas will be visiting tonight, but it takes him a long time to get around all the children and he likes to make sure they are asleep before he visits them. Isn't that right James?" said Liza.

"Absolutely," said James. "I know that I must soon go to bed, or Father Christmas won't be able to visit me, and it's the same for Susan, isn't it?"

"That's right," said Susan. "I must be asleep before Father Christmas delivers my presents."

"Oh," said Zara.

"Would you like me to take you to bed now?" asked Liza and Zara nodded vigorously so they slowly walked up the stairs together and Liza lifted her into her bed and covered her warmly. Christina was asleep so Liza whispered a little story to her about Father Christmas and before long Zara was sound asleep with a beautiful smile on her face.

James and Susan had disappeared when Liza made her way back to the drawing room. Diana asked if everything was alright.

"Zara was waiting for Father Christmas, but I managed to persuade her that he would only visit when all children were asleep," smiled Liza. "She's settled and is asleep now."

"You are right to try and make it a happy time for the children," said Douglas. "The children at the Palace naturally won't be that lucky."

"Well, I think that I had better get to my bed," smiled the Duke, "otherwise Father Christmas won't visit me."

"I should also. I'm sorry that Tricia can't be with us this year, but I think it is going to be some time before she will be able to return home and indeed have any form of private life," said Douglas.

"I suppose we will have to wear some form of mourning dress tomorrow for church," said Diana.

"I believe it will be expected of us," said Liza. "I shall be wearing grey with black accessories and the boys and girls will be wearing black armbands. I have plenty of armbands for those who need them."

"Yes, I have brought a black cloak with me, and I also have a grey outfit," said Diana. "I'll have an armband for Thomas if I may Liza."

"I have the mourning clothes I wore for the funeral," said Anthony.

The Duke and Douglas also agreed that they had their mourning suits with them.

"We can change into something more festive when we return," said Jamie and with that all the guests made their way to their various rooms, leaving Jamie and Liza relaxing in the drawing room.

"I suppose we ought to make our way to bed, otherwise Father Christmas won't visit us either," smiled Jamie.

"It's nice just the two of us here now; let's wait until everyone has settled although that's keeping Susan and Roberts up later than necessary," said Liza.

Jamie asked what was happening with the staff on Christmas Day and she told him that lunch would be ready by midday and hopefully they would be finished by three o'clock. The staff would have their Christmas lunch at around four o'clock, having already arranged cold cuts and salads for those who needed afternoon tea.

"Will Ken be there with his girls?" asked Jamie.

"Yes, and I'd like to encourage them to come up and visit Christina and Zara at some time during the afternoon or early evening," said Liza. "They all play together well and of course it will help Christina with her first day at school, and the younger ones are helping Zara with her language and showing her how to play."

"We've heard nothing further of Ken's problems with his father, but I have no doubt that we will. From what I have been told, the Earl of Graystead doesn't give up easily," said Jamie.

"Have you sorted out the problem with your farmer, Jeb Wickes, wasn't it?" asked Liza.

Jamie laughed, "I wondered how long it would take you to ask about him. One of our workers is married and in fact he and his wife have already moved into the Wickes farm. They wanted to be organised for Christmas. Mr and Mrs Wickes were not overly happy with the suggestion that they share their house with strangers, but when they realised who they were they found that they knew them, and Mr Wickes seemed quite flattered that he was needed to help with the instruction of a young farmer."

"So Jeb Wickes thinks that he is doing a favour for the young couple," said Liza. "Well done, Jamie. It often works that people think that they have come up with a brilliant idea. I hope they all get on well together and I'm sure in the fullness of time Mr and Mrs Wickes will realise that they need the assistance of the young couple. What's their name?"

"Their surname is Stebbs; I believe his name is Lawrence; I don't know his wife's name, but apparently she is a very good cook," said Jamie.

"Well, I hope she gets on with Mrs Wickes, because two women in a kitchen can create problems," said Liza. "I think everyone has settled, so we can make our way up to bed now and look forward to tomorrow with our boys and Christina, Zara and Thomas."

Before they went to their rooms, they crept into Christina and Zara's room and carefully hung stockings on the ends of their beds with small presents in them, and then on to Thomas' and did the same. They grinned as they also went into the boys' room and hung their stockings on each bed and then on to Nicholas and Richard's room.

When they finally made their way to their room Jamie said that he wished that he had had a childhood such as these children had.

"But you're happy now aren't you Jamie, and surely you'll get pleasure from hearing the sounds from all our charges tomorrow morning.

"I'm very happy now Liza, and as you say there is no point in dwelling on an unhappy childhood. We'll make sure that everyone enjoys their time with us tomorrow," said Jamie.

***

They woke up on Christmas morning to the sounds of laughter and shouts of pleasure and Jamie commented that he assumed that the stockings and presents had been found.

516

Breakfast was a happy and noisy time with everyone except Bella at the table. The church service later that morning was necessarily sombre, but the boys were pleased to see Derek and Christopher and they arranged to meet up the following day. The sermon was not overly long, and it did ask that all parishioners remember the Royal Family on this day which was a celebration of the birth of Christ but would be an unhappy one in the Royal household.

All the talk around the dinner table was light-hearted with the boys being the main leaders in any conversation. Then after lunch came the time for present giving whilst the staff enjoyed their Christmas lunch. Party games followed and by the time they were over, the staff had finished their lunch. Liza then took Christina and Zara down to the kitchen to visit Ken's daughters and invite them up to their bedroom to play for a while. Thomas had been invited to join them, but he was quite happy just sitting in the same room as Matthew.

Time was getting on and Harper came to say that Ken was contemplating taking his family home and Ernie was going to drive them. Ken was waiting in the hall as Liza came from the drawing room and she asked him how he had enjoyed the day and as they were talking Douglas came into the hall and he stopped and stared at Ken and nodded to him.

"I'm sure I know you from somewhere," said Douglas. "I thought I did when I saw you once before, but I can't for the life of me remember where. Can you enlighten me?"

"I've worked in many places Sir," said Ken. "I'm sure you must have seen me in one of them."

Liza was smiling but saying nothing.

"Possibly, but your face stayed in my mind last time I saw you here," said Douglas. "It's probably my mind playing tricks on me."

Christina and Zara then came down the stairs with Ken's four girls and Douglas looked at them and said what pretty girls they were and as he said it Liza could see that realisation was dawning on him, and he looked back at Ken but said nothing before disappearing into the drawing room.

"I believe that he has just realised who I am," said Ken quietly.

"Yes, I think you're right, but there is no problem with that," said Liza. "Lord Carlton is no troublemaker, and you have nothing to be ashamed or afraid of. I hope you and your girls have had a nice time. It has been a rather difficult Christmas, but I'm pleased that all the children have enjoyed their day. You do know that I am planning a party for them on New Year's Day; I hope you and your girls will be able join us then."

"Thank you, my girls will be pleased to," said Ken. "Whether I will be able to does depend on the tasks I have to carry out on that day."

Ken and his girls left, and Liza joined everyone in the drawing room where Douglas was in conversation with Jamie. Liza went over to them and said to Douglas that it was obvious that he had recognised Ken.

"I was just asking Jamie if he knew who he was, and I now realise that you do. There have been many rumours about him, but I believe that they have come mainly from his own family," said Douglas.

"Yes, we've heard many stories, but all are unfounded," said Liza. "He is honest and an excellent worker. There have been no problems with him, and he is devoted to his daughters."

"Where is his wife?" asked Douglas.

"She died some time ago," said Jamie.

"That's sad," said Douglas. "I saw her once before they were married. She was one of the Earl's groom's daughters. She was an extremely pretty girl; you could not help noticing her. The children look very like her, which is why I recognised him. Their marriage created a rift in the family, although it would not have been difficult to create a rift; the Earl is a strange and very domineering man. I have never been easy in his company, and I have only been in contact with him when it has been necessary."

Susan brought Christina and Zara in to say goodnight to everyone and they prettily went around everyone thanking them for a lovely day and when they came to Liza and Jamie, Christina put her arms around Liza and kissed her and Zara followed suit. Liza said that she would be up to see them shortly.

Thomas' nurse came to fetch him, and he too went around everyone saying goodnight and thank you. Matthew said that he would see him when he was tucked up in bed which made Thomas leave the room quickly and he could be heard running up the stairs.

"You're very kind Matthew," said Diana.

"He's no trouble. He's a very happy little boy and a pleasure to see," said Matthew. "It's no effort to say goodnight to him."

Finally the day was drawing to a close but before everyone went to their rooms the Duke thanked Liza and Jamie for making their Christmas a happy one, not just for the children but also for all the adults, as it had been a difficult time for the whole country.

Once again Jamie and Liza were left by themselves in the drawing room.

"Today worked out better than I had expected it to be," said Jamie. "The boys and the young ones enjoyed themselves and I believe everyone else did also. I was surprised that Douglas recognised Ken; he didn't seem too enthusiastic about the character of his father. Do you know how long our guests are staying?"

"Anthony, Diana and Rose will be with us until after the New Year, and I have a feeling that Bella and her boys will also stay until that time. I have no idea about the Duke and Douglas, but they do tend to amuse themselves, so they are not a problem. I believe that the Major and Jennifer and Lily and Joseph will visit tomorrow. They were going to visit today but decided that tomorrow would be a better day as they wanted to make sure that the children in the Homes were not too distressed by the Prince's death. Those children have enough problems without taking on the problems of the nation," said Liza.

"You look tired Liza," said Jamie. "I think we ought to make our way to bed now. Are you coming to my room tonight, or am I going to yours?"

"The choice is yours," said Liza. "Which would you prefer?"

"I like it when you come to me," said Jamie.

"Then that's what I shall do," smiled Liza.

***

The following week passed quickly. The Duke left after Boxing Day, but Douglas decided to stay until after the New Year.

All the children from the village and farms were invited to the party on New Year's Day and they all appeared to be looking forward to it. The boys were commissioned with the task of thinking up games for the children to play. Mrs Lambert was in her element making food suitable for youngsters and Liza had to remind her that it would seem that at least one parent would be accompanying their child, so it would really be catering for adults also. It was not a problem as Mrs Lambert was used to providing food for those at the cricket matches and it appeared that the children's party was an excuse for all the adults to get together also.

The Major and Jennifer would also be joining them on that day, and Liza was hoping that Lily and Joseph could also come as they were very good at entertaining children. Penny and Randolph had also intimated that they would like to help at the party. Liza remembered that Penny and Ken seemed to get on well together and she wondered whether Penny knew Ken's origins.

The day before the party Anthony, Diana and Douglas helped Mr Lambert and Ken arrange the dining room and adjoining drawing room to accommodate the number of children and adults who were coming, and that number seemed to be increasing at an alarming rate.

"This is no longer a party for children," said a worried Liza. "I'd better see Mrs Lambert again to make sure that we will have enough food for everyone. I knew what the children would drink, but I haven't arranged very much for the adults."

519

Jamie was standing and smiling at her, "Liza you should have known that nobody wants to miss out on one of your gatherings. It will all be organised by tomorrow; you've never failed in the past, there's no reason why you should fail tomorrow."

Harper said that he would arrange with Mr Rogers to organise what drink he thought should be consumed, but he would also arrange that there were some large punch bowls, some alcoholic and some not. Liza thanked him and then she disappeared down to the kitchen to consult with Mrs Lambert.

Miranda and Lucinda were finding the situation quite amusing; they had seen how all the people in the area never missed a chance to come to the house and join in any celebrations.

They all quietly saw in the New Year and in everyone's minds was the thought that it could only be better than the previous year.

After breakfast the house seemed to miraculously become organised ready to receive an unknown number of guests. Nobody had time for lunch, but as food would be ready as the guests arrived, they would be able to eat then.

The Major and Jennifer arrived early as did Lily and Joseph and they also brought Penny and Randolph and they all helped to put the final touches to the rooms, even Bella put her mark on one or two tables.

The Reverend Bernard Collins was next to arrive, and he said that if there were no objections, he would like to make a short speech, but they were not to worry as he would not make it too depressing. Liza reminded him that it was a party for children, although it did seem that the whole village, along with those from the farms, had decided that they would be attending. Bernard smiled and commented that the people enjoyed such gatherings, and they were happy to see Liza and Jamie safely back home and wanted to show how pleased they were.

Liza hoped that there were enough places set at the table for all the children. The adults were capable of standing and eating or waiting until the children had finished.

The boys were watching each dish as Mrs Lambert and the maids brought them up from the kitchen and Matthew asked if places had been set for them at the table.

"I'm not sure how many children are coming Matthew. I'll make sure that Thomas, Christina and Zara are seated with Ken's girls, but apart from that the children can sit where they like and if there's room then, yes, you can sit at the table, if that is what you really want," said Liza.

"I think that we ought to try to supervise the children, rather than sitting with them," said James.

520

"Yes, I suppose we are a little old for a children's party," said Matthew.

"We're organising games for them after they've eaten," said Nicholas. "We can stand and eat and make sure that all the children have what they want."

"Please do not encourage them to play any games that are too energetic soon after they've eaten. We do not want to have to mop up after any of them," said Liza.

"Yes, that's a thought, I think we had better rearrange the order in which the games are played," said Matthew thoughtfully and the others agreed with him.

Derek and Christopher arrived with Mrs Price, shortly followed by Adam and April. They had all come to help, and everything had become a hive of activity with everyone happily getting in one another's way and laughing about it.

Adam commented that he hoped that the children would not be unnerved by the fact that all their teachers were also present.

As three o'clock approached they could hear many people walking up the drive and Jamie told Harper to open the front doors so that they knew they were welcome to come in that way.

Ken had already arrived with his daughters, and they made their way to Christina and Zara. Many of the other children there were friends of Ken's daughters and they pulled Christina and Zara over to them and could be seen introducing them. *At least Christina will know a few more children when she starts school,* thought Liza. *And little Zara is also meeting some other children.*

Thomas was eyeing up one or two of the younger boys, but he was reluctant to leave Matthew's side, but Matthew knew some of the children and he was gradually easing him towards them.

Liza was standing at the door to the dining room welcoming everyone, Jamie was nearby, and Liza was aware that he was smiling broadly at four people who were just arriving.

He moved towards them and said, "Liza, this is Mr Jeb Wickes and Mr Lawrence Stebbs, I'm afraid I don't yet know your wives' names."

"My wife is Elsie and Lawrence's wife is Irene," said Jeb Wickes.

"I'm really pleased to meet you all; I understand that you now have some assistance working your farm Mr Wickes," said Liza. "It will give you a little more time to yourself."

"I'm training Lawrence in some of the more specialised aspects of farming," said Jeb Wickes.

"Yes, I had heard that Mr Wickes, and how are you getting on Mr Stebbs? I trust that he's not too much of a task master," said Liza.

"We're all getting on very well, and I know I still have a lot to learn," said Lawrence Stebbs.

"There's always a great deal to learn Mr Stebbs," said Liza. "We all have something to learn every day of our lives; that's what makes life so exciting."

"We know that this is really a party for the children, but we wanted to come to tell you how pleased we are that you are both back with us safely, and we didn't want to impose on you as we don't have any children, so we have brought some food with us and we hope we are not insulting you by doing this," said Jeb Wickes and he continued, "my wife and Irene are very good cooks."

"I'm sure they are, and I am not insulted. Thank you for your thoughtfulness," said Liza and she called Mrs Lambert over and explained about the food that the Wickes and Stebbs had brought with them.

"That's wonderful," said Mrs Lambert. "Shall we go and put it out on the table," she added to Elsie Wickes and Irene, which they did, and Liza noticed that others had done the same, and the tables were now loaded with food. *I needn't have worried; nobody will be leaving here hungry today.*

Liza and Jamie were gradually working their way around all the guests and Miranda and Lucinda were helping to get the children settled at the table. Bella was also helping along with the Major and Jennifer and Liza noticed that Penny was talking to Ken. Everyone seemed relaxed and happy to be there.

Bernard called everyone to order and when silence had fallen, he made a short speech:

"I am not going to take up much of your time; I would just like to say one or two things to everyone. I know that you are all happy to be here and I know that you are also all very pleased to see Lord Jamie and Lady Liza back home safely. I had the opportunity to see just about everyone whilst they were being held in America and I would like to tell you both that there was not one person who did not show concern or ask constantly if I knew of how you were faring. They also showed great concern for your boys and all members of your family. When we heard that you had managed to reach New York it was the first time that we knew that you were free; there had been a question of whether you were in fact alive. I think that you can see the high esteem that you are held in from the number of people here today and I know that they are here to let you know how proud they feel of you and their relief at seeing you both back with us."

Everyone agreed with him and clapped, and Liza and Jamie nodded and said thank you.

"I would just like to add one thing," said Bernard. "We are having a very happy and enjoyable afternoon here today; I would just ask you for a minute's silence while we remember Prince Albert and the sadness that our Queen and her family are feeling at this moment, and indeed the rest of our nation."

Everyone looked down and remained silent for the requested minute, after which the children's enthusiasm made the sadness pass and the afternoon proceeded as all good parties should, with a great deal of fun and laughter. The boys had excelled with their organisation of the games for the children, although many of the adults decided that it was a good idea to join in and chaos ensued, led mainly by Joseph. This reminded Liza of past Christmases in Belfast, with Joseph and Edward creating havoc whilst Peter stayed aloof, much to the amusement of everyone there.

Both punch bowls ran out and Mr Rogers was seen filling them again with whatever he had to hand; Diana was watching him closely so that she knew what was alcoholic and what was not.

Rose, David and Douglas were sitting and watching all that was going on with bemused smiles on their faces, whilst Randolph, Lily and Grace made sure that all adults were well catered for.

The Major, Jennifer and Anthony were encouraging the competition in the children's games. Liza noticed that Ken and Penny were once again deep in conversation, and she again wondered if Penny knew of Ken's origins.

John was helping Zara to join in the games, and she seemed to be enjoying it. Christina needed no help, but Thomas had to be encouraged by Matthew to leave his side and join in the fun.

In the middle of all this the Duke arrived. "I trust I am not intruding on you Liza, but I have finished the business that I needed to carry out and I was intrigued by what you were planning for today, so I am imposing myself upon you once again. I do hope that I am not putting you to too much trouble."

"Of course not," said Liza. "I'll just see Mrs Frances, but I think that your room is ready for you. Do you have your valet with you?"

"Yes, he's here," said the Duke.

"Well when he's sorted out your belongings, he must come and join us here. This is open house to everyone," said Liza.

Mrs Frances had pre-empted the Duke's return, both she and Liza had previously discussed such a possibility, so his room was ready for him. Whether Bella was pleased, nobody would ever know as they seemed to spend their lives in a very cordial relationship.

Seven o'clock came and went and it was not until nine o'clock that those with young children decided to leave. Liza was sitting with a sleeping Zara on her lap. Christina was still having a nice time with some of the other children. Susan said goodbye to her mother and brother, and they left with Christopher; Susan then took Zara up to her bed.

Ken gathered all his children together and he had arranged that Ernie would take them home. At the same time Penny and Randolph left with Lily and Joseph. The Major and Jennifer were staying the night and they settled down chatting with Miranda, Lucinda and Rose. Grace, David and Bernard were rounding up some of the stragglers, after which Bernard would be taken to his vicarage by Mr and Mrs Rogers.

Liza and Jamie looked at one another and Jamie commented that this was the first time that Liza did not have to arrange how people were getting to their homes; it had all be arranged by the guests themselves and many of the guests had also helped to clear the rooms and take everything down to the kitchen.

Finally all the guests had left and those within the house had gone to their rooms. The drawing and dining rooms still looked a little chaotic, but Liza knew that by the morning all would be back in its proper place, she had no doubt about that.

"Did you enjoy yourself Liza," asked Jamie when they were alone in his bedroom.

"I did Jamie, and I think that everyone else did also. It was a nice speech by Bernard; not too long, a little embarrassing but well meant. I think that his referral to the Prince was right and respectful, and I believe it made everyone appreciate how lucky we all are," said Liza.

Liza lay back thinking. She realised that it probably seemed that she had forgotten what had happened on that day nine years before but there were moments when she felt that it had been a mistake to organise what had turned out to be such a large gathering. Matthew, John, James and Simon had found her in her bedroom that morning and they all had kissed her and shown that they also remembered what day it was, with Matthew adding that no matter what they did they would always spend time on that day thinking about their daddy Patrick.

When they had left, Liza had sat appreciating how thoughtful her sons and Simon were. Matthew returned and asked her if she was now truly happy.

"Yes, Matthew, I am. My life with Jamie is different, but we love and look after one another. I will never forget Patrick, he loved us and gave us a wonderful life, but we are lucky that we managed to find someone who loves us all and makes sure that we are happy, and I know that we all love him also," said Liza.

"He's always loved you, hasn't he Mother?" said Matthew.

"Yes, since I was around your age, Matthew. It's a very long time and I'm very lucky to have someone who loves me and loves you also," said Liza.

With that Matthew had left and Liza had brushed herself down and got ready for a very long but entertaining day.

Chapter 15

As Jamie was taking the boys back to Cambridge a week after the beginning of the year, Liza was getting Christina ready for her first day at school. She was a little nervous but she now knew several the school children so it was not quite as daunting as it would otherwise have been.

Zara was a little upset that Christina would be away for the day, but Liza was going to take her to see Cora and Libby Wallace at Mrs Price's house once she had taken Christina to school.

Liza was ushered into Adam's office where Christopher was also waiting for them.

"I see you've brought your lunch with you Christina," said Christopher putting the little girl at ease. Liza smiled and nodded at him, and Christina answered that she had, and she told him exactly what was in her lunch box. Zara was watching closely, and she wasn't looking too happy. She whispered to Liza that she wanted to go to school with Christina.

"When you're a little older you can, but when we have finished here, you're going to visit your friends Cora and Libby," said Liza.

"I'll take you to your class now Christina and settle you in. You already know most of the children there, so it won't be too difficult for you," said Christopher. "Will your Aunt Liza be picking you up later?"

"Yes, she will," said Christina quietly as she was led out of Adam's room.

"Has Christina had a sound education prior to coming here?" asked Adam.

"The school in Benson was well run and the main teacher could recognise talent when she saw it. I don't think that Christina has a particular talent apart from kindness, but she has been described as good at most subjects and very keen to learn. I believe that she will eventually excel at helping others to learn; she has helped Zara in so many ways, not least with the English language, but that is all in the future. Things can change with time," said Liza.

"You know that we will look after her and encourage her in whatever she chooses as a future," said Adam. "You could easily have employed a governess for her, but I understand that she has been used to mixing at school, so it is probably a wise decision to send her here."

"Thank you, Adam," said Liza. "I feel happy that she is in your care, and in a couple of years you will have Zara under your wing."

Adam showed them out and Liza made her way to Mrs Price's home so that Zara could spend some time with Cora and Libby. Mrs Price said that Zara could stay for lunch and Liza said that she would call for her later when she came back to collect Christina from school.

"Are you happy to stay with Cora and Libby until we pick Christina up?" Liza asked Zara and her reply was to smile happily and run off to join the girls who were playing in the sitting room.

"This is very good of you Mrs Price," said Liza. "It's the first time that Zara has been away from Christina. They became inseparable when they both had to leave their homes in America. I'm pleased that Christina is at school as she needs to have a little independence from Zara, although they do love one another."

"Don't you worry about little Zara," said Mrs Price. "I'll make sure she enjoys her day with the girls. They are very well mannered and caring of one another; I'm sure they will also be caring of Zara. You go on; I know you always have a great deal to do."

On her way back, Liza called in to see Bernard Collins to check that his cupboards had enough supplies in them, and she made a list of what she thought he needed.

"Liza, you are very kind," said Bernard. "I do try to look after myself, but as you know I do sometimes forget."

"I haven't heard what the forecast is yet," said Liza. "But I'll have your room ready in case we have another bad winter."

"My vicarage is quite comfortable," said Bernard.

"I know it is Bernard, but if we have a winter as we did a few years ago you will be hard pressed to keep the place warm enough. Everyone loves you and we don't want you to die of hypothermia," said Liza.

"Well let's hope we have a bad winter as I enjoy my time with you," smiled Bernard.

"You're always welcome," said Liza and she carried on her way home.

She waved to David who was tidying his garden and then stopped at Miranda and Lucinda's.

They enquired how Christina had felt starting at school and how little Zara coped with leaving her there.

"They both are fine. It is giving Christina a break from looking after Zara, because that is what she has done ever since they met in Benson. Also Zara will not be so dependent on her because the time will come when Christina must go back to her grandparents. If the war finishes next week, then she will be leaving us shortly. I've become very fond of her and will miss her when the time comes," said Liza.

"She is a very charming child," said Lucinda. "Her colouring seems quite unique. I don't think that I have ever seen such red hair on such a sallow complexion, but of course her father is quite similar, only not so noticeable. I know that you are friends with her grandparents, did you know her mother?"

"Her mother is dead," said Liza and Lucinda realised that to ask anything further was intruding on something that Liza did not want to answer.

Over refreshments they discussed the weather and Liza said that she must ask Jamie to find out what the farmers think as they were normally very accurate in their forecasts.

As Liza finally made her way up the drive, she was overtaken by Hendry driving Jamie home from taking the boys back to university and they entered a very quiet house together.

"I know what you are going to say Liza," said Jamie. "This house is normally rather noisy and to walk into this quietness is somewhat unsettling. We ought to make the most of it because Christina will be anxious to tell us all about her first day at school, and Zara will be full of her time with the little Wallace girls. You won't have a minute to yourself when they get home."

"You're right Jamie," said Liza. "By the way, have you heard the forecast from any of the farmers yet?"

"Apparently it is not going to be as bad as a few years ago, but we are in for a week or so of heavy snowfall," said Jamie. "I suppose we had better make plans for it now."

"Yes, I've already seen Bernard and told him that much as his vicarage is quite comfortable, it is not that warm, and I'll have a room made ready for him. Your mother and Lucinda and their staff will probably be warm enough in their home, but the choice is theirs; I would be happier if they came here as well as David and Grace, but once again they can make that choice nearer the time. I'll just make sure that they at least have enough food and firewood should they wish to stay in their homes," said Liza.

"It's going to be quite a sparse house without them, but we'll survive. No doubt Bella will turn up and stay for the duration although the Duke has spent a fortune updating their house and making it warm and watertight. Douglas also normally turns up when the weather turns cold, so I think it would be strange for us to be on our own at such a time," smiled Jamie.

"I wish the boys were home, but I suppose they will be quite cosy where they are," said Liza. "I'll check with Mr and Mrs Rogers, Mrs Price, Adam and April and Ken, that they are all prepared."

Jamie smiled at Liza and said that he thought that people were quite capable of preparing themselves for winter.

"I know, but I'd only worry about them if I didn't check," said Liza.

"I have to say that it really is what the Lord and Lady of the manor should do with their tenants, although it is sadly lacking in many areas and was in my father's day, and in my early time here," said Jamie.

"I hadn't thought of it like that. It was something that we all did in Benson, and the winters there were much fiercer than here, apart from the other year which was rather extraordinary," said Liza. "I suppose the Wickes and the Stebbs are well prepared."

"That's working out quite well for both families," said Jamie. "I'm glad you thought of that."

"It wasn't me," said Liza. "You thought of it, not me."

"You put the germ of an idea in my mind, and I'm sure you would have said it if I hadn't," said Jamie.

"There are always solutions to every problem, but it just sometimes takes a little while to find them," said Liza.

"I think I'll take advantage of the opportunity to read my newspaper whilst it is quiet," said Jamie. "Do you want to join me?"

"No, I'd only start talking to you, which would take away your concentration," smiled Liza. "I have some correspondence to catch up on; I presume Grace is here already."

"I'll see you at lunchtime," said Jamie. "I'll come with you to pick up Christina and Zara. I'll drive you."

"Thank you, Jamie, I'll enjoy that," said Liza as she moved towards her study where she knew Grace would be.

Both girls were full of excitement when Liza and Jamie picked them up from school and Mrs Price's house, and they kept up a constant chatter on their way home, and then they both went running up the stairs to tell Susan what they had been doing that day.

"That seems to have been a successful day for both of them," commented Jamie and then after a short while they could be heard making their way down to the kitchen for their supper.

"This is just as it was when the boys were younger," said Liza. "I think they were a little noisier, but they seemed to instinctively know when supper was ready and it would appear that Christina and Zara do also."

Two weeks later the snow arrived. The school closed and Bernard moved in with them. During a particularly heavy snowfall Bella arrived. The Duke would be staying at his club for the duration and their staff had moved into the small house in their grounds. Initially David and Grace were going to stay in their home, but the farmers were saying that it was going to be a short but extremely sharp couple of weeks, so they decided to spend their time with Liza and Jamie. Miranda and Lucinda spent two days in their own home, but in a lull in the snowstorm they trudged their way over to the main house bringing their staff and all their food and fuel with them.

"I hope the boys are comfortable," said a worried Liza.

"They will be fine," smiled Jamie. "They will be out playing snowballs and their headmaster will not allow them to be cold. They are all in the same dormitory; they will look out for one another and probably enjoy not having their mother fussing over them."

"I saw Ken stacking loads of wood and other fuel outside his home and also outside Mrs Price's. Adam also has plenty of fuel and I know that April was stockpiling food; they are so cosy in their little house. I'm happy that your mother and Lucinda have joined us, I was concerned about them, and looking out of the window now, we would not have been able to reach them in an emergency," said Liza.

"Yes, you are right. I don't like to think about it, but neither of them are getting any younger and winter is a bad time for older people," said Jamie.

"That is a terrible thought; in fact I'm not going to think about it," said Liza.

The farmers had been right and the cold and blizzards only lasted ten days, but it had been very severe. As the thaw set in there was still plenty of snow around for Christina and Zara to make snowmen and throw a few snowballs at whoever was around. At least that year Liza was not as bombarded as she usually had been, although she did not get away with it completely.

Everyone was emerging from their homes. Ken made his way to the house and helped Mr Lambert and several others to clear the driveway and on down to the church. Fires were lit in the vicarage, but Bernard would not be moving back until after the weekend.

"Did your girls enjoy the snow, Ken?" asked Liza.

"We were very warm and comfortable in our home and as soon as they could they started building snowmen. It is so nice to see them doing things that children should be doing. For so many years my two eldest had responsibilities that no child should have. They are very happy. They managed to catch Christopher and Derek with some snowballs. I think Adam and April knew what would happen if they emerged from their home, so they stayed out of the way," laughed Ken and Liza thought how nice it was to see him laughing, for so long he had had a haunted look on his face but that had now gone.

The Duke arrived for the weekend, and he made it clear to Bella that he had arranged that their house is prepared ready for their return on Monday. Bella did not seem too happy at the prospect but she had no excuse to stay longer.

Miranda, Lucinda and their staff would also be staying until after the weekend, and their house also was being warmed for their return, as was David's and Grace's house.

"It would appear that we will have a mass exodus of people on Monday," said Jamie. "I presume that the school will also be opening on that day."

"So Ken tells me," said Liza. "I haven't seen Adam myself, but all should be in order for Monday."

Jamie and Liza were alone in the library and Jamie took advantage of the opportunity to kiss Liza and tell her that much as he enjoyed his visitors, he could not wait for Monday to arrive when they would have their home to themselves.

"Through the next week I will have to visit our farms to see how they have fared and find out if anything is needed by them, so after Monday I shall be busy," said Jamie. "But no doubt you will be also. Do you have much to catch up on?"

"Grace and I managed to spend a little time each day on work," said Liza. "Bella doesn't appear until well into the morning and your mother and Lucinda manage to occupy themselves quite happily without my help, as does David and Bernard, so I have caught up with much of the business in the last ten days. It was nice to have some children around the house, Susan is very good with them, but I did manage to spend quite some time with them."

Gradually through the course of Monday their guests left. First to go was Bernard followed by Miranda, Lucinda and their staff. David and Grace went after Grace had finalised a few letters for Liza. It was not until well after lunch that the Duke and Bella left with Bella grumbling that she hoped that the Duke was right that their house would be ready to receive them and if not, she was going to turn around and come straight back. As always Bella never asked, she just assumed that she would be welcome.

Liza sat back and reflected on the past year which had started out with such happy plans but for a while had turned into a nightmare. She was very concerned for all her friends in America and all she could do to assist was to love and look after the two girls who had been placed in her care. The whole country was still in mourning for Prince Albert, but Liza was determined that at least the girls would not be made to feel too sad, Christina had enough to contend with worrying about those that she loved in Benson; Zara was too young to understand.

"You're deep in thought Liza," said Jamie.

"Yes; I know I have probably said it before, but I was just thinking that all our exciting plans last year became a disaster. The only good to come out of it was that we have Christina and little Zara to care for and love. I pray that all our friends in America are safe. We must make a good life for the girls as we do for our boys," said Liza.

"We will Liza, and we will also try to have an uncomplicated life; something that we have yet to achieve," smiled Jamie.

EPILOGUE

Eddy had tried not to appear overly keen when he negotiated the sale of the old company offices and the rent of the warehouses.

"If I keep pushing the prospective buyers, they might think that there is something wrong with them and we are too anxious to palm off on to them premises with too many problems," said Eddy.

"Come on Eddy, they are old premises so they can't expect them to be in pristine condition. I know that the warehouses have been updated on occasion, but it is quite some years since the offices have been renovated and a while since we had any tenants in part of them," said Ellie.

"It's just as well that we never had tenants in the offices where the old safe was housed, otherwise we may not have found all Liza's possessions," said Eddy.

"When do you think that the sale will be finalised?" asked Ellie.

"It's going to be at least another couple of weeks," said Eddy. "It does seem to be taking a lot longer than the twenty-eight days originally quoted, but I'm assured that it is still all in order. I really would have liked to have booked our tickets to both Surrey and then on to America. Have you found out where Benson is, or was?"

"Yes, I believe I have," said Ellie. "It appears to be part of a much larger town now, but from what I have found they have kept part of it almost as it was, and people have guided tours. There are some street names that seem to be relating to Liza such as Kelly Avenue I believe and Bradley Lakeside. It's going to be exciting to see it. I looked further into Liza's belongings and found an engraved silver key which states that it's the key to the town. You remember that I wrote that Liza was presented with it the year before Patrick died and she never felt that she deserved it."

"She did though, didn't she? She did a great deal for the people of the town," said Eddy. "I wonder if we should take it with us and if they have a proper museum then we should let them have it so that it can be displayed where it should be. It is more theirs than ours, but we must make sure that it is the right place and that it will be looked after properly and appreciated."

"Good idea. I have a feeling that we must take her jewellery with us, although that is a risk. I'll see what Jamie thinks; he may have some idea how to keep it safe," said Ellie.

"You like him, don't you Ell? He seems to quite like you also. Do you think that it could mean that I could be related to aristocracy in the future?" laughed Eddy.

"I think that you are joking," said Ellie. "Yes, I do like him, but I've only met him on a few occasions, and he probably has women falling over themselves to be with him, and they all probably have titles and posh accents."

"I shall be happy when we can see that Liza is laid to rest properly next to her husband. I still cannot understand why her adopted son, James, allowed that to happen. By all accounts he loved her; he certainly did not want to be with his natural mother and yet he let her move Liza from her resting place and wanted her obliterated from memory. I wonder whether he had mental problems. I bet he suffered with dementia; how can we find that out?"

"There should be some old medical records which would answer that question. It's probably best not to mention that to Jamie, people don't like to think that it could be in the family," said Eddy.

"It's accepted more nowadays, but I will handle that gently," said Ellie. "I wonder if we will be able to visit South Carolina whilst we're in America. It would be good to see the Enderby plantation, or where it was. The graveyard in Benson will be very poignant; I felt really choked when writing about Rufus Denton and Paul Southern. It was such a correct decision to put Rufus in his proper uniform and lay him to rest next to Paul."

"Don't get too sad Ellie, or you'll never be able to finish Liza's story because it doesn't take a genius to know that it has to end when she dies," said Eddy.

"There are many things that seem to link with happenings that occurred long after she had gone which will probably eventually explain why she carried out some of her manipulations. So there is much that seems to relate to what appeared to be unfathomable reasons for some of her actions. Her story will end when all questions have been answered," said Ellie.

"What's the next part of her story, and has she told you the title yet?" asked Eddy.

"Well, she and Jamie are back from being caught up in the American Civil War and the country is immediately faced with the death of Prince Albert, but they try to make that Christmas a good time for the family and friends. She was looking forward to having a time where she could just concentrate on Jamie, her family and home. Naturally her business comes into that, but she just wanted the rest of her life to be contented and uncomplicated. However it seems that it was not to be and something serious happens to her, but as yet I don't know what that is," said Ellie.

"That sounds interesting, and do you have a title?" asked Eddy.

"Yes, it's 'Friends and Enemies' which gives away a little of what happens to her," said Ellie.

"That's intriguing. Will you be able to carry on writing whilst we are away? I suppose that we are lucky that we live in this day and age with all the technology that we have, which means that we no longer have to be tied to a desk to work," said Eddy.

Ellie nodded and prepared to contact Jamie, giving him an update on how they were progressing with the sale of the offices.

***